EVERYMAN'S LIBRARY

EVERYMAN,
I WILL GO WITH THEE,
AND BE THY GUIDE,
IN THY MOST NEED
TO GO BY THY SIDE

ANNE BRONTË

AGNES GREY

THE TENANT OF WILDFELL HALL

WITH AN INTRODUCTION
BY LUCY HUGHES-HALLETT

EVERYMAN'S LIBRARY
Alfred A. Knopf New York London Toronto

343

THIS IS A BORZOI BOOK
PUBLISHED BY ALFRED A. KNOPF

First included in Everyman's Library, 1914 (*The Tenant of Wildfell Hall*),
1953 (*Agnes Grey*)
New edition 2012
Introduction Copyright © 2012 by Lucy Hughes-Hallett
Bibliography and Chronology Copyright © 2012 by Everyman's Library
Typography by Peter B. Willberg

US website: www.randomhouse.com/everymans

ISBN: 978-0-307-95780-1 (US)
978-1-84159-343-2 (UK)

A CIP catalogue reference for this book is available from the
British Library

Book design by Barbara de Wilde and Carol Devine Carson

Typeset in the UK by AccComputing, North Barrow, Somerset

Printed and bound in Germany by GGP Media GmbH, Pössneck

CONTENTS

v

INTRODUCTION

Mr Hattersley, his face purple, his laughter manic, has Lord Lowborough by the arm and is trying to drag him out of the drawing-room. Lowborough has been first a gambler and then an alcoholic, but he is now reformed, and struggles, pale with anger, to resist Hattersley's proclaimed intent to make him drunk again. Two further wine-sodden gentlemen are present, one sprawling legless in an armchair laughing uproariously, the other holding forth to nobody about his manly capacity for boozing while he mistakes a saucer for a tea cup and a cup for the sugar basin. Women are variously sneering at or weeping over their sottish spouses. The wrestling men are deadlocked until Lord Lowborough shouts for a candle and burns Hattersley's hands with it. The latter lets go, 'roaring like a wild beast', and collapses onto an ottoman from which he begins to taunt and threaten his miserable wife, eventually staggering to his feet to knock her down.

No wonder some of their contemporaries were shocked by the lack of veiling sentimentality in the Brontës' fiction. No wonder Charlotte thought *The Tenant of Wildfell Hall*, Anne's second and best novel – from which this deplorable scene is taken – best forgotten. In 1850, two years after the book's first publication, one year after Anne's death from tuberculosis, Charlotte wrote '*Wildfell Hall*, it hardly appears to me desirable to preserve. The choice of subject in that work is a mistake.' That subject, she declared, was ill-suited to Anne's 'naturally sensitive, reserved and dejected nature'.

Charlotte, the last surviving sister, was the only one of the Brontës to live long enough to have a hand in the shaping of their reputation. She was driven to defend herself and her sisters against repeated charges of 'coarseness'. But in trying to protect Anne's reputation by overstating her feminine mildness and gentility, and in particular in declining to reissue her best book, she did her a grave disservice. The idea that Anne Brontë is the quiet one, perhaps even the dull one, among the Brontës, has persisted. A recent critic, Stevie Davies, has described

Anne's first novel, *Agnes Grey*, as having 'the beauty and sadness of music scored in a minor key'. The graphic artist Kate Beaton, in a witty cartoon strip 'Dude Watchin' with the Brontës', has Charlotte and Emily ogling surly Heathcliffean or Rochesterish hunks while Anne priggishly refuses to play the game. 'So passionate! . . . So mysterious!' coo the elder sisters. 'If you like alcoholic dickbags,' says killjoy Anne. Unfair. Charlotte wanted us to believe that her youngest sister was a 'gentle, retiring inexperienced writer'. But posterity, in taking her word for it, has done so only by ignoring the evidence of Anne's work.

There was nothing anodyne or 'inexperienced' about Anne Brontë. The narrator-heroine of *Agnes Grey*, far from being 'retiring', is a sharp critic of her employers and a woman who craves, above all things, to be 'noticed' (the word recurs persistently). Anne Brontë had seen a bit of the world, and, finding a lot to dislike there, described it with satiric energy. She wrote frankly about childish cruelty and adult self-indulgence, about alcoholism and about violence, both domestic and public. She tackled hard subjects and she approached them, not in a 'dejected' posture of prim distress, but with a tough wit and an intelligent clarity which gives her analyses of marriage, of employment and of the mutually destructive relationships between a group of hell-bent drunkards a bracing vigour.

*

To read Anne Brontë's novels alongside those of Charlotte and Emily is to see both how much they had in common (her plots are full of echoes of *Jane Eyre* and *Villette*, her patterning of disparate narrative voices recalls *Wuthering Heights*) but also how distinct was her particular gift. There is a trainspotters' pleasure to be had from noticing the correspondences between the sisters' works. The tortured animals in *Agnes Grey* irresistibly recall the hanged puppies in *Wuthering Heights*; *The Tenant of Wildfell Hall* takes the form – like Charlotte's *The Professor* – of a series of letters written by a male narrator. Arthur Huntingdon is at once a rake like *Jane Eyre*'s Mr Rochester, and a debauchee whose death – like that of Rochester's first wife – is a necessary condition of the happy ending. But, in the words of the critic Jill Matus, 'It is as if each Brontë sister broke off a piece of the same large clump of creative clay and set to kneading and shaping it in her own way.' Anne's way was distinctive. She has her own voice and her own sensibility.

She was the most devout of the sisters, but her religious faith wasn't of the meek-and-mild variety: rather it gives her fiction a fiery edge. She earnestly believed in the rewards and punishments of the Christian vision of the afterlife. When her characters – ignorant cottager or reckless gentleman alike – become frantic with fear of damnation, they are not thinking metaphorically. They are taking scriptural warnings as literally, and seriously, as the author herself did. Such a way of thinking is alien to many twenty-first century readers, but Anne Brontë wasn't a bigot. She was morally rigorous, but she was also tolerant. She persuaded herself that redemption was offered to all. Her understanding of psychology is subtle. She refuses to reduce any of her characters, however ill-behaved, to the simple status of out-and-out villain.

Pious as she was, she was also the funniest of the Brontë sisters. The 'Glass Town' stories, on which she and Emily collaborated in childhood, play ironic games with clashing viewpoints and incompatible narratives. Her adult fiction employs similar strategies. These books repeatedly burst the confines of their genres (feminist romance, Gothic mystery, didactic tale). Brontë's dialogue is as racy as that of the great eighteenth-century comic dramatists, and brilliantly reveals that which her characters might prefer to conceal. Her chronically unreliable narrators' self-delusions are subtly conveyed. Over a century before the word 'teenager' became current, Brontë created in Fergus Markham a hilarious picture of a disgruntled adolescent, a rude boy puncturing his elders' romantic pretensions with deliciously ribald disrespect.

Brontë's ability to convey the shock of physical violence (a governess yanking her little charge's hair, an otherwise decent young farmer assaulting a rival and leaving his victim semiconscious by the roadside) makes her novels electric. Her satirical humour grounds them, and gives them a kind of robust energy which prefigures the great realist novels of the next generation. For too long she has been undervalued as the thirdbest Brontë. She may not be quite the match of her sisters (with the exceptions of Dickens and Thackeray, no English author then publishing was) but her fiction, exploring the lamentably still current themes of addiction and domestic violence and the abuse of vulnerable women working away from home, has a vigour and a bracing satirical intelligence which places her in the first rank of what is arguably the greatest ever generation of novelists in English.

*

According to Elizabeth Gaskell, Charlotte Brontë described *Agnes Grey* as 'the novel in which her sister Anne pretty literally describes her own experience as a governess'. Again Charlotte was underestimating her sister's creativity. *Agnes Grey* is not just about the predicament of one mid-nineteenth-century British governess. It is that rare thing, a novel about work. It examines – as fiction rarely does – relations between employers and employees, and it does so through a sequence of vividly dramatic scenes.

'Married life is woman's profession, and to this life her training – that of dependence – is modelled. Of course by not getting a husband, or losing him, she may find that she is without resources. All that can be said of her is, she has failed in business': thus a contributor to the *Saturday Review*, writing in the decade after *Agnes Grey* was published. All of the Brontës rebelled against such a definition of woman's 'business', but they all knew from experience that the 'right to work,' so vociferously and optimistically claimed by feminists throughout the next century, was no guarantee of self-fulfilment, let alone of happiness. To work for one's living is to become the subordinate of people who may be, in every sense but the financial one, one's inferior. All the Brontë sisters had been fagged and underprized as governesses or student-teachers. All of them fantasized about running their own school, about becoming bosses themselves. In *Agnes Grey* Anne Brontë reinforces that fantasy with the depiction of two dismal alternatives: Agnes's humiliation at the hand of employers who never 'notice' her, and her charge Rosalie's bleak mercenary marriage. *Agnes Grey* offers a feminist critique of the nineteenth-century marriage-market, but it is also a commentary on the multifarious ways in which humans have been, and still are, obliged to sacrifice their self-respect for financial security.

First and foremost, though, it is a story, full of striking episodes. Many of the most memorable involve dumb creatures. Bidding goodbye to her home, Agnes takes her pet pigeons in her lap, stroking and kissing her favourite fantails. The next day odious little Tom Bloomfield is demonstrating how far he is from sharing her gentleness by showing her his bird traps, and boasting of how he has pulled off the legs and wings and heads of baby sparrows. 'Uncle Robson . . . laughed, and said I was a fine boy.' This 'fine boy' – miniature model of a deplorable ideal of masculinity – thrashes his rocking horse. Soon he has got hold of another nestful of fledglings. He stands over it in a childish travesty of a 'manly' posture, 'his legs wide apart, his hands thrust into his breeches-pockets', and exults, 'But you shall see me fettle 'em off. My word, but I *will* wallop 'em!'

When Agnes moves from the Bloomfields' household to the Murrays' the nature of Brontë's story shifts from horrific caricature to acute social comedy. Rosalie Murray, Agnes's pupil, rival and almost-friend, is at once disgraceful, pathetic and very funny. She is her mother's creation and instrument. (There is poignancy in the importance the motherless Brontë attached to maternal influence.) Rosalie has been raised to preen and flirt and marry well. She is utterly cynical, but yet pitiably naive. She knows her husband-to-be is an 'ugly beast' but 'mama says I should not mind that after a few months' acquaintance'. Soon she knows, as well, that he is a 'scamp' but 'he'll be all right when he's married, as mama says.'

Mama is wrong. Rosalie's story ends dismally. Agnes, visiting her after her marriage, looks out of an upstairs window of the grand house which is Rosalie's compensation for being tied for life to a gloomy drunkard and – in a fine piece of plangent expressionist description – watches as the sun goes down and the shadow of a high wall gradually engulfs the scene 'so lately bathed in glorious light'. Rosalie has her just reward for her husband-hunting and her heartless flirtations with other beaux, but there is a great sadness in seeing her brightness so extinguished. The extended passages of dialogue between her and Agnes, who is revealed in speech and action as a far livelier

xi

and bolder character than she is in her own self-descriptions, are full of vitality and humour and the warmth of unspoken affections. Brontë aficionados will see a premonition here of the relationship between *Villette*'s Lucy Snowe and Ginevra Fanshawe. Other readers will respond simply to the beguiling vitality of the image presented us of two young women, so different in their circumstances and their morality, so alike in their wit and their determination to find some pleasure wherever it may be allowed.

For both, though, that pleasure is hard to find. Rosalie sells herself for the position of chatelaine to a great house, and will yawn away her evenings for all the years to come while her husband 'sots over his wine'. But at least she has social status. She will never have to endure the humiliations to which Agnes is exposed day after day. As a governess, an employee, Agnes is slighted, patronized and ignored. Mr and Mrs Bloomfield quarrel in her presences as though they were alone. Young ladies and gentlemen talk across and through her, as though she were so much mist. She is of as little account as the footman who stands motionless while Rosalie wails indiscreetly about the irritations attendant on sharing a house with her mother-in-law. When Agnes reproaches her, Rosalie exclaims 'They're mere automatons...It would be a pretty thing indeed, if we were to be tongue-tied by our servants!' As a governess Agnes is another such automaton, a thing to be bought and used without thought of its emotional needs. Until the curate – perfect husband-material – appears to bring sunlight into her 'quiet, drab-colour life', the only person, or thing, which seems to 'notice' her fully is Snap the dog. There is a good reason why animals play such an important role in this story: they test humans' capacity for loving-kindness. The rector who kicks old Nancy's dog also shuts the carriage door in Agnes Grey's face. The curate who adopts Snap notices Agnes and, liking what he sees, marries her.

*

The Tenant of Wildfell Hall begins as it will go on – with a peremptory claim on the reader's attention. 'You must' [no diffidence from this narrator, no pretty pleases] 'go back with me to the autumn of 1827'. The voice is that of Gilbert Markham, who has revealed himself before the end of the first chapter, to be – at the time of the events described – a cocky, self-satisfied and self-deluding young farmer who thinks he is fit for a great place in the world, but busies himself in the meanwhile 'whacking' his younger brother, choking with laughter at silly jokes over his teatime toast and fancying himself in love with the rector's spiteful daughter. Though he's charming, we might quickly tire of him, but that Anne Brontë allows us to see him with triple vision. He is – at the time of the supposed writing – an older and (slightly) wiser man, recounting in a sequence of letters (hence the informal directness of the tone) the events which culminated in his marriage, while at once indulgently condescending to, and wryly apologizing for, his young self. But even as a mature narrator, Gilbert is far from being perfect or impartial. Nor, even in retrospect, does he understand his own story half as well as we quickly begin to. A third consciousness, the author's own, shapes his narrative, and displays his sweetness to the reader along with his worse qualities, which include vanity and a propensity for violence. The three levels of perception hum and crackle like crossed wires. This is (to start with) a simple rural comedy, but one with a multiplicity of layers of significance.

Gilbert's narrative tone is breezy, man-to-man. Other voices are even more energetic. 'Go it like bricks!' says his naughty brother Fergus. 'Mind you don't leave her one stone upon another!' Fergus is addressing two young ladies who have been trading slanderous innuendoes about a third. The blend of boyish slang with biblical imprecation is an instance of Anne Brontë's flexible command of language, and the skill with which she matches voice to character. There are long passages of dialogue, in which characters reveal themselves without any comment from the narrative voice (which, given how obtuse Gilbert often is, would probably be misleading). Voices chime and clash: fussy Mrs Markham being as irritating to her doted-upon eldest son as doting mothers inevitably are; Eliza with her bitchy barbs all wrapped up in coy girlish sweetness; Lawrence, the young squire who knows a secret, but only adds to everybody's perplexity by his cagey hints. There are passages full of absurd misunderstandings of which Sheridan might have been proud, and beneath all the comical verbal business there is a pulse of kindliness which warms the comedy of manners into a forgiving *comédie humaine*.

Once we hear tell – as we very soon do – that a beautiful young widow has moved into Wildfell Hall, the storytelling becomes even more complex. The heroine of a Gothic mystery steps out of her own genre to attend a tea-party full of village gossips among whom Jane Austen's Miss Bates would have felt at home. An outing to a beauty spot echoes the pivotal trip to Box Hill in Austen's *Emma*. But the enigmatic Mrs Graham, with her air of cultivated melancholy, her dark ringlets and her daring independence has blown in from a different literary landscape.

Down in the Markham household we are in a cosy world where young people flirt and squabble and read the *Farmer's Magazine*. Up at the Hall we are in a domain of picturesquely overgrown topiary and lofty deserted rooms through whose dusty casements a mysterious figure can dimly be seen. It is no accident that the book which Gilbert offers Helen is Sir Walter Scott's *Marmion*, defining text of late Romanticism. Gilbert frequently makes the walk from the village up to the semi-ruined hilltop Hall and arrives agitated, as well he might, having travelled not only from an intensely farmed valley to a bleak moor, but also from one genre to another, from realist social comedy to Romantic melodrama.

Helen and Gilbert fall in love, but there is a mysterious impediment to their relationship. She is enigmatic. He is hasty. There are misunderstandings, near-declarations, outbursts of temper, floods of tears. At last, apparently unequal to the task of explaining herself, she (rather improbably) gives him her diary. He keeps it and, years later, sends it (equally improbably) to the recipient of his long narrative letters. And so we find ourselves entering not only a different milieu but also a different kind of fiction. Leaving behind the playfulness of Gilbert's account and his simple rural life, we are seeing a more sophisticated society through the eyes of a solemn, initially naive, young woman.

*

The Brontë children read with interest about the depraved goings-on of regency roués. Thomas Moore's *Life of Lord Byron* was one of their favourite books. The heroes of their juvenilia are frequently Byronic, even diabolical. They felt the glamour of noble spirits darkened by ill-defined 'vice'. By the time Anne wrote *The Tenant of Wildfell Hall*, though, she had too much knowledge of the reality of bad behaviour to fool herself by romanticizing it.

Her brother Branwell was an alcoholic and a drug-user. His 'vice', all too specific and sordidly material, ruined his own life, and cast a gloom over all of his sisters'. For Anne, in particular, it was disastrous. After a miserable first job as governess, she found a happier one in the household of a clergyman, the Reverend Robinson. After three years there, she was joined by Branwell, who was to tutor the Robinsons' son. In 1845 Anne left, and shortly thereafter Branwell was turned out of the house, having apparently attempted to seduce Mrs Robinson. His self-indulgence had not only disgraced him: it had deprived Anne of a livelihood and a home from home.

At the Robinsons' and back at Haworth she was able to observe his deterioration, and she drew on it to create, in *The Tenant of Wildfell Hall*, an account of addiction, and the havoc it plays with the lives of all those touched by it, written with a candour which shocked her contemporaries and with a degree of penetration few modern therapists could match. The young men described in *The Tenant of Wildfell Hall* are not stereotypical rakes: they are alcoholics whose compulsion is described with the first-hand knowledge of one who had watched her brilliant brother reduce himself to a state of numb idiocy. Brontë shows us their pathetic neediness, their bullying, the joylessness of their 'jollifications'. She is perceptive about the ambivalent feelings of the women who fear, despise, but try to love them. Far from being crudely censorious, she points out, as few other commentators had, that these 'degenerates' are enacting, in exaggerated terms, faults endemic in society.

*

Helen's story begins with a situation as old as fiction. A beautiful young woman must chose between three suitors. The three initially appear to be mere types from a pattern book of comic convention. Mr Boarham is nothing but a name (we really don't need Helen to tell us she privately hears it as Bore 'em). Mr Wilmot is nothing but an age – too old. But Arthur Huntingdon, who begins by being every girl's dream of a dashing romantic lead before revealing himself to be a heartless rake, soon becomes a great deal more interesting than either stereotype could have made him.

He and Helen are not yet married when he displays his true nature by means of the story of Lord Lowborough's fall. Again Brontë is varying her narrative tone with long passages of dialogue, both direct and reported, and layering her story with multiple viewpoints. Helen, recording Huntingdon's account of his conversations with Lowborough, becomes – innocent as she still is – the conduit for a shocking story. Huntingdon is boasting of having been a pitiless witness as Lowborough came near to ruining himself at gambling, and then – worse – of having drawn him into alcoholism. It is a story of a Satanic temptation, but it also demonstrates the kind of pressure that Huntingdon, the tempter, is himself subject to. His friends have greeted the news of his engagement with 'bitter execrations'. 'They say there'll be no more fun now...I was the very life and prop of the community, they do me the honour to say, and I have shamefully betrayed my trust.' We will repeatedly see how the 'jovial band' resist any of their fellows' attempts at reform.

To drink is to be bold and manly. To abstain is to be a killjoy. When Huntingdon describes himself and his fellow-topers surreptitiously filling Lowborough's glass despite all the latter's protestations that he doesn't want to drink, he feels justified by the code of good fellowship which entraps him too, just as surely Lowborough is entrapped. We understand now why Helen, in hiding at Wildfell Hall, gave her little boy doctored wine as a kind of aversion therapy. More, we see that the good Mrs Markham's protest that she was thereby turning him into a 'milksop' is on the cosy and acceptable end of a spectrum at whose darker extreme is the violence with which Huntingdon and his friends bar the door to any of their number who would prefer to leave the dining-room before drinking himself stupid.

*

Wicked rakes and their innocent young female victims swarm through the fiction and drama of the century preceding this novel's publication. But Anne Brontë takes the old story in a new direction. Convention decreed that it was the woman's role to play the good angel to her erring partner. Mozart's Countess Almaviva, catching her husband betraying her in the shrubbery, magnanimously forgives him. Not so, in a similar, but far more darkly-toned situation, Helen Huntingdon. She asks for her money back, and for her child and her freedom. Denied the first two, and therefore unable to claim the third, she stays unwillingly, but from now on she despises and avoids her husband.

Brontë puts into the brutal Mr Hattersley's voice her own arguments against the code of wifely behaviour which required a woman to be forever patient. Hattersley is rough with his wife Milicent. The closest he comes to a caress is a tug at her hair. When Helen reproaches him he explains that sweet, submissive Milicent is as trying as soft sand. 'If you plod along, for half an hour, over this soft, easy carpet . . . you'll find it rather wearisome work, and be glad enough to come to a bit of good, firm rock, that won't budge an inch.' It's a striking image. Anne Brontë is certainly not inviting us to condone Hattersley's sadism, but when he says 'How can I help teasing her when she's so invitingly meek and mim – when she lies down like a spaniel at my feet?' she is plainly telling us that Milicent's conformity with the ideal of the ever-loyal, all-forgiving wife, is poor strategy. It is only when Helen hardens her heart against her husband that she regains her self-respect. It is only when she leaves him that the long progress towards a happy ending can begin.

Arthur Huntingdon is about as bad as a husband can be. He is drunken, promiscuous, and idle. Any kindly emotions he may feel are so smothered by his fear of appearing weak that he is incapable of addressing his young wife with any tenderness. His wooing is all facetious. So extreme is his misogyny that even as he watches his mistress hurrying back from their clandestine tryst in the shrubbery, Huntingdon is sneering at her under his breath. But Brontë makes it plain that Huntingdon's short-comings are not merely his own personal failings. The honour code of his social group forbids him to acknowledge any affection or respect he might feel for Helen. 'It's all these cursed women!' says the detestable Grimsby. 'They're the very bane of the world!' To disagree would be to transgress against the rules of masculinity and to be outcast.

Huntingdon and his friends are delinquent in their drinking and gambling and failure to take care of their wealth, but Brontë suggests that their attitude to women is fully endorsed by the society in which they live. In Gilbert Markham's framing narrative Mrs Markham laughs at Helen for wanting to keep her little boy near her and supervise his education. 'You'll spoil his spirit, and make a mere Miss Nancy of him.' There is an obvious irony in this – Mrs Markham is a great spoiler of her own boy. Gilbert's sister Rose complains that the household revolves around him and his brother. 'If there's anything particularly nice at table, Mamma winks and nods at me . . . she whispers, "Don't eat so much of that, Rose, Gilbert will like it for his supper.' But women's duty to cherish and indulge their menfolk is no joke. It is a function of their powerlessness. They must dote and submit and pander to their brothers' and husbands' wishes because they are totally dependent on them. When Helen asks Huntingdon to let her go he says, simply, 'No'. No need for him to argue, to justify himself or explain. She is his wife, his property. She will do as he pleases. After another unhappy year has gone by he has begun to offer her to his friends, as one might offer around any other outworn possession. 'Any one among you, that can fancy her, may have her and welcome!'

Brontë set her novel (published in 1848) some twenty years before the time of writing, and therefore before the act of 1839, which permitted a wife to petition for custody of her children under the age of seven (provided she had not been found guilty of adultery and provided she could afford the legal costs). Helen has no claim whatsoever over her dowry, or over her son. The nervousness which puzzles Gilbert Markham is fully justified. When she sees Gilbert helping little Arthur down from a wall her apparent overreaction is in fact the proportionate response of a mother whose husband is doing his utmost to abduct the boy with the law's blessing. She is in hiding because she is an outlaw in a state which decrees that a man like Huntingdon is inevitably her superior, simply because he is a man.

And so to Gilbert. Once he's read the diary there's no impediment to his love for Helen, but for the tiresome fact of her husband's continued existence. As Gilbert says, in a cunning bit of pre-emption on Brontë's part, it is uncomfortable, indeed 'morally evil' to base one's hopes of happiness on the death of another. All the same, just as no reader of *Jane Eyre* has ever hoped for Bertha Rochester to survive her fall from the flaming battlements, so readers of *The Tenant of Wildfell Hall* cannot but be delighted to hear that Arthur Huntingdon is gravely ill. Helen redeems herself in the eyes of the conventional by nursing him. He duly dies, and at last the way lies open to the inevitable happy ending. Inevitable, that is, but for Gilbert's obstructive masculinity.

He may not be a sot who feels he has to prove his virile boldness by debauchery, but Gilbert, all the same, finds it almost as hard to compromise his masculine prerogative by submitting to love as Arthur Huntingdon did before him. He cannot even accept Helen's pretty offer of a Christmas rose, signifying (as he really ought not to need telling) her heart. She has always been more refined, more articulate, more grown-up than him. ('She thinks me an impudent puppy,' he reflects, on first seeing her in church: we do too.) Now she is also very much richer: Brontë has made her proprietress of not one, but two estates. In marrying her, Gilbert will have to accept a subordinate role.

He balks at the prospect. What he calls 'delicacy' and readers see as stupid pride comes near to scuppering the courtship. Helen is the dominant partner now, and accordingly she lays claim to him while he shies and repeatedly backs off like a nervous pony. He wins love and lands and fortune, but he does so as his wife's dependant, what his mother might have called a 'Miss Nancy'.

The Tenant of Wildfell Hall was written simultaneously with *Jane Eyre*. Often Anne and Charlotte Brontë must have been working in the same room, even at the same table. Both were writing compelling romances which were also trenchant analyses of the problematic areas of human experience where the desires for love, independence and money overlap. Both conclude their novels with ostensibly happy endings which are actually profoundly equivocal. Like the blind and mutilated Mr Rochester marrying a newly independent Jane Eyre, Gilbert Markham gains love at the cost of his male dominance.

When he was younger and cockier, Gilbert ducked out of an argument in which Helen was besting him by exclaiming that the ladies 'must always have the last word'. He has the last word in this novel, relating the final scenes from his own blinkered viewpoint – and little good it does him. With a subtlety commensurate with her sister's, Anne Brontë lets us know how his longed-for marriage reduces and unmans him, and how profoundly flawed is the ideal of manhood which makes his marvellous good fortune so hard to take. Anne Brontë could certainly write word-music in a plangent minor key, but she also had the intelligence, the insight into her own culture and the imaginative power of a major novelist.

Lucy Hughes-Hallett

SELECT BIBLIOGRAPHY

BIOGRAPHY AND BACKGROUND

BARKER, JULIET, *The Brontës*, 1994, revised 2nd edition, Abacus, London, 2010.

FRASER, REBECCA, *Charlotte Brontë and her Family*, 1988, reissued as *Charlotte Brontë*, Vintage, London, 2003 and *Charlotte Brontë: A Writer's Life*, Pegasus, New York, 2008.

GASKELL, ELIZABETH, *The Life of Charlotte Brontë*, Penguin Books, London, 1997; Penguin USA, New York, 1998. The classic work, first published in 1857, which inaugurated the Brontë legend. The author was a close friend of Charlotte Brontë's and her book contains much information on Anne.

GÉRIN, WINIFRED, *Anne Brontë: A Biography*, Nelson, London, 1959, revised edition Allen Lane, London, 1976.

MILLER, LUCASTA, *The Brontë Myth*, Jonathan Cape, London, 2001; Alfred A. Knopf, New York, 2003.

VICINUS, MARTHA, *Suffer and Be Still: Women in the Victorian Age*, Indiana University Press, Bloomington, 1972; John Wiley, London, 1972.

CRITICISM

ALLOTT, MIRIAM, ed., *The Brontës: The Critical Heritage*, Routledge, London, 1974.

CRAIK, W. A., *The Brontë Novels*, 1968, reissued Routledge, London and New York, 2011.

EAGLETON, TERRY, *Myths of Power: A Marxist Study of the Brontës*, Macmillan, London and New York, 1975, revised edition 2005.

EWBANK, INGA-STINA, *Their Proper Sphere: A Study of the Brontë Sisters as Early Victorian Female Novelists*, Edward Arnold, London, 1965; Harvard University Press, Cambridge, 1966.

GILBERT, SANDRA M. and GUBAR, SUSAN, *The Madwoman in the Attic: The Woman Writer and the Nineteenth Century Literary Imagination*, Yale University Press, New Haven, 1979.

GLEN, HEATHER, ed., *The Cambridge Companion to the Brontës*, Cambridge University Press, Cambridge and New York, 2002.

KAPLAN, CORA, *Victoriana: Histories, Fictions, Criticisms*, Edinburgh University Press Edinburgh, 2007; Columbia University Press, New York, 2007.

SHOWALTER, ELAINE, *A Literature of their Own: British Women Novelists from Brontë to Lessing*, Princeton University Press, 1977; Virago, London, 1982.

CHRONOLOGY

DATE	AUTHOR'S LIFE	LITERARY CONTEXT
1815		
1817		Death of Jane Austen.
1818		Byron completes *Childe Harold's Pilgrimage.* Scott: *Ivanhoe.* Mary Shelley: *Frankenstein.*
1819		Birth of George Eliot.
1820	Anne Brontë born, 17 January, at Thornton, sixth and last child of Patrick Brontë, a Yorkshire parson, and his wife Maria. Sisters: Maria (b. 1813), Elizabeth (b. 1815), Charlotte (b. 1816), Emily (b. 1818); and brother Branwell (b. 1817). The family moves to Haworth.	Keats: *Lamia . . . and Other Poems.* Shelley: *Prometheus Unbound.* Lamb: *Essays of Elia* (to 1823).
1821	Death of Anne's mother. Her sister, Elizabeth Branwell, comes to Haworth to keep house and look after the children.	Scott: *Kenilworth.* Death of Keats.
1822		De Quincey: *Confessions of an English Opium Eater.* Death of Shelley.
1823		Death of Ann Radcliffe.
1824	The four eldest Brontë girls are sent to Cowan Bridge School.	Landor: *Imaginary Conversations* (to 1837). Hogg: *Confessions of a Justified Sinner.* Wordsworth: *Poetical Works* (4 vols). Carlyle's translation of Goethe: *Wilhelm Meister's Apprenticeship.* Death of Byron at Missolonghi.
1825	Death of Maria and Elizabeth. Charlotte and Emily return home.	Hazlitt: *The Spirit of the Age.*

Battle of Waterloo. End of Napoleonic Wars. Corn Law passed. Lord
Liverpool, Prime Minister since 1812, leads Tory government until 1827.

Congress of Aix-la-Chapelle.

Birth of Queen Victoria. Peterloo massacre followed by repressive Six Acts.
Factory Act restricts child labour.
Death of George III; accession of George IV. Trial of Queen Caroline.

Death of Napoleon on St Helena. Greek War of Independence begins.

First unions allowed in Britain. George IV induces government to purchase
the Angerstein Collection of old masters as nucleus of the National Gallery.

First steam locomotive railway opens (Stockton–Darlington).

DATE	AUTHOR'S LIFE	LITERARY CONTEXT
1826	Patrick Brontë gives the children a set of wooden soldiers about which they begin telling and writing stories.	Scott: *Woodstock.*
1828		
1829		Balzac: *La Comédie humaine* (to 1848). Carlyle: *Signs of the Times.*
1830		Stendhal: *Le Rouge et le noir.* Tennyson: *Poems, Chiefly Lyrical.* Moore's biography of Byron published. Cobbett: *Rural Rides.* Lyell: *Principles of Geology* (to 1833).
1831		Hugo: *Notre-Dame de Paris.*
1832		George Sand: *Indiana.* Death of Goethe and Sir Walter Scott.
1833		Carlyle: *Sartor Resartus.*
1834	Emily and Anne writing poems and stories about their fantasy world of Gondal.	Bulwer Lytton: *The Last Days of Pompeii.* Moore completes his *Irish Melodies.* Death of Coleridge.
1835	Emily a pupil at Roe Head School, Mirfield, where Charlotte is a teacher, but leaves after a few months; Anne takes her place.	
1837	Around this time Anne suffers a serious illness which brings on a religious crisis. She leaves the school in December.	Carlyle: *History of the French Revolution.* Dickens: *Pickwick Papers.*
1838		Dickens: *Oliver Twist.*
1839	In April, Anne takes up a post as governess to the children of Joshua Ingram at Blake Hall, Mirfield. She leaves by the end of the year.	Carlyle: *Chartism.* Darwin: *The Voyage of the Beagle.* Dickens: *Nicholas Nickleby.* Harriet Martineau: *Deerbrook.*
1840	Anne becomes governess to the children of Rev. Edmund Robinson at Thorp Green Hall, Little Ouseburn.	Dickens: *The Old Curiosity Shop* (to 1841).

CHRONOLOGY

DATE	AUTHOR'S LIFE	LITERARY CONTEXT
1841	Charlotte, Emily and Anne plan to start their own school.	Carlyle: *On Heroes, Hero-Worship and the Heroic in History.*
1842	Death of Anne's aunt, Elizabeth Branwell.	Tennyson: *Poems.* Browning: *Dramatic Lyrics.*
1843	Branwell joins Anne at Thorp Green Hall to take over the education of the son of the family.	Carlyle: *Past and Present.* Ruskin: *Modern Painters* (vol. 1). Death of Southey.
1844		Dumas *père*: *Les trois Mousquetaires.* Elizabeth Barrett Browning: *Poems.* Leigh Hunt: *Poetical Works*; *Imagination and Fancy.*
1845	Leaves Thorp Green Hall in July. Branwell is dismissed from his post as tutor and returns to Haworth where he becomes dependent on opium and alcohol. Anne writing *Agnes Grey*, Emily *Wuthering Heights* and Charlotte *The Professor*.	Disraeli: *Sybil.* Dumas *père*: *Le comte de Monte-Cristo.* Mérimée: *Carmen.* Poe: *Tales of Mystery and Imagination.*
1846	The sisters' novels are offered in vain to various publishers. Publication of *Poems by Currer, Ellis and Acton Bell.*	Strauss: *The Life of Jesus*, tr. George Eliot.
1847	Charlotte's *Jane Eyre* is published by Smith, Elder (October); *Agnes Grey* and *Wuthering Heights* are published together in three volumes by Thomas Cautley Newby (December).	Thackeray: *Vanity Fair* (to 1848). Tennyson: *The Princess.*
1848	*The Tenant of Wildfell Hall*, Anne's second novel, is published in June, with a second edition in August to which she writes a Preface. Anne and Charlotte visit Smith, Elder in London to prove their separate identities. Branwell dies in September, and Emily in December.	Mill: *Principles of Political Economy.* Dickens: *Dombey and Son.* Elizabeth Gaskell: *Mary Barton.* Thackeray: *Pendennis* (to 1850). George Sand: *François le Champi*; *La petite Fadette.*

CHRONOLOGY

ANNE BRONTË

DATE	AUTHOR'S LIFE	LITERARY CONTEXT
1849	Anne seriously ill with TB. In May she decides to visit Scarborough, scene of happy summer holidays with the Robinsons, in the hope that it will improve her health. Charlotte and a friend, Ellen Nussey, accompany her. She dies on 28 May and is buried in St Mary's churchyard. Charlotte publishes *Shirley*.	Macaulay: *History of England* (and 1855). Dickens: *David Copperfield* (to 1850). Kingsley: *Alton Locke*. Dinah Craik: *The Ogilvies*. Margaret Oliphant: *Passages in the Life of Mrs Margaret Maitland*.
1850	Charlotte brings out a second edition of *Wuthering Heights* and *Agnes Grey* with an 'Editor's Preface' to the former and a 'Biographical Notice of Ellis and Acton Bell'.	Tennyson: *In Memoriam*. Death of Wordsworth. Wordsworth: *The Prelude*. Elizabeth Barrett Browning: *Sonnets from the Portuguese*.

CHRONOLOGY

Mazzini's short-lived Roman republic falls to French army. Other European revolutions suppressed and period of reaction follows.

Don Pacifico incident: Palmerston's 'Civis Romanus Sum' speech. Public Libraries Act leads to foundation of municipal libraries throughout Great Britain. Foundation of the North London Collegiate School, the first independent school for girls, offering girls the same education as boys.

AGNES GREY

CONTENTS

CHAPTER I

THE PARSONAGE

ALL TRUE HISTORIES contain instruction; though, in some, the treasure may be hard to find, and when found, so trivial in quantity that the dry, shrivelled kernel scarcely compensates for the trouble of cracking the nut. Whether this be the case with my history or not, I am hardly competent to judge; I sometimes think it might prove useful to some, and entertaining to others, but the world may judge for itself: shielded by my own obscurity, and by the lapse of years, and a few fictitious names, I do not fear to venture, and will candidly lay before the public what I would not disclose to the most intimate friend.

My father was a clergyman of the north of England, who was deservedly respected by all who knew him, and, in his younger days, lived pretty comfortably on the joint income of a small incumbency, and a snug little property of his own. My mother, who married him against the wishes of her friends, was a squire's daughter, and a woman of spirit. In vain it was represented to her that, if she became the poor parson's wife, she must relinquish her carriage and her lady's-maid, and all the luxuries and elegancies of affluence, which to her were little less than the necessaries of life. A carriage and a lady's-maid were great conveniences; but, thank Heaven, she had feet to carry her, and hands to minister to her own necessities. An elegant house and spacious grounds were not to be despised, but she would rather live in a cottage with Richard Grey, than in a palace with any other man in the world.

Finding arguments of no avail, her father, at length, told the lovers they might marry if they pleased, but, in so doing, his daughter would forfeit every fraction of her fortune. He expected this would cool the ardour of both; but he was mistaken. My father knew too well my mother's superior worth, not to be sensible that she was a valuable fortune in herself; and if she would but consent to embellish his humble hearth, he should be happy to take her on any terms; while she, on her part, would rather labour with her own hands than be divided from the man she loved, whose happiness it would be her joy to make, and who was already one with her in heart and soul. So her fortune went to swell the purse of a wiser sister, who had married a rich nabob, and she, to the wonder and compassionate regret of all who knew her, went to bury herself in the homely village parsonage among the hills of —. And yet, in spite of all this, and in spite of my mother's high spirit, and my father's whims, I believe you might search all England through, and fail to find a happier couple.

Of six children, my sister Mary and myself were the only two that survived the perils of infancy and early childhood. I, being the younger by five or six years, was always regarded as the *child*, and the pet of the family – father, mother, and sister, all combined to spoil me – not by foolish indulgence to render me fractious and ungovernable, but by ceaseless kindness to make me too helpless and dependent, too unfit for buffeting with the cares and turmoils of life.

Mary and I were brought up in the strictest seclusion. My mother, being at once highly accomplished, well informed, and fond of employment, took the whole charge of our education on herself, with the exception of Latin – which my father undertook to teach us – so that we never even went to school; and as there was no society in the neighbourhood, our only intercourse with the world consisted in a stately tea-party, now and then, with the principal farmers and tradespeople of the vicinity, just to avoid being stigmatized as too proud to consort with our neighbours, and an annual visit to our paternal grandfather's,

where himself, our kind grandmamma, a maiden aunt, and two
or three elderly ladies and gentlemen were the only persons we
ever saw. Sometimes our mother would amuse us with stories
and anecdotes of her younger days, which, while they entertained us amazingly, frequently awoke – in *me*, at least – a vague
and secret wish to see a little more of the world.

I thought she must have been very happy; but she never
seemed to regret past times. My father, however, whose temper
was neither tranquil nor cheerful by nature, often unduly vexed
himself with thinking of the sacrifices his dear wife had made
for him, and troubled his head with revolving endless schemes
for the augmentation of his little fortune, for her sake, and ours.
In vain my mother assured him she was quite satisfied, and if
he would but lay by a little for the children, we should all have
plenty, both for time present and to come: but saving was not
my father's forte: he would not run in debt, (at least, my mother
took good care he should not,) but while he had money, he
must spend it; he liked to see his house comfortable, and his
wife and daughters well clothed, and well attended; and besides,
he was charitably disposed, and liked to give to the poor, according to his means, or, as some might think, beyond them.

At length, however, a kind friend suggested to him a means
of doubling his private property at one stroke; and further
increasing it, hereafter, to an untold amount. This friend was a
merchant, a man of enterprising spirit and undoubted talent;
who was somewhat straitened in his mercantile pursuits for
want of capital, but generously proposed to give my father a
fair share of his profits, if he would only intrust him with what
he could spare, and he thought he might safely promise that
whatever sum the latter chose to put into his hands, it should
bring him in cent per cent. The small patrimony was speedily
sold, and the whole of its price was deposited in the hands of
the friendly merchant, who as promptly proceeded to ship his
cargo, and prepare for his voyage.

My father was delighted, so were we all, with our brightening prospects: for the present, it is true, we were reduced to the narrow income of the curacy; but my father seemed to think there was no necessity for scrupulously restricting our expenditure to that: so, with a standing bill at Mr Jackson's, another at Smith's, and a third at Hobson's, we got along even more comfortably than before: though my mother affirmed we had better keep within bounds, for our prospects of wealth were but precarious after all; and if my father would only trust everything to her management, he should never feel himself stinted; but he, for once, was incorrigible.

What happy hours Mary and I have past, while sitting at our work by the fire, or wandering on the heath-clad hills, or idling under the weeping birch, (the only considerable tree in the garden,) talking of future happiness to ourselves and our parents, of what we would do, and see, and possess; with no firmer foundation for our goodly superstructure, than the riches that were expected to flow in upon us from the success of the worthy merchant's speculations. Our father was nearly as bad as ourselves; only, that he affected not to be so much in earnest, expressing his bright hopes and sanguine expectations in jests and playful sallies that always struck me as being exceedingly witty and pleasant. Our mother laughed with delight to see him so hopeful and happy; but still she feared he was setting his heart too much upon the matter; and once, I heard her whisper as she left the room,

'God grant he be not disappointed! I know not how he would bear it.'

Disappointed he was; and bitterly too. It came like a thunder-clap on us all that the vessel which contained our fortune had been wrecked, and gone to the bottom with all its stores, together with several of the crew, and the unfortunate merchant himself. I was grieved for him; I was grieved for the overthrow of all our air-built castles; but, with the elasticity of youth, I soon recovered the shock.

Though riches had charms, poverty had no terrors for an

inexperienced girl like me. Indeed, to say the truth, there was something exhilarating in the idea of being driven to straits, and thrown upon our own resources. I only wished papa, mama, and Mary were all of the same mind as myself and then, instead of lamenting past calamities, we might all cheerfully set to work to remedy them; and the greater the difficulties, the harder our present privations – the greater should be our cheerfulness to endure the latter, and our vigour to contend against the former.

Mary did not lament, but she brooded continually over the misfortune, and sank into a state of dejection from which no effort of mine could rouse her. I could not possibly bring her to regard the matter on its bright side as I did; and indeed I was so fearful of being charged with childish frivolity, or stupid insensibility, that I carefully kept most of my bright ideas and cheering notions to myself, well knowing they could not be appreciated.

My mother thought only of consoling my father, and paying our debts and retrenching our expenditure by every available means; but my father was completely overwhelmed by the calamity – health, strength, and spirits sunk beneath the blow; and he never wholly recovered them. In vain my mother strove to cheer him by appealing to his piety, to his courage, to his affection for herself and us. That very affection was his greatest torment: it was for our sakes he had so ardently longed to increase his fortune – it was our interest that had lent such brightness to his hopes, and that imparted such bitterness to his present distress. He now tormented himself with remorse at having neglected my mother's advice, which would at least have saved him from the additional burden of debt – he vainly reproached himself for having brought her from the dignity, the ease, the luxury of her former station to toil with him through the cares and toils of poverty. It was gall and worm-wood to his soul to see that splendid, highly accomplished woman, once so courted and admired, transformed into an active managing housewife, with hands and head continually occupied with household labours and household economy. The very willingness with which she performed these duties, the cheerfulness with which she bore her reverses, and the kindness which withheld her from imputing the smallest blame to him, were all perverted by this ingenious self-tormentor into further aggravations of his sufferings. And thus the mind preyed upon the body, and disordered the system of the nerves, and they in turn increased the troubles of the mind, till by action, and re-action, his health was seriously impaired; and not one of us could convince him that the aspect of our affairs was not half so gloomy, so utterly hopeless as his morbid imagination represented it to be.

The useful pony phaeton was sold, together with the stout well-fed pony – the old favourite that we had fully determined should end its days in peace, and never pass from our hands; the little coach-house and stable were let, the servant boy, and the more efficient (being the more expensive) of the two maid servants were dismissed. Our clothes were mended, turned, and darned to the utmost verge of decency; our food, always plain, was now simplified to an unprecedented degree – except my father's favourite dishes: our coals and candles were painfully economized – the pair of candles reduced to one, and that most sparingly used: the coals carefully husbanded in the half empty grate, especially when my father was out on his parish duties, or confined to bed through illness – then we sat with our feet on the fender, scraping the perishing embers together from time to time, and occasionally adding a slight scattering of the dust and fragments of coal, just to keep them alive. As for our carpets, they in time were worn threadbare, and patched and darned even to a greater extent than our garments. To save the expense of a gardener, Mary and I undertook to keep the garden in order; and all the cooking and household work, that could not easily be managed by one servant girl, was done by my mother and sister, with a little occasional help from me – only a little, because, though a woman in my own estimation, I was still a child in theirs; and my mother, like most active, managing women, was not gifted with very active daughters; for this reason – that being so clever and diligent herself, she was never tempted to trust her affairs to a deputy, but on the contrary, was willing to act and think for others as well as for number one; and whatever was the business in hand, she was apt to think that no one could do it so well as herself; so that whenever I offered to assist her, I received such an answer as – 'No, love, you cannot indeed – there's nothing here you can do. Go and help your sister, or get her to take a walk with you – tell her she must not sit so much, and stay so constantly in the house as she does – she may well look thin and dejected.'

'Mary, mama says I'm to help you; or get you to take a walk with me; she says you may well look thin and dejected, if you sit so constantly in the house.'

'Help me you cannot, Agnes; and I cannot go out with *you* – I have far too much to do.'

'Then let me help you.'

'You cannot indeed, dear child. Go and practise your music, or play with the kitten.'

There was always plenty of sewing on hand; but I had not been taught to cut out a single garment; and except plain hemming and seaming, there was little I could do, even in that line; for they both asserted, that it was far easier to do the work themselves, than to prepare it for me; and besides they liked better to see me prosecuting my studies, or amusing myself – it was time enough for me to sit bending over my work like a grave matron, when my favourite little pussy was become a steady old cat. Under such circumstances, although I was not many degrees more useful than the kitten, my idleness was not entirely without excuse.

Through all our troubles, I never but once heard my mother complain of our want of money. As summer was coming on, she observed to Mary and me,

'What a desirable thing it would be for your papa to spend

a few weeks at a watering place. I am convinced the sea air and the change of scene would be of incalculable service to him. But then you see there's no money,' she added with a sigh.

We both wished exceedingly that the thing might be done, and lamented greatly that it could not.

'Well, well!' said she, 'it's no use complaining. Possibly something might be done to further the project after all. Mary, you are a beautiful drawer. What do you say to doing a few more pictures, in your best style, and getting them framed, with the water-colour drawings you have already done, and trying to dispose of them to some liberal picture-dealer, who has the sense to discern their merits?'

'Mama, I should be delighted, if you think they *could* be sold; and for anything worth while.'

'It's worth while trying, however, my dear: do you procure the drawings, and I'll endeavour to find a purchaser.'

'I wish *I* could do something,' said I.

'You, Agnes! well, who knows? You draw pretty well too; if you choose some simple piece for your subject, I dare say you will be able to produce something we shall all be proud to exhibit.'

'But I have another scheme in my head, mama, and have had long ... only I did not like to mention it.'

'Indeed! pray tell us what it is.'

'I should like to be a governess.'

My mother uttered an exclamation of surprise, and laughed. My sister dropped her work in astonishment, exclaiming, '*You* a governess, Agnes! What *can* you be dreaming of?'

'Well! I don't see anything so *very* extraordinary in it. I do not pretend to be able to instruct great girls; but surely I could teach little ones ... and I should like it *so* much ... I am so fond of children. Do let me, mama!'

'But my love, you have not learnt to take care of *yourself* yet; and young children require more judgment and experience to manage than elder ones.'

'But mama, I am above eighteen, and quite able to take care of myself, and others too. You do not know half the wisdom and prudence I possess, because I have never been tried.'

'Only think,' said Mary, 'what would you do in a house full of strangers, without me or mama to speak and act for you ... with a parcel of children, besides yourself, to attend to; and no one to look to for advice? You would not even know what clothes to put on.'

'You think, because I always do as you bid me, I have no judgment of my own: but only try me – that is all I ask – and you shall see what I can do.'

At that moment my father entered, and the subject of our discussion was explained to him.

'What, my little Agnes, a governess!' cried he, and, in spite of his dejection, he laughed at the idea.

'Yes, papa, don't *you* say anything against it; I should like it *so* much; and I'm sure I could manage delightfully.'

'But, my darling, we could not spare you.' And a tear glistened in his eye as he added – 'No, no! afflicted as we are, surely we are not brought to that pass yet.'

'Oh, no!' said my mother. 'There is no necessity, whatever, for such a step; it is merely a whim of her own. So you must hold your tongue, you naughty girl, for though you are so ready to leave *us*, you know very well, we cannot part with *you*.'

I was silenced for that day, and for many succeeding ones; but still, I did not wholly relinquish my darling scheme. Mary got her drawing materials, and steadily set to work. I got mine too; but while I drew, I thought of other things.

How delightful it would be to be a governess! To go out into the world; to enter upon a new life; to act for myself; to exercise my unused faculties; to try my unknown powers; to earn my own maintenance, and something to comfort and help my father, mother, and sister, besides exonerating them from the provision of my food and clothing; to show papa what his little Agnes could do; to convince mama and Mary that I was not quite the helpless, thoughtless being they supposed. And then, how charming to be intrusted with the care and education of children! Whatever others said, I felt I was fully competent to the task: the clear remembrance of my own thoughts and feelings in early childhood would be a surer guide than the instructions of the most mature adviser. I had but to turn from my little pupils to myself at their age, and I should know, at once, how to win their confidence and affections; how to waken the contrition of the erring; how to embolden the timid, and console the afflicted; how to make Virtue practicable, Instruction desirable, and Religion lovely and comprehensible.

> ' – Delightful task!
> To teach the young idea how to shoot!'

To train the tender plants, and watch their buds unfolding day by day! Influenced by so many inducements, I determined still to persevere; though the fear of displeasing my mother, or distressing my father's feelings, prevented me from resuming the subject for several days. At length, again, I mentioned it to my mother in private, and, with some difficulty, got her to promise to assist me with her endeavours. My father's reluctant consent was next obtained, and then, though Mary still sighed her disapproval, my dear, kind mother began to look out for a situation for me. She wrote to my father's relations, and consulted the newspaper advertisements – her own relations she had long dropped all communication with – a formal interchange of occasional letters was all she had ever had since her marriage, and she would not, at any time, have applied to them in a case of this nature. But so long and so entire had been my parent's seclusion from the world, that many weeks elapsed before a suitable situation could be procured. At last, to my great joy, it was decreed that I should take charge of the young family of a certain Mrs Bloomfield, whom my kind, prim Aunt Grey had known in her youth, and asserted to be a very nice woman. Her husband was a retired tradesman, who had realized a very comfortable fortune, but could not be prevailed upon to give a greater salary than twenty-five pounds to the instructress of his children. I, however, was glad to accept this, rather than refuse the situation – which my parents were inclined to think the better plan.

But some weeks more were yet to be devoted to preparation. How long, how tedious those weeks appeared to me! Yet they were happy ones in the main – full of bright hopes, and ardent expectations. With what peculiar pleasure I assisted at the making of my new clothes, and, subsequently, the packing of my trunks! But there was a feeling of bitterness mingling with the latter occupation too – and when it was done, when all was ready for my departure on the morrow, and the last night at home approached, a sudden anguish seemed to swell my heart. My dear friends looked so sad, and spoke so very kindly, that I could scarcely keep my eyes from overflowing; but I still affected to be gay. I had taken my last ramble with Mary on the moors, my last walk in the garden, and round the house; I had fed, with her, our pet pigeons for the last time – the pretty creatures that we had tamed to peck their food from our hands. I had given a farewell stroke to all their silky backs as they crowded in my lap. I had tenderly kissed my own peculiar favourites, the pair of snow-white fantails; I had played my last tune on the old familiar piano, and sung my last song to papa; not the last, I hoped, but the last for what appeared to me a very long time; and, perhaps, when I did these things again, it would be with different feelings; circumstances might be changed, and this house might never be my settled home again.

My dear little friend, the kitten, would certainly be changed; she was already growing a fine cat; and when I returned, even for a hasty visit at Christmas, would most likely have forgotten both her playmate and her merry pranks. I had romped with her for the last time; and when I stroked her soft bright fur, while she lay purring herself to sleep in my lap, it was with a feeling of sadness I could not easily disguise. Then, at bed-time,

when I retired with Mary to our quiet little chamber, where
already my drawers were cleared out, and my share of the book-
case was empty – and where, hereafter, she would have to sleep
alone, in dreary solitude, as she expressed it, my heart sunk
more than ever: I felt as if I had been selfish and wrong to
persist in leaving her; and when I knelt once more beside our
little bed, I prayed for a blessing on her, and on my parents,
more fervently than ever I had done before. To conceal my
emotion, I buried my face in my hands, and they were presently
bathed in tears. I perceived, on rising, that she had been crying
too; but neither of us spoke; and in silence we betook ourselves
to our repose, creeping more closely together, from the consciousness that we were to part so soon.

But the morning brought a renewal of hope and spirits. I was
to depart early, that the conveyance which took me (a gig, hired
from Mr Smith, the draper, grocer, and tea-dealer of the village)
might return the same day. I rose, washed, dressed, swallowed
a hasty breakfast, received the fond embraces of my father,
mother, and sister, kissed the cat, to the great scandal of Sally,
the maid, shook hands with her, mounted the gig, drew my veil
over my face, and then, but not till then, burst into a flood
of tears.

The gig rolled on – I looked back – my dear mother and
sister were still standing at the door, looking after me, and
waving their adieux: I returned their salute, and prayed God to
bless them from my heart: we descended the hill, and I could
see them no more.

'It's a coldish mornin' for you, Miss Agnes,' observed Smith;
'and a darksome un too; but we's, happen, get to yon' spot afore
there come much rain to signify.'

'Yes, I hope so,' replied I, as calmly as I could.

'It's comed a good sup last night too.'

'Yes.'

'But this cold wind ull, happen, keep it off.'

'Perhaps it will.'

Here ended our colloquy; we crossed the valley, and began to ascend the opposite hill. As we were toiling up, I looked back again: there was the village spire, and the old grey parsonage beyond it, basking in a slanting beam of sunshine – it was but a sickly ray, but the village and surrounding hills were all in sombre shade, and I hailed the wandering beam as a propitious omen to my home. With clasped hands, I fervently implored a blessing on its inhabitants, and hastily turned away; for I saw the sunshine was departing; and I carefully avoided another glance, lest I should see it in gloomy shadow like the rest of the landscape.

CHAPTER II

FIRST LESSONS IN THE ART
OF INSTRUCTION

As we drove along, my spirits revived again, and I turned, with pleasure, to the contemplation of the new life upon which I was entering; but, though it was not far past the middle of September, the heavy clouds and strong north-easterly wind combined to render the day extremely cold and dreary, and the journey seemed a very long one, for, as Smith observed, the roads were 'very heavy;' and, certainly, his horse was very heavy too; it crawled up the hills, and crept down them, and only condescended to shake its sides in a trot, where the road was at a dead level or a very gentle slope, which was rarely the case in those rugged regions: so that it was nearly one o'clock before we reached the place of our destination. Yet, after all, when we entered the lofty iron gateway, when we drove softly up the smooth, well-rolled carriage road, with the green lawn on each side, studded with young trees, and approached the new but stately mansion of Wellwood, rising above its mushroom poplar groves, my heart failed me, and I wished it were a mile or two farther off: for the first time in my life, I must stand alone – there was no retreating now – I must enter that house, and introduce myself among its strange inhabitants – but how was it to be done? True, I was near nineteen, but, thanks to my retired life, and the protecting care of my mother and sister, I well knew that many a girl of fifteen, or under, was gifted with a more womanly address, and greater ease and self-possession, than I was. Yet, if Mrs Bloomfield were a kind, motherly woman, I might do very well after all; and the children, of course, I should soon be at ease with them – and Mr Bloomfield, I hoped, I should have but little to do with.

'Be calm, be calm, whatever happens,' I said within myself, and truly I kept this resolution so well, and was so fully occupied in steadying my nerves, and stilling the rebellious flutter of my heart, that when I was admitted into the hall, and ushered into the presence of Mrs Bloomfield, I almost forgot to answer her polite salutation; and it afterwards struck me, that the little I did say was spoken in the tone of one half dead, or half asleep. The lady too was somewhat chilly in her manner, as I discovered when I had time to reflect. She was a tall, spare, stately woman, with black hair, cold grey eyes, and extremely sallow complexion.

With due politeness, however, she shewed me my bed-room, and left me there to take off my things, desiring me afterwards, to come down and take a little refreshment. I was somewhat dismayed at my appearance on looking in the glass ... the cold wind had swelled and reddened my hands, uncurled and entangled my hair, and dyed my face of a pale purple; add to this my collar was horridly crumpled, my frock splashed with mud, my feet clad in stout new boots, and as the trunks were not brought up, there was no remedy: so having smoothed my hair as well as I could, and repeatedly twitched my obdurate collar, I proceeded to clomp down the two flights of stairs, philosophizing as I went, and with some difficulty found my way into the room where Mrs Bloomfield awaited me.

She led me into the dining-room where the family luncheon had been laid out. Some beefsteaks and half cold potatoes were set before me; and while I dined upon these, she sat opposite, watching me (as I thought), and endeavouring to sustain something like a conversation – consisting chiefly of a succession of common-place remarks, expressed with frigid formality: but this might be more my fault than hers, for I really *could* not converse. In fact, my attention was almost wholly absorbed in my dinner; not from ravenous appetite, but from distress at the toughness of the beefsteaks, and the numbness of my hands, almost palsied by their five hours exposure to the bitter wind. I would gladly have eaten the potatoes and let the meat alone, but having got a large piece of the latter on to my plate, I could not be so impolite as to leave it; so, after many awkward and unsuccessful attempts to cut it with the knife, or tear it with the fork, or pull it asunder between them, sensible that the awful lady was a spectator to the whole transaction, I at last desperately grasped the knife and fork in my fists, like a child of two years old, and fell to work with all the little strength I possessed. But this needed some apology – with a feeble attempt at a laugh, I said, 'My hands are so benumbed with the cold that I can scarcely handle my knife and fork.'

'I dare say you would find it cold,' replied she with a cool, immutable gravity that did not serve to re-assure me.

When the ceremony was concluded, she led me into the sitting-room again, where she rung and sent for the children.

'You will find them not very far advanced in their attainments,' said she, 'for I have had so little time to attend to their education myself, and we have thought them too young for a governess till now; but I think they are clever children, and very apt to learn, especially the little boy; he is, I think, the flower of the flock – a generous, noble-spirited boy, one to be led, but not driven, and remarkable for always speaking the truth. He seems to scorn deception' (this was good news.) 'His sister, Mary Ann, will require watching,' continued she, 'but she is a very good girl upon the whole: though I wish her to be kept out of the nursery, as much as possible, as she is now almost six years old, and might acquire bad habits from the nurses. I have ordered her crib to be placed in your room, and if you will be so kind as to overlook her washing and dressing, and take charge of her clothes, she need have nothing further to do with the nursery-maid.'

I replied I was quite willing to do so; and at that moment my young pupils entered the apartment with their two younger sisters. Master Tom Bloomfield was a well-grown boy of seven, with a somewhat wiry frame, flaxen hair, blue eyes, small turned-up nose, and fair complexion. Mary Ann was a tall girl too, somewhat dark like her mother, but with a round, full face, and a high colour in her cheeks. The second sister was Fanny, a very pretty little girl; Mrs Bloomfield assured me she was a remarkably gentle child, and required encouragement: she had not learnt anything yet; but in a few days, she would be four years old, and then she might take her first lesson in the alphabet, and be promoted to the school-room. The remaining one was Harriet, a little broad, fat, merry, playful thing of scarcely two, that I coveted more than all the rest – but with her I had nothing to do.

I talked to my little pupils as well as I could, and tried to render myself agreeable; but with little success I fear, for their mother's presence kept me under an unpleasant restraint. They, however, were remarkably free from shyness. They seemed bold, lively children, and I hoped I should soon be on friendly terms with them – the little boy especially, of whom I had heard such a favourable character from his mama. In Mary Ann there was a certain affected simper, and a craving for notice, that I was sorry to observe. But her brother claimed all my attention to himself: he stood bolt upright between me and the fire, with his hands behind his back, talking away like an orator, occasionally interrupting his discourse with a sharp reproof to his sisters when they made too much noise.

'O Tom, what a darling you are!' exclaimed his mother. 'Come and kiss dear mama – and then won't you show Miss Grey your school-room – and your nice new books?'

'I won't kiss *you* mama; but I *will* show Miss Grey my school-room, and my new books.'

'And *my* school-room, and *my* new books, Tom,' said Mary Ann. 'They're mine too.'

'They're *mine*,' replied he decisively. 'Come along, Miss Grey – I'll escort you.'

When the room and books had been shown, with some

bickerings between the brother and sister that I did my utmost to appease or mitigate, Mary Ann brought me her doll, and began to be very loquacious on the subject of its fine clothes, its bed, its chest of drawers, and other appurtenances; but Tom told her to hold her clamour, that Miss Grey might see his rocking-horse, which, with a most important bustle, he dragged forth from its corner into the middle of the room, loudly calling on me to attend to it. Then, ordering his sister to hold the reins, he mounted, and made me stand for ten minutes, watching how manfully he used his whip and spurs. Meantime, however, I admired Mary Ann's pretty doll, and all its possessions; and then told Master Tom he was a capital rider, but I hoped he would not use his whip and spurs so much when he rode a real pony.

'Oh yes, I will!' said he, laying on with redoubled ardour. 'I'll cut into him like smoke! Eeh! my word! but he shall sweat for it.'

This was very shocking, but I hoped in time to be able to work a reformation.

'Now you must put on your bonnet and shawl,' said the little hero, 'and I'll show you my garden.'

'And *mine*,' said Mary Ann.

Tom lifted his fist with a menacing gesture, she uttered a loud, shrill scream, ran to the other side of me, and made a face at him.

'Surely Tom, you would not strike your sister! I hope I shall *never* see you do that.'

'You will sometimes, I'm obliged to do it now and then to keep her in order.'

'But it is not your business to keep her in order, you know – that is for –'

'Well, now go and put on your bonnet.'

'I don't know – it is so very cloudy and cold, it seems likely to rain; – and you know I have had a long drive.'

'No matter – you *must* come; I shall allow of no excuses,' replied the consequential little gentleman. And as it was the first day of our acquaintance, I thought I might as well indulge him. It was too cold for Mary Ann to venture out, so she stayed with her mama, to the great relief of her brother, who liked to have me all to himself.

The garden was a large one, and tastefully laid out; besides several splendid dahlias, there were some other fine flowers still in bloom; but my companion would not give me time to examine them: I must go with him, across the wet grass, to a remote, sequestered corner, the most important place in the grounds – because it contained *his* garden. There were two round beds, stocked with a variety of plants. In one, there was a pretty little rose tree. I paused to admire its lovely blossoms.

'Oh, never mind that!' said he contemptuously. 'That's only *Mary Ann's* garden: look, THIS is mine.'

After I had observed every flower, and listened to a disquisition on every plant, I was permitted to depart; but first, with great pomp, he plucked a polyanthus and presented it to me, as one conferring a prodigious favour. I observed, on the grass about his garden, certain apparatus of sticks and cord, and asked what they were.

'Traps for birds.'

'Why do you catch them?'

'Papa says they do harm.'

'And what do you do with them, when you catch them?'

'Different things. Sometimes I give them to the cat; sometimes I cut them in pieces with my penknife; but the next, I mean to roast alive.'

'And why do you mean to do such a horrible thing?'

'For two reasons; first, to see how long it will live – and then, to see what it will taste like.'

'But don't you know it is extremely wicked to do such things? Remember, the birds can feel as well as you, and think, how would you like it yourself?'

'Oh, that's nothing! I'm not a bird, and I can't feel what I do to them.'

'But you will have to feel it sometime, Tom – you have heard where wicked people go to when they die; and if you don't leave off torturing innocent birds, remember, you will have to go there, and suffer just what you have made them suffer.'

'Oh, pooh! I shan't. Papa knows how I treat them, and he never blames me for it; he says it's just what *he* used to do when *he* was a boy. Last Summer he gave me a nest full of young sparrows, and he saw me pulling off their legs and wings and heads, and never said anything, except that they were nasty things, and I must not let them soil my trousers; and uncle Robson was there too, and he laughed, and said I was a fine boy.'

'But what would your mama say?'

'Oh! she doesn't care – she says it's a pity to kill the pretty singing birds, but the naughty sparrows, and mice and rats, I may do what I like with. So now, Miss Grey, you see it is *not* wicked.'

'I still think it is, Tom; and perhaps your papa and mama would think so too, if they thought much about it. However,' I internally added, 'they may say what they please, but I am determined you shall do nothing of the kind, as long as I have power to prevent it.'

He next took me across the lawn to see his mole-traps, and then into the stack-yard to see his weasel-traps, one of which, to his great joy, contained a dead weasel; and then into the stable to see, not the fine carriage horses, but a little rough colt, which he informed me had been bred on purpose for him, and he was to ride it as soon as it was properly trained.

I tried to amuse the little fellow, and listened to all his chatter as complacently as I could; for I thought if he had any affections at all, I would endeavour to win them; and then, in time, I might be able to show him the error of his ways; but I looked in vain for that generous, noble spirit, his mother talked of; though I could see he was not without a certain degree of quickness and penetration, when he chose to exert it.

When we re-entered the house it was nearly tea-time. Master

Tom told me that, as papa was from home, he and I and Mary Ann were to have tea with mama for a treat; for, on such occasions, she always dined at luncheon time with them, instead of at six o'clock. Soon after tea, Mary Ann went to bed, but Tom favoured us with his company and conversation till eight. After he was gone, Mrs Bloomfield further enlightened me on the subject of her children's dispositions and acquirements, and on what they were to learn, and how they were to be managed, and cautioned me to mention their defects to no one but herself. My mother had warned me before, to mention them as little as possible to *her*, for people did not like to be told of their children's faults, and so I concluded I was to keep silence on them altogether. About half past nine, Mrs Bloomfield invited me to partake a frugal supper of cold meat and bread. I was glad when that was over, and she took her bed-room candlestick and retired to rest; for though I wished to be pleased with her, her company was extremely irksome to me, and I could not help feeling that she was cold, grave, and forbidding – the very opposite of the kind, warm-hearted matron my hopes had depicted her to be.

CHAPTER III

A FEW MORE LESSONS

I ROSE, NEXT MORNING, with a feeling of hopeful exhilaration, in spite of the disappointments already experienced; but I found the dressing of Mary Ann was no light matter, as her abundant hair was to be smeared with pomade, plaited in three long tails, and tied with bows of ribbon, a task my unaccustomed fingers found great difficulty in performing. She told me her nurse could do it in half the time, and, by keeping up a constant fidget of impatience, contrived to render me still longer. When all was done, we went into the school-room, where I met my other pupil, and chatted with the two till it was time to go down to breakfast. That meal being concluded, and a few civil words having been exchanged with Mrs Bloomfield, we repaired to the school-room again, and commenced the business of the day. I found my pupils very backward indeed; but Tom, though averse to every species of mental exertion, was not without abilities. Mary Ann could scarcely read a word, and was so careless and inattentive, that I could hardly get on with her at all. However, by dint of great labour and patience, I managed to get something done in the course of the morning, and then accompanied my young charge out into the garden and adjacent grounds, for a little recreation before dinner. There we got along tolerably together, except that I found they had no notion of going with *me*; I must go with *them* wherever they chose to lead me. I must run, walk, or stand exactly as it suited their fancy. This, I thought, was reversing the order of things; and I found it doubly disagreeable, as on this as well as subsequent occasions, they seemed to prefer the dirtiest places, and the most dismal occupations. But there was no remedy; either I must follow them, or keep entirely apart from them, and thus appear neglectful of my charge. To-day, they manifested a particular attachment to a well at the bottom of the lawn, where they persisted in dabbling with sticks and pebbles, for above half an hour. I was in constant fear that their mother would see them from the window, and blame me for allowing them thus to draggle their clothes, and wet their feet and hands, instead of taking exercise; but no arguments, commands, or intreaties could draw them away. If *she* did not see them some one else did – a gentleman on horseback had entered the gate, and was proceeding up the road; at the distance of a few paces from us, he paused, and calling to the children in a waspish penetrating tone, bade them 'keep out of that water.' 'Miss Grey,' said he, '(I suppose it *is* Miss Grey) I am surprised that you should allow them to dirty their clothes, in that manner – Don't you see how Miss Bloomfield has soiled her frock? – and that Master Bloomfield's socks are quite wet? – and both of them without gloves! Dear! dear! Let me *request* that in future you will keep them *decent*, at least!' so saying, he turned away, and continued his ride up to the house. This was Mr Bloomfield. I was surprised that he should nominate his children Master and Miss Bloomfield, and still more so, that he should speak so uncivilly to me – their governess, and a perfect stranger to himself. Presently the bell rung to summon us in. I dined with the children at one, while he and his lady took their luncheon at the same table. His conduct there did not greatly raise him in my estimation. He was a man of ordinary stature – rather below than above, and rather thin than stout, apparently between thirty and forty years of age: he had a large mouth, pale, dingy complexion, milky blue eyes, and hair the colour of a hempen cord. There was a roast leg of mutton before him: he helped Mrs Bloomfield, the children, and me, desiring me to cut up the children's meat, then, after twisting about the mutton in various directions, and eyeing it from different points, he pronounced it not fit to be eaten, and called for the cold beef.

'What is the matter with the mutton, my dear?' asked his mate.

'It is quite overdone. Don't you taste, Mrs Bloomfield, that all the goodness is roasted out of it? And can't you see that all that nice, red gravy is completely dried away?'

'Well, I think the *beef* will suit you.'

The beef was set before him, and he began to carve, but with the most rueful expressions of discontent.

'What is the matter with the *beef*, Mr Bloomfield? I'm sure I thought it was very nice.'

'And so it *was* very nice. A nicer joint could not be; but it is *quite* spoiled,' replied he, dolefully.

'How so?'

'How so! Why, don't you see how it is cut? Dear – dear! it is quite shocking!'

'They must have cut it wrong in the kitchen then, for I'm sure I carved it quite properly here, yesterday.'

'No *doubt* they cut it wrong in the kitchen – the savages! Dear – dear! Did ever anyone see such a fine piece of beef so completely ruined? But remember that, in future, when a decent dish leaves this table, they shall not *touch* it in the kitchen. Remember *that*, Mrs Bloomfield!'

Notwithstanding the ruinous state of the beef, the gentleman managed to cut himself some delicate slices, part of which he ate in silence. When he next spoke it was, in a less querulous tone, to ask what there was for dinner.

'Turkey and grouse,' was the concise reply.

'And what besides?'

'Fish.'

'What kind of fish?'

'I don't know.'

'*You don't know?*' cried he, looking solemnly up from his plate, and suspending his knife and fork in astonishment.

'No. I told the cook to get some fish – I did not particularize what.'

'Well, that beats every thing! A lady professes to keep house, and doesn't even know what fish is for dinner! professes to order fish, and doesn't specify what!'

'Perhaps, Mr Bloomfield, you will order dinner yourself in future.'

Nothing more was said; and I was very glad to get out of the room with my pupils; for I never felt so ashamed and uncomfortable in my life, for anything that was not my own fault.

In the afternoon we applied to lessons again; then went out again; then had tea in the school-room; then I dressed Mary Ann for dessert; and when she and her brother were gone down to the dining-room, I took the opportunity of beginning a letter to my dear friends at home; but the children came up before I had half completed it.

At seven, I had to put Mary Ann to bed; then I played with Tom till eight, when he too went, and I finished my letter, and unpacked my clothes, which I had hitherto found no opportunity for doing, and, finally, went to bed myself.

But this is a very favourable specimen of a day's proceedings.

My task of instruction and surveillance, instead of becoming easier as my charge and I got better accustomed to each other, became more arduous as their characters unfolded. The name of governess, I soon found, was a mere mockery as applied to me; my pupils had no more notion of obedience than a wild, unbroken colt. The habitual fear of their father's peevish temper, and the dread of the punishments he was wont to inflict when irritated, kept them generally within bounds in his immediate presence. The girls, too, had some fear of their mother's anger; and the boy might occasionally be bribed to do as she bid him by the hope of reward; but I had no rewards to offer, and as for punishments, I was given to understand, the parents reserved that privilege to themselves; and yet they expected me to keep my pupils in order. Other children might be guided by the fear of anger, and the desire of approbation; but neither the one nor the other had any effect upon these.

Master Tom, not content with refusing to be ruled, must needs set up as a ruler, and manifested a determination to keep, not only his sisters, but his governess in order, by violent manual and pedal applications; and, as he was a tall, strong boy of his years, this occasioned no trifling inconvenience. A few sound boxes in the ear, on such occasions, might have settled the matter easily enough: but as, in that case, he might make up some story to his mother, which she would be sure to believe, as she had such unshaken faith in his veracity – though I had already discovered it to be by no means unimpeachable – I determined to refrain from striking him even in self-defence; and, in his most violent moods, my only resource was to throw him on his back, and hold his hands and feet till the frenzy was somewhat abated.

To the difficulty of preventing him from doing what he ought not, was added that of forcing him to do what he ought. Often he would positively refuse to learn, or to repeat his lessons, or even to look at his book. Here again, a good birch rod might have been serviceable; but, as my powers were so limited, I must make the best use of what I had. As there were no settled hours for study and play, I resolved to give my pupils a certain task, which, with moderate attention, they could perform in a short time; and till this was done, however weary I was, or however perverse they might be, nothing short of parental interference should induce me to suffer them to leave the school-room; even if I should sit with my chair against the door to keep them in. Patience, Firmness, and Perseverance were my only weapons; and these I resolved to use to the utmost.

I determined always strictly to fulfil the threats and promises I made; and to that end, I must be cautious to threaten and promise nothing that I could not perform. Then, I would carefully refrain from all useless irritability and indulgence of my own ill-temper: when they behaved tolerably, I would be as kind and obliging as it was in my power to be, in order to make the widest possible distinction between good and bad conduct; I would reason with them, too, in the simplest and most effective manner. When I reproved them, or refused to gratify their wishes, after a glaring fault, it should be more in sorrow than in anger: their little hymns and prayers I would make plain and clear to their understanding; when they said their prayers at night, and asked pardon for their offences, I would remind them of the sins of the past day, solemnly, but in perfect kindness, to avoid raising a spirit of opposition; penitential hymns should be said by the naughty, cheerful ones by the comparatively good; and every kind of instruction I would convey to them, as much as possible, by entertaining discourse – apparently with no other object than their present amusement in view.

By these means I hoped, in time, both to benefit the children, and to gain the approbation of their parents; and also to convince my friends at home that I was not so wanting in skill and prudence as they supposed. I knew the difficulties I had to contend with were great; but I knew, (at least, I believed,) unremitting patience and perseverance could overcome them, and night and morning I implored Divine assistance to this end. But either the children were so incorrigible, the parents so unreasonable, or myself so mistaken in my views, or so unable to carry them out, that my best intentions and most strenuous efforts seemed productive of no better result, than sport to the children, dissatisfaction to their parents, and torment to myself.

The task of instruction was as arduous for the body as the mind. I had to run after my pupils, to catch them, to carry, or drag them to the table, and often forcibly to hold them there, till the lesson was done. Tom, I frequently put into a corner, seating myself before him in a chair, with the book which contained the little task that must be said or read, before he was released, in my hand. He was not strong enough to push both me and the chair away; so he would stand twisting his body and face into the most grotesque and singular contortions – laughable, no doubt, to an unconcerned spectator, but not to me – and uttering loud yells and doleful outcries, intended to represent weeping, but wholly without the accompaniment of tears. I knew this was done solely for the purpose of annoying me; and, therefore, however I might inwardly tremble with impatience and irritation, I manfully strove to suppress all visible signs of molestation, and affected to sit, with calm indifference, waiting till it should please him to cease this pastime, and prepare for a run in the garden, by casting his eye on the book, and reading or repeating the few words he was required to say.

Sometimes he would determine to do his writing badly; and I had to hold his hand to prevent him from purposely blotting or disfiguring the paper. Frequently I threatened that, if he did not do better, he should have another line: then he would stubbornly refuse to write this line; and I, to save my word, had finally to resort to the expedient of holding his fingers upon the pen, and forcibly drawing his hand up and down till, in spite of his resistance, the line was in some sort completed.

Yet Tom was by no means the most unmanageable of my pupils: sometimes, to my great joy, he would have the sense to see that his wisest policy was to finish his tasks, and go out and amuse himself till I and his sisters came to join him, which, frequently, was not at all, for Mary Ann seldom followed his example in this particular. She apparently preferred rolling on the floor to any other amusement. Down she would drop like a leaden weight; and when I, with great difficulty, had succeeded in rooting her thence, I had still to hold her up with one arm, while, with the other, I held the book from which she was to read or spell her lesson. As the dead weight of the big girl of six became too heavy for one arm to bear, I transferred it to the other; or, if both were weary of the burden, I carried her into a corner, and told her she might come out when she should find the use of her feet, and stand up; but she generally preferred lying there like a log till dinner or tea time, when, as I could not deprive her of her meals, she must be liberated, and would come crawling out with a grin of triumph on her round, red face.

Often she would stubbornly refuse to pronounce some particular word in her lesson; and I now regret the lost labour I have had in striving to conquer her obstinacy. If I had passed it over as a matter of no consequence, it would have been better for both parties than vainly striving to overcome it, as I did; but I thought it my absolute duty to crush this vicious tendency in the bud; and so it was, if I could have done it: and, had my powers been less limited, I might have enforced obedience; but as it was, it was but a trial of strength between her and me, in which she generally came off victorious; and every victory served to encourage and strengthen her for a future contest.

In vain I argued, coaxed, entreated, threatened, scolded; in vain I kept her in from play, or, if obliged to take her out, refused to play with her, or to speak kindly, or have anything to do with her; in vain I tried to set before her the advantages of doing as she was bid, and being loved, and kindly treated in consequence, and the disadvantages of persisting in her absurd perversity. Sometimes, when she asked me to do something for her, I would answer –

'Yes, I will, Mary Ann, if you will only say that word. Come! you'd better say it at once, and have no more trouble about it.'

'No.'

'Then, of course, I can do nothing for you!'

With me, at her age, or under, neglect and disgrace were the most dreadful of punishments; but on her they made no impression.

Sometimes, exasperated to the utmost pitch, I would shake her violently by the shoulders, or pull her long hair, or put her in the corner, – for which she punished me with loud, shrill, piercing screams, that went through my head like a knife. She knew I hated this, and when she had shrieked her utmost, would look into my face with an air of vindictive satisfaction, exclaiming –

'*Now* then! *that's* for you!'

And then shriek again and again, till I was forced to stop my ears. Often these dreadful cries would bring Mrs Bloomfield up to inquire what was the matter?

'Mary Ann is a naughty girl, ma'am.'

'But what are these shocking screams?'

'She is screaming in a passion.'

'I never heard such a dreadful noise! You might be killing her. Why is she not out with her brother?'

'I cannot get her to finish her lessons.'

'But Mary Ann must be a *good* girl, and finish her lessons.' This was blandly spoken to the child. 'And I hope I shall *never* hear such terrible cries again!'

And fixing her cold, stony eyes upon me with a look that could not be mistaken, she would shut the door, and walk away.

Sometimes I would try to take the little obstinate creature by surprise, and casually ask her the word while she was thinking of something else: frequently she would begin to say it, and then suddenly check herself, with a provoking look that seemed to say, 'Ah! I'm too sharp for you; you shan't trick it out of me either.'

On another occasion, I pretended to forget the whole affair; and talked and played with her as usual, till night, when I put her to bed; then bending over her, while she lay all smiles and good-humour, just before departing, I said, as cheerfully and kindly as before –

'Now, Mary Ann, just tell me that word before I kiss you good night: you are a good girl now, and, of course, you will say it.'

'No, I won't.'

'Then I can't kiss you!'

'Well, I don't care.'

In vain I expressed my sorrow; in vain I lingered for some symptom of contrition; she really 'didn't care,' and I left her alone, and in darkness, wondering most of all at this last proof of insensate stubbornness. In *my* childhood I could not imagine a more afflictive punishment, than for my mother to refuse to

kiss me at night: the very idea was terrible; more than the idea
I never felt, for, happily, I never committed a crime that was
deemed worthy of such a penalty; but once, I remember, for
some transgression of my sister's, our mother thought proper
to inflict it upon her; what *she* felt, I cannot tell; but my sympathetic tears and suffering for her sake, I shall not soon forget.

Another troublesome trait in Mary Ann, was her incorrigible
propensity to keep running into the nursery to play with her
little sisters and the nurse. This was natural enough, but, as it
was against her mother's express desire, I, of course, forbade her
to do so, and did my utmost to keep her with me, but that only
increased her relish for the nursery; and the more I strove to
keep her out of it, the oftener she went, and the longer she
stayed; to the great dissatisfaction of Mrs Bloomfield, who,
I well knew, would impute all the blame of the matter to me.

Another of my trials was the dressing in the morning: at one
time she would not be washed; at another she would not be
dressed, unless she might wear some particular frock that, I
knew, her mother would not like her to have; at another she
would scream, and run away if I attempted to touch her hair.
So that frequently when, after much trouble and toil, I had at
length succeeded in bringing her down, the breakfast was nearly
half over; and black looks from 'mama,' and testy observations
from 'papa,' spoken at me, if not to me, were sure to be my
meed; for few things irritated the latter so much as want of
punctuality at meal-times.

Then, among the minor annoyances, was my inability to
satisfy Mrs Bloomfield with her daughter's dress; and the child's
hair 'was never fit to be seen.' Sometimes, as a powerful reproach
to me, she would perform the office of tire-woman herself, and
then complain bitterly of the trouble it gave her.

When little Fanny came into the school-room, I hoped *she*
would be mild and inoffensive at least; but a few days, if not a
few hours, sufficed to destroy the illusion: I found her a mischievous, intractable little creature, given up to falsehood and

deception, young as she was, and alarmingly fond of exercising her two favourite weapons of offence and defence: that of spitting in the faces of those who incurred her displeasure, and bellowing like a bull when her unreasonable desires were not gratified. As she, generally, was pretty quiet in her parents' presence, and they were impressed with the notion of her being a remarkably gentle child, her falsehoods were readily believed, and her loud uproars led them to suspect harsh and injudicious treatment on my part; and when, at length, her bad disposition became manifest, even to their prejudiced eyes, I felt that the whole was attributed to me.

'What a naughty girl Fanny is getting,' Mrs Bloomfield would say to her spouse. 'Don't you observe, my dear, how she is altered since she entered the school-room? She will soon be as bad as the other two; and, I am sorry to say, they have quite deteriorated of late.'

'You may say that,' was the answer. 'I've been thinking that same myself. I thought when we got them a governess they'd improve; but, instead of that, they get worse and worse: I don't know how it is with their learning; but their habits, I know, make no sort of improvement; they get rougher, and dirtier, and more unseemly every day.'

I knew this was all pointed at me; and these and all similar innuendos affected me far more deeply than any open accusations would have done; for, against the latter, I should have been roused to speak in my own defence: now, I judged it my wisest plan to subdue every resentful impulse, suppress every sensitive shrinking, and go on perseveringly doing my best; for, irksome as my situation was, I earnestly wished to retain it. I thought, if I could struggle on with unremitting firmness and integrity, the children would, in time, become more humanized: every month would contribute to make them some little wiser, and, consequently, more manageable; for a child of nine or ten, as frantic and ungovernable as these at six and seven would be a maniac.

I flattered myself I was benefiting my parents and sister by my continuance here; for, small as the salary was, I still was earning something, and, with strict economy, I could easily manage to have something to spare for them, if they would favour me by taking it. Then, it was by my own will that I had got the place, I had brought all this tribulation on myself, and I was determined to bear it; nay, more than that, I did not even regret the step I had taken, and I longed to show my friends that, even now, I was competent to undertake the charge, and able to acquit myself honourably to the end; and if ever I felt it degrading to submit so quietly, or intolerable to toil so constantly, I would turn towards my home, and say within myself –

'They may crush, but they shall not subdue me;
'Tis of thee that I think, not of them.'

About Christmas I was allowed a visit home, but only of a fortnight's duration.

'For,' said Mrs Bloomfield, 'I thought, as you had seen your friends so lately, you would not care for a longer stay.'

I left her to think so still; but she little knew how long, how wearisome those fourteen weeks of absence had been to me, how intensely I had longed for my holidays, how greatly I was disappointed at their curtailment. Yet she was not to blame in this; I had never told her my feelings, and she could not be expected to divine them; I had not been with her a full term, and she was justified in not allowing me a full vacation.

CHAPTER IV

THE GRANDMAMMA

I SPARE MY READERS the account of my delight on coming home, my happiness while there – enjoying a brief space of rest and liberty in that dear, familiar place, among the loving and the loved – and my sorrow on being obliged to bid them, once more, a long adieu.

I returned, however, with unabated vigour to my work – a more arduous task than any one can imagine, who has not felt something like the misery of being charged with the care and direction of a set of mischievous, turbulent rebels, whom his utmost exertions cannot bind to their duty, while, at the same time, he is responsible for their conduct to a higher power, who exacts from him what cannot be achieved without the aid of the superior's more potent authority, which, either from indolence, or the fear of becoming unpopular with the said rebellious gang, the latter refuses to give. I can conceive few situations more harassing than that wherein, however you may long for success, however you may labour to fulfil your duty, your efforts are baffled and set at naught by those beneath you, and unjustly censured and misjudged by those above.

I have not enumerated half the vexatious propensities of my pupils, or half the troubles resulting from my heavy responsibilities, for fear of trespassing too much upon the reader's patience, as, perhaps, I have already done; but my design, in writing the few last pages, was not to amuse, but to benefit those whom it might concern: he that has no interest in such matters will doubtless have skipped them over with a cursory glance, and, perhaps, a malediction against the prolixity of the writer; but, if a parent has, therefrom, gathered any useful hint, or an unfortunate governess received thereby the slightest benefit, I am well rewarded for my pains.

To avoid trouble and confusion, I have taken my pupils one by one, and discussed their various qualities; but this can give no adequate idea of being worried by the whole three together, when, as was often the case, all were determined to 'be naughty, and to tease Miss Grey, and put her in a passion.'

Sometimes, on such occasions, the thought has suddenly occurred to me – 'If *they* could see me now!' meaning, of course, my friends at home, and the idea of how they would pity me, has made me pity myself – so greatly that I have had the utmost difficulty to restrain my tears; but I have restrained them, till my little tormentors were gone to dessert, or cleared off to bed, (my only prospects of deliverance,) and then, in all the bliss of solitude, I have given myself up to the luxury of an unrestricted burst of weeping. But this was a weakness I did not often indulge: my employments were too numerous, my leisure moments were too precious, to admit of much time being given to fruitless lamentations.

I particularly remember one wild, snowy afternoon, soon after my return in January – the children had all come up from dinner, loudly declaring that they meant 'to be naughty;' and they had well kept their resolution, though I had talked myself hoarse, and wearied every muscle in my throat, in the vain attempt to reason them out of it. I had got Tom pinned up in a corner, whence, I told him, he should not escape till he had done his appointed task. Meantime, Fanny had possessed herself of my work-bag, and was rifling its contents – and spitting into it besides. I told her to let it alone, but to no purpose, of course.

'Burn it, Fanny!' cried Tom; and *this* command she hastened to obey. I sprang to snatch it from the fire, and Tom darted to the door.

'Mary Ann, throw her desk out of the window!' cried he, and my precious desk, containing my letters and papers, my small amount of cash, and all my valuables, was about to be precipitated from the three-story window. I flew to rescue it. Meanwhile Tom had left the room, and was rushing down the stairs, followed by Fanny. Having secured my desk, I ran to catch them, and Mary Ann came scampering after. All three escaped me, and ran out of the house into the garden, where they plunged about in the snow, shouting and screaming in exultant glee.

What must I do? If I followed them, I should probably be unable to capture one, and only drive them farther away; if I did not, how was I to get them in? and what would their parents think of me, if they saw or heard the children rioting, hatless, bonnetless, gloveless, and bootless, in the deep, soft snow?

While I stood in this perplexity, just without the door, trying, by grim looks and angry words, to awe them into subjection, I heard a voice behind me, in harshly piercing tones, exclaiming,

'Miss Grey! Is it possible! What in the d—l's name, can you be thinking about?'

'I can't get them in, sir,' said I, turning round, and beholding Mr Bloomfield, with his hair on end and his pale blue eyes bolting from their sockets.

'But I INSIST upon their being got in!' cried he, approaching nearer, and looking perfectly ferocious.

'Then sir, you must call them yourself if you please, for they won't listen to me,' I replied, stepping back.

'Come in with you, you filthy brats; or I'll horsewhip you every one!' roared he; and the children instantly obeyed. 'There, you see! they come at the first word!'

'Yes, when *you* speak.'

'And it's very strange, that when you've the care of 'em, you've no better control over 'em than that! – Now there they are – gone up-stairs with their nasty, snowy feet! Do go after 'em and see them made decent, for Heaven's sake!'

That gentleman's mother was then staying in the house; and as I ascended the stairs, and passed the drawing-room door,

I had the satisfaction of hearing the old lady declaiming aloud to her daughter-in-law to this effect (for I could only distinguish the most emphatic words),

'Gracious Heavens!—never in all my life—! —get their death as sure as—! Do you think my dear she's a *proper person* –? Take my word for it—'

I heard no more; but that sufficed.

The senior Mrs Bloomfield had been very attentive and civil to me; and till now, I had thought her a nice, kind-hearted, chatty old body. She would often come to me and talk in a confidential strain, nodding, and shaking her head, and gesticulating with hands and eyes, as a certain class of old ladies are wont to do, though I never knew one that carried the peculiarity to so great an extent: she would even sympathise with me for the trouble I had with the children, and express at times, by half sentences, interspersed with nods and knowing winks, her sense of the injudicious conduct of their mama in so restricting my power, and neglecting to support me with her authority. Such a mode of testifying disapprobation was not much to my taste; and I generally refused to take it in, or understand anything more than was openly spoken; at least, I never went farther than an implied acknowledgment that, if matters were otherwise ordered, my task would be a less difficult one, and I should be better able to guide and instruct my charge; but now I must be doubly cautious. Hitherto, though I saw the old lady had her defects, (of which one was a proneness to proclaim her perfections,) I had always been wishful to excuse them, and to give her credit for all the virtues she professed, and even imagine others yet untold. Kindness, which had been the food of my life through so many years, had lately been so entirely denied me, that I welcomed with grateful joy the slightest semblance of it. No wonder then that my heart warmed to the old lady, and always gladdened at her approach, and regretted her departure.

But now the few words, luckily or unluckily heard in passing, had wholly revolutionized my ideas respecting her; now I looked upon her as hypocritical and insincere, a flatterer, and a spy upon my words and deeds. Doubtless it would have been my interest still to meet her with the same cheerful smile, and tone of respectful cordiality as before; but I could not, if I would; my manner altered with my feelings, and became so cold and shy that she could not fail to notice it. She soon did notice it, and *her* manner altered too: – the familiar nod was changed to a stiff bow, the gracious smile gave place to a glare of gorgon ferocity, her vivacious loquacity was entirely transferred from me to the 'darling boy and girls,' whom she flattered and indulged more absurdly than ever their mother had done.

I confess I was somewhat troubled at this change: I feared the consequences of her displeasure, and even made some efforts to recover the ground I had lost – and with better apparent success than I could have anticipated. At one time, I, merely in common civility, asked after her cough – immediately her long visage relaxed into a smile, and she favoured me with a particular history of that and her other infirmities, followed by an account of her pious resignation, delivered in the usual emphatic, declamatory style which no writing can pourtray.

'But there's one remedy for all, my dear, and that's resignation,' (a toss of the head) 'resignation to the will of Heaven!' (an uplifting of hands and eyes.) 'It has always supported me through all my trials, and always will do.' (a succession of nods.) 'But then, it isn't everybody that can say that,' (a shake of the head), 'but I'm one of the pious ones, Miss Grey!' (a very significant nod and toss) 'And, thank Heaven, I always was,' (another nod) 'and I glory in it!' (an emphatic clasping of the hands and shaking of the head) and with several texts of scripture, misquoted or misapplied, and religious exclamations so redolent of the ludicrous in the style of delivery, and manner of bringing in, if not in the expressions themselves, that I decline repeating them, she withdrew, tossing her large head in high good-humour – with herself at least – and left me hoping that, after all, she was rather weak than wicked.

At her next visit to Wellwood House, I went so far as to say I was glad to see her looking so well. The effect of this was magical: the words, intended as a mark of civility, were received as a flattering compliment; her countenance brightened up, and from that moment she became as gracious and benign as heart could wish – in outward semblance at least; and from what I now saw of her, and what I heard from the children, I knew that in order to gain her cordial friendship, I had but to utter a word of flattery at each convenient opportunity; but this was against my principles; and for lack of this, the capricious old dame soon deprived me of her favour again, and I believe did me much secret injury.

She could not greatly influence her daughter-in-law against me, because between that lady and herself there was a mutual dislike – chiefly shewn by her in secret detractions and calumniations, by the other, in an excess of frigid formality in her demeanour; and no fawning flattery of the elder could thaw away the wall of ice which the younger interposed between them. But with her son the old lady had better success: he would listen to all she had to say, provided she could soothe his fretful temper, and refrain from irritating him by her own asperities; and I have reason to believe, that she considerably strengthened his prejudice against me. She would tell him that I shamefully neglected the children, and even his wife did not attend to them as she ought, and that he must look after them himself or they would all go to ruin.

Thus urged, he would frequently give himself the trouble of watching them from the windows during their play; at times, he would follow them through the grounds, and too often came suddenly upon them while they were dabbling in the forbidden well, talking to the coachman in the stables, or revelling in the filth of the farm-yard – and I meanwhile stupidly standing by, having previously exhausted my energy in vain attempts to get them away; often too he would unexpectedly pop his head into the school-room while the young people were at meals and find them spilling their milk over the table and themselves, plunging their fingers into their own or each other's mugs, or quarrelling over their victuals like a set of tiger's cubs. If I were quiet at the moment, I was conniving at their disorderly conduct, if, (as was frequently the case,) I happened to be exalting my voice to enforce order, I was using undue violence, and setting the girls a bad example by such ungentleness of tone and language.

I remember one afternoon in Spring, when, owing to the rain, they could not go out; but, by some amazing good fortune, they had all finished their lessons, and yet abstained from running down to tease their parents – a trick that annoyed me greatly, but which, on rainy days, I seldom could prevent their doing; because, below, they found novelty and amusement – especially when visiters were in the house; and their mother, though she bid me keep them in the school-room, would never chide them for leaving it, or trouble herself to send them back; but to-day they appeared satisfied with their present abode, and what is more wonderful still, seemed disposed to play together without depending on me for amusement, and without quarrelling with each other. Their occupation was a somewhat puzzling one: they were all squatted together on the floor by the window, over a heap of broken toys, and a quantity of birds' eggs, or rather egg-shells, for the contents had luckily been abstracted; these shells they had broken up, and were pounding into small fragments, to what end, I could not imagine; but, so long as they were quiet, and not in positive mischief, I did not care; and, with a feeling of unusual repose, I sat by the fire, putting the finishing stitches to a frock for Mary Ann's doll, intending, when that was done, to begin a letter to my mother. But, suddenly, the door opened, and the dingy head of Mr Bloomfield looked in.

'All very quiet here! What are you doing?' said he.

'No harm *to-day*, at least,' thought I.

But he was of a different opinion. Advancing to the window, and seeing the children's occupation, he testily exclaimed –

'What in the world are you about?'

'We're grinding egg-shells, papa!' cried Tom.

'How *dare* you make such a mess, you little d—ls? Don't you see what confounded work you're making of the carpet?' (the carpet was a plain, brown drugget.) 'Miss Grey, did you know what they were doing?'

'Yes, sir.'

'*You knew* it?'

'Yes.'

'You *knew* it! and you actually sat there, and permitted them to go on, without a word of reproof!'

'I didn't think they were doing any harm.'

'Any harm! Why look there! Just look at that carpet, and see – was there ever anything like it in a Christian house before? No wonder your room is not fit for a pigsty – no wonder your pupils are worse than a litter of pigs! – no wonder – Oh! I declare, it puts me quite past my patience!' and he departed, shutting the door after him with a bang that made the children laugh.

'It puts *me* quite past my patience too!' muttered I, getting up; and, seizing the poker, I dashed it repeatedly into the cinders, and stirred them up with unwonted energy; thus easing my irritation, under pretence of mending the fire.

After this, Mr Bloomfield was continually looking in to see if the school-room was in order; and, as the children were continually littering the floor with fragments of toys, sticks, stones, stubble, leaves, and other rubbish which I could not prevent their bringing, or oblige them to gather up, and which the servants refused to 'clean after them,' I had to spend a considerable portion of my valuable leisure moments on my knees upon the floor, in painfully reducing things to order. Once I told them that they should not taste their supper till they had picked up everything from the carpet; Fanny might have hers when she had taken up a certain quantity, Mary Ann, when she had gathered twice as many, and Tom was to clear away the rest.

Wonderful to state, the girls did their part; but Tom was in such a fury that he flew upon the table, scattered the bread and milk about the floor, struck his sisters, kicked the coals out of the coal-pan, attempted to overthrow the table and chairs, and seemed inclined to make a Douglas-larder of the whole contents of the room; but I seized upon him, and, sending Mary Ann to call her mama, held him in spite of kicks, blows, yells, and execrations, till Mrs Bloomfield made her appearance.

'What is the matter with my boy?' said she.

And when the matter was explained to her, all she did was to send for the nursery-maid to put the room in order, and bring Master Bloomfield his supper.

'There now,' cried Tom, triumphantly, looking up from his viands with his mouth almost too full for speech. 'There now, Miss Grey! you see I have got my supper in spite of you: and I haven't picked up a single thing!'

The only person in the house who had any real sympathy for me was the nurse; for she had suffered like afflictions, though in a smaller degree, as she had not the task of teaching, nor was she so responsible for the conduct of her charge.

'Oh, Miss Grey!' she would say, 'you have some trouble with them childer!'

'I have indeed, Betty; and I dare say you know what it is.'

'Ay, I do so! But I don't vex myself o'er 'em as you do. And then, you see, I hit 'em a slap sometimes; and them little uns – I gives 'em a good whipping now and then – there's nothing else ull do for 'em, as what they say. Howsever, I've lost my place for it.'

'Have you, Betty? I heard you were going to leave.'

'Eh, bless you, yes! Missis gave me warning a three-wik sin'. She told me afore Christmas how it mud be, if I hit 'em again; but I couldn't hold my hand off 'em at nothing – I know not how *you* do, for Miss Mary Ann's worse by the half nor her sisters!'

CHAPTER V

THE UNCLE

Besides the old lady, there was another relative of the family, whose visits were a great annoyance to me – this was 'uncle Robson,' Mrs Bloomfield's brother, a tall, self-sufficient fellow, with dark hair and sallow complexion like his sister, a nose that seemed to disdain the earth, and little grey eyes, frequently half closed, with a mixture of real stupidity and affected contempt of all surrounding objects. He was a thick-set, strongly built man, but he had found some means of compressing his waist into a remarkably small compass, and that, together with the unnatural stiffness of his form, showed that the lofty-minded, manly Mr Robson, the scorner of the female sex, was not above the foppery of stays.

He seldom deigned to notice me; and, when he did, it was with a certain supercilious insolence of tone and manner that convinced me he was no gentleman, though it was intended to have a contrary effect. But it was not for that I disliked his coming, so much as for the harm he did the children – encouraging all their evil propensities, and undoing, in a few minutes, the little good it had taken me months of labour to achieve.

Fanny and little Harriet, he seldom condescended to notice; but Mary Ann was something of a favourite. He was continually encouraging her tendency to affectation, (which I had done my utmost to crush,) talking about her pretty face, and filling her head with all manner of conceited notions concerning her personal appearance, (which I had instructed her to regard as dust in the balance compared with the cultivation of her mind and manners); and I never saw a child so susceptible of flattery as she was. Whatever was wrong, in either her or her brother, he would encourage by laughing at, if not by actually praising; and people little know the injury they do to children by laughing at their faults, and making a pleasant jest of what their true friends have endeavoured to teach them to hold in grave abhorrence.

Though not a positive drunkard, Mr Robson habitually swallowed great quantities of wine, and took with relish an occasional glass of brandy and water. He taught his nephew to imitate him in this to the utmost of his ability, and to believe that the more wine and spirits he could take, and the better he liked them, the more he manifested his bold and manly spirit, and rose superior to his sisters. Mr Bloomfield had not much to say against it, for *his* favourite beverage was gin and water, of which he took a considerable portion every day, by dint of constant sipping – and to that, I chiefly attributed his dingy complexion and waspish temper.

Mr Robson likewise encouraged Tom's propensity to per-secute the lower creation, both by precept and example. As he frequently came to course or shoot over his brother-in-law's grounds, he would bring his favourite dogs with him, and he treated them so brutally that, poor as I was, I would have given a sovereign any day to see one of them bite him, provided the animal could have done it with impunity. Sometimes, when in a very complacent mood, he would go a-bird-nesting with the children, a thing that irritated and annoyed me exceedingly, as, by frequent and persevering attempts, I flattered myself I had partly shown them the evil of this pastime, and hoped, in time, to bring them to some general sense of justice and humanity; but ten minutes' bird-nesting with uncle Robson, or even a laugh from him at some relation of their former barbarities, was sufficient, at once, to destroy the effect of my whole elaborate course of reasoning and persuasion. Happily, however, during that Spring, they never, but once, got anything but empty nests, or eggs – being too impatient to leave them till the birds were hatched; that once, Tom, who had been with his uncle into the neighbouring plantation, came running in high glee into the garden with a brood of little callow nestlings in his hands.

Mary Ann and Fanny, whom I was just bringing out, ran to admire his spoils, and to beg each a bird for themselves.

'No, not one!' cried Tom. 'They're all mine: uncle Robson gave them to me – one, two, three, four, five – you shan't touch one of them! no, not one for your lives!' continued he, exultantly, laying the nest on the ground, and standing over it, with his legs wide apart, his hands thrust into his breeches-pockets, his body bent forward, and his face twisted into all manner of contortions in the ecstacy of his delight.

'But you shall see me fettle 'em off. My word, but I *will* wallop 'em! See if I don't now! By gum! but there's rare sport for me in that nest.'

'But, Tom,' said I, 'I shall not allow you to torture those birds. They must either be killed at once, or carried back to the place you took them from, that the old birds may continue to feed them.'

'But you don't know where that is, madam. It's only me and uncle Robson that knows that.'

'But if you don't tell me, I shall kill them myself – much as I hate it.'

'You daren't. You daren't touch them for your life! because you know papa and mama and uncle Robson would be angry. Ha, hah! I've caught you there, Miss!'

'I shall do what I think right in a case of this sort, without consulting any one. If your papa and mama don't happen to approve of it, I shall be sorry to offend them, but your uncle Robson's opinions, of course, are nothing to me.'

So saying – urged by a sense of duty – at the risk of both making myself sick, and incurring the wrath of my employers – I got a large flat stone, that had been reared up for a mouse-trap by the gardener, then, having once more vainly endeavoured to persuade the little tyrant to let the birds be carried back, I asked what he intended to do with them. With fiendish glee he commenced a list of torments, and while he was busied in the relation, I dropped the stone upon his intended victims, and crushed them flat beneath it.

Loud were the outcries, terrible the execrations, consequent upon this daring outrage; uncle Robson had been coming up the walk with his gun, and was, just then, pausing to kick his dog. Tom flew towards him, vowing he would make him kick me instead of Juno. Mr Robson leant upon his gun, and laughed excessively at the violence of his nephew's passion, and the bitter maledictions and opprobrious epithets he heaped upon me.

'Well, you *are* a good un!' exclaimed he, at length, taking up his weapon, and proceeding towards the house. 'Damme, but the lad has some spunk in him too! Curse me, if ever I saw a nobler little scoundrel than that! He's beyond petticoat govern- ment already: – by G—, he defies mother, granny, governess, and all! Ha, ha, ha! Never mind, Tom, I'll get you another brood to-morrow.'

'If you do, Mr Robson, I shall kill them too,' said I.

'Humph!' replied he, and having honoured me with a broad stare, which, contrary to his expectations, I sustained without flinching, he turned away with an air of supreme contempt, and stalked into the house.

Tom next went to tell his mama. It was not her way to say much on any subject; but, when she next saw me, her aspect and demeanour were doubly dark and chill.

After some casual remark about the weather, she observed –

'I am sorry, Miss Grey, you should think it necessary to inter- fere with Master Bloomfield's amusements; he was *very* much distressed about your destroying the birds.'

'When Master Bloomfield's amusements consist in injuring sentient creatures,' I answered, 'I think it my duty to interfere.'

'You seemed to have forgotten,' said she, calmly, 'that the creatures were all created for our convenience.'

I thought that doctrine admitted some doubt, but merely replied –

'If they were, we have no right to torment them for our amusement.'

'I think,' said she, 'a child's amusement is scarcely to be weighed against the welfare of a soulless brute.'

'But, for the child's own sake, it ought not to be encouraged to have such amusements,' answered I, as meekly as I could, to make up for such unusual pertinacity.

'Blessed are the merciful, for they shall obtain mercy.'

'Oh, of course! but that refers to our conduct towards each other.'

'The merciful man shews mercy to his beast,'

I ventured to add.

'I think *you* have not shewn much mercy,' replied she, with a short, bitter laugh; 'killing the poor birds by wholesale, in that shocking manner, and putting the dear boy to such misery, for a mere whim!'

I judged it prudent to say no more.

This was the nearest approach to a quarrel I ever had with Mrs Bloomfield, as well as the greatest number of words I ever exchanged with her at one time, since the day of my first arrival.

But Mr Robson and old Mrs Bloomfield were not the only guests whose coming to Wellwood House annoyed me; every visiter disturbed me more or less, not so much because they neglected me (though I did feel their conduct strange and dis-agreeable in that respect) as because I found it so impossible to keep my pupils away from them, as I was repeatedly desired to do: Tom must talk to them, and Mary Ann must be noticed by them. Neither the one nor the other knew what it was to feel any degree of shame-facedness, or even common modesty. They would indecently and clamorously interrupt the conversa-tion of their elders, tease them with the most impertinent ques-tions, roughly collar the gentlemen, climb their knees uninvited, hang about their shoulders, or rifle their pockets, pull the ladies' gowns, disorder their hair, tumble their collars, and importunately beg for their trinkets.

Mrs Bloomfield had the sense to be shocked and annoyed at all this, but she had not sense to prevent it. She expected me to prevent it; – and how could I – when the guests, with their fine clothes and new faces, continually flattered and indulged them out of complaisance to their parents – how could *I*, with my homely garments, every-day face, and honest words, draw them away? I strained every nerve to do so; – by striving to amuse them, I endeavoured to attract them to my side, by the exertion of such authority as I possessed, and by such severity as I dared to use, I tried to deter them from tormenting the guests; and by reproaching their unmannerly conduct, to make them ashamed to repeat it. But they knew no shame – they scorned authority which had no terrors to back it, and as for kindness and affection, either they had no hearts, or such as they had were so strongly guarded, and so well concealed, that I, with all my efforts, had not yet discovered how to reach them.

But soon my trials in this quarter came to a close – sooner than I either expected or desired; for one sweet evening towards the close of May, as I was rejoicing in the near approach of the holidays, and congratulating myself upon having made some progress with my pupils – as far as their learning went at least, for I *had* instilled *something* into their heads, and I had at length brought them to be a little – a very little – more rational about getting their lessons done in time to leave some space for recreation, instead of tormenting themselves and me all day long to no purpose, Mrs Bloomfield sent for me, and calmly told me that after Midsummer my services would be no longer required. She assured me that my character and general conduct were unexceptionable; but the children had made so little improvement since my arrival, that Mr Bloomfield and she felt it their duty to seek some other mode of instruction. Though superior to most children of their years in abilities, they were decidedly behind them in attainments, their manners were uncultivated, and their tempers unruly. And this she attributed to a want of sufficient firmness and diligent, persevering care on my part.

Unshaken firmness, devoted diligence, unwearied perseverance, unceasing care, were the very qualifications on which I had secretly prided myself, and by which I had hoped in time, to overcome all difficulties, and obtain success at last. I wished to say something in my own justification, but in attempting to speak, I felt my voice falter, and rather than testify any emotion, or suffer the tears to overflow, that were already gathering in my eyes, I chose to keep silence, and bear all, like a self-convicted culprit.

Thus was I dismissed, and thus I sought my home. Alas! what would they think of me? unable, after all my boasting, to keep my place, even for a single year, as governess to three small children, whose mother was asserted, by my own aunt, to be a 'very nice woman.' Having been thus weighed in the balance, and found wanting, I need not hope they would be willing to try me again. And this was an unwelcome thought, for vexed, harassed, disappointed as I had been, and greatly as I had learnt to love and value my home, I was not yet weary of adventure, nor willing to relax my efforts. I knew all parents were not like Mr and Mrs Bloomfield, and I was certain all children were not like theirs. The next family must be different, and any change must be for the better. I had been seasoned by adversity, and tutored by experience, and I longed to redeem my lost honour in the eyes of those whose opinion was more than that of all the world to me.

CHAPTER VI

THE PARSONAGE AGAIN

FOR A FEW MONTHS I remained peaceably at home, in the quiet enjoyment of liberty and rest, and genuine friendship, from all of which I had fasted so long, and in the earnest prosecution of my studies to recover what I had lost during my stay at Wellwood House, and to lay in new stores for future use.

My father's health was still very infirm, but not materially worse than when I last saw him, and I was glad I had it in my power to cheer him by my return, and to amuse him with singing his favourite songs.

No one triumphed over my failure, or said I had better have taken his or her advice, and quietly stayed at home. All were glad to have me back again, and lavished more kindness than ever upon me, to make up for the sufferings I had undergone; but not one would touch a shilling of what I had so cheerfully earned and so carefully saved, in the hope of sharing it with them. By dint of pinching here, and scraping there, our debts already were nearly paid. Mary had had good success with her drawings, but our father had insisted upon *her* likewise keeping all the produce of her industry to herself. All we could spare from the supply of our humble wardrobe, and our little casual expenses, he directed us to put into the savings' bank, saying we knew not how soon we might be dependent on that alone for support, for he felt he had not long to be with us, and what would become of our mother and us when he was gone, God only knew.

Dear papa! if he had troubled himself less about the afflictions that threatened us in case of his death, I am convinced that dreaded event would not have taken place so soon. My mother would never suffer him to ponder the subject if she could help it.

'Oh Richard!' exclaimed she, on one occasion, 'if you would but dismiss such gloomy subjects from your mind, you would live as long as any of us – at least you would live to see the girls married, and yourself a happy grandfather with a canty old dame for your companion.'

My mother laughed, and so did my father, but his laugh soon perished in a dreary sigh.

'*Them* married – poor penniless things!' said he, 'who will take them I wonder!'

'Why nobody shall, that isn't thankful for them. – Wasn't I penniless when you took me? and you *pretended*, at least, to be vastly pleased with your acquisition. – But it's no matter whether they get married or not: we can devise a thousand honest ways of making a livelihood; and I wonder, Richard, you can think of bothering your head about our *poverty* in case of your death, as if *that* would be anything compared with the calamity of losing you – an affliction that, you well know, would swallow up all others, and which you ought to do your utmost to preserve us from; and there is nothing like a cheerful mind for keeping the body in health.'

'I know, Alice, it is wrong to keep repining as I do, but I cannot help it; you must bear with me.'

'I *won't* bear with you, if I can alter you!' replied my mother: but the harshness of her words was outdone by the earnest affection of her tone and pleasant smile, that made my father smile again, less sadly, and less transiently than was his wont.

'Mama,' said I, as soon as I could find an opportunity of speaking with her alone, 'my money is but little, and cannot last long; if I could increase it, it would lessen papa's anxiety on one subject at least. I cannot draw like Mary, and so the best thing I could do would be to look out for another situation.'

'And so you would actually try again, Agnes!'

'Decidedly, I would.'

'Why, my dear, I should have thought you had had enough of it.'

'I know,' said I, 'everybody is not like Mr and Mrs Bloom-field —'

'Some are worse,' interrupted my mother.

'But not many, I think,' replied I, 'and I'm sure all children are not like theirs; for I and Mary were not; we always did as you bid us, didn't we?'

'Generally: but then, I did not spoil you; and you were not perfect angels after all: Mary had a fund of quiet obstinacy, and you were somewhat faulty in regard to temper; but you were very good children on the whole.'

'I know I was sulky sometimes, and I should have been glad to see these children sulky sometimes too; for then I could have understood them; but they never were; for they *could* not be offended, nor hurt, nor ashamed: they could not be unhappy in any way, except when they were in a passion.'

'Well, if you *could* not, it was not their fault; you cannot expect stone to be as pliable as clay.'

'No, but still, it is very unpleasant to live with such unim-pressible, incomprehensible creatures. You cannot love them, and if you could, your love would be utterly thrown away; they could neither return it, nor value, nor understand it. — But however, even if I should stumble on such a family again, which is quite unlikely, I have all this experience to begin with, and I should manage better another time; and the end and aim of this preamble is, let me try again.'

'Well, my girl, you are not easily discouraged, I see — I am glad of that — But, let me tell you, you are a good deal paler and thinner than when you first left home, and we cannot have you undermining your health to hoard up money either for yourself or others.'

'Mary tells me I am changed too; and I don't much wonder at it, for I was in a constant state of agitation and anxiety all day long; but next time I am determined to take things coolly.'

After some further discussion, my mother promised once more to assist me, provided I would wait and be patient; and I left her to broach the matter to my father, when and how she deemed it most advisable, never doubting her ability to obtain his consent.

Meantime, I searched, with great interest, the advertising columns of the newspapers, and wrote answers to every 'Wanted a Governess,' that appeared at all eligible; but all my letters, as well as the replies, when I got any, were dutifully shewn to my mother; and she, to my chagrin, made me reject the situations one after another – These were low people, these were too exacting in their demands, and these too niggardly in their remunerations.

'Your talents are not such as every poor clergyman's daughter possesses, Agnes,' she would say, 'and you must not throw them away. Remember, you promised to be patient – there is no need of hurry – you have plenty of time before you, and may have many chances yet.'

At length, she advised me to put an advertisement, myself, in the paper, stating my qualifications, &c.

'Music, Singing, Drawing, French, Latin, and German,' said she, 'are no mean assemblage; many will be glad to have so much in one instructor; and this time, you shall try your fortune in a somewhat higher family – in that of some genuine, thorough-bred gentleman, for such are far more likely to treat you with proper respect and consideration, than those purse-proud trades-people, and arrogant upstarts. I have known several among the higher ranks, who treated their governesses quite as one of the family; though some, I allow, are as insolent and exacting as any one else can be; for there are bad and good in all classes.'

The advertisement was quickly written and despatched. Of the two parties who answered it, but one would consent to give me fifty pounds, the sum my mother bade me name as the salary I should require; and here, I hesitated about engaging myself, as I feared the children would be too old, and their parents would require some one more showy, or more experienced, if not more accomplished than I; but my mother dissuaded me from declining it on that account: I should do vastly well, she said, if I would only throw aside my diffidence, and acquire a little more confidence in myself. I was just to give a plain, true statement of my acquirements and qualifications, and name what stipulations I chose to make, and then await the result.

The only stipulation I ventured to propose, was that I might be allowed two months' holidays during the year to visit my friends, at Midsummer and Christmas. The unknown lady, in her reply, made no objection to this, and stated that, as to my acquirements, she had no doubt I should be able to give satisfaction; but in the engagement of governesses, she considered those things as but subordinate points, as, being situated in the neighbourhood of O—, she could get masters to supply any deficiences in that respect, but, in her opinion, next to unimpeachable morality, a mild and cheerful temper and obliging disposition were the most essential requisites.

My mother did not relish this at all, and now made many objections to my accepting the situation, in which my sister warmly supported her; but, unwilling to be baulked again, I overruled them all; and, having first obtained the consent of my father, who had, a short time previously, been apprised of these transactions, I wrote a most obliging epistle to my unknown correspondent, and, finally, the bargain was concluded.

It was decreed that, on the last day of January, I was to enter upon my new office, as governess in the family of Mr Murray, of Horton Lodge, near O—, about seventy miles from our village – a formidable distance to me, as I had never been above twenty miles from home in all the course of my twenty years sojourn on earth, and as, moreover, every individual, in that family and in the neighbourhood, was utterly unknown to myself and all my acquaintances. But this rendered it only the more piquant to me: I had now, in some measure, got rid of the *mauvaise honte* that had formerly oppressed me so much; there was a pleasing excitement in the idea of entering these unknown regions, and making my way alone among its strange inhabitants; I now flattered myself I was going to see something of the world; Mr Murray's residence was near a large town, and not in a manufacturing district, where the people had nothing to do but to make money; his rank, from what I could gather, appeared to be higher than that of Mr Bloomfield, and, doubtless, he was one of those genuine thorough-bred gentry my mother spoke of, who would treat his governess with due consideration as a respectable, well educated lady, the instructor and guide of his children, and not a mere upper servant; then, my pupils, being older, would be more rational, more teachable, and less troublesome than the last, they would be less confined to the school-room, and not require that constant labour and incessant watching; and, finally – bright visions mingled with my hopes, with which the care of children and the mere duties of a governess had little or nothing to do. So that the reader will see I had no claim to be regarded as a martyr to filial piety, going forth to sacrifice peace and liberty for the sole purpose of laying up stores for the comfort and support of my parents; though, certainly, the comfort of my father, and the future support of my mother had a large share in my calculations, and fifty pounds appeared to me no ordinary sum. I must have decent clothes becoming my station, I must, it seemed, put out my washing, and also pay for my four annual journeys between Horton Lodge and home; but, with strict attention to economy, surely twenty pounds, or little more, would cover those expenses, and then there would be thirty for the bank, or little less; what a valuable addition to our stock! Oh! I *must* struggle to keep this situation, whatever it might be! both for my own honour among my friends, and for the solid services I might render them by my continuance there.

CHAPTER VII

HORTON LODGE

THE THIRTY-FIRST OF January was a wild, tempestuous day; there was a strong north wind, with a continual storm of snow drifting on the ground, and whirling through the air. My friends would have had me delay my departure, but fearful of prejudicing my employers against me by such want of punctuality at the commencement of my undertaking, I persisted in keeping the appointment.

I will not inflict upon my readers an account of my leaving home on that dark winter morning, the fond farewells, the long, long journey to O—, the solitary waitings in inns for coaches or trains – for there were some railways then – and, finally, the meeting at O— with Mr Murray's servant, who had been sent, with the phaeton, to drive me from thence to Horton Lodge.

I will just state that the heavy snow had thrown such impediments in the way of both horses and steam-engines, that it was dark some hours before I reached my journey's end, and that a most bewildering storm came on at last, which made the few miles' space between O— and Horton Lodge a long and formidable passage. I sat resigned, with the cold, sharp snow drifting through my veil, and filling my lap, seeing nothing, and wondering how the unfortunate horse and driver could make their way even as well as they did, and indeed it was but a toilsome, creeping style of progression to say the best of it.

At length we paused; and, at the call of the driver, some one unlatched and rolled back upon their creaking hinges what appeared to be the park gates. Then we proceeded along a smoother road, whence, occasionally, I perceived some huge, hoary mass gleaming through the darkness, which I took to be a portion of a snow-clad tree.

After a considerable time, we paused again, before the stately portico of a large house with long windows descending to the ground.

I rose with some difficulty from under the superincumbent snowdrift, and alighted from the carriage, expecting a kind and hospitable reception would indemnify me for the toils and hardships of the day. A gentlemanly person in black opened the door, and admitted me into a spacious hall lighted by an amber-coloured lamp suspended from the ceiling; he led me through this, along a passage, and, opening the door of a back room, told me that was the school-room. I entered, and found two young ladies and two young gentlemen, my future pupils, I supposed. After a formal greeting, the elder girl, who was trifling over a piece of canvass and a basket of German wools, asked if I should like to go up-stairs.

I replied in the affirmative, of course.

'Matilda, take a candle, and show her her room,' said she.

Miss Matilda, a strapping hoyden of about fourteen, with a short frock and trousers, shrugged her shoulders, and made a slight grimace, but took a candle and proceeded before me, up the back stairs, a long, steep, double flight, and through a long, narrow passage, to a small but tolerably comfortable room. She then asked me if I would take some tea or coffee. I was about to answer no, but, remembering that I had taken nothing since seven o'clock that morning, and feeling faint in consequence, I said I would take a cup of tea. Saying she would tell 'Brown,' the young lady departed; and by the time I had divested myself of my heavy, wet cloak, shawl, bonnet, &c., a mincing damsel came to say, the young ladies desired to know whether I would take my tea up there or in the school-room. Under the plea of fatigue, I chose to take it there. She withdrew; and, after a while, returned again with a small tea-tray, and placed it on the chest of drawers which served as a dressing-table. Having civilly thanked her, I asked at what time I should be expected to rise in the morning.

'The young ladies and gentlemen breakfast at half-past eight, ma'am,' said she; 'they rise early; but, as they seldom do any lessons before breakfast, I should think it will do if you rise soon after seven.'

I desired her to be so kind as to call me at seven; and, promising to do so, she withdrew. Then, having broken my long fast on a cup of tea, and a little thin bread and butter, I sat down beside the small, smouldering fire, and amused myself with a hearty fit of crying; after which, I said my prayers, and then, feeling considerably relieved, began to prepare for bed; but, finding that none of my luggage was brought up, I instituted a search for the bell; and failing to discover any signs of such a convenience in any corner of the room, I took my candle, and ventured through the long passage, and down the steep stairs, on a voyage of discovery. Meeting a well-dressed female on the way, I told her what I wanted, but not without considerable hesitation, as I was not quite sure whether it was one of the upper servants, or Mrs Murray herself. It happened, however, to be the lady's maid.

With the air of one conferring an unusual favour, she vouchsafed to undertake the sending up of my things; and when I had re-entered my room, and waited and wondered a long time, greatly fearing that she had forgotten or neglected to perform her promise, and doubting whether to keep waiting, or go to bed, or go down again, my hopes at length were revived by the sound of voices and laughter, accompanied by a tramp of feet along the passage, and, presently, the luggage was brought in by a rough-looking maid and a man, neither of them very respectful in their demeanour to me.

Having shut the door upon their retiring footsteps, and unpacked a few of my things, I at length betook myself to rest, gladly enough, for I was weary in body and mind.

It was with a strange feeling of desolation mingled with a

strong sense of the novelty of my situation, and a joyless kind of curiosity concerning what was yet unknown, that I awoke the next morning feeling like one whirled away by enchantment, and suddenly dropped from the clouds into a remote and unknown land, widely and completely isolated from all he had ever seen or known before; or like a thistle-seed borne on the wind to some strange nook of uncongenial soil, where it must lie long enough before it can take root and germinate, extracting nourishment from what appears so alien to its nature, if indeed it ever can; but this gives no proper idea of my feelings at all; and no one, that has not lived such a retired, stationary life as mine, can possibly imagine what they were – hardly even if he has known what it is to awake some morning and find himself at Port Nelson in New Zealand, with a world of waters between himself and all that knew him.

I shall not soon forget the peculiar feeling with which I raised my blind and looked out upon the unknown world – a wide, white wilderness was all that met my gaze, a waste of –

> 'Deserts tossed in snow,
> And heavy laden groves.'

I descended to the school-room with no remarkable eagerness to join my pupils, though not without some feeling of curiosity respecting what a further acquaintance would reveal. One thing, among others of more obvious importance, I determined with myself; I must begin with calling them Miss and Master. It seemed to me a chilling and unnatural piece of punctilio between the children of a family and their instructor and daily companion, especially where the former were in their early childhood, as at Wellwood House; but even there, my calling the little Bloomfields by their simple names had been regarded as an offensive liberty, as their parents had taken care to show me, by carefully designating them *Master* and *Miss* Bloomfield, &c., in speaking to me. I had been very slow to take the hint, because the whole affair struck me as so very absurd; but now

I determined to be wiser, and begin at once with as much form and ceremony as any member of the family would be likely to require; and indeed, the children being so much older, there would be less difficulty; though the little words Miss and Master seemed to have a surprising effect in repressing all familiar, open-hearted kindness, and extinguishing every gleam of cordiality that might arise between us.

As I cannot, like Dogberry, find it in my heart to bestow *all* my tediousness upon the reader, I will not go on to bore him with a minute detail of all the discoveries and proceedings of this and the following day. No doubt he will be amply satisfied with a slight sketch of the different members of the family, and a general view of the first year or two of my sojourn among them.

To begin with the head, Mr Murray was, by all accounts, a blustering, roystering country squire, a devoted fox-hunter, a skilful horse-jockey and farrier, an active, practical farmer, and a hearty *bon-vivant* – by all accounts I say, for, except on Sundays when he went to church, I never saw him from month to month, unless, in crossing the hall or walking in the grounds, the figure of a tall, stout gentleman, with scarlet cheeks and crimson nose, happened to come across me; on which occasions, if he passed near enough to speak, an unceremonious nod, accompanied by a 'Morning, Miss Grey,' or some such brief salutation, was usually vouchsafed. Frequently indeed, his loud laugh reached me from afar, and oftener still, I heard him swearing and blaspheming against the footmen, groom, coachman, or some other hapless dependant.

Mrs Murray was a handsome, dashing lady of forty, who certainly required neither rouge nor padding to add to her charms, and whose chief enjoyments were, or seemed to be, in giving or frequenting parties, and in dressing at the very top of the fashion.

I did not see her till eleven o'clock on the morning after my arrival, when she honoured me with a visit, just as my mother might step into the kitchen to see a new servant girl – yet not so, either, for my mother would have seen her immediately after her arrival, and not waited till the next day; and moreover, she would have addressed her in a more kind and friendly manner, and given her some words of comfort as well as a plain exposition of her duties; but Mrs Murray did neither the one nor the other. She just stepped into the school-room, on her return from ordering dinner in the housekeeper's room, bid me good morning, stood for two minutes by the fire, said a few words about the weather and the 'rather rough' journey I must have had yesterday, petted her youngest child – a boy of ten, who had just been wiping his mouth and hands on her gown, after indulging in some savoury morsel from the housekeeper's stores – told me what a sweet, good boy he was, and then sailed out, with a self-complacent smile upon her face, thinking, no doubt, that she had done quite enough for the present, and had been delightfully condescending into the bargain. Her children evidently held the same opinion, and I alone thought otherwise.

After this she looked in upon me once or twice, during the absence of my pupils, to enlighten me concerning my duties towards them. For the girls, she seemed anxious only to render them as superficially attractive, and showily accomplished, as they could possibly be made without present trouble or discomfort to themselves; and I was to act accordingly – to study and strive to amuse and oblige, instruct, refine, and polish, with the least possible exertion on their part, and no exercise of authority on mine. With regard to the two boys it was much the same, only instead of accomplishments, I was to get the greatest possible quantity of Latin grammar and Valpy's Delectus into their heads, in order to fit them for school – the greatest possible quantity at least, *without* trouble to themselves. John might be a 'little high-spirited,' and Charles might be a little 'nervous and tedious –'

'But at all events, Miss Grey,' said she, 'I hope *you* will keep your temper, and be mild and patient throughout; especially with the dear little Charles, he is so extremely nervous and susceptible, and so utterly unaccustomed to anything but the tenderest treatment. You will excuse my naming these things to you; for the fact is, I have hitherto found all the governesses, even the very best of them, faulty in this particular. They wanted that meek and quiet spirit which St Matthew, or some of them, says is better than the putting on of apparel – you will know the passage to which I allude, for you are a clergyman's daughter; but I have no doubt you will give satisfaction in this respect as well as the rest. And remember, on all occasions, when any of the young people do anything very improper, if persuasion and gentle remonstrance will not do, let one of the others come and tell me; for *I* can speak to them more plainly than it would be proper for you to do. And make them as happy as you can, Miss Grey, and I dare say you will do very well.'

I observed that while Mrs Murray was so extremely solicitous for the comfort and happiness of her children, and continually talking about it, she never once mentioned mine, though they were at home surrounded by friends, and I an alien among strangers; and I did not yet know enough of the world, not to be considerably surprised at this anomaly.

Miss Murray, otherwise Rosalie, was about sixteen when I came, and decidedly a very pretty girl; and in two years longer, as time more completely developed her form, and added grace to her carriage and deportment, she was positively beautiful; and that in no common degree. She was tall and slender, but not thin, perfectly formed, exquisitely fair, but not without a brilliant, healthy bloom; her hair, which she wore in a profusion of long ringlets, was of a very light brown, strongly inclining to yellow, her eyes were pale blue, but so clear and bright that few would wish them darker, the rest of her features were small, not quite regular, and not remarkably otherwise, but altogether you could not hesitate to pronounce her a very lovely girl. I wish I could say as much for her mind and disposition as I can for her form and face.

Yet think not I have any dreadful disclosures to make: she was lively, light-hearted, and could be very agreeable, with those who did not cross her will. Towards me, when I first came she was cold and haughty, then, insolent and overbearing; but on a further acquaintance, she gradually laid aside her airs, and in time became as deeply attached to me as it was possible for *her* to be to one of my character and position; for she seldom lost sight, for above half-an-hour at a time, of the fact of my being a hireling, and a poor curate's daughter; and yet, upon the whole, I believe she respected me more than she herself was aware of, because I was the only person in the house who steadily professed good principles, habitually spoke the truth, and generally endeavoured to make inclination bow to duty; and this I say, not of course in commendation of myself, but to show the unfortunate state of the family to which my services were, for the present, devoted. There was no member of it in whom I regretted this sad want of principle so much as Miss Murray herself; not only because she had taken a fancy to me, but because there was so much of what was pleasant and prepossessing in herself, that, in spite of her failings, I really liked her – when she did not rouse my indignation, or ruffle my temper by *too* great a display of her faults, which however, I would fain persuade myself, were rather the effect of her education than her disposition: she had never been properly taught the distinction between right and wrong; she had, like her brothers and sisters, been suffered from infancy to tyrannize over nurses, governesses, and servants; she had not been taught to moderate her desires, to control her temper or bridle her will, or to sacrifice her own pleasure for the good of others; her temper being naturally good, she was never violent or morose, but from constant indulgence and habitual scorn of reason, she was often testy and capricious; her mind had never been cultivated: her intellect at best was somewhat shallow; she possessed considerable vivacity, some quickness of perception, and some talent for music and the acquisition of languages, but till fifteen she had troubled herself to acquire nothing; – then the love of display had roused her faculties, and induced her to apply herself, but only to the more showy accomplishments; and when I came, it was the same – everything was neglected but French, German, music, singing, dancing, fancy-work, and a little drawing – such drawing as might produce the greatest show with the smallest labour, and the principal parts of which were generally done by me. For music and singing, besides my occasional instruction, she had the attendance of the best master the country afforded; and in them, as well as in dancing, she certainly attained great proficiency. To music, indeed, she devoted too much of her time, as, governess though I was, I frequently told her: but her mother thought that if *she* liked it, she *could* not give too much time to the acquisition of so attractive an accomplishment.

Of fancy-work I knew nothing but what I gathered from my pupil and my own observation; but no sooner was I initiated, than she made me useful in twenty different ways: all the tedious parts of her work were shifted onto my shoulders; such as, stretching the frames, stitching in the canvass, sorting the wools and silks, putting in the grounds, counting the stitches, rectifying mistakes, and finishing the pieces she was tired of.

At sixteen, Miss Murray was something of a romp, yet not more so than is natural and allowable for a girl of that age; but at seventeen, that propensity, like all other things, began to give way to the ruling passion, and soon was swallowed up in the all absorbing ambition, to attract and dazzle the other sex. But enough of her: now let us turn to her sister.

Miss Matilda Murray was a veritable hoyden, of whom little need be said. She was about two years and a half younger than her sister; her features were larger, her complexion much darker. She might possibly make a handsome woman, but she was far too big-boned and awkward ever to be called a pretty girl, and, at present, she cared little about it. Rosalie knew all her charms, and thought them even greater than they were, and valued them more highly than she ought to have done had they been three times as great; Matilda thought she was well enough, but cared little about the matter; still less did she care about the cultivation of her mind, and the acquisition of ornamental accomplishments. The manner in which she learnt her lessons and practised her music was calculated to drive any governess to despair. Short and easy as her tasks were, if done at all, they were slurred over at any time, and in any way, but generally at the least convenient times, and in the way least beneficial to herself, and least satisfactory to me; and the short half-hour of practising was horribly strummed through; she, meantime, unsparingly abusing me, either for interrupting her with corrections, or for not rectifying her mistakes before they were made, or something equally unreasonable.

Once or twice, I ventured to remonstrate with her seriously for such irrational conduct; but, on each of these occasions, I received such reprehensive expostulations from her mother, as convinced me that, if I wished to keep the situation, I must even let Miss Matilda go on in her own way.

When her lessons were over, however, her ill-humour was generally over too; while riding her spirited pony, or romping with the dogs, or her brothers and sister, but especially with her dear brother John, she was as happy as a lark.

As an animal, Matilda was all right, full of life, vigour, and activity; as an intelligent being, she was barbarously ignorant, indocile, careless, and irrational, and consequently very distressing to one who had the task of cultivating her understanding, reforming her manners, and aiding her to acquire those ornamental attainments which, unlike her sister, she despised as much as the rest: her mother was partly aware of her deficiencies, and gave me many a lecture as to how I should try to form her tastes, and endeavour to rouse and cherish her dormant vanity, and, by insinuating, skilful flattery, to win her attention to the desired objects – which I would not do – and how I should prepare and smooth the path of learning till she could glide along it without the least exertion to herself, which

I could not, for nothing can be taught to any purpose without some little exertion on the part of the learner.

As a moral agent, she was reckless, headstrong, violent, and unamenable to reason. One proof of the deplorable state of her mind, was that from her father's example, she had learnt to swear like a trooper.

Her mother was greatly shocked at the 'unlady-like trick,' and wondered 'how she had picked it up.'

'But you can soon break her of it, Miss Grey,' said she; 'it is only a habit; and if you will just gently remind her every time she does so, I am sure she will soon lay it aside.'

I not only 'gently reminded' her, but I tried to impress upon her how wrong it was, and how distressing to the ears of decent people; but all in vain, I was only answered by a careless laugh, and –

'Oh, Miss Grey, how shocked you are! I'm so glad!'

Or –

'Well! I can't help it; papa shouldn't have taught me: I learnt it all from him; and maybe a bit from the coachman.'

Her brother John, alias Master Murray, was about eleven when I came, a fine, stout, healthy boy, frank, and good-natured in the main, and might have been a decent lad, had he been properly educated, but now he was as rough as a young bear, boisterous, unruly, unprincipled, untaught, unteachable – at least, for a governess under his mother's eye; his masters at school might be able to manage him better – for to school he was sent, greatly to my relief, in the course of a year; in a state, it is true, of scandalous ignorance as to Latin, as well as the more useful, though more neglected things; and this, doubtless, would all be laid to the account of his education having been intrusted to an ignorant female teacher, who had presumed to take in hand what she was wholly incompetent to perform. I was not delivered from his brother till full twelve months after, when he also was despatched in the same state of disgraceful ignorance as the former.

Master Charles was his mother's peculiar darling. He was little more than a year younger than John, but much smaller, paler, and less active and robust; a pettish, cowardly, capricious, selfish little fellow, only active in doing mischief, and only clever in inventing falsehoods, not simply to hide his faults, but, in mere malicious wantonness, to bring odium upon others; in fact, Master Charles was a very great nuisance to me: it was a trial of patience to live with him peaceably; to watch over him was worse; and to teach him, or pretend to teach him, was inconceivable.

At ten years old, he could not read, correctly, the easiest line in the simplest book; and as, according to his mother's principle, he was to be told every word, before he had time to hesitate, or examine its orthography, and never even to be informed, as a stimulant to exertion, that other boys were more forward than he, it is not surprising that he made but little progress during the two years I had charge of his education.

His minute portions of Latin grammar, &c., were to be repeated over to him, till he chose to say he knew them; and then, he was to be helped to say them: if he made mistakes in his little easy sums in arithmetic, they were to be shewn him at once, and the sum done for him, instead of his being left to exercise his faculties in finding them out himself; so that, of course, he took no pains to avoid mistakes, but frequently set down his figures at random without any calculation at all.

Yet I did not invariably confine myself to these rules; it was against my conscience to do so; but I seldom could venture to deviate from them, in the slightest degree, without incurring the wrath of my little pupil, and subsequently of his mama, to whom he would relate my transgressions, maliciously exaggerated, or adorned with embellishments of his own; and often, in consequence, was I on the point of losing or resigning my situation; but, for their sakes at home, I smothered my pride and suppressed my indignation, and managed to struggle on till my little tormentor was despatched to school, his father declaring that home education was 'no go for him, it was plain; his mother spoiled him outrageously, and his governess could make no hand of him at all.'

A few more observations about Horton Lodge and its on-goings, and I have done with dry description for the present.

The house was a very respectable one, superior to Mr Bloom-field's both in age, size, and magnificence: the garden was not so tastefully laid out; but instead of the smooth-shaven lawn, the young trees guarded by palings, the grove of upstart poplars, and the plantation of firs, there was a wide park, stocked with deer, and beautified by fine old trees. The surrounding country itself was pleasant, as far as fertile fields, flourishing trees, quiet green lanes, and smiling hedges, with wild flowers scattered along their banks, could make it; but it was depressingly flat, to one born and nurtured among the rugged hills of —.

We were situated nearly two miles from the village church, and, consequently, the family carriage was put in requisition every Sunday morning, and sometimes oftener.

Mr and Mrs Murray generally thought it sufficient to show themselves at church once in the course of the day; but fre-quently the children preferred going a second time to wandering about the grounds all day with nothing to do.

If some of my pupils chose to walk and take me with them, it was well for me; for otherwise, my position in the carriage was, to be crushed into the corner farthest from the open win-dow, and with my back to the horses, a position which invari-ably made me sick; and if I were not actually obliged to leave the church in the middle of the service, my devotions were disturbed with a feeling of languor and sickliness, and the tormenting fear of its becoming worse; and a depressing head-ache was generally my companion throughout the day, which would otherwise have been one of welcome rest, and holy, calm enjoyment.

'It's very odd, Miss Grey, that the carriage should always make you sick; it never makes *me*,' remarked Miss Matilda.

'Nor me either,' said her sister; 'but I dare say it would, if I sat where she does – such a nasty, horrid place, Miss Grey; I wonder how you can bear it!'

I am obliged to bear it, since no choice is left me – I might have answered; but in tenderness for their feelings I only replied –

'Oh! it is but a short way, and if I am not sick in church, I don't mind it.'

If I were called upon to give a description of the usual divisions and arrangements of the day, I should find it a very difficult matter. I had all my meals in the school-room with my pupils, at such times as suited their fancy: sometimes they would ring for dinner before it was half cooked; sometimes they would keep it waiting on the table for above an hour, and then be out of humour because the potatoes were cold, and the gravy covered with cakes of solid fat; sometimes they would have tea at four; frequently, they would storm at the servants because it was not in precisely at five; and when these orders were obeyed, by way of encouragement to punctuality, they would keep it on the table till seven or eight.

Their hours of study were managed in much the same way: my judgment or convenience was never once consulted. Sometimes Matilda and John would determine 'to get all the plaguy business over before breakfast,' and send the maid to call me up at half-past five, without any scruple or apology; sometimes, I was told to be ready precisely at six, and, having dressed in a hurry, came down to an empty room; and after waiting a long time in suspense, discovered that they had changed their minds, and were still in bed; or, perhaps, if it were a fine summer morning, Brown would come to tell me that the young ladies and gentlemen had taken a holiday, and were gone out; and then, I was kept waiting for breakfast till I was almost ready to faint; they having fortified themselves with something before they went.

Often they would do their lessons in the open air, which I

had nothing to say against, except that I frequently caught cold
by sitting on the damp grass, or from exposure to the evening
dew, or some insidious draught, which seemed to have no such
injurious effect on them. It was quite right that they should be
hardy; yet, surely, they might have been taught some consideration for others who were less so. But I must not blame them
for what was, perhaps, my own fault; for I never made any
particular objections to sitting where they pleased, foolishly
choosing to risk the consequences, rather than trouble them for
my convenience.

Their indecorous manner of doing their lessons was quite as
remarkable as the caprice displayed in their choice of time and
place. While receiving my instructions, or repeating what they
had learnt, they would lounge upon the sofa, lie on the rug,
stretch, yawn, talk to each other, or look out of the window;
whereas I could not so much as stir the fire, or pick up the
handkerchief I had dropped, without being rebuked for inatten-
tion by one of my pupils, or told that 'mama would not like
me to be so careless.'

The servants, seeing in what little estimation the governess
was held by both parents and children, regulated their behaviour
by the same standard.

I frequently stood up for *them*, at the risk of some injury to
myself, against the tyranny and injustice of their young masters
and mistresses; and I always endeavoured to give them as little
trouble as possible; but they entirely neglected my comfort,
despised my requests, and slighted my directions. All servants,
I am convinced, would not have done so; but domestics in
general, being ignorant and little accustomed to reason and
reflection, are too easily corrupted by the carelessness and bad
example of those above them; and these, I think, were not of
the best order to begin with.

I sometimes felt myself degraded by the life I led, and
ashamed of submitting to so many indignities; and sometimes
I thought myself a precious fool for caring so much about them,

and feared I must be sadly wanting in Christian humility, or that charity which suffereth long and is kind, seeketh not her own, is not easily provoked, beareth all things, endureth all things.

But, with time and patience, matters began to be slightly ameliorated, slowly, it is true, and almost imperceptibly; but I got rid of my male pupils, (that was no trifling advantage,) and the girls, as I intimated before concerning one of them, became a little less insolent, and began to show some symptoms of esteem.

Miss Grey was a queer creature; she never flattered, and did not praise them half enough, but whenever she did speak favourably of them, or anything belonging to them, they could be quite sure her approbation was sincere.

She was very obliging, quiet, and peaceable in the main, but there were some things that put her out of temper; they did not much care for that, to be sure, but still, it was better to keep her in tune, as when she was in a good humour she would talk to them, and be very agreeable and amusing sometimes, in her way, which was quite different from mama's, but still very well for a change. She had her own opinions on every subject, and kept steadily to them – very tiresome opinions they often were, as she was always thinking of what was right and what was wrong, and had a strange reverence for matters connected with Religion, and an unaccountable liking to good people.

CHAPTER VIII

THE 'COMING OUT'

At eighteen, Miss Murray was to emerge from the quiet obscurity of the school-room into the full blaze of the fashionable world – as much of it, at least, as could be had out of London, for her papa could not be persuaded to leave his rural pleasures and pursuits, even for a few weeks' residence in town.

She was to make her debut on the third of January, at a magnificent ball, which her mama proposed to give to all the nobility and choice gentry of O— and its neighbourhood for twenty miles round. Of course, she looked forward to it with the wildest impatience, and the most extravagant anticipations of delight.

'Miss Grey,' said she one evening, a month before the all important day, as I was perusing a long and extremely interesting letter of my sister's which I had just glanced at, in the morning, to see that it contained no very bad news, and kept till now, unable before to find a quiet moment for reading it. 'Miss Grey, do put away that dull, stupid letter, and listen to me! I'm sure my talk must be far more amusing than that.'

She seated herself on the low stool at my feet; and I, suppressing a sigh of vexation, began to fold up the epistle.

'You should tell the good people at home not to bore you with such long letters,' said she; 'and above all, do bid them write on proper note-paper, and not on those great vulgar sheets! You should see the charming little lady-like notes mama writes to her friends.'

'The good people at home,' replied I, 'know very well that

the longer their letters are, the better I like them. I should be very sorry to receive a charming little lady-like note from any of them; and I thought you were too much of a lady yourself, Miss Murray, to talk about the "vulgarity" of writing on a large sheet of paper.'

'Well, I only said it to tease you. But now I want to talk about the ball; and to tell you that you positively must put off your holidays till it is over.'

'Why so? – I shall not be present at the ball.'

'No, but you will see the rooms decked out before it begins, and hear the music, and, above all, see me in my splendid new dress! I shall be so charming, you'll be ready to worship me – you really must stay.'

'I should like to see you very much; but I shall have many opportunities of seeing you equally charming on the occasion of some of the numberless balls and parties that are to be, and I cannot disappoint my friends by postponing my return so long.'

'Oh, never mind your friends! Tell them we won't let you go.'

'But, to say the truth, it would be a disappointment to myself: I long to see them as much as they to see me – perhaps more.'

'Well, but it is such a short time.'

'Nearly a fortnight by my computation; and, besides, I cannot bear the thoughts of a Christmas spent from home; and, moreover, my sister is going to be married.'

'Is she – when?'

'Not till next month; but I want to be there to assist her in making preparations, and to make the best of her company while we have her.'

'Why didn't you tell me before?'

'I've only got the news in this letter, which you stigmatize as dull and stupid, and won't let me read.'

'Who is she to be married to?'

'To Mr Richardson, the vicar of a neighbouring parish.'

'Is he rich?'

'No, – only comfortable.'

'Is he handsome?'

'No, – only decent.'

'Young?'

'No – only middling.'

'O mercy! what a wretch! What sort of a house is it?'

'A quiet little vicarage, with an ivy-clad porch, an old fashioned garden, and –'

'Oh stop! – you'll make me sick. How *can* she bear it?'

'I expect she'll not only be able to bear it, but to be very happy. You did not ask me if Mr Richardson were a good, wise, or amiable man; I could have answered yes, to all these questions – at least so Mary thinks, and I hope she will not find herself mistaken.'

'But – miserable creature! how can she think of spending her life there, cooped up with that nasty old man; and *no* hope of change?'

'He is not old; he's only six or seven and thirty; and she herself is twenty-eight, and as sober as if she were fifty.'

'Oh! that's better then – they're well matched; but do they call him the "worthy vicar"?'

'I don't know; but if they do, I believe he merits the epithet.'

'Mercy, how shocking! and will she wear a white apron, and make pies and puddings?'

'I don't know about the white apron, but I dare say she will make pies and puddings, now and then; but that will be no great hardship as she has done it before.'

'And will she go about in a plain shawl, and a large straw bonnet, carrying tracts and bone soup to her husband's poor parishioners?'

'I'm not clear about that, but I dare say she will do her best to make them comfortable in body and mind, in accordance with our mother's example.'

CHAPTER IX

THE BALL

'NOW MISS GREY,' exclaimed Miss Murray, immediately as I entered the school-room, after having taken off my outdoor garments, upon returning from my four weeks' recreation, 'Now shut the door, and sit down, and I'll tell you all about the ball.'

'No, – d— it no!' shouted Miss Matilda. 'Hold your tongue can't ye! and let me tell her about my new mare – *such* a splendour, Miss Grey! a fine blood mare –'

'Do be quiet, Matilda! and let me tell my news first.'

'No, no, Rosalie! you'll be such a d— long time over it – she *shall* hear me first – I'll be hanged if she doesn't!'

'I'm sorry to hear, Miss Matilda, that you've not got rid of that shocking habit yet.'

'Well, I can't help it; but I'll never say a wicked word again, if you'll only listen to me, and tell Rosalie to hold her confounded tongue.'

Rosalie remonstrated, and I thought I should have been torn in pieces between them; but, Miss Matilda having the loudest voice, her sister at length gave in, and suffered her to tell her story first: so I was doomed to hear a long account of her splendid mare, its breeding and pedigree, its paces, its action, its spirit, &c., and of her own amazing skill and courage in riding it, concluding with an assertion that she could clear a five-barred gate 'like winking,' that papa said she might hunt next time the hounds met, and mama had ordered a bright scarlet hunting-habit for her.

'Oh, Matilda! what stories you are telling!' exclaimed her sister.

'Well,' answered she, no whit abashed, 'I know I *could* clear a five-barred gate, if I tried, and papa *will* say I may hunt, and mama *will* order the habit when I ask them.'

'Well, now get along,' replied Miss Murray; 'and do, dear Matilda, try to be a little more lady-like. Miss Grey, I wish you *would* tell her not to use such shocking words; she *will* call her horse a mare; it is so *inconceivably* shocking! and then she uses such dreadful expressions in describing it: she *must* have learnt it from the grooms. It nearly puts me into fits when she begins.'

'I learnt it from papa, you ass! and his jolly friends,' said the young lady, vigorously cracking a hunting-whip, which she habitually carried in her hand. 'I'm as good a judge of horseflesh as the best of 'em.'

'Well now, get along, you shocking girl: I really shall take a fit if you go on in such a way. And now Miss Grey, attend to me; I'm going to tell you about the ball. You must be dying to hear about it, I know. Oh, *such* a ball! You never saw or heard, or read, or dreamt of anything like it in all your life! The decorations, the entertainment, the supper, the music were indescribable! and then the guests! There were two noblemen, three baronets, and five titled ladies! – and other ladies and gentlemen innumerable. The ladies, of course, were of no consequence to me, except to put me in a good humour with myself, by showing how ugly and awkward most of them were; and the best, mama told me, – the most transcendent beauties among them, were nothing to me. As for *me*, Miss Grey – I'm so *sorry* you didn't see me! I was *charming* – wasn't I, Matilda?'

'Middling.'

'No, but I really *was* – at least so mama said ... and Brown and Williamson. Brown said she was sure no gentleman could set eyes on me without falling in love that minute; and so I may be allowed to be a little vain. I know you think me a shocking, conceited, frivolous girl, but then you know, I don't attribute it *all* to my personal attractions: I give some praise to the hair-dresser, and some to my exquisitely lovely dress – you must see it to-morrow – white gauze over pink satin ... and so *sweetly* made! and a necklace and bracelets of beautiful, large pearls!'

'I have no doubt you looked very charming; but should that delight you so *very* much?'

'Oh, no! ... not that alone: but then, I was so much admired; and I made so *many* conquests in that one night – you'd be astonished to hear –'

'But what good will they do you?'

'What good! Think of any woman asking that!'

'Well, I should think one conquest would be enough, and too much, unless the subjugation were mutual.'

'Oh, but you know I never agree with you on those points. Now wait a bit, and I'll tell you my principal admirers – those who made themselves very conspicuous that night and after, for I've been to two parties since. Unfortunately the two noblemen, Lord G— and Lord F—, were married, or I might have condescended to be particularly gracious to *them*; as it was, I did not, though Lord F—, who hates his wife, was evidently much struck with me. He asked me to dance with him twice – he is a charming dancer, by the by, and so am I ... you can't think how well I did ... I was astonished at myself. My lord was very complimentary too – rather too much so in fact, and I thought proper to be a little haughty and repellent; but I had the pleasure of seeing his nasty, cross wife ready to perish with spite and vexation –'

'Oh Miss Murray! you don't mean to say that such a thing could really give you pleasure! However cross or –'

'Well, I know it's very wrong; – but never mind! I mean to be good sometime – only don't preach now, there's a good creature – I haven't told you half yet. . . . Let me see ... Oh! I was going to tell you how many unmistakable admirers I had: – Sir Thomas Ashby was one, – Sir Hugh Meltham and Sir Broadley Wilson are old codgers, only fit companions for papa and mama. Sir Thomas is young, rich, and gay, but an ugly beast nevertheless: however, mama says I should not mind that after a few months' acquaintance. Then, there was Harry Meltham, Sir Hugh's younger son, rather good-looking, and a pleasant fellow to flirt with; but *being* a younger son, that is all he is good for: then there was young Mr Green, rich enough, but of no family, and a great stupid fellow, a mere country booby; and then, our good rector Mr Hatfield: an *humble* admirer, he ought to consider himself; but I fear he has forgotten to number humility among his stock of Christian virtues.'

'Was Mr Hatfield at the ball?'

'Yes to be sure. Did you think he was too good to go?'

'I thought he might consider it unclerical.'

'By *no* means. He did not profane his cloth by dancing; but it was with difficulty he could refrain, poor man: he looked as if he were dying to ask my hand just for *one* set; and – Oh! by the by – he's got a new curate . . . that seedy old fellow Mr Bligh has got his long-wished-for living at last, and gone.'

'And what is the new one like?'

'Oh *such* a beast! Weston his name is. I can give you his description in three words . . . an insensate, ugly, stupid block-head. That's four, but no matter . . . enough of *him* now.'

Then she returned to the ball, and gave me a further account of her deportment there, and at the several parties she had since attended, and further particulars respecting Sir Thomas Ashby and Messrs Meltham, Green, and Hatfield, and the ineffaceable impression she had wrought upon each of them.

'Well, which of the four do you like best?' said I, suppressing my third or fourth yawn.

'I detest them all,' replied she, shaking her bright ringlets in vivacious scorn.

'That means, I suppose, I like them all – but which most?'

'No, I really do detest them all; but Harry Meltham is the handsomest and most amusing, and Mr Hatfield the cleverest, Sir Thomas the wickedest, and Mr Green the most stupid. But the one I'm to have, I suppose, if I'm doomed to have any of them, is Sir Thomas Ashby.'

'Surely not, if he's so wicked, and if you dislike him?'

'Oh, I don't mind his being wicked; he's all the better for that; and as for disliking him – I shouldn't greatly object to being Lady Ashby of Ashby Park, if I must marry; but if I could be always young, I would be always single. I should like to enjoy myself thoroughly, and coquet with all the world, till I am on the verge of being called an old maid; and then, to escape the infamy of that, after having made ten thousand conquests, to break all their hearts save one, by marrying some high-born, rich, indulgent husband, whom, on the other hand, fifty ladies were dying to have.'

'Well, as long as you entertain those views, keep single by all means, and never marry at all, not even to escape the infamy of old-maidenhood.'

CHAPTER X

THE CHURCH

'WELL, MISS GREY, what do you think of the new curate?' asked Miss Murray, on our return from church the Sunday after the re-commencement of my duties.

'I can scarcely tell,' was my reply: 'I have not even heard him preach.'

'Well, but you saw him, didn't you?'

'Yes; but I cannot pretend to judge of a man's character by a single, cursory glance at his face.'

'But, *isn't* he ugly?'

'He did not strike me as being particularly so; I don't dislike that cast of countenance: but the only thing I particularly noticed about him was his style of reading, which appeared to me good – infinitely better, at least, than Mr Hatfield's. He read the lessons as if he were bent on giving full effect to every passage: it seemed as if the most careless person could not have helped attending, nor the most ignorant have failed to under-stand; and the prayers, he read as if he were not reading at all, but praying, earnestly and sincerely from his own heart.'

'Oh, yes! that's all he is good for: he can plod through the service well enough; but he has not a single idea beyond it.'

'How do you know?'

'Oh! I know perfectly well; I'm an excellent judge in such matters. Did you see how he went out of church? stumping along, as if there was nobody there but himself – never looking to the right hand or the left, and evidently thinking of nothing but just getting out of the church, and, perhaps, home to his dinner – his great stupid head could contain no other idea.'

'I suppose you would have had him cast a glance into the squire's pew,' said I, laughing at the vehemence of her hostility.

'Indeed! I should have been highly indignant if he had dared to do such a thing!' replied she, haughtily tossing her head; then, after a moment's reflection, she added – 'Well, well! I suppose he's good enough for his place; but, I'm glad I'm not dependent on *him* for amusement – that's all. Did you see how Mr Hatfield hurried out to get a bow from me, and be in time to put us into the carriage?'

'Yes,' answered I, internally adding, 'and I thought it somewhat derogatory to his dignity as a clergyman to come flying from the pulpit in such eager haste to shake hands with the squire, and hand his wife and daughters into their carriage; and moreover I owe him a grudge for nearly shutting me out of it;' for, in fact, though I was standing before his face, close beside the carriage steps, waiting to get in, he would persist in putting them up, and closing the door, till one of the family stopped him by calling out that the governess was not in yet: then, without a word of apology, he departed, wishing them good morning, and leaving the footman to finish the business. *Nota bene.* – Mr Hatfield never spoke to me, neither did Sir Hugh or Lady Meltham, nor Mr Harry or Miss Meltham, nor Mr Green or his sisters, nor any other lady or gentleman who frequented that church, nor, in fact, any one that visited at Horton Lodge.

Miss Murray ordered the carriage again, in the afternoon, for herself and her sister: she said it was too cold for them to enjoy themselves in the garden; and, besides, she believed Harry Meltham would be at church.

'For,' said she, smiling slyly at her own fair image in the glass, 'he has been a most exemplary attendant at church these last few Sundays. You would think he was quite a good Christian. And you may go with us, Miss Grey, I want you to see him; he is so greatly improved since he returned from abroad – you can't think! And, besides, then you will have an opportunity of seeing the beautiful Mr Weston again, and of hearing him preach.'

I did hear him preach, and was decidedly pleased with the evangelical truth of his doctrine, as well as the earnest simplicity of his manner, and the clearness and force of his style.

It was truly refreshing to hear such a sermon, after being so long accustomed to the dry, prosy discourses of the former curate, and the still less edifying harangues of the rector, who would come sailing up the aisle, or rather sweeping along like a whirlwind, with his rich silk gown flying behind him and rustling against the pew doors, mount the pulpit like a conqueror ascending his triumphal car; then sinking on the velvet cushion in an attitude of studied grace, remain in silent prostration for a certain time; then, mutter over a Collect, and gabble through the Lord's Prayer, rise, draw off one bright lavender glove to give the congregation the benefit of his sparkling rings, lightly pass his fingers through his well-curled hair, flourish a cambric handkerchief, recite a very short passage, or, perhaps, a mere phrase of scripture, as a head-piece to his discourse, and, finally, deliver a composition which, as a composition, might be considered good, though far too studied and too artificial to be pleasing to me; the propositions were well laid down, the arguments logically conducted; and yet, it was sometimes hard to listen quietly throughout, without some slight demonstrations of disapproval or impatience.

His favourite subjects were church discipline, rites and ceremonies, apostolical succession, the duty of reverence and obedience to the clergy, the atrocious criminality of dissent, the absolute necessity of observing all the forms of godliness, the reprehensible presumption of individuals who attempted to think for themselves in matters connected with religion, or to be guided by their own interpretations of Scripture, and, occasionally, (to please his wealthy parishioners,) the necessity of deferential obedience from the poor to the rich – supporting his maxims and exhortations throughout with quotations from the Fathers, with whom he appeared to be far better acquainted than with the Apostles and Evangelists, and whose importance he seemed to consider at least equal to theirs.

But now and then he gave us a sermon of a different order – what some would call a very good one, but sunless and severe, representing the Deity as a terrible task-master, rather than a benevolent father. Yet, as I listened, I felt inclined to think the man was sincere in all he said; he must have changed his views, and become decidedly religious, gloomy and austere, but still devout: but such illusions were usually dissipated, on coming out of church, by hearing his voice in jocund colloquy with some of the Melthams or Greens, or, perhaps, the Murrays themselves, probably laughing at his own sermon, and hoping that he had given the rascally people something to think about; perchance, exulting in the thoughts that old Betty Holmes would now lay aside the sinful indulgence of her pipe which had been her daily solace for upwards of thirty years, that George Higgins would be frightened out of his Sabbath evening walks, and Thomas Jackson would be sorely troubled in his conscience, and shaken in his sure and certain hope of a joyful resurrection at the last day.

Thus, I could not but conclude that Mr Hatfield was one of those who bind heavy burdens, and grievous to be borne, and lay them upon men's shoulders, while they themselves will not move them with one of their fingers, and that make the word of God of none effect by their traditions, teaching for doctrines the commandments of men. I was well pleased to observe that the new curate resembled him, as far as I could see, in none of these particulars.

'Well, Miss Grey! what do you think of him now?' said Miss Murray, as we took our places in the carriage after service.

'No harm still,' replied I.

'No harm!' repeated she in amazement. 'What do you mean?'

'I mean, I think no worse of him than I did before.'

'No worse! I should think not indeed – quite the contrary! Is he not greatly improved?'

'Oh, yes! very much indeed,' replied I; for I had now discovered that it was Harry Meltham she meant, not Mr Weston.

That gentleman had eagerly come forward to speak to the young ladies, a thing he would hardly have ventured to do had their mother been present; he had likewise politely handed them into the carriage – he had not attempted to shut me out like Mr Hatfield; neither, of course, had he offered me his assistance, (I should not have accepted it if he had,) but as long as the door remained open he had stood smirking and chatting with them, and then lifted his hat and departed to his own abode; – but I had scarcely noticed him all the time. My companions, however, had been more observant; and, as we rolled along, they discussed between them not only his looks, words, and actions, but every feature of his face, and every article of his apparel.

'You shan't have him all to yourself, Rosalie,' said Miss Matilda, at the close of this discussion; 'I like him: I know he'd make a nice, jolly companion for me.'

'Well, you're quite welcome to him, Matilda,' replied her sister, in a tone of affected indifference.

'And I'm sure,' continued the other, 'he admires me quite as much as he does you – doesn't he, Miss Grey?'

'I don't know; I'm not acquainted with his sentiments.'

'Well, but he *does* though!'

'My *dear* Matilda! nobody will ever admire you till you get rid of your rough, awkward manners.'

'Oh stuff! Harry Meltham likes such manners; and so do papa's friends.'

'Well, you *may* captivate old men, and younger sons; but nobody else, I'm sure, will ever take a fancy to you.'

'I don't care: I'm not always grubbing after money, like you and mama. If my husband is able to keep a few good horses and dogs, I shall be quite satisfied; and all the rest may go to the devil!'

'Well, if you use such shocking expressions, I'm sure no real gentleman will ever venture to come near you – really, Miss Grey, you should not let her do so!'

'I can't possibly prevent it, Miss Murray.'

'And you're quite mistaken, Matilda, in supposing that Harry Meltham admires you: I assure you he does nothing of the kind.'

Matilda was beginning an angry reply; but, happily our journey was now at an end; and the contention was cut short by the footman's opening the carriage door, and letting down the steps for our descent.

CHAPTER XI

THE COTTAGERS

As I had now only one regular pupil – though she contrived to give me as much trouble as three or four ordinary ones, and though her sister still took lessons in German and drawing – I had considerably more time at my own disposal than I had ever been blessed with before, since I had taken upon me the governess's yoke; which time I devoted partly to correspondence with my friends, partly to reading, study, and the practice of music, singing, &c., partly to wandering in the grounds or adjacent fields, with my pupils, if they wanted me, alone if they did not.

Often, when they had no more agreeable occupation at hand, the Misses Murray would amuse themselves with visiting the poor cottagers on their father's estate to receive their flattering homage, or to hear the old stories or gossiping news of the garrulous old women; or, perhaps, to enjoy the purer pleasure of making the poor people happy with their cheering presence, and their occasional gifts, so easily bestowed, so thankfully received. Sometimes, I was called upon to accompany one or both of the sisters in these visits; and, sometimes, I was desired to go alone to fulfil some promise, which they had been more ready to make than to perform, to carry some small donation, or read to one who was sick, or seriously disposed: and thus I made a few acquaintances among the cottagers; and, occasionally, I went to see them on my own account.

I generally had more satisfaction in going alone than with either of the young ladies, for they, chiefly owing to their defective education, comported themselves towards their inferiors in a manner that was highly disagreeable for me to witness. They never in thought exchanged places with them; and, consequently, had no consideration for their feelings, regarding them as an order of beings entirely distinct from themselves.

They would watch the poor creatures at their meals, making uncivil remarks about their food, and their manner of eating; they would laugh at their simple notions and provincial expressions, till some of them scarcely durst venture to speak; they would call the grave, elderly men and women old fools and silly old blockheads to their faces; and all this without meaning to offend.

I could see that the people were often hurt and annoyed by such conduct, though their fear of the 'grand ladies' prevented them from testifying any resentment; but *they* never perceived it. They thought that, as these cottagers were poor and untaught, they must be stupid and brutish; and as long as they, their superiors, condescended to talk to them, and to give them shillings and half-crowns, or articles of clothing, they had a right to amuse themselves, even at their expense; and the people must adore them as angels of light, condescending to minister to their necessities, and enlighten their humble dwellings.

I made many and various attempts to deliver my pupils from these delusive notions without alarming their pride, which was easily offended and not soon appeased, but with little apparent result; and I know not which was the more reprehensible of the two: Matilda was more rude and boisterous; but from Rosalie's womanly age and lady-like exterior better things were expected: yet she was as provokingly careless and inconsiderate as a giddy child of twelve.

One bright day in the last week of February, I was walking in the park, enjoying the threefold luxury of solitude, a book, and pleasant weather, for Miss Matilda had set out on her daily ride, and Miss Murray was gone in the carriage with her mama to pay some morning calls. But it struck me that I ought to leave these selfish pleasures, and the park with its glorious canopy of bright blue sky, the west wind sounding through its yet leafless branches, the snow-wreaths still lingering in its hollows, but melting fast beneath the sun, and the graceful deer browsing on its moist herbage, already assuming the freshness and verdure of Spring ... and go to the cottage of one Nancy Brown, a widow, whose son was at work all day in the fields, and who was afflicted with an inflammation in the eyes which had, for some time, incapacitated her from reading, to her own great grief, for she was a woman of a serious, thoughtful turn of mind.

I accordingly went, and found her alone, as usual, in her little close, dark cottage, redolent of smoke and confined air, but as tidy and clean as she could make it. She was seated beside her little fire (consisting of a few red cinders and a bit of stick), busily knitting, with a small sackcloth cushion at her feet, placed for the accommodation of her gentle friend the cat who was seated thereon, with her long tail half encircling her velvet paws, and her half-closed eyes dreamily gazing on the low, crooked fender.

'Well, Nancy, how are you to-day?'

'Why, middling, Miss, i' myseln – my eyes is no better, but I'm a deal easier i' my mind nor I have been,' replied she, rising to welcome me with a contented smile which I was glad to see, for Nancy had been somewhat afflicted with religious melancholy.

I congratulated her upon the change. She agreed that it was a great blessing, and expressed herself 'right down thankful for it,' adding, 'If it please God to spare my sight, and make me so as I can read my Bible again, I think I shall be as happy as a queen.'

'I hope He will, Nancy,' replied I; 'and, meantime, I'll come and read to you now and then, when I have a little time to spare.'

With expressions of grateful pleasure, the poor woman moved to get me a chair; but, as I saved her the trouble, she busied herself with stirring the fire, and adding a few more sticks to the decaying embers; and then, taking her well-used Bible from the shelf, dusted it carefully, and gave it to me. On my asking if there was any particular part she should like me to read, she answered –

'Well, Miss Grey, if it's all the same to you, I'd like to hear that chapter in the First Epistle of Saint John, that says, "God is love, and he that dwelleth in love dwelleth in God, and God in him."'

With a little searching I found these words in the fourth chapter. When I came to the seventh verse she interrupted me, and with needless apologies for such a liberty, desired me to read it very slowly, that she might take it all in, and dwell on every word; hoping I would excuse her as she was but a simple body.

'The wisest person,' I replied, 'might think over each of these verses for an hour, and be all the better for it; and I would rather read them slowly than not.'

Accordingly, I finished the chapter as slowly as need be, and at the same time as impressively as I could. My auditor listened most attentively all the while, and sincerely thanked me when I had done. I sat still about half a minute to give her time to reflect upon it; when, somewhat to my surprise, she broke the pause by asking me how I liked Mr Weston?

'I don't know,' I replied, a little startled by the suddenness of the question; 'I think he preaches very well.'

'Ay, he does so; and talks well too!'

'Does he?'

'He does. May be you haven't seen him – not to talk to much, yet?'

'No, I never see any one to talk to – except the young ladies of the hall.'

'Ah; they're nice, kind young ladies; but they can't talk as he does!'

'Then he comes to see you, Nancy?'

'He does, Miss; and I'se thankful for it. He comes to see all us poor bodies a deal ofter nor Maister Bligh, or th' rector ever did; an' it's well he does, for he's always welcome; and we can't say as much for th' rector – there is 'at says they're fair feared on him. When he comes into a house, they say he's sure to find summut wrong, and begin a calling 'em as soon as he crosses th' doorstuns: but may-be, he thinks it is his duty like to tell 'em what's wrong; and very oft, he comes o' purpose to reprove folk for not coming to church, or not kneeling an' standing when other folks does, or going to th' Methody chapel, or summut o' that sort; but I can't say 'at he ever fund much fault wi' me. He came to see me once or twice, afore Maister Weston come, when I was so ill troubled in my mind; and as I had only very poor health besides, I made bold to send for him – and he came right enough. I was sore distressed, Miss Grey – thank God it's owered now – but when I took my Bible I could get no comfort of it at all. That very chapter 'at you've just been reading troubled me as much as aught – "He that loveth not, knoweth not God." It seemed fearsome to me; for I felt that I loved neither God nor man as I should do, and could not, if I tried ever so. And th' chapter afore, where it says "He that is born of God cannot commit sin." And another place where it says "Love is the fulfilling of the Law." And many – many others, Miss; I should fair weary you out, if I was to tell them all. – But all seemed to condemn me, and to shew me 'at I was not in the right way; and as I knew not how to get into it, I sent our Bill to beg Maister Hatfield to be as kind as look in on me some day; and when he came, I told him all my troubles.'

'And what did he say, Nancy?'

'Why Miss, he like seemed to scorn me. I might be mista'en – but he like gave a sort of a whistle, and I saw a bit of a smile on his face; and he said, "Oh it's all stuff! You've been among the Methodists, my good woman." But I told him I'd never been near the Methodies. And then he said,

' "Well," says he, "you must come to church, where you'll hear the scriptures properly explained, instead of sitting poring over your Bible at home."

'But I told him, I always used coming to church when I had my health; but this very cold winter weather I hardly durst venture so far – and me so bad i' th' rheumatiz' an' all.

'But he says, "It'll do your rheumatiz' good to hobble to church; there's nothing like exercise for the rheumatiz'. You can walk about the house well enough; why can't you walk to church? The fact is," says he, "you're getting too fond of your ease. It's always easy to find excuses for shirking one's duty."

'But then, you know, Miss Grey, it wasn't so. However I telled him I'd try. "But please sir," says I, "if I do go to church, what the better shall I be? I want to have my sins blotted out, and to feel that they are remembered no more against me, and that the love of God is shed abroad in my heart; and if I can get no good by reading my Bible, an' saying my prayers at home, what good shall I get by going to church?"

' "The church," says he, "is the place appointed by God for His worship. It's your duty to go there as often as you can. If you want comfort, you must seek it in the path of duty" – an' a deal more he said, but I cannot remember all his fine words. However, it all came to this, that I was to come to church as oft as ever I could, and bring my prayer-book with me, an' read up all the sponsers after th' clerk, an' stand an' kneel an' sit an' do – all as I should, an' take the Lord's supper at every opportunity, an' hearken his sermons an' Maister Bligh's, an' it 'ud be all right: if I went on doing my duty, I should get a blessing at last.

' "But if you get no comfort that way," says he, "it's all up."

' "Then sir," says I, "should you think I'm a reprobate?"

' "Why," says he – he says "if you do your best to get to Heaven and can't manage it, you must be one of those that seek to enter in at the strait gate and shall not be able."

'An' then he asked me if I'd seen any of the ladies o' th' Hall about that mornin'; so I telled him where I'd seen the young Misses go on th' moss-lane; – an' he kicked my poor cat right across th' floor, an' went off after 'em as gay as a lark; but I was very sad. That last word o' his fair sunk into my heart, an' lay there like a lump o' lead, till I was weary to bear it.

'Howsever, I follered his advice: I thought he meant it all for th' best though he *had* a queer way with him – but you know, Miss, he's rich an' young, and such like cannot right understand the thoughts of a poor old woman such as me. But howsever, I did my best to do all as he bade me – but may-be I'm plaguing you, Miss, wi' my chatter.'

'Oh, no Nancy! Go on, and tell me all.'

'Well, my rheumatiz' got better – I know not whether wi' going to church or not, but one frosty Sunday I got this cold i' my eyes. Th' inflammation didn't come on all at once like, but bit by bit – but I wasn't going to tell you about my eyes, I was talking about my trouble o' mind; – and to tell the truth, Miss Grey, I don't think it was any-ways eased by coming to church – naught to speak on at least: I like got my health better; but that didn't mend my soul. I hearkened and hearkened the ministers, and read an' read at my prayer-book; but it was all like sounding brass, and a tinkling cymbal: the sermons I couldn't understand, an' th' prayer-book only served to shew me how wicked I was, that I could read such good words, an' never be no better for it, and oftens feel it a sore labour an' a heavy task beside, instead of a blessing and a privilege as all good Christians does. It seemed like as all were barren an' dark to me. And then, them dreadful words "Many shall seek to enter in, and shall not be able." They like as they fair dried up my sperrit.

'But one Sunday, when Maister Hatfield gave out about the sacrament, I noticed where he said, "If there be any of you that cannot quiet his own conscience, but requireth further comfort or counsel, let him come to me, or some other discreet and learned minister of God's word, and open his grief." So next Sunday morning, afore service, I just looked into th' vestry, an' began a talking to th' rector again ... I hardly could fashion to take such a liberty, but I thought when my soul was at stake, I shouldn't stick at a trifle. But he said he hadn't time to attend to me then.

' "And indeed," says he, "I've nothing to say to you, but what I've said before ... take the sacrament of course, and go on doing your duty; and if that won't serve you, nothing will. So don't bother me any more."

'So then, I went away. But I heard Maister Weston . . . Maister Weston was there, Miss – this was his first Sunday at Horton you know, an' he was i' th' vestry in his surplice, helping th' rector on with his gown.'

'Yes, Nancy.'

'And I heard him ask Maister Hatfield who I was; an' he said, "Oh! she's a canting old fool."'

'And I was very ill grieved, Miss Grey; but I went to my seat, and I tried to do my duty as aforetime; but I like got no peace. An' I even took the sacrament; but I felt as though I were eating an' drinking to my own damnation all th' time. So I went home, sorely troubled.

'But next day, afore I'd gotten fettled up – for indeed Miss, I'd no heart to sweeping an' fettling, an' washing pots; so I sat me down i' th' muck – but who should come in but Maister Weston! I started siding stuff then, an' sweeping an' doing; an' I expected he'd begin a calling me for my idle ways as Maister Hatfield would a' done; but I was mista'en: he only bid me good mornin' like, in a quiet dacent way. So I dusted him a chair, an' fettled up th' fire-place a bit; but I hadn't forgotten th' rector's words, so says I,

' "I wonder, sir, you should give yourself that trouble, to come so far to see a 'canting old fool,' such as me."

'He like seemed taken aback at that; but he would fain persuade me 'at th' rector was only in jest; and when that wouldn't do, he says,

' "Well Nancy, you shouldn't think so much about it: Mr Hatfield was a little out of humour just then; you know we're none of us perfect – even Moses spoke unadvisedly with his lips. But now sit down a minute, if you can spare the time, and tell me all your doubts and fears; and I'll try to remove them."

'So I sat me down anent him. He was quite a stranger you know, Miss Grey, and even *younger* nor Maister Hatfield, I believe; an' I had thought him not so pleasant looking as him, and rather a bit crossish, at first, to look at; but he spake so civil like – and when th' cat, poor thing, jumped on to his knee, he only stroked her, and gave a bit of a smile: so I thought that was a good sign; for once, when she did so to th' rector, he knocked her off, like as it might be in scorn and anger, poor thing. But you can't expect a cat to know manners like a Christian, you know, Miss Grey.'

'No of course not, Nancy. But what did Mr Weston say then?'

'He said naught; but he listened to me as steady an' patient as could be, an' never a bit o' scorn about him; so I went on, an' told him all, just as I've told you – an' more too.

' "Well," says he, "Mr Hatfield was quite right in telling you to persevere in doing your duty; but in advising you to go to church, and attend to the service, and so on, he didn't mean that was the whole of a Christian's duty; he only thought you might there learn what more was to be done, and be led to take delight in those exercises, instead of finding them a task and a burden. And if you had asked him to explain those words that trouble you so much, I think he would have told you that, if many shall seek to enter in at the strait gate and shall not be able, it is their own sins that hinder them; just as a man with a large sack on his back, might wish to pass through a narrow doorway, and find it impossible to do so, unless he would leave his sack behind him. But you, Nancy, I dare say, have no sins that you would not gladly throw aside, if you knew how?"

' "Indeed sir, you speak truth," says I.

' "Well," says he, "you know the first, and great commandment – and the second which is like unto it – on which two commandments hang all the law and the prophets? You say you cannot love God; but it strikes me, that if you rightly consider who and what He is, you cannot help it. He is your father, your best friend; every blessing, everything good, pleasant, or useful comes from Him; and everything evil, everything you have reason to hate, to shun, or to fear comes from Satan, *His* enemy as well as ours; and for *this* cause was God manifest in the flesh, that He might destroy the works of the devil: in one word God

IS LOVE; and the more of love we have within us, the nearer we are to Him, and the more of His spirit we possess."

' "Well sir," I said, "if I can always think on these things, I think I might well love God; but how can I love my neighbours – when they vex me, and be so contrairy and sinful as some on 'em is?"

' "It may seem a hard matter," says he, "to love our neighbours, who have so much of what is evil about them, and whose faults so often awaken the evil that lingers within ourselves, but remember, that *He* made them, and *He* loves them; and whosoever loved him that begat, loveth him that is begotten also. And if God so loveth us, that He gave His only begotten son to die for us, we ought also to love one another. But if you cannot feel positive affection for those who do not care for you, you can at least try to do to them as you would they should do unto you; you can endeavour to pity their failings and excuse their offences, and to do all the good you can to those about you. And if you accustom yourself to this, Nancy, the very effort itself will make you love them in some degree – to say nothing of the goodwill your kindness would beget in them, though they might have little else that is good about them. If we love God and wish to serve Him, let us try to be like Him, to do His work, to labour for His glory, which is the good of man, to hasten the coming of His kingdom, which is the peace and happiness of all the world – however powerless we may seem to be, in doing all the good we can through life, the humblest of us may do much towards it; and let us dwell in love, that He may dwell in us, and we in Him. The more happiness we bestow, the more we shall receive, even here, and the greater will be our reward in Heaven when we rest from our labours."

'I believe, Miss, them is his very words, for I've thought 'em ower many a time. An' then he took that Bible, an' read bits here and there, an' explained 'em as clear as the day: and it seemed like as a new light broke in on my soul; an' I felt fair a glow about my heart, an' only wished poor Bill an' all the world could a' been there an' heard it all, and rejoiced wi' me.

'After he was gone, Hannah Rogers, one o' th' neighbours, came in and wanted me to help her to wash. I telled her I couldn't just then, for I hadn't set on th' potaties for th' dinner, nor washed up th' breakfast stuff yet. So then she began a calling me for my nasty, idle ways. I was a little bit vexed at first; but I never said nothing wrong to her: I only telled her, like all in a quiet way, 'at I'd had th' new parson to see me; but I'd get done as quick as ever I could, an' then come an' help her. So then she softened down; and my heart like as it warmed towards her, an' in a bit, we was very good friends.

'An' so it is, Miss Grey, "a soft answer turneth away wrath; but grievous words stir up anger." It isn't only in them you speak to, but in yourself.'

'Very true, Nancy, if we could always remember it.'

'Ay, if we could!'

'And did Mr Weston ever come to see you again?'

'Yes, many a time; and since my eyes has been so bad, he's sat an' read to me by the half hour together; but you know, Miss, he has other folks to see, and other things to do – God bless him! An' that next Sunday he preached *such* a sermon! his text was "Come unto me all ye that labour and are heavy laden, and I will give you rest," and them two blessed verses that follows. You wasn't there, Miss, you was with your friends then – but it made me *so* happy! and I *am* happy now, thank God! an' I take a pleasure, now, in doing little bits o' jobs for my neighbours – such as a poor old body 'ats half blind can do . . . and they take it kindly of me, just as he said. You see, Miss, I'm knitting a pair o' stockings now: – they're for Thomas Jackson: he's a queerish old body, an' we've had many a bout at threaping one anent t'other; an' at times we've differed sorely. So I thought I couldn't do better nor knit him a pair o' warm stockings; an' I've felt to like him a deal better, poor old man, sin' I began. It's turned out just as Maister Weston said.'

'Well, I'm very glad to see you so happy, Nancy, and so wise: but I must go now; I shall be wanted at the Hall,' said I; and bidding her good-bye, I departed, promising to come again when I had time, and feeling nearly as happy as herself.

At another time, I went to read to a poor labourer who was in the last stage of a consumption. The young ladies had been to see him, and somehow a promise of reading to him had been extracted from them; but it was too much trouble, so they begged *me* to do it instead. I went, willingly enough, and there too I was gratified with the praises of Mr Weston, both from the sick man and his wife. The former told me that he derived great comfort and benefit from the visits of the new parson, who frequently came to see him, and was 'another guess sort of man,' to Mr Hatfield, who before the other's arrival at Horton had now and then paid him a visit, on which occasions he would always insist upon having the cottage door kept open to admit the fresh air for his own convenience, without considering how it might injure the sufferer, and having opened his prayer-book, and hastily read over a part of the service for the sick, would hurry away again, if he did not stay to administer some harsh rebuke to the afflicted wife, or to make some thoughtless, not to say heartless, observation rather calculated to increase than diminish the troubles of the suffering pair.

'Whereas,' said the man, 'Maister Weston 'ull pray with me quite in a different fashion, an' talk to me as kind as owt, an' oft read to me too, an' sit beside me just like a brother.'

'Just for all the world!' exclaimed his wife, 'an' about a three wik sin', when he seed how poor Jem shivered wi' cold, an' what pitiful fires we kept, he axed if wer stock o' coals was nearly done. I told him it was, an' we was ill set to get more – but you know mum I didn't think o' him helping us – but howsever, he sent us a sack o' coals next day; an' we've had good fires ever sin'; an' a great blessing it is, this winter time. But that's his way, Miss Grey – when he comes into a poor body's house a seein' sick folk, he like notices what they most stand i' need on, an' if he thinks they can't readily get it therseln, he never says nowt about it, but just gets it for 'em: – an' it isn't everybody 'at 'ud do that, 'at has as little as he has; for you know mum, he's now't at all to live on, but what he gets fro' th' rector; an' that's little enough they say.'

I remembered then, with a species of exultation, that he had frequently been styled a vulgar brute by the amiable Miss Murray, because he sported a silver watch, and clothes not quite so bright and fresh as Mr Hatfield's.

In returning to the lodge, I felt very happy, and thanked God that I had now something to think about, something to dwell on as a relief from the weary monotony, the lonely drudgery of my present life – for I *was* lonely – never, from month to month, from year to year, except during my brief intervals of rest at home, did I see one creature to whom I could open my heart, or freely speak my thoughts with any hope of sympathy, or even comprehension; never one, unless it were poor Nancy Brown, with whom I could enjoy a single moment of real social inter-course, or whose conversation was calculated to render me better, wiser, or happier than before; or who, as far as I could see, could be greatly benefited by mine. My only companions had been unamiable children, and ignorant, wrong-headed girls, from whose fatiguing folly, unbroken solitude was often a relief most earnestly desired, and dearly prized. But to be restricted to such associates was a serious evil, both in its imme-diate effects, and the consequences that were likely to ensue.

Never a new idea or a stirring thought came to me from without; and such as rose within me were, for the most part, miserably crushed at once, or doomed to sicken and fade away, because they could not see the light.

Habitual associates are known to exercise a great influence over each other's minds and manners. Those whose actions are for ever before our eyes, whose words are ever in our ears, will naturally lead us, albeit against our will – slowly – gradually – imperceptibly, perhaps, to act and speak as they do. I will not presume to say how far this irresistible power of assimilation extends; but if one civilized man were doomed to pass a dozen years amid a race of intractable savages, unless he had power to improve them, I greatly question whether, at the close of that period, he would not have become, at least, a barbarian himself. And I, as I could not make my young companions better, feared exceedingly that they would make me worse – would gradually bring my feelings, habits, capacities to the level of their own, without, however, imparting to me their light-heartedness and cheerful vivacity. Already, I seemed to feel my intellect deteriorating, my heart petrifying, my soul contracting, and I trembled lest my very moral perceptions should become deadened, my distinctions of right and wrong confounded, and all my better faculties be sunk, at last, beneath the baleful influence of such a mode of life. The gross vapours of earth were gathering round me, and closing in upon my inward heaven; and thus it was that Mr Weston rose at length upon me, appearing like the morning star in my horizon, to save me from the fear of utter darkness; and I rejoiced that I had now a subject for contemplation, that was above me, not beneath. I was glad to see that all the world was not made up of Bloomfields, Murrays, Hatfields, Ashbys, &c.; and that human excellence was not a mere dream of the imagination. When we hear a little good and no harm of a person, it is easy and pleasant to imagine more – in short, it is needless to analyze all my thoughts, but Sunday was now become a day of peculiar delight to me, (I was now almost broken in to the back corner in the carriage,) for I liked to hear him – and I liked to see him too, though I knew he was not handsome, or even what is called agreeable, in outward aspect; but, certainly, he was not ugly.

In stature, he was a little – a very little – above the middle size; perfectly symmetrical in figure, deep-chested, and strongly built; the outline of his face would be pronounced too square for beauty, but, to me, it announced decision of character; his dark brown hair was not carefully curled, like Mr Hatfield's, but simply brushed aside over a broad, white forehead; the eyebrows, I suppose, were too projecting, but from under those dark brows there gleamed an eye of singular power, brown in colour, not large, and somewhat deepset, but strikingly brilliant, and full of expression; there was character, too, in the mouth, something that bespoke a man of firm purpose, and an habitual thinker, and when he smiled – but I will not speak of that yet, for, at the time I mention, I had never seen him smile; and, indeed, his general appearance did not impress me with the idea of a man given to such a relaxation, nor of such an individual as the cottagers described him. I had early formed my opinion of him, and, in spite of Miss Murray's objurgations, was fully convinced that he was a man of strong sense, firm faith, and ardent piety, but thoughtful and stern: and when I found that, to his other good qualities, was added that of true benevolence, and gentle, considerate kindness, the discovery, perhaps, delighted me the more, as I had not been prepared to expect it.

CHAPTER XII

THE SHOWER

THE NEXT VISIT I paid to Nancy Brown was in the second week in March, for, though I had many spare minutes during the day, I seldom could look upon an hour as entirely my own, since, where everything was left to the caprices of Miss Matilda and her sister, there could be no order or regularity, and whatever occupation I chose, when not actually busied about them or their concerns, I had, as it were, to keep my loins girded, my shoes on my feet, and my staff in my hand; for, not to be immediately forthcoming when called for, was regarded as a grave and inexcusable offence, not only by my pupils and their mother, but by the very servant who came in breathless haste to call me, exclaiming –

'You're to go to the school-room *directly*, mum – the young ladies is WAITING!!'

Climax of horror! actually waiting for their governess!!!

But this time I was pretty sure of an hour or two to myself, for Matilda was preparing for a long ride, and Rosalie was dressing for a dinner party at Lady Ashby's: so I took the opportunity of repairing to the widow's cottage, where I found her in some anxiety about her cat, which had been absent all day. I comforted her with as many anecdotes of that animal's roving propensities as I could recollect.

'I'm feared o' th' gamekeepers,' said she, 'that's all 'at I think on. If th' young gentlemen had been at home, I should a' thought they'd been setting their dogs at her, an' worried her, poor thing, as they did *many* a poor body's cat; but I haven't that to be feared on now.'

Nancy's eyes were better, but still far from well: she had been trying to make a Sunday shirt for her son, but told me she could only bear to do a little bit at it now and then; so that it progressed but slowly, though the poor lad wanted it sadly. So I proposed to help her a little, after I had read to her, for I had plenty of time that evening, and need not return till dusk. She thankfully accepted the offer.

'An' you'll be a bit o' company for me too, Miss,' said she, 'I like as I feel lonesome without my cat.'

But when I had finished reading, and done the half of a seam, with Nancy's capacious brass thimble fitted on to my finger by means of a roll of paper, I was disturbed by the entrance of Mr Weston with the identical cat in his arms. I now saw that he could smile, and very pleasantly too.

'I've done you a piece of good service, Nancy,' he began; then seeing me, he acknowledged my presence by a slight bow. I should have been invisible to Mr Hatfield, or any other gentleman of those parts. 'I've delivered your cat,' he continued, 'from the hands, or rather the gun, of Mr Murray's gamekeeper.'

'God bless you sir,' cried the grateful old woman, ready to weep for joy as she received her favourite from his arms.

'Take care of it,' said he, 'and don't let it go near the rabbit warren, for the gamekeeper swears he'll shoot it, if he sees it there again. He would have done so to-day, if I had not been in time to stop him. I believe it is raining, Miss Grey,' added he, more quietly, observing that I had put aside my work and was preparing to depart. 'Don't let me disturb you – I shan't stay two minutes.'

'You'll *both* stay while this shower gets owered,' said Nancy as she stirred the fire, and placed another chair beside it; 'what! there's room for all.'

'I can see better here, thank you Nancy,' replied I, taking my work to the window, where she had the goodness to suffer me to remain unmolested, while she got a brush to remove the cat's hairs from Mr Weston's coat, carefully wiped the rain from his hat, and gave the cat its supper, busily talking all the time; now thanking her clerical friend for what he had done; now wondering how the cat had found out the warren; and now lamenting the probable consequences of such a discovery. He listened with a quiet, good-natured smile, and at length took a seat in compliance with her pressing invitations, but repeated that he did not mean to stay.

'I have another place to go to,' said he, 'and I see' (glancing at the book on the table) 'some one else has been reading to you.'

'Yes sir, Miss Grey has been as kind as read me a chapter; an' now she's helping me with a shirt for our Bill – but I'm feared she'll be cold there. Won't you come to th' fire, Miss?'

'No, thank you Nancy, I'm quite warm. I must go as soon as this shower is over.'

'Aw, Miss! You said you could stop while dusk!' cried the provoking old woman, and Mr Weston seized his hat.

'Nay sir,' exclaimed she, 'pray don't go now, while it rains so fast!'

'But, it strikes me I'm keeping your visiter away from the fire.'

'No you're not, Mr Weston,' replied I, hoping there was no harm in a falsehood of that description.

'No, sure!' cried Nancy. 'What, there's lots o' room!'

'Miss Grey,' said he, half jestingly, as if he felt it necessary to change the present subject, whether he had anything particular to say or not, 'I wish you would make my peace with the squire, when you see him. He was by when I rescued Nancy's cat, and did not quite approve of the deed. I told him I thought he might better spare all his rabbits than she her cat, for which audacious assertion he treated me to some rather ungentlemanly language, and, I fear, I retorted a trifle too warmly.'

'Oh lawful, sir! I hope you didn't fall out wi' th' maister for sake o' my cat! he cannot bide answering again – can th' maister.'

'Oh! it's no matter, Nancy: I don't care about it, really: I said nothing *very* uncivil; and I suppose Mr Murray is accustomed to use rather strong language when he's heated.'

'Ay sir: it's a pity!'

'And now, I really must go. I have to visit a place a mile beyond this; and you would not have me to return in the dark: besides, it has nearly done raining now – so good evening Nancy. – Good evening Miss Grey.'

'Good evening Mr Weston ... but don't depend upon me for making your peace with Mr Murray, for I never see him – to speak to.'

'Don't you? it can't be helped then!' replied he in dolorous resignation: then, with a peculiar half smile, he added, 'But never mind; I imagine the squire has more to apologize for than I,' and left the cottage.

I went on with my sewing as long as I could see; and then bid Nancy good evening, checking her too lively gratitude by the undeniable assurance, that I had only done for her what she would have done for me, if she had been in my place and I in hers, and hastened back to Horton Lodge; where, having entered the school-room, I found the tea-table all in confusion, the tray flooded with slops, and Miss Matilda in a most ferocious humour.

'Miss Grey, whatever have you been about? I've had tea half an hour ago, and had to make it myself, and drink it all alone! I wish you *would* come in sooner!'

'I've been to see Nancy Brown. I thought you would not be back from your ride.'

'How could I ride in the rain, I should like to know? That d—d pelting shower was vexatious enough – coming on when I was just in full swing; and then to come and find nobody in to tea! – and you *know* I can't make the tea as I like it.'

'I didn't think of the shower,' replied I, (and, indeed, the thought of its driving her home had never entered my head.)

'No, of course, you were under shelter yourself, and you never thought of other people.'

I bore her coarse reproaches with astonishing equanimity, even with cheerfulness; for I was sensible that I had done more good to Nancy Brown, than harm to her; and perhaps some other thoughts assisted to keep up my spirits, and impart a relish to the cup of cold, overdrawn tea, and a charm to the otherwise unsightly table, and – I had almost said – to Miss Matilda's unamiable face. But she soon betook herself to the stables, and left me to the quiet enjoyment of my solitary meal.

CHAPTER XIII

THE PRIMROSES

MISS MURRAY NOW always went twice to church, for she so loved admiration that she could not bear to lose a single opportunity of obtaining it; and she was so sure of it, wherever she showed herself, that whether Harry Meltham and Mr Green were there or not, there was certain to be somebody present who would be not insensible to her charms, besides the rector, whose official capacity generally obliged him to attend.

Usually, also, if the weather permitted, both she and her sister would walk home; Matilda because she hated the confinement of the carriage; she, because she disliked the privacy of it, and enjoyed the company that generally enlivened the first mile of the journey in walking from the church to Mr Green's park-gates, near which commenced the private road to Horton Lodge, which lay in the opposite direction; while the highway conducted in a straight-forward course to the still more distant mansion of Sir Hugh Meltham. Thus, there was always a chance of being accompanied, so far, either by Harry Meltham, with or without Miss Meltham, or Mr Green, with perhaps one or both of his sisters, and any gentlemen visiters they might have.

Whether I walked with the young ladies or rode with their parents, depended entirely upon their own capricious will: if they chose to 'take' me, I went; if, for reasons best known to themselves, they chose to go alone, I took my seat in the carriage: I liked walking better, but a sense of reluctance to obtrude my presence on any one who did not desire it, always kept me passive on these and similar occasions; and I never inquired into the causes of their varying whims. And indeed this was the best policy – for to submit and oblige was the governess's part, to consult their own pleasure was that of the pupils. But when I did walk, this first half of the journey was generally a great nuisance to me. As none of the before-mentioned ladies and gentlemen ever noticed me, it was disagreeable to walk beside them, as if listening to what they said, or wishing to be thought one of them, while they talked over me or across, and if their eyes, in speaking, chanced to fall on me, it seemed as if they looked on vacancy – as if they either did not see me, or were very desirous to make it appear so.

It was disagreeable, too, to walk behind, and thus appear to acknowledge my own inferiority; for in truth, I considered myself pretty nearly as good as the best of them, and wished them to know that I did so, and not to imagine that I looked upon myself as a mere domestic, who knew her own place too well to walk beside such fine ladies and gentlemen as they were . . . though her young ladies might choose to have her with them, and even condescend to converse with her, when no better company were at hand.

Thus – I am almost ashamed to confess it – but indeed I gave myself no little trouble in my endeavours (if I did keep up with them) to appear perfectly unconscious or regardless of their presence, as if I were wholly absorbed in my own reflections or the contemplation of surrounding objects; or if I lingered behind, it was some bird or insect, some tree or flower, that attracted my attention, and having duly examined that, I would pursue my walk alone, at a leisurely pace, until my pupils had bid adieu to their companions, and turned off into the quiet, private road.

One such occasion I particularly well remember, it was a lovely afternoon about the close of March; Mr Green and his sisters had sent their carriage back empty, in order to enjoy the bright sunshine and balmy air in a sociable walk home along with their visiters Captain Somebody and Lieutenant Somebody else (a couple of military fops,) and the Misses Murray, who, of course, contrived to join them.

Such a party was highly agreeable to Rosalie; but not finding it equally suitable to my taste, I presently fell back, and began to botanize and entomologize along the green banks and budding hedges, till the company was considerably in advance of me, and I could hear the sweet song of the happy lark: then my spirit of misanthropy began to melt away beneath the soft, pure air, and genial sunshine; but sad thoughts of early childhood, and yearnings for departed joys, or for a brighter future lot, arose instead.

As my eyes wandered over the steep banks covered with young grass and green-leaved plants, and surmounted by budding hedges, I longed intensely for some familiar flower that might recall the woody dales or green hillsides of home – the brown moorlands, of course, were out of the question. Such a discovery would make my eyes gush out with water, no doubt; but that was one of my greatest enjoyments now.

At length I descried, high up between the twisted roots of an oak, three lovely primroses, peeping so sweetly from their hiding-place that the tears already started at the sight, but they grew so high above me, that I tried in vain to gather one or two to dream over and to carry with me; I could not reach them, unless I climbed the bank, which I was deterred from doing by hearing a footstep at that moment behind me, and was therefore about to turn away, when I was startled by the words, 'Allow me to gather them for you, Miss Grey,' spoken in the grave, low tones of a well-known voice.

Immediately the flowers were gathered, and in my hand. It was Mr Weston of course – who else would trouble himself to do so much for *me*?

I thanked him; whether warmly or coldly, I cannot tell: but certain I am, that I did not express half the gratitude I felt. It was foolish, perhaps, to feel any gratitude at all, but it seemed to me, at that moment, as if this were a remarkable instance of his good nature, an act of kindness which I could not repay, but never should forget: so utterly unaccustomed was I to receive such civilities, so little prepared to expect them – from any one within fifty miles of Horton Lodge.

Yet this did not prevent me from feeling a little uncomfortable in his presence; and I proceeded to follow my pupils at a much quicker pace than before; though perhaps, if Mr Weston had taken the hint and let me pass without another word, I might have repented it an hour after: but he did not. A somewhat rapid walk for me, was but an ordinary pace for him.

'Your young ladies have left you alone,' said he.

'Yes; they are occupied with more agreeable company.'

'Then don't trouble yourself to overtake them.'

I slackened my pace; but next moment regretted having done so; my companion did not speak: and I had nothing in the world to say, and feared he might be in the same predicament. At length, however, he broke the pause by asking, with a certain quiet abruptness peculiar to himself, if I liked flowers.

'Yes, very much,' I answered, 'wild flowers especially.'

'*I* like wild flowers,' said he, 'others I don't care about, because I have no particular associations connected with them – except one or two. What are your favourite flowers?'

'Primroses, blue-bells, and heath-blossoms.'

'Not violets?'

'No, because, as you say, I have no particular associations connected with them; for there are no sweet violets among the hills and valleys round my home.'

'It must be a great consolation to you, to have a home, Miss Grey,' observed my companion after a short pause, 'however remote, or however seldom visited, still it is something to look to.'

'It is so much, that I think I could not live without it,' replied I, with an enthusiasm of which I immediately repented, for I thought it must have sounded essentially silly.

'O yes, you could!' said he with a thoughtful smile. 'The ties that bind us to life are tougher than you imagine, or than any one can, who has not felt how roughly they may be pulled without breaking. You might be miserable without a home, but even *you* could live, and no *so* miserably as you suppose. The human heart is like Indian-rubber, a little swells it, but a great deal will not burst it. If "little more than nothing" will disturb it, "little less than all things will suffice" to break it. As in the outer members of our frame, there is a vital power inherent in itself, that strengthens it against external violence. Every blow that shakes it, will serve to harden it against a future stroke; as constant labour thickens the skin of the hand, and strengthens its muscles instead of wasting them away: so that a day of arduous toil, that might excoriate a lady's palm, would make no sensible impression on that of a hardy ploughman.

'I speak from experience – partly my own. There was a time when I thought as you do – at least, I was fully persuaded that Home and its affections were the only things that made life tolerable ... that if deprived of these, existence would become a burden hard to be endured; but now, I have no home ... unless you would dignify my two hired rooms at Horton by such a name; ... and not twelve months ago, I lost the last and dearest of my early friends: and yet, not only I live, but I am not wholly destitute of hope and comfort, even for this life; though I must acknowledge that I can seldom enter even an humble cottage, at the close of day, and see its inhabitants peaceably gathered round their cheerful hearth, without a feeling *almost* of envy at their domestic enjoyment.'

'You don't know what happiness lies before you yet,' said I, 'you are now only in the commencement of your journey.'

'The best of happiness,' replied he, 'is mine already ... the power and the will to be useful.'

We now approached a stile communicating with a footpath that conducted to a farm-house, where I suppose Mr Weston purposed to make himself 'useful,' for he presently took leave of me, crossed the stile, and traversed the path with his usual firm, elastic tread, leaving me to ponder his words as I continued my course alone.

I had heard before that he had lost his mother not many months before he came. She then, was the last and dearest of his early friends; and he had *no home*. I pitied him from my heart; I almost wept for sympathy. And this, I thought, accounted for the shade of premature thoughtfulness that so frequently clouded his brow, and obtained for him the reputation of a morose and sullen disposition with the charitable Miss Murray and all her kin.

'But,' thought I, 'he is not so miserable as I should be under such a deprivation: he leads an active life; and a wide field for useful exertion lies before him, he can *make* friends – and he can make a home too, if he pleases, and doubtless he will please sometime; and God grant the partner of that home may be worthy of his choice, and make it a happy one . . . such a home as he deserves to have! And how delightful it would be to –' But no matter what I thought.

I began this book with the intention of concealing nothing, that those who liked might have the benefit of perusing a fellow creature's heart: but we have *some* thoughts that all the angels in heaven are welcome to behold – but not our brother-men – not even the best and kindest amongst them.

By this time the Greens had taken themselves to their own abode, and the Murrays had turned down the private road, whither I hastened to follow them. I found the two girls lost in an animated discussion on the respective merits of the two young officers; but on seeing me Rosalie broke off in the middle of a sentence to exclaim, with malicious glee,

'Oh ho, Miss Grey! you're come at last, are you? No *wonder* you lingered so long behind! and no *wonder* you always stand up so vigorously for Mr Weston when I abuse him – Ah, ha! I see it all now!'

'Now come, Miss Murray, don't be foolish,' said I, attempting a good-natured laugh, 'you know such nonsense can make no impression on me.'

But she still went on talking such intolerable stuff – her sister helping her with appropriate fictions coined for the occasion – that I thought it necessary to say something in my own justification.

'What humbug all this is!' I exclaimed. 'If Mr Weston's road happened to be the same as mine for a few yards, and if he chose to exchange a word or two in passing, what is there so remarkable in that? I assure you I never spoke to him before; except once.'

'Where? where? and when?' cried they eagerly.

'In Nancy's cottage.'

'Ah ha! you've met him there, have you?' exclaimed Rosalie, with exultant laughter. 'Ah! now Matilda, I've found out why she's so fond of going to Nancy Brown's! she goes there to flirt with Mr Weston!'

'Really that is not worth contradicting! ... I only saw him there once, I tell you ... and how could I know he was coming?'

Irritated as I was at their foolish mirth and vexatious imputations, the uneasiness did not continue long: when they had had their laugh out, they returned again to the Captain and Lieutenant; and, while they disputed and commented upon them, my indignation rapidly cooled; the cause of it was quickly forgotten, and I turned my thoughts into a pleasanter channel.

Thus we proceeded up the park, and entered the hall; and as I ascended the stairs to my own chamber, I had but one thought within me, my heart was filled to overflowing with one single earnest wish. Having entered the room, and shut the door, I fell upon my knees and offered up a fervent but not impetuous prayer: 'Thy will be done,' I strove to say throughout, but, 'Father, all things are possible with Thee, and may it be Thy will,' was sure to follow. That wish ... that prayer both men and women would have scorned me for ... 'But Father, *Thou* wilt *not* despise!' I said – and felt that it was true. It seemed to me that another's welfare was at least as ardently implored for as my own – nay, even that *that* was the principal object of my heart's desire. I might have been deceiving myself, but that idea gave me confidence to ask, and power to hope I did not ask in vain.

As for the primroses, I kept two of them in a glass in my room until they were completely withered, and the housemaid threw them out, and the petals of the other I pressed between the leaves of my Bible – I have them still, and mean to keep them always.

CHAPTER XIV

THE RECTOR

THE FOLLOWING DAY was as fine as the preceding one. Soon after breakfast, Miss Matilda, having galloped and blundered through a few unprofitable lessons, and vengeably thumped the piano for an hour, in a terrible humour with both me and it, because her mama would not give her a holiday, had betaken herself to her favourite places of resort, the yards, the stables, and the dog-kennels: and Miss Murray was gone forth to enjoy a quiet ramble with a new fashionable novel for her companion, leaving me in the school-room, hard at work upon a water-colour drawing I had promised to do for her, and which she insisted upon my finishing that day.

At my feet lay a little rough terrier. It was the property of Miss Matilda; but she hated the animal, and intended to sell it, alleging that it was quite spoiled. It was really an excellent dog of its kind; but she affirmed it was fit for nothing, and had not even the sense to know its own mistress.

The fact is, she had purchased it when but a small puppy, insisting, at first, that no one should touch it but herself; but, soon becoming tired of so helpless and troublesome a nursling, she had gladly yielded to my entreaties to be allowed to take charge of it; and I, by carefully nursing the little creature from infancy to adolescence, of course, had obtained its affections; a reward I should have greatly valued and looked upon as far outweighing all the trouble I had had with it, had not poor Snap's grateful feelings exposed him to many a harsh word and many a spiteful kick and pinch from his owner, and were he not now in danger of being 'put away' in consequence, or transferred to some rough, stony-hearted master. But how could I help it? I could not make the dog hate me by cruel treatment; and she would not propitiate him by kindness.

However, while I thus sat, working away at my pencil, Mrs Murray came, half sailing, half bustling, into the room.

'Miss Grey,' she began, – 'Dear! how can you sit at your drawing such a day as this?' (she thought I was doing it for my own pleasure) 'I *wonder* you don't put on your bonnet and go out with the young ladies.'

'I think, ma'am, Miss Murray is reading; and Miss Matilda is amusing herself with her dogs.'

'If you would try to amuse Miss Matilda yourself a little more, I think she would not be *driven* to seek amusement in the companionship of dogs and horses, and grooms, so much as she is; and if you would be a little more cheerful and conversable with Miss Murray, she would not so often go wandering in the fields with a book in her hand. However, I don't want to vex you,' added she, seeing, I suppose, that my cheeks burned and my hand trembled with some unamiable emotion. 'Do, pray, try not to be so touchy! – there's no speaking to you else. And tell me if you know where Rosalie is gone: and why she likes to be so much alone?'

'She says she likes to be alone when she has a new book to read.'

'But why can't she read it in the park or the garden; – why should she go into the fields and lanes? and how is that that Mr Hatfield so often finds her out? She told me last week he'd walked his horse by her side all up Moss-lane; and now I'm sure it was he I saw from my dressing-room window, walking so briskly past the park-gates, and on towards the field where she so frequently goes. I wish you would go and see if she is there; and just gently remind her that it is not proper for a young lady of her rank and prospects to be wandering about by herself in that manner, exposed to the attentions of any one that presumes to address her, like some poor neglected girl that has no park to walk in, and no friends to take care of her; and tell her that her papa would be extremely angry if he knew of her treating Mr Hatfield in that familiar manner that I fear she does; and – Oh! if you – if *any* governess had but half a mother's watch-fulness – half a mother's anxious care – I should be saved this trouble; and you would see at once the necessity of keeping your eye upon her, and making your company agreeable to – Well, go – go; there's no time to be lost,' cried she, seeing that I had put away my drawing materials, and was waiting in the door-way for the conclusion of her address.

According to her prognostications, I found Miss Murray in her favourite field just without the park; and, unfortunately, not alone; for the tall, stately figure of Mr Hatfield was slowly sauntering by her side.

Here was a poser for me. It was my duty to interrupt the *tête à-tête*: but how was it to be done? Mr Hatfield could not be driven away by so insignificant a person as I; and to go and place myself on the other side of Miss Murray, and intrude my unwelcome presence upon her without noticing her compan-ion, was a piece of rudeness I could not be guilty of: neither had I the courage to cry aloud from the top of the field that she was wanted elsewhere. So I took the intermediate course of walking slowly, but steadily towards them, resolving, if my approach failed to scare away the beau, to pass by and tell Miss Murray her mama wanted her.

She certainly looked very charming as she strolled lingeringly along under the budding horse-chestnut trees that stretched their long arms over the park-palings, with her closed book in one hand, and in the other a graceful sprig of myrtle which served her as a very pretty plaything ... her bright ringlets escaping profusely from her little bonnet, and gently stirred by the breeze, her fair cheek flushed with gratified vanity, her smiling blue eyes, now slyly glancing towards her admirer, now gazing downward at her myrtle sprig. But Snap, running before me, interrupted her in the midst of some half pert, half playful repartee, by catching hold of her dress and vehemently tugging thereat, till Mr Hatfield with his cane administered a resounding thwack upon the animal's skull, and sent it yelping back to me, with a clamorous outcry that afforded the reverend gentleman great amusement; but seeing me so near, he thought, I suppose, he might as well be taking his departure; and as I stooped to caress the dog, with ostentatious pity to shew my disapproval of his severity, I heard him say,

'When shall I see you again, Miss Murray?'

'At church, I suppose,' replied she, 'unless your business chance to bring you here again, at the precise moment when I happen to be walking by.'

'I could always manage to have business here, if I knew precisely when and where to find you.'

'But if I would, I could not inform you, for I am so immethodical I never can tell to-day what I shall do to-morrow.'

'Then give me that, meantime, to comfort me,' said he, half jestingly and half in earnest, extending his hand for the sprig of myrtle.

'No indeed, I shan't!'

'Do! *Pray* do! I shall be the most miserable of men if you don't. You cannot be so cruel as to deny me a favour so easily granted and yet so highly prized!' pleaded he as ardently as if his life depended on it.

By this time, I stood within a very few yards of them, impatiently waiting his departure.

'There then! take it and go,' said Rosalie.

He joyfully received the gift, murmured something that made her blush and toss aside her head, but with a little laugh that shewed her displeasure was entirely affected; and then with a courteous salutation withdrew.

'Did you ever see such a man, Miss Grey?' said she, turning to me, 'I'm so *glad* you came! I thought I never *should* get rid of him; – and I was so terribly afraid of papa seeing him.'

'Has he been with you long?'

'No, not long, but he's so extremely impertinent: and he's always hanging about, pretending his business or his clerical duties require his attendance in these parts, and really watching for poor me, and pouncing upon me wherever he sees me.'

'Well, your mama thinks you ought not to go beyond the park or garden without some discreet, matronly person like me to accompany you, and keep off all intruders. She descried Mr Hatfield hurrying past the park-gates, and forthwith dispatched me with instructions to seek you up and to take care of you, and likewise to warn –'

'Oh, mama's so tiresome! As if I couldn't take care of myself! She bothered me before about Mr Hatfield; and I told her she might trust me – I never should forget my rank and station for the most delightful man that ever breathed. – I wish he would go down on his knees to-morrow, and implore me to be his wife, that I might just shew her how mistaken she is in supposing that I could ever – Oh! it provokes me so – To think that I could be such a fool as to fall in *love*! It is quite beneath the dignity of a woman to do such a thing. Love! I detest the word! as applied to one of our sex, I think it a perfect insult! a preference I *might* acknowledge; but never for one like poor Mr Hatfield who has not seven hundred a year to bless himself with. I like to talk to him, because he's so clever and amusing – I wish Sir Thomas Ashby were half as nice – besides, I must have *somebody* to flirt with, and no one else has the sense to come here; and when we go out, mama won't let me flirt with anybody but Sir Thomas – if he's there, and if he's *not* there, I'm bound hand and foot, for fear somebody should go and make up some exaggerated story, and put it into his head that I'm engaged, or likely to be engaged, to somebody else; or, what is more probable, for fear his nasty old mother should see or hear of my ongoings, and conclude that I'm not a fit wife for her excellent son; as if the said son were not the greatest scamp in Christendom; and as if any woman of common decency were not a world too good for him.'

'Is it really so, Miss Murray? and does your mama know it, and yet wish you to marry him?'

'To be sure she does! She knows more against him than I do, I believe: she keeps it from me lest I should be discouraged; not knowing how little I care about such things. For it's no great matter really: he'll be all right when he's married, as mama says; and reformed rakes make the best husbands, *every* body knows. I only wish he were not so ugly – *that's* all *I* think about – but then there's no choice here in the country, and papa *will not* let us go to London –'

'But I should think Mr Hatfield would be far better.'

'And so he would if he were lord of Ashby Park – there's not a doubt of it; but the fact is, I *must* have Ashby Park, whoever shares it with me.'

'But Mr Hatfield thinks you like him all this time; you don't consider how bitterly he will be disappointed when he finds himself mistaken.'

'*No* indeed! It will be a proper punishment for his presumption – for ever *daring* to think I could like him. I should enjoy nothing so much as lifting the veil from his eyes.'

'The sooner you do it the better then.'

'No; – I tell you, I like to amuse myself with him. Besides, he doesn't really think I like him. I take good care of that; you don't know how cleverly I manage. He may presume to think he can *induce* me to like him, for which I shall punish him as he deserves.'

'Well, mind you don't give too much reason for such presumption – that's all,' replied I.

But all my exhortations were in vain: they only made her somewhat more solicitous to disguise her wishes and her thoughts from me. She talked no more to me about the rector; but I could see that her mind, if not her heart, was fixed upon him still, and that she was intent upon obtaining another interview; for though, in compliance with her mother's request, I was now constituted the companion of her rambles for a time, she still persisted in wandering in the fields and lanes that lay in the nearest proximity to the road; and, whether she talked to me, or read the book she carried in her hand, she kept continually pausing to look round her, or gaze up the road to see if any one was coming; and if a horseman trotted by, I could tell by her unqualified abuse of the poor equestrian, whoever he might be, that she hated him *because* he was not Mr Hatfield.

'Surely,' thought I, 'she is not so indifferent to him as she believes herself to be, or would have others to believe her; and her mother's anxiety is not so wholly causeless as she affirms.'

Three days passed away, and he did not make his appearance. On the afternoon of the fourth, as we were walking beside the park palings in the memorable field, each furnished with a book, (for I always took care to provide myself with something to be doing when she did not require me to talk), she suddenly interrupted my studies by exclaiming,

'Oh! Miss Grey, do be so kind as to go and see Mark Wood, and take his wife half a crown from me – I should have given or sent it a week ago, but quite forgot. There!' said she, throwing me her purse, and speaking very fast – 'Never mind getting it out now, but take the purse and give them what you like – I would go with you, but I want to finish this volume. I'll come and meet you when I've done it. Be quick will you – and – Oh wait; hadn't you better read to him a bit? Run to the house and get some sort of a good book – Anything will do.'

I did as I was desired; but, suspecting something from her hurried manner and the suddenness of the request, I just glanced back before I quitted the field, and there was Mr Hatfield about to enter at the gate below. By sending me to the house for a book, she had just prevented my meeting him on the road.

'Never mind!' thought I, 'there'll be no great harm done. Poor Mark will be glad of the half-crown, and perhaps of the good book too; and if the rector does steal Miss Rosalie's heart, it will only humble her pride a little; and if they do get married at last, it will only save her from a worse fate; and she will be quite a good enough partner for him, and he for her.'

Mark Wood was the consumptive labourer whom I mentioned before. He was now rapidly wearing away. Miss Murray, by her liberality, obtained literally the blessing of him that was ready to perish; for though the half-crown could be of very little service to him, he was glad of it for the sake of his wife and children, so soon to be widowed and fatherless.

After I sat a few minutes, and read a little for the comfort and edification of himself and his afflicted wife, I left them; but I had not proceeded fifty yards before I encountered Mr Weston, apparently on his way to the same abode.

He greeted me in his usual quiet, unaffected way, stopped to inquire about the condition of the sick man and his family, and with a sort of unconscious, brotherly disregard to ceremony, took from my hand the book out of which I had been reading, turned over the pages, made a few brief, but very sensible remarks, and restored it; then told me about some poor sufferer he had just been visiting, talked a little about Nancy Brown, made a few observations upon my little rough friend the terrier, that was frisking at his feet, and finally upon the beauty of the weather, and departed.

I have omitted to give a detail of his words from a notion that they would not interest the reader as they did me, and not because I have forgotten them. No; I remember them well; for I thought them over and over again in the course of that day and many succeeding ones, I know not how often, and recalled every intonation of his deep, clear voice, every flash of his quick, brown eye, and every gleam of his pleasant, but too transient smile. Such a confession will look very absurd, I fear – but no matter – I have written it; and they that read it will not know the writer.

While I was walking along, happy within, and pleased with all around, Miss Murray came hastening to meet me; her buoyant step, flushed cheek, and radiant smiles shewing that she, too, was happy, in her own way. Running up to me, she put her arm in mine, and without waiting to recover breath, began –

'Now Miss Grey, think yourself highly honoured, for I'm come to tell you my news before I've breathed a word of it to any one else.'

'Well, what is it?'

'Oh, *such* news! In the first place, you must know that Mr Hatfield came upon me just after you were gone. I was in *such* a way for fear papa or mama should see him! – but you know I couldn't call you back again; and so I – Oh dear! I can't tell you all about it now, for there's Matilda, I see, in the park, and I must go and open my budget to her. But however, Hatfield was most uncommonly audacious, unspeakably complimentary, and unprecedentedly tender – tried to be so at least – he didn't succeed very well in *that*, because it's not his vein. I'll tell you all he said another time.'

'But what did *you* say – I'm more interested in that?'

'I'll tell you that, too, at some future period. I happened to be in a very good humour just then; but, though I was complaisant and gracious enough, I took care not to compromise myself in any possible way. But, however, the conceited wretch chose to interpret my amiability of temper his own way, and at length presumed upon my indulgence so far, that – what do you think? – he actually – made me an offer!'

'And you –'

'I proudly drew myself up, and with the greatest coolness expressed my astonishment at such an occurrence, and hoped he had seen nothing in my conduct to justify his expectations. You should have *seen* how his countenance fell! He went perfectly white in the face. I assured him that I esteemed him and all that, but could not possibly accede to his proposals; and if I did, papa and mama could never be brought to give their consent.

' "But if they could," said he, "would yours be wanting?"

' "Certainly, Mr Hatfield," I replied, with a cool decision which quelled all hope at once. Oh, if you had seen how dreadfully mortified he was – how crushed to the earth by his disappointment! really, I almost pitied him myself!

'One more desperate attempt, however, he made. After a silence of considerable duration, during which he struggled to be calm, and I to be grave – for I felt a strong propensity to laugh – which would have ruined all – he said, with the ghost of a smile –

' "But tell me plainly, Miss Murray; if I had the wealth of Sir Hugh Meltham, or the prospects of his eldest son, would you still refuse me? answer me truly, upon your honour."

' "Certainly," said I. "That would make no difference whatever."

'It was a great lie, but he looked so confident in his own attractions still, that I determined not to leave him one stone upon another. He looked me full in the face; but I kept my countenance so well that he could not imagine I was saying anything more than the actual truth.

' "Then it's all over, I suppose," he said, looking as if he could have died on the spot with vexation and the intensity of his despair. But he was angry as well as disappointed. There was he, suffering so unspeakably, and there was I, the pitiless cause of it all, so utterly impenetrable to all the artillery of his looks and words, so calmly cold and proud, he could not but feel some resentment; and with singular bitterness he began,

' "I certainly did not expect this, Miss Murray. I might say something about your past conduct, and the hopes you have led me to foster; but I forbear, on condition –"

' "No conditions, Mr Hatfield!" said I, now truly indignant at his insolence.

' "Then let me beg it as a favour," he replied, lowering his voice at once, and taking an humbler tone; "let me entreat that you will not mention this affair to any one whatever. If you will keep silence about it, there need be no unpleasantness on either side – nothing, I mean, beyond what is quite unavoidable: for my own feelings I will endeavour to keep to myself, if I cannot annihilate; I will try to forgive, if I cannot forget the cause of my sufferings. I will not suppose, Miss Murray, that you know how deeply you have injured me. I would not have you aware of it; but if, in addition to the injury you have already done me – pardon me, but whether innocently or not, you *have* done it – and if you add to it by giving publicity to this unfortunate affair, or naming it *at all*, you will find that I too can speak; and though you scorned my love, you will hardly scorn my—"

'He stopped, but he bit his bloodless lip and looked so terribly fierce that I was quite frightened. However, my pride upheld me still, and I answered disdainfully,

' "I do not know what motive you suppose I could have for naming it to any one, Mr Hatfield; but if I were disposed to do so, you would not deter me by threats; and it is scarcely the part of a gentleman to attempt it."

' "Pardon me, Miss Murray," said he, "I have loved you so intensely – I do still adore you so deeply that I would not willingly offend you; but though I never have loved, and never *can* love any woman as I have loved you, it is equally certain that I never was so ill-treated by any. On the contrary, I have always found your sex the kindest, and most tender and obliging of God's creation, till now." (Think of the conceited fellow saying that!) "And the novelty and harshness of the lesson you have taught me to-day, and the bitterness of being disappointed in the only quarter on which the happiness of my life depended, must excuse any appearance of asperity. If my presence is disagreeable to you, Miss Murray," he said, (for I was looking about me to show how little I cared for him, so he thought I was tired of him, I suppose,) "If my presence is disagreeable to you, Miss Murray, you have only to promise me the favour I named, and I will relieve you at once. There are many ladies – some even in this parish – that would be delighted to accept what you have so scornfully trampled under your feet. They would be naturally inclined to hate one whose surpassing loveliness has so completely estranged my heart from them and blinded me to their attractions; and a single hint of the truth, from me to one of these, would be sufficient to raise such a talk against you as would seriously injure your prospects, and diminish your chance of success with any other gentleman you or your mama might design to entangle."

' "What do you mean, sir?" said I, ready to stamp with passion.

' "I mean that this affair from beginning to end appears to me like a case of arrant – flirtation, to say the least of it – such a case as you would find it rather inconvenient to have blazoned through the world – especially with the additions and exaggerations of your female rivals, who would be too glad to publish the matter, if I only gave them a handle to it. But I promise you, on the faith of a gentleman, that no word or syllable that could tend to your prejudice shall ever escape my lips, provided you will –"

' "Well, well, I won't mention it," said I. "You may rely upon my silence, if that can afford you any consolation."

' "You promise it?"

' "Yes," I answered, for I wanted to get rid of him now.

' "Farewell, then!" said he, in a most doleful heart-sick tone; and with a look where pride vainly struggled against despair, he turned and went away, longing, no doubt, to get home, that he might shut himself up in his study and cry – if he doesn't burst into tears before he gets there.'

'But you have broken your promise already!' said I, truly horrified at her perfidy.

'Oh! it's only to you – I know you won't repeat it.'

'Certainly I shall not; but you say you are going to tell your sister; and she will tell your brothers when they come home, and Brown immediately, if you do not tell her yourself, and Brown will blazon it, or be the means of blazoning it throughout the country.'

'No, indeed she won't – We shall not tell her at all, unless it be under promise of the strictest secrecy.'

'But how can you expect her to keep her promises better than her more enlightened mistress?'

'Well, well, she shan't hear it then,' said Miss Murray, some-what snappishly.

'But you will tell your mama, of course,' pursued I; 'and she will tell your papa.'

'Of course I shall tell mama: that is the very thing that pleases me so much. I shall now be able to convince her how mistaken she was in her fears about me.'

'Oh, *that's* it, is it? I was wondering what it was that delighted you so much.'

'Yes; and another thing is, that I've humbled Mr Hatfield so charmingly; and another – why, you must allow me some share of female vanity; I don't pretend to be without that most essential attribute of our sex – and if you had seen poor Hatfield's intense eagerness in making his ardent declaration and his flattering proposal, and his agony of mind, that no effort of pride could conceal, on being refused, you would have allowed I had some cause to be gratified.'

'The greater his agony, I should think, the less your cause for gratification.'

'Oh, nonsense!' cried the young lady, shaking herself with vexation. 'You either can't understand me, or you won't. If I had not confidence in your magnanimity, I should think you envied me. But you will perhaps comprehend *this* cause of pleasure – which is as great as any – namely, that I am delighted with myself for my prudence, my self-command, my *heartlessness*, if you please; I was not a bit taken by surprise, not a bit confused, or awkward, or foolish; I just acted and spoke as I ought to have done, and was completely my own mistress throughout. And here was a man, decidedly good-looking – Jane and Susan Green call him bewitchingly handsome – I suppose they're two of the ladies he pretends would be so glad to have him – but, however, he was certainly a very clever, witty, agreeable companion – not what *you* call clever, but just enough to make him entertaining; and a man one needn't be ashamed of anywhere, and would not soon grow tired of; and – to confess the truth, I rather liked him – better even, of late, than Harry Meltham – and he evidently idolized me; and yet, though he came upon me all alone and unprepared, I had the wisdom, and the pride, and the strength to refuse him – and so scornfully and coolly as I did: I have good reason to be proud of that!'

'And you are equally proud of having told him that his having the wealth of Sir Hugh Meltham would make no difference to you when that was not the case; and of having promised to tell no one of his misadventure, apparently without the slightest intention of keeping your promise?'

'Of course! what else could I do? You would not have had me – but I see, Miss Grey, you're not in a good temper. – Here's Matilda; I'll see what she and mama have to say about it.'

She left me, offended at my want of sympathy, and thinking, no doubt, that I envied her. I did not – at least, I firmly believe I did not. I was sorry for her; I was amazed, disgusted at her heartless vanity; I wondered why so much beauty should be given to those who made so bad a use of it, and denied to some who would make it a benefit to both themselves and others.

But, God knows best, I concluded. There are, I suppose, some men as vain, as selfish, and as heartless as she is, and perhaps such women may be useful to punish them.

CHAPTER XV

THE WALK

'O DEAR! I WISH Hatfield had not been so precipitate!' said Rosalie next day at four p.m., as, with a portentous yawn, she laid down her worsted-work and looked listlessly towards the window.

'There's no inducement to go out now; and nothing to look forward to. The days will be so long and dull when there are no parties to enliven them; and there are none this week, or next either, that I know of.'

'Pity you were so cross to him,' observed Matilda, to whom this lamentation was addressed. 'He'll never come again; and I suspect you liked him after all. I hoped you would have taken him for your beau, and left dear Harry to me.'

'Humph! my beau must be an Adonis indeed, Matilda, the admired of all beholders, if I am to be contented with him alone. I'm sorry to lose Hatfield, I confess; but the first decent man, or number of men, that come to supply his place, will be more than welcome. It's Sunday to-morrow – I do wonder how he'll look, and whether he'll be able to go through the service. Most likely he'll pretend he's got a cold and make Mr Weston do it all.'

'Not he!' exclaimed Matilda, somewhat contemptuously. 'Fool as he is, he's not so soft as that comes to.'

Her sister was slightly offended; but the event proved Matilda was right. The disappointed lover performed his pastoral duties as usual. Rosalie, indeed, affirmed he looked very pale and dejected: he might be a little paler, but the difference, if any, was scarcely perceptible. As for his dejection, I certainly did not hear his laugh ringing from the vestry as usual, nor his voice loud in hilarious discourse, though I did hear it uplifted in rating the sexton in a manner that made the congregation stare; and in his transits to and from the pulpit and the communion-table there was more of solemn pomp, and less of that irreverent, self-confident, or rather self-delighted imperiousness with which he usually swept along – that air that seemed to say, 'You all reverence and adore me, I know; but if any one does not, I defy him to the teeth!'

But the most remarkable change was that he never once suffered his eyes to wander in the direction of Mr Murray's pew, and did not leave the church till we were gone.

Mr Hatfield had doubtless received a very severe blow; but his pride impelled him to use every effort to conceal the effects of it. He had been disappointed in his certain hope of obtaining not only a beautiful and, to him, highly attractive wife, but one whose rank and fortune might give brilliance to far inferior charms: he was likewise, no doubt, intensely mortified by his repulse, and deeply offended at the conduct of Miss Murray throughout.

It would have given him no little consolation to have known how disappointed she was to find him apparently so little moved, and to see that he was able to refrain from casting a single glance at her throughout both the services, though, she declared, it showed he was thinking of her all the time, or his eyes would have fallen upon her, if it were only by chance; but if they had so chanced to fall, she would have affirmed it was because they could not resist the attraction. It might have pleased him too, in some degree, to have seen how dull and dissatisfied she was throughout that week, (the greater part of it, at least,) for lack of her usual source of excitement; and how often she regretted having 'used him up so soon,' like a child that, having devoured its plum-cake too hastily, sits sucking its fingers, and vainly lamenting its greediness.

At length, I was called upon, one fine morning, to accompany her in a walk to the village. Ostensibly she went to get some shades of Berlin wool at a tolerably respectable shop that was chiefly supported by the ladies of the vicinity: really – I trust there is no breach of charity in supposing that she went with the idea of meeting either with the rector himself, or some other admirer by the way; for as we went along, she kept wondering, 'what Hatfield would do or say if we met him,' &c., &c.; as we passed Mr Green's park-gates, she 'wondered whether he was at home – great stupid blockhead;' as Lady Meltham's carriage passed us she 'wondered what Mr Harry was doing this fine day;' and then began to abuse his elder brother for being 'such a fool as to get married and go and live in London.'

'Why,' said I, 'I thought you wanted to live in London yourself.'

'Yes, because it's so dull here; but then he makes it still duller by taking himself off and if he were not married I might have him instead of that odious Sir Thomas.'

Then, observing the prints of a horse's feet on the somewhat miry road, she 'wondered whether it was a gentleman's horse,' and finally concluded it was, for the impressions were too small to have been made by a 'great, clumsy cart-horse;' and then she 'wondered who the rider could be,' and whether we should meet him coming back, for she was sure he had only passed that morning; and lastly, when we entered the village and saw only a few of its humble inhabitants moving about, she 'wondered why the stupid people couldn't keep in their houses; she was sure she didn't want to see their ugly faces, and dirty, vulgar clothes – it wasn't for that she came to Horton!'

Amid all this, I confess, I wondered too, in secret, whether we should meet, or catch a glimpse of somebody else; and as we passed his lodgings, I even went so far as to wonder whether he was at the window.

On entering the shop, Miss Murray desired me to stand in the doorway while she transacted her business, and tell her if any one passed. But alas! there was no one visible besides the villagers, except Jane and Susan Green coming down the single street, apparently returning from a walk.

'Stupid things!' muttered she, as she came out after having concluded her bargain. 'Why couldn't they have their dolt of a brother with them? even *he* would be better than nothing!'

She greeted them, however, with a cheerful smile, and protestations of pleasure at the happy meeting equal to their own. They placed themselves one on each side of her; and all three walked away chatting and laughing as young ladies do when they get together, if they be but on tolerably intimate terms. But I, feeling myself to be one too many, left them to their merriment and lagged behind, as usual on such occasions: I had no relish for walking beside Miss Green or Miss Susan like one deaf and dumb, who could neither speak nor be spoken to.

But this time I was not long alone. It struck me, at first, as very odd, that just as I was thinking about Mr Weston he should come up and accost me; but afterwards, on due reflection, I thought there was nothing odd about it, unless it were the fact of his speaking to me, for, on such a morning, and so near his own abode, it was natural enough that he should be about; and as for my thinking of him, I had been doing that, with little intermission, ever since we set out on our journey; so there was nothing remarkable in that.

'You are alone again, Miss Grey,' said he.

'Yes.'

'What kind of people are those ladies – the Misses Green?'

'I really don't know.'

'That's strange – when you live so near and see them so often!'

'Well, I suppose they are lively, good-tempered girls; but I imagine you must know them better than I do, yourself, for I never exchanged a word with either of them.'

'Indeed! They don't strike me as being particularly reserved.'

'Very likely they are not so to people of their own class; but they consider themselves as moving in quite a different sphere from me!'

He made no reply to this; but after a short pause, he said,

'I suppose it's these things, Miss Grey, that make you think you could not live without a home?'

'Not exactly. The fact is I am too socially disposed to be able to live contentedly without a friend, and as the only friends I have, or am likely to have, are at home, if it – or rather, if they were gone – I will not say I could not live – but I would rather not live in such a desolate world.'

'But why do you say the only friends you are likely to have? Are you so unsociable that you cannot make friends?'

'No, but I never made one yet; and in my present position there is no possibility of doing so, or even of forming a common acquaintance. The fault may be partly in myself, but I hope not altogether.'

'The fault is partly in society, and partly, I should think, in your immediate neighbours, and partly, too, in yourself; for many ladies, in your position, would *make* themselves be noticed and accounted of. But your pupils should be companions for you in some degree; they cannot be many years younger than yourself.'

'Oh yes, they are good company sometimes; but I cannot call them friends, nor would they think of bestowing such a name on me – they have other companions better suited to their tastes.'

'Perhaps you are too wise for them. How do you amuse yourself when alone – do you read much?'

'Reading is my favourite occupation when I have leisure for it, and books to read.'

From speaking of books in general, he passed to different books in particular, and proceeded by rapid transitions from topic to topic, till several matters, both of taste and opinion, had been discussed considerably within the space of half an hour, but without the embellishment of many observations from himself; he being evidently less bent upon communicating his own thoughts and predilections, than on discovering mine.

He had not the tact or the art to effect such a purpose by skilfully drawing out my sentiments or ideas through the real or apparent statement of his own, or leading the conversation by imperceptible gradations to such topics as he wished to advert to. But such gentle abruptness, and such single-minded straightforwardness could not possibly offend me.

'And why should he interest himself at all in my moral and intellectual capacities: what is it to him what I think or feel?' I asked myself.

And my heart throbbed in answer to the question.

But Jane and Susan Green soon reached their home. As they stood parleying at the park-gates, attempting to persuade Miss Murray to come in, I wished Mr Weston would go, that she might not see him with me when she turned round; but, unfortunately, his business, which was to pay one more visit to poor Mark Wood, led him to pursue the same path as we did, till nearly the close of our journey.

When, however, he saw that Rosalie had taken leave of her friends, and I was about to join her, he would have left me and passed on at a quicker pace; but, as he civilly lifted his hat in passing her, to my surprise, instead of returning the salute with a stiff, ungracious bow, she accosted him with one of her sweetest smiles, and, walking by his side, began to talk to him with all imaginable cheerfulness and affability; and so we proceeded all three together.

After a short pause in the conversation, Mr Weston made some remark addressed particularly to me, as referring to something we had been talking of before; but, before I could answer, Miss Murray replied to the observation and enlarged upon it: he rejoined; and, from thence to the close of the interview, she engrossed him entirely to herself.

It might be partly owing to my own stupidity, my want of tact and assurance; but I felt myself wronged; I trembled with apprehension; and I listened with envy to her easy, rapid flow of utterance, and saw with anxiety the bright smile with which she looked into his face from time to time, for she was walking a little in advance for the purpose (as I judged) of being seen as well as heard.

If her conversation was light and trivial, it was amusing, and she was never at a loss for something to say, or for suitable words to express it in. There was nothing pert or flippant in her manner now, as when she walked with Mr Hatfield; there was only a gentle, playful kind of vivacity which I thought must be peculiarly pleasing to a man of Mr Weston's disposition and temperament.

When he was gone she began to laugh, and muttered to herself.

'I thought I could do it!'

'Do what?' I asked.

'Fix that man.'

'What in the world do you mean?'

'I mean that he will go home and dream of me. I have shot him through the heart!'

'How do you know?'

'By many infallible proofs: more especially the look he gave me when he went away. It was not an impudent look – I exonerate him from that – it was a look of reverential, tender adoration. Ha, ha! he's not quite such a stupid blockhead as I thought him!'

I made no answer, for my heart was in my throat, or something like it, and I could not trust myself to speak.

'Oh, God, avert it!' I cried, internally – 'for his sake, not for mine!'

Miss Murray made several trivial observations as we passed up the park, to which, (in spite of my reluctance to let one glimpse of my feelings appear,) I could only answer by monosyllables.

Whether she intended to torment me, or merely to amuse herself, I could not tell – and did not much care; but I thought of the poor man and his one lamb, and the rich man with his thousand flocks; and I dreaded I knew not what for Mr Weston, independently of my own blighted hopes.

Right glad was I to get into the house, and find myself alone once more in my own room. My first impulse was to sink into the chair beside the bed, and laying my head on the pillow, to seek relief in a passionate burst of tears: there was an imperative craving for such an indulgence; but alas! I must restrain and swallow back my feelings still: there was the bell – the odious bell for the school-room dinner; and I must go down with a calm face, and smile, and laugh, and talk nonsense – yes, and eat too, if possible, as if all were right, and I were just returned from a pleasant walk.

CHAPTER XVI

THE SUBSTITUTION

NEXT SUNDAY WAS one of the gloomiest of April days, a day of thick, dark clouds, and heavy showers. None of the Murrays were disposed to attend church in the afternoon, excepting Rosalie: she was bent upon going as usual; so she ordered the carriage, and I went with her, nothing loth of course, for at church I might look without fear of scorn or censure upon a form and face more pleasing to me than the most beautiful of God's creations; I might listen without disturbance to a voice more charming than the sweetest music to my ears; I might seem to hold communion with that soul in which I felt so deeply interested, and imbibe its purest thoughts and holiest aspirations, with no alloy to such felicity, except the secret reproaches of my conscience which would too often whisper that I was deceiving my own self, and mocking God with the service of a heart more bent upon the creature than the creator.

Sometimes such thoughts would give me trouble enough; but sometimes I could quiet them with thinking,

It is not the man, it is his goodness that I love.

'Whatsoever things are pure, whatsoever things are lovely, whatsoever things are honest and of good report, think on these things.'

We do well to worship God in His works; and I know none of them in which so many of His attributes – so much of His own spirit shines, as this His faithful servant, whom to know and not to appreciate, were obtuse insensibility in me, who have so little else to occupy my heart.

Almost immediately after the conclusion of the service, Miss

Murray left the church. We had to stand in the porch; for it was raining, and the carriage was not yet come. I wondered at her coming forth so hastily, for neither young Meltham nor Squire Green were there; but I soon found it was to secure an interview with Mr Weston as he came out, which he presently did, and, having saluted us both, would have passed on, but she detained him; first with observations upon the disagreeable weather, and then with asking if he would be so kind as to come sometime to-morrow to see the granddaughter of the old woman who kept the porter's lodge, for the girl was ill of a fever, and wished to see him. He promised to do so.

'And at what time will you be most likely to come, Mr Weston? The old woman will like to know when to expect you – you know such people think more about having their cottages in order when decent people come to see them than we are apt to suppose.'

Here was a wonderful instance of consideration from the thoughtless Miss Murray.

Mr Weston named an hour in the morning at which he would endeavour to be there. By this time the carriage was ready, and the footman was waiting, with an open umbrella, to escort Miss Murray through the church-yard. I was about to follow; but Mr Weston had an umbrella too, and offered me the benefit of its shelter, for it was raining heavily.

'No, thank you, I don't mind the rain,' I said.

I always lacked common sense when taken by surprise.

'But you don't *like* it I suppose? – an umbrella will do you no harm at any rate,' he replied, with a smile that shewed he was not offended, as a man of worse temper or less penetration would have been at such a refusal of his aid.

I could not deny the truth of his assertion, and so went with him to the carriage; he even offered me his hand on getting in, an unnecessary piece of civility, but I accepted that too for fear of giving offence. One glance he gave, one little smile at parting – it was but for a moment, but therein I read, or thought

I read, a meaning that kindled in my heart a brighter flame of hope than had ever yet arisen.

'I would have sent the footman back for you, Miss Grey, if you'd waited a moment – you needn't to have taken Mr Weston's umbrella,' observed Rosalie, with a very unamiable cloud upon her pretty face.

'I would have come without an umbrella, but Mr Weston offered me the benefit of his and I could not have refused it, more than I did, without offending him,' replied I, smiling placidly, for my inward happiness made that amusing, which would have wounded me at another time.

The carriage was now in motion. Miss Murray bent forwards, and looked out of the window as we were passing Mr Weston. He was pacing homewards along the causeway, and did not turn his head.

'Stupid ass!' cried she, throwing herself back again in the seat. 'You don't know *what* you've lost by not looking this way!'

'What has he lost?'

'A bow from me, that would have raised him to the seventh heaven!'

I made no answer. I saw she was out of humour, and I derived a secret gratification from the fact; not that she was vexed, but that she thought she had reason to be so. It made me think my hopes were not entirely the offspring of my wishes and imagination.

'I mean to take up Mr Weston instead of Mr Hatfield,' said my companion after a short pause, resuming something of her usual cheerfulness. 'The ball at Ashby Park takes place on Tuesday you know; and mama thinks it very likely that Sir Thomas will propose to me then – such things are often done in the privacy of the ball-room, when gentlemen are most easily en-snared, and ladies most enchanting: – but if I am to be married so soon, I must make the best of the present time: I am deter-mined Hatfield shall not be the only man who shall lay his heart at my feet, and implore me to accept the worthless gift in vain.'

'If you mean Mr Weston to be one of your victims,' said I, with affected indifference, 'you will have to make such overtures yourself, that you will find it difficult to draw back when he asks you to fulfil the expectations you have raised.'

'I don't suppose he will ask me to *marry* him – nor should I desire it ... that would be *rather* too much presumption! but I intend him to feel my power – he has felt it already, indeed – but he shall *acknowledge* it too; and what visionary hopes he may have, he must keep to himself, and only amuse me with the result of them – for a time.'

'Oh! that some kind spirit would whisper those words in his ear!' I inwardly exclaimed. I was far too indignant to hazard a reply to her observation aloud; and nothing more was said about Mr Weston that day, by me or in my hearing.

But next morning, soon after breakfast, Miss Murray came into the school-room where her sister was employed with me at her studies ... or rather her lessons, for studies they were not ... and said,

'Matilda, I want you to take a walk with me about eleven o'clock.'

'Oh, I can't, Rosalie! I've got to give orders about my new bridle and saddle-cloth, and to speak to the rat-catcher about his dogs ... Miss Grey must go with you.'

'No, I want *you*,' said Rosalie; and calling her sister to the window, she whispered an explanation in her ear, upon which the latter consented to go.

I remembered that eleven was the hour at which Mr Weston proposed to come to the porter's lodge; and remembering that, I beheld the whole contrivance.

Accordingly at dinner, I was entertained with a long account of how Mr Weston had overtaken them as they were walking along the road; and how they had had a long walk and talk with him, and really found him quite an agreeable companion; and how he must have been, and evidently was, delighted with them and their amazing condescension, &c., &c.

CHAPTER XVII

CONFESSIONS

As I am in the way of confessions, I may as well acknowledge that, about this time, I paid more attention to dress than ever I had done before ... this is not saying much, for hitherto I had been a little neglectful in that particular ... but now, also, it was no uncommon thing to spend as much as two minutes in the contemplation of my own image in the glass; though I never could derive any consolation from such a study: I could discover no beauty in those marked features, that pale hollow cheek, and ordinary dark brown hair; there might be intellect in the forehead, there might be expression in the dark grey eyes, but what of that? ... a low Grecian brow, and large black eyes devoid of sentiment would be esteemed far preferable.

It is foolish to wish for beauty. Sensible people never either desire it for themselves or care about it in others. If the mind be but well cultivated, and the heart well disposed, no one ever cares for the exterior.

So said the teachers of our childhood; and so say we to the children of the present day. All very judicious and proper no doubt; but are such assertions supported by actual experience?

We are naturally disposed to love what gives us pleasure, and what more pleasing than a beautiful face ... when we know no harm of the possessor at least? A little girl loves her bird ... Why? ... Because it lives and feels, because it is helpless and harmless. A toad, likewise, lives and feels, and is equally helpless and harmless; but though she would not hurt a toad, she cannot love it like the bird, with its graceful form, soft feathers, and bright, speaking eyes. If a woman is fair and amiable, she is praised for both qualities, but especially the former, by the bulk of mankind: if, on the other hand, she is disagreeable in person and character, her plainness is commonly inveighed against as her greatest crime, because to common observers, it gives the greatest offence; while, if she is plain and good, provided she is a person of retired manners and secluded life, no one ever knows of her goodness, except her immediate connections; others, on the contrary, are disposed to form unfavourable opinions of her mind and disposition, if it be but to excuse themselves for their instinctive dislike of one so unfavoured by nature; and *vice versa* with her whose angel form conceals a vicious heart, or sheds a false, deceitful charm over defects and foibles that would not be tolerated in another.

They that have beauty, let them be thankful for it, and make a good use of it, like any other talent: they that have it not, let them console themselves, and do the best they can without it – certainly, though liable to be over-estimated, it is a gift of God, and not to be despised. Many will feel this, who have felt that they could love, and whose hearts tell them they are worthy to be loved again, while yet they are debarred, by the lack of this, or some such seeming trifle from giving and receiving that happiness they seem almost made to feel and to impart. As well might the humble glow-worm despise that power of giving light, without which the roving fly might pass her and repass her a thousand times, and never light beside her; she might hear her winged darling buzzing over and around her; he vainly seeking her, she longing to be found, but with no power to make her presence known, no voice to call him, no wings to follow his flight; ... the fly must seek another mate, the worm must live and die alone.

Such were some of my reflections about this period. I might go on prosing more and more, I might dive much deeper, and disclose other thoughts, propose questions the reader might be puzzled to answer, and deduce arguments that might startle his prejudices, or perhaps provoke his ridicule, because he could not comprehend them; but I forbear.

Now, therefore, let us return to Miss Murray. She accompanied her mama to the ball on Tuesday; of course, splendidly attired, and delighted with her prospects and her charms. As Ashby Park was nearly ten miles distant from Horton Lodge, they had to set out pretty early, and I intended to have spent the evening with Nancy Brown, whom I had not seen for a long time; but my kind pupil took care I should spend it neither there nor anywhere else beyond the limits of the school-room by giving me a piece of music to copy, which kept me closely occupied till bed-time.

About eleven next morning, as soon as she had left her room, she came to tell me her news. Sir Thomas had indeed proposed to her at the ball, an event which reflected great credit on her mama's sagacity, if not upon her skill in contrivance; I rather incline to the belief that she had first laid her plans, and then predicted their success.

The offer had been accepted of course, and the bridegroom elect was coming that day to settle matters with Mr Murray.

Rosalie was pleased with the thoughts of becoming mistress of Ashby Park; she was elated with the prospect of the bridal ceremony and its attendant splendour and eclat, the honeymoon spent abroad, and the subsequent gaieties she expected to enjoy in London and elsewhere; she appeared pretty well pleased too, for the time being, with Sir Thomas himself, because she had so lately seen him, danced with him, and been flattered by him; but, after all, she seemed to shrink from the idea of being so soon united: she wished the ceremony to be delayed some months, at least; and I wished it too. It seemed a horrible thing to hurry on the inauspicious match, and not to give the poor creature time to think and reason on the irrevocable step she was about to take. I made no pretension to 'a mother's watchful, anxious care,' but I was amazed and horrified at Mrs Murray's heartlessness, or want of thought for the real good of her child; and, by my unheeded warnings and exhortations, I vainly strove to remedy the evil. Miss Murray only laughed at what I said; and I soon found that her reluctance to an immediate union arose chiefly from a desire to do what execution she could among the young gentlemen of her acquaintance before she was incapacitated from further mischief of the kind. It was for this cause that, before confiding to me the secret of her engagement, she had extracted a promise that I would not mention a word on the subject to any one. And when I saw this, and when I beheld her plunge more recklessly than ever into the depths of heartless coquetry, I had no more pity for her.

'Come what will,' I thought, 'she deserves it. Sir Thomas cannot be too bad for her; and the sooner she is incapacitated from deceiving and injuring others the better.'

The wedding was fixed for the first of June. Between that and the critical ball was little more than six weeks; but, with Rosalie's accomplished skill and resolute exertion, much might be done, even within that period, especially as Sir Thomas spent most of the interim in London, whither he went up, it was said, to settle affairs with his lawyer, and make other preparations for the approaching nuptials.

He endeavoured to supply the want of his presence by a pretty constant fire of billets-doux; but these did not attract the neighbours' attention, and open their eyes as personal visits would have done; and old Lady Ashby's haughty, sour spirit of reserve withheld her from spreading the news, while her indifferent health prevented her coming to visit her future daughter-in-law; so that, altogether, this affair was kept far closer than such things usually are.

Rosalie would sometimes shew her lover's epistles to me to convince me what a kind, devoted husband he would make. She shewed me the letters of another individual too, the unfortunate Mr Green, who had not the courage, or, as she expressed it, the 'spunk' to plead his cause in person, but whom one denial would not satisfy; he must write again and again.

He would not have done so if he could have seen the grimaces his fair idol made over his moving appeals to her feelings, and heard her scornful laughter, and the opprobrious epithets she heaped upon him for his perseverance.

'Why don't you tell him, at once, that you are engaged?' I asked.

'Oh, I don't want him to know that!' replied she. 'If he knew it, his sisters and everybody would know it, and then there would be an end of my – ahem – And besides, if I told him that, he would think my engagement was the only obstacle, and that I would have him if I were free, which I could not bear that any man should think, and he, of all others, the least. Besides, I don't care for his letters,' she added, contemptuously; 'he may write as often as he pleases, and look as great a calf as he likes when I meet him; it only amuses *me*.'

Meantime, young Meltham was pretty frequent in his visits to the house or transits past it; and, judging by Matilda's execrations and reproaches, her sister paid more attention to him than civility required – in other words she carried on as animated a flirtation as the presence of her parents would admit.

She made some attempts to bring Mr Hatfield once more to her feet; but finding them unsuccessful, she repaid his haughty indifference with still loftier scorn, and spoke of him with as much disdain and detestation as she had formerly done of his curate.

But, amid all this, she never for a moment lost sight of Mr Weston. She embraced every opportunity of meeting him, tried every art to fascinate him, and pursued him with as much perseverance as if she really loved him – and no other, and the happiness of her life depended upon eliciting a return of affection. Such conduct was beyond my comprehension. Had I seen it depicted in a novel I should have thought it unnatural; had I heard it described by others, I should have deemed it a mistake or an exaggeration; but when I saw it with my own eyes, and suffered from it too, I could only conclude that excessive vanity, like drunkenness, hardens the heart, enslaves the faculties, and perverts the feelings, and that dogs are not the only creatures which, when gorged to the throat, will yet gloat over what they cannot devour, and grudge the smallest morsel to a starving brother.

She now became extremely beneficent to the poor cottagers. Her acquaintance among them was more widely extended, her visits to their humble dwellings were more frequent and excursive than they had ever been before. Hereby she earned among them the reputation of a condescending and very charitable young lady; and their encomiums were sure to be repeated to Mr Weston, whom also she had thus a daily chance of meeting in one or other of their abodes, or in her transits to and fro; and often, likewise, she could gather, through their gossip, to what places he was likely to go at such and such a time, whether to baptise a child, or to visit the aged, the sick, the sad, or the dying; and most skilfully she laid her plans accordingly.

In these excursions she would sometimes go with her sister, whom, by some means, she had persuaded or bribed to enter into her schemes, sometimes alone, never, now, with me; so that I was debarred the pleasure of seeing Mr Weston, or hearing his voice, even in conversation with another, which would certainly have been a very great pleasure, however hurtful or however fraught with pain.

I could not even see him at church, for Miss Murray, under some trivial pretext, chose to take possession of that corner in the family pew, which had been mine ever since I came; and, unless I had the presumption to station myself between Mr and Mrs Murray, I must sit with my back to the pulpit, which I accordingly did.

Now, also, I never walked home with my pupils: they said their mama thought it did not look well to see three people out of the family walking, and only two going in the carriage; and, as they greatly preferred walking in fine weather, I should be honoured by going with the seniors.

'And besides,' said they, 'you can't walk as fast as we do; you know you're always lagging behind.'

I knew these were false excuses, but I made no objections, and never contradicted such assertions, well knowing the motives which dictated them.

And in the afternoons, during those six memorable weeks, I never went to church at all. If I had a cold, or any slight indisposition, they took advantage of that to make me stay at home; and often they would tell me they were not going again that day, themselves, and then pretend to change their minds, and set off without telling me, so managing their departure that I never discovered the change of purpose till too late.

Upon their return home, on one of these occasions, they entertained me with an animated account of a conversation they had had with Mr Weston as they came along.

'And he asked if you were ill, Miss Grey,' said Matilda; 'but we told him you were quite well, only you didn't want to come to church – so he'll think you're turned wicked.'

All chance meetings on week-days were likewise carefully prevented; for, lest I should go to see poor Nancy Brown or any other person, Miss Murray took good care to provide sufficient employment for all my leisure hours. There was always some drawing to finish, some music to copy, or some work to do, sufficient to incapacitate me from indulging in anything beyond a short walk about the grounds, however she or her sister might be occupied.

One morning, having sought and waylaid Mr Weston, they returned in high glee to give me an account of their interview.

'And he asked after you again,' said Matilda, in spite of her sister's silent, but imperative intimation that she should hold her tongue. 'He wondered why you were never with us, and thought you must have delicate health as you came out so seldom.'

'He didn't, Matilda – what nonsense you're talking!'

'Oh, Rosalie, what a lie! He did, you know; and you said – Don't, Rosalie – hang it! – I won't be pinched so! And, Miss Grey, Rosalie told him you were quite well, but you were always so buried in your books that you had no pleasure in anything else.'

'What an idea he must have of me!' I thought.

'And,' I asked, 'does old Nancy ever inquire about me?'

'Yes, and we tell her you are so fond of reading and drawing that you can do nothing else.'

'That is not the case though; if you had told her I was so busy I *could* not come to see her, it would have been nearer the truth.'

'I don't think it would,' replied Miss Murray, suddenly kindling up; 'I'm sure you have plenty of time to yourself now, when you have so little teaching to do.'

It was no use beginning to dispute with such indulged, unreasoning creatures; so I held my peace. I was accustomed, now, to keeping silence when things distasteful to my ear were uttered; and now, too, I was used to wearing a placid smiling countenance when my heart was bitter within me. Only those who have felt the like can imagine my feelings, as I sat with an assumption of smiling indifference, listening to the accounts of those meetings and interviews with Mr Weston, which they seemed to find such pleasure in describing to me, and hearing things asserted of him which, from the character of the man, I knew to be exaggerations and perversions of the truth, if not entirely false – things derogatory to him, and flattering to them – especially to Miss Murray – which I burned to contradict, or, at least, to show my doubts about, but dared not, lest, in expressing my disbelief, I should display my interest too.

Other things I heard, which I felt or feared were indeed too true; but I must still conceal my anxiety respecting him, my indignation against them, beneath a careless aspect; others again – mere hints of something said or done, which I longed to hear more of – but could not venture to inquire.

So passed the weary time. I could not even comfort myself with saying, 'She will soon be married; and then, there may be hope.'

Soon after her marriage the holidays would come; and when I returned from home, most likely, Mr Weston would be gone, for I was told that he and the rector could not agree, (the rector's fault, of course,) and he was about to remove to another place.

No – besides my hope in God, my only consolation was in thinking that, though he knew it not, I was more worthy of his love than Rosalie Murray, charming and engaging as she was; for I could appreciate his excellence, which she could not; I would devote my life to the promotion of his happiness; she would destroy his happiness for the momentary gratification of her own vanity.

'Oh, if he could but know the difference!' I would earnestly exclaim. 'But no! I would not have him see my heart – but if he could but know her hollowness, her worthless, heartless frivolity – he would then be safe, and I should be – *almost* happy, though I might never see him more!'

I fear, by this time, the reader is well nigh disgusted with the folly and weakness I have so freely laid before him. I never disclosed it then, and would not have done so had my own sister or my mother been with me in the house.

I was a close and resolute dissembler – in this one case at least. My prayers, my tears, my wishes, fears, and lamentations were witnessed by myself and Heaven alone.

When we are harassed by sorrows or anxieties, or long oppressed by any powerful feelings which we must keep to ourselves, for which we can obtain and seek no sympathy from any living creature, and which yet we cannot, or will not wholly crush, we often naturally seek relief in poetry – and often find it too – whether in the effusions of others, which seem to harmonize with our existing case, or in our own attempts to give utterance to those thoughts and feelings in strains less musical, perchance, but more appropriate, and therefore more penetrating and sympathetic, and, for the time, more soothing, or more powerful to rouse and to unburden the oppressed and swollen heart.

Before this time, at Wellwood House and here, when suffering from home-sick melancholy, I had sought relief twice or thrice at this secret source of consolation; and now I flew to it again, with greater avidity than ever, because I seemed to need

it more. I still preserve those relics of past sufferings and experience, like pillars of witness set up, in travelling through the vale
of life, to mark particular occurrences.

The footsteps are obliterated now; the face of the country
may be changed, but the pillar is still there to remind me how
all things were when it was reared.

Lest the reader should be curious to see any of these effusions,
I will favour him with one short specimen: cold and languid as
the lines may seem, it was almost a passion of grief to which
they owed their being.

> 'O, they have robbed me of the hope
>   My spirit held so dear;
> They will not let me hear that voice
>   My soul delights to hear.
>
> 'They will not let me see that face
>   I so delight to see;
> And they have taken all thy smiles,
>   And all thy love from me.
>
> 'Well, let them seize on all they can; –
>   One treasure still is mine, –
> A heart that loves to think on thee,
>   And feels the worth of thine.'

Yes! at least, they could not deprive me of that; I could think
of him day and night; and I could feel that he was worthy to
be thought of. Nobody knew him as I did; nobody could
appreciate him as I did; nobody could love him as I ... could,
if I might; but there was the evil. What business had I to think
so much of one that never thought of me? Was it not foolish?
... was it not wrong?

Yet, if I found such deep delight in thinking of him, and if
I kept those thoughts to myself, and troubled no one else with
them, where was the harm of it? I would ask myself.

And such reasoning prevented me from making any sufficient effort to shake off my fetters.

But, if those thoughts brought delight, it was a painful, troubled pleasure, too near akin to anguish; and one that did me more injury than I was aware of. It was an indulgence that a person of more wisdom or more experience would doubtless have denied herself.

And yet . . . how dreary to turn my eyes from the contemplation of that bright object, and force them to dwell on the dull, grey, desolate prospect around, the joyless, hopeless, solitary path that lay before me.

It was wrong to be so joyless, so desponding; I should have made God my friend, and to do His will the pleasure and the business of my life; but Faith was weak, and Passion was too strong.

In this time of trouble I had two other causes of affliction. The first may seem a trifle, but it cost me many a tear: Snap, my little dumb, rough-visaged, but bright-eyed, warm-hearted companion, the only thing I had to love me, was taken away, and delivered over to the tender mercies of the village rat-catcher, a man notorious for his brutal treatment of his canine slaves.

The other was serious enough: my letters from home gave intimation that my father's health was worse. No boding fears were expressed, but I was grown timid and despondent, and could not help fearing that some dreadful calamity awaited us there. I seemed to see the black clouds gathering round my native hills, and to hear the angry muttering of a storm that was about to burst, and desolate our hearth.

CHAPTER XVIII

MIRTH AND MOURNING

THE FIRST OF June arrived at last; and Rosalie Murray was transmuted into Lady Ashby. Most splendidly beautiful she looked in her bridal costume.

Upon her return from church after the ceremony, she came flying into the school-room, flushed with excitement, and laughing ... half in mirth, and half in reckless desperation ... as it seemed to me.

'Now, Miss Grey, I'm Lady Ashby!' she exclaimed. 'It's done! my fate is sealed ... there's no drawing back now! I'm come to receive your congratulations, and bid you good-bye; and then I'm off ... for Paris ... Rome ... Naples ... Switzerland ... London ... Oh dear! what a deal I shall see and hear before I come back again! But don't forget me; I shan't forget you, though I've been a naughty girl. Come! why don't you congratulate me?'

'I cannot congratulate you,' I replied, 'till I know whether this change is really for the better; but I sincerely hope it is; and I wish you true happiness and the best of blessings.'

'Well good-bye – the carriage is waiting, and they're calling me.'

She gave me a hasty kiss, and was hurrying away, but, suddenly returning, embraced me with more affection than I thought her capable of evincing, and departed with tears in her eyes.

Poor girl! I really loved her then; and forgave her from my heart all the injury she had done me – and others also; she had not half known it, I was sure; and I prayed God to pardon her too.

During the remainder of that day of festal sadness, I was left to my own devices. Being too much unhinged for any steady occupation, I wandered about with a book in my hand for several hours – more thinking than reading, for I had many things to think about; and in the evening, I made use of my liberty to go and see my old friend Nancy once again; to apologize for my long absence, which must have seemed so neglectful and unkind, by telling her how busy I had been, and to talk, or read, or work for her, whichever might be most acceptable; and also of course, to tell her the news of this important day, and perhaps to obtain a little information from her in return, respecting Mr Weston's expected departure. But of this, she seemed to know nothing, and I hoped, as she did, that it was all a false report.

She was very glad to see me; but, happily, her eyes were now so nearly well that she was almost independent of my services. She was deeply interested in the wedding; but while I amused her with the details of the festive day, the splendours of the bridal party and of the bride herself, she often sighed and shook her head, and wished good might come of it: she seemed like me to regard it rather as a theme for sorrow than rejoicing. I sat a long time talking to her about that and other things; – but *no one came*.

Shall I confess – that I sometimes looked towards the door with a half expectant wish to see it open and give entrance to Mr Weston, as had happened once before? and that, returning through the lanes and fields, I often paused to look round me, and walked more slowly than was at all necessary – for, though a fine evening, it was not a hot one – and, finally, felt a sense of emptiness and disappointment at having reached the house without meeting or even catching a distant glimpse of any one, except a few labourers returning from their work?

Sunday however was approaching: I should see him then; for now that Miss Murray was gone, I could have my old corner again – I should see him; and by look, speech, and manner

I might judge whether the circumstance of her marriage had very much afflicted him.

Happily I could perceive no shadow of a difference: he wore the same aspect as he had worn two months ago – voice, look, manner – all alike unchanged: there was the same keen-sighted, unclouded truthfulness in his discourse, the same forcible clearness in his style, the same earnest simplicity in all he said and did, that made itself, not marked by the eye and ear, but felt upon the hearts of his audience.

I walked home with Miss Matilda, but *he did not join us*. Matilda was now sadly at a loss for amusement, and wofully in want of a companion. Her brothers at school – her sister married and gone – she too young to be admitted into society, for which, from Rosalie's example, she was in some degree beginning to acquire a taste – a taste at least for the company of certain classes of gentlemen – at this dull time of the year – no hunting going on ... no shooting even ... for, though she might not join in that, it was *something* to see her father or the gamekeeper go out with the dogs, and to talk with them, on their return, about the different birds they had bagged. Now also she was denied the solace which the companionship of the coachman, groom, horses, greyhounds and pointers might have afforded; for her mother, having notwithstanding the disadvantages of a country life so satisfactorily disposed of her elder daughter, the pride of her heart, had begun seriously to turn her attention to the younger, and being truly alarmed at the roughness of her manners, and thinking it high time to work a reform, had been roused at length to exert her authority, and prohibited entirely the yards, stables, kennels, and coach-house. Of course, she was not implicitly obeyed; but indulgent as she had hitherto been, when once her spirit was roused, her temper was not so gentle as she required that of her governesses to be, and her will was not to be thwarted with impunity; and after many a scene of contention between mother and daughter, many a violent outbreak which I was ashamed to witness, in which the father's authority was often called in to confirm, with oaths and threats, the mother's slighted prohibitions . . . for even *he* could see that 'Tilly,' though she would have made a fine lad, was not quite what a young lady ought to be – Matilda at length found that her easiest plan was to keep clear of the forbidden regions, unless she could now and then steal a visit without her watchful mother's knowledge.

Amid all this, let it not be imagined that I escaped without many a reprimand, and many an implied reproach that lost none of its sting from not being openly worded, but rather wounded the more deeply, because from that very reason it seemed to preclude self-defence. Frequently, I was told to amuse Miss Matilda with other things, and to *remind* her of her mother's precepts and prohibitions. I did so to the best of my power; but she would not be amused against her will, and could not against her taste; and though I went beyond mere remind-ing, such gentle remonstrances as I could use were utterly ineffectual.

'*Dear* Miss Grey! it is the *strangest* thing – I suppose you can't help it, if it's not in your nature – but I *wonder* you can't win the confidence of that girl, and make your society at *least* as agreeable to her as that of Robert or Joseph!'

'They can talk the best about the things in which she is most interested,' I replied.

'Well! that is a strange confession, *however*, to come from her *governess*! Who is to form a young lady's tastes, I wonder, if the governess doesn't do it! I *have* known governesses who have so completely identified themselves with the reputation of their young ladies for elegance and propriety in mind and manners, that they would *blush* to speak a word against them; and to hear the slightest blame imputed to their pupils was worse than to be censured in their own persons, – and I really think it very natural, for my part.'

'Do you, ma'am?'

'Yes: of course, the young lady's proficiency and elegance is of more consequence to the governess than her own, as well as to the world. If she wishes to prosper in her vocation she must devote all her energies to her business; all her ideas and all her ambition will tend to the accomplishment of that one object. When we wish to decide upon the merits of a governess, we naturally look at the young ladies she professes to have educated, and judge accordingly. The *judicious* governess knows this; she knows that, while she lives in obscurity herself, her pupils' virtues and defects will be open to every eye, and that unless she loses sight of herself in their cultivation, she need not hope for success. You see, Miss Grey, it is just the same as any other trade or profession; they that wish to prosper must devote themselves body and soul to their calling, and if they begin to yield to indolence or self-indulgence they are speedily distanced by wiser competitors: there is little to choose between a person that ruins her pupils by neglect, and one that corrupts them by her example. You will excuse my dropping these little hints . . . you know it is all for your own good. Many ladies would speak to you much more strongly; and many would not trouble themselves to speak at all, but quietly look out for a substitute. That, of course, would be the *easiest* plan; but I know the advantages of a place like this to a person in your situation; and I have no desire to part with you, as I am sure you would do very well if you will only think of these things and try to exert yourself a *little* more; and then, I am convinced, you would *soon* acquire that delicate tact which alone is wanting to give you a proper influence over the mind of your pupil.'

I was about to give the lady some idea of the fallacy of her expectations; but she sailed away as soon as she had concluded her speech. Having said what she wished, it was no part of her plan to await my answer: it was my business to hear, and not to speak.

However, as I have said, Matilda at length yielded, in some degree, to her mother's authority (pity it had not been exerted before), and being thus deprived of almost every source of amusement, there was nothing for it but to take long rides with the groom and long walks with the governess, and to visit the cottages and farm-houses on her father's estate, to kill time in chatting with the old men and women that inhabited them.

In one of these walks, it was our chance to meet Mr Weston. This was what I had long desired; but now, for a moment, I wished either he or I were away: I felt my heart throb so violently that I dreaded lest some outward signs of emotion should appear; but I think he hardly glanced at me, and I was soon calm enough. After a brief salutation to both, he asked Matilda if she had lately heard from her sister.

'Yes,' replied she. 'She was at Paris when she wrote, and very well and very happy.'

She spoke the last word emphatically, and with a glance impertinently sly. He did not seem to notice it, but replied, with equal emphasis, and very seriously, 'I hope she will continue to be so.'

'Do you think it likely?' I ventured to inquire, for Matilda had started off in pursuit of her dog, that was chasing a leveret.

'I cannot tell,' replied he. 'Sir Thomas may be a better man than I suppose, but, from all I have heard and seen, it seems a pity that one so young, and gay, and ... and *interesting*, to express many things by one ... whose greatest, if not her only fault, appears to be thoughtlessness ... no trifling fault to be sure, since it renders the possessor liable to almost every other, and exposes him to so many temptations; but it seems a pity that she should be thrown away on such a man. It was her mother's wish, I suppose?'

'Yes; and her own too, I think, for she always laughed at my attempts to dissuade her from the step.'

'You did attempt it? Then, at least, you will have the satisfaction of knowing that it is no fault of yours, if any harm should come of it; as for Mrs Murray, I don't know how she can justify her conduct; if I had sufficient acquaintance with her I'd ask her.'

'It seems unnatural; but some people think rank and wealth the chief good; and, if they can secure that to their children, they think they have done their duty.'

'True; but is it not strange that persons of experience who have been married themselves should judge so falsely?'

Matilda now came panting back, with the lacerated body of the young hare in her hand.

'Was it your intention to kill that hare, or to save it, Miss Murray?' asked Mr Weston, apparently puzzled at her gleeful countenance.

'I pretended to want to save it,' she answered, honestly enough, 'as it was so glaringly out of season; but I was better pleased to see it killed. However, you can both witness that I couldn't help it; Prince was determined to have her; and he clutched her by the back, and killed her in a minute! Wasn't it a noble chase?'

'Very! for a young lady after a leveret.'

There was a quiet sarcasm in the tone of his reply which was not lost upon her; she shrugged her shoulders, and, turning away with a significant 'Humph!' asked me how I had enjoyed the fun.

I replied that I saw no fun in the matter; but admitted that I had not observed the transaction very narrowly.

'Didn't you see how it doubled – just like an old hare? and didn't you hear it scream?'

'I'm happy to say I did not.'

'It cried out just like a child.'

'Poor little thing! What will you do with it?'

'Come along – I shall leave it in the first house we come to – I don't want to take it home, for fear papa should scold me for letting the dog kill it.'

Mr Weston was now gone, and we too went on our way; but as we returned, after having deposited the hare in a farm-house, and demolished some spice cake and currant wine in exchange, we met him returning also from the execution of his mission, whatever it might be. He carried in his hand a cluster of beautiful bluebells which he offered to me, observing, with a smile, that though he had seen so little of me for the last two months, he had not forgotten that bluebells were numbered among my favourite flowers.

It was done as a simple act of good will, without compliment, or remarkable courtesy, or any look that could be construed into 'reverential, tender adoration,' (vide Rosalie Murray); but still, it was something to find my unimportant saying so well remembered; it was something that he had noticed so accurately the time I had ceased to be visible.

'I was told,' said he, 'that you were a perfect book-worm, Miss Grey, so completely absorbed in your studies that you were lost to every other pleasure.'

'Yes, and it's quite true!' cried Matilda.

'No, Mr Weston; don't believe it; it's a scandalous libel. These young ladies are too fond of making random assertions at the expense of their friends; and you ought to be careful how you listen to them.'

'I hope *this* assertion is groundless, at any rate.'

'Why? Do you particularly object to ladies' studying?'

'No; but I object to any one so devoting himself or herself to study, as to lose sight of everything else. Except under peculiar circumstances, I consider very close and constant study as a waste of time, and an injury to the mind as well as the body.'

'Well, I have neither the time nor the inclination for such transgressions.'

We parted again.

Well! what is there remarkable in all this? Why have I recorded it? Because, reader, it was important enough to give me a cheerful evening, a night of pleasing dreams, and a morning of felicitous hopes. Shallow-brained cheerfulness – foolish dreams – unfounded hopes – you would say; and I will not venture to deny it: suspicion to that effect arose too frequently in my own mind; but our wishes are like tinder: the flint and steel of circumstances are continually striking out sparks, which vanish immediately, unless they chance to fall upon the tinder of our wishes; then, they instantly ignite, and the flame of hope is kindled in a moment.

But alas! that very morning, my flickering flame of hope was dismally quenched by a letter from my mother, which spoke so seriously of my father's increasing illness, that I feared there was little or no chance of his recovery; and, close at hand as the holidays were, I almost trembled lest they should come too late for me to meet him in this world. Two days after, a letter from Mary told me his life was despaired of, and his end seemed fast approaching.

Then, immediately, I sought permission to anticipate the vacation, and go without delay.

Mrs Murray stared, and wondered at the unwonted energy and boldness with which I urged the request, and thought there was no occasion to hurry; but finally gave me leave, stating, however, that there was 'no need to be in such agitation about the matter – it might prove a false alarm after all; and if not – why, it was only in the common course of nature; we must all die sometime; and I was not to suppose myself the only afflicted person in the world;' and concluding with saying I might have the phaeton to take me to O—.

'And instead of *repining*, Miss Grey, be thankful for the *privileges* you enjoy. There's many a poor clergyman whose family would be plunged into *ruin* by the event of his death; but *you*, you see, have influential friends ready to continue their patronage, and to show you every consideration.'

I thanked her for her 'consideration,' and flew to my room to make some hurried preparations for my departure. My bonnet and shawl being on, and a few things hastily crammed into my largest trunk, I descended. But I might have done the work more leisurely, for no one else was in a hurry; and I had still a considerable time to wait for the phaeton.

At length it came to the door, and I was off; but oh, what a dreary journey was that! how utterly different from my former passages homewards!

Being too late for the last coach to —, I had to hire a cab for ten miles, and then a car to take me over the rugged hills. It was half-past ten before I reached home. They were not in bed.

My mother and sister both met me in the passage – sad – silent – pale! I was so much shocked and terror-stricken I could not speak to ask the information I so much longed yet dreaded to obtain.

'Agnes,' said my mother, struggling to repress some strong emotion.

'Oh, Agnes!' cried Mary, and burst into tears.

'How is he?' I asked, gasping for the answer.

'Dead!'

It was the reply I had anticipated; but the shock seemed none the less tremendous.

CHAPTER XIX

THE LETTER

M Y FATHER'S MORTAL remains had been consigned to the tomb; and we, with sad faces and sombre garments, sat lingering over the frugal breakfast-table, revolving plans for our future life.

My mother's strong mind had not given way beneath even this affliction: her spirit, though crushed, was not broken. Mary's wish was that I should go back to Horton Lodge, and that our mother should come and live with her and Mr Richardson at the vicarage: she affirmed that he wished it no less than herself, and that such an arrangement could not fail to benefit all parties, for my mother's society and experience would be of inestimable value to them, and they would do all they could to make her happy. But no arguments or entreaties could prevail: my mother was determined not to go; not that she questioned, for a moment, the kind wishes and intentions of her daughter; but she affirmed that so long as God spared her health and strength, she would make use of them to earn her own livelihood, and be chargeable to no one, whether her dependence would be felt as a burden or not. If she could afford to reside as a lodger in — vicarage, she would choose that house before all others as the place of her abode; but, not being so circumstanced, she would never come under its roof, except as an occasional visiter, unless sickness or calamity should render her assistance really needful, or until age or infirmity made her incapable of maintaining herself.

'No Mary,' said she, 'if Richardson and you have anything to spare, you must lay it aside for your family; and Agnes and I must gather honey for ourselves. Thanks to my having had daughters to educate, I have not forgotten my accomplishments . . . God willing I will check this vain repining,' – she said, while the tears coursed one another down her cheeks in spite of her efforts; but she wiped them away, and resolutely shaking back her head, continued, 'I will exert myself and look out for a small house commodiously situated in some populous but healthy district, where we will take a few young ladies to board and educate – if we can get them – and as many day-pupils as will come, or as we can manage to instruct. Your father's relations and old friends will be able to send us some pupils or to assist us with their recommendations, no doubt: I shall not apply to my own. What say you to it, Agnes – will you be willing to leave your present situation and try?'

'Quite willing, mama; and the money I have saved will do to furnish the house. It shall be taken from the bank directly.'

'When it is wanted: we must get the house, and settle all preliminaries first.'

Mary offered to lend the little she possessed; but my mother declined it, saying that we must begin on an economical plan, and she hoped that the whole or part of mine added to what we could get by the sale of the furniture, and what little our dear papa had contrived to lay aside for her since the debts were paid, would be sufficient to last us till Christmas, when, it was hoped, something would accrue from our united labours.

It was finally settled that this should be our plan; and that inquiries and preparations should immediately be set on foot; and while my mother busied herself with these, I should return to Horton Lodge at the close of my four weeks' vacation, and give notice for my final departure when things were in train for the speedy commencement of our school.

We were discussing these affairs on the morning I have mentioned, about a fortnight after my father's death, when a letter was brought in for my mother, on beholding which the colour mounted to her face – lately pale enough with anxious watchings and excessive sorrow.

'From my father!' murmured she, as she hastily tore off the cover.

It was many years since she had heard from any of her own relations before. Naturally wondering what the letter might contain, I watched her countenance while she read it, and was somewhat surprised to see her bite her lip and knit her brows as if in anger. When she had done, she somewhat irreverently cast it on the table, saying with a scornful smile,

'Your grandpapa has been so kind as to write to me. He says he has no doubt I have long repented of my "unfortunate marriage," and if I will only acknowledge this, and confess I was wrong in neglecting his advice, and that I have justly suffered for it, he will make a lady of me once again – if that be possible after my long degradation – and remember my girls in his will. Get my desk, Agnes, and send these things away – I will answer the letter directly – but first, as I may be depriving you both of a legacy, it is just that I should tell you what I mean to say.

'I shall say that he is mistaken in supposing that I can regret the birth of my daughters, (who have been the pride of my life, and are likely to be the comfort of my old age), or the thirty years I have passed in the company of my best and dearest friend; – that, had our misfortunes been three times as great as they were, (unless they had been my bringing on,) I should still the more rejoice to have shared them with your father, and administered what consolation I was able; and, had his sufferings in illness been ten times what they were, I could not regret having watched over and laboured to relieve them – that, if he had married a richer wife, misfortunes and trials would no doubt have come upon him still, while – I am an egotist enough to imagine that no other woman could have cheered him through them so well – not that I am superior to the rest, but I was made for him, and he for me; and I can no more repent the hours – days – years of happiness we have spent together, and which neither could have had without the other, than I can the privilege of having been his nurse in sickness, and his comfort in affliction.

'Will this do, children? – or shall I say we are all very sorry for what has happened during the last thirty years; and my daughters wish they had never been born; but since they have had that misfortune, they will be thankful for any trifle their grandpapa will be kind enough to bestow?'

Of course, we both applauded our mother's resolution; Mary cleared away the breakfast things; I brought the desk; the letter was quickly written and despatched; and, from that day, we heard no more of our grandfather till we saw his death announced in the newspaper a considerable time after – all his worldly possessions, of course, being left to our wealthy, unknown cousins.

CHAPTER XX

THE FAREWELL

A HOUSE IN A—, the fashionable watering place, was hired for our seminary; and a promise of two or three pupils was obtained to commence with. I returned to Horton Lodge about the middle of July, leaving my mother to conclude the bargain for the house, to obtain more pupils, to sell off the furniture of our old abode, and to fit out the new one.

We often pity the poor, because they have no leisure to mourn their departed relatives, and necessity obliges them to labour through their severest afflictions; but is not active employment the best remedy for overwhelming sorrow . . . the surest antidote for despair? It may be a rough comforter: it may seem hard to be harassed with the cares of life when we have no relish for its enjoyments, to be goaded to labour when the heart is ready to break, and the vexed spirit implores for rest only to weep in silence; but is not labour better than the rest we covet? and are not those petty, tormenting cares less hurtful than a continual brooding over the great affliction that oppresses us? – Besides, we cannot have cares, and anxieties, and toil, without hope – if it be but the hope of fulfilling our joyless task, accomplishing some needful project, or escaping some further annoyance.

At any rate, I was glad my mother had so much employment for every faculty of her action-loving frame. Our kind neighbours lamented that she, once so exalted in wealth and station, should be reduced to such extremity in her time of sorrow; but I am persuaded that she would have suffered thrice as much had she been left in affluence, with liberty to remain in that house, the scene of her early happiness and late affliction, and no stern necessity to prevent her from incessantly brooding over and lamenting her bereavement.

I will not dilate upon the feelings with which I left the old house, the well-known garden, the little village church – then doubly dear to me, because my father, who for thirty years had taught and prayed within its walls, lay slumbering now beneath its flags – and the old bare hills, delightful in their very desolation, with the narrow vales between, smiling in green wood and sparkling water – the house where I was born, the scene of all my early associations, the place where, throughout life, my earthly affections had been centred; – and left them to return no more! True, I was going back to Horton Lodge where, amid many evils, one source of pleasure yet remained; but it was pleasure mingled with excessive pain, and my stay, alas! was limited to six weeks.

And even of that precious time, day after day slipped by and I did not see him: – except at church, I never saw him for a fortnight after my return. It seemed a long time to me: and, as I was often out with my rambling pupil, of course hopes would keep rising, and disappointments would ensue; and then I would say to my own heart, 'Here is a convincing proof – if you would but have the sense to see it, or the candour to acknowledge it – that he does not care for you. If he only thought *half* as much about you, as you do about him, he would have contrived to meet you many times ere this – you must know that by consulting your own feelings. Therefore have done with this nonsense; you have no ground for hope; dismiss, at once, these hurtful thoughts and foolish wishes from your mind and turn to your own duty and the dull, blank life that lies before you. You might have *known* such happiness was not for you.'

But I saw him at last. He came suddenly upon me as I was crossing a field in returning from a visit to Nancy Brown, which I had taken the opportunity of paying while Matilda Murray was riding her matchless mare.

He must have heard of the heavy loss I had sustained; he expressed no sympathy, offered no condolence, but almost the first words he uttered were, 'How is your mother?' and this was no matter of course question, for I never told him that I *had* a mother, he must have learnt the fact from others, if he knew it at all – and besides, there was sincere good-will, and even deep, touching, unobtrusive sympathy in the tone and manner of the inquiry.

I thanked him with due civility, and told him she was as well as could be expected.

'What will she do?' was the next question. Many would have deemed it an impertinent one, and given an evasive reply; but such an idea never entered my head, and I gave a brief, but plain statement of my mother's plans and prospects.

'Then you will leave this place shortly?' said he.

'Yes, in a month.'

He paused a minute, as if in thought. When he spoke again I hoped it would be to express his concern at my departure; but it was only to say,

'I should think you will be willing enough to go?'

'Yes – for some things,' I replied.

'For *some* things only – I wonder what should make you regret it!'

I *was* annoyed at this, in some degree because it embarrassed me; I had only one reason for regretting it; and that was a profound secret, which he had no business to trouble me about.

'Why,' said I – 'why should you suppose that I dislike the place?'

'You told me so yourself,' was the decisive reply. 'You said, at least, that you could not live contentedly without a friend; and that you had no friend here, and no possibility of making one – and besides, I know you *must* dislike it.'

'But, if you remember rightly, I said – or meant to say – I could not live contentedly without a friend in the *world*: I was not so unreasonable as to require one always near me. I think

I could be happy in a house full of enemies if –' but no; that sentence must not be continued – I paused, and hastily added, 'And besides, we cannot well leave a place where we have lived for two or three years, without some feeling of regret.'

'Will you regret to part with Miss Murray ... your sole remaining pupil and companion?'

'I dare say I shall in some degree – it was not without sorrow I parted with her sister.'

'I can imagine that.'

'Well, Miss Matilda is quite as good ... better in one respect.'

'What is that?'

'She's honest.'

'And the other is not?'

'I should not call her *dis*honest; but it must be confessed, she's a little artful.'

'*Artful* is she? – I saw she was giddy and vain – and now,' he added, after a pause, 'I can well believe she was artful too, but so excessively so as to assume an aspect of extreme simplicity and unguarded openness. Yes,' continued he musingly, 'that accounts for some little things that puzzled me a trifle before.'

After that, he turned the conversation to more general subjects. He did not leave me till we had nearly reached the park-gates: he had certainly stepped a little out of his way to accompany me so far, for he now went back and disappeared down Moss-lane, the entrance of which we had passed some time before. Assuredly, I did not regret this circumstance: if sorrow had any place in my heart, it was that he was gone at last ... that he was no longer walking by my side, and that short interval of delightful intercourse was at an end. He had not breathed a word of love, or dropped one hint of tenderness or affection, and yet I had been supremely happy. To be near him, to hear him talk ... as he did talk; and to feel that he thought me worthy to be so spoken to ... capable of understanding and duly appreciating such discourse ... was enough.

'Yes Edward Weston, I could indeed be happy in a house full

of enemies, if I had but one friend who truly, deeply, and faithfully loved me, and if that friend were you – though we might be far apart . . . seldom to hear from each other, still more seldom to meet . . . though toil, and trouble, and vexation might surround me, still . . . it would be too much happiness for me to dream of! Yet who can tell,' said I within myself, as I proceeded up the park, 'who can tell what this one month may bring forth? I have lived nearly three and twenty years, and I have suffered much, and tasted little pleasure yet: is it likely my life all through will be so clouded? Is it not possible that God may hear my prayers, disperse these gloomy shadows, and grant me some beams of heaven's sunshine yet? Will He entirely deny to me those blessings which are so freely given to others, who neither ask them nor acknowledge them when received? May I not still hope and trust?'

I did hope and trust – for a while; but alas, alas! the time ebbed away; one week followed another, and, excepting one distant glimpse, and two transient meetings during which scarcely anything was said – while I was walking with Miss Matilda – I saw nothing of him, except, of course, at church.

And now, the last Sunday was come, and the last service. I was often on the point of melting into tears during the sermon – the last I was to hear from him . . . the best I should hear from any one, I was well assured. It was over . . . the congregation were departing; and I must follow . . . I had then seen him and heard his voice too, probably for the last time.

In the church-yard, Matilda was pounced upon by the two Misses Green. They had many inquiries to make about her sister, and I know not what besides. I only wished they would have done, that we might hasten back to Horton Lodge: I longed to seek the retirement of my own room, or some sequestered nook in the grounds, that I might deliver myself up to my feelings to weep my last farewell, and lament my false hopes and vain delusions . . . only this once and then adieu to fruitless dreaming . . . thenceforth, only sober, solid, sad reality should occupy my mind; but while I thus resolved, a low voice close beside me said,

'I suppose you are going this week, Miss Grey?'

'Yes,' I replied. I was very much startled; and had I been at all hysterically inclined, I certainly should have committed myself in some way then. Thank God I was not.

'Well,' said Mr Weston, 'I want to bid you good-bye ... it is not likely I shall see you again before you go.'

'Good-bye Mr Weston,' I said ... Oh, how I struggled to say it calmly! I gave him my hand. He retained it a few seconds in his.

'It is possible we may meet again,' said he, 'will it be of any consequence to you whether we do or not?'

'Yes, I should be very glad to see you again.'

I *could* say no less. He kindly pressed my hand, and went. Now I was happy again ... though more inclined to burst into tears than ever. If I had been forced to speak at that moment, a succession of sobs would have inevitably ensued; and as it was, I could not keep the water out of my eyes. I walked along with Miss Murray, turning aside my face and neglecting to notice several successive remarks, till she bawled out I was either deaf or stupid, and then (having recovered my self-possession) as one awakened from a fit of abstraction, I suddenly looked up and asked what she had been saying.

CHAPTER XXI

THE SCHOOL

I LEFT HORTON LODGE, and went to join my mother in our new abode at A——. I found her well in health, resigned in spirit, and even cheerful, though subdued and sober, in her general demeanour. We had only three boarders and half-a-dozen day-pupils to commence with; but by due care and diligence we hoped ere long to increase the number of both.

I set myself with befitting energy to discharge the duties of this new mode of life – I call it *new*, for there was, indeed, a considerable difference between working with my mother in a school of our own, and working as a hireling among strangers, despised and trampled upon by old and young; and for the first few weeks I was by no means unhappy. 'It is possible we may meet again,' and 'Will it be of any consequence to you whether we do or not?' – Those words still rang in my ear and rested on my heart; they were my secret solace and support.

'I shall see him again. – He will come; or he will write.' No promise, in fact, was too bright or too extravagant for Hope to whisper in my ear. I did not believe half of what she told me; I pretended to laugh at it all; but I was far more credulous than I myself supposed: otherwise, why did my heart leap up when a knock was heard at the front door, and the maid, who opened it, came to tell my mother a gentleman wished to see her? and why was I out of humour for the rest of the day, because it proved to be a music-master come to offer his services to our school? and what stopped my breath for a moment, when the postman having brought a couple of letters, my mother said, 'Here Agnes, this is for you,' and threw one of them to me? and what made the hot blood rush into my face when I saw it was directed in a gentleman's hand? and why – Oh! why did that cold, sickening sense of disappointment fall upon me, when I had torn open the cover and found it was *only* a letter from Mary, which, for some reason or other, her husband had directed for her?

Was it then come to this – that I should be *disappointed* to receive a letter from my only sister; and because it was not written by a comparative stranger? Dear Mary! and she had written it so kindly – and thinking I should be so pleased to have it! – I was not worthy to read it!

And I believe, in my indignation against myself, I should have put it aside till I had schooled myself into a better frame of mind, and was become more deserving of the honour and privilege of its perusal; but there was my mother looking on, and wishful to know what news it contained; so I read it and delivered it to her, and then went into the school-room to attend to the pupils; but amidst the cares of copies and sums – in the intervals of correcting errors here, and reproving derelictions of duty there, I was inwardly taking myself to task with far sterner severity.

'What a fool you must be,' said my head to my heart, or my sterner to my softer self; – 'how could you ever dream that he would write to *you*? What grounds have you for such a hope – or that he will see you, or give himself any trouble about you – or even think of you again?'

'What grounds? –' and then Hope set before me that last, short interview and repeated the words I had so faithfully treasured in my memory.

'Well, and what was there in that? ... Who ever hung his hopes upon so frail a twig? What was there in those words that any common acquaintance might not say to another? Of course, it was possible you might meet again; he might have said so if you had been going to New Zealand; but that did not imply any *intention* of seeing you – and then, as to the question that followed, any one might ask that; and how did you answer? – Merely with a stupid, commonplace reply, such as you would have given to Master Murray, or any one else you had been on tolerably civil terms with.'

'But then,' persisted Hope, 'the tone and manner in which he spoke.'

'Oh, that is nonsense! he always speaks impressively; and at that moment there were the Greens and Miss Matilda Murray just before, and other people passing by, and he was obliged to stand close beside you, and to speak very low, unless he wished everybody to hear what he said, which – though it was nothing at all particular – of course, he would rather not.'

'But then, above all, that emphatic, yet gentle pressure of the hand, which seemed to say, "*Trust me*," and many other things besides – too delightful, almost too flattering, to be repeated, even to one's self.'

'Egregious folly – too absurd to require contradiction ... mere inventions of the imagination, which you ought to be ashamed of. If you would but consider your own unattractive exterior, your unamiable reserve, your foolish diffidence, which must make you appear cold, dull, awkward, and perhaps ill-tempered too; ... if you had but rightly considered these from the beginning, you would never have harboured such presumptuous thoughts; and now that you have been so foolish, pray repent and amend, and let us have no more of it!'

I cannot say that I implicitly obeyed my own injunctions; but such reasoning as this became more and more effective as time wore on and nothing was seen or heard of Mr Weston; until at last, I gave up hoping, for even my heart acknowledged it was all in vain. But still, I would think of him; I would cherish his image in my mind; and treasure every word, look, and gesture that my memory could retain; and brood over his excellences, and his peculiarities, and, in fact, all I had seen, heard, or imagined respecting him.

'Agnes, this sea air and change of scene do *you* no good,

I think; I never saw you look so wretched. It must be that you sit too much, and allow the cares of the school-room to worry you: – you must learn to take things easy, and to be more active and cheerful; you must take exercise whenever you can get it, and leave the most tiresome duties to me: they will only serve to exercise my patience, and, perhaps, try my temper a little.'

So said my mother as we sat at work one morning during the Easter holidays. I assured her that my employments were not at all oppressive, that I was well, or if there was anything amiss, it would be gone as soon as the trying months of Spring were over; when Summer came I should be as strong and hearty as she could wish to see me; but inwardly her observation startled me. I knew my strength was declining, my appetite had failed, and I was grown listless and desponding; – and if indeed he could never care for me, and I could never see him more – if I was forbidden to minister to his happiness, forbidden, for ever, to taste the joys of love, to bless and to be blessed, then life must be a burden, and if my heavenly Father would call me away, I should be glad to rest; but it would not do to die and leave my mother – Selfish, unworthy daughter, to forget her for a moment! Was not her happiness committed in a great measure to my charge – and the welfare of our young pupils too? Should I shrink from the work that God had set before me, because it was not fitted to my taste? Did not He know best what I should do, and where I ought to labour? and should I long to quit His service before I had finished my task, and expect to enter into His rest without having laboured to earn it? 'No; by His help I will arise and address myself diligently to my appointed duty. If happiness in this world is not for me, I will endeavour to promote the welfare of those around me, and my reward shall be hereafter.'

So said I in my heart, and from that hour I only permitted my thoughts to wander to Edward Weston – or at least to dwell upon him now and then ... as a treat for rare occasions; and whether it was really the approach of Summer, or the effect of these good resolutions, or the lapse of time, or all together, tranquillity of mind was soon restored, and bodily health and vigour began likewise, slowly but surely, to return.

Early in June, I received a letter from Lady Ashby, late Miss Murray. She had written to me twice or thrice before, from the different stages of her bridal tour, always in good spirits, and professing to be very happy. I wondered every time that she had not forgotten me in the midst of so much gaiety and variety of scene. At length however, there was a pause; and it seemed she had forgotten me, for upwards of seven months passed away, and no letter. Of course, I did not break my heart about *that*, though I often wondered how she was getting on; and when this last epistle so unexpectedly arrived, I was glad enough to receive it.

It was dated from Ashby Park where she was come to settle down at last, having previously divided her time between the Continent and the Metropolis. She made many apologies for having neglected me so long, assured me she had not forgotten me, and had often intended to write, &c., &c., but always been prevented by something. She acknowledged that she had been leading a very dissipated life, and I should think her very wicked and very thoughtless, but notwithstanding that, she thought a great deal, and among other things, that she should vastly like to see me.

'We have been several days here already,' wrote she. 'We have not a single friend with us, and are likely to be very dull. You know I never had a fancy for living with my husband like two turtles in a nest, were he the most delightful creature that ever wore a coat, so do take pity upon me and come. I suppose your Midsummer holidays commence in June, the same as other people's, therefore you cannot plead want of time, and you must and shall come – in fact I shall die if you don't. I want you to visit me as a *friend*, and stay a long time. There is nobody with me, as I told you before, but Sir Thomas and old Lady Ashby; but you needn't mind them – they'll trouble us but little with their company; and you shall have a room to yourself, whenever you like to retire to it, and plenty of books to read when my company is not sufficiently amusing. I forget whether you like babies; if you do, you may have the pleasure of seeing mine ... the most charming child in the world, no doubt ... and all the more so, that I am not troubled with nursing it – I was determined I wouldn't be bothered with that – Unfortunately it is a girl, and Sir Thomas has never forgiven me; but however, if you will only come, I promise you shall be its governess as soon as it can speak, and you shall bring it up in the way it should go, and make a better woman of it than its mama; – and you shall see my poodle too, a splendid little charmer imported from Paris, and two fine Italian paintings of great value ... I forget the artist ... doubtless you will be able to discover prodigious beauties in them, which you must point out to me, as I only admire by hearsay, ... and many elegant curiosities besides, which I purchased at Rome and elsewhere; ... and, finally, you shall see my new home – the splendid house and grounds I used to covet so greatly. Alas! how far the promise of anticipation exceeds the pleasure of possession! ... There's a fine sentiment! I assure you I am become quite a grave old matron: ... pray come, if it be only to witness the wonderful change. Write by return of post, and tell me when your vacation commences, and say that you will come the day after, and stay till the day before it closes ... in mercy to

Yours affectionately
Rosalie Ashby.'

I shewed this strange epistle to my mother, and consulted her on what I ought to do. She advised me to go; and I went – willing enough to see Lady Ashby – and her baby too – and to do anything I could to benefit her by consolation or advice, for I imagined she must be unhappy, or she would not have applied to me thus – but feeling, as may readily be conceived, that, in accepting the invitation, I made a great sacrifice for her, and did violence to my feelings in many ways, instead of being delighted with the honourable distinction of being entreated by the baronet's lady to visit her as a friend.

However, I determined my visit should be only for a few days at most; and I will not deny that I derived some consolation from the idea that as Ashby Park was not very far from Horton, I might possibly see Mr Weston, or, at least, hear something about him.

CHAPTER XXII

THE VISIT

A SHBY PARK WAS certainly a very delightful residence. The mansion was stately without, commodious and elegant within, the park was spacious and beautiful – chiefly on account of its magnificent old trees, its stately herds of deer, its broad sheet of water, and the ancient woods that stretched beyond it, for there was no broken ground to give variety to the landscape, and but very little of that undulating swell which adds so greatly to the charm of park scenery.

And so – this was the place Rosalie Murray had so longed to call her own, that she must have a share of it on whatever terms it might be offered, whatever price was to be paid for the title of mistress, and whoever was to be her partner in the honour and bliss of such a possession! Well – I am not disposed to censure her now.

She received me very kindly; and, though I was a poor clergyman's daughter, a governess, and a school-mistress, she welcomed me with unaffected pleasure to her home; and – what surprised me rather – took some pains to make my visit agreeable. I could see, it is true, that she expected me to be greatly struck with the magnificence that surrounded her; and, I confess, I was rather annoyed at her evident efforts to reassure me, and prevent me from being overwhelmed by so much grandeur; too much awed at the idea of encountering her husband and mother-in-law, or too much ashamed of my own humble appearance – I was not ashamed of it at all; for, though plain, I had taken good care not to be shabby or mean, and should have been pretty considerably at my ease, if my condescending hostess had not taken such manifest pains to make me so; and, as for the magnificence that surrounded her, nothing that met my eyes struck me, or affected me half so much as her own altered appearance.

Whether from the influence of fashionable dissipation, or some other evil – a space of little more than twelve months, had had the effect that might be expected from as many years, in reducing the plumpness of her form, the freshness of her complexion, the vivacity of her movements, and the exuberance of her spirits.

I wished to know if she was unhappy; but I felt it was not my province to inquire; I might endeavour to win her confidence; but, if she chose to conceal her matrimonial cares from me, I would trouble her with no obtrusive questions.

I, therefore, at first, confined myself to a few general inquiries about her health and welfare, and a few commendations on the beauty of the park, and of the little girl that should have been a boy, a small delicate infant of seven or eight weeks old, whom its mother seemed to regard with no remarkable degree of interest or affection, though full as much as I expected her to show.

Shortly after my arrival, she commissioned her maid to conduct me to my room and see that I had everything I wanted: it was a small, unpretending, but sufficiently comfortable apartment.

When I descended thence – having divested myself of all travelling encumbrances, and arranged my toilet with due consideration for the feelings of my lady hostess – she conducted me herself to the room I was to occupy when I chose to be alone, or when she was engaged with visiters, or obliged to be with her mother-in-law, or otherwise prevented, as she said, from enjoying the pleasure of my society. It was a quiet, tidy little sitting-room, and I was not sorry to be provided with such a harbour of refuge.

'And sometime,' said she, 'I will show you the library; I never examined its shelves, but, I dare say, it is full of wise books, and you may go and burrow among them whenever you please; and now you shall have some tea – it will soon be dinner time, but

I thought, as you were accustomed to dine at one, you would perhaps like better to have a cup of tea about this time, and to dine when we lunch; and then, you know, you can have your tea in this room, and that will save you from having to dine with Lady Ashby and Sir Thomas, which would be rather awkward – at least, not awkward, but rather – a – you know what I mean – I thought you mightn't like it so well – especially as we may have other ladies and gentlemen to dine with us occasionally.'

'Certainly,' said I, 'I would much rather have it as you say; and, if you have no objection, I should prefer having all my meals in this room.'

'Why so?'

'Because, I imagine, it would be more agreeable to Lady Ashby and Sir Thomas.'

'Nothing of the kind!'

'At any rate it would be more agreeable to me.'

She made some faint objections, but soon conceded; and I could see that the proposal was a considerable relief to her.

'Now, come into the drawing-room,' said she. 'There's the dressing-bell; but I won't go yet; it's no use dressing when there's no one to see you; and I want to have a little discourse.'

The drawing-room was certainly an imposing apartment, and very elegantly furnished; but I saw its young mistress glance towards me as we entered, as if to notice how I was impressed by the spectacle, and, accordingly, I determined to preserve an aspect of stony indifference, as if I saw nothing at all remarkable – but this was only for a moment: immediately conscience whispered, 'Why should I disappoint her to save my pride? No – rather let me sacrifice my pride to give her a little innocent gratification.' And I honestly looked round, and told her it was a noble room, and very tastefully furnished. She said little, but I saw she was pleased.

She shewed me her fat French poodle that lay curled up on a silk cushion, and the two fine Italian paintings, which, however, she would not give me time to examine, but, saying I must look at them some other day, insisted upon my admiring the little jewelled watch she had brought from Geneva, and then took me round the room to point out sundry other articles of vertu she had imported from Italy, an elegant little time-piece, and several busts, small, graceful figures, and vases, all beautifully carved in white marble. She spoke of these with animation, and heard my admiring comments with a smile of pleasure, that soon, however, vanished, and was followed by a melancholy sigh, as if in consideration of the insufficiency of all such baubles to the happiness of the human heart, and their woful inability to supply its insatiate demands.

Then, stretching herself upon a couch, she motioned me to a capacious easy chair that stood opposite – not before the fire, but before a wide open window – for it was Summer, be it remembered – a sweet, warm evening in the latter half of June; and I sat for a moment in silence, enjoying the still, pure air, and the delightful prospect of the park that lay before me, rich in verdure and foliage, and basking in yellow sunshine relieved by the long shadows of declining day. But I must take advantage of this pause: I had inquiries to make, and, like the substance of a lady's postscript, the most important must come last.

So I began with asking after Mr and Mrs Murray, and Miss Matilda and the young gentlemen.

I was told that papa had got the gout which made him very ferocious, and that he would not give up his choice wines, and his substantial dinners and suppers, and had quarrelled with his physician, because the latter had dared to say, that no medicine could cure him while he lived so freely; that mama and the rest were well: Matilda was still wild and reckless, but she had got a fashionable governess, and was considerably improved in her manners, and soon to be introduced to the world; and that John and Charles, (now at home for the holidays,) were, by all accounts, 'fine, bold, unruly, mischievous boys.'

'And how are the other people getting on?' said I – 'the Greens, for instance?'

'Ah! Mr Green is heart-broken, you know,' replied she, with a languid smile; 'he hasn't got over his disappointment yet, and never will, I suppose. He's doomed to be an old bachelor; and his sisters are doing their best to get married.'

'And the Melthams?'

'Oh, they're jogging on as usual, I suppose; but I know very little about any of them – except Harry,' said she, blushing slightly, and smiling again; 'I saw a great deal of him while we were in London; for, as soon as he heard we were there, he came up under pretence of visiting his brother, and either followed me, like a shadow, wherever I went, or met me, like a reflection, at every turn. But you needn't look so shocked, Miss Grey; I was very discreet, I assure you; but, you know, one can't help being admired. Poor fellow! He was not my only worshipper, but he was certainly the most conspicuous, and, I think, the most devoted among them all. And that detestable – ahem – and Sir Thomas chose to take offence at him – or my profuse expenditure, or something – I don't exactly know what – and hurried me down to the country, at a moment's notice, where I'm to play the hermit, I suppose, for life.'

And she bit her lip, and frowned vindictively upon the fair domain she had once so coveted to call her own.

'And Mr Hatfield,' said I, 'what is become of him?'

Again, she brightened up, and answered gaily –

'Oh! he made up to an elderly spinster, and married her, not long since, weighing her heavy purse against her faded charms, and expecting to find that solace in gold which was denied him in love, ha, ha!'

'Well, and I think that's all – except Mr Weston – what is *he* doing?'

'I don't know I'm sure. He's gone from Horton.'

'How long since; and where is he gone to?'

'I know nothing about him,' replied she, yawning – 'except that he went about a month ago – I never asked where,' (I would have asked whether it was to a living or merely another curacy, but thought it better not,) 'and the people made a great rout about his leaving,' continued she, 'much to Mr Hatfield's displeasure, for Hatfield didn't like him, because he had too much influence with the common people, and because he was not sufficiently tractable and submissive to him – and for some other unpardonable sins, I don't know what. But now I positively must go and dress; the second bell will ring directly, and if I come to dinner in this guise, I shall never hear the end of it from Lady Ashby. It's a strange thing one can't be mistress in one's own house! Just ring the bell, and I'll send for my maid, and tell them to get you some tea. Only think of that intolerable woman –'

'Who – your maid?'

'No, my mother-in-law – and my unfortunate mistake! Instead of letting her take herself off to some other house, as she offered to do when I married, I was fool enough to ask her to live here still, and direct the affairs of the house for me; because, in the first place, I hoped we should spend the greater part of the year in Town, and in the second place, being so young and inexperienced, I was frightened at the idea of having a houseful of servants to manage, and dinners to order, and parties to entertain, and all the rest of it, and I thought she might assist me with her experience; never dreaming that she would prove a usurper, a tyrant, an incubus, a spy, and everything else that's detestable. I wish she was dead!'

She then turned to give her orders to the footman, who had been standing bolt upright within the door for the last half minute, and had heard the latter part of her animadversions, and, of course, made his own reflections upon them, notwithstanding the inflexible, wooden countenance he thought proper to preserve in the drawing-room.

On my remarking afterwards that he must have heard her, she replied,

'Oh, no matter! I never care about the footmen; they're mere automatons – it's nothing to them what their superiors say or do; they won't dare to repeat it; and as to what they think – if they presume to think at all – of course, nobody cares for that. It would be a pretty thing indeed, if we were to be tongue-tied by our servants!'

So saying, she ran off to make her hasty toilet, leaving me to pilot my way back to my sitting-room, where, in due time, I was served with a cup of tea; and, after that, I sat musing on Lady Ashby's past and present condition; and on what little information I had obtained respecting Mr Weston, and the small chance there was of ever seeing or hearing anything more of him throughout my quiet, drab-colour life, which, hence-forth, seemed to offer no alternative between positive rainy days, and days of dull, grey clouds without downfall.

At length, however, I began to weary of my thoughts, and to wish I knew where to find the library my hostess had spoken of, and to wonder whether I was to remain there, doing nothing till bed-time.

As I was not rich enough to possess a watch, I could not tell how time was passing, except by observing the slowly lengthen-ing shadows from the window, which presented a side view, including a corner of the park, a clump of trees, whose topmost branches had been colonized by an innumerable company of noisy rooks, and a high wall with a massive wooden gate, no doubt communicating with the stable yard, as a broad carriage-road swept up to it from the park. The shadow of this wall soon took possession of the whole of the ground as far as I could see, forcing the golden sunlight to retreat inch by inch, and at last take refuge in the very tops of the trees. At last, even they were left in shadow – the shadow of the distant hills, or of the earth itself; and, in sympathy for the busy citizens of the rookery, I regretted to see their habitation, so lately bathed in glorious light, reduced to the sombre, worky-day hue of the lower world, or of my own world within. For a moment, such birds as soared above the rest might still receive the lustre on their wings, which imparted to their sable plumage the hue and brilliance of deep red gold; at last, that too departed. Twilight came stealing on – the rooks became more quiet – I became more weary, and wished I were going home to-morrow.

At length it grew dark; and I was thinking of ringing for a candle, and betaking myself to bed, when my hostess appeared, with many apologies for having neglected me so long, and laying all the blame upon that 'nasty old woman,' as she called her mother-in-law.

'If I didn't sit with her in the drawing-room while Sir Thomas is taking his wine,' said she, 'she would never forgive me; and then, if I leave the room the instant he comes – as I have done once or twice – it is an unpardonable offence against her dear Thomas. *She* never shewed such disrespect to *her* husband – and as for affection, wives never think of that now-a-days, she supposes; but things were different in *her* time – As if there was any good to be done by staying in the room, when he does nothing but grumble and scold when he's in a bad humour, talk disgusting nonsense when he's in a good one, and go to sleep on the sofa when he's too stupid for either, which is most frequently the case now, when he has nothing to do but to sot over his wine.'

'But could you not try to occupy his mind with something better; and engage him to give up such habits? I'm sure you have powers of persuasion, and qualifications for amusing a gentleman, which many ladies would be glad to possess.'

'And so you think I would lay myself out for his amusement! No; that's not *my* idea of a wife. It's the husband's part to please the wife, not hers to please him; and if he isn't satisfied with her as she is – and thankful to possess her too – he isn't worthy of her – that's all. And as for persuasion, I assure you I shan't trouble myself with that: I've enough to do to bear with him as he is, without attempting to work a reform. But, I'm sorry I left you so long alone, Miss Grey. How have you passed the time?'

'Chiefly in watching the rooks.'

'Mercy, how dull you must have been! I really must shew you

the library; and you must ring for everything you want, just as you would in an inn, and make yourself comfortable. I have selfish reasons for wishing to make you happy, because I want you to stay with me, and not fulfil your horrid threat of running away in a day or two.'

'Well, don't let me keep you out of the drawing-room any longer to-night, for at present I am tired, and wish to go to bed.'

CHAPTER XXIII

THE PARK

I CAME DOWN a little before eight, next morning, as I knew by the striking of a distant clock. There was no appearance of breakfast. I waited above an hour before it came, still vainly longing for access to the library; and, after that lonely repast was concluded, I waited again about an hour and a half in great suspense and discomfort, uncertain what to do.

At length, Lady Ashby came to bid me good morning. She informed me she had only just breakfasted, and now wanted me to take an early walk with her in the park. She asked how long I had been up, and, on receiving my answer, expressed the deepest regret, and again promised to shew me the library.

I suggested she had better do so at once, and then there would be no further trouble either with remembering or forgetting. She complied, on condition that I would not think of reading, or bothering with the books now, for she wanted to shew me the gardens, and take a walk in the park with me, before it became too hot for enjoyment, which, indeed, was nearly the case already. Of course, I readily assented; and we took our walk accordingly.

As we were strolling in the park, talking of what my companion had seen and heard during her travelling experience, a gentleman on horseback rode up and passed us. As he turned, in passing, and stared me full in the face, I had a good opportunity of seeing what he was like. He was tall, thin, and wasted, with a slight stoop in the shoulders, a pale face, but somewhat blotchy, and disagreeably red about the eye-lids, plain features, and a general appearance of languor and flatness, relieved by a sinister expression about the mouth and the dull, soulless eyes.

'I detest that man!' whispered Lady Ashby with bitter emphasis, as he slowly trotted by.

'Who is it?' I asked, unwilling to suppose that she should so
speak of her husband.

'Sir Thomas Ashby,' she replied with dreary composure.

'And do you *detest* him, Miss Murray?' said I, for I was too
much shocked to remember her name at the moment.

'Yes, I do, Miss Grey – and despise him too! and if you knew
him, you would not blame me.'

'But you knew what he was before you married him.'

'No; I only thought so; – I did not half know him really.
I know you warned me against it; and I wish I had listened to
you – but it's too late to regret that now – and besides mama
ought to have known better than either of us; and she never said
anything against it – quite the contrary – And then I thought he
adored me, and would let me have my own way – he did pretend
to do so at first; but now he does not care a bit about me. But
I should not care for that; he might do as he pleased, if I might
only be free to amuse myself and to stay in London, or have a
few friends down here … but *he will* do as he pleases – and
I must be a prisoner and a slave. The moment he saw I could
enjoy myself without him, and that others knew my value better
than himself, the selfish wretch began to accuse me of coquetry
and extravagance, and to abuse Harry Meltham whose shoes he
was not worthy to clean; – and then, he must needs have me
down in the country to lead the life of a nun, lest I should
dishonour him or bring him to ruin, as if he had not been ten
times worse every way – with his betting book, and his gaming
table, and his opera girls, and his Lady this and Mrs that – yes
and his bottles of wine, and glasses of brandy and water too –
filthy beast! Oh, I would give ten thousand worlds to be Miss
Murray again! It is *too* bad to feel life, health, and beauty wasting
away, unfelt and unenjoyed, for such a brute as that!' exclaimed
she, fairly bursting into tears in the bitterness of her vexation.

Of course, I pitied her exceedingly, as well for her false idea of happiness and disregard of duty, as for the wretched partner with whom her fate was linked.

I said what I could to comfort her, and offered such counsels as I thought she most required, advising her, first, by gentle reasoning, by kindness, example, and persuasion to try to ameliorate her husband; and then, when she had done all she could, if she still found him incorrigible, to endeavour to abstract herself from him – to wrap herself up in her own integrity, and trouble herself as little about him as possible. I exhorted her to seek consolation in doing her duty to God and man, to put her trust in Heaven, and solace herself with the care and nurture of her little daughter, assuring her she would be amply rewarded by witnessing its progress in strength and wisdom, and receiving its genuine affection.

'But I can't devote myself entirely to a child,' said she, 'it may die – which is not at all improbable.'

'But with care, many a delicate infant has become a strong man or woman.'

'But it may grow so intolerably like its father that I shall hate it.'

'That is not likely; it is a little girl, and strongly resembles its mother.'

'No matter – I should like it better if it were a boy – only that its father will leave it no inheritance that he can possibly squander away. What pleasure can I have in seeing a girl grow up to eclipse me, and enjoy those pleasures that I am for ever debarred from? But supposing I could be so generous as to take delight in this, still it is *only* a child; and I can't centre all my hopes in a child; that is only one degree better than devoting one's self to a dog. And as for all the wisdom and goodness you have been trying to instil into me – that is all very right and proper, I dare say; and if I were some twenty years older, I might fructify by it; but people must enjoy themselves when they're young – and if others won't let them – why, they must hate them for it!'

'The best way to enjoy yourself is to do what is right, and hate nobody. The end of Religion is not to teach us how to die, but how to live; and the earlier you become wise and good, the more of happiness you secure. And now Lady Ashby, I have one more piece of advice to offer you, which is that you will not make an enemy of your mother-in-law. Don't get into the way of holding her at arm's length and regarding her with jealous distrust. I never saw her, but I have heard good as well as evil respecting her, and I imagine that, though cold and haughty in her general demeanour, and even exacting in her requirements, she has strong affections for those who can reach them; and, though so blindly attached to her son, she is not without good principles, or incapable of hearing reason; and if you would but conciliate her a little, and adopt a friendly, open manner – and even confide your grievances to her ... *real* grievances, such as you have a right to complain of ... it is my firm belief that she would, in time, become your faithful friend, and a comfort and support to you, instead of the incubus you describe her.'

But I fear my advice had little effect upon the unfortunate young lady; and, finding I could render myself so little serviceable, my residence at Ashby Park became doubly painful. But still, I must stay out that day and the following one, as I had promised to do so; though, resisting all intreaties and inducements to prolong my visit further, I insisted upon departing the next morning, affirming that my mother would be lonely without me, and that she impatiently expected my return.

Nevertheless, it was with a heavy heart that I bid adieu to poor Lady Ashby and left her in her princely home. It was no slight additional proof of her unhappiness, that she should so cling to the consolation of my presence, and earnestly desire the company of one whose general tastes and ideas were so little congenial to her own, whom she had completely forgotten in her hours of prosperity, and whose presence would be rather a nuisance than a pleasure, if she could but have half her heart's desire.

CHAPTER XXIV

THE SANDS

OUR SCHOOL WAS not situated in the heart of the town: on entering A— from the north-west there is a row of respectable looking houses, on each side of the broad, white road, with narrow slips of garden ground before them, Venetian blinds to the windows, and a flight of steps leading to each trim, brass-handled door. In one of the largest of these habitations dwelt my mother and I, with such young ladies as our friends and the public chose to commit to our charge. Consequently, we were a considerable distance from the sea, and divided from it by a labyrinth of streets and houses. But the sea was my delight; and I would often gladly pierce the town to obtain the pleasure of a walk beside it, whether with the pupils, or alone or with my mother during the vacations. It was delightful to me at all times and seasons, but especially in the wild commotion of a rough sea-breeze, and in the brilliant freshness of a Summer morning.

I awoke early on the third morning after my return from Ashby Park ... the sun was shining through the blind, and I thought how pleasant it would be to pass through the quiet town and take a solitary ramble on the sands while half the world was in bed. I was not long in forming the resolution, nor slow to act upon it. Of course I would not disturb my mother, so I stole noiselessly down stairs, and quietly unfastened the door. I was dressed, down, and out when the church clock struck a quarter to six.

There was a feeling of freshness and vigour in the very streets; and when I got free of the town, when my foot was on the sands and my face towards the broad, bright bay ... no language can describe the effect of the deep, clear azure of the sky and ocean, the bright morning sunshine on the semi-circular barrier of craggy cliffs surmounted by green swelling hills, and on the smooth, wide sands, and the low rocks out at sea ... looking, with their clothing of weeds and moss, like little grass-grown islands – and above all, on the brilliant, sparkling waves. And then, the unspeakable purity and freshness of the air! there was just enough heat to enhance the value of the breeze, and just enough wind to keep the whole sea in motion, to make the waves come bounding to the shore, foaming and sparkling, as if wild with glee. Nothing else was stirring – no living creature was visible besides myself. My footsteps were the first to press the firm, unbroken sands; – nothing before had trampled them since last night's flowing tide had obliterated the deepest marks of yesterday, and left it fair and even, except where the subsiding water had left behind it the traces of dimpled pools, and little running streams.

Refreshed, delighted, invigorated, I walked along, forgetting all my cares, feeling as if I had wings to my feet, and could go at least forty miles without fatigue, and experiencing a sense of exhilaration to which I had been an entire stranger since the days of early youth. About half-past six, however, the grooms began to come down to air their master's horses – first one, and then another, till there were some dozen horses and five or six riders; but that need not trouble me, for they would not come as far as the low rocks which I was now approaching. When I had reached these, and walked over the moist, slippery sea-weed, (at the risk of floundering into one of the numerous pools of clear, salt water that lay between them,) to a little mossy promontory with the sea splashing round it, I looked back again to see who next was stirring. Still, there were only the early grooms with their horses, and one gentleman with a little dark speck of a dog running before him, and one water-cart coming out of the town to get water for the baths. In another minute or two, the distant bathing machines would begin to move: and then the elderly gentlemen of regular habits, and sober quaker ladies would be coming to take their salutary morning walks. But however interesting such a scene might be, I could not wait to witness it, for the sun and the sea so dazzled my eyes in that direction, that I could but afford one glance; and then I turned again to delight myself with the sight and the sound of the sea dashing against my promontory – with no prodigious force, for the swell was broken by the tangled sea-weed and the unseen rocks beneath; otherwise I should soon have been deluged with spray.

But the tide was coming in; the water was rising; the gulfs and lakes were filling; the straits were widening: it was time to seek some safer footing; so I walked, skipped, and stumbled back to the smooth, wide sands, and resolved to proceed to a certain bold projection in the cliffs, and then return.

Presently, I heard a snuffling sound behind me, and then a dog came frisking and wriggling to my feet. It was my own Snap – the little dark, wire-haired terrier! When I spoke his name, he leapt up in my face, and yelled for joy.

Almost as much delighted as himself, I caught the little creature in my arms, and kissed him repeatedly. But how came he to be there? He could not have dropped from the sky, or come all that way alone: it must be either his master, the rat-catcher, or somebody else that had brought him; so, repressing my extravagant caresses, and endeavouring to repress his likewise, I looked round, and beheld – Mr Weston!

'Your dog remembers you well, Miss Grey,' said he, warmly grasping the hand I offered him without clearly knowing what I was about.

'You rise early.'

'Not often so early as this,' I replied, with amazing composure, considering all the circumstances of the case.

'How far do you purpose to extend your walk?'

'I was thinking of returning – it must be almost time, I think.'

He consulted his watch – a gold one now – and told me it was only five minutes past seven.

'But doubtless, you have had a long enough walk,' said he, turning towards the town, to which I now proceeded leisurely to retrace my steps; and he walked beside me.

'In what part of the town do you live?' asked he. 'I never could discover.'

Never could discover? Had he endeavoured to do so then? I told him the place of our abode.

He asked how we prospered in our affairs; I told him we were doing very well, – that we had had a considerable addition to our pupils after the Christmas vacation, and expected a still further increase at the close of this.

'You must be an accomplished instructor,' he observed.

'No, it is my mother,' I replied, 'she manages things so well, and is so active, and clever, and kind.'

'I should like to know your mother – Will you introduce me to her sometime if I call?'

'Yes, willingly.'

'And will you allow me the privilege of an old friend, of looking in upon you now and then?'

'Yes, if – I suppose so.'

This was a very foolish answer, but the truth was, I considered that I had no right to invite any one to my mother's house without her knowledge; and if I had said, 'yes, if my mother does not object,' it would appear as if, by his question, I understood more than was expressed, so, *supposing* she would not, I added, 'I suppose so,' but of course I should have said something more sensible and more polite if I had had my wits about me. We continued our walk for a minute in silence, which, however, was shortly relieved, (no small relief to me,) by Mr Weston commenting upon the brightness of the morning, and the beauty of the bay, and then, upon the advantages A— possessed over many other fashionable places of resort.

'You don't ask what brings me to A—,' said he. 'You can't suppose I'm rich enough to come for my own pleasure.'

'I heard you had left Horton.'

'You didn't hear then, that I had got the living of F—?'

F— was a village about two miles distant from A—.

'No,' said I; 'we live so completely out of the world, even here, that news seldom reaches me from any quarter – except through the medium of the — Gazette. But I hope you like your new parish; and that I may congratulate you on the acquisition?'

'I expect to like my parish better a year or two hence, when I have worked certain reforms I have set my heart upon – or, at least, progressed some steps towards such an achievement; but you may congratulate me now, for I find it very agreeable to *have* a parish all to myself with nobody to interfere with me – to thwart my plans or cripple my exertions; and besides, I have a respectable house in a rather pleasant neighbourhood, and three hundred pounds a year; and, in fact, I have nothing but solitude to complain of, and nothing but a companion to wish for.'

He looked at me as he concluded; and the flash of his dark eyes seemed to set my face on fire, greatly to my own disconcertion, for to evince confusion at such a juncture was intolerable.

I made an effort, therefore, to remedy the evil, and disclaim all personal application of the remark, by a hasty, ill-expressed reply to the effect that, if he waited till he was well known in the neighbourhood, he might have numerous opportunities for supplying his want among the residents of F—, and its vicinity, or the visiters of A—, if he required so ample a choice; not considering the compliment implied by such an assertion, till his answer made me aware of it.

'I am not so presumptuous as to believe that,' said he, 'though you tell it me; but if it were so – I am rather particular in my notions of a companion for life, and perhaps I might not find one to suit me among the ladies you mention.'

'If you require perfection, you never will.'

'I do not – I have no right to, as being so far from perfect myself.'

Here the conversation was interrupted by a water-cart lumbering past us, for we were now come to the busy part of the sands;

and, for the next eight or ten minutes, between carts and horses, and asses, and men, there was little room for social intercourse, till we had turned our backs upon the sea, and begun to ascend the precipitous road leading into the town. Here my companion offered me his arm, which I accepted, though not with the intention of using it as a support.

'You don't often come on to the sands, I think,' said he, 'for I have walked there many times, both morning and evening, since I came, and never seen you till now; and several times, in passing through the town, too, I have looked about for your school – but I did not think of the — road; and once or twice I made inquiries, but without obtaining the requisite information.'

When we had surmounted the acclivity, I was about to withdraw my arm from his, but by a slight tightening of the elbow was tacitly informed that such was not his will, and accordingly desisted.

Discoursing on different subjects, we entered the town, and passed through several streets; I saw that he was going out of his way to accompany me, notwithstanding the long walk that was yet before him; and, fearing that he might be inconveniencing himself from motives of politeness, I observed –

'I fear I am taking you out of your way, Mr Weston – I believe the road to F— lies quite in another direction.'

'I'll leave you at the end of the next street,' said he.

'And when will you come to see mama?'

'To-morrow – God willing.'

The end of the next street was nearly the conclusion of my journey. He stopped there, however, bid me good morning, and called Snap, who seemed a little doubtful whether to follow his old mistress or his new master, but trotted away upon being summoned by the latter.

'I won't offer to restore him to you, Miss Grey,' said Mr Weston, smiling, 'because I like him.'

'Oh, I don't want him,' replied I; 'now that he has a good master, I'm quite satisfied.'

'You take it for granted that I *am* a good one then?'

The man and the dog departed, and I returned home, full of gratitude to Heaven for so much bliss, and praying that my hopes might not again be crushed.

CHAPTER XXV

CONCLUSION

'WELL, AGNES, YOU must not take such long walks again before breakfast,' said my mother, observing that I drank an extra cup of coffee and ate nothing – pleading the heat of the weather, and the fatigue of my long walk as an excuse.

I certainly did feel feverish, and tired too.

'You always do things by extremes: now, if you had taken a *short* walk every morning, and would continue to do so, it would do you good.'

'Well, mama, I will.'

'But this is worse than lying in bed, or bending over your books; you have quite put yourself into a fever.'

'I won't do it again,' said I.

I was racking my brains with thinking how to tell her about Mr Weston, for she must know he was coming to-morrow. However, I waited till the breakfast things were removed, and I was more calm and cool; and then, having sat down to my drawing, I began –

'I met an old friend on the sands to-day, mama.'

'An old friend! Who could it be?'

'Two old friends indeed. One was a dog,' and then I reminded her of Snap, whose history I had recounted before, and related the incident of his sudden appearance and remarkable recognition, 'and the other,' continued I, 'was Mr Weston, the Curate of Horton.'

'Mr Weston! I never heard of him before.'

'Yes, you have: I've mentioned him several times, I believe, but you don't remember.'

'I've heard you speak of Mr Hatfield.'

'Mr Hatfield was the rector, and Mr Weston the curate; I used to mention him sometimes in contradistinction to Mr Hatfield, as being a more efficient clergyman. However, he was on the sands this morning with the dog – he had bought it, I suppose, from the rat-catcher; and he knew me as well as it did – probably through its means; and I had a little conversation with him, in the course of which, as he asked about our school, I was led to say something about you and your good management; and he said he should like to know you, and asked if I would introduce him to you, if he should take the liberty of calling to-morrow, so I said I would. Was I right?'

'Of course. What kind of a man is he?'

'A very respectable man, I think; but you will see him to-morrow. He is the new vicar of F—, and as he has only been there a few weeks, I suppose he has made no friends yet, and wants a little society.'

The morrow came. What a fever of anxiety and expectation I was in from breakfast till noon – at which time he made his appearance.

Having introduced him to my mother, I took my work to the window, and sat down to await the result of the interview.

They got on extremely well together, greatly to my satisfaction, for I had felt very anxious about what my mother would think of him. He did not stay long that time; but when he rose to take leave, she said she should be happy to see him, whenever he might find it convenient to call again; and when he was gone, I was gratified by hearing her say, –

'Well! I think he's a very sensible man. But why did you sit back there, Agnes,' she added, 'and talk so little?'

'Because you talked so well, mama, I thought you required no assistance from me; and, besides, he was your visitor, not mine.'

After that, he often called upon us – several times in the course of a week. He generally addressed most of his conversation to my mother; and no wonder, for she *could* converse. I almost envied the unfettered, vigorous fluency of her discourse, and the strong sense evinced by everything she said – and yet, I did not, for though I occasionally regretted my own deficiencies for his sake, it gave me very great pleasure to sit and hear the two beings I loved and honoured above every one else in the world, discoursing together so amicably, so wisely, and so well.

I was not always silent, however; nor was I at all neglected. I was quite as much noticed as I would wish to be: there was no lack of kind words and kinder looks, no end of delicate attentions, too fine and subtle to be grasped by words, and, therefore, indescribable – but deeply felt at heart.

Ceremony was quickly dropped between us, Mr Weston came as an expected guest, welcome at all times, and never deranging the economy of our household affairs. He even called me 'Agnes;' the name had been timidly spoken at first, but, finding it gave no offence in any quarter, he seemed greatly to prefer that appellation to 'Miss Grey,' and so did I.

How tedious and gloomy were those days in which he did not come! and yet not miserable, for I had still the remembrance of the last visit and the hope of the next to cheer me. But when two or three days passed without my seeing him, I certainly felt very anxious – absurdly, unreasonably so, for, of course, he had his own business and the affairs of his parish to attend to: and I dreaded the close of the holidays, when my business also would begin, and I should be sometimes unable to see him, and sometimes . . . when my mother was in the school-room – obliged to be with him alone, a position I did not at all desire . . . in the house, though to meet him out of doors, and walk beside him had proved by no means disagreeable.

One evening, however, in the last week of the vacation, he arrived – unexpectedly, for a heavy and protracted thunder shower during the afternoon had almost destroyed my hopes of seeing him that day; but now the storm was over, and the sun was shining brightly.

'A beautiful evening, Mrs Grey!' said he, as he entered. 'Agnes,

I want you to take a walk with me to —' (he named a certain part of the coast ... a bold hill on the land side, and towards the sea, a steep precipice, from the summit of which a glorious view is to be had.) 'The rain has laid the dust, and cooled and cleared the air, and the prospect will be magnificent. Will you come?'

'Can I go, mama?'

'Yes, to be sure.'

I went to get ready, and was down again in a few minutes, though, of course, I took a little more pains with my attire than if I had merely been going out on some shopping expedition alone.

The thunder shower had certainly had a most beneficial effect upon the weather, and the evening was most delightful. Mr Weston would have me to take his arm: he said little during our passage through the crowded streets, but walked very fast, and appeared grave and abstracted.

I wondered what was the matter, and felt an indefinite dread that something unpleasant was on his mind; and vague surmises, concerning what it might be, troubled me not a little, and made me grave and silent enough. But these fantasies vanished upon reaching the quiet outskirts of the town, for as soon as we came within sight of the venerable old church, and the — hill, with the deep blue sea beyond it, I found my companion was cheerful enough.

'I'm afraid I've been walking too fast for you, Agnes,' said he; 'in my impatience to be rid of the town, I forgot to consult your convenience; but now, we'll walk as slowly as you please: I see, by those light clouds in the west, there will be a brilliant sunset, and we shall be in time to witness its effect upon the sea, at the most moderate rate of progression.'

When we had got about half-way up the hill, we fell into silence again, which, as usual, he was the first to break.

'My house is desolate yet, Miss Grey,' he smilingly observed, 'and I am acquainted now with all the ladies in my parish, and several in this town too; and many others I know by sight and by report; but not one of them will suit me for a companion ... in fact, there is only one person in the world that will; and that is yourself; and I want to know your decision?'

'Are you in earnest, Mr Weston?'

'In earnest! How could you think I should jest on such a subject?'

He laid his hand on mine that rested on his arm: he must have felt it tremble ... but it was no great matter now.

'I hope I have not been too precipitate,' he said, in a serious tone. 'You must have known that it was not my way to flatter and talk soft nonsense, or even to speak the admiration that I felt; and that a single word or glance of mine meant more than the honied phrases and fervent protestations of most other men.'

I said something about not liking to leave my mother, and doing nothing without her consent.

'I settled everything with Mrs Grey while you were putting on your bonnet,' replied he. 'She said I might have her consent if I could obtain yours; and I asked her, in case I should be so happy, to come and live with us – for I was sure you would like it better; but she refused, saying she could now afford to employ an assistant, and would continue the school till she could purchase an annuity sufficient to maintain her in comfortable lodgings; and meantime she would spend her vacations alternately with us and your sister, and should be quite contented if you were happy. And so now I have overruled your objections on her account. Have you any other?'

'No – none.'

'You love me then?' said he, fervently pressing my hand.

'Yes.'

* * *

Here I pause. My diary, from which I compiled these pages, goes but little farther. I could go on for years; but I will content myself with adding, that I shall never forget that glorious Summer evening, and always remember with delight that steep, rugged hill, and the edge of the precipice where we stood together watching the splendid sun-set mirrored on the restless world of waters at our feet – with hearts filled with gratitude to Heaven, and happiness, and love – almost too full for speech.

A few weeks after that, when my mother had supplied herself with an assistant, I became the wife of Edward Weston, and never have found cause to repent it, and am certain that I never shall. We have had trials, and we know that we must have them again; but we bear them well together, and endeavour to fortify ourselves and each other against the final separation – that greatest of all afflictions to the survivor; but, if we keep in mind the glorious heaven beyond, where both may meet again, and sin and sorrow are unknown, surely that too may be borne; and meantime, we endeavour to live to the glory of Him who has scattered so many blessings in our path.

Edward, by his strenuous exertions, has worked surprising reforms in his parish, and is esteemed and loved by its inhabitants – as he deserves – for whatever his faults may be as a man, (and no one is entirely without,) I defy anybody to blame him as a pastor, a husband, or a father.

Our children, Edward, Agnes, and little Mary, promise well; their education, for the time being, is chiefly committed to me; and they shall want no good thing that a mother's care can give.

Our modest income is amply sufficient for our requirements; and by practising the economy we learnt in harder times, and never attempting to imitate our richer neighbours, we manage not only to enjoy comfort and contentment ourselves, but to have every year something to lay by for our children, and something to give to those who need it.

And now I think I have said sufficient.

THE END

THE TENANT OF
WILDFELL HALL

PREFACE TO THE
SECOND EDITION

WHILE I ACKNOWLEDGE the success of the present work to have been greater than I anticipated, and the praises it has elicited from a few kind critics to have been greater than it deserved, I must also admit that from some other quarters it has been censured with an asperity which I was as little prepared to expect, and which my judgment as well as my feelings, assures me is more bitter than just. It is scarcely the province of an author to refute the arguments of his censors and vindicate his own productions, but I may be allowed to make here a few observations with which I would have prefaced the first edition had I foreseen the necessity of such precautions against the misapprehensions of those who would read it with a prejudiced mind or be content to judge it by a hasty glance.

My object in writing the following pages, was not simply to amuse the Reader, neither was it to gratify my own taste, nor yet to ingratiate myself with the Press and the Public: I wished to tell the truth, for truth always conveys its own moral to those who are able to receive it. But as the priceless treasure too frequently hides at the bottom of a well, it needs some courage to dive for it, especially as he that does so will be likely to incur more scorn and obloquy for the mud and water into which he has ventured to plunge, than thanks for the jewel he procures; as, in like manner, she who undertakes the cleansing of a careless bachelor's apartment will be liable to more abuse for the dust she raises, than commendation for the clearance she effects. Let it not be imagined, however, that I consider myself competent to reform the errors and abuses of society, but only that I would fain contribute my humble quota towards so good an aim, and if I can gain the public ear at all, I would rather whisper a few wholesome truths therein than much soft nonsense.

As the story of 'Agnes Grey' was accused of extravagant over-colouring in those very parts that were carefully copied from the life, with a most scrupulous avoidance of all exaggeration, so, in the present work, I find myself censured for depicting con amore, with 'a morbid love of the coarse, if not of the brutal,' those scenes which, I will venture to say, have not been more painful for the most fastidious of my critics to read, than they were for me to describe. I may have gone too far, in which case I shall be careful not to trouble myself or my readers in the same way again; but when we have to do with vice and vicious characters, I maintain it is better to depict them as they really are than as they would wish to appear. To represent a bad thing in its least offensive light is, doubtless, the most agreeable course for a writer of fiction to pursue; but is it the most honest, or the safest? Is it better to reveal the snares and pitfalls of life to the young and thoughtless traveller, or to cover them with branches and flowers? O Reader! if there were less of this delicate concealment of facts – this whispering 'Peace, peace,' when there is no peace, there would be less of sin and misery to the young of both sexes who are left to wring their bitter knowledge from experience.

I would not be understood to suppose that the proceedings of the unhappy scapegrace, with his few profligate companions I have here introduced, are a specimen of the common practices of society: the case is an extreme one, as I trusted none would fail to perceive; but I know that such characters do exist, and if I have warned one rash youth from following in their steps, or prevented one thoughtless girl from falling into the very natural error of my heroine, the book has not been written in vain. But, at the same time, if any honest reader shall have derived more pain than pleasure from its perusal, and have closed the last volume with a disagreeable impression on his mind, I humbly crave his pardon, for such was far from my intention; and I will endeavour to do better another time, for I love to give innocent pleasure. Yet, be it understood, I shall not limit my ambition to this, – or even to producing 'a perfect work of art:' time and talents so spent, I should consider wasted and misapplied. Such humble talents as God has given me I will endeavour to put to their greatest use; if I am able to amuse I will try to benefit too; and when I feel it my duty to speak an unpalatable truth, with the help of God, I will speak it, though it be to the prejudice of my name and to the detriment of my reader's immediate pleasure as well as my own.

One word more, and I have done. Respecting the author's identity, I would have it to be distinctly understood that Acton Bell is neither Currer nor Ellis Bell, and therefore let not his faults be attributed to them. As to whether the name be real or fictitious, it cannot greatly signify to those who know him only by his works. As little, I should think, can it matter whether the writer so designated is a man, or a woman, as one or two of my critics profess to have discovered. I take the imputation in good part, as a compliment to the just delineation of my female characters; and though I am bound to attribute much of the severity of my censors to this suspicion, I make no effort to refute it, because, in my own mind, I am satisfied that if a book is a good one, it is so whatever the sex of the author may be. All novels are or should be written for both men and women to read, and I am at a loss to conceive how a man should permit himself to write anything that would be really disgraceful to a woman, or why a woman should be censured for writing any-thing that would be proper and becoming for a man.

July 22nd, 1848.

CONTENTS

TO J. HALFORD, ESQ.

DEAR HALFORD,

When we were together last, you gave me a very particular and interesting account of the most remarkable occurrences of your early life, previous to our acquaintance; and then you requested a return of confidence from me. Not being in a story-telling humour at the time, I declined, under the plea of having nothing to tell, and the like shuffling excuses, which were regarded as wholly inadmissible by you; for though you instantly turned the conversation, it was with the air of an uncomplaining, but deeply injured man, and your face was overshadowed with a cloud which darkened it to the end of our interview, and, for what I know, darkens it still; for your letters have, ever since, been distinguished by a certain dignified, semi-melancholy stiffness and reserve, that would have been very affecting, if my conscience had accused me of deserving it.

Are you not ashamed, old boy – at your age, and when we have known each other so intimately and so long, and when I have already given you so many proofs of frankness and confidence, and never resented your comparative closeness and taciturnity? – But there it is, I suppose; you are not naturally communicative, and you thought you had done great things, and given an unparalleled proof of friendly confidence on that memorable occasion – which, doubtless, you have sworn shall be the last of the kind, – and you deemed that the smallest return I could make for so mighty a favour, would be to follow your example without a moment's hesitation. –

Well! – I did not take up my pen to reproach you, nor to

defend myself, not to apologize for past offences, but, if possible, to atone for them.

It is a soaking, rainy day, the family are absent on a visit, I am alone in my library, and have been looking over certain musty old letters and papers, and musing on past times; so that I am now in a very proper frame of mind for amusing you with an old world story; – and, having withdrawn my well-roasted feet from the hobs, wheeled round to the table, and indited the above lines to my crusty old friend, I am about to give him a sketch – no not a sketch, – a full and faithful account of certain circumstances connected with the most important event of my life – previous to my acquaintance with Jack Halford at least; – and when you have read it, charge me with ingratitude and unfriendly reserve if you can.

I know you like a long story, and are as great a stickler for particularities and circumstantial details as my grandmother, so I will not spare you: my own patience and leisure shall be my only limits.

Among the letters and papers I spoke of, there is a certain faded old journal of mine, which I mention by way of assurance that I have not my memory alone – tenacious as it is – to depend upon; in order that your credulity may not be too severely taxed in following me through the minute details of my narrative. – To begin then, at once, with Chapter first, – for it shall be a tale of many chapters. –

CHAPTER I

A DISCOVERY

YOU MUST GO back with me to the autumn of 1827.

My father, as you know, was a sort of gentleman farmer in —shire; and I, by his express desire, succeeded him in the same quiet occupation, not very willingly, for ambition urged me to higher aims, and self-conceit assured me that, in disregarding its voice, I was burying my talent in the earth, and hiding my light under a bushel. My mother had done her utmost to persuade me that I was capable of great achievements; but my father, who thought ambition was the surest road to ruin, and change but another word for destruction, would listen to no scheme for bettering either my own condition, or that of my fellow mortals. He assured me it was all rubbish, and exhorted me, with his dying breath, to continue in the good old way, to follow his steps, and those of his father before him, and let my highest ambition be, to walk honestly through the world, looking neither to the right hand nor to the left, and to transmit the paternal acres to my children in, at least, as flourishing a condition as he left them to me.

'Well! – an honest and industrious farmer is one of the most useful members of society; and if I devote my talents to the cultivation of my farm, and the improvement of agriculture in general, I shall thereby benefit, not only my own immediate connections and dependants, but in some degree, mankind at large: – hence I shall not have lived in vain.'

With such reflections as these, I was endeavouring to console myself, as I plodded home from the fields, one cold, damp, cloudy evening towards the close of October. But the gleam of a bright red fire through the parlour window, had more effect in cheering my spirits, and rebuking my thankless repinings, than all the sage reflections and good resolutions I had forced my mind to frame; – for I was young then, remember – only four and twenty – and had not acquired half the rule over my own spirit, that I now possess – trifling as that may be.

However, that haven of bliss must not be entered till I had exchanged my miry boots, for a clean pair of shoes, and my rough surtout for a respectable coat, and made myself generally presentable before decent society; for my mother, with all her kindness, was vastly particular on certain points.

In ascending to my room, I was met upon the stairs by a smart, pretty girl of nineteen, with a tidy, dumpy figure, a round face, bright, blooming cheeks, glossy, clustering curls, and little merry brown eyes. I need not tell you this was my sister Rose. She is, I know, a comely matron still, and, doubtless, no less lovely – in *your* eyes – than on the happy day you first beheld her. Nothing told me then, that she, a few years hence, would be the wife of one – entirely unknown to me as yet, but destined hereafter to become a closer friend than even herself, more intimate than that unmannerly lad of seventeen, by whom I was collared in the passage, on coming down, and wellnigh jerked off my equilibrium, and who, in correction for his impudence, received a resounding whack over the sconce, which, however, sustained no serious injury from the infliction; as besides being more than commonly thick, it was protected by a redundant shock of short, reddish curls, that my mother called auburne.

On entering the parlour, we found that honoured lady seated in her arm-chair at the fire side, working away at her knitting, according to her usual custom, when she had nothing else to do. She had swept the hearth, and made a bright blazing fire for our reception; the servant had just brought in the tea-tray; and Rose was producing the sugar-basin and tea-caddy, from the cupboard in the black, oak sideboard, that shone like polished ebony, in the cheerful parlour twilight.

'Well! here they both are,' cried my mother, looking round upon us without retarding the motion of her nimble fingers and glittering needles. 'Now shut the door, and come to the fire, while Rose gets the tea ready; I'm sure you must be starved; – and tell me what you've been about all day; I like to know what my children have been about.'

'I've been breaking in the grey colt – no easy business that – directing the ploughing of the last wheat stubble – for the ploughboy has not the sense to direct himself – and carrying out a plan for the extensive and efficient draining of the low meadow-lands.'

'That's my brave boy! – and Fergus – what have you been doing?'

'Badger-baiting.'

And here he proceeded to give a particular account of his sport, and the respective traits of prowess evinced by the badger and the dogs; my mother pretending to listen with deep attention, and watching his animated countenance with a degree of maternal admiration I thought highly disproportioned to its object.

'It's time you should be doing something else, Fergus,' said I, as soon as a momentary pause in his narration, allowed me to get in a word.

'What *can* I do?' replied he; 'my mother won't let me go to sea or enter the army; and I'm determined to do nothing else – except make myself such a nuisance to you all, that you will be thankful to get rid of me, on any terms.'

Our parent soothingly stroked his stiff, short curls. He growled, and tried to look sulky, and then, we all took our seats at the table, in obedience to the thrice repeated summons of Rose.

'Now take your tea,' said she; 'and I'll tell you what *I've* been doing. I've been to call on the Wilsons; and it's a *thousand* pities you didn't go with me, Gilbert, for Eliza Millward was there!'

'Well! what of her?'

'Oh, nothing! – I'm not going to tell you about her; – only that she's a nice, amusing little thing, when she is in a merry humour, and I shouldn't mind calling her —'

'Hush, hush, my dear! your brother has no such idea!' whispered my mother earnestly, holding up her finger.

'Well,' resumed Rose; 'I was going to tell you an important piece of news I heard there – I've been bursting with it ever since. You know it was reported a month ago, that some body was going to take Wildfell Hall – and – what do you think? It has actually been inhabited above a week! – and we never knew!'

'Impossible!' cried my mother.

'Preposterous!!!' shrieked Fergus.

'It has indeed! – and by a single lady!'

'Good gracious, my dear! The place is in ruins!'

'She has had two or three rooms made habitable; and there she lives, all alone – except an old woman for a servant!'

'Oh dear! that spoils it – I'd hoped she was a witch,' observed Fergus, while carving his inch-thick slice of bread and butter.

'Nonsense, Fergus! But isn't it strange, mamma?'

'Strange! I can hardly believe it.'

'But you may believe it; for Jane Wilson has seen her. She went with her mother, who, of course, when she heard of a stranger being in the neighbourhood, would be on pins and needles till she had seen her and got all she could out of her. She is called Mrs Graham, and she is in mourning – not widow's weeds, but slightish mourning – and she is quite young, they say, – not above five or six and twenty, – but *so* reserved! They tried all they could to find out who she was, and where she came from, and all about her, but neither Mrs Wilson, with her pertinacious and impertinent home thrusts, nor Miss Wilson, with her skilful manœuvring, could manage to elicit a single satisfactory answer, or even a casual remark, or chance expression calculated to allay their curiosity, or throw the faintest ray of light upon her history, circumstances, or connexions. Moreover, she was barely civil to them, and evidently better pleased to say "good-bye," than "how do you do." But Eliza Millward says her father intends to call upon her soon, to offer some pastoral advice, which he fears she needs, as, though she is known to have entered the neighbourhood early last week, she did not make her appearance at church on Sunday; and she – Eliza, that is – will beg to accompany him, and is sure *she* can succeed in wheedling something out of her – you know, Gilbert, *she* can do anything. And *we* should call some time, mamma; it's only proper, you know.'

'Of course, my dear. Poor thing! how lonely she must feel!'

'And pray be quick about it; and mind you bring me word how much sugar she puts in her tea, and what sort of caps and aprons she wears, and all about it; for I don't know how I can live till I know,' said Fergus, very gravely.

But if he intended the speech to be hailed as a master-stroke of wit, he signally failed, for nobody laughed. However, he was not much disconcerted at that; for when he had taken a mouthful of bread and butter, and was about to swallow a gulp of tea, the humour of the thing burst upon him with such irresistible force, that he was obliged to jump up from the table, and rush snorting and choking from the room; and a minute after, was heard screaming in fearful agony in the garden.

As for me, I was hungry, and contented myself with silently demolishing the tea, ham, and toast, while my mother and sister went on talking, and continued to discuss the apparent, or non-apparent circumstances, and probable or improbable history of the mysterious lady; but I must confess that, after my brother's misadventure, I once or twice, raised the cup to my lips, and put it down again without daring to taste the contents, lest I should injure my dignity by a similar explosion.

The next day, my mother and Rose hastened to pay their compliments to the fair recluse; and came back but little wiser than they went; though my mother declared she did not regret the journey, for if she had not gained much good, she flattered herself she had imparted some, and that was better: she had given some useful advice, which, she hoped, would not be thrown away; for Mrs Graham, though she said little to any purpose, and appeared somewhat self-opinionated, seemed not incapable of reflection, – though she did not know where she had been all her life, poor thing, for she betrayed a lamentable ignorance on certain points, and had not even the sense to be ashamed of it.

'On what points, mother?' asked I.

'On household matters, and all the little niceties of cookery, and such things, that every lady ought to be familiar with, whether she be required to make a practical use of her knowledge or not. I gave her some useful pieces of information, however, and several excellent receipts, the value of which, she evidently could not appreciate, for she begged I would not trouble myself, as she lived in such a plain, quiet way, that she was sure she should never make use of them. "No matter, my dear," said I; "it is what every respectable female ought to know; – and besides, though you are alone now, you will not be always so; you *have* been married, and probably – I might say almost certainly – will be again." "You are mistaken there Ma'am," said she, almost haughtily; "I am certain I never shall." – But I told her *I* knew better.'

'Some romantic young widow, I suppose,' said I, 'come there to end her days in solitude, and mourn in secret for the dear departed – but it won't last long.'

'No, I think not,' observed Rose; 'for she didn't seem *very* disconsolate after all; and she's excessively pretty – handsome rather – you must see her Gilbert; you will call her a perfect beauty, though you could hardly pretend to discover a resemblance between her and Eliza Millward.'

'Well, I can imagine many faces more beautiful than Eliza's, though not more charming. I allow she has small claims to perfection; but then, I maintain that, if she were more perfect, she would be less interesting.'

'And so you prefer her faults to other people's perfections?'

'Just so – saving my mother's presence.'

'Oh, my dear Gilbert, what nonsense you talk! – I know you don't mean it; it's quite out of the question,' said my mother, getting up, and bustling out of the room, under pretence of household business, in order to escape the contradiction that was trembling on my tongue.

After that, Rose favoured me with further particulars respecting Mrs Graham. Her appearance, manners, and dress, and the very furniture of the room she inhabited, were all set before me, with rather more clearness and precision than I cared to see them; but, as I was not a very attentive listener, I could not repeat the description if I would.

The next day was Saturday; and, on Sunday, everybody wondered whether or not the fair unknown would profit by the vicar's remonstrance, and come to church. I confess, I looked with some interest myself towards the old family pew, appertaining to Wildfell Hall, where the faded crimson cushions and lining had been unpressed and unrenewed so many years, and the grim escutcheons, with their lugubrious borders of rusty black cloth, frowned so sternly from the wall above.

And there I beheld a tall, lady-like figure, clad in black. Her face was towards me, and there was something in it, which, once seen, invited me to look again. Her hair was raven black, and disposed in long glossy ringlets, a style of coiffure, rather unusual in those days, but always graceful and becoming; her complexion was clear and pale; her eyes I could not see, for being bent upon her prayer-book they were concealed by their drooping lids and long black lashes, but the brows above were expressive and well defined, the forehead was lofty and intellectual, the nose, a perfect aquiline, and the features in general, unexceptionable – only there was a slight hollowness about the cheeks and eyes, and the lips, though finely formed, were a little too thin, a little too firmly compressed, and had something about them that betokened, I thought, no very soft or amiable temper; and I said in my heart –

'I would rather admire you from this distance, fair lady, than be the partner of your home.'

Just then, she happened to raise her eyes, and they met mine; I did not choose to withdraw my gaze, and she turned again to her book, but with a momentary, indefinable expression of quiet scorn, that was inexpressibly provoking to me.

'She thinks me an impudent puppy,' thought I. 'Humph! – she shall change her mind before long, if I think it worth while.'

But then, it flashed upon me that these were very improper thoughts for a place of worship, and that my behaviour, on the present occasion, was anything but what it ought to be. Previous, however, to directing my mind to the service, I glanced round the church to see if any one had been observing me; – but no, – all, who were not attending to their prayer-books, were attending to the strange lady, – my good mother and sister among the rest, and Mrs Wilson and her daughter; and even Eliza Millward was slyly glancing from the corners of her eyes towards the object of general attraction. Then, she glanced at me, simpered a little, and blushed, – modestly looked at her prayer-book, and endeavoured to compose her features.

Here I was transgressing again; and this time I was made sensible of it by a sudden dig in the ribs, from the elbow of my pert brother. For the present, I could only resent the insult by pressing my foot upon his toes, deferring further vengeance till we got out of church.

Now, Halford, before I close this letter, I'll tell you who Eliza Millward was: she was the vicar's younger daughter, and a very engaging little creature, for whom I felt no small degree of partiality; – and she knew it, though I had never come to any direct explanation, and had no definite intention of so doing, for my mother, who maintained there was no one good enough for me, within twenty miles round, could not bear the thoughts of my marrying that insignificant, little thing, who, in addition to her numerous other disqualifications, had not twenty pounds to call her own. Eliza's figure was at once slight and plump, her face small, and nearly as round as my sister's, – complexion, something similar to hers, but more delicate and less decidedly blooming, – nose, *retroussé*, – features, generally irregular; – and, altogether, she was rather charming than pretty. But her eyes – I must not forget those remarkable features, for therein her chief attraction lay – in outward aspect at least; – they were long and narrow in shape, the irids black, or very dark brown, the expression various, and ever changing, but always either preternaturally – I had almost said *diabolically* – wicked, or irresistibly bewitching – often both. Her voice was gentle and childish, her tread light and soft as that of a cat; – but her manners more frequently resembled those of a pretty, playful kitten, that is now pert and roguish, now timid and demure, according to its own sweet will.

Her sister, Mary, was several years older, several inches taller, and of a larger, coarser build – a plain, quiet, sensible girl who had patiently nursed their mother, through her last long, tedious illness, and been the housekeeper, and family drudge, from thence to the present time. She was trusted and valued by her father, loved and courted by all dogs, cats, children, and poor people, and slighted and neglected by everybody else.

The Reverend Michael Millward, himself, was a tall, ponderous, elderly gentleman, who placed a shovel hat above his large, square, massive-featured face, carried a stout walking stick in his hand, and incased his still powerful limbs in knee breeches and gaiters, – or black silk stockings on state occasions. He was a man of fixed principles, strong prejudices, and regular habits, – intolerant of dissent in any shape, acting under a firm conviction that *his* opinions were always right, and whoever differed from them, must be, either most deplorably ignorant, or wilfully blind.

In childhood, I had always been accustomed to regard him with a feeling of reverential awe – but lately, even now, surmounted, for, though he had a fatherly kindness for the well-behaved, he was a strict disciplinarian, and had often sternly reproved our juvenile failings and peccadillos; and moreover, in those days whenever he called upon our parents, we had to stand up before him, and say our catechism, or repeat 'How doth the little busy bee,' or some other hymn, or – worse than all – be questioned about his last text and the heads of the discourse, which we never could remember. Sometimes, the worthy gentleman would reprove my mother for being over indulgent to her sons, with a reference to old Eli, or David and Absalom, which was particularly galling to her feelings; and, very highly as she respected him, and all his sayings, I once heard her exclaim, 'I wish to goodness he had a son himself! He wouldn't be so ready with his advice to other people then; – he'd see what it *is* to have a couple of boys to keep in order.'

He had a laudable care for his own bodily health – kept very early hours, regularly took a walk before breakfast, was vastly particular about warm and dry clothing, had never been known to preach a sermon without previously swallowing a raw egg – albeit he was gifted with good lungs and a powerful voice, – and was, generally, extremely particular about what he eat and drank, though by no means abstemious, and having a mode of dietary peculiar to himself, – being a great despiser of tea and such slops, and a patron of malt liquors, bacon and eggs, ham, hung beef, and other strong meats, which agreed well enough with his digestive organs, and therefore were maintained by him to be good and wholesome for everybody, and confidently recommended to the most delicate convalescents or dyspeptics, who, if they failed to derive the promised benefit from his prescriptions, were told it was because they had not persevered, and if they complained of inconvenient results therefrom, were assured it was all fancy.

I will just touch upon two other persons whom I have mentioned, and then bring this long letter to a close. These are Mrs Wilson and her daughter. The former was the widow of a substantial farmer, a narrow-minded, tattling old gossip, whose character is not worth describing. She had two sons, Robert, a rough countrified farmer, and Richard, a retiring, studious young man, who was studying the classics with the vicar's assistance, preparing for college, with a view to enter the church.

Their sister Jane was a young lady of some talents and more ambition. She had at her own desire, received a regular boarding-school education, superior to what any member of the family had obtained before. She had taken the polish well, acquired considerable elegance of manners, quite lost her provincial accent, and could boast of more accomplishments than the vicar's daughters. She was considered a beauty besides; but never for a moment could she number me amongst her admirers. She was about six and twenty, rather tall and very slender, her hair was neither chestnut nor auburne, but a most decided, bright, light red, her complexion was remarkably fair and brilliant, her head small, neck long, chin well turned, but very short, lips thin and red, eyes clear hazel, quick, and penetrating, but entirely destitute of poetry or feeling. She had, or might have had many suitors in her own rank of life, but scornfully repulsed or rejected them all; for none but a gentleman could please her refined taste, and none but a rich one could satisfy her soaring ambition. One gentleman there was, from whom she had lately received some rather pointed attentions, and upon whose heart, name, and fortune, it was whispered, she had serious designs. This was Mr Lawrence, the young squire whose family had formerly occupied Wildfell Hall, but had deserted it, some fifteen years ago, for a more modern and commodious mansion in the neighbouring parish.

Now Halford, I bid you adieu for the present. This is the first instalment of my debt. If the coin suits you, tell me so, and I'll send you the rest at my leisure: if you would rather remain my creditor than stuff your purse with such ungainly, heavy pieces, – tell me still, and I'll pardon your bad taste, and willingly keep the treasure to myself.

Yours immutably,

GILBERT MARKHAM.

CHAPTER II

AN INTERVIEW

I PERCEIVE, WITH JOY, my most valued friend, that the cloud of your displeasure has past away; the light of your countenance blesses me once more, and you desire the continuation of my story: therefore, without more ado, you shall have it.

I think the day I last mentioned, was a certain Sunday, the latest in the October of 1827. On the following Tuesday I was out with my dog and gun, in pursuit of such game as I could find within the territory of Linden-car; but finding none at all, I turned my arms against the hawks and carrion crows, whose depredations, as I suspected, had deprived me of better prey. To this end, I left the more frequented regions, the wooded valleys, the cornfields, and the meadowlands, and proceeded to mount the steep acclivity of Wildfell, the wildest and the loftiest eminence in our neighbourhood, where, as you ascend, the hedges, as well as the trees, become scanty and stunted, the former, at length, giving place to rough stone fences, partly greened over with ivy and moss, the latter to larches and Scotch fir-trees, or isolated black thorns. The fields, being rough and stony and wholly unfit for the plough, were mostly devoted to the pasturing of sheep and cattle; the soil was thin and poor: bits of grey rock here and there peeped out from the grassy hillocks; bilberry plants and heather – relics of more savage wildness, – grew under the walls; and in many of the enclosures, ragweeds and rushes usurped supremacy over the scanty herbage; – but these were not *my* property.

Near the top of this hill, about two miles from Linden-car,

stood Wildfell Hall, a superannuated mansion of the Eliza-
bethan era, built of dark grey stone, – venerable and picturesque
to look at, but doubtless, cold and gloomy enough to inhabit,
with its thick stone mullions and little latticed panes, its time-
eaten air-holes, and its too lonely, too unsheltered situation, –
only shielded from the war of wind and weather by a group of
Scotch firs, themselves half blighted with storms, and looking
as stern and gloomy as the Hall itself. Behind it lay a few desolate fields, and then the brown heath-clad summit of the hill;
before it (enclosed by stone walls, and entered by an iron gate
with large balls of grey granite – similar to those which deco-
rated the roof and gables – surmounting the gate-posts), was a
garden, – once, stocked with such hardy plants and flowers as
could best brook the soil and climate, and such trees and shrubs
as could best endure the gardener's torturing shears, and most
readily assume the shapes he chose to give them, – now, having
been left so many years, untilled and untrimmed, abandoned
to the weeds and the grass, to the frost and the wind, the rain
and the drought, it presented a very singular appearance indeed.
The close green walls of privet, that had bordered the principal
walk, were two-thirds withered away, and the rest grown beyond
all reasonable bounds; the old boxwood swan, that sat beside
the scraper, had lost its neck and half its body; the castellated
towers of laurel in the middle of the garden, the gigantic warrior
that stood on one side of the gateway, and the lion that guarded
the other, were sprouted into such fantastic shapes as resembled
nothing either in Heaven or earth, or in the waters under the
earth; but, to my young imagination, they presented all of them
a goblinish appearance, that harmonized well with the ghostly
legends and dark traditions our old nurse had told us respecting
the haunted Hall and its departed occupants.

I had succeeded in killing a hawk and two crows when I came
within sight of the mansion; and then, relinquishing further
depredations, I sauntered on, to have a look at the old place, and
see what changes had been wrought in it by its new inhabitant.

I did not like to go quite to the front and stare in at the gate; but I paused beside the garden wall, and looked, and saw no change – except in one wing, where the broken windows and dilapidated roof had evidently been repaired, and where a thin wreath of smoke was curling up from the stack of chimneys.

While I thus stood, leaning on my gun, and looking up at the dark gables, sunk in an idle reverie, weaving a tissue of wayward fancies, in which old associations and the fair young hermit, now within those walls, bore a nearly equal part, I heard a slight rustling and scrambling just within the garden; and, glancing in the direction whence the sound proceeded, I beheld a tiny hand elevated above the wall: it clung to the topmost stone, and then another little hand was raised to take a firmer hold, and then appeared a small white forehead, surmounted with wreaths of light brown hair, with a pair of deep blue eyes beneath, and the upper portion of a diminutive ivory nose.

The eyes did not notice me, but sparkled with glee on behold-ing Sancho, my beautiful black and white setter, that was cours-ing about the field with its muzzle to the ground. The little creature raised its face and called aloud to the dog. The good-natured animal paused, looked up, and wagged his tail, but made no further advances. The child (a little boy, apparently about five years old) scrambled up to the top of the wall and called again and again; but finding this of no avail, apparently made up his mind, like Mahomet, to go to the mountain since the mountain would not come to him, and attempted to get over; but a crabbed old cherry tree, that grew hard by, caught him by the frock in one of its crooked scraggy arms that stretched over the wall. In attempting to disengage himself, his foot slipped, and down he tumbled – but not to the earth; – the tree still kept him suspended. There was a silent struggle, and then a piercing shriek; – but, in an instant, I had dropped my gun on the grass, and caught the little fellow in my arms.

I wiped his eyes with his frock, told him he was all right, and called Sancho to pacify him. He was just putting his little hand on the dog's neck and beginning to smile through his tears, when I heard, behind me, a click of the iron gate and a rustle of female garments, and lo! Mrs Graham darted upon me, – her neck uncovered, her black locks streaming in the wind.

'Give me the child!' she said in a voice scarce louder than a whisper, but with a tone of startling vehemence, and, seizing the boy, she snatched him from me, as if some dire contamination were in my touch, and then stood with one hand firmly clasping his, the other on his shoulder, fixing upon me her large, luminous, dark eyes – pale, breathless, quivering with agitation.

'I was not harming the child Madam,' said I, scarce knowing whether to be most astonished or displeased; 'he was tumbling off the wall there; and I was so fortunate as to catch him, while he hung suspended headlong from that tree, and prevent I know not what catastrophe.'

'I beg your pardon sir,' stammered she; – suddenly calming down, – the light of reason seeming to break upon her beclouded spirit and a faint blush mantling on her cheek – 'I did not know you; – and I thought –'

She stooped to kiss the child, and fondly clasped her arm round his neck.

'You thought I was going to kidnap your son, I suppose?'

She stroked his head with a half-embarrassed laugh, and replied, –

'I did not know he had attempted to climb the wall – I have the pleasure of addressing Mr Markham, I believe?' she added somewhat abruptly.

I bowed, but ventured to ask how she knew me.

'Your sister called here, a few days ago, with Mrs Markham.'

'Is the resemblance so strong then?' I asked in some surprise, and not so greatly flattered at the idea as I ought to have been.

'There is a likeness about the eyes and complexion I think,' replied she, somewhat dubiously surveying my face; – 'and I think I saw you at church on Sunday.'

I smiled. – There was something either in that smile or the

recollections it awakened that was particularly displeasing to her, for she suddenly assumed again that proud, chilly look that had so unspeakably roused my corruption at church – a look of repellent scorn, so easily assumed, and so entirely without the least distortion of a single feature that, while there, it seemed like the natural expression of the face, and was the more provoking to me, because I could not think it affected.

'Good morning, Mr Markham,' said she; and without another word or glance, she withdrew with her child into the garden; and I returned home, angry and dissatisfied – I could scarcely tell you why – and therefore will not attempt it.

I only stayed to put away my gun and powder-horn, and give some requisite directions to one of the farming-men, and then repaired to the vicarage, to solace my spirit and soothe my ruffled temper with the company and conversation of Eliza Millward.

I found her, as usual, busy with some piece of soft embroidery (the mania for Berlin wools had not yet commenced), while her sister was seated at the chimney-corner, with the cat on her knee, mending a heap of stockings.

'Mary – Mary! put them away!' Eliza was hastily saying just as I entered the room.

'Not I, indeed!' was the phlegmatic reply; and my appearance prevented further discussion.

'You're *so* unfortunate, Mr Markham!' observed the younger sister, with one of her arch, sidelong glances. 'Papa's just gone out into the parish, and not likely to be back for an hour!'

'Never mind; I can manage to spend a few minutes with his daughters, if they'll allow me,' said I, bringing a chair to the fire, and seating myself therein, without waiting to be asked.

'Well, if you'll be very good and amusing, we shan't object.'

'Let your permission be unconditional, pray; for I came not to give pleasure, but to seek it,' I answered.

However, I thought it but reasonable to make some slight exertion to render my company agreeable; and what little effort I made, was apparently pretty successful, for Miss Eliza was never in a better humour. We seemed, indeed, to be mutually pleased with each other, and managed to maintain between us a cheerful and animated, though not very profound conversation. It was little better than a *tête-à-tête*, for Miss Millward never opened her lips, except occasionally to correct some random assertion or exaggerated expression of her sister's, and once to ask her to pick up the ball of cotton, that had rolled under the table. I did this myself, however, as in duty bound.

'Thank you, Mr Markham,' said she, as I presented it to her. 'I would have picked it up myself; only I did not want to disturb the cat.'

'Mary, dear, *that* won't excuse you in Mr Markham's eyes,' said Eliza; 'he hates cats, I dare say, as cordially as he does old maids – like all other gentlemen – don't you Mr Markham?'

'I believe it is natural for our unamiable sex, to dislike the creatures,' replied I; 'for you ladies lavish so many caresses upon them.'

'Bless them – little darlings!' cried she, in a sudden burst of enthusiasm, turning round and overwhelming her sister's pet with a shower of kisses.

'Don't Eliza!' said Miss Millward, somewhat gruffly as she impatiently pushed her away.

But it was time for me to be going: make what haste I would, I should still be too late for tea; and my mother was the soul of order and punctuality.

My fair friend was evidently unwilling to bid me adieu. I tenderly squeezed her little hand at parting; and she repaid me with one of her softest smiles and most bewitching glances. I went home very happy, with a heart brimful of complacency for myself, and overflowing with love for Eliza.

CHAPTER III

A CONTROVERSY

Two days after, Mrs Graham called at Linden-car, contrary to the expectation of Rose, who entertained an idea that the mysterious occupant of Wildfell Hall would wholly disregard the common observances of civilized life, – in which opinion she was supported by the Wilsons, who testified that neither their call nor the Millwards' had been returned as yet. Now however, the cause of that omission was explained, though not entirely to the satisfaction of Rose. Mrs Graham had brought her child with her, and on my mother's expressing surprise that he could walk so far, she replied, –

'It is a long walk for him; but I must have either taken him with me, or relinquished the visit altogether; for I never leave him alone; and I think, Mrs Markham, I must beg you to make my excuses to the Millwards and Mrs Wilson, when you see them, as I fear I cannot do myself the pleasure of calling upon them till my little Arthur is able to accompany me.'

'But you have a servant,' said Rose; 'could you not leave him with her?'

'She has her own occupations to attend to; and besides, she is too old to run after a child, and he is too mercurial to be tied to an elderly woman.'

'But you left him to come to church.'

'Yes, once; but I would not have left him for any other purpose; and I think, in future, I must contrive to bring him with me, or stay at home.'

'Is he so mischievous?' asked my mother, considerably shocked.

'No,' replied the lady, sadly smiling, as she stroked the wavy locks of her son, who was seated on a low stool at her feet; 'but he is my only treasure; and I am his only friend, so we don't like to be separated.'

'But my dear, I call that doting,' said my plain-spoken parent. 'You should try to suppress such foolish fondness, as well to save your son from ruin as yourself from ridicule.'

'*Ruin*, Mrs Markham!'

'Yes; it is spoiling the child. Even at *his* age, he ought not to be always tied to his mother's apron string; he should learn to be ashamed of it.'

'Mrs Markham, I beg you will not say such things in *his* presence, at least. I trust my son will *never* be ashamed to love his mother!' said Mrs Graham, with a serious energy that startled the company.

My mother attempted to appease her by an explanation; but she seemed to think enough had been said on the subject, and abruptly turned the conversation.

'Just as I thought,' said I to myself: 'the lady's temper is none of the mildest, notwithstanding her sweet, pale face and lofty brow, where thought and suffering seem equally to have stamped their impress.'

All this time, I was seated at a table on the other side of the room, apparently immersed in the perusal of a volume of the Farmer's Magazine, which I happened to have been reading at the moment of our visitor's arrival; and, not choosing to be over civil, I had merely bowed as she entered, and continued my occupation as before.

In a little while, however, I was sensible that some one was approaching me, with a light, but slow and hesitating tread. It was little Arthur, irresistibly attracted by my dog Sancho, that was lying at my feet. On looking up, I beheld him standing about two yards off, with his clear blue eyes wistfully gazing on the dog, transfixed to the spot, not by fear of the animal, but by a timid disinclination to approach its master. A little encouragement, however, induced him to come forward. The child, though shy, was not sullen. In a minute he was kneeling on the carpet, with his arms round Sancho's neck, and in a minute or two more, the little fellow was seated on my knee, surveying with eager interest the various specimens of horses, cattle, pigs, and model farms portrayed in the volume before me. I glanced at his mother now and then, to see how she relished the new-sprung intimacy; and I saw, by the unquiet aspect of her eye, that for some reason or other, she was uneasy at the child's position.

'Arthur,' said she, at length, 'come here. You are troublesome to Mr Markham: he wishes to read.'

'By no means, Mrs Graham; pray let him stay. I am as much amused as he is,' pleaded I. But still, with hand and eye, she silently called him to her side.

'No, mamma,' said the child; 'let me look at these pictures first; and then I'll come, and tell you all about them.'

'We are going to have a small party on Monday, the fifth of November,' said my mother; 'and I hope you will not refuse to make one, Mrs Graham. You can bring your little boy with you, you know – I dare say we shall be able to amuse him; – and then you can make your own apologies to the Millwards and Wilsons, – they will all be here I expect.'

'Thank you, I never go to parties.'

'Oh! but this will be quite a family concern – early hours, and nobody here but ourselves, and just the Millwards and Wilsons, most of whom you already know, and Mr Lawrence, your landlord, whom you ought to make acquaintance with.'

'I do know something of him – but you must excuse me this time; for the evenings, now, are dark and damp, and Arthur, I fear, is too delicate to risk exposure to their influence with impunity. We must defer the enjoyment of your hospitality, till the return of longer days and warmer nights.'

Rose, now, at a hint from my mother, produced a decanter of wine, with accompaniments of glasses and cake, from the cupboard and the oak sideboard, and the refreshment was duly presented to the guests. They both partook of the cake, but obstinately refused the wine, in spite of their hostess's hospitable attempts to force it upon them. Arthur especially shrank from the ruby nectar as if in terror and disgust, and was ready to cry when urged to take it.

'Never mind, Arthur,' said his mamma; 'Mrs Markham thinks it will do you good, as you were tired with your walk; but she will not oblige you to take it; – I dare say you will do very well without. He detests the very sight of wine,' she added, 'and the smell of it almost makes him sick. I have been accustomed to make him swallow a little wine or weak spirits-and-water, by way of medicine when he was sick, and, in fact, I have done what I could to make him hate them.'

Everybody laughed, except the young widow and her son.

'Well, Mrs Graham,' said my mother, wiping the tears of merriment from her bright, blue eyes – 'well, you surprise me! I really gave you credit for having more sense – the poor child will be the veriest milksop that ever was sopped! Only think what a man you will make of him, if you persist in –'

'I think it a very excellent plan,' interrupted Mrs Graham with imperturbable gravity. 'By that means I hope to save him from one degrading vice at least. I wish I could render the incentives to every other equally innoxious in his case.'

'But by such means,' said I, 'you will never render him virtuous. – What is it that constitutes virtue, Mrs Graham? Is it the circumstance of being able and willing to resist temptation; or that of having no temptations to resist? – Is he a strong man that overcomes great obstacles and performs surprising achievements, though by dint of great muscular exertion, and at the risk of some subsequent fatigue, or he that sits in his chair all day, with nothing to do more laborious than stirring the fire, and carrying his food to his mouth? If you would have your son to walk honourably through the world, you must not attempt to clear the stones from his path, but teach him to walk firmly over them – not insist upon leading him by the hand, but let him learn to go alone.'

'I will lead him by the hand, Mr Markham, till he has strength to go alone; and I will clear as many stones from his path as I can, and teach him to avoid the *rest* – or walk firmly over them, as you say; – for when I have done my utmost, in the way of clearance, there will still be plenty left to exercise all the agility, steadiness, and circumspection he will ever have. – It is all very well to talk about noble resistance, and trials of virtue; but for fifty – or five hundred men that have yielded to temptation, shew me one that has had virtue to resist. And why should I take it for granted that my son will be one in a thousand? – and not rather prepare for the worst, and suppose he will be like his — like the rest of mankind, unless I take care to prevent it?'

'You are very complimentary to us all,' I observed.

'I know nothing about *you* – I speak of those I do know – and when I see the whole race of mankind (with a few rare exceptions), stumbling and blundering along the path of life, sinking into every pitfall, and breaking their shins over every impediment that lies in their way, shall I not use all the means in my power to ensure for him, a smoother and a safer passage?'

'Yes, but the surest means will be, to endeavour to fortify him *against* temptation, not to remove it out of his way.'

'I will do both, Mr Markham. God knows he will have temptations enough to assail him, both from within and without, when I have done all I can to render vice as uninviting to him, as it is abominable in its own nature. – I myself, have had, indeed, but few incentives to what the world calls vice, but yet, I have experienced temptations and trials of another kind, that have required, on many occasions, more watchfulness and firmness to resist, than I have hitherto been able to muster against them. And this, I believe, is what most others would acknowledge who are accustomed to reflection, and wishful to strive against their natural corruptions.'

'Yes,' said my mother, but half apprehending her drift; 'but you would not judge of a boy by yourself – and my dear Mrs Graham, let me warn you in good time against the error – the fatal error, I may call it – of taking that boy's education upon yourself. – Because you are clever, in some things, and well informed, you may fancy yourself equal to the task; but indeed you are not; and if you persist in the attempt, believe me, you will bitterly repent it when the mischief is done.'

'I am to send him to school, I suppose, to learn to despise his mother's authority and affection!' said the lady, with rather a bitter smile.

'Oh, *no*! – But if you would have a boy to despise his mother, let her keep him at home, and spend her life in petting him up, and slaving to indulge his follies and caprices.'

'I perfectly agree with you Mrs Markham; but nothing can be further from my principles and practice than such criminal weakness as that.'

'Well, but you will treat him like a girl – you'll spoil his spirit, and make a mere Miss Nancy of him – you will, indeed, Mrs Graham, whatever you may think. – But I'll get Mr Millward to talk to you about it: – *he'll* tell you the consequences; – he'll set it before you as plain as the day; – and tell you what you ought to do, and all about it; – and, I don't doubt, he'll be able to convince you in a minute.'

'No occasion to trouble the vicar,' said Mrs Graham, glancing at me – I suppose I was smiling at my mother's unbounded confidence in that worthy gentleman – 'Mr Markham here, thinks his powers of conviction at least equal to Mr Millward's. If I hear not him, neither should I be convinced though one rose from the dead, he would tell you. – Well, Mr Markham, you that maintain that a boy should not be shielded from evil, but sent out to battle against it, alone and unassisted – not taught to avoid the snares of life, but boldly to rush into them, or over them, as he may – to seek danger rather than shun it, and feed his virtue by temptation, – would you –'

'I beg your pardon, Mrs Graham – but you get on too fast. I have not yet said that a boy should be taught to rush into the snares of life, – or even wilfully to seek temptation for the sake of exercising his virtue by overcoming it; – I only say that it is better to arm and strengthen your hero, than to disarm and enfeeble the foe; – and if you were to rear an oak sapling in a hot-house, tending it carefully night and day, and shielding it from every breath of wind, you could not expect it to become a hardy tree, like that which has grown up on the mountain-side, exposed to all the action of the elements, and not even sheltered from the shock of the tempest.'

'Granted; – but would you use the same argument with regard to a girl?'

'Certainly not.'

'No; you would have her to be tenderly and delicately nurtured, like a hot-house plant – taught to cling to others for direction and support, and guarded, as much as possible, from the very knowledge of evil. But will you be so good as to inform me, why you make this distinction? Is it that you think she *has* no virtue?'

'Assuredly not.'

'Well, but you affirm that virtue is only elicited by temptation; – and you think that a woman cannot be too little exposed to temptation, or too little acquainted with vice, or any thing connected therewith. – It *must* be, either, that you think she is essentially so vicious, or so feeble-minded, that she *cannot* withstand temptation, – and though she may be pure and innocent as long as she is kept in ignorance and restraint, yet, being destitute of *real* virtue, to teach her how to sin, is at once to make her a sinner, and the greater her knowledge, the wider her liberty, the deeper will be her depravity, – whereas, in the nobler sex, there is a natural tendency to goodness, guarded by a superior fortitude, which, the more it is exercised by trials and dangers, is only the further developed –'

'Heaven forbid that I should think so!' I interrupted her at last.

'Well then, it must be that you think they are *both* weak and prone to err, and the slightest error, the merest shadow of pollution will ruin the one, while the character of the other will be strengthened and embellished – his education properly finished by a little practical acquaintance with forbidden things. Such experience, to him (to use a trite simile), will be like the storm to the oak, which, though it may scatter the leaves, and snap the smaller branches, serves but to rivet the roots, and to harden and condense the fibres of the tree. You would have us encourage our sons to prove all things by their own experience, while our daughters must not even profit by the experience of others. Now *I* would have both so to benefit by the experience of others, and the precepts of a higher authority, that they should know beforehand to refuse the evil and choose the good, and require no experimental proofs to teach them the evil of transgression. I would not send a poor girl into the world, unarmed against her foes, and ignorant of the snares that beset her path: nor would I watch and guard her, till, deprived of self-respect and self-reliance, she lost the power, or the will to watch and guard herself; – and as for my son – if I thought he would grow up to be what you call a man of the world – one that has "*seen life*," and glories in his experience, even though he should so far profit by it, as to sober down, at length, into a useful and respected member of society – I would rather that he died to-morrow! – rather a thousand times!' she earnestly repeated, pressing her darling to her side and kissing his forehead with intense affection. He had, already, left his new companion, and been standing for some time beside his mother's knee, looking up into her face, and listening in silent wonder to her incomprehensible discourse.

'Well! you ladies must always have the last word, I suppose,' said I, observing her rise, and begin to take leave of my mother.

'You may have as many words as you please, – only I can't stay to hear them.'

'No; that is the way: you hear just as much of an argument as you please; and the rest may be spoken to the wind.'

'If you are anxious to say anything more on the subject,' replied she, as she shook hands with Rose, 'you must bring your sister to see me some fine day, and I'll listen, as patiently as you could wish, to whatever you please to say. I would rather be lectured by you than the vicar, because, I should have less remorse in telling you, at the end of the discourse, that I preserve my own opinion precisely the same as at the beginning – as would be the case, I am persuaded, with regard to either logician.'

'Yes, of course,' replied I, determined to be as provoking as herself, 'for, when a lady does consent to listen to an argument against her own opinions, she is always predetermined to withstand it – to listen only with her bodily ears, keeping the mental organs resolutely closed against the strongest reasoning.'

'Good morning, Mr Markham,' said my fair antagonist with a pitying smile; and deigning no further rejoinder, she slightly bowed, and was about to withdraw; but her son, with childish impertinence, arrested her by exclaiming,

'Mamma, you have not shaken hands with Mr Markham!'

She laughingly turned round, and held out her hand. I gave it a spiteful squeeze; for I was annoyed at the continual injustice she had done me from the very dawn of our acquaintance. Without knowing anything about my real disposition and principles, she was evidently prejudiced against me, and seemed bent upon showing me that her opinions respecting me, on every particular, fell far below those I entertained of myself. I was naturally touchy, or, it would not have vexed me so much. Perhaps, too, I was a little bit spoiled by my mother and sister, and some other ladies of my acquaintance; – and yet, I was by no means a fop – of that I am fully convinced, whether *you* are or not.

CHAPTER IV

THE PARTY

OUR PARTY, ON the fifth of November, passed off very well in spite of Mrs Graham's refusal to grace it with her presence. Indeed, it is probable that, had she been there, there would have been less cordiality, freedom, and frolic amongst us than there was without her.

My mother, as usual, was cheerful and chatty, full of activity and good nature, and only faulty in being too anxious to make her guests happy, thereby forcing several of them to do what their soul abhorred, in the way of eating or drinking, sitting opposite the blazing fire, or talking when they would be silent. Nevertheless, they bore it very well, being all in their holiday humours.

Mr Millward was mighty in important dogmas and sententious jokes, pompous anecdotes and oracular discourses, dealt out for the edification of the whole assembly in general, and of the admiring Mrs Markham, the polite Mr Lawrence, the sedate Mary Millward, the quiet Richard Wilson, and the matter of fact Robert, in particular, – as being the most attentive listeners.

Mrs Wilson was more brilliant than ever, with her budgets of fresh news and old scandal, strung together with trivial questions and remarks, and old repeated observations, uttered apparently for the sole purpose of denying a moment's rest to her inexhaustible organs of speech. She had brought her knitting with her, and it seemed as if her tongue had laid a wager with her fingers, to outdo them in swift and ceaseless motion.

Her daughter Jane was, of course, as graceful and elegant, as witty and seductive, as she could possibly manage to be; for here were all the ladies to outshine, and all the gentlemen to charm, – and Mr Lawrence, especially, to capture and subdue. Her little arts to effect his subjugation were too subtle and impalpable to attract my observation; but I thought there was a certain *refined* affectation of superiority, and an ungenial self-consciousness about her, that negatived all her advantages, and after she was gone Rose interpreted to me her various looks, words, and actions with a mingled acuteness and asperity that made me wonder, equally, at the lady's artifice and my sister's penetration, and ask myself if she too had an eye to the squire – but never mind, Halford; she had not.

Richard Wilson, Jane's younger brother, sat in a corner, apparently good-tempered, but silent and shy, desirous to escape observation, but willing enough to listen and observe: and, although somewhat out of his element, he would have been happy enough in his own quiet way, if my mother could only have let him alone; but in her mistaken kindness, she would keep persecuting him with her attentions – pressing upon him all manner of viands, under the notion that he was too bashful to help himself, and obliging him to shout across the room his monosyllabic replies to the numerous questions and observations by which she vainly attempted to draw him into conversation.

Rose informed me that he never would have favoured us with his company, but for the importunities of his sister Jane, who was most anxious to show Mr Lawrence that she had at least one brother more gentlemanly and refined than Robert. That worthy individual she had been equally solicitous to keep away; but he affirmed that he saw no reason why he should not enjoy a crack with Markham and the old lady (my mother was not old really), and bonny Miss Rose and the parson, as well as the best; – and he was in the right of it too. So he talked commonplace with my mother and Rose, and discussed parish affairs with the vicar, farming matters with me, and politics with us both.

Mary Millward was another mute, – not so much tormented with cruel kindness as Dick Wilson, because she had a certain short, decided way of answering and refusing, and was supposed to be rather sullen than diffident. However that might be, she certainly did not give much pleasure to the company; – nor did she appear to derive much from it. Eliza told me she had only come because her father insisted upon it, having taken it into his head that she devoted herself too exclusively to her household duties, to the neglect of such relaxations and innocent enjoyments as were proper to her age and sex. She seemed, to me, to be good-humoured enough on the whole. Once or twice she was provoked to laughter by the wit or the merriment of some favoured individual amongst us; and then I observed she sought the eye of Richard Wilson, who sat over against her. As he studied with her father, she had some acquaintance with him, in spite of the retiring habits of both, and I suppose there was a kind of fellow-feeling established between them.

My Eliza was charming beyond description, coquettish without affectation, and evidently more desirous to engage my attention than that of all the room besides. Her delight in having me near her, seated or standing by her side, whispering in her ear, or pressing her hand in the dance, was plainly legible in her glowing face and heaving bosom, however belied by saucy words and gestures. But I had better hold my tongue: if I boast of these things now, I shall have to blush hereafter.

To proceed then, with the various individuals of our party; Rose was simple and natural as usual, and full of mirth and vivacity.

Fergus was impertinent and absurd; but his impertinence and folly served to make others laugh, if they did not raise himself in their estimation.

And finally (for I omit myself), Mr Lawrence was gentlemanly and inoffensive to all, and polite to the vicar and the ladies, especially his hostess and her daughter, and Miss Wilson – misguided man; he had not the taste to prefer Eliza Millward. Mr Lawrence and I were on tolerably intimate terms. Essentially of reserved habits, and but seldom quitting the secluded place of his birth, where he had lived in solitary state since the death of his father, he had neither the opportunity nor the inclination for forming many acquaintances; and, of all he had ever known, I (judging by the results) was the companion most agreeable to his taste. I liked the man well enough, but he was too cold, and shy, and self-contained, to obtain my cordial sympathies. A spirit of candour and frankness, when wholly unaccompanied with coarseness, he admired in others, but he could not acquire it himself. His excessive reserve upon all his own concerns was, indeed, provoking and chilly enough; but I forgave it, from a conviction that it originated, less in pride and want of confidence in his friends, than in a certain morbid feeling of delicacy, and a peculiar diffidence, that he was sensible of, but wanted energy to overcome. His heart was like a sensitive plant, that opens for a moment in the sunshine, but curls up and shrinks into itself at the slightest touch of the finger, or the lightest breath of wind. And, upon the whole, our intimacy was rather a mutual predilection than a deep and solid friendship, such as has since arisen between myself and you, Halford, whom, in spite of your occasional crustiness, I can liken to nothing so well as an old coat, unimpeachable in texture, but easy and loose – that has conformed itself to the shape of the wearer, and which he may use as he pleases, without being bothered with the fear of spoiling it; – whereas Mr Lawrence was like a new garment, all very neat and trim to look at, but so tight in the elbows that you would fear to split the seams by the unrestricted motion of your arms, and so smooth and fine in surface that you scruple to expose it to a single drop of rain.

Soon after the arrival of the guests, my mother mentioned Mrs Graham, regretted she was not there to meet them, and explained to the Millwards and Wilsons, the reasons she had given for neglecting to return their calls, hoping they would excuse her, as she was sure she did not mean to be uncivil, and would be glad to see them at any time; –

'But she is a very singular lady, Mr Lawrence,' added she; 'we don't know what to make of her – but I dare say you can tell us something about her; for she is your tenant, you know, – and she said she knew you a little.'

All eyes were turned to Mr Lawrence. I thought he looked unnecessarily confused at being so appealed to.

'I, Mrs Markham!' said he; 'you are mistaken – I don't – that is – I have seen her certainly; but I am the last person you should apply to for information respecting Mrs Graham.'

He then immediately turned to Rose, and asked her to favour the company with a song, or a tune on the piano.

'No,' said she, 'you must ask Miss Wilson: she outshines us all in singing, and music too.'

Miss Wilson demurred.

'*She'll* sing readily enough,' said Fergus, 'if you'll undertake to stand by her, Mr Lawrence, and turn over the leaves for her.'

'I shall be most happy to do so, Miss Wilson; will you allow me?'

She bridled her long neck and smiled, and suffered him to lead her to the instrument, where she played and sang, in her very best style, one piece after another; while he stood patiently by, leaning one hand on the back of her chair, and turning over the leaves of her book with the other. Perhaps, he was as much charmed with her performance as she was. It was all very fine in its way; but I cannot say that it moved me very deeply. There was plenty of skill and execution, but precious little feeling.

But we had not done with Mrs Graham yet.

'I don't take wine, Mrs Markham,' said Mr Millward, upon the introduction of that beverage; 'I'll take a little of your home-brewed ale. I always prefer your home-brewed to anything else.'

Flattered at this compliment, my mother rang the bell, and a china jug of our best ale was presently brought, and set before the worthy gentleman who so well knew how to appreciate its excellencies.

'Now THIS is the thing!' cried he, pouring out a glass of the same in a long stream, skilfully directed from the jug to the tumbler, so as to produce much foam without spilling a drop; and, having surveyed it for a moment opposite the candle, he took a deep draught, and then smacked his lips, drew a long breath, and refilled his glass, my mother looking on with the greatest satisfaction.

'There's nothing like this, Mrs Markham!' said he. 'I always maintain that there's nothing to compare with your home-brewed alc.'

'I'm sure I'm glad you like it, sir. I always look after the brewing myself, as well as the cheese and the butter – I like to have things well done, while we're about it.'

'*Quite right*, Mrs Markham!'

'But then, Mr Millward, you don't think it *wrong* to take a little wine now and then – or a little spirits either!' said my mother, as she handed a smoking tumbler of gin and water to Mrs Wilson, who affirmed that wine sat heavy on her stomach, and whose son Robert was at that moment helping himself to a pretty stiff glass of the same.

'By no means!' replied the oracle with a Jove-like nod; 'these things are all blessings and mercies, if we only knew how to make use of them.'

'But Mrs Graham doesn't think so. You shall just hear now, what she told us the other day – I *told* her I'd tell you.'

And my mother favoured the company with a particular account of that lady's mistaken ideas and conduct regarding the matter in hand, concluding with, 'Now don't you think it is wrong?'

'Wrong!' repeated the vicar, with more than common solemnity – 'criminal, I should say – criminal! – Not only is it making a fool of the boy, but it is despising the gifts of Providence, and teaching him to trample them under his feet.'

He then entered more fully into the question, and explained at large the folly and impiety of such a proceeding. My mother heard him with profoundest reverence; and even Mrs Wilson vouchsafed to rest her tongue for a moment, and listen in silence, while she complacently sipped her gin and water. Mr Lawrence sat with his elbow on the table, carelessly playing with his half-empty wine-glass, and covertly smiling to himself.

'But don't you think, Mr Millward,' suggested he, when at length that gentleman paused in his discourse, 'that when a child may be naturally prone to intemperance – by the fault of its parents or ancestors, for instance – some precautions are advisable?' (Now it was generally believed that Mr Lawrence's father had shortened his days by intemperance.)

'Some precautions, it may be; but temperance, sir, is one thing, and abstinence another.'

'But I have heard that, with some persons, temperance – that is moderation – is almost impossible; and if abstinence be an evil (which some have doubted), no one will deny that excess is a greater. Some parents have entirely prohibited their children from tasting intoxicating liquors; but a parent's authority cannot last for ever; children are naturally prone to hanker after forbidden things; and a child, in such a case, would be likely to have a strong curiosity to taste, and try the effect of what has been so lauded and enjoyed by others, so strictly forbidden to himself – which curiosity would generally be gratified on the first convenient opportunity; and the restraint once broken, serious consequences might ensue. I don't pretend to be a judge of such matters, but it seems to me, that this plan of Mrs Graham's, as you describe it, Mrs Markham, extraordinary as it may be, is not without its advantages; for here you see the child is delivered at once from temptation; he has no secret curiosity, no hankering desire; he is as well acquainted with the tempting liquors as he ever wishes to be; and is thoroughly disgusted with them, without having suffered from their effects.'

'And is that right, sir? Have I not proven to you how wrong it is – how contrary to Scripture and to reason, to teach a child to look with contempt and disgust upon the blessings of Providence, instead of to use them aright?'

'You may consider laudanum a blessing of Providence, sir,'

replied Mr Lawrence, smiling; 'and yet, you will allow that most of us had better abstain from it, even in moderation; but,' added he, 'I would not desire you to follow out my simile too closely – in witness whereof I finish my glass.'

'And take another, I hope, Mr Lawrence,' said my mother, pushing the bottle towards him.

He politely declined, and pushing his chair a little away from the table, leant back towards me – I was seated a trifle behind, on the sofa beside Eliza Millward – and carelessly asked me if I knew Mrs Graham.

'I have met her once or twice,' I replied.

'What do you think of her?'

'I cannot say that I like her much. She is handsome – or rather I should say distinguished and interesting – in her appearance, but by no means amiable – a woman liable to take strong prejudices, I should fancy, and stick to them through thick and thin, twisting everything into conformity with her own preconceived opinions – too hard, too sharp, too bitter for my taste.'

He made no reply, but looked down and bit his lip, and shortly after rose and sauntered up to Miss Wilson, as much repelled by me, I fancy, as attracted by her. I scarcely noticed it at the time, but afterwards, I was led to recall this and other trifling facts, of a similar nature, to my remembrance, when – but I must not anticipate.

We wound up the evening with dancing – our worthy pastor thinking it no scandal to be present on the occasion, though one of the village musicians was engaged to direct our evolutions with his violin. But Mary Millward obstinately refused to join us; and so did Richard Wilson, though my mother earnestly entreated him to do so, and even offered to be his partner.

We managed very well without them, however. With a single set of quadrilles, and several country dances, we carried it on to a pretty late hour; and at length, having called upon our musician to strike up a waltz, I was just about to whirl Eliza round in that delightful dance, accompanied by Lawrence and Jane

Wilson, and Fergus and Rose, when Mr Millward interposed with, –

'No, no; I don't allow that! Come, it's time to be going now.'

'Oh, no, papa!' pleaded Eliza.

'High time my girl – high time! – Moderation in all things, remember! That's the plan – "Let your moderation be known unto all men!"'

But in revenge, I followed Eliza into the dimly lighted passage, where under pretence of helping her on with her shawl, I fear I must plead guilty to snatching a kiss behind her father's back, while he was enveloping his throat and chin in the folds of a mighty comforter. But alas! in turning round, there was my mother close beside me. The consequence was, that no sooner were the guests departed, than I was doomed to a very serious remonstrance, which unpleasantly checked the galloping course of my spirits, and made a disagreeable close to the evening.

'My dear Gilbert,' said she, 'I wish you wouldn't do so! You know how deeply I have your advantage at heart, how I love you and prize you above everything else in the world, and how much I long to see you well settled in life – and how bitterly it would grieve me to see you married to that girl – or any other in the neighbourhood. What you *see* in her I don't know. It isn't only the want of money that I think about – nothing of the kind – but there's neither beauty, nor cleverness, nor goodness, nor anything else that's desirable. If you knew your own value, as I do, you wouldn't dream of it. Do wait awhile and see! If you bind yourself to her, you'll repent it all your life-time when you look round and see how many better there are. Take my word for it, you will.'

'Well, mother, do be quiet! – I hate to be lectured! – I'm not going to marry yet, I tell you; but – dear me! mayn't I enjoy myself at *all*?'

'Yes, my dear boy, but not in that way. Indeed, you shouldn't do such things. You would be wronging the girl, if she were what she ought to be; but I assure you she is as artful a little hussy as anybody need wish to see; and you'll get entangled in her snares before you know where you are. And if you *do* marry her, Gilbert, you'll break my heart – so there's an end of it.'

'Well, don't cry about it, mother,' said I, for the tears were gushing from her eyes; 'there, let that kiss efface the one I gave Eliza; don't abuse her any more, and set your mind at rest; for I'll promise never to – that is, I'll promise to – to think twice before I take any important step you seriously disapprove of.'

So saying, I lighted my candle, and went to bed, considerably quenched in spirit.

CHAPTER V

THE STUDIO

IT WAS ABOUT the close of the month, that, yielding at length to the urgent importunities of Rose, I accompanied her in a visit to Wildfell Hall. To our surprise, we were ushered into a room where the first object that met the eye was a painter's easel, with a table beside it covered with rolls of canvass, bottles of oil and varnish, palette, brushes, paints, &c. Leaning against the wall were several sketches in various stages of progression, and a few finished paintings – mostly of landscapes and figures.

'I must make you welcome to my studio,' said Mrs Graham; 'there is no fire in the sitting-room to-day, and it is rather too cold to shew you into a place with an empty grate.'

And disengaging a couple of chairs from the artistical lumber that usurped them, she bid us be seated, and resumed her place beside the easel – not facing it exactly, but now and then glancing at the picture upon it while she conversed, and giving it an occasional touch with her brush, as if she found it impossible to wean her attention entirely from her occupation to fix it upon her guests. It was a view of Wildfell Hall, as seen at early morning from the field below, rising in dark relief against a sky of clear silvery blue, with a few red streaks on the horizon, faithfully drawn and coloured, and very elegantly and artistically handled.

'I see your heart is in your work, Mrs Graham,' observed I: 'I must beg you to go on with it; for if you suffer our presence to interrupt you, we shall be constrained to regard ourselves as unwelcome intruders.'

'Oh, no!' replied she, throwing her brush on to the table, as if startled into politeness. 'I am not so beset with visitors, but that I can readily spare a few minutes to the few that do favour me with their company.'

'You have almost completed your painting,' said I, approaching to observe it more closely, and surveying it with a greater degree of admiration and delight than I cared to express. 'A few more touches in the foreground will finish it, I should think. – But why have you called it Fernley Manor, Cumberland, instead of Wildfell Hall, —shire?' I asked, alluding to the name she had traced in small characters at the bottom of the canvass.

But immediately I was sensible of having committed an act of impertinence in so doing; for she coloured and hesitated; but after a moment's pause, with a kind of desperate frankness, she replied, –

'Because I have friends – acquaintances at least – in the world, from whom I desire my present abode to be concealed; and as they might see the picture, and might possibly recognize the style in spite of the false initials I have put in the corner, I take the precaution to give a false name to the place also, in order to put them on a wrong scent, if they should attempt to trace me out by it.'

'Then you don't intend to keep the picture?' said I, anxious to say anything to change the subject.

'No; I cannot afford to paint for my own amusement.'

'Mamma sends all her pictures to London,' said Arthur; 'and somebody sells them for her there, and sends us the money.'

In looking round upon the other pieces, I remarked a pretty sketch of Lindenhope from the top of the hill; another view of the old hall basking in the sunny haze of a quiet summer afternoon; and a simple but striking little picture of a child brooding with looks of silent, but deep and sorrowful regret, over a handful of withered flowers, with glimpses of dark low hills and autumnal fields behind it, and a dull beclouded sky above.

'You see there is a sad dearth of subjects,' observed the fair artist. 'I took the old hall once on a moonlight night, and I suppose I must take it again on a snowy winter's day, and then again on a dark cloudy evening; for I really have nothing else to paint. I have been told that you have a fine view of the sea somewhere in the neighbourhood – is it true? – and is it within walking distance?'

'Yes, if you don't object to walking four miles, – or nearly so – little short of eight miles, there and back – and over a somewhat rough, fatiguing road.'

'In what direction does it lie?'

I described the situation as well as I could, and was entering upon an explanation of the various roads, lanes, and fields to be traversed in order to reach it, the goings straight on, and turnings to the right, and the left, when she checked me with, –

'Oh, stop! – don't tell me now: I shall forget every word of your directions before I require them. I shall not think about going till next spring; and then, perhaps, I may trouble you. At present we have the winter before us, and –'

She suddenly paused, with a suppressed exclamation started up from her seat, and saying, 'Excuse me one moment,' hurried from the room, and shut the door behind her.

Curious to see what had startled her so, I looked towards the window, – for her eyes had been carelessly fixed upon it the moment before – and just beheld the skirts of a man's coat vanishing behind a large holly bush that stood between the window and the porch.

'It's Mamma's friend,' said Arthur.

Rose and I looked at each other.

'I don't know what to make of her, at all,' whispered Rose.

The child looked at her in grave surprise. She straightway began to talk to him on indifferent matters, while I amused myself with looking at the pictures. There was one in an obscure corner that I had not before observed. It was a little child, seated on the grass with its lap full of flowers. The tiny features and large, blue eyes, smiling through a shock of light brown curls, shaken over the forehead as it bent above its treasure, bore sufficient resemblance to those of the young gentleman before me, to proclaim it a portrait of Arthur Graham in his early infancy.

In taking this up to bring it to the light, I discovered another behind it, with its face to the wall. I ventured to take that up too. It was the portrait of a gentleman in the full prime of youthful manhood – handsome enough, and not badly executed; but if done by the same hand as the others, it was evidently some years before; for there was far more careful minuteness of detail, and less of that freshness of colouring and freedom of handling, that delighted and surprised me in them. Nevertheless, I surveyed it with considerable interest. There was a certain individuality in the features and expression that stamped it, at once, a successful likeness. The bright, blue eyes regarded the spectator with a kind of lurking drollery – you almost expected to see them wink; the lips – a little too voluptuously full – seemed ready to break into a smile; the warmly tinted cheeks were embellished with a luxuriant growth of reddish whiskers; while the bright chestnut hair, clustering in abundant, wavy curls, trespassed too much upon the forehead, and seemed to intimate that the owner thereof was prouder of his beauty than his intellect – as perhaps, he had reason to be; – and yet he looked no fool.

I had not had the portrait in my hands two minutes before the fair artist returned.

'Only some one come about the pictures,' said she, in apology for her abrupt departure: 'I told him to wait.'

'I fear it will be considered an act of impertinence,' said I, 'to presume to look at a picture that the artist has turned to the wall; but may I ask –'

'It *is* an act of very great impertinence, sir; and therefore, I beg you will ask nothing about it, for your curiosity will not be gratified,' replied she, attempting to cover the tartness of her rebuke with a smile; – but I could see, by her flushed cheek and kindling eye, that she was seriously annoyed.

'I was only going to ask if you had painted it yourself,' said I, sulkily resigning the picture into her hands; for without a grain of ceremony, she took it from me; and quickly restoring it to the dark corner, with its face to the wall, placed the other against it as before, and then turned to me and laughed.

But I was in no humour for jesting. I carelessly turned to the window, and stood looking out upon the desolate garden, leaving her to talk to Rose for a minute or two; and then, telling my sister it was time to go, shook hands with the little gentleman, coolly bowed to the lady, and moved towards the door. But, having bid adieu to Rose, Mrs Graham presented her hand to me, saying, with a soft voice, and by no means a disagreeable smile, –

'Let not the sun go down upon your wrath, Mr Markham. I'm sorry I offended you by my abruptness.'

When a lady condescends to apologize, there is no keeping one's anger of course; so we parted good friends for once; and *this* time I squeezed her hand with a cordial, not a spiteful pressure.

CHAPTER VI

PROGRESSION

D URING THE NEXT four months, I did not enter Mrs Graham's house, nor she mine; but still, the ladies continued to talk about her, and still, our acquaintance continued, though slowly, to advance. As for their talk, I paid but little attention to that (when it related to the fair hermit, I mean), and the only information I derived from it, was that, one fine, frosty day, she had ventured to take her little boy as far as the vicarage, and that, unfortunately, nobody was at home but Miss Millward; nevertheless, she had sat a long time, and, by all accounts, they had found a good deal to say to each other, and parted with a mutual desire to meet again. – But Mary liked children, and fond mammas like those who can duly appreciate their treasures.

But sometimes, I saw her myself, – not only when she came to church, but when she was out on the hills with her son, whether taking a long, purpose-like walk, or – on specially fine days – leisurely rambling over the moor or the bleak pasturelands, surrounding the old hall, herself with a book in her hand, her son gambolling about her; and, on any of these occasions, when I caught sight of her in my solitary walks or rides, or while following my agricultural pursuits, I generally contrived to meet or overtake her; for I rather liked to see Mrs Graham, and to talk to her, and I decidedly liked to talk to her little companion, whom, when once the ice of his shyness was fairly broken, I found to be a very amiable, intelligent, and entertaining little fellow; and we soon became excellent friends – how much to the gratification of his mamma, I cannot undertake to say.

I suspected at first, that she was desirous of throwing cold water on this growing intimacy – to quench, as it were, the kindling flame of our friendship – but discovering, at length, in spite of her prejudice against me, that I was perfectly harmless, and even well-intentioned, and that, between myself and my dog, her son derived a great deal of pleasure from the acquaintance, that he would not otherwise have known, she ceased to object, and even welcomed my coming with a smile.

As for Arthur, he would shout his welcome from afar, and run to meet me fifty yards from his mother's side. If I happened to be on horseback, he was sure to get a canter or a gallop; or, if there was one of the draught horses within an available distance, he was treated to a steady ride upon that, which served his turn almost as well; but his mother would always follow and trudge beside him – not so much, I believe, to ensure his safe conduct, as to see that I instilled no objectionable notions into his infant mind; for she was ever on the watch, and never would allow him to be taken out of her sight. What pleased her best of all, was to see him romping and racing with Sancho, while I walked by her side – not, I fear, for love of my company (though I sometimes deluded myself with that idea), so much as for the delight she took in seeing her son thus happily engaged in the enjoyment of those active sports, so invigorating to his tender frame, yet so seldom exercised for want of playmates suited to his years; and, perhaps, her pleasure was sweetened, not a little, by the fact of my being with *her* instead of with *him*; and therefore, – incapable of doing him any injury directly or indirectly, designedly or otherwise – small thanks to her for that same.

But sometimes, I believe, she really had some little gratification in conversing with me; and one bright February morning, during twenty minutes' stroll along the moor, she laid aside her usual asperity and reserve, and fairly entered into conversation with me, discoursing with so much eloquence, and depth of thought and feeling, on a subject, happily coinciding with my own ideas, and looking so beautiful withal, that I went home enchanted; and on the way (morally) started to find myself thinking that, after all, it would, perhaps, be better to spend one's days with such a woman than with Eliza Millward; – and then, I (figuratively) blushed for my inconstancy.

On entering the parlour, I found Eliza there, with Rose and no one else. The surprise was not altogether so agreeable as it ought to have been. We chatted together a long time; but I found her rather frivolous, and even a little insipid, compared with the more mature and earnest Mrs Graham. – Alas, for human constancy!

'However,' thought I, 'I ought not to marry Eliza since my mother so strongly objects to it, and I ought not to delude the girl with the idea that I intended to do so. Now, if this mood continue, I shall have less difficulty in emancipating my affections from her soft, yet unrelenting sway; and, though Mrs Graham might be equally objectionable, I may be permitted, like the doctors, to cure a greater evil by a less; for I shall not fall seriously in love with the young widow, I think, – nor she with me – that's certain – but if I find a little pleasure in her society, I may surely be allowed to seek it; and if the star of her divinity be bright enough to dim the lustre of Eliza's, so much the better; but I scarcely can think it.'

And thereafter, I seldom suffered a fine day to pass without paying a visit to Wildfell, about the time my new acquaintance usually left her hermitage; but so frequently was I balked in my expectations of another interview, so changeable was she in her times of coming forth and in her places of resort, so transient were the occasional glimpses I was able to obtain, that I felt half inclined to think she took as much pains to avoid my company, as I to seek hers; but this was too disagreeable a supposition to be entertained a moment after it could, conveniently, be dismissed.

One calm, clear afternoon, however, in March, as I was superintending the rolling of the meadow-land, and the repairing of a hedge in the valley, I saw Mrs Graham down by the brook, with a sketchbook in her hand, absorbed in the exercise of her favourite art, while Arthur was putting on the time with constructing dams and breakwaters in the shallow, stony stream. I was rather in want of amusement, and so rare an opportunity was not to be neglected; so, leaving both meadow and hedge, I quickly repaired to the spot, – but not before Sancho, who, immediately upon perceiving his young friend, scoured at full gallop the intervening space, and pounced upon him with an impetuous mirth that precipitated the child almost into the middle of the beck; but, happily, the stones preserved him from any serious wetting, while their smoothness prevented his being too much hurt to laugh at the untoward event.

Mrs Graham was studying the distinctive characters of the different varieties of trees in their winter nakedness, and copying, with a spirited, though delicate touch, their various ramifications. She did not talk much; but I stood and watched the progress of her pencil: it was a pleasure to behold it so dexterously guided by those fair and graceful fingers. But ere-long their dexterity became impaired, they began to hesitate, to tremble slightly, and make false strokes, and, then, suddenly came to a pause, while their owner laughingly raised her face to mine, and told me that her sketch did not profit by my superintendence.

'Then,' said I, 'I'll talk to Arthur till you've done.'

'I should like to have a ride, Mr Markham, if Mamma will let me,' said the child.

'What on, my boy?'

'I think there's a horse in that field,' replied he, pointing to where the strong black mare was pulling the roller.

'No, no, Arthur; it's too far,' objected his mother.

But I promised to bring him safe back, after a turn or two up and down the meadow; and when she looked at his eager face, she smiled and let him go. It was the first time she had even allowed me to take him so much as half a field's length from her side.

Enthroned upon his monstrous steed, and solemnly proceeding up and down the wide, steep field, he looked the very incarnation of quiet, gleeful satisfaction and delight. The rolling, however, was soon completed; but when I dismounted the gallant horseman, and restored him to his mother, she seemed rather displeased at my keeping him so long. She had shut up her sketch-book, and been, probably, for some minutes, impatiently waiting his return.

It was now high time to go home, she said, and would have bid me good evening; but I was not going to leave her yet: I accompanied her half way up the hill. She became more sociable; and I was beginning to be very happy; but, on coming within sight of the grim old Hall, she stood still and turned towards me while she spoke, as if expecting I should go no further, that the conversation would end here, and I should now take leave and depart – as, indeed, it was time to do; for 'the clear, cold eve' was fast 'declining,' the sun had set, and the gibbous moon was visibly brightening in the pale grey sky; but a feeling almost of compassion riveted me to the spot. It seemed hard to leave her to such a lonely, comfortless home. I looked up at it. Silent and grim it frowned before us. A faint, red light was gleaming from the lower windows of one wing; but all the other windows were in darkness, and many exhibited their black, cavernous gulfs, entirely destitute of glazing or frame work.

'Do you not find it a desolate place to live in?' said I, after a moment of silent contemplation.

'I do, sometimes,' replied she. 'On winter evenings, when Arthur is in bed, and I am sitting there alone, hearing the bleak wind moaning round me and howling through the ruinous old chambers, no books or occupations can repress the dismal thoughts and apprehensions that come crowding in – but it is folly to give way to such weakness I know. – If Rachel is satisfied with such a life, why should not I? – Indeed I cannot be too thankful for such an asylum, while it is left me.'

The closing sentence was uttered in an under tone, as if spoken rather to herself than to me. She then bid me good evening and withdrew.

I had not proceeded many steps on my way homewards, when I perceived Mr Lawrence, on his pretty grey pony, coming up the rugged lane that crossed over the hill top. I went a little out of my way to speak to him; for we had not met for some time.

'Was that Mrs Graham you were speaking to just now?' said he, after the first few words of greeting had passed between us.

'Yes.'

'Humph! I thought so.' He looked contemplatively at his horse's mane, as if he had some serious cause of dissatisfaction with it, or something else.

'Well! what then?'

'Oh, nothing!' replied he. 'Only I thought you disliked her,' he quietly added, curling his classic lip with a slightly sarcastic smile.

'Suppose I did; mayn't a man change his mind on further acquaintance?'

'Yes, of course,' returned he, nicely reducing an entanglement in the pony's redundant, hoary mane. Then suddenly turning to me, and fixing his shy, hazel eyes upon me with a steady penetrating gaze, he added, 'Then you *have* changed your mind?'

'I can't say that I have exactly. No; I think I hold the same opinion respecting her as before – but slightly ameliorated.'

'Oh.' He looked round for something else to talk about; and glancing up at the moon, made some remark upon the beauty of the evening, which I did not answer, as being irrelevant to the subject.

'Lawrence,' said I, calmly looking him in the face, 'are you in love with Mrs Graham?'

Instead of his being deeply offended at this, as I more than

half expected he would, the first start of surprise, at the audacious question, was followed by a tittering laugh, as if he was
highly amused at the idea.

'*I* in love with her!' repeated he. 'What makes you dream of
such a thing?'

'From the interest you take in the progress of my acquaintance with the lady, and the changes of my opinion concerning
her, I thought you might be jealous.'

He laughed again. 'Jealous! no – but I thought you were
going to marry Eliza Millward.'

'You thought wrong, then; I am not going to marry either
one or the other – that I know of.'

'Then I think you'd better let them alone.'

'Are you going to marry Jane Wilson?'

He coloured, and played with the mane again, but answered, –
'No, I think not.'

'Then you had better let her alone.'

She won't let me alone – he might have said; but he only
looked silly and said nothing for the space of half a minute,
and then, made another attempt to turn the conversation; and,
this time, I let it pass; for he had borne enough: another word
on the subject would have been like the last atom that breaks
the camel's back.

I was too late for tea; but my mother had kindly kept the
tea-pot and muffin warm upon the hobs, and, though she
scolded me a little, readily admitted my excuses; and when I
complained of the flavour of the overdrawn tea, she poured the
remainder into the slop-basin, and bade Rose put some fresh
into the pot, and reboil the kettle, which offices were performed
with great commotion, and certain remarkable comments.

'Well! – if it had been *me* now, I should have had no tea at
all – if it had been Fergus, even, he would have had to put up
with such as there was, and been told to be thankful, for it was
far too good for him; but *you* – we can't do too much for you. –
It's always so – if there's anything particularly nice at table,

Mamma winks and nods at me, to abstain from it, and if I don't attend to that, she whispers, "Don't eat so much of that, Rose, Gilbert will like it for his supper" – *I'm* nothing at all – in the parlour, it's "Come Rose, put away your things, and let's have the room nice and tidy against they come in; and keep up a good fire; Gilbert likes a cheerful fire." In the kitchen – "Make that pie a large one, Rose; I dare say the boys'll be hungry; – and don't put so much pepper in, they'll not like it I'm sure" – or, "Rose, don't put so many spices in the pudding, Gilbert likes it plain," – or, "Mind you put plenty of currants in the cake, Fergus likes plenty." If I say, "Well mamma, *I* don't," I'm told I ought not to think of myself – "You know, Rose, in all household matters, we have only two things to consider, first, what's proper to be done, and secondly, what's most agreeable to the gentlemen of the house – any thing will do for the ladies." '

'And very good doctrine too,' said my mother. 'Gilbert thinks so, I'm sure.'

'Very convenient doctrine, for us, at all events,' said I; 'but if you would really study my pleasure, Mother, you must consider your own comfort and convenience a little more than you do – as for Rose, I have no doubt she'll take care of herself; and when-ever she does make a sacrifice or perform a remarkable act of devotedness, she'll take good care to let me know the extent of it. But for *you*, I might sink into the grossest condition of self-indulgence and carelessness about the wants of others, from the mere habit of being constantly cared for myself, and having all my wants anticipated or immediately supplied, while left in total ignorance of what is done for me, – if Rose did not enlighten me now and then; and I should receive all your kindness as a matter of course, and never know how much I owe you.'

'Ah! and you never *will* know, Gilbert, till you're married. Then, when you've got some trifling, self-conceited girl like Eliza Millward, careless of everything but her own immediate pleasure and advantage, or some misguided, obstinate woman like Mrs Graham, ignorant of her principal duties, and clever only in what concerns her least to know – then, you'll find the difference.'

'It will do me good Mother; I was not sent into the world merely to exercise the good capacities and good feelings of others – was I? – but to exert my own towards them; and when I marry, I shall expect to find more pleasure in making my wife happy and comfortable, than in being made so by her: I would rather give than receive.'

'Oh! that's all nonsense, my dear – it's mere boy's talk that! You'll soon tire of petting and humouring your wife, be she ever so charming, and *then* comes the trial.'

'Well, then, we must bear one another's burdens.'

'Then, you must fall each into your proper place. You'll do your business, and she, if she's worthy of you, will do hers; but it's your business to please yourself, and hers to please you. I'm sure your poor, dear father was as good a husband as ever lived, and after the first six months or so were over, I should as soon have expected him to fly, as to put himself out of his way to pleasure me. He always said I was a good wife, and did my duty; and he always did his – bless him! – he was steady and punctual, seldom found fault without a reason, always did justice to my good dinners, and hardly ever spoiled my cookery by delay – and that's as much as any woman can expect of any man.'

Is it so Halford? Is that the extent of *your* domestic virtues; and does your happy wife exact no more?

CHAPTER VII

THE EXCURSION

Not many days after this, on a mild sunny morning – rather soft under foot; for the last fall of snow was only just wasted away, leaving yet a thin ridge, here and there, lingering on the fresh green grass beneath the hedges; but beside them already, the young primroses were peeping from among their moist, dark foliage, and the lark above was singing of summer, and hope, and love, and every heavenly thing – I was out on the hill-side, enjoying these delights, and looking after the well-being of my young lambs and their mothers, when, on glancing round me, I beheld three persons ascending from the vale below. They were Eliza Millward, Fergus and Rose; so I crossed the field to meet them; and, being told they were going to Wildfell Hall, I declared myself willing to go with them, and offering my arm to Eliza, who readily accepted it in lieu of my brother's, told the latter he might go back, for I would accompany the ladies.

'I beg *your* pardon!' exclaimed he – 'it's the ladies that are accompanying me, not I them. You had all had a peep at this wonderful stranger, but me, and I could endure my wretched ignorance no longer – come what would, I must be satisfied; so I begged Rose to go with me to the Hall, and introduce me to her at once. She swore she would not, unless Miss Eliza would go too; so I ran to the vicarage and fetched her; and we've come hooked all the way, as fond as a pair of lovers – and now you've taken her from me; and you want to deprive me of my walk and my visit besides. – Go back to your fields and your cattle, you lubberly fellow; you're not fit to associate with ladies and gentlemen, like us, that have nothing to do but to run snooking about to our neighbours' houses, peeping into their private corners; and scenting out their secrets, and picking holes in their coats, when we don't find them ready made to our hands – you don't understand such refined sources of enjoyment.'

'Can't you both go?' suggested Eliza, disregarding the latter half of the speech.

'Yes, both to be sure!' cried Rose; 'the more the merrier – and I'm sure we shall want all the cheerfulness we can carry with us to that great, dark, gloomy room, with its narrow latticed windows, and its dismal old furniture – unless she shews us into her studio again.'

So we went all in a body; and the meager old maidservant, that opened the door, ushered us into an apartment, such as Rose had described to me as the scene of her first introduction to Mrs Graham, a tolerably spacious and lofty room, but obscurely lighted by the old-fashioned windows, the ceiling, panels, and chimney-piece of grim black oak – the latter elaborately, but not very tastefully carved, – with tables and chairs to match, an old bookcase on one side of the fire-place, stocked with a motley assemblage of books, and an elderly cabinet piano on the other.

The lady was seated in a stiff, high-backed arm-chair, with a small, round table, containing a desk and a work basket, on one side of her, and her little boy on the other, who stood leaning his elbow on her knee, and reading to her, with wonderful fluency, from a small volume that lay in her lap; while she rested her hand on his shoulder, and abstractedly played with the long, wavy curls that fell on his ivory neck. They struck me as forming a pleasing contrast to all the surrounding objects; but of course their position was immediately changed on our entrance; I could only observe the picture during the few brief seconds that Rachel held the door for our admittance.

I do not think Mrs Graham was particularly delighted to see us: there was something indescribably chilly in her quiet, calm civility; but I did not talk much to her. Seating myself near the window, a little back from the circle, I called Arthur to me, and he and I and Sancho amused ourselves very pleasantly together, while the two young ladies baited his mother with small talk, and Fergus sat opposite with his legs crossed, and his hands in his breeches pockets, leaning back in his chair, and staring now up at the ceiling, now straight forward at his hostess (in a manner that made me strongly inclined to kick him out of the room), now whistling sotto voce to himself a snatch of a favourite air, now interrupting the conversation, or filling up a pause (as the case might be), with some most impertinent question or remark. At one time it was –

'It amazes me, Mrs Graham, how you could choose such a dilapidated, rickety old place as this to live in. If you couldn't afford to occupy the whole house, and have it mended up, why couldn't you take a neat little cottage?'

'Perhaps I was too proud, Mr Fergus,' replied she, smiling; 'perhaps I took a particular fancy for this romantic, old-fashioned place – but indeed, it has many advantages over a cottage – in the first place, you see, the rooms are larger and more airy; in the second place, the unoccupied apartments, which I don't pay for, may serve as lumber-rooms, if I have anything to put in them; and they are very useful for my little boy to run about in on rainy days when he can't go out; and then, there is the garden for him to play in, and for me to work in. You see I have effected some little improvement already,' continued she, turning to the window. 'There is a bed of young vegetables in that corner, and here are some snowdrops and primroses already in bloom – and there, too, is a yellow crocus just opening in the sunshine.'

'But then how can you bear such a situation – your nearest neighbours two miles distant, and nobody looking in or passing by? – Rose would go stark mad in such a place. She can't put on life unless she sees half a dozen fresh gowns and bonnets a day – not to speak of the faces within; but you might sit watching at these windows all day long, and never see so much as an old woman carrying her eggs to market.'

'I am not sure the loneliness of the place was not one of its chief recommendations – I take no pleasure in watching people pass the windows; and I like to be quiet.'

'Oh! as good as to say, you wish we would all of us mind our own business, and let you alone.'

'No, I dislike an extensive acquaintance; but if I have a few friends, of course I am glad to see them occasionally. No one can be happy in eternal solitude. Therefore, Mr Fergus, if you choose to enter my house as a friend, I will make you welcome; if not, I must confess, I would rather you kept away.' She then turned and addressed some observation to Rose or Eliza.

'And, Mrs Graham,' said he again, five minutes after, 'we were disputing, as we came along, a question that you can readily decide for us, as it mainly regarded yourself – and indeed, we often hold discussions about you; for some of us have nothing better to do than to talk about our neighbours' concerns, and we, the indigenous plants of the soil, have known each other so long, and talked each other over so often, that we are quite sick of that game; so that a stranger coming amongst us makes an invaluable addition to our exhausted sources of amusement. Well, the question, or questions you are requested to solve –'

'Hold your tongue, Fergus!' cried Rose, in a fever of apprehension and wrath.

'I won't I tell you. The questions you are requested to solve are these: – First, concerning your birth, extraction, and previous residence. Some will have it that you are a foreigner, and some an Englishwoman; some a native of the north country, and some of the south; some say –'

'Well, Mr Fergus, I'll tell you. I'm an Englishwoman – and I don't see why any one should doubt it – and I was born in the country neither in the extreme north nor south of our happy isle; and in the country I have chiefly passed my life, and now,

I hope, you are satisfied; for I am not disposed to answer any more questions at present.'

'Except this —'

'No, not one more!' laughed she, and, instantly quitting her seat, she sought refuge at the window by which I was seated, and, in very desperation, to escape my brother's persecutions, endeavoured to draw me into conversation.

'Mr Markham,' said she, her rapid utterance and heightened colour too plainly evincing her disquietude; 'have you forgotten the fine sea view we were speaking of some time ago? I think I must trouble you, now, to tell me the nearest way to it; for if this beautiful weather continue, I shall, perhaps, be able to walk there, and take my sketch; I have exhausted every other subject for painting, and I long to see it.'

I was about to comply with her request; but Rose would not suffer me to proceed.

'Oh, don't tell her Gilbert!' cried she; 'she shall go with us. It's — Bay you are thinking about I suppose, Mrs Graham. It is a very long walk, too far for you, and out of the question for Arthur. But we were thinking about making a pic-nic to see it, some fine day; and, if you will wait till the settled fine weather comes, I'm sure we shall all be delighted to have you amongst us.'

Poor Mrs Graham looked dismayed, and attempted to make excuses, but Rose, either compassionating her lonely life, or anxious to cultivate her acquaintance, was determined to have her; and every objection was overruled. She was told it would only be a small party, and all friends, and that the best view of all was from — Cliffs, full five miles distant.

'Just a nice walk for the gentlemen,' continued Rose; 'but the ladies will drive and walk by turns; for we shall have our pony-carriage, which will be plenty large enough to contain little Arthur and three ladies, together with your sketching apparatus, and our provisions.'

So the proposal was finally acceded to; and, after some further discussion respecting the time and manner of the projected excursion, we rose, and took our leave.

But this was only March: a cold, wet April, and two weeks of May passed over before we could venture forth on our expedition with the reasonable hope of obtaining that pleasure we sought in pleasant prospects, cheerful society, fresh air, good cheer, and exercise, without the alloy of bad roads, cold winds, or threatening clouds. Then, on a glorious morning, we gathered our forces and set forth. The company consisted of Mrs and Master Graham, Mary and Eliza Millward, Jane and Richard Wilson, and Rose, Fergus, and Gilbert Markham.

Mr Lawrence had been invited to join us, but, for some reason best known to himself, had refused to give us his company. I had solicited the favour myself. When I did so, he hesitated, and asked who were going. Upon my naming Miss Wilson among the rest, he seemed half inclined to go, but when I mentioned Mrs Graham, thinking it might be a further inducement, it appeared to have a contrary effect, and he declined it altogether, and, to confess the truth, the decision was not displeasing to me, though I could scarcely tell you why.

It was about mid-day, when we reached the place of our destination. Mrs Graham walked all the way to the cliffs; and little Arthur walked the greater part of it too; for he was now much more hardy and active than when he first entered the neighbourhood, and he did not like being in the carriage with strangers, while all his four friends, Mamma, and Sancho, and Mr Markham, and Miss Millward, were on foot, journeying far behind, or passing through distant fields and lanes.

I have a very pleasant recollection of that walk, along the hard, white, sunny road, shaded here and there with bright green trees, and adorned with flowery banks and blossoming hedges of delicious fragrance; or through pleasant fields and lanes, all glorious in the sweet flowers, and brilliant verdure of delightful May. It was true, Eliza was not beside me; but she was with her friends in the pony-carriage, as happy, I trusted, as I was; and even when we pedestrians, having forsaken the highway for a short cut across the fields, beheld the little carriage far away, disappearing amid the green, imbowering trees, I did not hate those trees for snatching the dear little bonnet and shawl from my sight, nor did I feel that all those intervening objects lay between my happiness and me; for, to confess the truth, I was too happy in the company of Mrs Graham to regret the absence of Eliza Millward.

The former, it is true, was most provokingly unsociable at first – seemingly bent upon talking to no one but Mary Mill-ward and Arthur. She and Mary journeyed along together, generally with the child between them; – but where the road permitted, I always walked on the other side of her, Richard Wilson taking the other side of Miss Millward, and Fergus roving here and there according to his fancy; and, after a while, she became more friendly, and at length, I succeeded in securing her attention, almost entirely to myself – and then I was happy indeed; for whenever she did condescend to converse, I liked to listen. Where her opinions and sentiments tallied with mine, it was her extreme good sense, her exquisite taste and feeling that delighted me; where they differed, it was still her un-compromising boldness in the avowal or defence of that differ-ence – her earnestness and keenness that piqued my fancy: and even when she angered me by her unkind words or looks, and her uncharitable conclusions respecting me, it only made me the more dissatisfied with myself for having so unfavourably impressed her, and the more desirous to vindicate my character and disposition in her eyes, and if possible, to win her esteem.

At length our walk was ended. The increasing height and boldness of the hills had for some time intercepted the prospect; but, on gaining the summit of a steep acclivity, and looking downward, an opening lay before us – and the blue sea burst upon our sight! – deep violet blue – not deadly calm, but covered with glinting breakers – diminutive white specks twinkling on its bosom, and scarcely to be distinguished, by the keenest vision, from the little sea-mews that sported above, their white wings glittering in the sunshine: only one or two vessels were visible; and those were far away.

I looked at my companion to see what she thought of this glorious scene. She said nothing: but she stood still, and fixed her eyes upon it with a gaze that assured me she was not disappointed. She had very fine eyes by the by – I don't know whether I've told you before, but they were full of soul, large, clear, and nearly black – not brown, but very dark grey. A cool, reviving breeze blew from the sea – soft, pure, salubrious: it waved her drooping ringlets, and imparted a livelier colour to her usually too pallid lip and cheek. She felt its exhilarating influence, and so did I – I felt it tingling through my frame, but dared not give way to it while she remained so quiet. There was an aspect of subdued exhilaration in her face, that kindled into almost a smile of exalted, glad intelligence as her eye met mine. Never had she looked so lovely: never had my heart so warmly cleaved to her as now. Had we been left two minutes longer, standing there alone, I cannot answer for the consequences. Happily for my discretion, perhaps for my enjoyment during the remainder of the day, we were speedily summoned to the repast – a very respectable collation, which Rose, assisted by Miss Wilson and Eliza, who, having shared her seat in the carriage, had arrived with her a little before the rest, had set out upon an elevated platform overlooking the sea, and sheltered from the hot sun by a shelving rock and overhanging trees.

Mrs Graham seated herself at a distance from me. Eliza was my nearest neighbour. She exerted herself to be agreeable, in her gentle, unobtrusive way, and was, no doubt, as fascinating and charming as ever, if I could only have felt it. But soon, my heart began to warm towards her once again; and we were all very merry and happy together – as far as I could see – throughout the protracted social meal.

When that was over, Rose summoned Fergus to help her to gather up the fragments, and the knives, dishes, &c. and restore them to the baskets; and Mrs Graham took her camp-stool and drawing materials; and having begged Miss Millward to take charge of her precious son, and strictly enjoined him not to wander from his new guardian's side, she left us and proceeded along the steep, stony hill, to a loftier, more precipitous eminence at some distance, whence a still finer prospect was to be had, where she preferred taking her sketch, though some of the ladies told her it was a frightful place, and advised her not to attempt it.

When she was gone, I felt as if there was to be no more fun – though it is difficult to say what she had contributed to the hilarity of the party. No jests, and little laughter had escaped her lips; but her smile had animated my mirth, a keen observation or a cheerful word from her had insensibly sharpened my wits, and thrown an interest over all that was done and said by the rest. Even my conversation with Eliza had been enlivened by her presence, though I knew it not; and now that she was gone, Eliza's playful nonsense ceased to amuse me – nay, grew wearisome to my soul, and I grew weary of amusing her: I felt myself drawn by an irresistible attraction to that distant point where the fair artist sat and plied her solitary task – and not long did I attempt to resist it: while my little neighbour was exchanging a few words with Miss Wilson, I rose and cannily slipped away. A few rapid strides, and a little active clambering, soon brought me to the place where she was seated – a narrow ledge of rock at the very verge of the cliff which descended with a steep, precipitous slant, quite down to the rocky shore.

She did not hear me coming: the falling of my shadow across her paper, gave her an electric start; and she looked hastily round – any other lady of my acquaintance would have screamed under such a sudden alarm.

'Oh! I didn't know it was you – why did you startle me so?' said she, somewhat testily, 'I hate anybody to come upon me so unexpectedly.'

'Why, what did you take me for?' said I, 'if I had known you were so nervous, I would have been more cautious; but —'

'Well, never mind. What did you come for? are they all coming?'

'No; this little ledge could scarcely contain them all.'

'I'm glad, for I'm tired of talking.'

'Well then, I won't talk. I'll only sit and watch your drawing.'

'Oh, but you know I don't like that.'

'Then I'll content myself with admiring this magnificent prospect.'

She made no objection to this; and, for some time, sketched away in silence. But I could not help stealing a glance, now and then, from the splendid view at our feet to the elegant white hand that held the pencil, and the graceful neck and glossy raven curls that drooped over the paper.

'Now,' thought I, 'if I had but a pencil and a morsel of paper, I could make a lovelier sketch than hers, admitting I had the power to delineate faithfully what is before me.'

But, though this satisfaction was denied me, I was very well content to sit beside her there, and say nothing.

'Are you there still, Mr Markham?' said she at length looking round upon me – for I was seated a little behind on a mossy projection of the cliff. – 'Why don't you go and amuse yourself with your friends?'

'Because I am tired of them, like you; and I shall have enough of them to-morrow – or at any time hence; but you, I may not have the pleasure of seeing again for I know not how long.'

'What was Arthur doing when you came away?'

'He was with Miss Millward where you left him – all right, but hoping mamma would not be long away. You didn't intrust him to me, by the by,' I grumbled, 'though I had the honour of a much longer acquaintance; but Miss Millward has the art of conciliating and amusing children,' I carelessly added, 'if she is good for nothing else.'

'Miss Millward has many estimable qualities, which such as you cannot be expected to perceive or appreciate. Will you tell Arthur that I shall come in a few minutes?'

'If that be the case, I will wait, with your permission, till those few minutes are past; and then I can assist you to descend this difficult path.'

'Thank you – I always manage best, on such occasions, without assistance.'

'But, at least, I can carry your stool and sketchbook.'

She did not deny me this favour; but I was rather offended at her evident desire to be rid of me, and was beginning to repent of my pertinacity, when she somewhat appeased me by consulting my taste and judgment about some doubtful matter in her drawing. My opinion, happily, met her approbation, and the improvement I suggested was adopted without hesitation.

'I have often wished in vain,' said she, 'for another's judgment to appeal to when I could scarcely trust the direction of my own eye and head, they having been so long occupied with the contemplation of a single object, as to become almost incapable of forming a proper idea respecting it.'

'That,' replied I, 'is only one of many evils to which a solitary life exposes us.'

'True,' said she; and again we relapsed into silence.

About two minutes after, however, she declared her sketch completed and closed the book.

On returning to the scene of our repast, we found all the company had deserted it, with the exception of three – Mary Millward, Richard Wilson, and Arthur Graham. The younger gentleman lay fast asleep with his head pillowed on the lady's lap; the other was seated beside her with a pocket edition of some classic author in his hand. He never went anywhere without such a companion wherewith to improve his leisure moments: all time seemed lost that was not devoted to study, or exacted, by his physical nature, for the bare support of life. Even now, he could not abandon himself to the enjoyment of that pure air and balmy sunshine – that splendid prospect, and those soothing sounds, the music of the waves and of the soft wind in the sheltering trees above him – not even with a lady by his side (though not a very charming one, I will allow) – he must pull out his book, and make the most of his time while digesting his temperate meal, and reposing his weary limbs, unused to so much exercise.

Perhaps, however, he spared a moment to exchange a word or a glance with his companion now and then – at any rate, she did not appear at all resentful of his conduct; for her homely features wore an expression of unusual cheerfulness and serenity, and she was studying his pale, thoughtful face with great complacency when we arrived.

The journey homeward was by no means so agreeable, to me, as the former part of the day; for now Mrs Graham was in the carriage, and Eliza Millward was the companion of my walk. She had observed my preference for the young widow, and evidently felt herself neglected. She did not manifest her chagrin by keen reproaches, bitter sarcasms, or pouting sullen silence – any or all of these I could easily have endured, or lightly laughed away; but she showed it by a kind of gentle melancholy, a mild, reproachful sadness that cut me to the heart. I tried to cheer her up, and apparently succeeded in some degree, before the walk was over; but in the very act my conscience reproved me, knowing, as I did, that, sooner or later, the tie must be broken, and this was only nourishing false hopes, and putting off the evil day.

When the pony-carriage had approached as near Wildfell Hall as the road would permit – unless, indeed, it proceeded up the long rough lane, which Mrs Graham would not allow – the young widow and her son alighted, relinquishing the driver's seat to Rose; and I persuaded Eliza to take the latter's place. Having put her comfortably in, bid her take care of the evening air, and wished her a kind good-night, I felt considerably relieved, and hastened to offer my services to Mrs Graham to carry her apparatus up the fields, but she had already hung her camp-stool on her arm and taken her sketchbook in her hand; and insisted upon bidding me adieu then and there, with the rest of the company. But this time, she declined my proffered aid in so kind and friendly a manner, that I almost forgave her.

CHAPTER VIII

THE PRESENT

Six weeks had passed away. It was a splendid morning about the close of June. Most of the hay was cut, but the last week had been very unfavourable; and now that fine weather was come at last, being determined to make the most of it, I had gathered all hands together into the hayfield, and was working away myself, in the midst of them, in my shirt sleeves, with a light, shady straw hat on my head, catching up armfuls of moist, reeking grass, and shaking it out to the four winds of Heaven, at the head of a goodly file of servants and hirelings – intending so to labour, from morning to night, with as much zeal and assiduity as I could look for from any of them, as well to prosper the work by my own exertion as to animate the workers by my example – when, lo! my resolutions were overthrown in a moment, by the simple fact of my brother's running up to me and putting into my hand a small parcel, just arrived from London, which I had been for some time expecting. I tore off the cover, and disclosed an elegant and portable edition of 'Marmion.'

'I guess I know who that's for,' said Fergus, who stood looking on while I complacently examined the volume. 'That's for Miss Eliza, now.'

He pronounced this with a tone and look so prodigiously knowing, that I was glad to contradict him.

'You're wrong my lad,' said I; and taking up my coat, I deposited the book in one of its pockets, and then put it on (i.e. the coat). 'Now come here you idle dog, and make yourself useful for once,' I continued. – 'Pull off your coat, and take my place in the field till I come back.'

'Till you come back? – and where are you going, pray?'

'No matter – *where* – the *when* is all that concerns you; – and I shall be back by dinner, at least.'

'Oh ho! and I'm to labour away till then, am I – and to keep all these fellows hard at it besides? – Well, well! I'll submit – for once in a way. – Come my lads, you must look sharp: *I*'m come to help you now; – and wo be to that man, or woman either, that pauses for a moment amongst you – whether to stare about him, to scratch his head, or blow his nose – no pretext will serve – nothing but work, work, work in the sweat of your face,' – &c. &c.

Leaving him thus haranguing the people, more to their amusement than edification, I returned to the house, and having made some alteration in my toilet, hastened away to Wildfell Hall, with the book in my pocket; for it was destined for the shelves of Mrs Graham.

'What, then, had she and you got on so well together as to come to the giving and receiving of presents?' – Not precisely, old buck; this was my first experiment in that line; and I was very anxious to see the result of it.

We had met several times since the —— Bay excursion, and I had found she was not averse to my company, provided, I confined my conversation to the discussion of abstract matters, or topics of common interest; – the moment I touched upon the sentimental or the complimentary, or made the slightest approach to tenderness in word or look, I was not only punished by an immediate change in her manner at the time, but doomed to find her more cold and distant, if not entirely inaccessible, when next I sought her company. This circumstance did not greatly disconcert me however, because, I attributed it, not so much to any dislike of my person, as to some absolute resolution against a second marriage formed prior to the time of our acquaintance, whether from excess of affection for her late husband, or because she had had enough of him and the matrimonial state together. At first, indeed, she had seemed to take a pleasure in mortifying my vanity and crushing my presumption – relentlessly nipping off bud by bud as they ventured to appear; and then, I confess, I was deeply wounded, though, at the same time, stimulated to seek revenge; – but latterly finding, beyond a doubt, that I was not that empty-headed coxcomb she had first supposed me, she had repulsed my modest advances in quite a different spirit. It was a kind of serious, almost sorrowful displeasure, which I soon learnt carefully to avoid awakening.

'Let me first establish my position as a friend,' thought I, – 'the patron and playfellow of her son, the sober, solid, plain-dealing friend of herself, and then, when I have made myself fairly necessary to her comfort and enjoyment in life (as I believe I can), we'll see what next may be effected.'

So we talked about painting, poetry, and music, theology, geology, and philosophy: once or twice I lent her a book, and once she lent me one in return: I met her in her walks as often as I could; I came to her house as often as I dared. My first pretext for invading the sanctum, was to bring Arthur a little waddling puppy of which Sancho was the father, and which delighted the child beyond expression, and, consequently, could not fail to please his mamma. My second was to bring him a book, which, knowing his mother's particularity, I had carefully selected, and which I submitted for her approbation before presenting it to him. Then, I brought her some plants for her garden, in my sister's name – having previously persuaded Rose to send them. Each of these times I inquired after the picture she was painting from the sketch taken on the cliff, and was admitted into the studio, and asked my opinion or advice respecting its progress.

My last visit had been to return the book she had lent me; and then it was, that, in casually discussing the poetry of Sir Walter Scott, she had expressed a wish to see 'Marmion,' and I had conceived the presumptuous idea of making her a present of it, and, on my return home, instantly sent for the smart little volume I had this morning received. But an apology for invading the hermitage was still necessary; so I had furnished myself with a blue morocco collar for Arthur's little dog; and that being given and received, with much more joy and gratitude, on the part of the receiver, than the worth of the gift, or the selfish motive of the giver deserved, I ventured to ask Mrs Graham for one more look at the picture, if it was still there.

'Oh, yes! come in,' said she (for I had met them in the garden). 'It is finished and framed, all ready for sending away; but give me your last opinion, and if you can suggest any further improvement, it shall be – duly considered, at least.'

The picture was strikingly beautiful; it was the very scene itself, transferred as if by magic to the canvass; but I expressed my approbation in guarded terms, and few words, for fear of displeasing her. She, however, attentively watched my looks, and her artist's pride was gratified, no doubt, to read my heartfelt admiration in my eyes. But, while I gazed, I thought upon the book, and wondered how it was to be presented. My heart failed me; but I determined not to be such a fool as to come away without having made the attempt. It was useless waiting for an opportunity, and useless trying to concoct a speech for the occasion. The more plainly and naturally the thing was done, the better, I thought; so I just looked out of the window to screw up my courage, and then pulled out the book, turned round, and put it into her hand, with this short explanation:

'You were wishing to see "Marmion," Mrs Graham; and here it is, if you will be so kind as to take it.'

A momentary blush suffused her face – perhaps, a blush of sympathetic shame for such an awkward style of presentation: she gravely examined the volume on both sides; then silently turned over the leaves, knitting her brows the while, in serious cogitation; then closed the book, and, turning from it to me, quietly asked the price of it. – I felt the hot blood rush to my face.

'I'm sorry to offend you, Mr Markham,' said she, 'but unless I pay for the book, I cannot take it.' And she laid it on the table.

'Why cannot you?'

'Because,' – she paused, and looked at the carpet.

'Why cannot you?' I repeated with a degree of irascibility that roused her to lift her eyes, and look me steadily in the face.

'Because, I don't like to put myself under obligations that I can never repay – I *am* obliged to you already for your kindness to my son; but his grateful affection, and your own good feelings must reward you for that.'

'Nonsense!' ejaculated I.

She turned her eyes on me again, with a look of quiet, grave surprise, that had the effect of a rebuke, whether intended for such or not.

'Then you won't take the book?' I asked, more mildly than I had yet spoken.

'I will gladly take it, if you will let me pay for it.'

I told her the exact price, and the cost of the carriage besides, in as calm a tone as I could command – for in fact, I was ready to weep with disappointment and vexation.

She produced her purse, and coolly counted out the money, but hesitated to put it into my hand. Attentively regarding me, in a tone of soothing softness she observed, –

'You think yourself insulted, Mr Markham – I wish I could make you understand that – that I –'

'I do understand you, perfectly,' I said. 'You think that if you were to accept that trifle from me now, I should presume upon it hereafter; but you are mistaken: – if you will only oblige me by taking it, believe me, I shall build no hopes upon it, and consider this no precedent for future favours: – and it is nonsense to talk about putting yourself under obligations to *me* when you must know that in such a case the obligation is entirely on my side, – the favour on yours.'

'Well then I'll take you at your word,' she answered, with a most angelic smile, returning the odious money to her purse – 'but *remember!*'

'I will remember – what I have said; – but do not you punish my presumption by withdrawing your friendship entirely from me, – or expect me to atone for it by being *more* distant than before,' said I, extending my hand to take leave, for I was too much excited to remain.

'Well then! let us be as we were,' replied she, frankly placing her hand in mine; and while I held it there, I had much difficulty to refrain from pressing it to my lips; – but that would be suicidal madness: I had been bold enough already, and this premature offering had well-nigh given the death-blow to my hopes.

It was with an agitated, burning heart and brain that I hurried homewards, regardless of that scorching noon-day sun – forgetful of everything but her I had just left – regretting nothing but her impenetrability, and my own precipitancy and want of tact – fearing nothing but her hateful resolution, and my inability to overcome it – hoping nothing – but halt, – I will not bore you with my conflicting hopes and fears – my serious cogitations and resolves.

CHAPTER IX

A SNAKE IN THE GRASS

Though my affections might now be said to be fairly weaned from Eliza Millward, I did not yet entirely relinquish my visits to the vicarage, because I wanted, as it were, to let her down easy; without raising much sorrow, or incurring much resentment, – or making myself the talk of the parish; and besides, if I had wholly kept away, the vicar, who looked upon my visits as paid chiefly, if not entirely to himself, would have felt himself decidedly affronted by the neglect. But when I called there the day after my interview with Mrs Graham, he happened to be from home – a circumstance by no means so agreeable to me now as it had been on former occasions. Miss Millward was there, it is true, but she, of course, would be little better than a non-entity. However, I resolved to make my visit a short one, and to talk to Eliza in a brotherly, friendly sort of way, such as our long acquaintance might warrant me in assuming, and which, I thought, could neither give offence nor serve to encourage false hopes.

It was never my custom to talk about Mrs Graham either to her or any one else; but I had not been seated three minutes, before she brought that lady on to the carpet herself, in a rather remarkable manner.

'Oh, Mr Markham!' said she, with a shocked expression and voice subdued almost to a whisper – 'what do you think of these shocking reports about Mrs Graham? – can you encourage us to disbelieve them?'

'What reports?'

'Ah, now! *you* know!' she slyly smiled and shook her head.

'I know nothing about them – what in the world do you mean, Eliza?'

'Oh, don't ask *me*! – I can't explain it.' She took up the cambric handkerchief which she had been beautifying with a deep lace border, and began to be very busy.

'What is it, Miss Millward? what does she mean?' said I, appealing to her sister, who seemed to be absorbed in the hemming of a large, coarse sheet.

'I don't know,' replied she. – 'Some idle slander, somebody has been inventing, I suppose. I never heard it till Eliza told me, the other day, – but if all the parish dinned it in my ears, I shouldn't believe a word of it – I know Mrs Graham too well!'

'Quite right Miss Millward! – and so do I – whatever it may be.'

'Well,' observed Eliza, with a gentle sigh – 'it's well to have such a comfortable assurance regarding the worth of those we love. – I only wish you may not find your confidence misplaced.'

And she raised her face, and gave me such a look of sorrowful tenderness as might have melted my heart, but within those eyes there lurked a something that I did not like; and I wondered how I ever could have admired them: her sister's honest face and small grey optics appeared far more agreeable; – but I was out of temper with Eliza, at that moment, for her insinuations against Mrs Graham – which were false, I was certain, whether she knew it or not.

I said nothing more on the subject, however, at the time, and but little on any other; for, finding I could not well recover my equanimity, I presently rose and took leave, excusing myself under the plea of business at the farm; – and to the farm I went – not troubling my mind one whit about the possible truth of these mysterious reports, but only wondering what they were, by whom originated, and on what foundations raised, – and how they could the most effectually be silenced or disproved.

A few days after this, we had another of our quiet little parties, to which the usual company of friends and neighbours had been invited, and Mrs Graham among the number. She could not now absent herself under the plea of dark evenings or inclement weather, and, greatly to my relief, she came. Without her I should have found the whole affair an intolerable bore; but the moment of her arrival brought new life to the house; and though I might not neglect the other guests for her, or expect to engross much of her attention and conversation to myself alone, I anticipated an evening of no common enjoyment.

Mr Lawrence came too. He did not arrive till some time after the rest were assembled. I was curious to see how he would comport himself to Mrs Graham. A slight bow was all that passed between them on his entrance; and having politely greeted the other members of the company, he seated himself quite aloof from the young widow, between my mother and Rose.

'Did you ever see such art!' whispered Eliza, who was my nearest neighbour. 'Would you not say they were perfect strangers?'

'Almost; – but what then?'

'What then! – why you can't pretend to be ignorant?'

'Ignorant of *what*?' demanded I, so sharply that she started and replied, –

'Oh, hush! don't speak so loud.'

'Well, tell me then,' I answered in a lower tone, 'what is it you mean? I hate enigmas.'

'Well you know, I don't vouch for the truth of it – indeed, far from it – but haven't you heard –'

'I've heard *nothing*, except from you.'

'You must be wilfully deaf then; for any one will tell you that – but I shall only anger you by repeating it, I see; so I had better hold my tongue.'

She closed her lips and folded her hands before her with an air of injured meekness.

'If you had wished not to anger me, you should have held your tongue from the beginning; or else spoken out plainly and honestly all you had to say.'

She turned aside her face, pulled out her handkerchief, rose, and went to the window, where she stood for some time, evidently dissolved in tears. I was astounded, provoked, ashamed – not so much of my harshness as for her childish weakness. However, no one seemed to notice her, and shortly after, we were summoned to the tea-table; in those parts it was customary to sit to the table at tea-time on all occasions, and make a meal of it; for we dined early. On taking my seat, I had Rose on one side of me, and an empty chair on the other.

'May I sit by you?' said a soft voice at my elbow.

'If you like,' was the reply; and Eliza slipped into the vacant chair; then looking up in my face with a half sad, half playful smile, she whispered –

'You're so stern, Gilbert.'

I handed down her tea with a slightly contemptuous smile, and said nothing, for I had nothing to say.

'What have I done to offend you?' said she, more plaintively. 'I wish I knew.'

'Come, take your tea Eliza, and don't be foolish,' responded I, handing her the sugar and cream.

Just then, there arose a slight commotion on the other side of me, occasioned by Miss Wilson's coming to negotiate an exchange of seats with Rose.

'Will you be so good as to exchange places with me, Miss Markham?' said she; 'for I don't like to sit by Mrs Graham. If your mamma thinks proper to invite such persons to her house, she cannot object to her daughter's keeping company with them.'

This latter clause was added in a sort of soliloquy when Rose was gone; but I was not polite enough to let it pass:

'Will you be so good as to tell me what you mean, Miss Wilson?' said I.

The question startled her a little, but not much.

'Why Mr Markham,' replied she coolly, having quickly recovered her self-possession, 'it surprises me rather that Mrs Markham should invite such a person as Mrs Graham to her house; but, perhaps, she is not aware that the lady's character is considered scarcely respectable.'

'She is not, nor am I; and therefore, you would oblige me by explaining your meaning a little further.'

'This is scarcely the time or the place for such explanations; but I think you can hardly be so ignorant as you pretend: you must know her as well as I do.'

'I think I do, perhaps a little better; and therefore, if you will inform me what you have heard, or imagined against her, I shall, perhaps, be able to set you right.'

'Can you tell me, then, who was her husband; or if she ever had any?'

Indignation kept me silent. At such a time and place I could not trust myself to answer.

'Have you never observed,' said Eliza, 'what a striking likeness there is between that child of hers and –'

'And whom?' demanded Miss Wilson, with an air of cold, but keen severity.

Eliza was startled: the timidly spoken suggestion had been intended for my ear alone.

'Oh, I beg your pardon!' pleaded she, 'I may be mistaken – perhaps I *was* mistaken.' But she accompanied the words with a sly glance of derision directed to me from the corner of her disingenuous eye.

'There's no need to ask *my* pardon,' replied her friend; 'but I see no one here that at all resembles that child, except his mother; and when you hear ill-natured reports, Miss Eliza, I will thank you – that is, I think you will do well to refrain from repeating them. I presume the person you allude to is Mr Lawrence; but I think I can assure you that your suspicions, in that respect, are utterly misplaced; and if he has any particular connection with the lady at all (which no one has a right to assert), at least, he has (what cannot be said of some others) sufficient sense of propriety to withhold him from acknowledging anything more than a bowing acquaintance in the presence of respectable persons – he was evidently both surprised and annoyed to find her here.'

'Go it!' cried Fergus, who sat on the other side of Eliza, and was the only individual who shared that side of the table with us; 'go it like bricks! mind you don't leave her one stone upon another.'

Miss Wilson drew herself up with a look of freezing scorn, but said nothing. Eliza would have replied, but I interrupted her by saying as calmly as I could, though in a tone which betrayed, no doubt, some little of what I felt within, –

'We have had enough of this subject: if we can only speak to slander our betters, let us hold our tongues.'

'I think you'd better,' observed Fergus; 'and so does our good parson: he has been addressing the company in his richest vein all the while, and eyeing you, from time to time, with looks of stern distaste, while you sat there, irreverently whispering and muttering together; and once he paused in the middle of a story – or a sermon, I don't know which, and fixed his eyes upon you, Gilbert, as much as to say, "When Mr Markham has done flirting with those two ladies I will proceed!"'

What more was said at the tea-table I cannot tell; nor how I found patience to sit till the meal was over. I remember, how-ever, that I swallowed with difficulty the remainder of the tea that was in my cup, and eat nothing; and that the first thing I did was to stare at Arthur Graham, who sat beside his mother on the opposite side of the table, and the second to stare at Mr Lawrence, who sat below; and, first, it struck me that there *was* a likeness; but, on further contemplation, I concluded it was only in imagination. Both, it is true, had more delicate features and smaller bones than commonly fall to the lot of individuals of the rougher sex, and Lawrence's complexion was pale and clear, and Arthur's delicately fair; but Arthur's tiny, somewhat snubby nose could never become so long and straight as Mr Lawrence's, and the outline of his face, though not full enough to be round, and too finely converging to the small, dimpled chin to be square, could never be drawn out to the long oval of the other's; while the child's hair was evidently of a lighter, warmer tint than the elder gentleman's had ever been, and his large, clear blue eyes, though prematurely serious at times, were utterly dissimilar to the shy hazel eyes of Mr Lawrence, whence the sensitive soul looked so distrustfully forth, as ever ready to retire within, from the offences of a too rude, too uncongenial world. Wretch that I was to harbour that detestable idea for a moment! Did I not know Mrs Graham? Had I not seen her, conversed with her time after time? Was I not certain that she, in intellect, in purity and elevation of soul, was immeasurably superior to any of her detractors; that she was, in fact, the noblest, the most adorable, of her sex I had ever beheld, or even imagined to exist? Yes, and I would say with Mary Millward (sensible girl as she was) that if all the parish, ay, or all the world should din these horrible lies in my ears, I would not believe them; for I knew her better than they.

Meantime, my brain was on fire with indignation, and my heart seemed ready to burst from its prison with conflicting passions. I regarded my two fair neighbours with a feeling of abhorrence and loathing I scarcely endeavoured to conceal: I was rallied from several quarters for my abstraction and ungallant neglect of the ladies; but I cared little for that: all I cared about, besides that one grand subject of my thoughts, was to see the cups travel up to the tea-tray, and not come down again. I thought Mr Millward never *would* cease telling us that he was no tea-drinker, and that it was highly injurious to keep loading the stomach with slops to the exclusion of more wholesome sustenance, and so give himself time to finish his fourth cup.

At length it was over; and I rose and left the table and the guests, without a word of apology – I could endure their company no longer. I rushed out to cool my brain in the balmy evening air, and to compose my mind, or indulge my passionate thoughts in the solitude of the garden.

To avoid being seen from the windows, I went down a quiet

little avenue, that skirted one side of the inclosure, at the bottom
of which was a seat embowered in roses and honeysuckles. Here
I sat down to think over the virtues and wrongs of the lady of
Wildfell Hall; but I had not been so occupied two minutes,
before voices and laughter, and glimpses of moving objects
through the trees, informed me that the whole company had
turned out to take an airing in the garden too. However, I
nestled up in a corner of the bower, and hoped to retain possession of it, secure alike from observation and intrusion. But no –
confound it – there was some one coming down the avenue!
Why couldn't they enjoy the flowers and sunshine of the open
garden, and leave that sunless nook to me, and the gnats and
midges?

But peeping through my fragrant screen of the interwoven
branches to discover who the intruders were (for a murmur of
voices told me it was more than one), my vexation instantly
subsided, and far other feelings agitated my still unquiet soul;
for there was Mrs Graham, slowly moving down the walk with
Arthur by her side, and no one else. Why were they alone? Had
the poison of detracting tongues already spread through all; and
had they all turned their backs upon her? I now recollected
having seen Mrs Wilson, in the early part of the evening, edging
her chair close up to my mother, and bending forward, evidently
in the delivery of some important confidential intelligence; and
from the incessant wagging of her head, the frequent distortions
of her wrinkled physiognomy, and the winking and malicious
twinkle of her little ugly eyes, I judged it was some spicy piece
of scandal that engaged her powers; and from the cautious
privacy of the communication, I supposed some person then
present, was the luckless object of her calumnies; and from all
these tokens, together with my mother's looks and gestures of
mingled horror and incredulity, I now concluded that object to
have been Mrs Graham. I did not emerge from my place of
concealment, till she had nearly reached the bottom of the walk,
lest my appearance should drive her away; and when I did step

forward she stood still and seemed inclined to turn back as it was.

'Oh, don't let us disturb you, Mr Markham!' said she. 'We came here to seek retirement ourselves; not to intrude on your seclusion.'

'I am no hermit, Mrs Graham – though I own it looks rather like it, to absent myself in this uncourteous fashion from my guests.'

'I feared you were unwell,' said she with a look of real concern.

'I was rather, but it's over now. Do sit here a little, and rest, and tell me how you like this arbour,' said I, and, lifting Arthur by the shoulders, I planted him in the middle of the seat by way of securing his mamma, who, acknowledging it to be a tempting place of refuge, threw herself back in one corner, while I took possession of the other.

But that word refuge disturbed me. Had their unkindness then really driven her to seek for peace in solitude?

'Why have they left you alone?' I asked.

'It is I who have left them,' was the smiling rejoinder. 'I was wearied to death with small talk – nothing wears me out like that. I cannot imagine how they *can* go on as they do.'

I could not help smiling at the serious depth of her wonderment.

'Is it that they think it a *duty* to be continually talking,' pursued she, 'and so never pause to think, but fill up with aimless trifles and vain repetitions, when subjects of real interest fail to present themselves, or do they really take a pleasure in such discourse?'

'Very likely they do,' said I: 'their shallow minds can hold no great ideas, and their light heads are carried away by trivialities, that would not move a better furnished skull; – and their only alternative to such discourse, is to plunge over head and ears into the slough of scandal – which is their chief delight.'

'Not all of them, surely?' cried the lady, astonished at the bitterness of my remark.

'No, certainly; I exonerate my sister from such degraded tastes – and my mother too, if you included *her* in your animadversions.'

'I meant no animadversions against any one, and certainly intended no disrespectful allusions to your mother. I have known some sensible persons great adepts in that style of conversation, when circumstances impelled them to it; but it is a gift I cannot boast the possession of. I kept up my attention, on this occasion, as long as I could, but when my powers were exhausted, I stole away, to seek a few minutes' repose in this quiet walk. I hate talking where there is no exchange of ideas or sentiments, and no good given or received.'

'Well,' said I, 'if ever I trouble you with my loquacity, tell me so at once, and I promise not to be offended; for I possess the faculty of enjoying the company of those I — of my friends as well in silence as in conversation.'

'I don't quite believe you; but if it were so, you would exactly suit me for a companion.'

'I am all you wish, then, in other respects?'

'No, I don't mean that. How beautiful those little clusters of foliage look, where the sun comes through behind them!' said she, on purpose to change the subject.

And they did look beautiful, where at intervals the level rays of the sun penetrating the thickness of trees and shrubs on the opposite side of the path before us, relieved their dusky verdure by displaying patches of semitransparent leaves of resplendent golden green.

'I almost wish I were not a painter,' observed my companion.

'Why so? one would think at such a time you would most exult in your privilege of being able to imitate the various brilliant and delightful touches of nature.'

'No; for instead of delivering myself up to the full enjoyment of them as others do, I am always troubling my head about how I could produce the same effect upon canvass; and as that can never be done, it is mere vanity and vexation of spirit.'

'Perhaps you cannot do it to satisfy yourself, but you may and do succeed in delighting others with the result of your endeavours.'

'Well, after all, I should not complain: perhaps few people gain their livelihood with so much pleasure in their toil as I do. Here is some one coming.'

She seemed vexed at the interruption.

'It is only Mr Lawrence and Miss Wilson,' said I, 'coming to enjoy a quiet stroll. They will not disturb us.'

I could not quite decipher the expression of her face; but I was satisfied there was no jealousy therein. What business had I to look for it?

'What sort of a person is Miss Wilson?' she asked.

'She is elegant and accomplished above the generality of her birth and station; and some say she is lady-like and agreeable.'

'I thought her somewhat frigid, and rather supercilious in her manner to-day.'

'Very likely she might be so to you. She has possibly taken a prejudice against you, for I think she regards you in the light of a rival.'

'Me? Impossible, Mr Markham!' said she, evidently astonished and annoyed.

'Well, I know nothing about it,' returned I, rather doggedly; for I thought her annoyance was chiefly against myself.

The pair had now approached within a few paces of us. Our arbour was set snugly back in a corner, before which, the avenue at its termination, turned off into the more airy walk along the bottom of the garden. As they approached this, I saw, by the aspect of Jane Wilson, that she was directing her companion's attention to us; and, as well by her cold, sarcastic smile, as by the few isolated words of her discourse that reached me, I knew full well that she was impressing him with the idea that we were strongly attached to each other. I noticed that he coloured up to the temples, gave us one furtive glance in passing, and walked on, looking grave, but seemingly offering no reply to her remarks.

It was true, then, that he *had* some designs upon Mrs Graham; and, were they honourable, he would not be so anxious to conceal them. *She* was blameless, of course, but he was detestable beyond all count.

While these thoughts flashed through my mind, my companion abruptly rose, and calling her son, said they would now go in quest of the company, and departed up the avenue. Doubtless she had heard or guessed something of Miss Wilson's remarks, and therefore, it was natural enough she should choose to continue the *tête-à-tête* no longer, especially as at that moment my cheeks were burning with indignation against my former friend, the token of which she might mistake for a blush of stupid embarrassment. For this I owed Miss Wilson yet another grudge; and still the more I thought upon her conduct, the more I hated her.

It was late in the evening before I joined the company. I found Mrs Graham already equipped for departure, and taking leave of the rest, who were now returned to the house. I offered – nay, begged to accompany her home. Mr Lawrence was standing by at the time conversing with some one else. He did not look at us, but, on hearing my earnest request, he paused in the middle of a sentence to listen for her reply, and went on, with a look of quiet satisfaction the moment he found it was to be a denial.

A denial it was, decided, though not unkind. She could not be persuaded to think there was danger for herself or her child in traversing those lonely lanes and fields without attendance. It was daylight still, and she should meet no one; or if she did, the people were quiet and harmless she was well assured. In fact, she would not hear of any one's putting himself out of the way to accompany her, though Fergus vouchsafed to offer his services, in case they should be more acceptable than mine, and my mother begged she might send one of the farming-men to escort her.

When she was gone, the rest was all a blank, or worse. Lawrence attempted to draw me into conversation, but I snubbed him, and went to another part of the room. Shortly after, the party broke up, and he himself took leave. When he came to me, I was blind to his extended hand, and deaf to his good night till he repeated it a second time; and then, to get rid of him, I muttered an inarticulate reply accompanied by a sulky nod.

'What is the matter, Markham?' whispered he.

I replied by a wrathful and contemptuous stare.

'Are you angry because Mrs Graham would not let you go home with her?' he asked with a faint smile that nearly exasperated me beyond controul.

But, swallowing down all fiercer answers, I merely demanded, –

'What business is it of yours?'

'Why, none,' replied he with provoking quietness; 'only,' and he raised his eyes to my face, and spoke with unusual solemnity, 'only let me tell you, Markham, that if you have any designs in that quarter they will certainly fail; and it grieves me to see you cherishing false hopes, and wasting your strength in useless efforts, for –'

'Hypocrite!' I exclaimed, and he held his breath, and looked very blank, turned white about the gills, and went away without another word.

I had wounded him to the quick; and I was glad of it.

CHAPTER X

A CONTRACT AND A QUARREL

WHEN ALL WERE gone, I learnt that the vile slander had indeed been circulated throughout the company, in the very presence of the victim. Rose, however, vowed she did not and would not believe it, and my mother made the same declaration, though not, I fear, with the same amount of real, unwavering incredulity. It seemed to dwell continually on her mind, and she kept irritating me from time to time by such expressions as – 'Dear, dear, who would have thought it! – Well! I always thought there was something odd about her. – You see what it is for women to affect to be different to other people.' And once it was, –

'I misdoubted that appearance of mystery from the very first – I *thought* there would no good come of it; but this is a sad, sad business, to be sure!'

'Why, mother, you said you didn't believe these tales,' said Fergus.

'No more I do, my dear; but then, you know, there must be some foundation.'

'The foundation is in the wickedness and falsehood of the world,' said I, 'and in the fact that Mr Lawrence has been seen to go that way once or twice of an evening – and the village gossips say he goes to pay his addresses to the strange lady, and the scandal mongers have greedily seized the rumour, to make it the basis of their own infernal structure.'

'Well, but Gilbert, there must be something in her *manner* to countenance such reports.'

'Did *you* see anything in her manner?'

'No, certainly; but then you know, I always said there was something strange about her.'

I believe it was on that very evening that I ventured on another invasion of Wildfell Hall. From the time of our party, which was upwards of a week ago, I had been making daily efforts to meet its mistress in her walks; and, always disappointed (she must have managed it so on purpose), had nightly kept revolving in my mind some pretext for another call. At length, I concluded that the separation could be endured no longer (by this time, you will see I was pretty far gone); and, taking from the book case an old volume that I thought she might be interested in, though, from its unsightly and somewhat dilapidated condition, I had not yet ventured to offer it for perusal, I hastened away, – but not without sundry misgivings as to how she would receive me, or how I could summon courage to present myself with so slight an excuse. But, perhaps, I might see her in the field or the garden, and then, there would be no great difficulty: it was the formal knocking at the door, with the prospect of being gravely ushered in, by Rachel, to the presence of a surprised, uncordial mistress, that so greatly disturbed me.

My wish, however, was not gratified. Mrs Graham, herself, was not to be seen; but there was Arthur playing with his frolicsome little dog in the garden. I looked over the gate and called him to me. He wanted me to come in; but I told him I could not without his mother's leave.

'I'll go and ask her,' said the child.

'No, no, Arthur, you mustn't do that, – but if she's not engaged, just ask her to come here a minute: tell her I want to speak to her.'

He ran to perform my bidding, and quickly returned with his mother. How lovely she looked with her dark ringlets streaming in the light summer breeze, her fair cheek slightly flushed, and her countenance radiant with smiles! – Dear Arthur! what did

I not owe to you for this and every other happy meeting? – Through him, I was at once delivered from all formality, and terror, and constraint. In love affairs, there is no mediator like a merry, simple-hearted child – ever ready to cement divided hearts, to span the unfriendly gulph of custom, to melt the ice of cold reserve, and overthrow the separating walls of dread formality and pride.

'Well, Mr Markham, what is it?' said the young mother, accosting me with a pleasant smile.

'I want you to look at this book, and, if you please, to take it, and peruse it at your leisure. I make no apology for calling you out on such a lovely evening though it *be* for a matter of no greater importance.'

'Tell him to come in, Mamma,' said Arthur.

'Would you like to come in?' asked the lady.

'Yes; I should like to see your improvements in the garden.'

'And how your sister's roots have prospered in my charge,' added she, as she opened the gate.

And we sauntered through the garden, and talked of the flowers, the trees, and the book, – and then of other things. The evening was kind and genial, and so was my companion. By degrees, I waxed more warm and tender than, perhaps, I had ever been before; but still, I said nothing tangible, and she attempted no repulse; until, in passing a moss rose-tree that I had brought her some weeks since, in my sister's name, she plucked a beautiful half open bud and bade me give it to Rose.

'May I not keep it myself?' I asked.

'No; but here is another for you.'

Instead of taking it quietly, I likewise took the hand that offered it, and looked into her face. She let me hold it for a moment, and I saw a flash of extatic brilliance in her eye, a glow of glad excitement on her face – I thought my hour of victory was come – but instantly, a painful recollection seemed to flash upon her; a cloud of anguish darkened her brow, a marble paleness blanched her cheek and lip; there seemed a moment of inward conflict, – and with a sudden effort, she withdrew her hand, and retreated a step or two back.

'Now Mr Markham,' said she, with a kind of desperate calmness, 'I must tell you plainly, that I cannot do with this. I like your company, because I am alone here, and your conversation pleases me more than that of any other person; but if you cannot be content to regard me as a friend – a plain, cold, motherly, or sisterly friend, I must beg you to leave me now, and let me alone hereafter – in fact, we must be strangers for the future.'

'I will, then – be your friend, – or brother, or anything you wish, if you will only let me continue to see you; but tell me why I cannot be anything more?'

There was a perplexed and thoughtful pause.

'Is it in consequence of some rash vow?'

'It is something of the kind,' she answered – 'some day I may tell you, but, at present you had better leave me; and never, Gilbert, put me to the painful necessity of repeating what I have just now said to you!' – she earnestly added, giving me her hand in serious kindness. How sweet, how musical my own name sounded in her mouth!

'I will not,' I replied. 'But you pardon *this* offence?'

'On condition that you never repeat it.'

'And may I come to see you now and then?'

'Perhaps, – occasionally; provided you never abuse the privilege.'

'I make no empty promises, but you shall see.'

'The moment you do, our intimacy is at an end, that's all.'

'And will you always call me Gilbert? – it sounds more sisterly, and it will serve to remind me of our contract.'

She smiled, and once more bid me go, – and, at length, I judged it prudent to obey; and she re-entered the house, and I went down the hill. But as I went, the tramp of horses' hoofs fell on my ear, and broke the stillness of the dewy evening; and, looking towards the lane, I saw a solitary equestrian coming up. Inclining to dusk as it was, I knew him at a glance: it was

Mr Lawrence on his grey pony. I flew across the field – leaped the stone fence – and then walked down the lane to meet him. On seeing me, he suddenly drew in his little steed, and seemed inclined to turn back, but on second thought, apparently judged it better to continue his course as before. He accosted me with a slight bow, and, edging close to the wall, endeavoured to pass on – but I was not so minded: seizing his horse by the bridle, I exclaimed: –

'Now Lawrence, I will have this mystery explained! Tell me where you are going, and what you mean to do – at once, and distinctly!'

'Will you take your hand off the bridle?' said he, quietly – 'you're hurting my pony's mouth.'

'You and your pony be —'

'What makes you so coarse and brutal, Markham? I'm quite ashamed of you.'

'You answer my questions – before you leave this spot! I *will* know what you mean by this perfidious duplicity?'

'I shall answer *no* questions till you let go the bridle, – if you stand till morning.'

'Now then,' said I, unclosing my hand, but still standing before him.

'Ask me some other time, when you can speak like a gentleman,' returned he, and he made an effort to pass me again; but I quickly recaptured the pony scarce less astonished than its master at such uncivil usage.

'Really, Mr Markham, this is *too* much!' said the latter. 'Can I not go to see my tenant on matters of business, without being assaulted in this manner by –'

'This is no time for business, sir! – I'll tell you, now, what I think of your conduct.'

'You'd better defer your opinion to a more convenient season,' interrupted he in a low tone – 'here's the vicar.'

And in truth, the vicar was just behind me, plodding homeward from some remote corner of his parish. I immediately released the squire; and he went on his way, saluting Mr Millward as he passed.

'What, quarrelling Markham?' cried the latter, addressing himself to me, – 'and about that young widow I doubt,' he added, reproachfully shaking his head. 'But let me tell you young man' (here he put his face into mine with an important, confidential air), 'she's not worth it!' and he confirmed the assertion by a solemn nod.

'Mr MILLWARD!' I exclaimed, in a tone of wrathful menace that made the reverend gentleman look round – aghast – astounded at such unwonted insolence, and stare me in the face, with a look that plainly said: 'What, this to me!' But I was too indignant to apologize, or to speak another word to him: I turned away, and hastened homewards, descending with rapid strides the steep, rough lane, and leaving him to follow as he pleased.

CHAPTER XI

THE VICAR AGAIN

YOU MUST SUPPOSE about three weeks past over. Mrs Graham and I were now established friends – or brother and sister as we rather chose to consider ourselves. She called me Gilbert, by my express desire, and I called her Helen, for I had seen that name written in her books. I seldom attempted to see her above twice a week; and still I made our meetings appear the result of accident as often as I could – for I found it necessary to be extremely careful – and, altogether, I behaved with such exceeding propriety that she never had occasion to reprove me once. Yet I could not but perceive that she was at times unhappy and dissatisfied with herself – or her position, and truly I myself was not quite contented with the latter: this assumption of brotherly nonchalance was very hard to sustain, and I often felt myself a most confounded hypocrite with it all; I saw too, or rather I felt, that, in spite of herself, 'I was not indifferent to her,' as the novel heroes modestly express it, and while I thankfully enjoyed my present good fortune, I could not fail to wish and hope for something better in future; but of course, I kept such dreams entirely to myself.

'Where are you going Gilbert?' said Rose, one evening, shortly after tea, when I had been busy with the farm all day.

'To take a walk,' was the reply.

'Do you always brush your hat so carefully, and do your hair so nicely, and put on such smart new gloves when you take a walk?'

'Not always.'

'You're going to Wildfell Hall, aren't you?'

'What makes you think so?'

'Because you look as if you were – but I wish you wouldn't go so often.'

'Nonsense child! I don't go once in six weeks – what do you mean?'

'Well, but if I were you, I wouldn't have so much to do with Mrs Graham.'

'Why Rose, are you, too, giving in to the prevailing opinion?'

'No,' returned she, hesitatingly – 'but I've heard so much about her lately, both at the Wilsons and the vicarage; – and besides, mamma says, if she were a proper person, she would not be living there by herself – and don't you remember last winter, Gilbert, all that about the false name to the picture; and how she explained it – saying she had friends or acquaintances from whom she wished her present residence to be concealed, and that she was afraid of their tracing her out; – and then, how suddenly she started up and left the room when that person came – whom she took good care not to let us catch a glimpse of, and who Arthur, with such an air of mystery, told us was his mamma's friend?'

'Yes Rose, I remember it all; and I can forgive your uncharitable conclusions; for perhaps, if I did not know her myself, I should put all these things together, and believe the same as you do; but thank God, I do know her; and I should be unworthy the name of a man, if I could believe anything that was said against her, unless I heard it from her own lips. – I should as soon believe such things of you, Rose.'

'Oh, Gilbert!'

'Well, do you think I *could* believe anything of the kind, – whatever the Wilsons and Millwards dared to whisper?'

'I should hope *not* indeed!'

'And why not? – Because I know you well, and I know her just as well.'

'Oh, no! you know nothing of her former life; and last year at this time, you did not know that such a person existed.'

'No matter. There is such a thing as looking through a person's eyes into the heart, and learning more of the height, and breadth, and depth of another's soul in one hour, than it might take you a life time to discover, if he or she were not disposed to reveal it, – or if you had not the sense to understand it.'

'Then you *are* going to see her this evening?'

'To be sure I am!'

'But what would mamma say, Gilbert!'

'Mamma needn't know.'

'But she must know some time, if you go on.'

'Go on! – there's no going on in the matter – Mrs Graham and I are two friends – and will be; and no man breathing shall hinder it, – or has a right to interfere between us.'

'But if you knew how they talk, you would be more careful – for her sake as well as for your own. Jane Wilson thinks your visits to the old Hall but another proof of her depravity –'

'Confound Jane Wilson!'

'And Eliza Millward is quite grieved about you.'

'I hope she is.'

'But I wouldn't if I were you.'

'Wouldn't what? – How do they know that I go there?'

'There's nothing hid from them: they spy out everything.'

'O, I never thought of this! – And so they dare to turn my friendship into food for further scandal against her! – That proves the falsehood of their other lies, at all events, if any proof were wanting. – Mind you contradict them Rose, whenever you can.'

'But they don't speak openly to me about such things: it is only by hints and innuendoes, and by what I hear others say, that I know what they think.'

'Well, then, I won't go to-day, as it's getting latish. But oh, deuce take their cursed envenomed tongues!' I muttered, in the bitterness of my soul.

And just at that moment, the vicar entered the room: we had been too much absorbed in our conversation to observe his knock. After his customary, cheerful and fatherly greeting of Rose, who was rather a favourite with the old gentleman, he turned somewhat sternly to me: –

'Well sir!' said he, 'you're quite a stranger. It is – let – me – see,' he continued, slowly, as he deposited his ponderous bulk in the arm-chair that Rose officiously brought towards him, 'it is just – six – weeks – by my reckoning, since you darkened – my – door!' He spoke it with emphasis, and struck his stick on the floor.

'Is it, sir?' said I.

'Ay! It is so!' He added an affirmatory nod, and continued to gaze upon me with a kind of irate solemnity, holding his substantial stick between his knees, with his hands clasped upon its head.

'I have been busy,' I said, for an apology was evidently demanded.

'Busy!' repeated he derisively.

'Yes you know I've been getting in my hay; and now the harvest is beginning.'

'Humph!'

Just then my mother came in, and created a diversion in my favour, by her loquacious and animated welcome of the reverend guest. She regretted deeply that he had not come a little earlier, in time for tea, but offered to have some immediately prepared, if he would do her the favour to partake of it.

'Not any for me, I thank you,' replied he; 'I shall be at home in a few minutes.'

'Oh, but do stay and take a little! it will be ready in five minutes.'

But he rejected the offer, with a majestic wave of the hand.

'I'll tell you what I'll take, Mrs Markham,' said he: 'I'll take a glass of your excellent ale.'

'With pleasure!' cried my mother, proceeding with alacrity to pull the bell and order the favoured beverage.

'I thought,' continued he, 'I'd just look in upon you as I passed, and taste your home-brewed ale. I've been to call on Mrs Graham.'

'Have you indeed?'

He nodded gravely, and added with awful emphasis –

'I thought it incumbent upon me to do so.'

'Really!' ejaculated my mother.

'Why so, Mr Millward?' asked I. He looked at me with some severity, and turning again to my mother, repeated –

'I thought it incumbent upon me!' and struck his stick on the floor again. My mother sat opposite, an awe-struck but admiring auditor.

' "Mrs Graham," said I,' he continued, shaking his head as he spoke, ' "these are terrible reports!" "What sir?" says she, affecting to be ignorant of my meaning. "It is my – duty – as – your pastor," said I, "to tell you both everything that I myself see reprehensible in your conduct, and all I have reason to suspect, and what others tell me concerning you." – So I told her!'

'You did sir?' cried I, starting from my seat, and striking my fist on the table. He merely glanced towards me, and continued – addressing his hostess: –

'It was a painful duty, Mrs Markham – but I told her!'

'And how did she take it?' asked my mother.

'Hardened, I fear – hardened!' he replied, with a despondent shake of the head; 'and at the same time, there was a strong display of unchastened, misdirected passions. She turned white in the face, and drew her breath through her teeth in a savage sort of way; – but she offered no extenuation or defence; and with a kind of shameless calmness – shocking indeed to witness, in one so young – as good as told me that my remonstrance was unavailing, and my pastoral advice quite thrown away upon her – nay, that my very *presence* was displeasing while I spoke such things. And I withdrew at length, too plainly seeing that nothing could be done – and sadly grieved to find her case so hopeless. But I am fully determined, Mrs Markham, that *my* daughters – shall – not – consort with her. Do you adopt the same resolution with regard to yours! – As for your sons – as for *you*, young man,' he continued, sternly turning to me.

'As for ME, sir,' – I began, but checked by some impediment in my utterance, and finding that my whole frame trembled with fury, I said no more – but took the wiser part of snatching up my hat and bolting from the room, slamming the door behind me, with a bang that shook the house to its foundations, and made my mother scream – and gave a momentary relief to my excited feelings.

The next minute saw me hurrying with rapid strides in the direction of Wildfell Hall – to what intent or purpose I could scarcely tell, but I must be moving somewhere, and no other goal would do – I must see her too, and speak to her – that was certain, but what to say or how to act, I had no definite idea. Such stormy thoughts – so many different resolutions crowded in upon me, that my mind was little better than a chaos of conflicting passions.

CHAPTER XII

A *TÊTE-À-TÊTE* AND A DISCOVERY

In little more than twenty minutes, the journey was accomplished. I paused at the gate to wipe my streaming forehead, and recover my breath and some degree of composure. Already the rapid walking had somewhat mitigated my excitement; and with a firm and steady tread, I paced the garden walk. In passing the inhabited wing of the building, I caught a sight of Mrs Graham, through the open window, slowly pacing up and down her lonely room.

She seemed agitated, and even dismayed at my arrival, as if she thought, I too was coming to accuse her. I had entered her presence intending to condole with her upon the wickedness of the world, and help her to abuse the vicar and his vile informants, but now I felt positively ashamed to mention the subject, and determined not to refer to it, unless she led the way.

'I am come at an unseasonable hour,' said I, assuming a cheerfulness I did not feel, in order to reassure her; 'but I won't stay many minutes.'

She smiled upon me, faintly it is true, but most kindly – I had almost said thankfully, as her apprehensions were removed.

'How dismal you are, Helen! Why have you no fire?' I said, looking round on the gloomy apartment.

'It is summer yet,' she replied.

'But *we always* have a fire in the evenings – if we can bear it; – and you especially require one in this cold house and dreary room.'

'You should have come a little sooner, and I would have had

one lighted for you; but it is not worth while now – you won't stay many minutes you say, and Arthur is gone to bed.'

'But I have a fancy for a fire, nevertheless. Will you order one, if I ring?'

'Why Gilbert, you don't *look* cold!' said she, smilingly regarding my face, which no doubt seemed warm enough.

'No,' replied I, 'but I want to see you comfortable before I go.'

'Me comfortable!' repeated she, with a bitter laugh, as if there were something amusingly absurd in the idea. 'It suits me better as it is,' she added, in a tone of mournful resignation.

But determined to have my own way I pulled the bell.

'There now, Helen!' I said, as the approaching steps of Rachel were heard in answer to the summons. There was nothing for it but to turn round and desire the maid to light the fire.

I owe Rachel a grudge to this day for the look she cast upon me ere she departed on her mission – the sour, suspicious, inquisitorial look that plainly demanded, 'what are *you* here for, I wonder?' Her mistress did not fail to notice it, and a shade of uneasiness darkened her brow.

'You must not stay long Gilbert,' said she, when the door was closed upon us.

'I'm not going to,' said I, somewhat testily, though without a grain of anger in my heart against any one but the meddling old woman. 'But Helen, I've something to say to you before I go.'

'What is it?'

'No, not now – I don't know yet precisely what it is – or how to say it,' replied I, with more truth than wisdom; and then, fearing lest she should turn me out of the house, I began talking about indifferent matters in order to gain time. Meanwhile Rachel came in to kindle the fire, which was soon effected by thrusting a red-hot poker between the bars of the grate, where the fuel was already disposed for ignition. She honoured me with another of her hard, inhospitable looks in departing, but, little moved thereby, I went on talking; and setting a chair for Mrs Graham on one side of the hearth and one for myself on the other, I ventured to sit down, though half suspecting she would rather see me go.

In a little while we both relapsed into silence, and continued for several minutes gazing abstractedly into the fire – she intent upon her own sad thoughts, and I reflecting how delightful it would be to be seated thus beside her with no other presence to restrain our intercourse – not even that of Arthur, our mutual friend, without whom we had never met before – if only I could venture to speak my mind, and disburden my full heart of the feelings that had so long oppressed it, and which it now struggled to retain, with an effort that it seemed impossible to continue much longer, – and revolving the pros and cons for opening my heart to her there and then, and imploring a return of affection, the permission to regard her thenceforth as my own, and the right and the power to defend her from the calumnies of malicious tongues. On the one hand, I felt a new-born confidence in my powers of persuasion – a strong conviction that my own fervour of spirit would grant me eloquence – that my very determination – the absolute necessity for succeeding that I felt – must win me what I sought; while on the other, I feared to lose the ground I had already gained with so much toil and skill, and destroy all future hope by one rash effort, when time and patience might have won success. It was like setting my life upon the cast of a die; and yet I was ready to resolve upon the attempt. At any rate I would entreat the explanation she had half promised to give me before: I would demand the reason of this hateful barrier, this mysterious impediment to my happiness, and, as I trusted, to her own.

But while I considered in what manner I could best frame my request, my companion wakened from her reverie with a scarcely audible sigh, and looking towards the window where the blood-red harvest moon, just rising over one of the grim, fantastic evergreens, was shining in upon us, said, –

'Gilbert, it is getting late.'

'I see,' said I. 'You want me to go, I suppose.'

'I think you ought. If my kind neighbours get to know of this visit – as no doubt they will – they will not turn it much to my advantage.'

It was with what the Vicar would doubtless have called a savage sort of smile that she said this.

'Let them turn it as they will,' said I. 'What are their thoughts to you or me, so long as we are satisfied with ourselves – and each other? Let them go to the deuce with their vile constructions, and their lying inventions!'

This outburst brought a flush of colour to her face.

'You have heard, then, what they say of me?'

'I heard some detestable falsehoods; but none but fools would credit them for a moment, Helen, so don't let them trouble you.'

'I did not think Mr Millward a fool, and he believes it all; but however little you may value the opinions of those about you – however little you may esteem them as individuals, it is not pleasant to be looked upon as a liar and a hypocrite, to be thought to practice what you abhor, and to encourage the vices you would discountenance, to find your good intentions frustrated, and your hands crippled by your supposed unworthiness, and to bring disgrace on the principles you profess.'

'True; and if I, by my thoughtlessness and selfish disregard to appearances, have at all assisted to expose you to these evils, let me entreat you not only to pardon me, but to enable me to make reparation; authorize me to clear your name from every imputation: give me the right to identify your honour with my own, and to defend your reputation as more precious than my life!'

'Are you hero enough to unite yourself to one whom you know to be suspected and despised by all around you, and identify your interests and your honour with hers? Think! it is a serious thing.'

'I should be proud to do it Helen! – most happy – delighted beyond expression! – and if that be all the obstacle to our union, it is demolished, and you must – you shall be mine!'

And starting from my seat in a frenzy of ardour, I seized her hand and would have pressed it to my lips, but she as suddenly caught it away, exclaiming in the bitterness of intense affliction: –

'No, no, it is not all!'

'What is it then? You promised I should know some time, and –'

'You shall know some time – but not now – my head aches terribly,' she said, pressing her hand to her forehead, 'and I must have some repose – and surely, I have had misery enough to-day!' she added, almost wildly.

'But it could not harm you to tell it,' I persisted: 'it would ease your mind; and I should then know how to comfort you.'

She shook her head despondingly. 'If you knew all, you, too, would blame me – perhaps even more than I deserve – though I have cruelly wronged you,' she added in a low murmur, as if she mused aloud.

'*You*, Helen? Impossible!'

'Yes, not willingly; for I did not know the strength and depth of your attachment – I thought – at least I endeavoured to think your regard for me was as cold and fraternal as you professed it to be.'

'Or as yours?'

'Or as mine – ought to have been – of such a light and selfish, superficial nature, that –'

'*There*, indeed, you wronged me.'

'I know I did; and, sometimes, I suspected it then; but I thought, upon the whole, there could be no great harm in leaving your fancies and your hopes to dream themselves to nothing – or flutter away to some more fitting object, while your friendly sympathies remained with me; but if I had known the depth of your regard, the generous disinterested affection you seem to feel –'

'*Seem*, Helen?'

'That you *do* feel, then, I would have acted differently.'

'How? You *could* not have given me less encouragement, or

treated me with greater severity than you did! And if you think you have wronged me by giving me your friendship, and occasionally admitting me to the enjoyment of your company and conversation, when all hopes of closer intimacy were vain – as indeed you always gave me to understand – if you think you have wronged me by this, you are mistaken; for such favours, in themselves alone, are not only delightful to my heart, but purifying, exalting, ennobling to my soul; and I would rather have your friendship than the love of any other woman in the world!'

Little comforted by this, she clasped her hands upon her knee, and glancing upward, seemed, in silent anguish, to implore divine assistance; then turning to me, she calmly said –

'To-morrow, if you meet me on the moor about mid-day, I will tell you all you seek to know; and perhaps you will then see the necessity of discontinuing our intimacy – if, indeed, you do not willingly resign me as one no longer worthy of regard.'

'I can safely answer no, to that: you cannot have such grave confessions to make – you must be trying my faith, Helen.'

'No, no, no,' she earnestly repeated – 'I wish it were so! Thank Heaven,' she added, 'I have no great crime to confess; but I have more than you will like to hear, or, perhaps, can readily excuse, – and more than I can tell you now; so let me entreat you to leave me!'

'I will; but answer me this one question first: – do you love me?'

'I will not answer it!'

'Then I will conclude you do; and so good night.'

She turned from me to hide the emotion she could not quite controul; but I took her hand and fervently kissed it.

'Gilbert, *do* leave me!' she cried, in a tone of such thrilling anguish that I felt it would be cruel to disobey.

But I gave one look back before I closed the door, and saw her leaning forward on the table, with her hands pressed against her eyes, sobbing convulsively; yet I withdrew in silence. I felt

that to obtrude my consolations on her then would only serve
to aggravate her sufferings.

To tell you all the questionings and conjectures – the fears,
and hopes, and wild emotions that jostled and chased each
other through my mind as I descended the hill, would almost
fill a volume in itself. But before I was half way down a sentiment of strong sympathy for her I had left behind me had
displaced all other feelings, and seemed imperatively to draw
me back: I began to think, 'Why am I hurrying so fast in this
direction? Can I find comfort or consolation – peace, certainty,
contentment, all – or anything that I want at home? and can
I leave all perturbation, sorrow and anxiety behind me there?'

And I turned to look at the old Hall. There was little besides
the chimneys visible above my contracted horizon. I walked
back to get a better view of it. When it rose in sight, I stood
still a moment to look, and then continued moving towards the
gloomy object of attraction. Something called me nearer –
nearer still – and why not, pray? Might I not find more benefit in the contemplation of that venerable pile with the full moon
in the cloudless heaven shining so calmly above it – with that
warm yellow lustre peculiar to an August night – and the mistress of my soul within, than in returning to my home where all
comparatively was light, and life, and cheerfulness, and therefore
inimical to me in my present frame of mind, – and the more so
that its inmates all were more or less imbued with that detestable
belief the very *thought* of which made my blood boil in my
veins – and how could I endure to hear it openly declared – or
cautiously insinuated – which was worse? – I had had trouble
enough already, with some babbling fiend that would keep
whispering in my ear, 'It may be true,' till I had shouted aloud,
'It is false! I defy you to make me suppose it!'

I could see the red fire-light dimly gleaming from her parlour
window. I went up to the garden wall, and stood leaning over it,
with my eyes fixed upon the lattice, wondering what she was
doing, thinking, or suffering now, and wishing I could speak to

her but one word, or even catch one glimpse of her, before I went.

I had not thus looked, and wished, and wondered long, before I vaulted over the barrier, unable to resist the temptation of taking one glance through the window, just to see if she were more composed than when we parted; – and if I found her still in deep distress, perhaps I might venture to attempt a word of comfort – to utter one of the many things I should have said before, instead of aggravating her sufferings by my stupid impetuosity. I looked. Her chair was vacant: so was the room. But at that moment some one opened the outer door, and a voice – *her* voice – said, –

'Come out – I want to see the moon, and breathe the evening air: they will do me good – if anything will.'

Here, then, were she and Rachel coming to take a walk in the garden. I wished myself safe back over the wall. I stood, however, in the shadow of the tall holly bush, which, standing between the window and the porch, at present screened me from observation, but did not prevent me from seeing two figures come forth into the moonlight: Mrs Graham followed by another – *not* Rachel, but a young man, slender and rather tall. Oh Heavens, how my temples throbbed! Intense anxiety darkened my sight; but I thought – yes, and the voice confirmed it – it was Mr Lawrence.

'You should not let it worry you so much, Helen,' said he; 'I will be more cautious in future; and in time –'

I did not hear the rest of the sentence; for he walked close beside her and spoke so gently that I could not catch the words. My heart was splitting with hatred; but I listened intently for her reply. I heard it plainly enough.

'But I must leave this place, Frederick,' she said – 'I never can be happy here, – nor anywhere else, indeed,' she added, with a mirthless laugh, – 'but I cannot rest here.'

'But where could you find a better place?' replied he, – 'so secluded – so near me, if you think anything of that.'

'Yes,' interrupted she, 'it is all I could wish, if they could only have left me alone.'

'But wherever you go, Helen, there will be the same sources of annoyance. I cannot consent to lose you: I must go with you, or come to you; and there are meddling fools elsewhere, as well as here.'

While thus conversing they had sauntered slowly past me, down the walk, and I heard no more of their discourse; but I saw him put his arm round her waist, while she lovingly rested her hand on his shoulder; – and then, a tremulous darkness obscured my sight, my heart sickened and my head burned like fire. I half rushed, half staggered from the spot where horror had kept me rooted, and leaped or tumbled over the wall – I hardly know which – but I know that, afterwards, like a passionate child, I dashed myself on the ground and lay there in a paroxysm of anger and despair – how long, I cannot undertake to say; but it must have been a considerable time; for when, having partially relieved myself by a torment of tears, and looked up at the moon, shining so calmly and carelessly on, as little influenced by my misery as I was by its peaceful radiance, and earnestly prayed for death or forgetfulness, I had risen and journeyed homewards – little regarding the way, but carried instinctively by my feet to the door, I found it bolted against me, and every one in bed except my mother, who hastened to answer my impatient knocking, and received me with a shower of questions and rebukes.

'Oh, Gilbert! how *could* you do so? Where *have* you been? Do come in and take your supper – I've got it all ready, though you don't deserve it, for keeping me in such a fright, after the strange manner you left the house this evening. Mr Millward was quite – Bless the boy! how ill he looks! Oh, gracious! what is the matter?'

'Nothing, nothing – give me a candle.'

'But won't you take some supper?'

'No, I want to go to bed,' said I, taking a candle and lighting it at the one she held in her hand.

'Oh, Gilbert, how you tremble!' exclaimed my anxious parent. 'How white you look! – Do tell me what it is? Has anything happened?'

'It's nothing,' cried I, ready to stamp with vexation because the candle would not light. Then, suppressing my irritation, I added, 'I've been walking too fast, that's all. Good night,' and marched off to bed, regardless of the 'Walking too fast! where have you been?' that was called after me from below.

My mother followed me to the very door of my room with her questionings and advice concerning my health and my conduct; but I implored her to let me alone till morning; and she withdrew, and at length, I had the satisfaction to hear her close her own door. There was no sleep for me, however, that night, as I thought; and instead of attempting to solicit it, I employed myself in rapidly pacing the chamber – having first removed my boots lest my mother should hear me. But the boards creaked, and she was watchful. I had not walked above a quarter of an hour before she was at the door again.

'Gilbert, why are you not in bed – you said you wanted to go?'

'Confound it! I'm going,' said I.

'But why are you so long about it? you must have something on your mind –'

'For Heaven's sake, let me alone, and get to bed yourself!'

'Can it be that Mrs Graham that distresses you so!'

'No, no, I tell you – it's nothing.'

'I wish to goodness it mayn't!' murmured she, with a sigh, as she returned to her own apartment, while I threw myself on the bed, feeling most undutifully disaffected towards her for having deprived me of what seemed the only shadow of a consolation that remained, and chained me to that wretched couch of thorns.

Never did I endure so long, so miserable a night as that. And yet, it was not wholly sleepless: towards morning my distracting thoughts began to lose all pretensions to coherency, and shape themselves into confused and feverish dreams, and, at length, there followed an interval of unconscious slumber. But then the dawn of bitter recollection that succeeded – the waking to find life a blank, and worse than a blank – teeming with torment and misery – not a mere barren wilderness, but full of thorns and briars – to find myself deceived, duped, hopeless, my affections trampled upon, my angel not an angel, and my friend a fiend incarnate – it was worse than if I had not slept at all.

It was a dull, gloomy morning, the weather had changed like my prospects, and the rain was pattering against the window. I rose nevertheless, and went out; not to look after the farm, though that would serve as my excuse, but to cool my brain, and regain, if possible, a sufficient degree of composure to meet the family at the morning meal without exciting inconvenient remarks. If I got a wetting, that, in conjunction with a pretended over exertion before breakfast, might excuse my sudden loss of appetite; and if a cold ensued, the severer the better, it would help to account for the sullen moods and moping melancholy likely to cloud my brow for long enough.

CHAPTER XIII

A RETURN TO DUTY

'MY DEAR GILBERT, I wish you *would* try to be a little more amiable,' said my mother one morning after some display of unjustifiable ill humour on my part. 'You say there is nothing the matter with you, and nothing has happened to grieve you, and yet, I never *saw* any one so altered as you within these last few days: you haven't a good word for any body-friends and strangers, equals and inferiors – it's all the same. I do wish you'd try to check it.'

'Check what?'

'Why, your strange temper. You don't know *how* it spoils you. I'm sure a finer disposition than yours, by nature, could not be, if you'd let it have fair play; so you've no excuse *that* way.'

While she thus remonstrated, I took up a book, and laying it open on the table before me, pretended to be deeply absorbed in its perusal; for I was equally unable to justify myself, and unwilling to acknowledge my errors; and I wished to have nothing to say on the matter. But my excellent parent went on lecturing, and then came to coaxing, and began to stroke my hair; and I was getting to feel quite a good boy, but my mischievous brother who was idling about the room, revived my corruption by suddenly calling out: –

'Don't touch him mother! he'll bite! He's a very tiger in human form. *I've* given him up, for my part – fairly disowned him – cast him off, root and branch. It's as much as my life is worth to come within six yards of him. The other day he nearly fractured my skull for singing a pretty, inoffensive love song, on purpose to amuse him.'

'Oh, Gilbert! how could you?' exclaimed my mother.

'I told you to hold your noise first, you know Fergus,' said I.

'Yes, but when I assured you it was no trouble, and went on with the next verse, thinking you might like it better, you clutched me by the shoulder and dashed me away, right against the wall there, with such force, that I thought I had bitten my tongue in two, and expected to see the place plastered with my brains; and when I put my hand to my head and found my skull not broken, I thought it was a miracle and no mistake. But poor fellow!' added he, with a sentimental sigh – 'his heart's broken – that's the truth of it – and his head's –'

'Will you be silent NOW?' cried I, starting up, and eyeing the fellow so fiercely that my mother, thinking I meant to inflict some grievous bodily injury, laid her hand on my arm, and besought me to let him alone, and he walked leisurely out, with his hands in his pockets, singing provokingly – 'Shall I because a woman's fair,' &c.

'I'm not going to defile my fingers with him,' said I, in answer to the maternal intercession. 'I wouldn't touch him with the tongs.'

I now recollected that I had business with Robert Wilson, concerning the purchase of a certain field adjoining my farm – a business I had been putting off from day to day; for I had no interest in anything now; and besides, I was misanthropically inclined, and, moreover, had a particular objection to meeting Jane Wilson or her mother; for though I had too good reason, now, to credit their reports concerning Mrs Graham, I did not like *them* a bit the better for it – or Eliza Millward either – and the thought of meeting them was the more repugnant to me, that I could not, now, defy their seeming calumnies and triumph in my own convictions as before. But to-day, I determined to make an effort to return to my duty. Though I found no pleasure in it, it would be less irksome than idleness – at all events it would be more profitable. If life promised no enjoyment within my vocation, at least it offered no allurements out of it; and henceforth, I would put my shoulder to the wheel and toil away, like any poor drudge of a cart-horse that was fairly broken in to its labour, and plod through life, not wholly useless if not agreeable, and uncomplaining if not contented with my lot.

Thus resolving, with a kind of sullen resignation, if such a term may be allowed, I wended my way to Ryecote Farm, scarcely expecting to find its owner within at this time of day, but hoping to learn in what part of the premises he was most likely to be found.

Absent he was, but expected home in a few minutes; and I was desired to step into the parlour and wait. Mrs Wilson was busy in the kitchen, but the room was not empty; and I scarcely checked an involuntary recoil as I entered it; for there sat Miss

Wilson chattering with Eliza Millward. However, I determined to be cool and civil. Eliza seemed to have made the same resolution on her part. We had not met since the evening of the tea party; but there was no visible emotion either of pleasure or pain, no attempt at pathos, no display of injured pride: she was cool in temper, civil in demeanour. There was even an ease and cheerfulness about her air and manner that I made no pretension to; but there was a depth of malice in her too expressive eye, that plainly told me I was not forgiven; for, though she no longer hoped to win me to herself, she still hated her rival, and evidently delighted to wreak her spite on me. On the other hand, Miss Wilson was as affable and courteous as heart could wish, and though I was in no very conversable humour myself, the two ladies between them managed to keep up a pretty continuous fire of small talk. But Eliza took advantage of the first convenient pause to ask if I had lately seen Mrs Graham, in a tone of merely casual inquiry, but with a sidelong glance – intended to be playfully mischievous – really, brimful and running over with malice.

'Not lately,' I replied, in a careless tone, but sternly repelling her odious glances with my eyes; for I was vexed to feel the colour mounting to my forehead, despite my strenuous efforts to appear unmoved.

'What! are you beginning to tire already? I thought so noble a creature would have power to attach you for a year at least!'

'I would rather not speak of her now.'

'Ah! then you are convinced at last, of your mistake – you have at length discovered that your divinity is not quite the immaculate –'

'I desired you not to speak of her, Miss Eliza.'

'Oh, I beg your pardon! I perceive Cupid's arrows have been too sharp for you: the wounds being more than skin-deep, are not yet healed and bleed afresh at every mention of the loved one's name.'

'Say rather,' interposed Miss Wilson, 'that Mr Markham feels that name is unworthy to be mentioned in the presence of right-minded females. I wonder Eliza, you should think of referring to that unfortunate person – you might know the mention of her would be anything but agreeable to any one here present.'

How could this be borne? I rose and was about to clap my hat upon my head and burst away, in wrathful indignation, from the house; but recollecting – just in time to save my dignity – the folly of such a proceeding, and how it would only give my fair tormentors a merry laugh at my expense, for the sake of one I acknowledged in my own heart to be unworthy of the slightest sacrifice – though the ghost of my former reverence and love so hung about me still, that I could not bear to hear her name aspersed by others – I merely walked to the window, and having spent a few seconds in vengibly biting my lips and sternly repressing the passionate heavings of my chest, I observed to Miss Wilson, that I could see nothing of her brother, and added that, as my time was precious, it would perhaps be better to call again to-morrow, at some time when I should be sure to find him at home.

'Oh, no!' said she; 'if you wait a minute, he will be sure to come; for he has business at L—' (that was our market town) 'and will require a little refreshment before he goes.'

I submitted accordingly, with the best grace I could; and happily, I had not long to wait. Mr Wilson soon arrived, and, indisposed for business as I was at that moment, and little as I cared for the field or its owner, I forced my attention to the matter in hand, with very creditable determination, and quickly concluded the bargain – perhaps more to the thrifty farmer's satisfaction, than he cared to acknowledge. Then, leaving him to the discussion of his substantial 'refreshment,' I gladly quitted the house, and went to look after my reapers.

Leaving them busy at work on the side of the valley, I ascended the hill, intending to visit a corn-field in the more elevated regions, and see when it would be ripe for the sickle. But I did *not* visit it that day; for, as I approached, I beheld at no great distance, Mrs Graham and her son coming down in the opposite direction. They saw me; and Arthur, already, was running to meet me; but I immediately turned back and walked steadily homeward; for I had fully determined never to encounter his mother again; and regardless of the shrill voice in my ear, calling upon me to 'wait a moment,' I pursued the even tenor of my way; and he soon relinquished the pursuit as hopeless, or was called away by his mother. At all events, when I looked back, five minutes after, not a trace of either was to be seen.

This incident agitated and disturbed me most unaccountably – unless you would account for it by saying that Cupid's arrows not only had been too sharp for me, but they were barbed and deeply rooted, and I had not yet been able to wrench them from my heart. However that be, I was rendered doubly miserable for the remainder of the day.

CHAPTER XIV

AN ASSAULT

NEXT MORNING, I bethought me, I, too, had business at L—; so I mounted my horse and set forth on the expedition, soon after breakfast. It was a dull, drizzly day; but that was no matter: it was all the more suitable to my frame of mind. It was likely to be a lonely journey; for it was no market-day, and the road I traversed was little frequented at any other time; but that suited me all the better too.

As I trotted along, however, chewing the cud of – *bitter* fancies, I heard another horse at no great distance behind me; but I never conjectured who the rider might be – or troubled my head about him, till on slackening my pace to ascend a gentle acclivity – or rather suffering my horse to slacken his pace into a lazy walk; for, lost in my own reflexions, I was letting it jog on as leisurely as it thought proper – I lost ground, and my fellow traveller overtook me. He accosted me by name; for it was no stranger – it was Mr Lawrence! Instinctively the fingers of my whip-hand tingled, and grasped their charge with convulsive energy; but I restrained the impulse, and answering his salutation with a nod, attempted to push on; but he pushed on beside me and began to talk about the weather and the crops. I gave the briefest possible answers to his queries and observations, and fell back. He fell back too, and asked if my horse was lame. I replied, with a *look* – at which he placidly smiled.

I was as much astonished as exasperated at this singular pertinacity and imperturbable assurance on his part. I had thought the circumstances of our last meeting would have left such an impression on his mind as to render him cold and distant ever after: instead of that, he appeared not only to have forgotten all former offences, but to be impenetrable to all present incivilities. Formerly, the slightest hint, or mere fancied coldness in tone or glance, had sufficed to repulse him: now, positive rudeness could not drive him away. Had he heard of my disappointment; and was he come to witness the result, and triumph in my despair? I grasped my whip with more determined energy than before – but still forbore to raise it, and rode on in silence, waiting for some more tangible cause of offence, before I opened the floodgates of my soul, and poured out the dammed up fury that was foaming and swelling within.

'Markham,' said he, in his usual quiet tone, 'why do you quarrel with your friends, because you have been disappointed in one quarter? You have found your hopes defeated; but how am *I* to blame for it? I warned you beforehand, you know, but you would not –'

He said no more; for, impelled by some fiend at my elbow, I had seized my whip by the small end, and – swift and sudden as a flash of lightning – brought the other down upon his head. It was not without a feeling of savage satisfaction that I beheld the instant, deadly pallor that overspread his face, and the few red drops that trickled down his forehead, while he reeled a moment in his saddle, and then fell backward to the ground. The pony, surprised to be so strangely relieved of its burden, started and capered, and kicked a little, and then made use of its freedom to go and crop the grass of the hedge bank; while its master lay as still and silent as a corpse. Had I killed him? – an icy hand seemed to grasp my heart and check its pulsation, as I bent over him, gazing with breathless intensity upon the ghastly, upturned face. But no; he moved his eyelids and uttered a slight groan. I breathed again – he was only stunned by the fall. It served him right – it would teach him better manners in future. Should I help him to his horse? No. For any other combination of offences I would; but his were too unpardonable. He might mount it himself, if he liked – in a while: already he was beginning to stir and look about him – and there it was for him, quietly browsing on the road-side.

So with a muttered execration, I left the fellow to his fate, and clapping spurs to my own horse, galloped away, excited by a combination of feelings it would not be easy to analyze; and perhaps, if I did so, the result would not be very creditable to my disposition; for I am not sure that a species of exultation in what I had done, was not one principal concomitant.

Shortly, however, the effervescence began to abate, and not many minutes elapsed before I had turned and gone back to look after the fate of my victim. It was no generous impulse – no kind relentings that led me to this – nor even the fear of what might be the consequences to myself, if I finished my assault upon the squire by leaving him thus neglected, and exposed to further injury; it was, simply, the voice of conscience; and I took great credit to myself for attending so promptly to its dictates – and judging the merit of the deed by the sacrifice it cost, I was not far wrong.

Mr Lawrence and his pony had both altered their positions, in some degree. The pony had wandered eight or ten yards farther away; and he had managed, somehow, to remove himself from the middle of the road: I found him seated in a recumbent position on the bank, – looking very white and sickly still, and holding his cambric handkerchief (now more red than white) to his head. It must have been a powerful blow; but half the credit – or the blame of it (which you please) must be attributed to the whip, which was garnished with a massive horse's head of plated metal. The grass, being sodden with rain, afforded the young gentleman a rather inhospitable couch; his clothes were considerably bemired; and his hat was rolling in the mud, on the other side of the road. But his thoughts seemed chiefly bent upon his pony, on which he was wistfully gazing – half in helpless anxiety, and half in hopeless abandonment to his fate.

I dismounted, however, and having fastened my own animal to the nearest tree, first picked up his hat, intending to clap it on his head; but either he considered his head unfit for a hat, or the hat, in its present condition, unfit for his head; for shrinking away the one, he took the other from my hand, and scornfully cast it aside.

'It's good enough for *you*,' I muttered.

My next good office was to catch his pony and bring it to him, which was soon accomplished; for the beast was quiet enough in the main, and only winced and flirted a trifle, till I got hold of the bridle, – but then, I must see him in the saddle.

'Here, you fellow – scoundrel – dog – give me your hand, and I'll help you to mount.'

No; he turned from me in disgust. I attempted to take him by the arm. He shrank away as if there had been contamination in my touch.

'What, you won't? Well you may sit there till doomsday, for what I care. But I suppose you don't want to lose all the blood in your body – I'll just condescend to bind that up for you.'

'Let me alone, if you please.'

'Humph! with all my heart. You may go to the d—l if you choose – and say I sent you.'

But before I abandoned him to his fate, I flung his pony's bridle over a stake in the hedge, and threw him my handkerchief, as his own was now saturated with blood. He took it and cast it back to me, in abhorrence and contempt, with all the strength he could muster. It wanted but this to fill the measure of his offences. With execrations not loud but deep, I left him to live or die as he could, well satisfied that I had done my duty in attempting to save him – but forgetting how I had erred in bringing him into such a condition, and how insultingly my after-services had been offered – and sullenly prepared to meet the consequences if he should choose to say I had attempted to murder him, – which I thought not unlikely, as it seemed probable he was actuated by some such spiteful motives in so perseveringly refusing my assistance.

Having remounted my horse, I just looked back to see how he was getting on, before I rode away. He had risen from the ground, and grasping his pony's mane, was attempting to resume his seat in the saddle; but scarcely had he put his foot in the stirrup, when a sickness or dizziness seemed to overpower him: he leant forward a moment, with his head drooped on the animal's back, and then made one more effort, which proving ineffectual, he sank back on the bank, where I left him, reposing his head on the oozy turf, and, to all appearance, as calmly reclining as if he had been taking his rest on his sofa at home.

I ought to have helped him in spite of himself – to have bound up the wound he was unable to staunch, and insisted upon getting him on his horse and seeing him safe home; but, besides my bitter indignation against himself, there was the question what to say to his servants, – and what to my own family. Either I should have to acknowledge the deed, which would set me down as a madman, unless I acknowledged the motive too – and that seemed impossible, – or I must get up a lie, which seemed equally out of the question – especially as

Mr Lawrence would probably reveal the whole truth, and thereby bring me to tenfold disgrace, – unless I were villain enough, presuming on the absence of witnesses, to persist in my own version of the case, and make him out a still greater scoundrel than he was. No; he had only received a cut above the temple, and perhaps, a few bruises from the fall, or the hoofs of his own pony: that could not kill him if he lay there half the day; and, if he could not help himself, surely some one would be coming by: it would be impossible that a whole day should pass and no one traverse the road but ourselves. As for what he might choose to say hereafter, I would take my chance about it: if he told lies, I would contradict him; if he told the truth, I would bear it as best I could. I was not *obliged* to enter into explanations, further than I thought proper. Perhaps, he might choose to be silent on the subject, for fear of raising inquiries as to the cause of the quarrel, and drawing the public attention to his connection with Mrs Graham, which, whether for her sake or his own, he seemed so very desirous to conceal.

Thus reasoning, I trotted away to the town, where I duly transacted my business, and performed various little commissions for my mother and Rose, with very laudable exactitude, considering the different circumstances of the case. In returning home, I was troubled with sundry misgivings about the unfortunate Lawrence. The question, what if I should find him lying, still on the damp earth, fairly dying of cold and exhaustion – or already stark and chill? thrust itself most unpleasantly upon my mind, and the appalling possibility pictured itself with painful vividness to my imagination as I approached the spot where I had left him. But no; thank Heaven, both man and horse were gone, and nothing was left to witness against me but two objects – unpleasant enough in themselves, to be sure, and presenting a very ugly, not to say murderous, appearance – in one place, the hat saturated with rain and coated with mud, indented and broken above the brim by that villainous whip-handle; in another, the crimson handkerchief, soaking in a deeply tinctured pool of water – for much rain had fallen in the interim.

Bad news fly fast: it was hardly four o'clock when I got home, but my mother gravely accosted me with –

'Oh, Gilbert! – *Such* an accident! Rose has been shopping in the village, and she's heard that Mr Lawrence has been thrown from his horse and brought home dying!'

This shocked me a trifle, as you may suppose; but I was comforted to hear that he had frightfully fractured his skull and broken a leg; for, assured of the falsehood of this, I trusted the rest of the story was equally exaggerated; and when I heard my mother and sister so feelingly deploring his condition, I had considerable difficulty in preventing myself from telling them the real extent of the injuries, as far as I knew them.

'You must go and see him to-morrow,' said my mother.

'Or to-day,' suggested Rose: 'there's plenty of time; and you can have the pony, as your horse is tired. Won't you Gilbert – as soon as you've had something to eat?'

'No, no – how can we tell that it isn't all a false report? It's highly im—'

'Oh, I'm sure it isn't; for the village is all alive about it; and I saw two people that had seen others that had seen the man that found him. That sounds far fetched; but it isn't so, when you think of it.'

'Well, but Lawrence is a good rider; it is not likely he would fall from his horse at all; and if he did, it is highly improbable he should break his bones in that way. It must be a gross exaggeration at least.'

'No, but the horse kicked him – or something.'

'What, his quiet little pony?'

'How do you know it was that?'

'He seldom rides any other.'

'At any rate,' said my mother, 'you will call to-morrow. Whether it be true or false, exaggerated or otherwise, we shall like to know how he is.'

'Fergus may go.'

'Why not you?'

'He has more time. I am busy just now.'

'Oh! but, Gilbert, how can you be so composed about it? You won't mind business for an hour or two, in a case of this sort – when your friend is at the point of death!'

'He is *not*, I tell you.'

'For anything you know, he *may* be: you can't tell till you have seen him. – At all events, he must have met with some terrible accident, and you ought to see him: he'll take it very unkind of you if you don't.'

'Confound it! I can't. He and I have not been on good terms, of late.'

'O my *dear* boy! Surely, surely you are not so unforgiving as to carry your little differences to such a length as –'

'Little differences, indeed!' I muttered.

'Well, but only remember the occasion! Think how –'

'Well, well, don't bother me now – I'll see about it,' I replied.

And my seeing about it, was to send Fergus next morning, with my mother's compliments, to make the requisite inquiries; for, of course, my going was out of the question – or sending a message, either. He brought back intelligence that the young squire was laid up with the complicated evils of a broken head and certain contusions (occasioned by a fall – of which he did not trouble himself to relate the particulars – and the subsequent misconduct of his horse), and a severe cold, the consequence of lying on the wet ground in the rain; but there were no broken bones, and no immediate prospects of dissolution.

It was evident then, that, for Mrs Graham's sake, it was not his intention to criminate me.

CHAPTER XV

AN ENCOUNTER AND ITS CONSEQUENCES

THAT DAY WAS rainy like its predecessor; but towards evening it began to clear up a little, and the next morning was fair and promising. I was out on the hill with the reapers. A light wind swept over the corn; and all nature laughed in the sunshine. The lark was rejoicing among the silvery floating clouds. The late rain had so sweetly freshened and cleared the air, and washed the sky, and left such glittering gems on branch and blade, that not even the farmers could have the heart to blame it. But no ray of sunshine could reach my heart, no breeze could freshen it; nothing could fill the void my faith, and hope, and joy in Helen Graham had left, or drive away the keen regrets, and bitter dregs of lingering love that still oppressed it.

While I stood, with folded arms, abstractedly gazing on the undulating swell of the corn not yet disturbed by the reapers, something gently pulled my skirts, and a small voice, no longer welcome to my ears, aroused me with the startling words: –

'Mr Markham, mamma wants you.'

'Wants *me*, Arthur?'

'Yes. Why do you look so queer?' said he, half laughing, half frightened at the unexpected aspect of my face in suddenly turning towards him – 'and why have you kept so long away? – Come! – Won't you come?'

'I'm busy just now,' I replied, scarce knowing what to answer.

He looked up in childish bewilderment; but before I could speak again, the lady herself was at my side.

'Gilbert, I *must* speak with you!' said she in a tone of suppressed vehemence.

I looked at her pale cheek and glittering eye, but answered nothing.

'Only for a moment,' pleaded she. 'Just step aside into this other field' – she glanced at the reapers, some of whom were directing looks of impertinent curiosity towards her – 'I won't keep you a minute.'

I accompanied her through the gap.

'Arthur, darling, run and gather those bluebells,' said she, pointing to some that were gleaming, at some distance, under the hedge along which we walked. The child hesitated, as if unwilling to quit my side. 'Go, love!' repeated she more urgently, and in a tone, which, though not unkind, demanded prompt obedience, and obtained it.

'Well, Mrs Graham?' said I, calmly and coldly; for, though I saw she was miserable, and pitied her, I felt glad to have it in my power to torment her.

She fixed her eyes upon me with a look that pierced me to the heart; – and yet, it made me smile.

'I don't ask the reason of this change, Gilbert,' said she with bitter calmness. – 'I know it too well; but though I could see myself suspected and condemned by every one else, and bear it with calmness, I cannot endure it from you. – Why did you not come to hear my explanation on the day I appointed to give it?'

'Because, I happened, in the interim, to learn all you would have told me, – and a trifle more I imagine.'

'Impossible, for I would have told you all!' cried she, passionately. – 'But I won't now, for I see you are not worthy of it!'

And her pale lips quivered with agitation.

'Why not, may I ask?'

She repelled my mocking smile with a glance of scornful indignation.

'Because, you never understood me, or you would not soon have listened to my traducers – my confidence would be misplaced in you – you are not the man I thought you. – Go! I won't care *what* you think of me.'

She turned away, and I went; for I thought that would torment her as much as anything; and I believe I was right; for, looking back a minute after, I saw her turn half round, as if hoping or expecting to find me still beside her; and then she stood still, and cast one look behind. It was a look less expressive of anger than of bitter anguish and despair; but I immediately assumed an aspect of indifference, and affected to be gazing carelessly round me, and I suppose she went on; for after lingering awhile to see if she would come back or call, I ventured one more glance, and saw her a good way off, moving rapidly up the field with little Arthur running by her side and apparently talking as he went; but she kept her face averted from him, as if to hide some uncontrollable emotion. And I returned to my business.

But I soon began to regret my precipitancy in leaving her so soon. It was evident she loved me – probably, she was tired of Mr Lawrence, and wished to exchange him for me; and if I had loved and reverenced her less to begin with, the preference might have gratified and amused me; but now, the contrast between her outward seeming and her inward mind, as I supposed, – between my former and my present opinion of her, was so harrowing – so distressing to my feelings, that it swallowed up every lighter consideration.

But still, I was curious to know what sort of an explanation she would have given me, – or would give now, if I pressed her for it – how much she would confess, and how she would endeavour to excuse herself. I longed to know what to despise, and what to admire in her, how much to pity, and how much to hate; – and, what was more, I *would* know. I would see her once more, and fairly satisfy myself in what light to regard her, before we parted. Lost to me she was, for ever, of course; but still, I could not bear to think that we had parted, for the last time, with so much unkindness and misery on both sides. That last look of hers had sunk into my heart; I could not forget it. – But what a fool I was! – Had she not deceived me, injured me

– blighted my happiness for life? – 'Well, I'll see her, however,' was my concluding resolve, – 'but not to-day: to-day and to-night, she may think upon her sins, and be as miserable as she will: to-morrow, I will see her once again, and know something more about her. The interview may be serviceable to her, or it may not. – At any rate, it will give a breath of excitement to the life she has doomed to stagnation, and may calm with certainty some agitating thoughts.'

I did go on the morrow; but not till towards evening, after the business of the day was concluded, that is between six and seven; and the westering sun was gleaming redly on the old Hall, and flaming in the latticed windows, as I reached it, imparting to the place a cheerfulness not its own. I need not dilate upon the feelings with which I approached the shrine of my former divinity – that spot teeming with a thousand delightful recollections and glorious dreams – all darkened now, by one disastrous truth.

Rachel admitted me into the parlour, and went to call her mistress, for she was not there; but there was her desk left open on the little round table beside the high-backed chair, with a book laid upon it. Her limited but choice collection of books was almost as familiar to me as my own; but this volume I had not seen before. I took it up. It was Sir Humphrey Davy's 'Last days of a Philosopher,' and on the first leaf was written, – 'Frederick Lawrence.' I closed the book, but kept it in my hand, and stood facing the door, with my back to the fire-place, calmly waiting her arrival; for I did not doubt she would come. And soon I heard her step in the hall. My heart was beginning to throb, but I checked it with an internal rebuke, and maintained my composure – outwardly, at least. She entered, calm, pale, collected.

'To what am I indebted for this favour, Mr Markham?' said she, with such severe but quiet dignity as almost disconcerted me; but I answered with a smile, and impudently enough:

'Well, I am come to hear your explanation.'

'I told you I would not give it,' said she. 'I said you were unworthy of my confidence.'

'Oh, very well,' replied I, moving to the door.

'Stay a moment,' said she. 'This is the last time I shall see you: don't go just yet.'

I remained, awaiting her further commands.

'Tell me,' resumed she, 'on what grounds you believe these things against me; who told you; and what did they say?'

I paused a moment. She met my eye as unflinchingly as if her bosom had been steeled with conscious innocence. She was resolved to know the worst, and determined to dare it too. 'I can crush that bold spirit,' thought I. But while I secretly exulted in my power, I felt disposed to dally with my victim like a cat. Showing her the book that I still held, in my hand, and pointing to the name on the fly leaf, but fixing my eye upon her face, I asked, –

'Do you know that gentleman?'

'Of course I do,' replied she; and a sudden flush suffused her features – whether of shame or anger I could not tell: it rather resembled the latter. 'What next, sir?'

'How long is it since you saw him?'

'Who gave you the right to catechize me, on this or any other subject?'

'Oh, no one! – it's quite at your option whether to answer or not. – And now, let me ask – have you heard what has lately befallen this friend of yours? – because, if you have not –'

'I will not be insulted Mr Markham!' cried she, almost infuriated at my manner. – 'So you had better leave the house at once, if you came only for that.'

'I did not come to insult you: I came to hear your explanation.'

'And I tell you I won't give it!' retorted she, pacing the room in a state of strong excitement, with her hands clasped tightly together, breathing short, and flashing fires of indignation from her eyes. 'I will not condescend to explain myself to one that can make a jest of such horrible suspicions, and be so easily led to entertain them.'

'I do not make a jest of them, Mrs Graham,' returned I, dropping at once, my tone of taunting sarcasm. 'I heartily wish I could find them a jesting matter! And as to being easily led to suspect, God only knows what a blind, incredulous fool I have hitherto been, perseveringly shutting my eyes and stopping my ears against everything that threatened to shake my confidence in you, till proof itself confounded my infatuation!'

'What proof, sir?'

'Well, I'll tell you. You remember that evening when I was here last?'

'I do.'

'Even then, you dropped some hints that might have opened the eyes of a wiser man; but they had no such effect upon me: I went on trusting and believing, hoping against hope, and adoring where I could not comprehend. – It so happened, how-ever, that after I left you, I turned back – drawn by pure depth of sympathy, and ardour of affection – not daring to intrude my presence openly upon you, but unable to resist the tempta-tion of catching one glimpse through the window, just to see how you were; for I had left you apparently in great affliction, and I partly blamed my own want of forbearance and discretion as the cause of it. If I did wrong, love alone was my incentive, and the punishment was severe enough; for it was just as I had reached that tree, that you came out into the garden with your friend. Not choosing to shew myself, under the circumstances, I stood still, in the shadow, till you had both passed by.'

'And how much of our conversation did you hear?'

'I heard quite enough, Helen. And it was well for me that I did hear it; for nothing less could have cured my infatuation. I always said and thought, that I would never believe a word against you, unless I heard it from your own lips. All the hints and affirmations of others I treated as malignant, baseless slan-ders; your own self accusations I believed to be overstrained;

and all that seemed unaccountable in your position, I trusted that you could account for if you chose.'

Mrs Graham had discontinued her walk. She leant against one end of the chimney piece, opposite that near which I was standing, with her chin resting on her closed hand, her eyes – no longer burning with anger, but gleaming with restless excitement – sometimes glancing at me while I spoke, then coursing the opposite wall, or fixed upon the carpet.

'You should have come to me, after all,' said she, 'and heard what I had to say in my own justification. It was ungenerous and wrong to withdraw yourself so secretly and suddenly, immediately after such ardent protestations of attachment, without ever assigning a reason for the change. You should have told me all – no matter *how* bitterly – It would have been better than this silence.'

'To what end should I have done so? – You could not have enlightened me farther, on the subject which alone concerned me; nor could you have made me discredit the evidence of my senses. I desired our intimacy to be discontinued at once, as you yourself had acknowledged would probably be the case if I knew all; but I did not wish to upbraid you, – though (as you also acknowledged) you had deeply wronged me. – Yes; you have done me an injury you can never repair – or any other either – you have blighted the freshness and promise of youth, and made my life a wilderness! I might live a hundred years, but I could never recover from the effects of this withering blow – and never forget it! Hereafter – You smile, Mrs Graham,' said I, suddenly stopping short, checked in my passionate declamation by unutterable feelings to behold her actually *smiling* at the picture of the ruin she had wrought.

'Did I?' replied she, looking seriously up, 'I was not aware of it. If I did, it was not for pleasure at the thoughts of the harm I had done you – Heaven knows I have had torment enough at the bare possibility of that! – it was for joy to find that you had some depth of soul and feeling after all, and to hope that I had not been utterly mistaken in your worth. But smiles and tears are so alike with me; they are neither of them confined to any particular feelings: I often cry when I am happy, and smile when I am sad.'

She looked at me again, and seemed to expect a reply; but I continued silent.

'Would you be *very* glad,' resumed she, 'to find that you were mistaken in your conclusions?'

'How can you ask it, Helen?'

'I don't say I can clear myself altogether,' said she, speaking low and fast, while her heart beat visibly and her bosom heaved with excitement, – 'but would you be glad to discover I was better than you think me?'

'Anything that could, in the least degree, tend to restore my former opinion of you, to excuse the regard I still feel for you, and alleviate the pangs of unutterable regret that accompany it, would be only too gladly – too eagerly received!'

Her cheeks burned and her whole frame trembled, now, with excess of agitation. She did not speak, but flew to her desk, and snatching thence what seemed a thick album or manuscript volume, hastily tore away a few leaves from the end, and thrust the rest into my hand, saying, 'You needn't read it all; but take it home with you,' – and hurried from the room. But when I had left the house, and was proceeding down the walk, she opened the window and called me back. It was only to say, –

'Bring it back when you have read it; and don't breathe a word of what it tells you to any living being – I trust to your honour.'

Before I could answer, she had closed the casement and turned away. I saw her cast herself back in the old oak chair, and cover her face with her hands. Her feelings had been wrought to a pitch that rendered it necessary to seek relief in tears.

Panting with eagerness, and struggling to suppress my hopes, I hurried home, and rushed up stairs to my room, – having first provided myself with a candle, though it was scarcely twilight yet, – then, shut and bolted the door, determined to tolerate no interruption, and sitting down before the table, opened out my prize and delivered myself up to its perusal – first, hastily turning over the leaves and snatching a sentence here and there, and then, setting myself steadily to read it through.

I have it now before me; and though you could not, of course, peruse it with half the interest that I did, I know you would not be satisfied with an abbreviation of its contents and you shall have the whole, save, perhaps, a few passages here and there of merely temporal interest to the writer, or such as would serve to encumber the story rather than elucidate it. It begins somewhat abruptly, thus – but we will reserve its commencement for another chapter, and call it, –

CHAPTER XVI

THE WARNINGS OF EXPERIENCE

JUNE 1ST, 1821. – We have just returned to Staningley – that is, we returned some days ago, and I am not yet settled, and feel as if I never should be. We left town sooner than was intended, in consequence of my uncle's indisposition – I wonder what would have been the result if we had stayed the full time. I am quite ashamed of my new-sprung distaste for country life. All my former occupations seem so tedious and dull, my former amusements so insipid and unprofitable. I cannot enjoy my music, because there is no one to hear it. I cannot enjoy my walks, because there is no one to meet. I cannot enjoy my books, because they have not power to arrest my attention: my head is so haunted with the recollections of the last few weeks that I cannot attend to them. My drawing suits me best, for I can draw and think at the same time; and if my productions cannot now be seen by any one but myself and those who do not care about them, they, possibly, may be, hereafter. But then, there is one face I am always trying to paint or to sketch, and always without success; and that vexes me. As for the owner of that face, I cannot get him out of my mind – and, indeed, I never try. I wonder whether he ever thinks of me; and I wonder whether I shall ever see him again. And then might follow a train of other wonderments, questions for time and fate to answer, concluding with: – supposing all the rest be answered in the affirmative, I wonder whether I shall ever repent it – as my aunt would tell me I should, if she knew what I was thinking about. How distinctly I remember our conversation that evening before our departure for town, when we were sitting together over the fire, my uncle having gone to bed with a slight attack of the gout.

'Helen,' said she, after a thoughtful silence, 'do you ever think about marriage?'

'Yes aunt, often.'

'And do you ever contemplate the possibility of being married yourself, or engaged, before the season is over?'

'Sometimes; but I don't think it at all likely that I *ever* shall.'

'Why so?'

'Because, I imagine there must be only a very, very few men in the world, that I should like to marry; and of those few, it is ten to one I may never be acquainted with one; or if I should, it is twenty to one, he may not happen to be single, or to take a fancy to me.'

'That is no argument at all. It may be very true – and I hope is true, that there are very few men whom you would choose to marry, of yourself. – It is not, indeed, to be supposed that you would *wish* to marry *any* one, till you were asked: a girl's affections should never be won unsought. But when they *are* sought – when the citadel of the heart is fairly besieged, it is apt to surrender sooner than the owner is aware of, and often against her better judgment, and in opposition to all her preconceived ideas of what she could have loved, unless she be extremely careful and discreet. Now I want to warn you, Helen, of these things, and to exhort you to be watchful and circumspect from the very commencement of your career, and not to suffer your heart to be stolen from you by the first foolish or unprincipled person that covets the possession of it. – You know, my dear, you are only just eighteen; there is plenty of time before you, and neither your uncle nor I are in any hurry to get you off our hands; and, I may venture to say, there will be no lack of suitors; for you can boast a good family, a pretty considerable fortune and expectations, and, I may as well tell you likewise – for if I don't others will – that you have a fair share of beauty, besides – and I hope you may never have cause to regret it! –'

'I hope not, aunt; but why should you fear it?'

'Because, my dear, beauty is that quality which, next to money, is generally the most attractive to the worst kinds of men; and, therefore, it is likely to entail a great deal of trouble on the possessor.'

'Have *you* been troubled in that way, aunt?'

'No, Helen,' said she, with reproachful gravity, 'but I know many that have; and some, through carelessness, have been the wretched victims of deceit; and some, through weakness, have fallen into snares and temptations terrible to relate.'

'Well, I shall be neither careless nor weak.'

'Remember Peter, Helen! Don't boast, but *watch*. Keep a guard over your eyes and ears as the inlets of your heart, and over your lips as the outlet, lest they betray you in a moment of unwariness. Receive, coldly and dispassionately, every attention, till you have ascertained and duly considered the worth of the aspirant; and let your affections be consequent upon approbation alone. First study; then approve; then love. Let your eyes be blind to all external attractions, your ears deaf to all the fascinations of flattery and light discourse. – These are nothing – and worse than nothing – snares and wiles of the tempter, to lure the thoughtless to their own destruction. Principle is the first thing, after all; and next to that, good sense, respectability, and moderate wealth. If you should marry the handsomest, and most accomplished and superficially agreeable man in the world, you little know the misery that would overwhelm you, if, after all, you should find him to be a worthless reprobate, or even an impracticable fool.'

'But what are all the poor fools and reprobates to do, aunt? If everybody followed your advice the world would soon come to an end.'

'Never fear, my dear! the male fools and reprobates will never want for partners while there are so many of the other sex to match them; but do *you* follow my advice. And this is no subject for jesting, Helen, I am sorry to see you treat the matter in that light way. Believe me, *matrimony is a serious thing.*' And she spoke it *so* seriously that one might have fancied she had known it to her cost; but I asked no more impertinent questions, and merely answered, –

'I know it is; and I know there is truth and sense in what you say; but you need not fear me, for I not only should think it *wrong* to marry a man that was deficient in sense or in principle, but I should never be *tempted* to do it; for I could not like him, if he were ever so handsome, and ever so charming, in other respects; I should hate him – despise him – pity him – anything but love him. My affections not only *ought* to be founded on approbation, but they will and must be so: for, without approving I cannot love. It is needless to say I ought to be able to respect and honour the man I marry as *well* as love him, for I cannot love him without. So set your mind at rest.'

'I hope it may be so,' answered she.

'I *know* it *is* so,' persisted I.

'You have not been tried yet, Helen: we can but hope,' said she, in her cold, cautious way.

I was vexed at her incredulity; but I am not sure her doubts were entirely without sagacity; I fear I have found it much easier to remember her advice than to profit by it – indeed, I have sometimes been led to question the soundness of her doctrines on those subjects. Her counsels may be good, as far as they go – in the main points, at least; – but there are some things she has overlooked in her calculations. I wonder if *she* was ever in love.

I commenced my career – or my first campaign, as my uncle calls it – kindling with bright hopes and fancies – chiefly raised by this conversation – and full of confidence in my own discretion. At first, I was delighted with the novelty and excitement of our London life; but, soon, I began to weary of its mingled turbulence and constraint, and sigh for the freshness and freedom of home. My new acquaintances, both male and female, disappointed my expectations, and vexed and depressed me by turns; for I soon grew tired of studying their peculiarities, and laughing at their foibles – particularly as I was obliged to keep my criticisms to myself, for my aunt would not hear them – and they – the ladies especially – appeared so provokingly mindless, and heartless, and artificial. The gentlemen seemed better, but perhaps, it was because I knew them less, perhaps, because they flattered me; but I did not fall in love with any of them, and if their attentions pleased me one moment, they provoked me the next, because they put me out of humour with myself, by revealing my vanity and making me fear I was becoming like some of the ladies I so heartily despised.

There was one elderly gentleman that annoyed me very much; a rich old friend of my uncle's who, I believe, thought I could not do better than marry him; but, besides being old, he was ugly and disagreeable, – and wicked, I am sure, though my aunt scolded me for saying so; but she allowed he was no saint. And there was another, less hateful, but still *more* tiresome, because she favoured him, and was always thrusting him upon me, and sounding his praises in my ears, Mr Boarham, by name, Bore'em as I prefer spelling it, for a terrible bore he was: I shudder still, at the remembrance of his voice, drone, drone, drone, in my ear, while he sat beside me, prosing away by the half-hour together, and beguiling himself with the notion that he was improving my mind by useful information, or, impressing his dogmas upon me, and reforming my errors of judgment, or perhaps, that he was talking down to my level, and amusing me with entertaining discourse. Yet he was a decent man enough, in the main, I dare say; and if he had kept his distance, I never would have hated him. As it was, it was almost impossible to help it; for he not only bothered me with the infliction of his own presence, but he kept me from the enjoyment of more agreeable society.

One night, however, at a ball, he had been more than usually tormenting, and my patience was quite exhausted. – It appeared as if the whole evening was fated to be insupportable: I had just had one dance with an empty-headed coxcomb, and then Mr Boarham had come upon me, and seemed determined to cling to me for the rest of the night. He never danced himself, and there he sat, poking his head in my face, and impressing all beholders with the idea that he was a confirmed, acknowledged lover; my aunt looking complacently on, all the time, and wishing him God-speed. In vain I attempted to drive him away by giving a loose to my exasperated feelings, even to positive rudeness: nothing could convince him that his presence was disagreeable. Sullen silence was taken for rapt attention, and gave him greater room to talk; sharp answers were received as smart sallies of girlish vivacity, that only required an indulgent rebuke; and flat contradictions were but as oil to the flames, calling forth new strains of argument to support his dogmas, and bringing down upon me endless floods of reasoning to overwhelm me with conviction.

But there was one present who seemed to have a better appreciation of my frame of mind. A gentleman stood by, who had been watching our conference for some time, evidently much amused at my companion's remorseless pertinacity and my manifest annoyance, and laughing to himself at the asperity and uncompromising spirit of my replies. At length, however, he withdrew, and went to the lady of the house, apparently for the purpose of asking an introduction to me, for, shortly after, they both came up, and she introduced him as Mr Huntingdon, the son of a late friend of my uncle's. He asked me to dance. I gladly consented, of course; and he was my companion during the remainder of my stay, which was not long, for my aunt, as usual, insisted upon an early departure.

I was sorry to go, for I had found my new acquaintance a very lively and entertaining companion. There was a certain graceful ease and freedom about all he said and did, that gave a sense of repose and expansion to the mind, after so much constraint and formality as I had been doomed to suffer. There might be, it is true, a little too much careless boldness in his manner and address, but I was in so good a humour, and so grateful for my late deliverance from Mr Boarham, that it did not anger me.

'Well, Helen, how do you like Mr Boarham now?' said my aunt, as we took our seats in the carriage and drove away.

'Worse than ever,' I replied.

She looked displeased but said no more on that subject.

'Who was the gentleman you danced with last,' resumed she, after a pause – 'that was so officious in helping you on with your shawl?'

'He was not officious at all, aunt: he never *attempted* to help me, till he saw Mr Boarham coming to do so; and then he stepped laughingly forward and said, "Come, I'll preserve you from that infliction." '

'Who was it, I ask?' said she, with frigid gravity.

'It was Mr Huntingdon, the son of uncle's old friend.'

'I have heard your uncle speak of young Mr Huntingdon. I've heard him say, "He's a fine lad, that young Huntingdon, but a bit wildish, I fancy." So I'd have you beware.'

'What does "a bit wildish" mean?' I enquired.

'It means destitute of principle, and prone to every vice that is common to youth.'

'But I've heard uncle say he was a sad wild fellow himself, when he was young.'

She sternly shook her head.

'He was jesting then, I suppose,' said I, 'and here he was speaking at random – at least, I cannot believe there is any harm in those laughing blue eyes.'

'False reasoning, Helen!' said she with a sigh.

'Well, we ought to be charitable, you know, aunt – besides, I don't think it *is* false: I am an excellent physiognomist, and I always judge of people's characters by their looks – not by whether they are handsome or ugly, but by the general cast of the countenance. For instance, I should know by your countenance that you were not of a cheerful, sanguine disposition; and I should know by Mr Wilmot's that he was a worthless old reprobate, and by Mr Boarham's that he was not an agreeable companion, and by Mr Huntingdon's that he was neither a fool nor a knave, though, possibly, neither a sage nor a saint – but that is no matter to me, as I am not likely to meet him again – unless as an occasional partner in the ballroom.'

It was not so, however, for I met him again next morning. He came to call upon my uncle, apologizing for not having done so before, by saying he was only lately returned from the continent, and had not heard, till the previous night, of my uncle's arrival in town; and after that, I often met him; sometimes in public, sometimes at home; for he was very assiduous in paying his respects to his old friend, who did not, however, consider himself greatly obliged by the attention.

'I wonder what the deuce the lad means by coming so often,' he would say, – 'can *you* tell, Helen? – Hey? He wants none o' my company, nor I his – that's certain.'

'I wish you'd tell him so, then,' said my aunt.

'Why, what for? If I don't want him, somebody does, mayhap'

(winking at me). 'Besides, he's a pretty tidy fortune, Peggy, you know – not such a catch as Wilmot; but then Helen won't hear of that match; for, somehow, these old chaps don't go down with the girls – with *all* their money – and their experience to boot. I'll bet anything she'd rather have this young fellow without a penny, than Wilmot with his house full of gold – wouldn't you Nell?'

'Yes, uncle; but that's not saying much for Mr Huntingdon, for I'd rather be an old maid and a pauper than Mrs Wilmot.'

'And Mrs Huntingdon? What would you rather be than Mrs Huntingdon? eh?'

'I'll tell you when I've considered the matter.'

'Ah! it needs consideration then. – But come now – would you rather be an old maid – let alone the pauper?'

'I can't tell till I'm asked.'

And I left the room immediately, to escape further examination. But five minutes after, in looking from my window, I beheld Mr Boarham coming up to the door. I waited nearly half an hour in uncomfortable suspense, expecting every minute to be called, and vainly longing to hear him go. Then, footsteps were heard on the stairs, and my aunt entered the room with a solemn countenance, and closed the door behind her.

'Here is Mr Boarham, Helen,' said she. 'He wishes to see you.'

'Oh, aunt! Can't you tell him I'm indisposed? – I'm sure I am – to see *him*.'

'Nonsense, my dear! this is no trifling matter. He is come on a very important errand – to ask your hand in marriage, of your uncle and me.'

'I hope my uncle and you told him it was not in your power to give it. What right had he to ask *any* one before me?'

'Helen!'

'What did my uncle say?'

'He said he would not interfere in the matter; if you liked to accept Mr Boarham's obliging offer, you –'

'Did he say obliging offer?'

'No; he said if you liked to take him you might; and if not, you might please yourself.'

'He said right; and what did you say?'

'It is no matter what I said. What will *you* say? – that is the question. He is now waiting to ask you himself, but consider well before you go; and if you intend to refuse him, give me your reasons.'

'I *shall* refuse him, of course, but you must tell me how, for I want to be civil and yet decided – and when I've got rid of him, I'll give you my reasons afterwards.'

'But stay Helen; sit down a little and compose yourself. Mr Boarham is in no particular hurry, for he has little doubt of your acceptance; and I want to speak with you. Tell me, my dear, what are your objections to him? Do you deny that he is an upright, honourable man?'

'No.'

'Do you deny that he is sensible, sober, respectable?'

'No; he may be all this, but –'

'*But* Helen! How many such men do you expect to meet with in the world? Upright, honourable, sensible, sober, respectable! – Is *this* such an every day character, that you should reject the possessor of such noble qualities, without a moment's hesitation? – Yes, *noble* I may call them; for, think of the full meaning of each, and how many inestimable virtues they include (and I might add many more to the list), and consider that all this is laid at your feet: it is in your power to secure this inestimable blessing for life – a worthy and excellent husband, who loves you tenderly, but not too fondly so as to blind him to your faults, and will be your guide throughout life's pilgrimage, and your partner in eternal bliss! Think how –'

'But I hate him, aunt,' said I, interrupting this unusual flow of eloquence.

'Hate him, Helen! Is this a Christian spirit? – *you hate him?* – and he so good a man!'

'I don't hate him as a man, but as a husband. As a man, I love him so much, that I wish him a better wife than I – one as good as himself, or better – if you think that possible – provided she could like him; – but I never could, and therefore –'

'But why not? What objection do you find?'

'Firstly, he is, at least, forty years old – considerably more I should think, and I am but eighteen; secondly, he is narrow-minded and bigoted in the extreme; thirdly, his tastes and feelings are wholly dissimilar to mine; fourthly, his looks, voice, and manner are particularly displeasing to me; and finally, I have an aversion to his whole person that I never can surmount.'

'Then you ought to surmount it! And please to compare him for a moment with Mr Huntingdon, and, good looks apart (which contribute nothing to the merit of the man, or to the happiness of married life, and which you have so often professed to hold in light esteem), tell me which is the better man.'

'I have no doubt Mr Huntingdon is a much better man than you think him, – but we are not talking about him, now, but about Mr Boarham; and as I would rather grow, live and die in single blessedness than be his wife, it is but right that I should tell him so at once, and put him out of suspense – so let me go.'

'But don't give him a flat denial; he has no idea of such a thing, and it would offend him greatly: say you have no thoughts of matrimony, at present –'

'But I *have* thoughts of it.'

'Or that you desire a further acquaintance.'

'But I don't desire a further acquaintance – quite the contrary.'

And without waiting for further admonitions, I left the room and went to seek Mr Boarham. He was walking up and down the drawing-room, humming snatches of tunes, and nibbling the end of his cane.

'My dear young lady,' said he, bowing and smirking with great complacency, 'I have your kind guardian's permission –'

'I know, sir,' said I, wishing to shorten the scene as much as possible, 'and I am greatly obliged for your preference, but must beg to decline the honour you wish to confer; for, I think, we were not made for each other – as you yourself would shortly discover if the experiment were tried.'

My aunt was right: it was quite evident he had had little doubt of my acceptance, and no idea of a positive denial. He was amazed – astounded at such an answer, but too incredulous to be much offended; and after a little humming and hawing, he returned to the attack.

'I know, my dear, that there exists a considerable disparity between us in years, in temperament, and perhaps some other things, but let me assure you, I shall not be severe to mark the faults and foibles of a young and ardent nature such as yours, and while I acknowledge them to myself, and even rebuke them with all a father's care, believe me, no youthful lover could be more tenderly indulgent towards the object of his affections, than I to you; and, on the other hand, let me hope that my more experienced years and graver habits of reflection will be no disparagement in your eyes, as I shall endeavour to make them all conducive to your happiness. Come now! What do you say? – Let us have no young lady's affectations and caprices, but speak out at once!'

'I will, but only to repeat what I said before, that I am certain we were not made for each other.'

'You really think so?'

'I do.'

'But you don't know me – you wish for a further acquaint-ance – a longer time to –'

'No, I don't. I know you as well as I ever shall, and better than you know me, or you would never dream of uniting yourself to one so incongruous – so utterly unsuitable to you in every way.'

'But my dear young lady, I don't look for perfection, I can excuse –'

'Thank you, Mr Boarham, but I won't trespass upon your goodness. You may save your indulgence and consideration for some more worthy object, that won't tax them so heavily.'

'But let me beg you to consult your aunt; that excellent lady, I am sure, will –'

'I have consulted her; and I know her wishes coincide with yours; but in such important matters, I take the liberty of judging for myself, and no persuasion can alter my inclinations, or induce me to believe that such a step would be conducive to my happiness, or yours – and I wonder that a man of your experience and discretion should think of choosing such a wife.'

'Ah, well!' said he – 'I have sometimes wondered at that myself. I have sometimes said to myself, "Now Boarham, what is this you're after? Take care man – look before you leap! This is a sweet, bewitching creature, but remember, the brightest attractions to the lover, too often prove the husband's greatest torments!" – I assure you my choice has not been made without much reasoning and reflection. The seeming imprudence of the match has cost me many an anxious thought by day, and many a sleepless hour by night; but at length, I satisfied myself, that it was not, in very deed, imprudent. I saw my sweet girl was not without her faults, but of these, her youth, I trusted, was not one, but rather an earnest of virtues yet unblown – a strong ground of presumption that her little defects of temper, and errors of judgment, opinion, or manner were not irremediable, but might easily be removed or mitigated by the patient efforts of a watchful and judicious adviser, and where I failed to enlighten and controul, I thought I might safely undertake to pardon, for the sake of her many excellencies. Therefore, my dearest girl, since *I* am satisfied, why should *you* object – on my account, at least?'

'But to tell you the truth, Mr Boarham, it is on my own account I principally object; so let us — drop the subject,' I would have said, 'for it is worse than useless to pursue it any further,' but he pertinaciously interrupted me with –

'But why so? I would love you, cherish you, protect you, &c. &c.'

I shall not trouble myself to put down all that passed between us. Suffice it to say, that I found him very troublesome, and very hard to convince that I really meant what I said, and really *was* so obstinate and blind to my own interests, that there was no shadow of a chance that either he or my aunt would ever be able to overcome my objections. Indeed, I am not sure that I succeeded after all; though wearied with his so pertinaciously returning to the same point and repeating the same arguments over and over again, forcing me to reiterate the same replies, I at length turned short and sharp upon him, and my last words were –

'I tell you plainly, that it cannot be. No consideration can induce me to marry against my inclinations. I respect you – at least, I would respect you, if you would behave like a sensible man – but I cannot love you, and never could – and the more you talk the farther you repel me; so pray don't say any more about it.'

Whereupon he wished me a good morning, and withdrew, disconcerted and offended, no doubt; but surely it was not my fault.

CHAPTER XVII

FURTHER WARNINGS

THE NEXT DAY I accompanied my uncle and aunt to a dinner party at Mr Wilmot's. He had two ladies staying with him, his niece Annabella, a fine dashing girl, or rather young woman, of some five and twenty, too great a flirt to be married, according to her own assertion, but greatly admired by the gentlemen, who universally pronounced her a splendid woman, – and her gentle cousin, Milicent Hargrave, who had taken a violent fancy to me, mistaking me for something vastly better than I was. And I in return, was very fond of her – I should entirely exclude poor Milicent in my general animad-versions against the ladies of my acquaintance. But it was not on her account, or her cousin's, that I have mentioned the party: it was for the sake of another of Mr Wilmot's guests, to wit Mr Huntingdon. I have good reason to remember his presence there, for this was the last time I saw him.

He did not sit near me at dinner; for it was his fate to hand in a capacious old dowager, and mine to be handed in by Mr Grimsby, a friend of his, but a man I very greatly disliked: there was a sinister cast in his countenance, and a mixture of lurking ferocity and fulsome insincerity in his demeanour, that I could not away with. What a tiresome custom that is, by the by – one among the many sources of factitious annoyance of this ultra civilized life. If the gentlemen *must* lead the ladies into the dining-room, why cannot they take those they like best?

I am not sure, however, that Mr Huntingdon would have taken me, if he *had* been at liberty to make his own selection. It is quite possible he might have chosen Miss Wilmot; for she seemed bent upon engrossing his attention to herself, and he seemed nothing loath to pay the homage she demanded. I thought so, at least, when I saw how they talked and laughed, and glanced across the table, to the neglect and evident umbrage of their respective neighbours – and afterwards, as the gentlemen joined us in the drawing-room, when she, immediately upon his entrance, loudly called upon him to be the arbiter of a dispute between herself and another lady, and he answered the summons with alacrity, and decided the question without a moment's hesitation in her favour – though, to my thinking, she was obviously in the wrong – and then stood chatting familiarly with her and a group of other ladies; while I sat with Milicent Har-grave, at the opposite end of the room, looking over the latter's drawings and aiding her with my critical observations and advice, at her particular desire. But in spite of my efforts to remain composed my attention wandered from the drawings to the merry group, and against my better judgment my wrath rose, and doubtless, my countenance lowered; for Milicent, observing that I must be tired of her daubs and scratches, begged I would join the company now, and defer the examination of the remainder to another opportunity. But while I was assuring her that I had no wish to join them, and was not tired, Mr Huntingdon himself came up to the little round table at which we sat.

'Are these yours?' said he, carelessly taking up one of the drawings.

'No, they are Miss Hargrave's.'

'Oh! well, let's have a look at them.'

And, regardless of Miss Hargrave's protestations, that they were not worth looking at, he drew a chair to my side, and receiving the drawings, one by one from my hand, successively scanned them over, and threw them on the table, but said not a word about them, though he was talking all the time. I don't know what Milicent Hargrave thought of such conduct, but *I* found his conversation extremely interesting, though as I afterwards discovered, when I came to analyze it, it was chiefly confined to quizzing the different members of the company present; and albeit he made some clever remarks, and some excessively droll ones, I do not think the whole would appear anything very particular, if written here, without the adventitious aids of look, and tone, and gesture, and that ineffable but indefinite charm, which cast a halo over all he did and said, and which would have made it a delight to look in his face, and hear the music of his voice, if he had been talking positive nonsense – and which, moreover, made me feel so bitter against my aunt when she put a stop to this enjoyment, by coming composedly forward, under pretence of wishing to see the drawings, that she cared and knew nothing about, and while making believe to examine them, addressing herself to Mr Huntingdon, with one of her coldest and most repellent aspects, and beginning a series of the most common place and formidably formal questions and observations, on purpose to wrest his attention from me – on purpose to vex me, as I thought: and having now looked through the portfolio, I left them to their *tête-à-tête*, and seated myself on a sofa, quite apart from the company – never thinking how strange such conduct would appear, but merely to indulge, at first, the vexation of the moment, and subsequently to enjoy my private thoughts.

But I was not left long alone, for Mr Wilmot, of all men the least welcome, took advantage of my isolated position to come and plant himself beside me. I had flattered myself that I had so effectually repulsed his advances on all former occasions, that I had nothing more to apprehend from his unfortunate predilection; but it seems I was mistaken: so great was his confidence, either in his wealth or his remaining powers of attraction, and so firm his conviction of feminine weakness, that he thought himself warranted to return to the siege, which he did with renovated ardour, enkindled by the quantity of wine he had drunk – a circumstance that rendered him infinitely the more disgusting; but greatly as I abhorred him at that moment, I did not like to treat him with rudeness, as I was now his guest and had just been enjoying his hospitality; and I was no hand at a polite but determined rejection, nor would it have greatly availed me if I had, for he was too coarse-minded to take any repulse that was not as plain and positive as his own effrontery. The consequence was, that he waxed more fulsomely tender, and more repulsively warm, and I was driven to the very verge of desperation, and about to say, I know not what, when I felt my hand, that hung over the arm of the sofa, suddenly taken by another and gently but fervently pressed. Instinctively, I guessed who it was, and on looking up, was less surprised than delighted, to see Mr Huntingdon smiling upon me. It was like turning from some purgatorial fiend to an angel of light, come to announce that the season of torment was past.

'Helen,' said he (he frequently called me Helen, and I never resented the freedom), 'I want you to look at this picture: Mr Wilmot will excuse you a moment, I'm sure.'

I rose with alacrity. He drew my arm within his, and led me across the room to a splendid painting of Vandyke's that I had noticed before, but not sufficiently examined. After a moment of silent contemplation, I was beginning to comment on its beauties and peculiarities, when, playfully pressing the hand he still retained within his arm, he interrupted me with –

'Never mind the picture, it was not for that I brought you here; it was to get you away from that scoundrelly old profligate yonder, who is looking as if he would like to challenge me for the affront.'

'I am very much obliged to you,' said I. 'This is twice you have delivered me from such unpleasant companionship.'

'Don't be too thankful,' he answered: 'it is not all kindness to you; it is partly from a feeling of spite to your tormentors that makes me delighted to do the old fellows a bad turn, though I don't think I have any great reason to dread them as rivals – have I Helen?'

'You know I detest them both.'

'And me?'

'I have no reason to detest *you*.'

'But what are your sentiments towards me? – Helen – Speak! – How do you regard me?'

And again he pressed my hand; but I feared there was more of conscious power than tenderness in his demeanour, and I felt he had no right to extort a confession of attachment from me when he had made no correspondent avowal himself, and knew not what to answer. At last I said –

'How do *you* regard *me*?'

'Sweet angel, I adore you! I –'

'Helen, I want you a moment,' said the distinct, low voice of my aunt, close beside us. And I left him, muttering maledictions against his evil angel.

'Well aunt, what is it? What do you want?' said I, following her to the embrasure of the window.

'I want you to join the company, when you are fit to be seen,' returned she, severely regarding me; 'but please to stay here a little till that shocking colour is somewhat abated, and your eyes have recovered something of their natural expression. I should be ashamed for anyone to see you in your present state.'

Of course, such a remark had no effect in reducing the 'shocking colour;' on the contrary, I felt my face glow with redoubled fires kindled by a complication of emotions, of which indignant, swelling anger was the chief. I offered no reply, however, but pushed aside the curtain and looked into the night – or rather, into the lamp-lit square.

'Was Mr Huntingdon proposing to you, Helen?' inquired my too watchful relative.

'No.'

'What was he saying then? I heard something very like it.'

'I don't know what he would have said, if you hadn't interrupted him.'

'And would you have accepted him, Helen, if he had proposed?'

'Of course not – without consulting uncle and you.'

'Oh! I'm glad, my dear, you have so much prudence left. Well, now,' she added, after a moment's pause, 'you have made yourself conspicuous enough for one evening. The ladies are directing inquiring glances towards us at this moment I see. I shall join them. Do you come too, when you are sufficiently composed to appear as usual.'

'I am so now.'

'Speak gently then; and don't look so malicious,' said my calm, but provoking aunt. 'We shall return home shortly, and then,' she added with solemn significance, 'I have much to say to you.'

So I went home prepared for a formidable lecture. Little was said by either party in the carriage during our short transit homewards; but when I had entered my room and thrown myself into an easy chair to reflect on the events of the day, my aunt followed me thither, and having dismissed Rachel, who was carefully stowing away my ornaments, closed the door; and placing a chair beside me, or rather at right angles with mine, sat down. With due deference I offered her my more commodious seat. She declined it, and thus opened the conference:

'Do you remember, Helen, our conversation the night but one before we left Staningley?'

'Yes aunt.'

'And do you remember how I warned you against letting your heart be stolen from you by those unworthy of its possession; and fixing your affections where approbation did not go before, and where reason and judgment withheld their sanction?'

'Yes, but *my* reason –'

'Pardon me – and do you remember assuring me that there was no occasion for uneasiness on your account; for you should never be *tempted* to marry a man who was deficient in sense or principle, however handsome or charming in other respects he might be, for you could not love him, you should hate – despise – pity – anything but love him – were not those your words?'

'Yes, but –'

'And did you not say that your affection *must* be founded on approbation; and that unless you could approve and honour and respect, you could not love?'

'Yes; but I do approve and honour, and respect –'

'How so, my dear? is Mr Huntingdon a good man?'

'He is a much better man than you think him.'

'That is nothing to the purpose. Is he a *good* man?'

'Yes – in some respects. He has a good disposition.'

'Is he a man of *principle*?'

'Perhaps not, exactly; but it is only for want of thought: if he had some one to advise him, and remind him of what is right –'

'He would soon learn, you think – and you yourself would

willingly undertake to be his teacher? But, my dear, he is, I believe, full ten years older than you – how is it that you are so before-hand in moral acquirements?'

'Thanks to you, aunt, I have been well brought up, and had good examples always before me, which he, most likely, has not; – and besides, he is of a sanguine temperament, and a gay, thoughtless temper, and I am naturally inclined to reflection.'

'Well, now you have made him out to be deficient in both sense and principle, by your own confession –'

'Then, my sense and my principle are at his service!'

'That sounds presumptuous, Helen! Do you think you have enough for both; and do you imagine your merry, thoughtless profligate would allow himself to be guided by a young girl like you?'

'No; I should not wish to guide him; but I think I might have influence sufficient to save him from some errors, and I should think my life well spent in the effort to preserve so noble a nature from destruction. He always listens attentively now, when I speak seriously to him (and I often venture to reprove his random way of talking), and sometimes he says that if he had me always by his side he should never do or say a wicked thing, and that a little daily talk with me would make him quite a saint. It may be partly jest and partly flattery, but still –'

'But still you think it may be truth?'

'If I do think there is any mixture of truth in it, it is not from confidence in my own powers, but in *his* natural good-ness. – And you have no right to call him a profligate, aunt; he is nothing of the kind.'

'Who told you so, my dear? What was that story about his intrigue with a married lady – Lady who was it? – Miss Wilmot herself was telling you the other day?'

'It was false – false!' I cried. 'I don't believe a word of it.'

'You think, then, that he is a virtuous, well-conducted young man?'

'I know nothing positive respecting his character. I only know that I have heard nothing definitive against it – nothing that could be proved, at least; and till people can prove their slanderous accusations, I will not believe them. And I know this, that if he has committed errors, they are only such as are common to youth, and such as nobody thinks anything about; for I see that everybody likes him, and all the mammas smile upon him, and their daughters – and Miss Wilmot herself – are only too glad to attract his attention.'

'Helen, the world *may* look upon such offences as venial; a few unprincipled mothers *may* be anxious to catch a young man of fortune without reference to his character; and thoughtless girls *may* be glad to win the smiles of so handsome a gentleman, without seeking to penetrate beyond the surface; but *you*, I trusted were better informed than to see with their eyes, and judge with their perverted judgment. I did not think *you* would call these venial errors!'

'Nor do I, aunt; but if I hate the sins I love the sinner, and would do much for his salvation, even supposing your suspicions to be mainly true – which I do not and will not believe.'

'Well, my dear, ask your uncle what sort of company he keeps, and if he is not banded with a set of loose, profligate young men, whom he calls his friends – his jolly companions, and whose chief delight is to wallow in vice, and vie with each other who can run fastest and farthest down the headlong road, to the place prepared for the devil and his angels.'

'Then, I will save him from them.'

'Oh, Helen, Helen! you little know the misery of uniting your fortunes to such a man!'

'I have such confidence in him, aunt, notwithstanding all you say, that I would willingly risk my happiness for the chance of securing his. I will leave better men to those who only consider their own advantage. If he has done amiss, I shall consider my life well spent in saving him from the consequences of his early errors, and striving to recall him to the path of virtue. – God grant me success!'

Here the conversation ended, for at this juncture my uncle's voice was heard, from his chamber, loudly calling upon my aunt to come to bed. He was in a bad humour that night; for his gout was worse. It had been gradually increasing upon him ever since we came to town; and my aunt took advantage of the circumstance, next morning, to persuade him to return to the country immediately, without waiting for the close of the season. His physician supported and enforced her arguments; and contrary to her usual habits, she so hurried the preparations for removal (as much for my sake as my uncle's, I think), that in a very few days we departed; and I saw no more of Mr Huntingdon. My aunt flatters herself I shall soon forget him – perhaps, she thinks I have forgotten him already, for I never mention his name; and she may continue to think so, till we meet again, – if ever that should be. I wonder if it will.

CHAPTER XVIII

THE MINIATURE

AUGUST 25TH. – I am now quite settled down to my usual routine of steady occupations and quiet amusements – tolerably contented and cheerful, but still looking forward to spring with the hope of returning to town, not for its gaieties and dissipations, but for the chance of meeting Mr Huntingdon once again; for still he is always in my thoughts and in my dreams. In all my employments, whatever I do, or see, or hear, has an ultimate reference to him; whatever skill or knowledge I acquire is some day to be turned to his advantage or amusement; whatever new beauties in nature or art I discover, are to be depicted to meet his eye, or stored in my memory to be told him at some future period. This, at least, is the hope that I cherish, the fancy that lights me on my lonely way. It may be only an ignis fatuus, after all, but it can do no harm to follow it with my eyes and rejoice in its lustre, as long as it does not lure me from the path I ought to keep; and I think it will not, for I have thought deeply on my aunt's advice, and I see clearly, now, the folly of throwing myself away on one that is unworthy of all the love I have to give, and incapable of responding to the best and deepest feelings of my inmost heart – *so* clearly that even if I should see him again, and if he should remember me and love me still (which, alas! is too little probable, consider-ing how he is situated, and by whom surrounded), and if he should ask me to marry him, – I am determined not to consent until I know for certain whether my aunt's opinion of him or mine is nearest the truth; for if mine is altogether wrong, it is not he that I love; it is a creature of my own imagination. But I think it is not wrong – no, no – there is a secret something – an inward instinct that assures me I am right. There *is* essential goodness in him; – and what delight to unfold it! If he has wandered, what bliss to recall him! If he is now exposed to the baneful influence of corrupting and wicked companions, what glory to deliver him from them! – Oh! if I could but believe that Heaven has designed me for this!

To-day is the first of September; but my uncle has ordered the gamekeeper to spare the partridges till the gentlemen come. 'What gentlemen?' I asked when I heard it – a small party he had invited to shoot. His friend Mr Wilmot was one, and my aunt's friend Mr Boarham another. This struck me as terrible news, at the moment, but all regret and apprehension vanished like a dream when I heard that Mr Huntingdon was actually to be a third! My aunt is greatly against his coming, of course: she earnestly endeavoured to dissuade my uncle from asking him; but he, laughing at her objections, told her it was no use talking for the mischief was already done: he had invited Huntingdon and his friend Lord Lowborough before we left London, and nothing now remained but to fix the day for their coming. So he is safe, and I am sure of seeing him. I cannot express my joy – I find it very difficult to conceal it from my aunt; but I don't wish to trouble her with my feelings till I know whether I ought to indulge them or not. If I find it my absolute duty to suppress them, they shall trouble no one but myself and if I can really feel myself justified in indulging this attachment, I can dare anything, even the anger and grief of my best friend, for its object – surely, I shall soon know. But they are not coming till about the middle of the month.

We are to have two lady visitors also: Mr Wilmot is to bring his niece and her cousin Milicent. I suppose my aunt thinks the latter will benefit me by her society and the salutary example of her gentle deportment, and lowly and tractable spirit; and the former, I suspect she intends as a species of counter-attraction to win Mr Huntingdon's attention from me. I don't thank her for this; but I shall be glad of Milicent's company: she is a sweet, good girl, and I wish I were like her – *more* like her, at least, than I am.

19th. They are come. They came the day before yesterday. The gentlemen are all gone out to shoot, and the ladies are with my aunt, at work, in the drawing-room. I have retired to the library, for I am very unhappy, and I want to be alone. Books cannot divert me; so having opened my desk, I will try what may be done by detailing the cause of my uneasiness. This paper will serve instead of a confidential friend into whose ear I might pour forth the overflowings of my heart. It will not sympathize with my distresses, but then, it will not laugh at them, and, if I keep it close, it cannot tell again; so it is, perhaps, the best friend I could have for the purpose.

First, let me speak of his arrival – how I sat at my window and watched for nearly two hours, before his carriage entered the park gates – for they all came before him, – and how deeply I was disappointed at every arrival, because it was not his. First came Mr Wilmot and the ladies. When Milicent had got into her room, I quitted my post a few minutes, to look in upon her and have a little private conversation, for she was now my intimate friend, several long epistles having passed between us since our parting. On returning to my window, I beheld another carriage at the door. Was it his? No; it was Mr Boarham's plain, dark chariot; and there stood he upon the steps, carefully superintending the dislodging of his various boxes and packages. What a collection! One would have thought he projected a visit of six months at least. A considerable time after, came Lord Lowborough in his barouche. Is he one of the profligate friends, I wonder? I should think not; for no one could call *him* a jolly companion, I'm sure, – and besides, he appears too sober and gentlemanly in his demeanour, to merit such suspicions. He is a tall, thin, gloomy-looking man, apparently between thirty and forty, and of a somewhat sickly, careworn aspect.

At last, Mr Huntingdon's light phaeton came bowling merrily up the lawn. I had but a transient glimpse of him, for the moment it stopped, he sprang out over the side on to the portico steps, and disappeared into the house.

I now submitted to be dressed for dinner – a duty which Rachel had been urging upon me for the last twenty minutes; and when that important business was completed, I repaired to the drawing-room where I found Mr and Miss Wilmot and Milicent Hargrave already assembled. Shortly after, Lord Lowborough entered, and then Mr Boarham, who seemed quite willing to forget and forgive my former conduct, and to hope that a little conciliation and steady perseverance on his part might yet succeed in bringing me to reason. While I stood at the window, conversing with Milicent, he came up to me, and was beginning to talk in nearly his usual strain, when Mr Huntingdon entered the room.

'How will he greet me, I wonder?' said my bounding heart; and instead of advancing to meet him, I turned to the window to hide or subdue my emotion. But having saluted his host and hostess, and the rest of the company, he came to me, ardently squeezed my hand, and murmured he was glad to see me once again. At that moment dinner was announced, my aunt desired him to take Miss Hargrave into the dining-room, and odious Mr Wilmot, with unspeakable grimaces, offered his arm to me; and I was condemned to sit between himself and Mr Boarham. But afterwards, when we were all again assembled in the drawing-room, I was indemnified for so much suffering by a few delightful minutes of conversation with Mr Huntingdon.

In the course of the evening, Miss Wilmot was called upon to sing and play for the amusement of the company, and I to exhibit my drawings, and, though he likes music, and she is an accomplished musician, I think I am right in affirming that he paid more attention to my drawings than to her music.

So far, so good; – but, hearing him pronounce, sotto voce, but with peculiar emphasis, concerning one of the pieces, 'THIS is better than all!' – I looked up, curious to see which it was, and, to my horror, beheld him complacently gazing at the *back* of the picture – it was his own face that I had sketched there and forgotten to rub out! To make matters worse, in the agony of the moment, I attempted to snatch it from his hand; – but he prevented me, and exclaiming, 'No – by George, I'll keep it!' placed it against his waistcoat and buttoned his coat upon it with a delighted chuckle.

Then, drawing a candle close to his elbow, he gathered all the drawings to himself, as well what he had seen as the others, and muttering, 'I must look at *both* sides now,' he eagerly commenced an examination, which I watched, at first, with tolerable composure, in the confidence that his vanity would not be gratified by any further discoveries; for, though I must plead guilty to having disfigured the backs of several with abortive attempts to delineate that too fascinating physiognomy, I was sure that, with that one unfortunate exception, I had carefully obliterated all such witnesses of my infatuation. But the pencil frequently leaves an impression upon cardboard that no amount of rubbing can efface. Such, it seems, was the case with most of these; and I confess I trembled when I saw him holding them so close to the candle, and poring so intently over the seeming blanks; but still, I trusted, he would not be able to make out these dim traces to his own satisfaction. I was mistaken however – having ended his scrutiny, he quietly remarked, –

'I perceive, the backs of young ladies' drawings, like the post-scripts of their letters, are the most important and interesting part of the concern.'

Then, leaning back in his chair, he reflected a few minutes in silence, complacently smiling to himself, and while I was concocting some cutting speech wherewith to check his grati-fication, he rose, and passing over to where Annabella Wilmot sat vehemently coquetting with Lord Lowborough, seated him-self on the sofa beside her, and attached himself to her for the rest of the evening.

'So then!' thought I – 'he despises me, because he knows I love him.'

And the reflection made me so miserable I knew not what to do. Milicent came and began to admire my drawings and make remarks upon them; but I could not talk to her – I could talk to no one; and upon the introduction of tea, I took advantage of the open door and the slight diversion caused by its entrance, to slip out – for I was sure I could not take any – and take refuge in the library. My aunt sent Thomas in quest of me, to ask if I were not coming to tea; but I bade him say l should not take any to-night; and happily she was too much occupied with her guests to make any further enquiries at the time.

As most of the company had travelled far that day, they retired early to rest; and having heard them all, as I thought, go up stairs, I ventured out, to get my candlestick from the drawing-room sideboard. But Mr Huntingdon had lingered behind the rest: he was just at the foot of the stairs when I opened the door; and hearing my step in the hall – though I could hardly hear it myself – he instantly turned back.

'Helen, is that you?' said he, 'why did you run away from us?'

'Good night, Mr Huntingdon,' said I, coldly, not choosing to answer the question. And I turned away to enter the drawing-room.

'But you'll shake hands, won't you?' said he, placing himself in the door-way before me. And he seized my hand and held it, much against my will.

'Let me go, Mr Huntingdon,' said I – 'I want to get a candle.'

'The candle will keep,' returned he.

I made a desperate effort to free my hand from his grasp.

'Why are you in such a hurry to leave me, Helen?' he said, with a smile of the most provoking self-sufficiency – 'you don't hate me, you *know*.'

'Yes, I do – at this moment.'

'Not you! It is Annabella Wilmot you hate, not me.'

'I have nothing to do with Annabella Wilmot,' said I, burning with indignation.

'But *I* have, you know,' returned he, with peculiar emphasis.

'That is nothing to me, sir!' I retorted.

'*Is* it nothing to you, Helen? – Will you swear it? – Will you?'

'No I won't, Mr Huntingdon! and I *will* go!' cried I, not knowing whether to laugh or to cry, or to break out into a tempest of fury.

'Go then, you vixen!' he said; but the instant he released my hand he had the audacity to put his arm round my neck and kiss me.

Trembling with anger and agitation – and I don't know what besides, I broke away, and got my candle, and rushed up stairs to my room. He would not have done so but for that hateful picture! And there he had it still in his possession, an eternal monument to his pride and my humiliation!

It was but little sleep I got that night; and in the morning I rose perplexed and troubled with the thoughts of meeting him at breakfast. I knew not how it was to be done; an assumption of dignified, cold indifference would hardly do after what he knew of my devotion – to his face, at least. Yet something must be done to check his presumption – I would not submit to be tyrannized over by those bright, laughing eyes. And accordingly, I received his cheerful morning salutation as calmly and coldly as my aunt could have wished, and defeated with brief answers his one or two attempts to draw me into conversation; while I comported myself with unusual cheerfulness and complaisance towards every other member of the party, especially Annabella Wilmot, and even her uncle and Mr Boarham were treated with an extra amount of civility on the occasion, not from any motives of coquetry, but just to show him that my particular coolness and reserve arose from no general ill-humour or depression of spirits.

He was not, however, to be repelled by such acting as this. He did not talk much to me, but when he did speak, it was with a degree of freedom and openness – and *kindliness* too – that plainly seemed to intimate he knew his words were music to my ears; and when his looks met mine, it was with a smile – presumptuous it might be – but oh, so sweet, so bright, so genial, that I could not possibly retain my anger; every vestige of displeasure soon melted away beneath it, like morning clouds before the summer sun.

Soon after breakfast all the gentlemen save one, with boyish eagerness, set out on their expedition against the hapless partridges; my uncle and Mr Wilmot on their shooting ponies, Mr Huntingdon and Lord Lowborough on their legs; the one exception being Mr Boarham, who, in consideration of the rain that had fallen during the night, thought it prudent to remain behind a little, and join them in a while, when the sun had dried the grass. And he favoured us all with a long and minute disquisition upon the evils and dangers attendant upon damp feet, delivered with the most imperturbable gravity, amid the jeers and laughter of Mr Huntingdon and my uncle, who, leaving the prudent sportsman to entertain the ladies with his medical discussions, sallied forth with their guns, bending their steps to the stables first, to have a look at the horses, and let out the dogs.

Not desirous of sharing Mr Boarham's company for the whole of the morning, I betook myself to the library; and there brought forth my easel, and began to paint. The easel and the painting apparatus would serve as an excuse for abandoning the drawing-room, if my aunt should come to complain of the desertion; and besides, I wanted to finish the picture. It was one I had taken great pains with, and I intended it to be my master-piece, though it was somewhat presumptuous in the design. By the bright azure of the sky, and by the warm and brilliant lights, and deep, long shadows, I had endeavoured to convey the idea of a sunny morning. I had ventured to give more of the bright verdure of spring or early summer to the grass and foliage, than is commonly attempted in painting. The scene represented was an open glade in a wood. A group of dark Scotch firs was introduced in the middle distance to relieve the prevailing fresh-ness of the rest; but in the foreground, were part of the gnarled trunk and of the spreading boughs of a large forest tree, whose foliage was of a brilliant golden green – not golden from autumn-al mellowness, but from the sunshine, and the very immaturity of the scarce expanded leaves. Upon this bough, that stood out in bold relief against the sombre firs, were seated an amorous pair of turtle doves, whose soft sad coloured plumage afforded a contrast of another nature; and beneath it, a young girl was kneeling on the daisy-spangled turf, with head thrown back and masses of fair hair falling on her shoulders, her hands clasped, lips parted, and eyes intently gazing upward in pleased, yet earnest contemplation of those feathered lovers – too deeply absorbed in each other to notice her.

I had scarcely settled to my work – which, however, wanted

but a few touches to the finishing – when the sportsmen passed the window on their return from the stables. It was partly open, and Mr Huntingdon must have seen me as he went by, for in half a minute he came back, and setting his gun against the wall, threw up the sash, and sprang in, and set himself before my picture.

'Very pretty, i'faith!' said he, after attentively regarding it for a few seconds – 'and a very fitting study for a young lady. – Spring just opening into summer – morning just approaching noon – girlhood just ripening into womanhood – and hope just verging on fruition. She's a sweet creature! but why didn't you make her black hair?'

'I thought light hair would suit her better. You see I have made her blue-eyed and plump, and fair and rosy.'

'Upon my word – a very Hebe! I should fall in love with her, if I hadn't the artist before me. Sweet innocent! she's thinking there will come a time when she will be wooed and won like that pretty hen-dove, by as fond and fervent a lover; and she's thinking how pleasant it will be, and how tender and faithful he will find her.'

'And perhaps,' suggested I, 'how tender and faithful she shall find him.'

'Perhaps – for there is no limit to the wild extravagance of hope's imaginings, at such an age.'

'Do you call *that*, then, one of her wild, extravagant delusions?'

'No; my heart tells me it is not. I might have thought so once, but now, I say, give me the girl I love, and I will swear eternal constancy to her and her alone, through summer and winter, through youth and age, and life and death! if age and death *must* come.'

He spoke this in such serious earnest that my heart bounded with delight; but the minute after he changed his tone, and asked, with a significant smile, if I had 'any more portraits.'

'No,' replied I, reddening with confusion and wrath. But my

portfolio was on the table; he took it up, and coolly sat down to examine its contents.

'Mr Huntingdon, those are my unfinished sketches,' cried I, 'and I never let any one see them.'

And I placed my hand on the portfolio to wrest it from him; but he maintained his hold, assuring me that he 'liked unfinished sketches of all things.'

'But I hate them to be seen,' returned I. 'I can't let you have it, indeed!'

'Let me have its bowels then,' said he; and just as I wrenched the portfolio from his hand, he deftly abstracted the greater part of its contents, and after turning them over a moment, he cried out, –

'Bless my stars, here's another!' and slipped a small oval of ivory paper into his waistcoat pocket – a complete miniature portrait, that I had sketched with such tolerable success, as to be induced to colour it with great pains and care. But I was determined he should not keep it.

'Mr Huntingdon,' cried I, 'I *insist* upon having that back! It is mine, and you have no *right* to take it. Give it me, directly – I'll never forgive you, if you don't!'

But the more vehemently I insisted, the more he aggravated my distress by his insulting, gleeful laugh. At length however, he restored it to me, saying –

'Well, well, since you value it so much, I'll not deprive you of it.'

To show him how I valued it, I tore it in two, and threw it into the fire. He was not prepared for this. His merriment suddenly ceasing, he stared in mute amazement at the consuming treasure; and then, with a careless 'Humph! I'll go and shoot now,' he turned on his heel and vacated the apartment by the window as he came, and setting on his hat with an air, took up his gun and walked away, whistling as he went – and leaving me not too much agitated to finish my picture; for I was glad, at the moment, that I had vexed him.

When I returned to the drawing-room, I found Mr Boarham had ventured to follow his comrades to the field; and shortly after lunch, to which they did not think of returning, I volunteered to accompany the ladies in a walk, and show Annabella and Milicent the beauties of the country. We took a long ramble and re-entered the park just as the sportsmen were returning from their expedition. Toil-spent and travel-stained, the main body of them crossed over the grass to avoid us; but Mr Huntingdon, all spattered and splashed as he was, and stained with the blood of his prey – to the no small offence of my aunt's strict sense of propriety – came out of his way to meet us, with cheerful smiles and words for all but me, and placing himself between Annabella Wilmot and myself, walked up the road and began to relate the various exploits and disasters of the day, in a manner that would have convulsed me with laughter, if I had been on good terms with him; but he addressed himself entirely to Annabella, and I, of course, left all the laughter and all the badinage to her, and affecting the utmost indifference to whatever passed between them, walked along a few paces apart, and looking every way but theirs; while my aunt and Milicent went before, linked arm in arm, and gravely discoursing together. At length, Mr Huntingdon turned to me, and addressing me in a confidential whisper, said –

'Helen, why did you burn my picture?'

'Because, I wished to destroy it,' I answered, with an asperity it is useless now to lament.

'Oh, very good!' was the reply; 'if *you* don't value me, I must turn to somebody that will.'

I thought it was partly in jest – a half playful mixture of mock resignation and pretended indifference; but immediately he resumed his place beside Miss Wilmot, and from that hour to this – during all that evening, and all the next day, and the next, and the next, and all this morning (the 22nd), he has never given me one kind word or one pleasant look – never spoken to me, but from pure necessity – never glanced towards me, but with a cold, unfriendly look I thought him quite incapable of assuming.

My aunt observes the change, and though she has not inquired the cause or made any remark to me on the subject, I see it gives her pleasure. Miss Wilmot observes it too, and triumphantly ascribes it to her own superior charms and blandishments; but I am truly miserable – more so than I like to acknowledge to myself. Pride refuses to aid me. It has brought me into the scrape, and will not help me out of it.

He meant no harm – it was only his joyous, playful spirit; and I, by my acrimonious resentment – so serious, so disproportioned to the offence – have so wounded his feelings – so deeply offended him, that I fear he will never forgive me – and all for a mere jest! He thinks I dislike him, – and he must continue to think so. I must lose him for ever; and Annabella may win him, and triumph as she will.

But it is not my loss, nor her triumph that I deplore so greatly as the wreck of my fond hopes for his advantage, and her unworthiness of his affection, and the injury he will do himself by trusting his happiness to her. *She* does not love him: she thinks only of herself. She cannot appreciate the good that is in him: she will neither see it, nor value it, nor cherish it. She will neither deplore his faults nor attempt their amendment, but rather aggravate them by her own. And I doubt whether she will not deceive him after all: I see she is playing double between him and Lord Lowborough, and while she amuses herself with the lively Huntingdon, she tries her utmost to enslave his moody friend; and should she succeed in bringing both to her feet, the fascinating commoner will have but little chance against the lordly peer. If he observes her artful by-play, it gives him no uneasiness, but rather adds new zest to his diversion by opposing a stimulating check to his otherwise too easy conquest.

Messrs Wilmot and Boarham have severally taken occasion by his neglect of me to renew their advances; and if I were like

Annabella and some others, I should take advantage of their perseverance to endeavour to pique him into a revival of affection; but, justice and honesty apart, I could not *bear* to do it; I am annoyed enough by their present persecutions without encouraging them farther; – and even if I did, it would have precious little effect upon him. He sees me suffering under the condescending attentions and prosaic discourses of the one, and the repulsive obtrusions of the other, without so much as a shadow of commiseration for me, or resentment against my tormentors. He never could have loved me, or he would not have resigned me so willingly, and he would not go on talking to everybody else so cheerfully as he does – laughing and jesting with Lord Lowborough and my uncle, teasing Milicent Hargrave, and flirting with Annabella Wilmot – as if nothing were on his mind. Oh, why can't I hate him? I must be infatuated, or I should *scorn* to regret him as I do! But I must rally all the powers I have remaining, and try to tear him from my heart. There goes the dinner bell – and here comes my aunt to scold me for sitting here at my desk all day, instead of staying with the company – I wish the company were – gone.

CHAPTER XIX

AN INCIDENT

Twenty-second. Night – What have I done? and what will be the end of it? I cannot calmly reflect upon it; I cannot sleep. I must have recourse to my diary again; I will commit it to paper to-night, and see what I shall think of it to-morrow.

I went down to dinner resolving to be cheerful and well-conducted, and kept my resolution very creditably, considering how my head ached, and how internally wretched I felt. – I don't know what is come over me of late; my very energies both mental and physical must be strangely impaired, or I should not have acted so weakly in many respects, as I have done; – but I have not been well this last day or two: I suppose it is with sleeping and eating so little, and thinking so much, and being so continually out of humour. But to return: I was exerting myself to sing and play for the amusement, and at the request of my aunt and Milicent, before the gentlemen came into the drawing-room (Miss Wilmot never likes to waste her musical efforts on ladies' ears alone): Milicent had asked for a little Scotch song, and I was just in the middle of it when they entered. The first thing Mr Huntingdon did, was to walk up to Annabella: –

'Now, Miss Wilmot, won't *you* give us some music to-night?' said he. 'Do now! I know you will, when I tell you that I have been hungering and thirsting all day, for the sound of your voice. Come! the piano's vacant.'

It was; for I had quitted it immediately upon hearing his petition. Had I been endowed with a proper degree of self-possession, I should have turned to the lady myself; and cheerfully joined my entreaties to his; whereby I should have disappointed his expectations, if the affront had been purposely given, or made him sensible of the wrong, if it had only arisen from thoughtlessness; but I felt it too deeply to do anything but rise from the music-stool, and throw myself back on the sofa, suppressing with difficulty the audible expression of the bitterness I felt within. I knew Annabella's musical talents were superior to mine, but that was no reason why I should be treated as a perfect nonentity. The time and the manner of his asking her, appeared like a gratuitous insult to me; and I could have wept with pure vexation.

Meantime, she exultantly seated herself at the piano, and favoured him with two of his favourite songs, in such superior style that even I soon lost my anger in admiration, and listened with a sort of gloomy pleasure to the skilful modulations of her full-toned and powerful voice, so judiciously aided by her rounded and spirited touch; and while my ears drank in the sound, my eyes rested on the face of her principal auditor, and derived an equal or superior delight from the contemplation of his speaking countenance, as he stood beside her – that eye and brow lighted up with keen enthusiasm, and that sweet smile passing and appearing like gleams of sunshine on an April day. No wonder he should hunger and thirst to hear her sing. I now forgave him, from my heart, his reckless slight of me, and I felt ashamed at my pettish resentment of such a trifle – ashamed too of those bitter envious pangs that gnawed my inmost heart, in spite of all this admiration and delight.

'There now!' said she, playfully running her fingers over the keys, when she had concluded the second song. 'What shall I give you next?'

But in saying this, she looked back at Lord Lowborough, who was standing a little behind leaning against the back of a chair – an attentive listener, too, experiencing, to judge by his countenance, much the same feelings of mingled pleasure and sadness as I did. But the look she gave him, plainly said, 'Do you choose for me now: I have done enough for him, and will gladly exert myself to gratify you;' and thus encouraged, his lordship came forward, and turning over the music, presently set before her a little song that I had noticed before, and read more than once, with an interest arising from the circumstance of my connecting it in my mind with the reigning tyrant of my thoughts. And now with my nerves already excited and half unstrung, I could not hear those words so sweetly warbled forth, without some symptoms of emotion I was not able to suppress. Tears rose unbidden to my eyes, and I buried my face in the sofa-pillow that they might flow unseen while I listened. The air was simple, sweet, and sad, it is still running in my head, – and so are the words: –

'Farewell to thee! but not farewell
   To all my fondest thoughts of thee:
Within my heart they still shall dwell;
   And they shall cheer and comfort me.

O' beautiful, and full of grace!
   If thou hadst never met mine eye,
I had not dreamed a living face
   Could fancied charms so far outvie.

If I may ne'er behold again
   That form and face, so dear to me,
Nor hear thy voice, still would I fain
   Preserve, for aye, their memory.

That voice, the magic of whose tone
   Can wake an echo in my breast,
Creating feelings that, alone,
   Can make my tranced spirit blest.

That laughing eye, whose sunny beam
   My memory would not cherish less; –
And oh, that smile! whose joyous gleam
   No mortal languish can express.

Adieu! but let me cherish, still,
   The hope with which I cannot part.
Contempt may wound, and coldness chill,
   But still it lingers in my heart.

And who can tell but Heaven, at last,
   May answer all my thousand prayers,
And bid the future pay the past
   With joy for anguish, smiles for tears?'

When it ceased, I longed for nothing so much as to be out of the room. The sofa was not far from the door, but I did not dare to raise my head, for I knew Mr Huntingdon was standing near me, and I knew by the sound of his voice, as he spoke in answer to some remark of Lord Lowborough's, that his face was turned towards me. Perhaps, a half suppressed sob had caught his ear, and caused him to look round – Heaven forbid! But with a violent effort, I checked all further signs of weakness, dried my tears, and, when I thought he had turned away again, rose, and instantly left the apartment, taking refuge in my favourite resort, the library.

There was no light there but the faint red glow of the neglected fire; – but I did not want a light; I only wanted to indulge my thoughts, unnoticed and undisturbed; and sitting down on a low stool before the easy chair, I sunk my head upon its cushioned seat, and thought, and thought, until the tears gushed out again, and I wept like any child. Presently, however, the door was gently opened and someone entered the room. I trusted it was only a servant, and did not stir. The door was closed again – but I was not alone: a hand gently touched my shoulder, and a voice said, softly –

'Helen, what is the matter?'

I could not answer at the moment.

'You must and shall tell me,' was added more vehemently, and the speaker threw himself on his knees, beside me on the rug, and forcibly possessed himself of my hand; but I hastily caught it away, and replied –

'It is nothing to you, Mr Huntingdon.'

'Are you sure it is nothing to me?' he returned, 'can you swear that you were not thinking of me while you wept?'

This was unendurable. I made an effort to rise, but he was kneeling on my dress.

'Tell me,' continued he – 'I want to know, – because, if you were, I have something to say to you, – and if not, I'll go.'

'Go then!' I cried; but, fearing he would obey too well, and never come again, I hastily added – 'Or say what you have to say, and have done with it!'

'But which?' said he – 'for I shall only say it if you really were thinking of me. So tell me, Helen.'

'You're excessively impertinent, Mr Huntingdon!'

'Not at all – too pertinent, you mean – so you won't tell me? – Well, I'll spare your woman's pride, and, construing your silence into "Yes," I'll take it for granted that I *was* the subject of your thoughts, and the cause of your affliction –'

'Indeed, sir –'

'If you deny it, I won't tell you my secret,' threatened he; and I did not interrupt him again – or even attempt to repulse him, though he had taken my hand once more, and half embraced me with his other arm – I was scarcely conscious of it, at the time.

'It is this,' resumed he: 'that Annabella Wilmot, in comparison with you, is like a flaunting peony compared with a sweet, wild rosebud gemmed with dew – and I love you to distraction! – Now, tell me if that intelligence gives you any pleasure. – Silence again? That means yes. – Then let me add, that I cannot live without you, and if you answer, No, to this last question, you will drive me mad. – Will you bestow yourself upon me? – you will!' he cried, nearly squeezing me to death in his arms.

'No, no!' I exclaimed, struggling to free myself from him – 'you must ask my uncle and aunt.'

'They won't refuse me, if you don't.'

'I'm not sure of that – my aunt dislikes you.'

'But *you* don't, Helen – say you love me, and I'll go.'

'I wish you *would* go!' I replied.

'I will, this instant, – if you'll only say you love me.'

'You know I do,' I answered. And again he caught me in his arms, and smothered me with kisses.

At that moment, my aunt opened wide the door, and stood before us, candle in hand, in shocked and horrified amazement, gazing alternately at Mr Huntingdon and me – for we had both started up, and now stood wide enough asunder. But *his* confusion was only for a moment. Rallying in an instant, with the most enviable assurance, he began –

'I beg ten thousand pardons, Mrs Maxwell! Don't be too severe upon me. I've been asking your sweet niece to take me for better, for worse; and she, like a good girl, informs me she cannot think of it without her uncle's and aunt's consent. So let me implore you not to condemn me to eternal wretchedness: if *you* favour my cause, I am safe; for Mr Maxwell, I am certain, can refuse you nothing.'

'We will talk of this to-morrow, sir,' said my aunt, coldly. 'It is a subject that demands mature and serious deliberation. At present, you had better return to the drawing-room.'

'But meantime,' pleaded he, 'let me commend my cause to your most indulgent –'

'No indulgence for you, Mr Huntingdon, must come between me and the consideration of my niece's happiness.'

'Ah, true! I know she is an angel, and I am a presumptuous dog to dream of possessing such a treasure; but, nevertheless, I would sooner die than relinquish her in favour of the best man that ever went to Heaven – and as for her happiness, I would sacrifice my body and soul –'

'Body and *soul* Mr Huntingdon – sacrifice your *soul*?'

'Well, I would lay down life –'

'You would not be required to lay it down.'

'I would spend it, then – devote my life – and all its powers to the promotion and preservation –'

'Another time, sir, we will talk of this – and I should have felt disposed to judge more favourably of your pretensions, if you too had chosen another time and place, and – let me add – another *manner* for your declaration.'

'Why, you see, Mrs Maxwell,' he began –

'Pardon me, sir,' said she, with dignity – 'The company are inquiring for you in the other room.' And she turned to me.

'Then *you* must plead for me, Helen,' said he, and at length withdrew.

'You had better retire to your room, Helen,' said my aunt, gravely. 'I will discuss this matter with you, too, to-morrow.'

'Don't be angry, aunt,' said I.

'My dear, I am not angry,' she replied: 'I am *surprised*. If it is true that you told him you could not accept his offer without our consent –'

'It *is* true,' interrupted I.

'Then how could you permit –'

'I couldn't help it, aunt,' I cried bursting into tears. They were not altogether the tears of sorrow, or of fear for her displeasure, but rather the outbreak of the general tumultuous excitement of my feelings. But my good aunt was touched at my agitation. In a softer tone, she repeated her recommendation to retire, and gently kissing my forehead, bade me good-night, and put her candle in my hand; and I went; – but my brain worked so, I could not think of sleeping. I feel calmer now that I have written all this; and I will go to bed, and try to win tired nature's sweet restorer.

END OF VOL. I

CHAPTER XX

PERSISTENCE

SEPTEMBER 24TH. – In the morning I rose, light and cheerful, nay, intensely happy. The hovering cloud cast over me by my aunt's views, and by the fear of not obtaining her consent, was lost in the bright effulgence of my own hopes, and the too delightful consciousness of requited love. It was a splendid morning; and I went out to enjoy it, in a quiet ramble in company with my own blissful thoughts. The dew was on the grass, and ten thousand gossamers were waving in the breeze; the happy red-breast was pouring out its little soul in song, and my heart overflowed with silent hymns of gratitude and praise to Heaven.

But I had not wandered far before my solitude was interrupted by the only person that could have disturbed my musings, at that moment, without being looked upon as an unwelcome intruder: Mr Huntingdon came suddenly upon me. So unexpected was the apparition, that I might have thought it the creation of an over-excited imagination, had the sense of sight alone borne witness to his presence; but immediately I felt his strong arm round my waist and his warm kiss on my cheek, while his keen and gleeful salutation, 'My own Helen!' was ringing in my ear.

'Not yours yet,' said I, hastily swerving aside from this too presumptuous greeting – 'remember my guardians. You will not easily attain my aunt's consent. Don't you see she is prejudiced against you?'

'I do, dearest; and you must tell me why, that I may best know how to combat her objections. I suppose she thinks I am a prodigal,' pursued he, observing that I was unwilling to reply, 'and concludes that I shall have but little worldly goods wherewith to endow my better half? If so, you must tell her that my property is mostly entailed, and I cannot get rid of it. There may be a few mortgages on the rest – a few trifling debts and encumbrances here and there, but nothing to speak of, and though I acknowledge I am not so rich as I might be – or have been – still, I think, we could manage pretty comfortably on what's left. My father, you know, was something of a miser, and in his latter days especially, saw no pleasure in life but to amass riches; and so it is no wonder that his son should make it his chief delight to spend them, which was accordingly the case, until my acquaintance with you, dear Helen, taught me other views and nobler aims. And the very idea of having you to care for under my roof, would force me to moderate my expenses and live like a Christian – not to speak of all the prudence and virtue you would instil into my mind by your wise counsels and sweet, attractive goodness.'

'But it is not that,' said I, 'it is not money my aunt thinks about. She knows better than to value worldly wealth above its price.'

'What is it then?'

'She wishes me to – to marry none but a really good man.'

'What, a man of "decided piety"? – ahem! – Well, come, I'll manage that too! It's Sunday to-day, isn't it? I'll go to church morning, afternoon, and evening, and comport myself in such a godly sort that she shall regard me with admiration and sisterly love, as a brand plucked from the burning. I'll come home sighing like a furnace, and full of the savour and unction of dear Mr Blatant's discourse –'

'Mr Leighton,' said I, dryly.

'Is Mr Leighton a "sweet preacher," Helen – a "dear, delightful, heavenly-minded man?"'

'He is a *good* man, Mr Huntingdon. I wish I could say half as much for you.'

'Oh, I forgot, you are a saint, too. I crave your pardon, dearest – but don't call me Mr Huntingdon, my name is Arthur.'

'I'll call you nothing – for I'll have nothing at all to do with you, if you talk in that way any more. If you really mean to deceive my aunt as you say, you are very wicked; and if not, you are very wrong to jest on such a subject.'

'I stand corrected,' said he, concluding his laugh with a sorrowful sigh. 'Now,' resumed he, after a momentary pause, 'let us talk about something else. And come nearer to me, Helen, and take my arm; and then I'll let you alone. I can't be quiet while I see you walking there.'

I complied; but said we must soon return to the house.

'No one will be down to breakfast yet, for long enough,' he answered. 'You spoke of your guardians just now, Helen, but is not your father still living?'

'Yes, but I always look upon my uncle and aunt as my guardians, for they are so, in deed, though not in name. My father has entirely given me up to their care. I have never seen him since dear mamma died when I was a very little girl, and my aunt, at her request, offered to take charge of me, and took me away to Staningley, where I have remained ever since; and I don't think he would object to anything for me, that she thought proper to sanction.'

'But would he sanction anything to which she thought proper to object?'

'No, I don't think he cares enough about me.'

'He is very much to blame – but he doesn't know what an angel he has for his daughter – which is all the better for me, as, if he did, he would not be willing to part with such a treasure.'

'And Mr Huntingdon,' said I, 'I suppose you *know* I am not an heiress?'

He protested he had never given it a thought, and begged I would not disturb his present enjoyment by the mention of such uninteresting subjects. I was glad of this proof of disinterested affection; for Annabella Wilmot is the probable heiress to all her uncle's wealth, in addition to her late father's property, which she has already in possession.

I now insisted upon retracing our steps to the house; but we walked slowly, and went on talking as we proceeded. I need not repeat all we said: let me rather refer to what passed between my aunt and me, after breakfast, when Mr Huntingdon called my uncle aside, no doubt to make his proposals, and she beckoned me into another room, where she once more commenced a solemn remonstrance which, however, entirely failed to convince me that her view of the case was preferable to my own.

'You judge him uncharitably, aunt, I know,' said I. 'His very friends are not half so bad as you represent them. There is Walter Hargrave, Milicent's brother, for one: he is but a little lower than the angels, if half she says of him is true. She is continually talking to me about him, and lauding his many virtues to the skies.'

'You will form a very inadequate estimate of a man's character,' replied she, 'if you judge by what a fond sister says of him. The worst of them generally know how to hide their misdeeds from their sister's eyes, and their mother's too.'

'And there is Lord Lowborough,' continued I, 'quite a decent man.'

'Who told you so? Lord Lowborough is a *desperate* man. He has dissipated his fortune in gambling and other things, and is now seeking an heiress to retrieve it. I told Miss Wilmot so; but you're all alike: she haughtily answered she was very much obliged to me, but she believed *she* knew when a man was seeking her for her fortune, and when for herself; she flattered herself she had had experience enough in those matters, to be justified in trusting to her own judgment – and as for his lordship's lack of fortune, she cared nothing about that, as she hoped her own would suffice for both; and as for his wildness, she supposed he was no worse than others – besides he was reformed now. – Yes, they can all play the hypocrite when they want to take in a fond, misguided woman!'

'Well, I think he's about as good as she is,' said I. 'But when Mr Huntingdon is married, he won't have many opportunities of consorting with his bachelor friends; – and the worse they are, the more I long to deliver him from them.'

'To be sure, my dear; and the worse *he* is, I suppose, the more you long to deliver him from himself.'

'Yes, provided he is not incorrigible – that is, the more I long to deliver him from his faults – to give him an opportunity of shaking off the adventitious evil got from contact with others worse than himself, and shining out in the unclouded light of his own genuine goodness – to do my utmost to help his better self against his worse, and make him what he would have been if he had not, from the beginning, had a bad, selfish, miserly father, who to gratify his own sordid passions, restricted him in the most innocent enjoyments of childhood and youth, and so disgusted him with every kind of restraint; – and a foolish mother who indulged him to the top of his bent, deceiving her husband for him, and doing her utmost to encourage those germs of folly and vice it was her duty to suppress, – and then, such a set of companions as you represent his friends to be –'

'Poor man!' said she, sarcastically, 'his kind have greatly wronged him!'

'They have!' cried I – 'and they shall wrong him no more – his wife shall undo what his mother did!'

'Well!' said she, after a short pause. 'I must say, Helen, I thought better of your judgment than this – and your taste too. How you can love such a man I cannot tell, or what pleasure you can find in his company; for "What fellowship hath light with darkness; or he that believeth with an infidel?" '

'He is not an infidel; – and I am not light, and he is not darkness, his worst and only vice is thoughtlessness.'

'And thoughtlessness,' pursued my aunt, 'may lead to every crime, and will but poorly excuse our errors in the sight of

God. Mr Huntingdon, I suppose, is not without the common faculties of men: he is not so light-headed as to be irresponsible: his Maker has endowed him with reason and conscience as well as the rest of us; the scriptures are open to him as well as to others; – and "If he hear not them, neither will he hear though one rose from the dead." And, remember, Helen,' continued she solemnly, ' "The wicked shall be turned into hell, and they that *forget* God!" And suppose, even, that he should continue to love you, and you him, and that you should pass through life together with tolerable comfort, – how will it be in the end, when you see yourselves parted for ever; you, perhaps, taken into eternal bliss, and he cast into the lake that burneth with unquenchable fire – there for ever to –'

'Not for ever,' I exclaimed, ' "only till he has paid the uttermost farthing;" for "If any man's work abide not the fire, he shall suffer loss, yet himself shall be saved, but so as by fire," and He that "is able to subdue all things to Himself, will have all men to be saved," and "will in the fulness of time, gather together in one all things in Christ Jesus, who tasted death for every man, and in whom God will reconcile all things to Himself, whether they be things in earth or things in Heaven." '

'Oh, Helen! where did you learn all this?'

'In the bible, aunt. I have searched it through, and found nearly thirty passages, all tending to support the same theory.'

'And is *that* the use you make of your bible? And did you find no passages tending to prove the danger and the falsity of such a belief?'

'No: I found indeed some passages that taken by themselves, might seem to contradict that opinion; but they will all bear a different construction to that which is commonly given, and in most the only difficulty is in the word which we translate "everlasting" or "eternal." I don't know the Greek, but I believe it strictly means for ages, and might signify either endless or long-enduring. And as for the danger of the belief, I would not publish it abroad, if I thought any poor wretch would be likely to presume upon it to his own destruction, but it is a glorious thought to cherish in one's own heart, and I would not part with it for all the world can give!'

Here our conference ended, for it was now high time to prepare for church. Every one attended the morning service, except my uncle, who hardly ever goes, and Mr Wilmot, who stayed at home with him to enjoy a quiet game of cribbage. In the afternoon Miss Wilmot and Lord Lowborough likewise excused themselves from attending; but Mr Huntingdon vouchsafed to accompany us again. Whether it was to ingratiate himself with my aunt I cannot tell, but, if so, he certainly should have behaved better. I must confess, I did not like his conduct during service at all. Holding his prayer-book upside down, or open at any place but the right, he did nothing but stare about him, unless he happened to catch my aunt's eye or mine, and then he would drop his own on his book, with a puritanical air of mock solemnity that would have been ludicrous, if it had not been too provoking. Once, during the sermon, after attentively regarding Mr Leighton for a few minutes, he suddenly produced his gold pencil case and snatched up a bible. Perceiving that I observed the movement, he whispered that he was going to make a note of the sermon; but instead of that – as I sat next him I could not help seeing that he was making a caricature of the preacher, giving to the respectable, pious, elderly gentleman, the air and aspect of a most absurd old hypocrite. And yet, upon his return, he talked to my aunt about the sermon with a degree of modest, serious discrimination that tempted me to believe he had really attended and profited by the discourse.

Just before dinner my uncle called me into the library for the discussion of a very important matter, which was dismissed in few words.

'Now Nell,' said he, 'this young Huntingdon has been asking for you: what must I say about it? Your aunt would answer "No" – but what say you?'

'I say yes, uncle,' replied I, without a moment's hesitation; for I had thoroughly made up my mind on the subject.

'Very good!' cried he. 'Now that's a good honest answer – wonderful for a girl! – Well, I'll write to your father to-morrow. He's sure to give his consent; so you may look on the matter as settled. You'd have done a deal better if you'd taken Wilmot, I can tell you; but that you won't believe. At your time of life, it's love that rules the roast: at mine, it's solid, serviceable gold. I suppose now, you'd never dream of looking into the state of your husband's finances, or troubling your head about settlements, or anything of that sort?'

'I don't think I should.'

'Well, be thankful, then, that you've wiser heads to think for you. I haven't had time, yet, to examine thoroughly into this young rascal's affairs, but I see that a great part of his father's fine property has been squandered away; – but still, I think there's a pretty fair share of it left, and a little careful nursing may make a handsome thing of it yet; and then we must persuade your father to give you a decent fortune, as he has only one besides yourself to care for; – and, if you behave well, who knows but what I may be induced to remember you in my will?' continued he, putting his finger to his nose, with a knowing wink.

'Thanks uncle, for that and all your kindness,' replied I.

'Well, and I questioned this young spark on the matter of settlements,' continued he; 'and he seemed disposed to be generous enough on that point –'

'I knew he would!' said I. 'But pray don't trouble your head – or his, or mine about that; for all I have will be his, and all he has will be mine; and what more could either of us require?' And I was about to make my exit, but he called me back.

'Stop, stop!' cried he – 'we haven't mentioned the time yet. When must it be? Your aunt would put it off till the Lord knows when, but he is anxious to be bound as soon as may be: he won't hear of waiting beyond next month; and you, I guess, will be of the same mind, so –'

'Not at all, uncle; on the contrary, I should like to wait till after Christmas, at least.'

'Oh! pooh, pooh! never tell me that tale – I know better,' cried he; and he persisted in his incredulity. Nevertheless, it is quite true. I am in no hurry at all. How can I be, when I think of the momentous change that awaits me, and of all I have to leave? It is happiness enough, to know that we *are* to be united; and that he really loves me, and I may love *him* as devotedly, and think of him as often as I please. However, I insisted upon consulting my aunt about the *time* of the wedding, for I determined her counsels should not be utterly disregarded; and no conclusions on that particular are come to yet.

CHAPTER XXI

OPINIONS

OCTOBER 1ST. – All is settled now. My father has given his consent, and the time is fixed for Christmas, by a sort of compromise between the respective advocates for hurry and delay. Milicent Hargrave is to be one bridesmaid, and Annabella Wilmot the other – not that I am particularly fond of the latter, but she is an intimate of the family, and I have not another friend.

When I told Milicent of my engagement, she rather provoked me by her manner of taking it. After staring a moment in mute surprise, she said —

'Well Helen, I suppose I ought to congratulate you – and I *am* glad to see you so happy; but I did not think you would take him; and I can't help feeling surprised that you should like him so much.'

'Why so?'

'Because you are so superior to him in every way, and there's something so bold – and reckless about him – so, I don't know how – but I always feel a wish to get out of his way, when I see him approach.'

'You are timid, Milicent, but that's no fault of his.'

'And then his look,' continued she. 'People say he's handsome, and of course he is, but *I* don't *like* that kind of beauty; and I wonder that you should.'

'Why so, pray?'

'Well, you know, I think there's nothing noble or lofty in his appearance.'

'In fact, you wonder that I can like any one so unlike the stilted heroes of romance? Well! give me my flesh and blood lover, and I'll leave all the Sir Herberts and Valentines to you – if you can find them.'

'I don't want them,' said she, 'I'll be satisfied with flesh and blood too – only the spirit must shine through and predominate. But don't you think Mr Huntingdon's face is too red?'

'No!' cried I, indignantly. 'It is not red at all. There is just a pleasant glow – a healthy freshness in his complexion, the warm, pinky tint of the whole harmonizing with the deeper colour of the cheeks, exactly as it ought to do. I hate a man to be red and white, like a painted doll – or all sickly white, or smoky black, or cadaverous yellow!'

'Well, tastes differ – but *I* like pale or dark,' replied she. 'But, to tell you the truth Helen, I had been deluding myself with the hope that you would one day be my sister. I expected Walter would be introduced to you next season; and I thought you would like him, and was certain he would like you; and I flattered myself I should thus have the felicity of seeing the two persons I like best in the world – except mamma – united in one. He mayn't be exactly what you would call handsome, but he's far more distinguished-looking, and nicer and better than Mr Huntingdon; – and I'm sure you would say so, if you knew him.'

'Impossible, Milicent! You think so, because you're his sister; and, on that account, I'll forgive you; but nobody else should so disparage Arthur Huntingdon to me with impunity.'

Miss Wilmot expressed her feelings on the subject, almost as openly.

'And so, Helen,' said she, coming up to me with a smile of no amiable import, 'you are to be Mrs Huntingdon, I suppose?'

'Yes,' replied I. 'Don't you envy me?'

'Oh, *dear*, no!' she exclaimed. 'I shall probably be Lady Low-borough some day, and then you know, dear, I shall be in a capacity to enquire, "Don't you envy *me*?"'

'Henceforth, I shall envy no one,' returned I.

'Indeed! Are you so happy then?' said she thoughtfully; and something very like a cloud of disappointment shadowed her face. 'And does he love you – I mean, does he idolize you as much as you do him?' she added, fixing her eyes upon me with ill-disguised anxiety for the reply.

'I don't want to be idolized,' I answered, 'but I am well assured that he *loves* me more than anybody else in the world – as I do him.'

'Exactly,' said she with a nod. 'I wish –' she paused.

'What do you wish?' asked I, annoyed at the vindictive expression of her countenance.

'I wish,' returned she, with a short laugh, 'that all the attractive points and desirable qualifications of the two gentlemen were united in one – that Lord Lowborough had Huntingdon's handsome face and good temper, and all his wit, and mirth and charm, or else that Huntingdon had Lowborough's pedigree, and title, and delightful old family seat, and I had him; and you might have the other and welcome.'

'Thank you, dear Annabella, I am better satisfied with things as they are, for my own part; and for you, I wish you were as well content with your intended, as I am with mine,' said I; and it was true enough; for, though vexed at first at her unami-able spirit, her frankness touched me, and the contrast between our situations was such, that I could well afford to pity her and wish her well.

Mr Huntingdon's acquaintances appear to be no better pleased with our approaching union than mine. This morning's post brought him letters from several of his friends, during the perusal of which, at the breakfast-table, he excited the attention of the company, by the singular variety of his grimaces. But he crushed them all into his pocket, with a private laugh, and said nothing till the meal was concluded. Then, while the company were hanging over the fire or loitering through the room, previous to settling to their various morning's avocations, he came and leant over the back of my chair, with his face in contact with my curls, and commencing with a quiet little kiss, poured forth the following complaints into my ear –

'Helen, you witch, do you know that you've entailed upon me the curses of all my friends? I wrote to them the other day, to tell them of my happy prospects, and now, instead of a bundle of congratulations, I've got a pocket-full of bitter execrations and reproaches. There's not one kind wish for me, or one good word for you among them all. They say there'll be no more fun now, no more merry days and glorious nights – and all my fault – I am the first to break up the jovial band, and others in pure despair, will follow my example. I was the very life and prop of the community, they do me the honour to say, and I have shamefully betrayed my trust –'

'You may join them again, if you like,' said I, somewhat piqued at the sorrowful tone of his discourse. 'I should be sorry to stand between any man – or body of men and so much happiness; and perhaps I can manage to do without you, as well as your poor deserted friends.'

'Bless you! no,' murmured he. 'It's "all for love or the world well lost," with me. Let them go to – where they belong, to speak politely. But if you saw how they abuse me, Helen, you would love me all the more, for having ventured so much for your sake.'

He pulled out his crumpled letters. I thought he was going to shew them to me, and told him I did not wish to see them.

'I'm not going to shew them to you, love,' said he. 'They're hardly fit for a lady's eyes – the most part of them. But look here. This is Grimsby's scrawl – only three lines, the sulky dog! He doesn't say much, to be sure, but his very silence implies more than all the others' words, and the less he says, the more he thinks – G—d—n him! – I beg your pardon, dearest – and this is Hargrave's missive. He is particularly grieved at me, because, forsooth, he had fallen in love with you from his sister's reports, and meant to have married you himself, as soon as he had sown his wild oats.'

'I'm vastly obliged to him,' observed I.

'And so am I,' said he. 'And look at this. This is Hattersley's – every page stuffed full of railing accusations, bitter curses, and lamentable complaints, ending up with swearing that he'll get married himself in revenge: he'll throw himself away on the first old maid that chooses to set her cap at him, – as if *I* cared what he did with himself.'

'Well,' said I, 'if you do give up your intimacy with these men, I don't think you will have much cause to regret the loss of their society; for it's my belief they never did you much good.'

'May be not; but we'd a merry time of it, too, though mingled with sorrow and pain, as Lowborough knows to his cost – ha, ha!' and while he was laughing at the recollection of Lowborough's troubles, my uncle came and clapped him on the shoulder.

'Come my lad!' said he. 'Are you too busy making love to my niece, to make war with the pheasants? – First of October remember! – Sun shines out – rain ceased – even Boarham's not afraid to venture in his waterproof boots; and Wilmot and I are going to beat you all. I declare, we old 'uns are the keenest sportsmen of the lot!'

'I'll shew you what I can do to-day, however,' said my companion. 'I'll murder your birds by wholesale, just for keeping me away from better company than either you or them.'

And so saying he departed; and I saw no more of him till dinner. It seemed a weary time: I wonder what I shall do without him.

It is very true that the three elder gentlemen have proved themselves much keener sportsmen than the two younger ones; for both Lord Lowborough and Arthur Huntingdon have of late, almost daily neglected the shooting excursions to accompany us in our various rides and rambles. But these merry times are fast drawing to a close. In less than a fortnight the party breaks up, much to my sorrow, for every day I enjoy it more and more – now that Messrs Boarham and Wilmot have ceased to tease me, and my aunt has ceased to lecture me, and I have ceased to be jealous of Annabella – and even to dislike her – and now that Mr Huntingdon is become *my* Arthur, and I may enjoy his society without restraint. – What *shall* I do without him, I repeat?

CHAPTER XXII

TRAITS OF FRIENDSHIP

OCTOBER 5TH. – My cup of sweets is not unmingled: it is dashed with a bitterness that I cannot hide from myself, disguise it as I will. I may try to persuade myself that the sweetness overpowers it; I may call it a pleasant aromatic flavour; but, say what I will, it is still there, and I cannot but taste it. I cannot shut my eyes to Arthur's faults; and the more I love him the more they trouble me. His very heart, that I trusted so, is, I fear, less warm and generous than I thought it. At least, he gave me a specimen of his character to-day, that seemed to merit a harder name than thoughtlessness. He and Lord Lowborough were accompanying Annabella and me in a long, delightful ride; he was riding by my side, as usual, and Annabella and. Lord Lowborough were a little before us, the latter bending towards his companion as if in tender and confidential discourse.

'Those two will get the start of us, Helen, if we don't look sharp,' observed Huntingdon. 'They'll make a match of it, as sure as can be. That Lowborough's fairly besotted. But he'll find himself in a fix when he's got her, I doubt.'

'And she'll find *her*self in a fix when she's got *him*,' said I, 'if what I've heard of him is true.'

'Not a bit of it. She knows what she's about; but he, poor fool, deludes himself with the notion that she'll make him a good wife, and because she has amused him with some rodo-montade about despising rank and wealth in matters of love and marriage, he flatters himself that she's devotedly attached to him; that she will not refuse him for his poverty, and does not court him for his rank, but loves him for himself alone.'

'But is not *he* courting *her* for her fortune?'

'No, not he. That was the first attraction, certainly; but now he has quite lost sight of it: it never enters his calculations, except merely as an essential without which, for the lady's own sake, he could not think of marrying her. No; he's fairly in love. He thought he never could be again, but he's in for it once more. He was to have been married before, some two or three years ago; but he lost his bride by losing his fortune. He got into a bad way among us in London: he had an unfortunate taste for gambling; and surely the fellow was born under an unlucky star, for he always lost thrice ere he gained once. That's a mode of self-torment I never was much addicted to, when I spend my money I like to enjoy the full value of it: I see no fun in wasting it on thieves and black-legs; and as for *gaining* money, hitherto I have always had sufficient; it's time enough to be clutching for more, I think, when you begin to see the end of what you have. But I have sometimes frequented the

gaming-houses just to watch the on-goings of those mad votar-
ies of chance – a very interesting study, I assure you, Helen,
and sometimes very diverting: I've had many a laugh at the
boobies and bedlamites. Lowborough was quite infatuated –
not willingly, but of necessity, – he was always resolving to give
it up, and always breaking his resolutions. Every venture was
the "just once more:" if he gained a little, he hoped to gain a
little more next time, and if he lost, it would not do to leave
off at that juncture; he must go on till he had retrieved that last
misfortune, at least: bad luck could not last for ever; and every
lucky hit was looked upon as the dawn of better times, till
experience proved the contrary. At length he grew desperate,
and we were daily on the look out for a case of felo-de-se – no
great matter, some of us whispered, as his existence had ceased
to be an acquisition to our club. At last, however, he came to a
check. He made a large stake which he determined should be
the last, whether he lost or won. He had often so determined
before, to be sure, and as often broken his determination; and
so it was this time. He lost; and while his antagonist smilingly
swept away the stakes, he, turning chalky white, drew back in
silence and wiped his forehead. I was present at the time; and
while he stood with folded arms and eyes fixed on the ground,
I knew well enough what was passing in his mind.

' "Is it to be the last, Lowborough?" said I, stepping up to him.

' "The last but ONE," he answered, with a grim smile; and
then, rushing back to the table, he struck his hand upon it, and
raising his voice high above all the confusion of jingling coins
and muttered oaths and curses in the room, he swore a deep
and solemn oath that, come what would, THIS trial *should* be
the last, and imprecated unspeakable curses on his head, if ever
he should shuffle a card or rattle a dice-box again. He then
doubled his former stake, and challenged any one present to
play against him. Grimsby instantly presented himself. Lowborough glared fiercely at him, for Grimsby was almost as celebrated for his luck as *he* was for his ill-fortune. However, they

fell to work. But Grimsby had much skill and little scruple, and whether he took advantage of the other's trembling, blinded eagerness to deal unfairly by him, I cannot undertake to say; but Lowborough lost again, and fell dead sick.

' "You'd better try once more," said Grimsby, leaning across the table. And then he winked at me.

' "I've nothing to try with," said the poor devil, with a ghastly smile.

' "Oh, Huntingdon will lend you what you want," said the other.

' "No; you heard my oath," answered Lowborough, turning away in quiet despair. And I took him by the arm and led him out.

' "Is it to be the last, Lowborough?" I asked, when I got him into the street.

' "The last," he answered, somewhat against my expectation. And I took him home – that is, to our club – for he was as submissive as a child, and plied him with brandy and water till he began to look rather brighter – rather more alive, at least.

' "Huntingdon, I'm ruined!" said he, taking the third glass from my hand – he had drunk the others in dead silence.

' "Not you!" said I. "You'll find a man can live without his money as merrily as a tortoise without its head, or a wasp without its body."

' "But I'm in debt," said he – "deep in debt! And I can never, *never* get out of it!"

' "Well, what of that? many a better man than you, has lived and died in debt, and they can't put you in prison, you know, because you're a peer." And I handed him his fourth tumbler.

' "But I hate to be in debt!" he shouted. "I wasn't born for it, and I cannot *bear* it!"

' "What can't be cured must be endured," said I, beginning to mix the fifth.

' "And then, I've lost my Caroline." And he began to snivel then, for the brandy had softened his heart.

' "No matter," I answered, "there are more Carolines in the world than one."

' "There's only one for me," he replied, with a dolorous sigh. "And if there were fifty more, who's to get them, I wonder, without money?"

' "Oh, somebody will take you for your title; and then you've your family estate yet; that's entailed, you know."

' "I wish to God I could sell it to pay my debts," he muttered.

' "And then," said Grimsby, who had just come in, "you can *try again*, you know. I *would* have one more chance if I were you. I'd never stop here."

' "I *won't*, I tell you!" shouted he. And he started up and left the room – walking rather unsteadily, for the liquor had got into his head. He was not so much used to it then, but after that, he took to it kindly to solace his cares.

'He kept his oath about gambling (not a little to the surprise of us all), though Grimsby did his utmost to tempt him to break it; but now he had got hold of another habit that bothered him nearly as much, for he soon discovered that the demon of drink was as black as the demon of play, and nearly as hard to get rid of – especially as his kind friends did all they could to second the promptings of his own insatiable cravings.'

'Then, they were demons themselves,' cried I, unable to contain my indignation. 'And you, Mr Huntingdon, it seems, were the first to tempt him.'

'Well, what could we do?' replied he, deprecatingly. – 'We meant it in kindness – we couldn't bear to see the poor fellow so miserable: – and besides, he was such a damper upon us, sitting there, silent and glum, when he was under the threefold influence of the loss of his sweetheart, the loss of his fortune, and the reaction of the lost night's debauch; whereas, when he had something in him, if he was not merry himself, he was an unfailing source of merriment to us. Even Grimsby could chuckle over his odd sayings: they delighted him far more than my merry jests or Hattersley's riotous mirth. But one evening, when we were sitting over our wine, after one of our club dinners, and had all been hearty together, – Lowborough giving us mad toasts, and hearing our wild songs and bearing a hand in the applause, if he did not help us to sing them himself, – he suddenly relapsed into silence, sinking his head on his hand, and never lifting his glass to his lips; – but this was nothing new; so we let him alone, and went on with our jollification, till, suddenly raising his head, he interrupted us in the middle of a roar of laughter, by exclaiming, –

' "Gentlemen, where is all this to end? – Will you just tell me *that* now? – Where is it all to end?"

' "In hell fire," growled Grimsby.

' "You've hit it – I thought so!" cried he. "Well then, I'll tell you what" – he rose.

' "A speech, a speech!" shouted we. "Hear, hear! Lowborough's going to give us a speech!"

'He waited calmly till the thunders of applause and gingling of glasses had ceased, and then proceeded, –

' "It's only this, gentlemen, – that I think we'd better go no further. We'd better stop while we can."

' "Just so!" cried Hattersley –

> "Stop poor sinner, stop and think
> 　　Before you further go,
> No longer sport upon the brink
> 　　Of everlasting woe."

' "Exactly!" replied his lordship, with the utmost gravity. "And if *you* choose to visit the bottomless pit, I won't go with you – we must part company, for I swear I'll not move another step towards it! – What's this?" he said, taking up his glass of wine.

' "Taste it," suggested I.

' "This is hell broth!" he exclaimed. "I renounce it for ever!" And he threw it out into the middle of the table.

' "Fill again!" said I, handing him the bottle – "and let us drink to your renunciation."

' "It's rank poison," said he, grasping the bottle by the neck, "and I forswear it! I've given up gambling, and I'll give up this too." He was on the point of deliberately pouring the whole contents of the bottle on to the table, but Hargrave wrested it from him. "On you be the curse, then!" said he. And backing from the room, he shouted, "Farewell, ye tempters!" and vanished amid shouts of laughter and applause.

'We expected him back among us the next day; but, to our surprise, the place remained vacant: we saw nothing of him for a whole week; and we really began to think he was going to keep his word. At last, one evening, when we were most of us assembled together again, he entered, silent and grim as a ghost, and would have quietly slipped into his usual seat at my elbow, but we all rose to welcome him, and several voices were raised to ask what he would have, and several hands were busy with bottle and glass to serve him; but I knew a smoking tumbler of brandy and water would comfort him best, and had nearly prepared it, when he peevishly pushed it away, saying,

' "Do let me alone, Huntingdon! Do be quiet, all of you! I'm not come to join you: I'm only come to be with you awhile, because I can't bear my own thoughts." And he folded his arms and leant back in his chair; so we let him be. But I left the glass by him; and after a while, Grimsby directed my attention towards it, by a significant wink; and, on turning my head, I saw it was drained to the bottom. He made me a sign to replenish, and quietly pushed up the bottle. I willingly complied; but Lowborough detected the pantomime, and, nettled at the intelligent grins that were passing between us, snatched the glass from my hand, dashed the contents of it in Grimsby's face, threw the empty tumbler at me, and then bolted from the room.'

'I hope he broke your head,' said I.

'No, love,' replied he, laughing immoderately at the recollection of the whole affair, 'he would have done so, – and perhaps spoilt my face, too, but, providentially, this forest of curls' (taking off his hat and shewing his luxuriant chestnut locks) 'saved my skull, and prevented the glass from breaking till it reached the table.

'After that,' he continued, 'Lowborough kept aloof from us a week or two longer. I used to meet him occasionally in the town; and then, as I was too good natured to resent his unmannerly conduct, and he bore no malice against me, – he was never unwilling to talk to me; on the contrary, he would cling to me and follow me anywhere, – but to the club, and the gaming-houses, and such like dangerous places of resort – he was so weary of his own moping, melancholy mind. At last, I got him to come in with me to the club, on condition that I would not tempt him to drink; and for some time, he continued to look in upon us pretty regularly of an evening, – still abstaining, with wonderful perseverance, from the "rank poison" he had so bravely forsworn. But some of our members protested against this conduct. They did not like to have him sitting there like a skeleton at a feast, instead of contributing his quota to the general amusement, casting a cloud over all, and watching, with greedy eyes, every drop they carried to their lips, they vowed it was not fair; and some of them maintained that he should either be compelled to do as others did or expelled from the society, and swore that, next time he shewed himself, they would tell him as much, and, if he did not take the warning, proceed to active measures. However, I befriended him on this occasion, and recommended them to let him be for a while, intimating that, with a little patience on our parts, he would soon come round again. – But, to be sure, it *was* rather provoking; for though he refused to drink like an honest Christian, it was well known to me, that he kept a private bottle of laudanum about him, which he was continually soaking at – or rather, holding off and on with, abstaining one day and exceeding the next, just like the spirits.

'One night, however, during one of our orgies – one of our high festivals, I mean – he glided in, like the ghost in Macbeth, and seated himself, as usual, a little back from the table, in the chair we always placed for "the spectre," whether it chose to fill it or not. I saw by his face that he was suffering from the effects of an overdose of his insidious comforter; but nobody spoke to him, and he spoke to nobody. A few sidelong glances, and a whispered observation that "the ghost was come," was all the notice he drew by his appearance, and we went on with our merry carousals as before, till he startled us all by suddenly drawing in his chair and leaning forward with his elbows on the table, and exclaiming with portentous solemnity, –

' "Well! it puzzles me what you can find to be so merry about. What *you* see in life I don't know – *I* see only the blackness of darkness and a fearful looking for of judgment and fiery indignation!"

'All the company simultaneously pushed up their glasses to him, and I set them before him in a semicircle, and, tenderly patting him on the back, bid him drink and he would soon see as bright a prospect as any of us; but he pushed them back, muttering, –

' "Take them away! I won't taste it, I tell you – I won't – I won't!" So I handed them down again to the owners; but I saw that he followed them with a glare of hungry regret as they departed. Then, he clasped his hands before his eyes to shut out the sight, and two minutes after, lifted his head again, and said, in a hoarse but vehement whisper, –

' "And yet I must! Huntingdon, get me a glass!"

' "Take the bottle, man!" said I, thrusting the brandy-bottle into his hand – but stop, I'm telling too much,' muttered the narrator, startled at the look I turned upon him. 'But no matter,' he recklessly added, and thus continued his relation: – 'In his desperate eagerness, he seized the bottle and sucked away, till he suddenly dropped from his chair, disappearing under the table amid a tempest of applause. The consequence of this imprudence was something like an apoplectic fit, followed by a rather severe brain fever –'

'And what did you think of *yourself*, sir?' said I, quickly.

'Of course, I was very penitent,' he replied. 'I went to see him once or twice – nay, twice or thrice – or by'r lady, some four times, – and when he got better, I tenderly brought him back to the fold.'

'What do you mean?'

'I mean, I restored him to the bosom of the club, and compassionating the feebleness of his health and extreme lowness of his spirits, I recommended him to "take a little wine for his stomach's sake," and, when he was sufficiently re-established, to embrace the media-via, ni-jamais-ni-toujours plan not to kill himself like a fool, and not to abstain like a ninny – in a word, to enjoy himself like a rational creature, and do as I did; – for don't think, Helen, that I'm a tippler; I'm nothing at all of the kind, and never was, and never shall be. I value my comfort far too much. I see that a man cannot give himself up to drinking without being miserable one half his days and mad the other; – besides, I like to enjoy my life at all sides and ends, which cannot be done by one that suffers himself to be the slave of a single propensity – and moreover, drinking spoils one's good looks,' he concluded, with a most conceited smile that ought to have provoked me more than it did.

'And did Lord Lowborough profit by your advice?' I asked.

'Why, yes, in a manner. For a while, he managed very well; indeed, he was a model of moderation and prudence – something too much so for the tastes of our wild community; – but, somehow, Lowborough had not the gift of moderation: if he stumbled a little to one side, he must go down before he could right himself: if he overshot the mark one night, the effects of it rendered him so miserable the next day that he must repeat the offence to mend it; and so on from day to day, till his clamorous conscience brought him to a stand. – And then, in his sober moments, he so bothered his friends with his remorse, and his terrors and woes, that they were obliged, in self-defence, to get him to drown his sorrows in wine, or any more potent

beverage that came to hand; and when his first scruples of conscience were overcome, he would need no more persuading, he
would often grow desperate, and be as great a blackguard as any
of them could desire – but only to lament his own unutterable
wickedness and degradation the more when the fit was over.

'At last, one day when he and I were alone together, after
pondering awhile in one of his gloomy, abstracted moods, with
his arms folded and his head sunk on his breast, – he suddenly
woke up, and vehemently grasping my arm, said, "Huntingdon,
this won't do! I'm resolved to have done with it."

' "What, are you going to shoot yourself?" said I.

' "No; I'm going to reform."

' "Oh, *that's* nothing new! You've been going to reform these
twelve months and more."

' "Yes, but you wouldn't let me; and I was such a fool I
couldn't live without you. But now I see what it is that keeps
me back, and what's wanted to save me; and I'd compass sea
and land to get it – only I'm afraid there's no chance." And he
sighed as if his heart would break.

' "What is it, Lowborough?" said I, thinking he was fairly
cracked at last.

' "A wife," he answered; "for I can't live alone, because my
own mind distracts me, and I can't live with you, because you
take the devil's part against me."

' "Who – I?"

' "Yes – all of you do, – and you more than any of them, you
know. But if I could get a wife, with fortune enough to pay off
my debts and set me straight in the world –"

' "To be sure," said I.

' "And sweetness and goodness enough," he continued, "to
make home tolerable, and to reconcile me to myself, – I think
I should do, yet. I shall never be in love again, that's certain;
but perhaps that would be no great matter, it would enable me
to choose with my eyes open, – and I should make a good
husband in spite of it; but could any one be in love with *me*?

– that's the question. – With *your* good looks and powers of fascination" (he was pleased to say) "I might hope; but as it is, Huntingdon, do you think *any* body would take me – ruined and wretched as I am?"

' "Yes, certainly."

' "Who?"

' "Why, any neglected old maid, fast sinking in despair, would be delighted to –"

' "No, no," said he – "it must be somebody that I can love."

' "Why, you just said you never could be in love again."

' "Well, love is not the word, – but somebody that I can like. – I'll search all England through, at all events!" he cried, with a sudden burst of hope, or desperation. "Succeed or fail, it will be better than rushing headlong to destruction at that d—d club: so farewell to it and you. Whenever I meet you on honest ground or under a Christian roof, I shall be glad to see you; but never more shall you entice me to that *devil's den*!"

'This was shameful language, but I shook hands with him, and we parted. He kept his word; and from that time forward, he has been a pattern of propriety, as far as I can tell; but, till lately, I have not had very much to do with him. He occasionally sought my company but as frequently shrunk from it, fearing lest I should wile him back to destruction, and I found his not very entertaining, especially, as he sometimes attempted to awaken my conscience and draw me from the perdition he considered himself to have escaped; but when I did happen to meet him, I seldom failed to ask after the progress of his matrimonial efforts and researches, and in general he could give me but a poor account. The mothers were repelled by his empty coffers and his reputation for gambling, and the daughters by his cloudy brow and melancholy temper, – besides, he didn't understand them; he wanted the spirit and assurance to carry his point.

'I left him at it when I went to the continent; and on my return, at the year's end, I found him still a disconsolate bachelor – though, certainly, looking somewhat less like an unblest exile from the tomb than before. The young ladies had ceased to be afraid of him, and were beginning to think him quite interesting; but the mammas were still unrelenting. It was about this time, Helen, that my good angel brought me into conjunction with you; and then I had eyes and ears for nobody else. But meantime, Lowborough became acquainted with our charming friend, Miss Wilmot – through the intervention of *his* good angel, no doubt he would tell you, though he did not dare to fix his hopes on one so courted and admired, till after they were brought into closer contact here at Staningley, and she, in the absence of her other admirers, indubitably courted his notice and held out every encouragement to his timid advances. Then indeed, he began to hope for a dawn of brighter days; and if for a while, I darkened his prospects by standing between him and his sun – and so, nearly plunged him again into the abyss of despair – it only intensified his ardour and strengthened his hopes when I chose to abandon the field in the pursuit of a brighter treasure. In a word, as I told you, he is fairly besotted. At first, he could dimly perceive her faults, and they gave him considerable uneasiness; but now his passion and her art together, have blinded him to everything but her perfections and his amazing good fortune. Last night, he came to me brim-full of his new-found felicity:

' "Huntingdon, I am not a cast-away!" said he, seizing my hand and squeezing it like a vice. "There is happiness in store for me, yet – even in this life – she loves me!"

' "Indeed!" said I. "Has she told you so?"

' "No, but I can no longer doubt it. Do you not see how pointedly kind and affectionate she is? And she knows the utmost extent of my poverty, and cares nothing about it! She knows all the folly and all the wickedness of my former life, and is not afraid to trust me – and my rank and title are no allurements to her; for them, she utterly disregards. She is the most generous, high-minded being that can be conceived of. She will save me, body and soul, from destruction. Already, she has ennobled me in my own estimation, and made me three times better, wiser, greater than I was. Oh! if I had but known her before, how much degradation and misery I should have been spared! But what have I done to deserve so magnificent a creature?"

'And the cream of the jest,' continued Mr Huntingdon, laughing, 'is that the artful minx loves nothing about him, but his title and pedigree, and "that delightful old family seat." '

'How do you know?' said I.

'She told me so herself; she said, "As for the man himself, I thoroughly despise him; but then, I suppose, it is time to be making my choice, and if I waited for some one capable of eliciting my esteem and affection, I should have to pass my life in single blessedness, for I detest you all!" Ha, ha! I suspect she was wrong there; – but however, it is evident she has no love for *him*, poor fellow.'

'Then you ought to tell him so.'

'What, and spoil all her plans and prospects, poor girl? No, no: that would be a breach of confidence, wouldn't it Helen? Ha, ha! Besides, it would break his heart.' And he laughed again.

'Well, Mr Huntingdon, I don't know what you see so amazingly diverting in the matter; *I* see nothing to laugh at.'

'I'm laughing at *you*, just now love,' said he, redoubling his cachinnations.

And leaving him to enjoy his merriment alone, I touched Ruby with the whip, and cantered on to rejoin our companions; for we had been walking our horses all this time, and were consequently a long way behind. Arthur was soon at my side again; but not disposed to talk to him, I broke into a gallop. He did the same; and we did not slacken our pace till we came up with Miss Wilmot and Lord Lowborough, which was within half a mile of the park gates. I avoided all further conversation with him, till we came to the end of our ride, when I meant to jump off my horse and vanish into the house, before he could offer his assistance; but while I was disengaging my habit from the crutch, he lifted me off, and held me by both hands, asserting that he would not let me go till I had forgiven him.

'I have nothing to forgive,' said I. 'You have not injured *me*.'

'No, darling – God forbid that I should! – but you are angry, because it was to me that Annabella confessed her lack of esteem for her lover.'

'No, Arthur, it is not *that* that displeases me: it is the whole system of your conduct towards your friend; and if you wish me to forget it, go, now, and tell him what sort of a woman it is, that he adores so madly, and on whom he has hung his hopes of future happiness.'

'I tell you, Helen, it would break his heart – it would be the death of him, – besides being a scandalous trick to poor Annabella. There is no help for him now; he is past praying for. Besides, she may keep up the deception to the end of the chapter; and then he will be just as happy in the illusion as if it were reality; or perhaps, he will only discover his mistake when he has ceased to love her; – and if not, it is much better that the truth should dawn gradually upon him. So now, my angel, I hope I have made out a clear case, and fully convinced you that I cannot make the atonement you require. What other requisition have you to make? Speak, and I will gladly obey.'

'I have none but this,' said I, as gravely as before: 'that, in future, you will never make a jest of the sufferings of others, and always use your influence with your friends for their own advantage against their evil propensities, instead of seconding their evil propensities against themselves.'

'I will do my utmost,' said he, 'to remember and perform the injunctions of my angel monitress,' and after kissing both my gloved hands, he let me go.

When I entered my room, I was surprised to see Annabella Wilmot standing before my toilet-table, composedly surveying her features in the glass, with one hand flirting her gold-mounted whip, and the other holding up her long habit.

'She certainly *is* a magnificent creature!' thought I, as I beheld

that tall, finely developed figure, and the reflection of the handsome face in the mirror before me, with the glossy dark hair,
slightly and not ungracefully disordered by the breezy ride, the
rich brown complexion glowing with exercise, and the black
eyes sparkling with unwonted brilliance. On perceiving me, she
turned round exclaiming, with a laugh that savoured more of
malice than of mirth, –

'Why, Helen! what *have* you been doing so long? – I came to
tell you my good fortune,' she continued, regardless of Rachel's
presence. 'Lord Lowborough has proposed, and I have been
graciously pleased to accept him. Don't you envy me, dear?'

'No, love,' said I – 'or him either,' I mentally added. 'And do
you like him Annabella?'

'Like him! yes, to be sure – over head and ears in love!'

'Well, I hope you'll make him a good wife.'

'Thank you, my dear! And what besides do you hope?'

'I hope you will both love each other, and both be happy.'

'Thanks; – and I hope you will make a *very* good wife to
Mr Huntingdon!' said she, with a queenly bow, and retired.

'Oh, Miss! how could you say so to her!' cried Rachel.

'Say what?' replied I.

'Why, that you hoped she would make him a good wife –
I never heard such a thing!'

'Because, I do hope it – or rather, I wish it – she's almost past
hope.'

'Well!' said she, 'I'm sure I hope he'll make *her* a good
husband. They tell queer things about him down stairs. They
were saying –'

'I know Rachel – I've heard all about him; but he's reformed
now. And they have no business to tell tales about their masters.'

'No mum – or else, they *have* said some things about Mr
Huntingdon too.'

'I won't hear them, Rachel; they tell lies.'

'Yes mum,' said she, quietly, as she went on arranging my hair.

'Do *you* believe them, Rachel?' I asked, after a short pause.

'No, Miss, not all. You know when a lot of servants gets together, they like to talk about their betters; and some, for a bit of swagger, likes to make it appear as though they knew more than they do, and to throw out hints and things, just to astonish the others. But I think, if I was you, Miss Helen, I'd look *very* well before I leaped. I do believe a young lady can't be too careful who she marries.'

'Of course not,' said I – 'but be quick, will you, Rachel? I want to be dressed.'

And indeed, I was anxious to be rid of the good woman, for I was in such a melancholy frame I could hardly keep the tears out of my eyes while she dressed me. It was not for Lord Lowborough – it was not for Annabella – it was not for myself – it was for Arthur Huntingdon that they rose.

13th. They are gone – and he is gone. We are to be parted for more than two months – above ten weeks! a long, long time to live and not to see him. But he has promised to write often, and made me promise to write still oftener, because he will be busy settling his affairs, and I shall have nothing better to do. Well, I think I shall always have plenty to say. – But O! for the time when we shall be always together, and can exchange our thoughts without the intervention of these cold go-betweens, pen, ink, and paper!

22nd. I have had several letters from Arthur, already. They are not long, but passing sweet, and just like himself – full of ardent affection, and playful, lively humour; but – there is always a *but* in this imperfect world – I do wish he would *sometimes* be serious. I cannot get him to write or speak in real, solid earnest. I don't much mind it now; but if it be always so, what shall I do with the serious part of myself?

CHAPTER XXIII

FIRST WEEKS OF MATRIMONY

FEB. 18TH, 1822. Early this morning, Arthur mounted his hunter and set off in high glee to meet the — hounds. He will be away all day; and so I will amuse myself with my neglected diary – if I can give that name to such an irregular composition. It is exactly four months since I opened it last.

I am married now, and settled down as Mrs Huntingdon of Grassdale Manor. I have had eight weeks' experience of matrimony. And do I regret the step I have taken? – No – though I must confess, in my secret heart, that Arthur is not what I thought him at first, and if I had known him in the beginning, as thoroughly as I do now, I probably never should have loved him, and if I had loved him first, and then made the discovery, I fear I should have thought it my duty not to have married him. To be sure, I might have known him, for every one was willing enough to tell me about him, and he himself was no accomplished hypocrite, but I was wilfully blind, and now, instead of regretting that I did not discern his full character before I was indissolubly bound to him, I am *glad*; for it has saved me a great deal of battling with my conscience, and a great deal of consequent trouble and pain; and, whatever I *ought* to have done, my duty, now, is plainly to love him and to cleave to him; and this just tallies with my inclination.

He is very fond of me – almost *too* fond. I could do with less caressing and more rationality: I should like to be less of a pet and more of a friend, if I might choose – but I won't complain of that: I am only afraid his affection loses in depth where it gains in ardour. I sometimes liken it to a fire of dry twigs and branches compared with one of solid coal, – very bright and hot, but if it should burn itself out and leave nothing but ashes behind, what shall I do? But it won't – it *shan't*, I am determined – and surely I have power to keep it alive. So let me dismiss *that* thought at once. But Arthur is selfish – I am constrained to acknowledge that; and, indeed, the admission gives me less pain than might be expected; for, since *I* love him so much, I can easily forgive him for loving himself: he likes to be pleased, and it is my delight to please him, – and when I regret this tendency of his, it is for his own sake, not for mine.

The first instance he gave was on the occasion of our bridal tour. He wanted to hurry it over, for all the continental scenes were already familiar to him: many had lost their interest in his eyes, and others had never had anything to lose. The consequence was, that, after a flying transit through part of France and part of Italy, I came back nearly as ignorant as I went, having made no acquaintance with persons and manners, and very little with things, – my head swarming with a motley confusion of objects and scenes – some, it is true, leaving a deeper and more pleasing impression than others, but these embittered by the recollection that my emotions had not been shared by my companion, but that, on the contrary, when I had expressed a particular interest in anything that I saw or desired to see, it had been displeasing to him in as much as it proved that I could take delight in anything disconnected with himself.

As for Paris, we only just touched at that, and he would not give me time to see one tenth of the beauties and interesting objects of Rome. He wanted to get me home, he said, to have me all to himself, and to see me safely installed as the mistress of Grassdale Manor, just as single-minded, as naive, and piquante as I was; and, as if I had been some frail butterfly, he expressed himself fearful of rubbing the silver off my wings by bringing me into contact with society, especially that of Paris and Rome; and, moreover, he did not scruple to tell me that there were ladies in both places that would tear his eyes out if they happened to meet him with me.

Of course I was vexed at all this; but, still, it was less the disappointment to myself that annoyed me, than the disappointment *in him*, and the trouble I was at to frame excuses to my friends for having seen and observed so little, without imputing one particle of blame to my companion. But when we got home – to my new, delightful home – I was so happy and he was so kind that I freely forgave him all; – and I was beginning to think my lot *too* happy, and my husband actually too good for me, if not too good for this world, when, on the second Sunday after our arrival, he shocked and horrified me by another instance of his unreasonable exaction. We were walking home from the morning service – for it was a fine frosty day, and, as we are so near the church, I had requested the carriage should not be used: –

'Helen,' said he, with unusual gravity, 'I am not quite satisfied with you.'

I desired to know what was wrong.

'But will you promise to reform, if I tell you?'

'Yes, if I can – and without offending a higher authority.'

'Ah! there it is, you see – you don't love me with all your heart.'

'I don't understand you, Arthur (at least, I hope I don't): pray tell me what I have done or said amiss?'

'It is nothing you have done or said; it is something that you *are*: you are too religious. Now I like a woman to be religious, and I think your piety one of your greatest charms, but then, like all other good things, it may be carried too far. To my thinking, a woman's religion ought not to lessen her devotion to her earthly lord. She should have enough to purify and etherealize her soul, but not enough to refine away her heart, and raise her above all human sympathies.'

'And am *I* above all human sympathies?' said I.

'No, darling; but you are making more progress towards that saintly condition than I like; for, all these two hours, I have been thinking of you and wanting to catch your eye, and you were so absorbed in your devotions that you had not even a glance to spare for me – I declare, it is enough to make one jealous of one's Maker – which is very wrong, you know; so don't excite such wicked passions again, for my soul's sake.'

'I will give my whole heart and soul to my Maker if I can,' I answered, 'and not one atom more of it to you than He allows. What are *you*, sir, that you should set yourself up as a god, and presume to dispute possession of my heart with Him to whom I owe all I have and all I am, every blessing I ever did or ever can enjoy – and yourself among the rest – if you *are* a blessing, which I am half inclined to doubt.'

'Don't be so hard upon me, Helen; and don't pinch my arm so, you're squeezing your fingers into the bone.'

'Arthur,' continued I, relaxing my hold of his arm, 'you don't love me half as much as I do you; and yet, if you loved me far less than you do, I would not complain, provided you loved your Maker more. I should *rejoice* to see you at any time, so deeply absorbed in your devotions that you had not a single thought to spare for me. But, indeed, I should lose nothing by the change, for the more you loved your God the more deep and pure and true would be your love to me.'

At this he only laughed, and kissed my hand, calling me a sweet enthusiast. Then taking off his hat, he added –

'But look here, Helen – what can a man do with such a head as this?'

The head looked right enough, but when he placed my hand on the top of it, it sunk in a bed of curls, rather alarmingly low, especially in the middle.

'You see I was not made to be a saint,' said he, laughing. 'If God meant me to be religious, why didn't He give me a proper organ of veneration?'

'You are like the servant,' I replied, 'who instead of employing his one talent in his master's service, restored it to him un-improved, alleging, as an excuse, that he knew him "to be a

hard man, reaping where he had not sown and gathering where
he had not strawed." Of him, to whom less is given, less will
be required; but our utmost exertions are required of us all. You
are not without the capacity of veneration, and faith and hope,
and conscience and reason, and every other requisite to a Christian's character, if you choose to employ them; but all our talents
increase in the using, and every faculty, both good and bad,
strengthens by exercise; therefore, if you choose to use the bad –
or those which tend to evil till they become your masters – and
neglect the good till they dwindle away, you have only yourself
to blame. But you *have* talents, Arthur – natural endowments,
both of heart and mind, and temper such as many a better
Christian would be glad to possess – if you would only employ
them in God's service. I should never expect to see you a
devotee, but it is quite possible to be a good Christian without
ceasing to be a happy, merry-hearted man.'

'You speak like an oracle, Helen, and all you say is indisput-
ably true; but listen here: I am hungry, and I see before me a
good substantial dinner; I am told that, if I abstain from this
to-day, I shall have a sumptuous feast to-morrow, consisting of
all manner of dainties and delicacies. Now in the first place,
I should be loath to wait till to-morrow, when I have the means
of appeasing my hunger already before me; in the second place,
the solid viands of to-day are more to my taste than the dainties
that are promised me; in the third place, I don't *see* to-morrow's
banquet, and how can I tell that it is not all a fable, got up by
the greasy-faced fellow that is advising me to abstain, in order
that he may have all the good victuals to himself? in the fourth
place, this table must be spread for somebody, and, as Solomon
says, "Who can eat, or who else can hasten hereunto more
than I?" and finally, with your leave, I'll sit down and satisfy
my cravings of to-day, and leave to-morrow to shift for itself –
who knows but what I may secure both this and that?'

'But you are not required to abstain from the substantial
dinner of to-day; you are only advised to partake of these coarser

viands in such moderation as not to incapacitate you from enjoying the choicer banquet of to-morrow. If, regardless of that counsel, you choose to make a beast of yourself now, and over-eat and over-drink yourself till you turn the good victuals into poison, who is to blame if, hereafter, while you are suffering the torments of yesterday's gluttony and drunkenness, you see more temperate men sitting down to enjoy themselves at that splendid entertainment which you are unable to taste?'

'Most true my patron saint; but again, our friend Solomon says, – "There is nothing better for a man than to eat and to drink, and to be merry."'

'And again,' returned I, 'he says, "Rejoice, O young man, in thy youth, and walk in the ways of thine heart and in the sight of thine eyes; but know thou that, for all these things, God will bring thee into judgment."'

'Well, but Helen, I'm sure I've been very good these last few weeks. What have you seen amiss in me; and what would you have me to do?'

'Nothing – more than you do, Arthur: your actions are all right, so far; but I would have your thoughts changed; I would have you to fortify yourself against temptation, and not to call evil good, and good, evil; I should wish you to think more deeply, to look further, and aim higher than you do.'

We now stood before our door, and I said no more; but, with an ardent and tearful embrace, I left him, and went into the house, and up stairs to take off my bonnet and mantle. I wished to say nothing more on that subject at the time, lest I should disgust him with both it and me.

CHAPTER XXIV

FIRST QUARREL

MARCH 25TH. – Arthur is getting tired – not of me I trust, but of the idle, quiet life he leads – and no wonder, for he has so few sources of amusement; he never reads anything but newspapers and sporting magazines; and when he sees me occupied with a book, he won't let me rest till I close it. In fine weather he generally manages to get through the time pretty well; but on rainy days, of which we have had a good many of late, it is quite painful to witness his ennui. I do all I can to amuse him, but it is impossible to get him to feel interested in what I most like to talk about; while, on the other hand, he likes to talk about things that cannot interest me – or even that annoy me – and these please him the most of all; for his favourite amusement is to sit or loll beside me on the sofa and tell me stories of his former amours, always turning upon the ruin of some confiding girl or the cozening of some unsuspecting husband; and when I express my horror and indignation, he lays it all to the charge of jealousy, and laughs till the tears run down his cheeks. I used to fly into passions or melt into tears at first, but seeing that his delight increased in proportion to my anger and agitation, I have since endeavoured to suppress my feelings and receive his revelations in the silence of calm contempt; but still, he reads the inward struggle in my face, and misconstrues my bitterness of soul for his unworthiness into the pangs of wounded jealousy; and when he has sufficiently diverted himself with that, or fears my displeasure will become too serious for his comfort, he tries to kiss and soothe me into smiles again – never were his caresses so little welcome as then! This is *double* selfishness, displayed to me and to the victims of his former love. There are times when, with a momentary pang – a flash of wild dismay, I ask myself, 'Helen, what have you done?' But I rebuke the inward questioner, and repel the obtrusive thoughts that crowd upon me; for, were he ten times as sensual and impenetrable to good and lofty thoughts, I well know I have no right to complain. And I don't and won't complain. I do and will love him still; and I do not and will not regret that I have linked my fate with his.

April 4th. – We have had a downright quarrel. The particulars are as follows: – Arthur had told me, at different intervals, the whole story of his intrigue with Lady F—, which I would not believe before. It was some consolation, however, to find that, in this instance, the lady had been more to blame than he; for he was very young at the time, and she had decidedly made the first advances, if what he said was true. I hated her for it, for it seemed as if she had chiefly contributed to his corruption, and when he was beginning to talk about her the other day, I begged he would not mention her, for I detested the very sound of her name.

'Not because you loved her, Arthur, mind, but because she injured you, and deceived her husband, and was altogether a very abominable woman, whom you ought to be ashamed to mention.'

But he defended her by saying that she had a doting old husband, whom it was impossible to love.

'Then why did she marry him?' said I.

'For his money,' was the reply.

'Then that was another crime, and her solemn promise to love and honour him was another, that only increased the enormity of the last.'

'You are too severe upon the poor lady,' laughed he. 'But never mind, Helen, I don't care for her now; and I never loved any of them half as much as I do you; so you needn't fear to be forsaken like them.'

'If you had told me these things before, Arthur, I never should have given you the chance.'

'*Wouldn't* you, my darling?'

'Most certainly not!'

He laughed incredulously.

'I wish I could convince you of it now!' cried I, starting up from beside him; and for the first time in my life, and I hope the last, I wished I had not married him.

'Helen,' said he, more gravely, 'do you know that if I believed you now, I should be very angry? – but thank Heaven I don't. Though you stand there with your white face and flashing eyes, looking at me like a very tigress, I know the heart within you, perhaps a trifle better than you know it yourself.'

Without another word, I left the room, and locked myself up in my own chamber. In about half an hour, he came to the door; and first he tried the handle, then he knocked.

'Won't you let me in, Helen?' said he.

'No; you have displeased me,' I replied, 'and I don't want to see your face or hear your voice again till the morning.'

He paused a moment, as if dumbfoundered or uncertain how to answer such a speech, and then turned and walked away. This was only an hour after dinner: I knew he would find it very dull to sit alone all the evening; and this considerably softened my resentment, though it did not make me relent. I was determined to shew him that my heart was not his slave, and I could live without him if I chose; and I sat down and wrote a long letter to my aunt – of course telling her nothing of all this. Soon after ten o'clock, I heard him come up again; but he passed my door and went straight to his own dressing-room, where he shut himself in for the night.

I was rather anxious to see how he would meet me in the morning, and not a little disappointed to behold him enter the breakfast-room with a careless smile.

'Are you cross still, Helen?' said he, approaching as if to salute me. I coldly turned to the table, and began to pour out the coffee, observing that he was rather late.

He uttered a low whistle and sauntered away to the window, where he stood for some minutes looking out upon the pleasing prospect of sullen, grey clouds, streaming rain, soaking lawn, and dripping, leafless trees – and muttering execrations on the weather, and then sat down to breakfast. While taking his coffee, he muttered it was 'd—d cold.'

'You should not have left it so long,' said I.

He made no answer, and the meal was concluded in silence. It was a relief to both when the letter-bag was brought in. It contained, upon examination, a newspaper and one or two letters for him, and a couple of letters for me, which he tossed across the table without a remark. One was from my brother, the other from Milicent Hargrave, who is now in London with her mother. His, I think, were business letters, and apparently not much to his mind, for he crushed them into his pocket with some muttered expletives, that I should have reproved him for at any other time. The paper, he set before him, and pretended to be deeply absorbed in its contents during the remainder of breakfast, and a considerable time after.

The reading and answering of my letters, and the direction of household concerns afforded me ample employment for the morning; after lunch, I got my drawing, and from dinner till bed-time, I read. Meanwhile, poor Arthur was sadly at a loss for something to amuse him or to occupy his time. He wanted to appear as busy and as unconcerned as I did: had the weather at all permitted, he would doubtless have ordered his horse and set off to some distant region – no matter where – immediately after breakfast, and not returned till night; had there been a lady anywhere within reach, of any age between fifteen and forty-five, he would have sought revenge and found employment in getting up – or trying to get up a desperate flirtation with her; but being, to my private satisfaction, entirely cut off from both these sources of diversion, his sufferings were truly deplorable. When he had done yawning over his paper and scribbling short answers to his shorter letters, he spent the remainder of the morning and the whole of the afternoon in fidgeting about from room to room, watching the clouds, cursing the rain, alternately petting, and teasing, and abusing his dogs, sometimes lounging on the sofa with a book that he could not force himself to read, and very often fixedly gazing at me, when he thought I did not perceive it, with the vain hope of detecting some traces of tears, or some tokens of remorseful anguish in my face. But I managed to preserve an undisturbed, though grave serenity throughout the day. I was not really angry: I felt for him all the time, and longed to be reconciled; but I determined he should make the first advances, or at least show some signs of an humble and contrite spirit, first; for, if I began, it would only minister to his self-conceit, increase his arrogance, and quite destroy the lesson I wanted to give him.

He made a long stay in the dining-room after dinner, and, I fear, took an unusual quantity of wine, but not enough to loosen his tongue; for when he came in and found me quietly occupied with my book, too busy to lift my head on his entrance, he merely murmured an expression of suppressed disapprobation, and shutting the door with a bang, went and stretched himself at full length on the sofa, and composed himself to sleep. But his favourite cocker, Dash, that had been lying at my feet, took the liberty of jumping upon him and beginning to lick his face. He struck it off with a smart blow; and the poor dog squeaked, and ran cowering back to me. When he woke up, about half an hour after, he called it to him again; but Dash only looked sheepish and wagged the tip of his tail. He called again, more sharply, but Dash only clung the closer to me, and licked my hand as if imploring protection. Enraged at this, his master snatched up a heavy book and hurled it at his head. The poor dog set up a piteous outcry and ran to the door. I let him out, and then quietly took up the book.

'Give that book to me,' said Arthur, in no very courteous tone. I gave it to him.

'Why did you let the dog out?' he asked. 'You knew I wanted him.'

'By what token?' I replied; 'by your throwing the book at him? but perhaps, it was intended for me?'

'No – but I see you've got a taste of it,' said he, looking at my hand, that had also been struck, and was rather severely grazed.

I returned to my reading; and he endeavoured to occupy himself in the same manner; but in a little while, after several portentous yawns, he pronounced *his* book to be 'cursed trash,' and threw it on to the table. Then followed eight or ten minutes of silence, during the greater part of which, I believe, he was staring at me. At last his patience was tired out.

'What *is* that book, Helen?' he exclaimed. I told him.

'Is it interesting?'

'Yes, very.'

'Humph!'

I went on reading – or pretending to read, at least – I cannot say there was much communication between my eyes and my brain; for, while the former ran over the pages, the latter was earnestly wondering when Arthur would speak next, and what he would say, and what I should answer. But he did not speak again till I rose to make the tea, and then it was only to say he should not take any. He continued lounging on the sofa, and alternately closing his eyes and looking at his watch and at me, till bed-time, when I rose, and took my candle and retired.

'Helen!' cried he, the moment I had left the room. I turned back, and stood awaiting his commands.

'What do you want, Arthur?' I said at length.

'Nothing,' replied he. 'Go!'

I went, but hearing him mutter something as I was closing the door, I turned again. It sounded very like 'confounded slut,' but I was quite willing it should be something else.

'Were you speaking Arthur?' I asked.

'No,' was the answer; and I shut the door and departed. I saw nothing more of him till the following morning at breakfast, when he came down a full hour after the usual time.

'You're very late,' was my morning's salutation.

'You needn't have waited for me,' was his; and he walked up to the window again. It was just such weather as yesterday.

'Oh, this confounded rain!' he muttered. But after studiously regarding it for a minute or two, a bright idea seemed to strike him, for he suddenly exclaimed, 'But I know what I'll do!' and then returned and took his seat at the table. The letter-bag was already there, waiting to be opened. He unlocked it and examined the contents, but said nothing about them.

'Is there anything for me?' I asked.

'No.'

He opened the newspaper and began to read.

'You'd better take your coffee,' suggested I; 'it will be cold again.'

'You may go,' said he, 'if you've done; I don't want you.'

I rose, and withdrew to the next room, wondering if we were to have another such miserable day as yesterday, and wishing intensely for an end of these mutually inflicted torments. Shortly after, I heard him ring the bell and give some orders about his wardrobe that sounded as if he meditated a long journey. He then sent for the coachman, and I heard something about the carriage and the horses, and London, and seven o'clock to-morrow morning, that startled and disturbed me not a little.

'I must not let him go to London, whatever comes of it,' said I to myself; 'he will run into all kinds of mischief, and I shall be the cause of it. But the question is, how am I to alter his purpose? – Well, I will wait awhile, and see if he mentions it.'

I waited most anxiously, from hour to hour; but not a word was spoken, on that or any other subject, to me. He whistled, and talked to his dogs, and wandered from room to room, much the same as on the previous day. At last I began to think I must introduce the subject myself, and was pondering how to bring it about, when John unwittingly came to my relief with the following message from the coachman.

'Please sir, Richard says one of the horses has got a very bad cold, and he thinks, sir, if you could make it convenient to go the day after to-morrow, instead of to-morrow, he could physic it to-day, so as –'

'Confound his impudence!' interjected the master.

'Please sir, he says it would be a deal better if you could,' persisted John, 'for he hopes there'll be a change in the weather shortly, and he says it's not *likely*, when a horse is so bad with a cold, and physicked and all –'

'Devil take the horse!' cried the gentleman. – 'Well, tell him I'll think about it,' he added, after a moment's reflection. He cast a searching glance at me, as the servant withdrew, expecting to see some token of deep astonishment and alarm; but, being previously prepared, I preserved an aspect of stoical indifference. His countenance fell as he met my steady gaze, and he turned away in very obvious disappointment, and walked up to the fire-place, where he stood in an attitude of undisguised dejection, leaning against the chimney-piece with his forehead sunk upon his arm.

'Where do you want to go, Arthur?' said I.

'To London,' replied he, gravely.

'What for?' I asked.

'Because I cannot be happy here.'

'Why not?'

'Because my wife doesn't love me.'

'She would love you with all her heart, if you deserved it.'

'What must I do to deserve it?'

This seemed humble and earnest enough; and I was so much affected, between sorrow and joy, that I was obliged to pause a few seconds before I could steady my voice to reply.

'If she gives you her heart,' said I, 'you must take it thankfully, and use it well, and not pull it in pieces, and laugh in her face, because she cannot snatch it away.'

He now turned round and stood facing me, with his back to the fire.

'Come then, Helen, are you going to be a good girl?' said he.

This sounded rather too arrogant, and the smile that accompanied it did not please me. I therefore hesitated to reply. Perhaps, my former answer had implied too much: he had heard my voice falter, and might have seen me brush away a tear.

'Are you going to forgive me, Helen?' he resumed, more humbly.

'Are *you* penitent?' I replied, stepping up to him and smiling in his face.

'Heart-broken!' he answered, with a rueful countenance – yet with a merry smile just lurking within his eyes and about the corners of his mouth; but this could not repulse me, and I flew into his arms. He fervently embraced me and though I shed a torrent of tears, I think I never was happier in my life than at that moment.

'Then you won't go to London, Arthur?' I said, when the first transport of tears and kisses had subsided.

'No, love, – unless you will go with me.'

'I will, gladly,' I answered, 'if you think the change will amuse you, and if you will put off the journey till next week.'

He readily consented, but said there was no need of much preparation, as he should not be for staying long, for he did not wish me to be Londonized, and to lose my country freshness and originality by too much intercourse with the ladies of the world. I thought this folly; but I did not wish to contradict him now: I merely said that I was of very domestic habits, as he well knew, and had no particular wish to mingle with the world.

So we are to go to London on Monday, the day after tomorrow. It is now four days since the termination of our quarrel, and I'm sure it has done us both good: it has made me like Arthur a great deal better and made him behave a great deal better to me. He has never once attempted to annoy me, since, by the most distant allusion to Lady F— or any of those disagreeable reminiscences of his former life – I wish I could blot them from my memory, or else get him to regard such matters in the same light as I do. Well! it is something, however, to have made him see that they are not fit subjects for a conjugal jest. He may see farther sometime – I will put no limits to my hopes; and, in spite of my aunt's forebodings and my own unspoken fears, I trust we shall be happy yet.

CHAPTER XXV

FIRST ABSENCE

ON THE EIGHTH of April, we went to London; on the eighth of May I returned, in obedience to Arthur's wish: very much against my own, because I left him behind. If he had come with me, I should have been very glad to get home again, for he led me such a round of restless dissipation, while there, that, in that short space of time, I was quite tired out. He seemed bent upon displaying me to his friends and acquaintances in particular, and the public in general, on every possible occasion and to the greatest possible advantage. It was something to feel that he considered me a worthy object of pride; but I paid dear for the gratification, for in the first place, to please him, I had to violate my cherished predilections – my almost rooted principles in favour of a plain, dark, sober style of dress; I must sparkle in costly jewels and deck myself out like a painted butterfly, just as I had, long since, determined I would never do – and this was no trifling sacrifice; – in the second place, I was continually straining to satisfy his sanguine expectations and do honour to his choice, by my general conduct and deportment, and fearing to disappoint him by some awkward misdemeanour, or some trait of inexperienced ignorance about the customs of society, especially when I acted the part of hostess, which I was not unfrequently called upon to do; and in the third place, as I intimated before, I was wearied of the throng and bustle, the restless hurry and ceaseless change of a life so alien to all my previous habits. At last, he suddenly discovered that the London air did not agree with me, and I was languishing for my country home and must immediately return to Grassdale.

I laughingly assured him that the case was not so urgent as he appeared to think it, but I was quite willing to go home if he was. He replied that he should be obliged to remain a week or two longer, as he had business that required his presence.

'Then I will stay with you,' said I.

'But I can't do with you, Helen,' was his answer: 'as long as you stay, I shall attend to you and neglect my business.'

'But I won't let you,' I returned: 'now that I know you have business to attend to, I shall insist upon your attending to it, and letting me alone – and, to tell you the truth, I shall be glad of a little rest. I can take my rides and walks in the park as usual; and your business cannot occupy all your time; I shall see you at mealtimes and in the evenings, at least, and that will be better than being leagues away and never seeing you at all.'

'But my love, I cannot let you stay. How can I settle my affairs when I know that you are here, neglected –'

'I shall not feel myself neglected: while you are doing your duty, Arthur, I shall never complain of neglect. If you had told me, before, that you had anything to do, it would have been half done before this; and now you must make up for lost time by redoubled exertions. Tell me what it is; and I will be your taskmaster, instead of being a hindrance.'

'No, no,' persisted the impracticable creature; 'you *must* go home, Helen; I must have the satisfaction of knowing that you are safe and well, though far away. Don't I see that you are looking quite rakish? – Your bright eyes are faded, and that tender, delicate bloom has quite deserted your cheek.'

'That is only with too much gaiety and fatigue.'

'It is not, I tell you; it is the London air: you are pining for the fresh breezes of your country home – and you shall feel them, before you are two days older. And remember your situation, dearest Helen; on your health, you know, depends the health, if not the life of our future hope.'

'Then you really wish to get rid of me?'

'Positively, I do; and I will take you down myself to Grassdale, and then return. I shall not be absent above a week – or fortnight at most.'

'But if I must go, I will go alone: if you must stay, it is needless to waste your time in the journey there and back.'

But he did not like the idea of sending me alone.

'Why, what helpless creature do you take me for,' I replied, 'that you cannot trust me to go a hundred miles in our own carriage with our own footman and maid to attend me? If you come with me I shall assuredly keep you. But tell me, Arthur, what *is* this tiresome business; and why did you never mention it before?'

'It is only a little business with my lawyer,' said he; and he told me something about a piece of property he wanted to sell in order to pay off a part of the encumbrances on his estate; but either the account was a little confused or I was rather dull of comprehension, for I could not clearly understand how that should keep him in town a fortnight after me. Still less can I now comprehend how it should keep him a month – for it is nearly that time since I left him, and no signs of his return as yet. In every letter he promises to be with me in a few days, and every time deceives me – or deceives himself. His excuses are vague and insufficient. I cannot doubt that he is got among his former companions again – oh, why did I leave him? I wish – I do intensely wish he would return!

June 29th: – No Arthur yet; and for many days I have been
looking and longing in vain for a letter. His letters, when they
come, are kind – if fair words and endearing epithets can give
them a claim to the title – but very short, and full of trivial
excuses and promises that I cannot trust; and yet how anxiously
I look forward to them! how eagerly I open and devour one of
those little, hastily scribbled returns for the three or four long
letters, hitherto unanswered, he has had from me!

Oh, it is cruel to leave me so long alone! He knows I have
no one but Rachel to speak to, for we have no neighbours here,
except the Hargraves, whose residence I can dimly descry from
these upper windows imbosomed among those low, woody hills
beyond the Dale. I was glad when I learnt that Milicent was so
near us; and her company would be a soothing solace to me
now, but she is still in town with her mother: there is no one
at the Grove but little Esther and her French governess, for
Walter is always away. I saw that paragon of manly perfections
in London: he seemed scarcely to merit the eulogiums of his
mother and sister, though he certainly appeared more conversable and agreeable than Lord Lowborough, more candid and
high-minded than Mr Grimsby, and more polished and gentlemanly than Mr Hattersley, Arthur's only other friend whom he
judged fit to introduce to me. – O Arthur, why won't you come!
why won't you write to me at least! You talked about my health –
how can you expect me to gather bloom and vigour here; pining
in solitude and restless anxiety from day to day? – It would
serve you right to come back and find my good looks entirely
wasted away. I would beg my uncle and aunt, or my brother to
come and see me, but I do not like to complain of my loneliness
to them, – and indeed, loneliness is the least of my sufferings;
but what is he doing – what is it that keeps him away? It is this
ever-recurring question and the horrible suggestions it raises
that distract me.

July 3rd. – My last bitter letter has wrung from him an answer
at last, – and a rather longer one than usual; but still, I don't

know what to make of it. He playfully abuses me for the gall and vinegar of my latest effusion, tells me I can have no conception of the multitudinous engagements that keep him away, but avers that, in spite of them all, he will assuredly be with me before the close of next week; though it is impossible for a man, so circumstanced as he is, to fix the precise day of his return: meantime, he exhorts me to the exercise of patience, 'that first of woman's virtues,' and desires me to remember the saying, 'Absence makes the heart grow fonder,' and comfort myself with the assurance that the longer he stays away, the better he shall love me when he returns; and till he does return, he begs I will continue to write to him constantly, for, though he is sometimes too idle and often too busy to answer my letters as they come, he likes to receive them daily, and if I fulfil my threat of punishing his seeming neglect by ceasing to write, he shall be so angry that he will do his utmost to forget me. He adds this piece of intelligence respecting poor Milicent Hargrave: –

'Your little friend Milicent is likely, before long, to follow your example, and take upon her the yoke of matrimony in conjunction with a friend of mine. Hattersley, you know, has not yet fulfilled his direful threat of throwing his precious person away on the first old maid that chose to evince a tenderness for him; but he still preserves a resolute determination to see himself a married man before the year is out. "Only," said he to me, "I must have somebody that will let me have my own way in everything – not like *your* wife, Huntingdon, she is a charming creature, but she looks as if she had a will of her own, and could play the vixen upon occasion" (I thought "you're right there, man," but I didn't say so). "I must have some good, quiet soul that will let me just do what I like and go where I like, keep at home or stay away, without a word of reproach or complaint; for I can't do with being bothered." "Well," said I, "I know somebody that will suit you to a tee, if you don't care for money, and that's Hargrave's sister, Milicent." He desired to be introduced to her forthwith, for he said he had plenty of the

needful himself – or should have, when his old governor chose
to quit the stage. So you see, Helen, I have managed pretty well,
both for your friend and mine.'

Poor Milicent! But I cannot imagine she will ever be led to
accept such a suitor – one so repugnant to all her ideas of a
man to be honoured and loved.

5th. – Alas! I was mistaken. I have got a long letter from her
this morning, telling me she is already engaged, and expects to
be married before the close of the month.

'I hardly know what to say about it,' she writes, 'or what to
think. To tell you the truth, Helen, I don't like the thoughts of
it at all. If I *am* to be Mr Hattersley's wife, I must try to love
him; and I do try with all my might; but I have made very little
progress yet; and the worst symptom of the case is, that the
further he is from me the better I like him: he frightens me with
his abrupt manners and strange hectoring ways, and I dread the
thoughts of marrying him. "Then why have you accepted him?"
you will ask; and I didn't know I had accepted him; but mamma
tells me I have, and he seems to think so too. I certainly didn't
mean to do so; but I did not like to give him a flat refusal for
fear mamma should be grieved and angry (for I knew she wished
me to marry him), and I wanted to talk to her first about it, so
I gave him what *I* thought was an evasive, half negative answer;
but she says it was as good as an acceptance, and he would think
me very capricious if I were to attempt to draw back – and
indeed, I was so confused and frightened at the moment, I can
hardly tell what I said. And next time I saw him, he accosted
me in all confidence as his affianced bride, and immediately
began to settle matters with mamma. I had not courage to
contradict them then, and how can I do it now? I cannot: they
would think me mad. Besides, mamma is so delighted with the
idea of the match; she thinks she has managed so well for me;
and I cannot bear to disappoint her. I do object sometimes, and
tell her what I feel, but you don't know *how* she talks. Mr
Hattersley, you know, is the son of a rich banker, and as Esther

and I have no fortunes and Walter very little, our dear mamma is very anxious to see us all well married, that is, united to rich partners – it is not *my* idea of being well married, but she means it all for the best. She says when I am safe off her hands it will be such a relief to her mind; and she assures me it will be a good thing for the family as well as for me. Even Walter is pleased at the prospect, and when I confessed my reluctance to him, he said it was all childish nonsense. Do *you* think it nonsense, Helen? I should not care if I could see any prospect of being able to love and admire him, but I can't. There is nothing about him to hang one's esteem and affection upon: he is so diametrically opposite to what I imagined my husband should be. Do write to me, and say all you can to encourage me. Don't attempt to dissuade me, for my fate is fixed: preparations for the important event are already going on around me; and don't say a word against Mr Hattersley, for I want to think well of him; and though I have spoken against him myself, it is for the last time: hereafter, I shall never permit myself to utter a word in his dispraise, however he may seem to deserve it; and whoever ventures to speak slightingly of the man I have promised to love, to honour, and obey, must expect my serious displeasure. After all, I think he is quite as good as Mr Huntingdon, if not better; and yet, you love *him*, and seem to be happy and contented; and perhaps I may manage as well. You must tell me, if you can, that Mr Hattersley is better than he seems – that he is upright, honourable, and open-hearted – in fact, a perfect diamond in the rough. He may be all this, but I don't know him – I know only the exterior and what I trust is the worst part of him.'

She concludes with 'Good-bye, dear Helen, I am waiting anxiously for your advice – but mind you let it be all on the right side.'

Alas! poor Milicent, what encouragement can I give you? – or what advice – except that it is better to make a bold stand now, though at the expense of disappointing and angering both mother and brother, and lover, than to devote your whole life, hereafter, to misery and vain regret?

Saturday, 13th. The week is over, and he is not come. All the sweet summer is passing away without one breath of pleasure to me or benefit to him. And I had all along been looking forward to this season with the fond, delusive hope that we should enjoy it so sweetly together; and that, with God's help and my exertions, it would be the means of elevating his mind, and refining his taste to a due appreciation of the salutary and pure delights of nature, and peace, and holy love. But now, – at evening, when I see the round, red sun sink quietly down behind those woody hills, leaving them sleeping in a warm, red, golden haze, I only think another lovely day is lost to him and me; – and at morning, when roused by the flutter and chirp of the sparrows, and the gleeful twitter of the swallows – all intent upon feeding their young, and full of life and joy in their own little frames – I open the window to inhale the balmy, soul-reviving air, and look out upon the lovely landscape, laughing in dew and sunshine, – I too often shame that glorious scene with tears of thankless misery, because *he* cannot feel its freshening influence; – and when I wander in the ancient woods, and meet the little wild-flowers smiling in my path, or sit in the shadow of our noble ash-trees by the water-side, with their branches gently swaying in the light summer breeze that murmurs through their feathery foliage – my ears full of that low music mingled with the dreamy hum of insects, my eyes abstractedly gazing on the glassy surface of the little lake before me, with the trees that crowd about its bank, some gracefully bending to kiss its waters, some rearing their stately heads high above, but stretching their wide arms over its margin, all faithfully mirrored far, far down in its glassy depth – though sometimes the images are partially broken by the sport of aquatic insects, and sometimes, for a moment, the whole is shivered into trembling fragments by a transient breeze that sweeps the surface too roughly, – still I have no pleasure; for the greater the happiness that nature sets before me, the more I lament that *he* is not here to taste it: the greater the bliss we might enjoy together, the more I feel our present wretchedness apart (yes, ours; he must be wretched, though he may not know it); and the more my senses are pleased, the more my heart is oppressed; for he keeps it with him confined amid the dust and smoke of London, – perhaps, shut up within the walls of his own abominable club.

But most of all, at night, when I enter my lonely chamber, and look out upon the summer moon, 'sweet regent of the sky,' floating above me in the 'black blue vault of heaven,' shedding a flood of silver radiance over park, and wood, and water, so pure, so peaceful, so divine, – and think, Where is he now? – what is he doing at this moment? – wholly unconscious of this heavenly scene, – perhaps, revelling with his boon companions, perhaps – God help me, it is too – *too* much!

23rd. Thank Heaven, he is come at last! But how altered! – flushed and feverish, listless and languid, his beauty strangely diminished, his vigour and vivacity quite departed. I have not upbraided him by word or look; I have not even asked him what he has been doing. I have not the heart to do it, for I think he is ashamed of himself – he must be so indeed, – and such enquiries could not fail to be painful to both. My forbearance pleases him – touches him even, I am inclined to think. He says he is glad to be home again, and God knows how glad I am to get him back, even as he is. He lies on the sofa nearly all day long; and I play and sing to him for hours together. I write his letters for him, and get him everything he wants; and sometimes I read to him, and sometimes I talk, and sometimes only sit by him and soothe him with silent caresses. I know he does not deserve it; and I fear I am spoiling him; but this once, I will forgive him, freely and entirely – I will shame him into virtue if I can, and I will never let him leave me again.

He is pleased with my attentions – it may be, grateful for them. He likes to have me near him; and though he is peevish and testy with his servants and his dogs, he is gentle and kind to me. What he would be, if I did not so watchfully anticipate his wants, and so carefully avoid, or immediately desist from doing anything that has a tendency to irritate or disturb him, with however little reason, I cannot tell. How intensely I wish he were worthy of all this care! Last night as I sat beside him, with his head in my lap, passing my fingers through his beautiful curls, this thought made my eyes overflow with sorrowful tears – as it often does, – but this time, a tear fell on his face and made him look up. He smiled, but not insultingly.

'Dear Helen!' he said – 'why do you cry? you know that I love you' (and he pressed my hand to his feverish lips), 'and what more could you desire?'

'Only, Arthur, that you would love *yourself*, as truly and as faithfully as you are loved by me.'

'That would be hard indeed!' he replied, tenderly squeezing my hand.

I don't know whether he fully understood my meaning, but he smiled – thoughtfully and even sadly – a most unusual thing with him; – and then he closed his eyes and fell asleep, looking as careless and sinless as a child. As I watched that placid slumber, my heart swelled fuller than ever, and my tears flowed unrestrained.

August 24. Arthur is himself again, as lusty and reckless, as light of heart and head as ever, and as restless and hard to amuse as a spoilt child, – and almost as full of mischief too, especially when wet weather keeps him within doors. I wish he had something to do, some useful trade, or profession, or employment – anything to occupy his head or his hands for a few hours a day, and give him something besides his own pleasure to think about. If he would play the country gentleman, and attend to the farm – but that he knows nothing about, and won't give his mind to consider, – or if he would take up with some literary study, or learn to draw or to play – as he is so fond of music, I often try to persuade him to learn the piano, but he is far too idle for such an undertaking: he has no more idea of exerting himself to overcome obstacles than he has of restraining his natural appetites; and these two things are the ruin of him. I lay them both to the charge of his harsh yet careless father and his madly indulgent mother. If ever I am a mother I will zealously strive against this *crime* of over indulgence – I can hardly give it a milder name when I think of the evils it brings.

Happily, it will soon be the shooting season, and then, if the weather permit, he will find occupation enough in the pursuit and destruction of the partridges and pheasants; we have no grouse, or he might have been similarly occupied at this moment, instead of lying under the acacia tree pulling poor Dash's ears. But he says it is dull work shooting alone; he must have a friend or two to help him.

'Let them be tolerably decent then, Arthur,' said I. – The word 'friend,' in his mouth makes me shudder: I know it was some of his 'friends' that induced him to stay behind me in London, and kept him away so long – indeed, from what he has unguardedly told me, or hinted from time to time, I cannot doubt that he frequently showed them my letters, to let them see how fondly his wife watched over his interests and how keenly she regretted his absence; and that they induced him to remain week after week, and to plunge into all manner of excesses to avoid being laughed at for a wife-ridden fool, and, perhaps, to show how far he could venture to go without danger of shaking the fond creature's devoted attachment. It is a hateful idea, but I cannot believe it is a false one.

'Well,' replied he, 'I thought of Lord Lowborough for one; but there is no possibility of getting him without his better half, our mutual friend Annabella; so we must ask them both. You're not afraid of her, are you Helen?' he asked, with a mischievous twinkle in his eyes.

'Of course not,' I answered: 'why should I? – And who besides?'

'Hargrave for one – he will be glad to come, though his own

place is so near, for he has little enough land of his own to
shoot over, and we can extend our depredations into it, if we
like; – and he is thoroughly respectable, you know, Helen, quite
a lady's man: – and I think, Grimsby for another: he's a decent,
quiet fellow enough – you'll not object to Grimsby?'

'I hate him: but however, if you wish it, I'll try to endure his
presence for a while.'

'All a prejudice Helen – a mere woman's antipathy.'

'No; I have solid grounds for my dislike. And is that all?'

'Why, yes, I think so. Hattersley will be too busy billing and
cooing with his bride to have much time to spare for guns
and dogs, at present,' he replied. – And that reminds me that
I have had several letters from Milicent since her marriage, and
that she either is or pretends to be quite reconciled to her lot.
She professes to have discovered numberless virtues and perfections in her husband, some of which, I fear, less partial eyes
would fail to distinguish, though they sought them carefully
with tears; and now that she is accustomed to his loud voice
and abrupt, uncourteous manners, she affirms she finds no
difficulty in loving him as a wife should do, and begs I will
burn that letter wherein she spoke so unadvisedly against him.
So that I trust she may yet be happy; but if she is, it will be
entirely the reward of her own goodness of heart; for had she
chosen to consider herself the victim of fate, or of her mother's
worldly wisdom, she might have been thoroughly miserable;
and if, for duty's sake, she had not made every effort to love her
husband, she would doubtless have hated him to the end of
her days.

CHAPTER XXVI

THE GUESTS

SEPT. 23RD. Our guests arrived about three weeks ago. Lord and Lady Lowborough have now been married above eight months; and I will do the lady the credit to say that her husband is quite an altered man: his looks, his spirits, and his temper are all perceptibly changed for the better since I last saw him. But there is room for improvement still. He is not always cheerful nor always contented, and she often complains of his ill-humour, which, however, of all persons, *she* ought to be the last to accuse him of, as he never displays it against her, except for such conduct as would provoke a saint. He adores her still, and would go to the world's end to please her. She knows her power, and she uses it too; but well knowing that to wheedle and coax is safer than to command, she judiciously tempers her despotism with flattery and blandishments enough to make him deem himself a favoured and a happy man. And yet, at times, a sombre shadow overclouds his brow even in her presence, but evidently the result of despondency rather than of ill-humour, and generally occasioned by some display of her ill-regulated temper or misguided mind – some wanton trampling upon his most cherished opinions – some reckless disregard of principle that makes him bitterly regret that she is not as good as she is charming and beloved. I pity him from my heart, for I know the misery of such regrets.

But she has another way of tormenting him, in which I am a fellow sufferer – or might be, if I chose to regard myself as such. This is by openly but not too glaringly coquetting with Mr Huntingdon, who is quite willing to be her partner in the game; but I don't care for it, because with him, I know there is nothing but personal vanity and a mischievous desire to excite my jealousy, and perhaps to torment his friend; and she, no doubt, is actuated by much the same motives; only there is more of malice and less of playfulness in *her* manœuvres. It is obviously, therefore, my interest to disappoint them both, as far as I am concerned, by preserving a cheerful, undisturbed serenity throughout; and accordingly I endeavour to show the fullest confidence in my husband and the greatest indifference to the arts of my attractive guest. I have never reproached the former but once, and that was for laughing at Lord Lowborough's depressed and anxious countenance one evening, when they had both been particularly provoking; and then, indeed, I said a good deal on the subject, and rebuked him sternly enough; but he only laughed, and said –

'You can feel for him, Helen – can't you?'

'I can feel for any one that is unjustly treated,' I replied, 'and I can feel for those that injure them too.'

'Why Helen, you are as jealous as he is!' cried he, laughing still more; and I found it impossible to convince him of his mistake. So from that time I have carefully refrained from any notice of the subject whatever, and left Lord Lowborough to take care of himself. He either has not the sense or the power to follow my example, though he does try to conceal his uneasiness as well as he can; but still, it will appear in his face, and his ill-humour will peep out at intervals, though not in the expression of open resentment – they never go far enough for that. But I confess I do feel jealous at times – most painfully, bitterly so – when she sings and plays to him, and he hangs over the instrument and dwells upon her voice with no affected interest; for then, I know he is really delighted, and I have no power to awaken similar fervour. I can amuse and please him with my simple songs, but not delight him thus.

I might retaliate if I chose, for Mr Hargrave is disposed to be very polite and attentive to me as his hostess – especially so when Arthur is the most neglectful, whether in mistaken compassion for me, or ambitious to show off his own good breeding by comparison with his friend's remissness, I cannot tell; but in either case, his civilities are highly distasteful to me. If Arthur is a little careless, of course it is unpleasant to have the fault exaggerated by contrast; and to be pitied as a neglected wife when I am not such, is an insult I can ill endure. But for hospitality's sake, I endeavour to suppress my impulse of scarcely reasonable resentment, and behave with decent civility to our guest, who, to give him his due, is by no means a disagreeable companion: he has good conversational powers and considerable information and taste, and talks about things that Arthur never could be brought to discuss, or to feel any interest in. But Arthur dislikes me to talk to him, and is visibly annoyed by his commonest acts of politeness; not that my husband has any unworthy suspicions of me – or of his friend either, as I believe – but he dislikes me to have any pleasure but in himself, any shadow of homage or kindness but such as he chooses to vouchsafe: he knows he is my sun, but when he chooses to withhold his light, he would have my sky to be all darkness; he cannot bear that I should have a moon to mitigate the deprivation. This is unjust; and I am sometimes tempted to tease him accordingly; but I won't yield to the temptation: if he should carry his trifling with my feelings too far, I shall find some other means of checking him.

28th. – Yesterday we all went to the Grove, Mr Hargrave's much neglected home. His mother frequently asks us over that she may have the pleasure of her dear Walter's company; and this time she had invited us to a dinner party, and got together as many of the country gentry as were within reach to meet us. The entertainment was very well got up; but I could not help thinking about the cost of it all the time. I don't like Mrs Hargrave; she is a hard, pretentious, worldly-minded woman. She has money enough to live very comfortably, if she only knew how to use it judiciously, and had taught her son to do the same; but she is ever straining to keep up appearances, with that despicable pride that shuns the semblance of poverty as of a shameful crime. She grinds her dependants, pinches her servants, and deprives even her daughters and herself of the real comforts of life, because she will not consent to yield the palm in outward show to those who have three times her wealth, and, above all, because she is determined her cherished son shall be enabled to 'hold up his head with the highest gentlemen in the land.' This same son, I imagine, is a man of expensive habits – no reckless spendthrift, and no abandoned sensualist, but one who likes to have 'everything handsome about him,' and to go to a certain length in youthful indulgences – not so much to gratify his own tastes as to maintain his reputation as a man of fashion in the world, and a respectable fellow among his own lawless companions; while he is too selfish to consider how many comforts might be obtained for his fond mother and sisters with the money he thus wastes upon himself: as long as they can contrive to make a respectable appearance once a year when they come to town, he gives himself little concern about their private stintings and struggles at home. This is a harsh judgment to form of 'dear, noble-minded, generous-hearted Walter,' but I fear it is too just.

Mrs Hargrave's anxiety to make good matches for her daughters is partly the cause and partly the result of these errors: by making a figure in the world and shewing them off to advantage, she hopes to obtain better chances for them; and by thus living beyond her legitimate means and lavishing so much on their brother, she renders them portionless, and makes them burdens on her hands. Poor Milicent, I fear, has already fallen a sacrifice to the manœuvrings of this mistaken mother, who congratulates herself on having so satisfactorily discharged her maternal duty, and hopes to do as well for Esther. But Esther is a child as yet – a little merry romp of fourteen: as honest-hearted, and as guileless and simple as her sister, but with a fearless spirit of her own, that I fancy, her mother will find some difficulty in bending to her purposes.

CHAPTER XXVII

A MISDEMEANOUR

OCTOBER 9TH. – While the gentlemen are ranging the woods and Lady Lowborough is busy writing her letters, I will return to my chronicle for the purpose of recording sayings and doings, the last of the kind I hope I shall ever have cause to describe.

It was on the night of the 4th, a little after tea, that Annabella had been singing and playing, with Arthur as usual at her side: she had ended her song, but still she sat at the instrument; and he stood leaning on the back of her chair, conversing in scarcely audible tones, with his face in very close proximity with hers. I looked at Lord Lowborough. He was at the other end of the room, talking with Messrs Hargrave and Grimsby; but I saw him dart towards his lady and his host, a quick, impatient glance, expressive of intense disquietude, at which Grimsby smiled. Determined to interrupt the *tête-à-tête*, I rose, and selecting a piece of music from the music-stand, stepped up to the piano, intending to ask the lady to play it; but I stood transfixed and speechless on seeing her seated there, listening with what seemed an exultant smile on her flushed face, to his soft murmurings, with her hand quietly surrendered to his clasp. The blood rushed first to my heart and then to my head – for there was more than this; almost at the moment of my approach, he cast a hurried glance over his shoulder towards the other occupants of the room, and then ardently pressed the unresisting hand to his lips. On raising his eyes he beheld me and dropped them again, confounded and dismayed. She saw me too, and confronted me with a look of hard defiance. I laid the music on the piano, and retired. I felt ill; but I did not leave the room: happily, it was getting late and could not be long before the company dispersed. I went to the fire and leant my head against the chimney-piece. In a minute or two, some one asked me if I felt unwell. I did not answer – indeed, at the time I knew not what was said – but I mechanically looked up, and saw Mr Hargrave standing beside me on the rug.

'Shall I get you a glass of wine?' said he.

'No, thank you,' I replied; and turning from him, I looked round. Lady Lowborough was beside her husband, bending over him as he sat, with her hand on his shoulder, softly talking and smiling in his face; and Arthur was at the table turning over a book of engravings. I seated myself in the nearest chair; and Mr Hargrave, finding his services were not desired, judiciously withdrew. Shortly after, the company broke up, and as the guests were retiring to their rooms, Arthur approached me, smiling with the utmost assurance.

'Are you *very* angry, Helen?' murmured he.

'This is no jest, Arthur,' said I seriously, but as calmly as I could – 'unless you think it a jest to lose my affection for ever.'

'What! so bitter?' he exclaimed, laughingly clasping my hand between both his; but I snatched it away, in indignation – almost in disgust, for he was obviously affected with wine.

'Then I must go down on my knees,' said he; and kneeling before me with clasped hands uplifted in mock humiliation, he continued imploringly – 'Forgive me, Helen! – dear Helen forgive me, and I'll *never* do it again!' and burying his face in his handkerchief, he affected to sob aloud.

Leaving him thus employed, I took my candle, and slipping quietly from the room, hastened up stairs as fast as I could. But he soon discovered that I had left him, and rushing up after me, caught me in his arms, just as I had entered the chamber, and was about to shut the door in his face.

'No, no, by Heaven, you shan't escape me so!' he cried. Then, alarmed at my agitation, he begged me not to put myself in such a passion, telling me I was white in the face, and should kill myself if I did so.

'Let me go then,' I murmured; and immediately he released me – and it was well he did, for I was really in a passion. I sunk into the easy-chair and endeavoured to compose myself, for I wanted to speak to him calmly. He stood beside me, but did not venture to touch me or to speak, for a few seconds; then approaching a little nearer, he dropped on one knee – not in mock humility, but to bring himself nearer my level, and leaning his hand on the arm of the chair, he began in a low voice –

'It is all nonsense, Helen – a jest, a mere nothing – not worth a thought. Will you *never* learn,' he continued more boldly, 'that you have nothing to fear from me? that I love you wholly and entirely? – or if,' he added with a lurking smile, 'I ever give a thought to another you may well spare it, for those fancies are here and gone like a flash of lightning, while my love for you burns on steadily, and for ever like the sun. You little exorbitant tyrant, will not *that* —'

'Be quiet a moment, will you Arthur,' said I, 'and listen to me – and don't think I'm in a jealous fury: I am perfectly calm. Feel my hand.' And I gravely extended it towards him – but closed it upon his with an energy that seemed to disprove the assertion, and made him smile. 'You needn't smile, sir,' said I, still tightening my grasp, and looking steadfastly on him till he almost quailed before me. 'You may think it all very fine, Mr Huntingdon, to amuse yourself with rousing my jealousy; but take care you don't rouse my hate instead. And when you have once extinguished my love, you will find it no easy matter to kindle it again.'

'Well Helen, I won't repeat the offence. But I meant nothing by it, I assure you. I had taken too much wine, and I was scarcely myself, at the time.'

'You often take too much; – and that is another practice I detest.' He looked up astonished at my warmth. 'Yes,' I continued. 'I never mentioned it before, because I was ashamed to do so; but now I'll tell you that it distresses me, and may disgust me, if you go on and suffer the habit to grow upon you, as it will, if you don't check it in time. But the whole system of your conduct to Lady Lowborough, is not referrible to wine; and this night you knew perfectly well what you were doing.'

'Well, I'm sorry for it,' replied he, with more of sulkiness than contrition: 'what more would you have?'

'You are sorry that I saw you, no doubt,' I answered coldly.

'If you had not seen me,' he muttered, fixing his eyes on the carpet, 'it would have done no harm.'

My heart felt ready to burst; but I resolutely swallowed back my emotion, and answered calmly, 'You think not?'

'No,' replied he, boldly. 'After all, what have I done? It's nothing – except as you choose to make it a subject of accusation and distress.'

'What would Lord Lowborough, your *friend* think, if he knew all? or what would you yourself think, if he or any other had acted the same part to me, throughout, as you have to Annabella?'

'I would blow his brains out.'

'Well then, Arthur, how can you call it nothing – an offence for which you would think yourself justified in blowing another man's brains out? Is it nothing to trifle with your friend's feelings and mine – to endeavour to steal a woman's affections from her husband – what he values more than his gold, and therefore what it is more dishonest to take? Are the marriage vows a jest; and is it nothing to make it your sport to break them, and to tempt another to do the same? Can I love a man that does such things, and coolly maintains it is nothing?'

'You are breaking your marriage vows yourself,' said he, indignantly rising and pacing to and fro. 'You promised to honour and obey me, and now you attempt to hector over me, and threaten and accuse me and call me worse than a highwayman. If it were not for your situation Helen, I would not submit to it so tamely. I won't be dictated to by a woman, though she be my wife.'

'What will you do then? Will you go on till I hate you, and then accuse me of breaking my vows?'

He was silent a moment, and then replied,

'You never will hate me.' Returning and resuming his former position at my feet, he repeated more vehemently – 'You cannot hate me, as long as I love you.'

'But how can I believe that you love me, if you continue to act in this way? Just imagine yourself in my place: would *you* think I loved *you*, if *I* did so? Would you believe my protestations, and honour and trust me under such circumstances?'

'The cases are different,' he replied. 'It is a woman's nature to be constant – to love one and one only, blindly, tenderly, and for ever – bless them, dear creatures! and you above them all – but you must have some commiseration for us, Helen; you must give us a little more licence, for as Shakespeare has it –

> "However we do praise ourselves,
> Our fancies are more giddy and unfirm,
> More longing, wavering, sooner lost and won
> Than women's are." '

'Do you mean by that, that your fancies are lost to me, and won by Lady Lowborough?'

'No; Heaven is my witness that I think her mere dust and ashes in comparison with you, – and shall continue to think so, unless you drive me from you by too much severity. She is a daughter of earth; you are an angel of Heaven; only be not too austere in your divinity, and remember that I am a poor, fallible mortal. Come now, Helen; won't you forgive me?' he said, gently taking my hand, and looking up with an innocent smile.

'If I do, you will repeat the offence.'

'I swear by –'

'Don't swear; I'll believe your word as well as your oath. I wish I could have confidence in either.'

'Try me then, Helen: only trust and pardon me this once, and you shall see! Come, I am in hell's torments till you speak the word.'

I did not speak it, but I put my hand on his shoulder and kissed his forehead, and then burst into tears. He embraced me tenderly; and we have been good friends ever since. He has been decently temperate at table, and well-conducted towards Lady Lowborough. The first day, he held himself aloof from her, as far as he could without any flagrant breach of hospitality: since that, he has been friendly and civil but nothing more – in my presence, at least, nor, I think, at any other time; for she seems haughty and displeased, and Lord Lowborough is manifestly more cheerful, and more cordial towards his host than before. But I shall be glad when they are gone, for I have so little love for Annabella that it is quite a task to be civil to her, and as she is the only woman here besides myself, we are necessarily thrown so much together. Next time Mrs Hargrave calls, I shall hail her advent as quite a relief. I have a good mind to ask Arthur's leave to invite the old lady to stay with us till our guests depart. I think I will. She will take it as a kind attention, and, though I have little relish for her society, she will be truly welcome as a third to stand between Lady Lowborough and me.

The first time the latter and I were alone together, after that unhappy evening, was an hour or two after breakfast on the following day, when the gentlemen were gone out after the usual time spent in the writing of letters, the reading of newspapers, and desultory conversation. We sat silent for two or three minutes. She was busy with her work and I was running over the columns of a paper from which I had extracted all the pith some twenty minutes before. It was a moment of painful embarrassment to me, and I thought it must be infinitely more so to her; but it seems I was mistaken. She was the first to speak; and, smiling with the coolest assurance, she began, –

'Your husband was merry last night, Helen: is he often so?'

My blood boiled in my face; but it was better she should seem to attribute his conduct to this than to anything else.

'No,' replied I, 'and never will be so again I trust.'

'You gave him a curtain lecture, did you?'

'No; but I told him I disliked such conduct, and he promised me not to repeat it.'

'I *thought* he looked rather subdued this morning,' she continued; 'and you, Helen; you've been weeping I see – that's our grand resource, you know – but doesn't it make your eyes smart? – and do you always find it to answer?'

'I never cry for effect; nor can I conceive how any one can.'

'Well, I don't know: I never had occasion to try it; – but I think if Lowborough were to commit such improprieties, I'd make *him* cry. I don't wonder at your being angry, for I'm sure I'd give my husband a lesson he would not soon forget for a lighter offence than that. But then he never *will* do anything of the kind; for I keep him in too good order for that.'

'Are you sure you don't arrogate too much of the credit to yourself? Lord Lowborough was quite as remarkable for his abstemiousness for some time before you married him, as he is now, I have heard.'

'Oh, about the *wine* you mean – yes, he's safe enough for that. And as to looking askance at another woman – he's safe enough for that too, while I live, for he worships the very ground I tread on.'

'Indeed! and are you sure you deserve it?'

'Why, as to that, I can't say: you know we're all fallible creatures, Helen; we none of us deserve to be worshipped. But are *you* sure your darling Huntingdon deserves all the love you give to *him*?'

I knew not what to answer to this. I was burning with anger; but I suppressed all outward manifestations of it, and only bit my lip and pretended to arrange my work.

'At any rate,' resumed she, pursuing her advantage, 'you can console yourself with the assurance that *you* are worthy of all the love he gives to you.'

'You flatter me,' said I; 'but at least, I can try to be worthy of it.' And then I turned the conversation.

CHAPTER XXVIII

PARENTAL FEELINGS

DECEMBER 25TH. – Last Christmas I was a bride, with a heart overflowing with present bliss, and full of ardent hopes for the future – though not unmingled with foreboding fears. Now I am a wife: my bliss is sobered, but not destroyed; my hopes diminished, but not departed; my fears increased but not yet thoroughly confirmed; – and, thank Heaven, I am a mother too. God has sent me a soul to educate for Heaven, and given me a new and calmer bliss, and stronger hopes to comfort me. But where hope rises fear *must* lurk behind, and when I clasp my little darling to my breast, or hang over his slumbers with unutterable delight, and a world of hope within my heart, one of two thoughts is ever at hand to check my swelling bliss; the one: He may be taken from me; the other: He may live to curse his own existence. In the first, I have this consolation: that the bud, though plucked, would not be withered, only transplanted to a fitter soil to ripen and blow beneath a brighter sun; and though I might not cherish and watch my child's unfolding intellect, he would be snatched away from all the suffering and sins of earth; and my understanding tells me this would be no great evil; but my heart shrinks from the contemplation of such a possibility, and whispers I could not bear to see him die, and relinquish to the cold and cruel grave this cherished form, now warm with tender life, flesh of my flesh and shrine of that pure spark which it should be my life's sweet labour to keep unsullied from the world, – and ardently implores that Heaven would spare him still, to be my comfort and my joy, and me to be his shield, instructor, friend – to guide him along the perilous path of youth, and train him to be God's servant while on earth, a blessed and honoured saint in Heaven. But in the other case, if he should live to disappoint my hopes, and frustrate all my efforts – to be a slave of sin, the victim of vice and misery, a curse to others and himself – Eternal Father, if Thou beholdest such a life before him, tear him from me now in spite of all my anguish, and take him from my bosom to Thine own, while he is yet a guileless, unpolluted lamb!

My little Arthur! There you lie in sweet, unconscious slumber, the tiny epitome of your father, but stainless yet as that pure snow, new fallen from Heaven – God shield thee from his errors! How will I watch and toil to guard thee from them! He wakes; his tiny arms are stretched towards me; his eyes unclose; they meet my gaze, but will not answer it. Little angel! you do not know me; you cannot think of me or love me yet; and yet how fervently my heart is knit to yours; how grateful I am for all the joy you give me! Would that your father could share it with me – that he could feel my love, my hope, and take an equal part in my resolves and projects for the future – nay, if he could but sympathize in half my views, and share one half my feelings, it would be indeed a blessing to both himself and me: it would elevate and purify his mind, and bind him closer to his home and me.

Perhaps, he will feel awakening interest and affection for his child as it grows older. At present, he is pleased with the acquisition, and hopes it will become a fine boy and a worthy heir; and that is nearly all I can say. At first, it was a thing to wonder and laugh at, not to touch: now, it is an object almost of indifference, except when his impatience is roused by its 'utter helplessness' and 'imperturbable stupidity' (as he calls it), or my too close attention to its wants. He frequently comes and sits beside me while I am busied with my maternal cares. I hoped at first it was for the pleasure of contemplating our priceless treasure; but I soon found it was only to enjoy my company, or escape the pains of solitude. He is kindly welcome of course, but the best compliment to a mother is to appreciate her little one. He shocked me very much on one occasion: it was about a fortnight after the birth of our son, and he was with me in the nursery. We had neither of us spoken for some time: I was lost in the contemplation of my nursling, and I thought he was similarly occupied – as far, at least, as I thought about him at all. But suddenly he startled me from my reverie by impatiently exclaiming, –

'Helen, I shall positively hate that little wretch, if you worship it so madly! You are absolutely infatuated about it.'

I looked up in astonishment, to see if he could be in earnest.

'You have not a thought to spare for anything else,' he continued in the same strain: 'I may go or come, be present or absent, cheerful or sad; it's all the same to you. As long as you have that ugly little creature to doat upon, you care not a farthing what becomes of me.'

'It is false, Arthur; when you enter the room, it always doubles my happiness; when you are near me, the sense of your presence delights me, though I don't look at you; and when I think about our child, I please myself with the idea that you share my thoughts and feelings, though I don't speak them.'

'How the devil can I waste my thoughts and feelings on a little worthless idiot like that?'

'It is your own son Arthur, – or, if that consideration has no weight with you, it is mine; and you ought to respect my feelings.'

'Well, don't be cross; it was only a slip of the tongue,' pleaded he. 'The little fellow is well enough, only I can't worship him as you do.'

'You shall nurse him for me, as a punishment,' said I, rising to put my baby in its father's arms.

'No, don't, Helen – don't!' cried he, in real disquietude.

'I will: you'll love him better, when you feel the little creature in your arms.'

I deposited the precious burden in his hands, and retreated to the other side of the room, laughing at the ludicrous, half embarrassed air with which he sat, holding it at arm's length, and looking upon it as if it were some curious being of quite a different species to himself.

'Come, take it, Helen; take it,' he cried at length. 'I shall drop it, if you don't.'

Compassionating his distress – or rather the child's unsafe position, I relieved him of the charge.

'Kiss it, Arthur; do – you've never kissed it yet!' said I, kneeling and presenting it before him.

'I would rather kiss its mother,' replied he, embracing me. 'There now; won't that do as well?'

I resumed my seat in the easy chair, and gave my little one a shower of gentle kisses to make up for its other parent's refusal.

'There goes!' cried the jealous father. 'That's more, in one minute, lavished on that little senseless, thankless, oyster, than you have given me these three weeks past.'

'Come here then, you insatiable monopolist, and you shall have as many as you like, incorrigible and undeserving as you are. – There now, won't that suffice? I have a good mind never to give you another till you have learnt to love my baby as a father should.'

'I like the little devil –'

'Arthur!'

'Well, the little angel – well enough,' and he pinched its delicate little nose to prove his affection, 'only I can't *love* it – what is there to love? It can't love me – or you either; it can't understand a single word you say to it, or feel one spark of gratitude for all your kindness. Wait till it can shew some little affection for me, and then I'll see about loving it. At present it is nothing more than a little selfish, senseless, sensualist, and if *you* see anything adorable in it, it's all very well – I only wonder how you can.'

'If you were less selfish yourself, Arthur, you would not regard it in that light.'

'Possibly not, love; but so it is: there's no help for it.'

CHAPTER XXIX

THE NEIGHBOUR

Dec. 25th, 1823. Another year is gone. My little Arthur lives and thrives. He is healthy but not robust, full of gentle playfulness and vivacity, already affectionate, and susceptible of passions and emotions it will be long ere he can find words to express. He has won his father's heart at last; and now my constant terror is, lest he should be ruined by that father's thoughtless indulgence. But I must beware of my own weakness too, for I never knew till now how strong are a parent's temptations to spoil an only child.

I have need of consolation in my son, for (to this silent paper I may confess it) I have but little in my husband. I love him still; and he loves me, in his own way – but oh, how different from the love I could have given, and once had hoped to receive! how little real sympathy there exists between us; how many of my thoughts and feelings are gloomily cloistered within my own mind; how much of my higher and better self is indeed unmarried – doomed either to harden and sour in the sunless shade of solitude, or to quite degenerate and fall away for lack of nutriment in this unwholesome soil! – But, I repeat, I have no right to complain: only let me state the truth – some of the truth at least, – and see hereafter, if any darker truths will blot these pages. We have now been full two years united – the 'romance' of our attachment must be worn away. Surely I have now got down to the lowest gradation in Arthur's affection, and discovered all the evils of his nature: if there be any further change, it must be for the better, as we become still more accustomed to each other: surely we shall find no lower depth than this. And, if so, I can bear it well – as well, at least, as I have borne it hitherto.

Arthur is not what is commonly called a *bad* man: he has many good qualities; but he is a man without self-restraint or lofty aspirations – a lover of pleasure, given up to animal enjoyments: he is not a bad husband, but his notions of matrimonial duties and comforts are not my notions. Judging from appearances, his idea of a wife, is a thing to love one devotedly and to stay at home – to wait upon her husband, and amuse him and minister to his comfort in every possible way, while he chooses to stay with her; and, when he is absent, to attend to his interests, domestic or otherwise, and patiently wait his return; no matter how he may be occupied in the meantime.

Early in spring, he announced his intention of going to London: his affairs there demanded his attendance, he said, and he could refuse it no longer. He expressed his regret at having to leave me, but hoped I would amuse myself with the baby till he returned.

'But why leave me?' I said. 'I can go with you: I can be ready at any time.'

'You would not take that child to town?'

'Yes – why not?'

The thing was absurd: the air of the town would be certain to disagree with him, and with me as a nurse; the late hours and London habits would not suit me under such circumstances; and altogether he assured me that it would be excessively troublesome, injurious, and unsafe. I overruled his objections as well as I could, for I trembled at the thoughts of his going alone, and would sacrifice almost anything for myself, much even for my child, to prevent it; but at length he told me, plainly, and somewhat testily, that he could not do with me: he was worn out with the baby's restless nights, and must have some repose. I proposed separate apartments; but it would not do.

'The truth is, Arthur,' I said at last, 'you are weary of my company, and determined not to have me with you. You might as well have said so at once.'

He denied it; but I immediately left the room, and flew to

the nursery to hide my feelings, if I could not soothe them, there.

I was too much hurt to express any further dissatisfaction with his plans, or at all to refer to the subject again, except for the necessary arrangements concerning his departure and the conduct of affairs during his absence, – till the day before he went, when I earnestly exhorted him to take care of himself and keep out of the way of temptation. He laughed at my anxiety, but assured me there was no cause for it, and promised to attend to my advice.

'I suppose it is no use asking you to fix a day for your return?' said I.

'Why, no: I hardly can, under the circumstances; but be assured, love, I shall not be long away.'

'I don't wish to keep you a prisoner at home,' I replied: 'I should not grumble at your staying whole months away – if you can be happy so long without me – provided, I knew you were safe; but I don't like the idea of your being there, among your friends, as you call them.'

'Pooh, pooh, you silly girl! Do you think I can't take care of myself?'

'You didn't last time. But THIS time, Arthur,' I added, earnestly, 'show me that you can, and teach me that I need not fear to trust you!'

He promised fair, but in such a manner as we seek to soothe a child. And did he keep his promise? No; – and, henceforth, *I can never trust his word*. Bitter, bitter confession! Tears blind me while I write. It was early in March that he went, and he did not return till July. This time, he did not trouble himself to make excuses as before, and his letters were less frequent, and shorter and less affectionate, especially after the first few weeks: they came slower and slower, and more terse and careless every time. But still, when *I* omitted writing he complained of my neglect. When I wrote sternly and coldly, as I confess I frequently did at the last, he blamed my harshness, and said it was enough to scare him from his home: when I tried mild persuasion, he was a little more gentle in his replies, and promised to return; but I had learnt, at last, to disregard his promises.

Those were four miserable months, alternating between intense anxiety, despair, and indignation; pity for him, and pity for myself. And yet, through all, I was not wholly comfortless; I had my darling, sinless, inoffensive little one to console me, but even this consolation was embittered by the constantly recurring thought, 'How shall I teach him, hereafter, to respect his father, and yet to avoid his example?'

But I remembered that I had brought all these afflictions, in a manner wilfully, upon myself; and I determined to bear them without a murmur. At the same time I resolved not to give myself up to misery for the transgressions of another, and endeavoured to divert myself as much as I could; and besides the companionship of my child and my dear, faithful Rachel, who evidently guessed my sorrows and felt for them, though she was too discreet to allude to them, – I had my books and pencil, my domestic affairs, and the welfare and comfort of Arthur's poor tenants and labourers to attend to; and I sometimes sought and obtained amusement in the company of my young friend Esther Hargrave: occasionally, I rode over to see her, and once or twice I had her to spend the day with me at the Manor. Mrs Hargrave did not visit London that season: having no daughter to marry, she thought it as well to stay at home and economize; and, for a wonder, Walter came down to join her in the beginning of June and stayed till near the close of August.

The first time I saw him was on a sweet, warm evening, when I was sauntering in the park with little Arthur and Rachel, who is head-nurse and lady's-maid in one – for, with my secluded life and tolerably active habits, I require but little attendance, and as she had nursed me and coveted to nurse my child, and was moreover so very trustworthy, I preferred committing the important charge to her, with a young nursery-maid under her directions, to engaging any one else: – besides it saves money;

and since I have made acquaintance with Arthur's affairs, I have learnt to regard that as no trifling recommendation; for, by my own desire, nearly the whole of the income of my fortune is devoted, for years to come, to the paying off of his debts, and the money he contrives to squander away in London is incomprehensible. – But to return to Mr Hargrave: – I was standing with Rachel beside the water, amusing the laughing baby in her arms, with a twig of willow laden with golden catkins, when greatly to my surprise, he entered the park, mounted on his costly black hunter, and crossed over the grass to meet me. He saluted me with a very fine compliment, delicately worded, and modestly delivered withal, which he had doubtless concocted as he rode along. He told me he had brought a message from his mother, who, as he was riding that way, had desired him to call at the Manor and beg the pleasure of my company to a friendly, family dinner to-morrow.

'There is no one to meet but ourselves,' said he; 'but Esther is very anxious to see you; and my mother fears you will feel solitary in this great house so much alone, and wishes she could persuade you to give her the pleasure of your company more frequently, and make yourself at home in our more humble dwelling, till Mr Huntingdon's return shall render this a little more conducive to your comfort.'

'She is very kind,' I answered, 'but I am not alone, you see; – and those, whose time is fully occupied, seldom complain of solitude.'

'Will you not come to-morrow, then? She will be sadly disappointed if you refuse.'

I did not relish being thus compassionated for my loneliness; but, however, I promised to come.

'What a sweet evening this is!' observed he, looking round upon the sunny park, with its imposing swell and slope, its placid water, and majestic clumps of trees. 'And what a paradise you live in!'

'It is a lovely evening,' answered I; and I sighed to think how little I had felt its loveliness, and how little of a paradise sweet Grassdale was to me – how still less to the voluntary exile from its scenes. Whether Mr Hargrave divined my thoughts, I cannot tell, but, with a half-hesitating, sympathizing seriousness of tone and manner, he asked if I had lately heard from Mr Huntingdon.

'Not lately,' I replied.

'I thought not,' he muttered, as if to himself, looking thoughtfully on the ground.

'Are you not lately returned from London?' I asked.

'Only yesterday.'

'And did you see him there?'

'Yes – I saw him.'

'Was he well?'

'Yes – that is,' said he, with increasing hesitation and an appearance of suppressed indignation, 'he was as well as – as he deserved to be, but under circumstances I should have deemed incredible for a man so favoured as he is.' He here looked up and pointed the sentence with a serious bow to me. I suppose my face was crimson.

'Pardon me, Mrs Huntingdon,' he continued, 'but I cannot suppress my indignation when I behold such infatuated blindness and perversion of taste; – but, perhaps you are not aware –' He paused.

'I am aware of nothing sir – except that he delays his coming longer than I expected; and if at present, he prefers the society of his friends to that of his wife, and the dissipations of the town to the quiet of country life, I suppose I have those friends to thank for it. *Their* tastes and occupations are similar to his, and I don't see why his conduct should awaken either their indignation or surprise.'

'You wrong me cruelly,' answered he: 'I have shared but little of Mr Huntingdon's society, for the last few weeks; and as for his tastes and occupations, they are quite beyond me – lonely wanderer as I am. Where I have but sipped and tasted, he drains the cup to the dregs; and if ever for a moment I have sought to drown the voice of reflection in madness and folly, or if I have wasted too much of my time and talents among reckless and dissipated companions, God knows I would gladly renounce them entirely and for ever, if I had but *half* the blessings that man so thanklessly casts behind his back – but *half* the inducements to virtue and domestic orderly habits that he despises – but *such* a home, and *such* a partner to share it! – It is infamous!' he muttered between his teeth. 'And don't think, Mrs Huntingdon,' he added aloud, 'that I could be guilty of inciting him to persevere in his present pursuits: on the contrary, I have remonstrated with him again and again; I have frequently expressed my surprise at his conduct and reminded him of his duties and his privileges – but to no purpose; he only –'

'Enough, Mr Hargrave; you ought to be aware that whatever my husband's faults may be, it can only aggravate the evil for me to hear them from a stranger's lips.'

'*Am* I then a stranger?' said he in a sorrowful tone. 'I am your nearest neighbour, your son's god-father, and your husband's friend; may I not be yours also?'

'Intimate acquaintance must precede real friendship: I know but little of you, Mr Hargrave, except from report.'

'Have you then forgotten the six or seven weeks I spent under your roof last autumn? *I* have not forgotten them. And I know enough of *you*, Mrs Huntingdon, to think that your husband is the most enviable man in the world, and I should be the next if you would deem me worthy of your friendship.'

'If you knew more of me, you would not think it – or if you did, you would not say it, and expect me to be flattered by the compliment.'

I stepped backward as I spoke. He saw that I wished the conversation to end; and immediately taking the hint, he gravely bowed, wished me good evening, and turned his horse towards the road. He appeared grieved and hurt at my unkind reception of his sympathizing overtures. I was not sure that I had done right in speaking so harshly to him; but at the time, I had felt irritated – almost insulted by his conduct; it seemed as if he was presuming upon the absence and neglect of my husband, and insinuating even more than the truth against him.

Rachel had moved on, during our conversation, to some yards' distance. He rode up to her, and asked to see the child. He took it carefully into his arms, looked upon it with an almost paternal smile, and I heard him say, as I approached –

'And this too, he has forsaken!'

He then tenderly kissed it, and restored it to the gratified nurse.

'Are you fond of children, Mr Hargrave?' said I, a little softened towards him.

'Not in general,' he replied, 'but that is such a *sweet* child – and so like its mother,' he added in a lower tone.

'You are mistaken there; it is its father it resembles.'

'Am I not right, nurse?' said he, appealing to Rachel.

'I think, sir, there's a bit of both,' she replied.

He departed; and Rachel pronounced him a very nice gentleman. I had still my doubts on the subject.

When I met him on the morrow, under his own roof, he did not offend me with any more of his virtuous indignation against Arthur or unwelcome sympathy for me; and, indeed, when his mother began, in guarded terms, to intimate her sorrow and surprise at my husband's conduct, he, perceiving my annoyance, instantly came to the rescue, and delicately turned the conversation, at the same time warning her, by a sidelong glance, not to recur to the subject again. He seemed bent upon doing the honours of his house in the most unexceptionable manner, and exerting all his powers for the entertainment of his guest, and the display of his own qualifications as a host, a gentleman, and a companion; and actually succeeded in making himself very agreeable – only that he was too polite. – And yet, Mr Hargrave, I don't much like you; there is a certain want of openness about you that does not take my fancy, and a lurking selfishness, at the bottom of all your fine qualities, that I do not intend to lose sight of. No; for, instead of combating my slight prejudice against you as uncharitable, I mean to cherish it, until I am convinced that I have no reason to distrust this kind, insinuating friendship you are so anxious to push upon me.

In the course of the following six weeks, I met him several times, but always, save once, in company with his mother or his sister, or both. When I called on them, he always happened to be at home, and when they called on me, it was always he that drove them over in the phaeton. His mother, evidently, was quite delighted with his dutiful attentions and newly acquired domestic habits.

The time that I met him alone was on a bright but not oppressively hot day in the beginning of July: I had taken little Arthur into the wood that skirts the park, and there seated him on the moss-cushioned roots of an old oak; and, having gathered a handful of bluebells and wild roses, I was kneeling before him, and presenting them, one by one, to the grasp of his tiny fingers; enjoying the heavenly beauty of the flowers, through the medium of his smiling eyes; forgetting, for the moment, all my cares, laughing at his gleeful laughter, and delighting myself with his delight, – when a shadow suddenly eclipsed the little space of sunshine on the grass before us; and, looking up, I beheld Walter Hargrave standing and gazing upon us.

'Excuse me, Mrs Huntingdon,' said he, 'but I was spellbound; I had neither the power to come forward and interrupt you, nor to withdraw from the contemplation of such a scene. – How vigorous my little godson grows! and how merry he is this morning.' He approached the child and stooped to take his hand; but, on seeing that his caresses were likely to produce tears and lamentations instead of a reciprocation of friendly demonstrations, he prudently drew back.

'What a pleasure and comfort that little creature must be to you, Mrs Huntingdon!' he observed with a touch of sadness in his intonation, as he admiringly contemplated the infant.

'It is,' replied I; and then I asked after his mother and sister. He politely answered my inquiries, and then returned again to the subject I wished to avoid; though with a degree of timidity that witnessed his fear to offend.

'You have not heard from Huntingdon lately?' he said.

'Not this week,' I replied. – Not these three weeks, I might have said.

'I had a letter from him this morning. I wish it were such a one as I could show to his lady.' He half drew from his waistcoat pocket a letter with Arthur's still beloved hand on the address, scowled at it, and put it back again, adding – 'But he tells me he is about to return next week.'

'He tells *me* so every time he writes.'

'Indeed! – Well, it is like him. – But to *me* he always avowed it his intention to stay till the present month.'

It struck me like a blow, this proof of premeditated transgression and systematic disregard of truth.

'It is only of a piece with the rest of his conduct,' observed Mr Hargrave, thoughtfully regarding me, and reading, I suppose, my feelings in my face.

'Then he is really coming next week?' said I, after a pause.

'You may rely upon it – if the assurance can give you any pleasure. – And is it *possible*, Mrs Huntingdon, that you can rejoice at his return?' he exclaimed, attentively perusing my features again.

'Of course, Mr Hargrave; is he not my husband?'

'Oh, Huntingdon; you know not *what* you slight!' he passionately murmured.

I took up my baby and, wishing him good morning, departed, to indulge my thoughts unscrutinized, within the sanctum of my home.

And *was* I glad? – Yes, delighted; – though I was angered by Arthur's conduct, and though I felt that he had wronged me, and was determined he should feel it too.

CHAPTER XXX

DOMESTIC SCENES

ON THE FOLLOWING morning, I received a few lines from him myself, confirming Hargrave's intimations respecting his approaching return. And he did come next week, but in a condition of body and mind even worse than before. I did not however intend to pass over his derelictions this time without a remark; – I found it would not do. But the first day, he was weary with his journey, and I was glad to get him back: I would not upbraid him then; I would wait till to-morrow. Next morning, he was weary still: I would wait a little longer. But at dinner, when, after breakfasting at twelve o'clock on a bottle of soda-water and a cup of strong coffee, and lunching at two on another bottle of soda-water mingled with brandy, he was finding fault with everything on the table and declaring we must change our cook – I thought the time was come.

'It is the same cook as we had before you went, Arthur,' said I. 'You were generally pretty well satisfied with her then.'

'You must have been letting her get into slovenly habits then, while I was away. It is enough to poison one – eating such a disgusting mess!' And he pettishly pushed away his plate, and leant back despairingly in his chair.

'I think it is you that are changed, not she,' said I, but with the utmost gentleness, for I did not wish to irritate him.

'It may be so,' he replied carelessly, as he seized a tumbler of wine and water, adding, when he had tossed it off – 'for I have an infernal fire in my veins, that all the waters of the ocean cannot quench!'

'What kindled it?' I was about to ask, but at that moment the butler entered and began to take away the things.

'Be quick Benson – do have done with that infernal clatter!' cried his master. – 'And *don't* bring the cheese! – unless you want to make me sick outright!'

Benson, in some surprise, removed the cheese, and did his best to effect a quiet and speedy clearance of the rest, but, unfortunately, there was a rumple in the carpet, caused by the hasty pushing back of his master's chair, at which he tripped and stumbled, causing a rather alarming concussion with the trayful of crockery in his hands, but no positive damage, save the fall and breaking of a sauce-tureen; – but, to my unspeakable shame and dismay, Arthur turned furiously around upon him, and swore at him with savage coarseness. The poor man turned pale, and visibly trembled as he stooped to pick up the fragments.

'He couldn't help it, Arthur,' said I; 'the carpet caught his foot – and there's no great harm done. Never mind the pieces now, Benson, you can clear them away afterwards.'

Glad to be released, Benson expeditiously set out the dessert and withdrew.

'What *could* you mean, Helen, by taking the servant's part against me,' said Arthur, as soon as the door was closed, 'when you knew I was distracted?'

'I did not know you were distracted, Arthur, and the poor man was quite frightened and hurt at your sudden explosion.'

'Poor man indeed! and do you think I could stop to consider the feelings of an insensate brute like that, when my own nerves were racked and torn to pieces by his confounded blunders?'

'I never heard you complain of your nerves before.'

'And why shouldn't I have nerves as well as you?'

'Oh, I don't dispute your claim to their possession, but *I* never complain of mine.'

'No – how should you, when you never do anything to try them?'

'Then why do you try yours, Arthur?'

'Do you think I have nothing to do but to stay at home and take care of myself like a woman?'

'Is it impossible then, to take care of yourself like a man when you go abroad? You told me that you could – and would too; and you promised –'

'Come, come, Helen, don't begin with that nonsense now; I can't bear it.'

'Can't bear what? – to be reminded of the promises you have broken?'

'Helen, you are cruel. If you knew how my heart throbbed, and how every nerve thrilled through me while you spoke, you would spare me. You can pity a dolt of a servant for breaking a dish; but you have no compassion for *me*, when my head is split in two and all on fire with this consuming fever.'

He leant his head on his hand, and sighed. I went to him and put my hand on his forehead. It was burning indeed.

'Then come with me into the drawing-room, Arthur; and don't take any more wine; you have taken several glasses since dinner, and eaten next to nothing all the day. How can *that* make you better?'

With some coaxing and persuasion, I got him to leave the table. When the baby was brought I tried to amuse him with that; but poor little Arthur was cutting his teeth, and his father could not bear his complaints; sentence of immediate banishment was passed upon him on the first indication of fretfulness; and, because, in the course of the evening, I went to share his exile for a little while, I was reproached, on my return, for preferring my child to my husband. I found the latter reclining on the sofa just as I had left him.

'Well!' exclaimed the injured man, in a tone of pseudo-resignation. 'I thought I wouldn't send for you; I thought I'd just see – how long it would please you to leave me alone.'

'I have not been *very* long, have I, Arthur? I have not been an hour, I'm sure.'

'Oh, of course, an hour is nothing to you, so pleasantly employed; but to *me* –'

'It has not been pleasantly employed,' interrupted I. 'I have been nursing our poor little baby, who is very far from well, and I could not leave him till I got him to sleep.'

'Oh to be sure, you're overflowing with kindness and pity for everything but me.'

'And why should I pity *you*? what is the matter with you?'

'Well! that passes everything! After all the wear and tear that I've had, when I come home sick and weary, longing for comfort, and expecting to find attention and kindness, at least, from my wife, – she calmly asks what is the matter with me!'

'There is *nothing* the matter with you,' returned I, 'except what you have wilfully brought upon yourself against my earnest exhortation and entreaty.'

'Now, Helen,' said he, emphatically, half rising from his recumbent posture, 'if you bother me with another word, I'll ring the bell and order six bottles of wine – and, by Heaven, I'll drink them dry before I stir from this place!'

I said no more but sat down before the table and drew a book towards me.

'Do let me have quietness at least!' continued he, 'if you deny me every other comfort,' and sinking back into his former position, with an impatient expiration between a sigh and a groan, he languidly closed his eyes as if to sleep.

What the book was, that lay open on the table before me, I cannot tell, for I never looked at it. With an elbow on each side of it, and my hands clasped before my eyes, I delivered myself up to silent weeping. But Arthur was not asleep: at the first slight sob, he raised his head and looked round, impatiently exclaiming –

'What are you crying for, Helen? What the deuce is the matter *now*?'

'I'm crying for you, Arthur,' I replied, speedily drying my tears; and starting up, I threw myself on my knees before him, and clasping his nerveless hand between my own, continued: 'Don't you know that you are a part of myself? And do you think you can injure and degrade yourself, and I not feel it?'

'*Degrade* myself, Helen?'

'Yes, degrade! What have you been doing all this time?'

'You'd better not ask,' said he with a faint smile.

'And you had better not tell – but you cannot deny that you *have* degraded yourself miserably. You have shamefully wronged yourself, body and soul – and me too; and I can't endure it quietly – and I won't!'

'Well, don't squeeze my hand so frantically and don't agitate me so, for Heaven's sake! Oh, Hattersley! you were right; this woman will be the death of me, with her keen feelings and her interesting force of character. – There, there, do spare me a little.'

'Arthur, you *must* repent!' cried I, in a frenzy of desperation, throwing my arms around him and burying my face in his bosom. 'You *shall* say you are sorry for what you have done!'

'Well, well, I am.'

'You are not! you'll do it again.'

'I shall never live to do it again, if you treat me so savagely,' replied he, pushing me from him. 'You've nearly squeezed the breath out of my body.' He pressed his hand to his heart, and looked really agitated and ill.

'Now get me a glass of wine,' said he, 'to remedy what you've done, you she tiger! I'm almost ready to faint.'

I flew to get the required remedy. It seemed to revive him considerably.

'What a shame it is,' said I, as I took the empty glass from his hand, 'for a strong young man like you to reduce yourself to such a state!'

'If you knew all, my girl, you'd say rather, "What a wonder it is you can bear it so well as you do!" I've lived more in these four months, Helen, than you have in the whole course of your existence, or will to the end of your days, if they numbered a hundred years; – so I must expect to pay for it in some shape.'

'You will have to pay a higher price than you anticipate, if you don't take care – there will be the total loss of your own health, and of my affection too – if *that* is of any value to you.'

'What, you're at that game of threatening me with the loss of your affection again, are you? I think it couldn't have been very genuine stuff to begin with, if it's so easily demolished. If you don't mind, my pretty tyrant, you'll make me regret my choice in good earnest, and envy my friend Hattersley, his meek little wife – she's quite a pattern to her sex, Helen; he had her with him in London all the season, and she was no trouble at all. He might amuse himself just as he pleased, in regular bachelor style, and she never complained of neglect; he might come home at any hour of the night or morning, or not come home at all; be sullen sober, or glorious drunk; and play the fool or the madman to his own heart's desire without any fear or botheration. She never gives him a word of reproach or complaint, do what he will. He says there's not such a jewel in all England, and swears he wouldn't take a kingdom for her.'

'But he makes her life a curse to her.'

'Not he! She has no will but his, and is always contented and happy as long as he is enjoying himself.'

'In that case, she is as great a fool as he is; but it is not so. I have several letters from her, expressing the greatest anxiety about his proceedings, and complaining that you incite him to commit those extravagances – one especially, in which she implores me to use my influence with you to get you away from London, and affirms that her husband never did such things before you came, and would certainly discontinue them as soon as you departed and left him to the guidance of his own good sense.'

'The detestable little traitor! Give me the letter, and he shall see it as sure as I'm a living man.'

'No, he shall not see it without her consent; but if he did, there is nothing there to anger him – nor in any of the others. She never speaks a word against him; it is only anxiety *for* him that she expresses. She only alludes to his conduct in the most delicate terms, and makes every excuse for him that she can possibly think of – and as for her own misery, I rather *feel* it than *see* it expressed in her letters.'

'But she abuses *me*; and no doubt you helped her.'

'No; I told her she over-rated my influence with you, that I would gladly draw you away from the temptations of the town if I could, but had little hope of success, and that I thought she was wrong in supposing that you enticed Mr Hattersley or any one else into error. I had, myself, held the *contrary* opinion at one time, but I now believed that you mutually corrupted each other; and, perhaps, if she used a little gentle, but serious remonstrance with her husband, it might be of some service, as though he was more rough-hewn than mine, I believed he was of a less impenetrable material.'

'And so *that* is the way you go on – heartening each other up to mutiny, and abusing each other's partners, and throwing out implications against your own, to the mutual gratification of both!'

'According to your own account,' said I, 'my evil counsel has had but little effect upon *her*. And as to abuse and aspersions, we are both of us far too deeply ashamed of the errors and vices of our other halves, to make them the common subject of our correspondence. Friends as we are, we would willingly keep your failings to ourselves – even *from* ourselves if we could, unless by knowing them we could deliver you from them.'

'Well, well! don't worry me about them: you'll never effect any good by that. Have patience with me, and bear with my languor and crossness a little while, till I get this cursed low fever out of my veins, and then you'll find me cheerful and kind as ever. Why can't you be gentle and good as you were last time? – I'm sure I was very grateful for it.'

'And what good did your gratitude do? I deluded myself with the idea that you were ashamed of your transgressions, and hoped you would never repeat them again; but now, you have left me nothing to hope!'

'My case is quite desperate, is it? A very blessed consideration, if it will only secure me from the pain and worry of my dear, anxious wife's efforts to convert me, and her from the toil and trouble of such exertions, and her sweet face and silver accents from the ruinous effects of the same. A burst of passion is a fine, rousing thing upon occasion, Helen, and a flood of tears is marvellously affecting, but, when indulged too often, they are both deuced plaguy things for spoiling one's beauty and tiring out one's friends.'

Thenceforth, I restrained my tears and passions as much as I could. I spared him my exhortations and fruitless efforts at conversion too, for I saw it was all in vain: God might awaken that heart supine and stupefied with self-indulgence, and remove the film of sensual darkness from his eyes, but I could not. His injustice and ill-humour towards his inferiors, who could not defend themselves, I still resented and withstood; but when I alone was their object, as was frequently the case, I endured it with calm forbearance, except at times when my temper, worn out by repeated annoyances, or stung to distraction by some new instance of irrationality, gave way in spite of myself, and exposed me to the imputations of fierceness, cruelty, and impatience. I attended carefully to his wants and amusements, but not, I own, with the same devoted fondness as before, because, I could not feel it: besides, I had now another claimant on my time and care – my ailing infant, for whose sake I frequently braved and suffered the reproaches and complaints of his unreasonably exacting father.

But Arthur is not naturally a peevish or irritable man – so far from it that there was something almost ludicrous in the incongruity of this adventitious fretfulness and nervous irritability, rather calculated to excite laughter than anger, if it were not for the intensely painful considerations attendant upon those symptoms of a disordered frame, – and his temper gradually improved as his bodily health was restored which was much sooner than would have been the case, but for my strenuous exertions; for there was still one thing about him that I did not give up in despair, and one effort for his preservation that I would not remit. His appetite for the stimulus of wine had increased upon him, as I had too well foreseen. It was now something more to him than an accessory to social enjoyment: it was an important source of enjoyment in itself. In this time of weakness and depression he would have made it his medicine and support, his comforter, his recreation, and his friend, – and thereby sunk deeper and deeper – and bound himself down for ever in the bathos whereinto he had fallen. But I determined this should never be, as long as I had any influence left; and though I could not prevent him from taking more than was good for him, still, by incessant perseverance, by kindness, and firmness, and vigilance, by coaxing, and daring, and determination, – I succeeded in preserving him from absolute bondage to that detestable propensity, so insidious in its advances, so inexorable in its tyranny, so disastrous in its effects.

And here, I must not forget that I am not a little indebted to his friend Mr Hargrave. About that time he frequently called at Grassdale, and often dined with us, on which occasions, I fear, Arthur would willingly have cast prudence and decorum to the winds and made 'a night of it,' as often as his friend would have consented to join him in that exalted pastime; and if the latter had chosen to comply, he might, in a night or two, have ruined the labour of weeks, and overthrown with a touch, the frail bulwark it had cost me such trouble and toil to construct. I was so fearful of this at first, that I humbled myself to intimate to him in private, my apprehensions of Arthur's proneness to these excesses and to express a hope that he would not encourage it. He was pleased with this mark of confidence, and certainly did not betray it. On that and every subsequent occasion, his presence served rather as a check upon his host, than an incitement to further acts of intemperance; and he always succeeded in bringing him from the dining-room in good time and in tolerably good condition; for if Arthur disregarded such intimations, as 'Well, I must not detain you from your lady,' or 'We must not forget that Mrs Huntingdon is alone,' he would insist upon leaving the table himself, to join me, and his host, however unwillingly, was obliged to follow.

Hence, I learned to welcome Mr Hargrave, as a real friend to the family, a harmless companion for Arthur, to cheer his spirits and preserve him from the tedium of absolute idleness and a total isolation from all society but mine, and a useful ally to me. I could not but feel grateful to him under such circumstances; and I did not scruple to acknowledge my obligation on the first convenient opportunity; yet, as I did so, my heart whispered all was not right, and brought a glow to my face, which he heightened by his steady, serious gaze, while, by his manner of receiving those acknowledgments, he more than doubled my misgivings. His high delight at being able to serve me, was chastened by sympathy for me and commiseration for himself – about I know not what, for I would not stay to inquire or suffer him to unburden his sorrows to me. His sighs and intimations of suppressed affliction seemed to come from a full heart; but either he must contrive to retain them within it, or breathe them forth in other ears than mine: there was enough of confidence between us already. It seemed wrong that there should exist a secret understanding between my husband's friend and me, unknown to him, of which he was the object. But my after thought was, 'If it is wrong, surely Arthur's is the fault, not mine.'

And indeed, I know not whether at the time, it was not for *him* rather than myself that I blushed; for, since he and I are one, I so identify myself with him, that I feel his degradation, his failings, and transgressions as my own; I blush for him, I fear for him; I repent for him, weep, pray, and feel for him as for myself; but I cannot act for him; and hence, I must be and I am debased, contaminated by the union, both in my own eyes, and in the actual truth. I am so determined to love him – so intensely anxious to excuse his errors, that I am continually dwelling upon them, and labouring to extenuate the loosest of his principles and the worst of his practices, till I am familiarized with vice and almost a partaker in his sins. Things that formerly shocked and disgusted me, now seem only natural. I know them to be wrong, because reason and God's word declare them to be so; but I am gradually losing that instinctive horror and repulsion which was given me by nature, or instilled into me by the precepts and example of my aunt. Perhaps, then, I was too severe in my judgments, for I abhorred the sinner as well as the sin; now, I flatter myself I am more charitable and considerate; but am I not becoming more indifferent and insensate too? Fool that I was to dream that I had strength and purity enough to save myself and him! Such vain presumption would be rightly served, if I should perish with him in the gulf from which I sought to save him! Yet, God preserve me from it! – and him too. Yes, poor Arthur, I will still hope and pray for you; and though I write as if you were some abandoned wretch, past hope and past reprieve, it is only my anxious fears – my strong desires that make me do so; one who loved you less would be less bitter – less dissatisfied.

His conduct has of late, been what the world calls irreproachable; but then I know his heart is still unchanged; – and I know that spring is approaching, and deeply dread the consequences.

As he began to recover the tone and vigour of his exhausted frame, and with it something of his former impatience of retirement and repose, I suggested a short residence by the seaside, for his recreation and further restoration, and for the benefit of our little one as well. But no; watering-places were so intolerably dull – besides, he had been invited by one of his friends to spend a month or two in Scotland for the better recreation of grouse-shooting and deer-stalking, and had promised to go.

'Then you will leave me again, Arthur?' said I.

'Yes, dearest, but only to love you the better when I come back, and make up for all past offences and short-comings; and you needn't fear me this time; there are no temptations on the mountains. And during my absence you may pay a visit to Staningley, if you like: your uncle and aunt have long been wanting us to go there, you know; but somehow, there's such a repulsion between the good lady and me, that I never could bring myself up to the scratch.'

I was perfectly willing to avail myself of this permission, though not a little apprehensive of my aunt's questions and comments concerning my matrimonial experience, regarding which I had been very reserved in my letters, for I had not much that was pleasant to communicate.

About the third week in August, Arthur set out for Scotland, and Mr Hargrave accompanied him thither, to my private satisfaction. Shortly after, I, with little Arthur and Rachel, went to Staningley, my dear old home, which, as well as my dear old friends its inhabitants, I saw again with mingled feelings of pleasure and pain so intimately blended that I could scarcely distinguish the one from the other, or tell to which to attribute the various tears, and smiles, and sighs awakened by those old familiar scenes, and tones, and faces. Not quite two years had past since I had seen and heard them last; but it seemed a far, far longer time; and well it might, for how immeasurably changed was I! how many things had I not seen, and felt, and learnt since then! My uncle too appeared perceptibly more aged and infirm, my aunt more sad and grave. I believe she thought I had repented of my rashness; though she did not openly express her conviction, or triumphantly remind me of her slighted counsels, as I had partly feared she would; but she observed me narrowly – more narrowly than I like to be observed – and seemed to mistrust my cheerfulness and unduly mark each little indication of sadness or serious thought, to notice all my casual observations, and silently draw her own inferences from them; while, by a system of quiet cross-questioning renewed from time to time, she drew from me many things I should not otherwise have told her, and laying this and that together, obtained, I fear, a pretty clear conception of my husband's faults and my afflictions, though not of my remaining sources of comfort and hope, for though I endeavoured to impress her strongly with

the notion of Arthur's redeeming qualities, of our mutual affection, and the many causes I had for thankfulness and self-
congratulation, she received all such intimations coldly and
calmly as if mentally making her own deductions – which
deductions, I am persuaded, were generally far beyond the
truth; though I certainly did exaggerate a little in attempting to
picture the bright side of my position. Was it pride that made
me so extremely anxious to appear satisfied with my lot, – or
merely a just determination to bear my self-imposed burden
alone, and preserve my best friend from the slightest partici-
pation in those sorrows from which she had striven so hard to
save me? It might have been something of each, but I am sure
the latter motive was predominant.

I did not much prolong my visit, for, not only did I feel my
aunt's relentless watchfulness and incredulity to be a restraint
upon me, and a silent reproach that oppressed me more than
she could well imagine, but I was sensible that my little Arthur
was an annoyance to his uncle, though the latter wished him
well, and no great amusement to his aunt, though an object of
her earnest affection and anxious solicitude.

Dear aunt! have you so tenderly reared me from infancy, so
carefully guided and instructed me in childhood and youth;
and could I give you no return but this – to disappoint your
hopes, oppose your wishes, scorn your warnings and advice,
and darken your latter years with anxious fears and sorrow for
the sufferings you cannot relieve? – It almost broke my heart to
think of it; and again and again I endeavoured to convince her
that I was happy and contented with my lot; but her last words,
as she embraced me and kissed the child in my arms, before
I entered the carriage, were, –

'Take care of your son, Helen, and there may be happy days
in store for you, yet. How great a comfort and treasure he is to
you now I can well imagine; but if you spoil him to gratify your
present feelings, it will be too late to repent it when your heart
is broken.'

Arthur did not come home till several weeks after my return to Grassdale; but I did not feel so anxious about him now: to think of him engaged in active sports among the wild hills of Scotland, was very different from knowing him to be immersed amid the corruptions and temptations of London. His letters now, though neither long nor lover-like, were more regular than ever they had been before; and when he did return, to my great joy instead of being worse than when he went, he was more cheerful and vigorous, and better in every respect. Since that time, I have had little cause to complain. He still has an unfortunate predilection for the pleasures of the table, against which I have to struggle and watch; but he has begun to notice his boy, and that is an increasing source of amusement to him within doors; while his fox-hunting and coursing are a sufficient occupation for him without, when the ground is not hardened by frost; so that he is not wholly dependent on me for entertainment. But it is now January: spring is approaching; and, I repeat, I dread the consequences of its arrival. That sweet season, I once so joyously welcomed as the time of hope and gladness, awakens, now, far other anticipations by its return.

CHAPTER XXXI

SOCIAL VIRTUES

MARCH 20TH, 1824. The dreaded time is come, and Arthur is gone, as I expected. This time he announced it his intention to make but a short stay in London, and pass over to the continent, where he should probably stay a few weeks; but I shall not expect him till after the lapse of many weeks: I now know that, with him, days signify weeks, and weeks months.

I was to have accompanied him, but, a little before the time arranged for our departure, he allowed – and even urged me, with an appearance of wonderful self-sacrifice, to go and see my unfortunate father, who is very ill, and my brother, who is very unhappy in consequence of both the illness and its cause, and whom I had not seen since the day our child was christened, when he stood sponsor along with Mr Hargrave and my aunt. Not willing to impose upon my husband's good-nature in thus allowing me to leave him, I made but a very short stay; but when I returned to Grassdale – he was gone.

He left a note to explain his so hasty departure, pretending that some sudden emergency had demanded his immediate presence in London, and rendered it impossible to await my return; adding that I had better not trouble myself to follow him, as he intended to make such a short stay, that it would hardly be worth while; and as, of course, he could travel alone at less than half the expense than if I accompanied him, it would perhaps be better to defer the excursion to another year, when he should have got our affairs into a rather more settled state, as he was now endeavouring to do.

Was it really so? – or was the whole a contrivance to ensure his going forth upon his pleasure-seeking excursion, without my presence to restrain him? It is painful to doubt the sincerity of those we love, but after so many proofs of falsity and utter disregard to principle how can I believe so improbable a story?

I have this one source of consolation left: – he had told me some time previously, that if ever he went to London or Paris again, he should observe more moderation in his indulgences than before, lest he should destroy his capacity for enjoyment altogether: he had no ambition to live to a prodigious old age, but he should like to have his share of life, and above all, to relish its pleasures to the last – to which end, he found it necessary to economize, for already, he feared, he was not so handsome a fellow as he had been, and young as he was, he had lately detected some grey hairs among his beloved chestnut locks; he suspected he was getting a trifle fatter too, than was quite desirable – but that was with good living and idleness; and for the rest, he trusted he was as strong and hearty as ever: only there was no saying what *another* such a season of unlimited madness and devilment, as the last, might not do towards bringing him down. Yes; he said this to *me* – with unblushing effrontery, and that same blythe, roguish twinkle of the eyes I once so loved to see, and that low, joyous laugh it used to warm my heart to hear.

Well! such considerations will doubtless have more weight with him than any that I could urge. We shall see what *they* can do towards his preservation, since no better hope remains.

July 30th. – He returned about three weeks ago, rather better in health, certainly, than before, but still worse in temper. And yet, perhaps, I am wrong: it is *I* that am less patient and forbearing. I am tired out with his injustice, his selfishness and hopeless *depravity* – I wish a milder word would do –; I am no angel and my corruption rises against it. My poor father died last week: Arthur was vexed to hear of it, because he saw that I was shocked and grieved, and he feared the circumstance would mar his comfort. When I spoke of ordering my mourning, he exclaimed –

'Oh, I hate black! But, however, I suppose you must wear it awhile, for form's sake; but I hope, Helen, you won't think it your bounden duty to compose your face and manners into conformity with your funereal garb. Why should you sigh and groan, and I be made uncomfortable because an old gentleman in —shire, a perfect stranger to us both, has thought proper to drink himself to death? – There now, I declare you're crying! Well, it must be affectation.'

He would not hear of my attending the funeral, or going for a day or two, to cheer poor Frederick's solitude. It was quite unnecessary, he said, and I was unreasonable to wish it. What was my father to me? I had never seen him, but once since I was a baby, and I well knew he had never cared a stiver about me; – and my brother too, was little better than a stranger. 'Besides, dear Helen,' said he, embracing me with flattering fondness, 'I cannot spare you for a single day.'

'Then how have you managed without me, these *many* days?' said I.

'Ah! then I was knocking about the world, now I am at home; and home without you, my household deity, would be intolerable.'

'Yes, as long as I am necessary to your comfort; but you did not say so before, when you urged me to leave you, in order that you might get away from your home without me,' retorted I; but before the words were well out of my mouth, I regretted having uttered them. It seemed so heavy a charge: if false, too gross an insult; if true, too humiliating a fact to be thus openly cast in his teeth. But I might have spared myself that momentary pang of self-reproach. The accusation awoke neither shame nor indignation in him: he attempted neither denial nor excuse, but only answered with a long, low, chuckling laugh as if he viewed the whole transaction as a clever, merry jest from beginning to end. Surely that man will make me dislike him at last!

> 'Sine as ye brew, my maiden fair,
> Keep mind that ye maun drink the yill.'

Yes; and I *will* drink it to the very dregs: and none but myself shall know how bitter I find it!

August 20th. – We are shaken down again to about our usual position. Arthur has returned to nearly his former condition and habits; and I have found it my wisest plan to shut my eyes against the past and future, as far as *he* at least is concerned, and live only for the present; to love him when I can; to smile (if possible) when he smiles, be cheerful when he is cheerful, and pleased when he is agreeable; and when he is not, to try to make him so – and if that won't answer, to bear with him, to excuse him, and forgive him, as well as I can, and restrain my own evil passions from aggravating his; and yet, while I thus yield and minister to his more harmless propensities to self-indulgence, to do all in my power to save him from the worse.

But we shall not be long alone together. I shall shortly be called upon to entertain the same select body of friends as we had the autumn before last, with the addition of Mr Hattersley and, at my special request, his wife and child. I long to see Milicent – and her little girl too. The latter is now above a year old; she will be a charming playmate for my little Arthur.

September 30th. – Our guests have been here a week or two; but I have had no leisure to pass any comments upon them till now. I cannot get over my dislike to Lady Lowborough. It is not founded on mere personal pique; it is the woman herself that I dislike, because I so thoroughly disapprove of her. I always avoid her company as much as I can without violating the laws of hospitality; but when we do speak or converse together, it is with the utmost civility – even apparent cordiality on her part; but preserve me from such cordiality! It is like handling brier-roses and may-blossoms – bright enough to the eye, and outwardly soft to the touch, but you know there are thorns beneath, and every now and then you feel them too; and perhaps resent the injury by crushing them in till you have destroyed their power, though somewhat to the detriment of your own fingers.

Of late, however, I have seen nothing in her conduct towards Arthur to anger or alarm me. During the first few days I thought she seemed very solicitous to win his admiration. Her efforts were not unnoticed by him: I frequently saw him smiling to himself at her artful manœuvres: but, to his praise be it spoken, her shafts fell powerless by his side. Her most bewitching smiles, her haughtiest frowns were ever received with the same immutable, careless good-humour; till, finding he was indeed impenetrable, she suddenly remitted her efforts, and became, to all appearance, as perfectly indifferent as himself. Nor have I since witnessed any symptom of pique on his part, or renewed attempts at conquest upon hers.

This is as it should be; but Arthur never will let me be satisfied with him. I have never, for a single hour since I married him, known what it is to realize that sweet idea, 'In quietness and confidence shall be your rest.' Those two detestable men Grimsby and Hattersley have destroyed all my labour against his love of wine. They encourage him daily to overstep the bounds of moderation, and, not unfrequently, to disgrace himself by positive excess. I shall not soon forget the second night after their arrival. Just as I had retired from the dining-room with the ladies, before the door was closed upon us, Arthur exclaimed –

'Now then, my lads, what say you to a regular jollification?'

Milicent glanced at me with a half reproachful look, as if *I* could hinder it; but her countenance changed when she heard Hattersley's voice shouting through door and wall:

'*I'm* your man! Send for more wine: here isn't *half* enough!'

We had scarcely entered the drawing-room before we were joined by Lord Lowborough.

'What *can* induce you to come so soon?' exclaimed his lady, with a most ungracious air of dissatisfaction.

'You know I never drink, Annabella,' replied he, seriously.

'Well, but you might stay with them a little: it looks so silly to be always dangling after the women – I wonder you can!'

He reproached her with a look of mingled bitterness and surprise, and sinking into a chair, suppressed a heavy sigh, bit his pale lips, and fixed his eyes upon the floor.

'You did right to leave them, Lord Lowborough,' said I. 'I trust you will always continue to honour us so early with your company. And if Annabella knew the value of true wisdom, and the misery of folly and – and intemperance, she would not talk such nonsense – even in jest.'

He raised his eyes while I spoke, and gravely turned them upon me with a half surprised, half abstracted look, and then bent them on his wife.

'At least,' said she, 'I know the value of a warm heart and a bold, manly spirit.'

And she pointed her words with a glance of triumph at me, which seemed to say, 'And that is more than *you* do,' and a look of scorn at her husband, that entered into his soul. I was intensely exasperated; but it was not for me to reprove her, or, as it seemed, to express my sympathy with her husband without insulting his feelings. All I could do, to obey my inward impulse, was to hand him a cup of coffee, bringing it to him myself, and before I served either of the ladies, by way of balancing her contempt by my exceeding deference. He took it mechanically from my hand, with a slight inclination, and, next minute, rose and placed it untasted on the table, looking, not at it, but at her.

'Well, Annabella,' said he, in a deep and hollow tone, 'since my presence is disagreeable to you, I will relieve you of it.'

'Are you going back to them, then?' said she, carelessly.

'No,' exclaimed he, with harsh and startling emphasis; 'I will NOT go back to them! And I will never stay with them one moment longer than I think right, for you or any other tempter! But you needn't mind that – I shall never trouble you again, by intruding my company upon you so unseasonably.'

He left the room, I heard the hall door open and shut, and immediately after, on putting aside the curtain, I saw him pacing down the park, in the comfortless gloom of the damp, cloudy twilight.

Such scenes as this are always disagreeable to witness. Our little party was completely silenced for a moment. Milicent played with her teaspoon, and looked confounded and uncomfortable. If Annabella felt any shame or uneasiness, she attempted to hide it by a short, reckless laugh, and calmly betook herself to her coffee.

'It would serve you right, Annabella,' said I at length, 'if Lord Lowborough were to return to his old habits, which had so nearly effected his ruin, and which it cost him such an effort to break. You would then see cause to repent such conduct as this.'

'Not at all, my dear! I should not mind if his lordship were to see fit to intoxicate himself every day: I should only the sooner be rid of him.'

'Oh, Annabella!' cried Milicent. 'How *can* you say such wicked things! It would indeed be a just punishment, as far as you are concerned, if Providence should take you at your word, and make you feel what others feel that –' She paused as a sudden burst of loud talking and laughter reached us from the dining-room, in which the voice of Hattersley was pre-eminently conspicuous, even to my unpractised ear.

'What *you* feel at this moment, I suppose?' said Lady Low-borough, with a malicious smile, fixing her eyes upon her cousin's distressed countenance.

The latter offered no reply, but averted her face and brushed away a tear. At that moment the door opened and admitted Mr Hargrave; just a little flushed, his dark eyes sparkling with unwonted vivacity.

'Oh, I'm so glad you're come, Walter!' cried his sister – 'But I wish you could have got Ralph to come too.'

'Utterly impossible, dear Milicent,' replied he, gaily. 'I had much ado to get away myself. Ralph attempted to keep me by violence; Huntingdon threatened me with the eternal loss of his friendship; and Grimsby, worse than all, endeavoured to make me ashamed of my virtue, by such galling sarcasms and innuendoes as he knew would wound me the most. So you see, ladies, you ought to make me welcome when I have braved and suffered so much for the favour of your sweet society.' He smilingly turned to me and bowed as he finished the sentence.

'Isn't he *handsome* now Helen?' whispered Milicent, her sis-terly pride overcoming, for the moment, all other considerations.

'He would be,' I returned, 'if that brilliance of eye, and lip, and cheek were natural to him; but look again, a few hours hence.'

Here the gentleman took a seat near me at the table, and petitioned for a cup of coffee.

'I consider this an apt illustration of Heaven taken by storm,' said he, as I handed one to him. 'I am in paradise now; but

I have fought my way through flood and fire to win it. Ralph Hattersley's last resource was to set his back against the door, and swear I should find no passage but through his body (a pretty substantial one too). Happily, however, that was not the only door, and I effected my escape by the side entrance, through the butler's pantry, to the infinite amazement of Benson, who was cleaning the plate.'

Mr Hargrave laughed, and so did his cousin; but his sister and I remained silent and grave.

'Pardon my levity, Mrs Huntingdon,' murmured he, more seriously, as he raised his eyes to my face. 'You are not used to these things: you suffer them to affect your delicate mind too sensibly. But I thought of you in the midst of those lawless roysterers; and I endeavoured to persuade Mr Huntingdon to think of you too; but to no purpose: I fear he is fully determined to enjoy himself this night; and it will be no use keeping the coffee waiting for him or his companions: it will be much if they join us at tea. Meantime, I earnestly wish I could banish the thoughts of them from your mind – and my own too, for I hate to think of them – yes – even of my dear friend Huntingdon, when I consider the power he possesses over the happiness of one so immeasurably superior to himself, and the use he makes of it – I positively *detest* the man!'

'You had better not say so to me, then,' said I; 'for, bad as he is, he is part of myself, and you cannot abuse him without offending me.'

'Pardon me, then, for I would sooner die than offend you. – But let us say no more of him for the present if you please.'

He then entirely changed the subject of discourse, and exerting all his powers to entertain our little circle, conversed on different topics with more than his usual brilliance and fluency, addressing himself, sometimes, exclusively to me, sometimes to the whole trio of ladies. Annabella cheerfully bore her part in the conversation; but I was sick at heart, – especially when loud bursts of laughter and incoherent songs, pealing through the triple doors of hall and ante-room, startled my ear and pierced my aching temples; – and Milicent partly shared my feelings; so that, to us, the evening appeared a very long one, in spite of Hargrave's apparently good-natured exertions to give it a contrary effect.

At last, they came; but not till after ten, when tea, which had been delayed for more than half an hour, was nearly over. Much as I had longed for their coming, my heart failed me at the riotous uproar of their approach; and Milicent turned pale and almost started from her seat as Mr Hattersley burst into the room with a clamorous volley of oaths in his mouth, which Hargrave endeavoured to check by entreating him to remember the ladies.

'Ah! you do well to remind me of the ladies, you dastardly deserter,' cried he, shaking his formidable fist at his brother-in-law; 'if it were not for them, you well know, I'd demolish you in the twinkling of an eye, and give your body to the fowls of Heaven and the lilies of the field!' Then, planting a chair by Lady Lowborough's side, he stationed himself in it, and began to talk to her with a mixture of absurdity and impudence that seemed rather to amuse than to offend her; though she affected to resent his insolence, and to keep him at bay with sallies of smart and spirited repartee.

Meantime, Mr Grimsby seated himself by me, in the chair vacated by Hargrave as they entered, and gravely stated that he would thank me for a cup of tea: and Arthur placed himself beside poor Milicent, confidentially pushing his head into her face, and drawing in closer to her as she shrank away from him. He was not so noisy as Hattersley, but his face was exceedingly flushed, he laughed incessantly, and while I blushed for all I saw and heard of him, I was glad that he chose to talk to his companion in so low a tone that no one could hear what he said but herself. It must have been intolerable nonsense at best, for she looked excessively annoyed, and first went red in the face, then indignantly pushed back her chair, and finally took refuge behind me on the sofa. Arthur's sole intention seemed to have been to produce some such disagreeable effects: he laughed immoderately on finding he had driven her away – drawing in his chair to the table, he leant his folded arms upon it, and delivered himself up to a paroxysm of weak, low, foolish laughter. When he was tired of this exercise he lifted his head and called aloud to Hattersley, and there ensued a clamorous contest between them about I know not what.

'What fools they are!' drawled Mr Grimsby, who had been talking away, at my elbow, with sententious gravity all the time; but I had been too much absorbed in contemplating the deplorable state of the other two – especially Arthur – to attend to him.

'Did you ever hear such nonsense as they talk, Mrs Huntingdon?' he continued. 'I'm quite ashamed of them for my part: they can't take so much as a bottle between them without its getting into their heads –'

'You are pouring the cream into your saucer, Mr Grimsby.'

'Ah! yes, I see, but we're almost in darkness here. Hargrave, snuff those candles, will you?'

'They're wax; they don't require snuffing,' said I.

' "The light of the body is the eye," ' observed Hargrave, with a sarcastic smile. ' "If thine eye be *single* thy whole body shall be full of light." '

Grimsby repulsed him with a solemn wave of the hand, and then, turning to me, continued, with the same drawling tones, and strange uncertainty of utterance and heavy gravity of aspect as before, 'But as I was saying, Mrs Huntingdon, – they have no head at all: they can't take half a bottle without being affected some way; whereas I – well, I've taken three times as much as they have to-night, and you see I'm perfectly steady. Now that may strike you as very singular, but I think I can explain it: – you see *their* brains – I mention no names, but you'll understand to whom I allude – *their* brains are light to begin with, and the fumes of the fermented liquor render them lighter still, and produce an entire light-headedness, or giddiness, resulting in intoxication; whereas *my* brains being composed of more solid materials will absorb a considerable quantity of this alcoholic vapour without the production of any sensible result –'

'I think you will find a sensible result produced on that tea,' interrupted Mr Hargrave, 'by the quantity of sugar you have put into it. Instead of your usual complement of one lump you have put in six.'

'Have I so?' replied the philosopher, diving with his spoon into the cup and bringing up several half-dissolved pieces in confirmation of the assertion. 'Um! I perceive. Thus, Madam, you see the evil of absence of mind – of thinking too much while engaged in the common concerns of life. Now if I had had my wits about me, like ordinary men, instead of within me like a philosopher, I should not have spoiled this cup of tea, and been constrained to trouble you for another. – With your permission, I'll turn this into the slop-basin'.

'That is the sugar-basin, Mr Grimsby. Now you have spoiled the sugar too; and I'll thank you to ring for some more – for here is Lord Lowborough, at last; and I hope his lordship will condescend to sit down with us, such as we are, and allow me to give him some tea.'

His lordship gravely bowed in answer to my appeal, but said nothing. Meantime, Hargrave volunteered to ring for the sugar, while Grimsby lamented his mistake, and attempted to prove that it was owing to the shadow of the urn and the badness of the lights.

Lord Lowborough had entered a minute or two before, unobserved by any one but me, and had been standing before the door, grimly surveying the company. He now stepped up to Annabella, who sat with her back towards him, with Hattersley still beside her, though not now attending to her, being occupied in vociferously abusing and bullying his host.

'Well, Annabella,' said her husband, as he leant over the back of her chair, 'which of these three "bold, manly spirits" would you have me to resemble?'

'By Heaven and earth, you shall resemble us all!' cried

Hattersley, starting up and rudely seizing him by the arm. 'Hallo Huntingdon!' he shouted – '*I've* got him! Come, man, and help me! And d—n me body and soul if I don't make him blind drunk before I let him go! He shall make up for all past delinquencies as sure as I'm a living soul!'

There followed a disgraceful contest; Lord Lowborough, in desperate earnest, and pale with anger, silently struggling to release himself from the powerful madman that was striving to drag him from the room. I attempted to urge Arthur to interfere in behalf of his outraged guest, but he could do nothing but laugh.

'Huntingdon, you fool, come and help me, can't you!' cried Hattersley, himself somewhat weakened by his excesses.

'I'm wishing you God-speed, Hattersley,' cried Arthur, 'and aiding you with my prayers: I can't do anything else if my life depended on it! I'm quite used up. Oh, ho!' and leaning back in his seat, he clapped his hands on his sides and groaned aloud.

'Annabella, give me a candle!' said Lowborough whose antagonist had now got him round the waist and was endeavouring to root him from the door-post to which he madly clung with all the energy of desperation.

'*I* shall take no part in your rude sports!' replied the lady, coldly drawing back. 'I wonder you can expect it.'

But I snatched up a candle and brought it to him. He took it and held the flame to Hattersley's hands till, roaring like a wild beast, the latter unclasped them and let him go. He vanished, I suppose to his own apartment, for nothing more was seen of him till the morning. Swearing and cursing like a maniac, Hattersley threw himself on to the ottoman beside the window. The door being now free, Milicent attempted to make her escape from the scene of her husband's disgrace; but he called her back, and insisted upon her coming to him.

'What do you want, Ralph?' murmured she, reluctantly approaching him.

'I want to know what's the matter with you,' said he, pulling her on to his knee like a child. 'What are you crying for Milicent? – Tell me!'

'I'm not crying.'

'You are,' persisted he, rudely pulling her hands from her face. 'How dare you tell such a lie!'

'I'm not crying now,' pleaded she.

'But you have been – and just this minute too; and I *will* know what for. Come now, you *shall* tell me!'

'Do let me alone Ralph! remember we are not at home.'

'No matter: you *shall* answer my question!' exclaimed her tormentor; and he attempted to extort the confession by shaking her and remorselessly crushing her slight arms in the gripe of his powerful fingers.

'Don't let him treat your sister in that way,' said I to Mr Hargrave.

'Come now, Hattersley, I can't allow that,' said that gentleman, stepping up to the ill-assorted couple. 'You let my sister alone, if you please.' And he made an effort to unclasp the ruffian's fingers from her arm, but was suddenly driven backward and nearly laid upon the floor by a violent blow on the chest accompanied with the admonition,

'Take that for your insolence! – and learn not to interfere between me and mine again.'

'If you were not beastly drunk, I'd have satisfaction for that!' gasped Hargrave, white and breathless as much from passion as from the immediate effects of the blow.

'Go to the devil!' – responded his brother-in-law. 'Now Milicent, tell me what you were crying for.'

'I'll tell you some other time,' murmured she, 'when we are alone.'

'Tell me now!' said he with another shake and a squeeze that made her draw in her breath and bite her lip to suppress a cry of pain.

'*I'll* tell you, Mr Hattersley,' said I. 'She was crying from pure shame and humiliation for you; because she could not bear to see you conduct yourself so disgracefully.'

'Confound you, Madam!' muttered he, with a stare of stupid

amazement at my 'impudence.' 'It was *not* that – was it Milicent?'

She was silent.

'Come, speak up child!'

'I can't tell now,' sobbed she.

'But you can say "yes" or "no" as well as "I can't tell" – come!'

'Yes,' she whispered, hanging her head and blushing at the awful acknowledgment.

'Curse you for an impertinent huzzy then!' cried he, throwing her from him with such violence that she fell on her side; but she was up again before either I or her brother could come to her assistance, and made the best of her way out of the room and, I suppose, up stairs, without loss of time.

The next object of assault was Arthur, who sat opposite, and had no doubt richly enjoyed the whole scene.

'Now Huntingdon,' exclaimed his irascible friend, 'I WILL NOT have you sitting there and laughing like an idiot!'

'Oh, Hattersley!' cried he, wiping his swimming eyes – 'you'll be the death of me.'

'Yes I will, but not as you suppose: I'll have the heart out of your body, man, if you irritate me with any more of that imbecile laughter! – What! are you at it yet? – There! see if that'll settle you!' cried Hattersley, snatching up a footstool and hurling it at the head of his host; but he missed his aim and the latter still sat collapsed and quaking with feeble laughter, with tears running down his face; a deplorable spectacle indeed.

Hattersley tried cursing and swearing, but it would not do; he then took a number of books from the table beside him and threw them, one by one, at the object of his wrath, but Arthur only laughed the more; and, finally, Hattersley rushed upon him in a phrensy, and, seizing him by the shoulders, gave him a violent shaking, under which he laughed and shrieked alarmingly. But I saw no more: I thought I had witnessed enough of my husband's degradation; and, leaving Annabella and the rest to follow when they pleased, I withdrew – but not to bed.

Dismissing Rachel to her rest, I walked up and down my room, in an agony of misery, for what had been done, and suspense, not knowing what might further happen or how or when that unhappy creature would come up to bed.

At last he came, slowly and stumblingly, ascending the stairs, supported by Grimsby and Hattersley, who neither of them walked quite steadily themselves, but were both laughing and joking at him, and making noise enough for all the servants to hear. He himself was no longer laughing now, but sick and stupid – I will write no more about *that*.

Such disgraceful scenes (or nearly such) have been repeated more than once. I don't say much to Arthur about it, for if I did, it would do more harm than good; but I let him know that I intensely dislike such exhibitions; and each time he has promised they should never again be repeated; but I fear he is losing the little self-command and self-respect he once possessed: formerly, he would have been ashamed to act thus – at least, before any other witnesses than his boon companions, or such as they. His friend Hargrave, with a prudence and self-government that I envy for *him*, never disgraces himself by taking more than sufficient to render him a little 'elevated,' and is always the first to leave the table, after Lord Lowborough, who, wiser still, perseveres in vacating the dining-room immediately after us; but never once, since Annabella offended him so deeply, has he entered the drawing-room before the rest; always spending the interim in the library, which I take care to have lighted for his accommodation – or, on fine moonlight nights, in roaming about the grounds. But I think she regrets her misconduct, for she has never repeated it since, and of late she has comported herself with wonderful propriety towards him, treating him with more uniform kindness and consideration than ever I have observed her to do before. I date the time of this improvement from the period when she ceased to hope and strive for Arthur's admiration.

CHAPTER XXXII

COMPARISONS: INFORMATION REJECTED

OCTOBER 5TH. – Esther Hargrave is getting a fine girl.
She is not out of the school-room yet, but her mother
frequently brings her over to call in the mornings when the
gentlemen are out, and sometimes she spends an hour or two
in company with her sister, and me, and the children; and when
we go to the Grove, I always contrive to see her, and talk more
to her than to any one else, for I am very much attached to my
little friend, and so is she to me. I wonder what she can see to
like in me though, for I am no longer the happy, lively girl
I used to be; but she has no other society – save that of her
uncongenial mother, and her governess (as artificial and conventional a person as that prudent mother could procure to rectify
the pupil's natural qualities), and, now and then, her subdued,
quiet sister. I often wonder what will be *her* lot in life – and so
does she; but *her* speculations on the future are full of buoyant
hope – so were mine once. I shudder to think of her being
awakened like me to a sense of their delusive vanity. It seems as
if I should feel her disappointment even more deeply than my
own: I feel, almost, as if I were born for such a fate, but *she* is
so joyous and fresh, so light of heart and free of spirit, and so
guileless and unsuspecting too – oh, it would be cruel to make
her feel as I feel now, and know what I have known!

Her sister trembles for her too. Yesterday morning, one of
October's brightest, loveliest days, Milicent and I were in the
garden enjoying a brief half-hour together with our children,
while Annabella was lying on the drawing-room sofa, deep
in the last new novel. We had been romping with the little

creatures, almost as merry and wild as themselves, and now paused in the shade of the tall copper beech, to recover breath and rectify our hair, disordered by the rough play and the frolicsome breeze – while they toddled together along the broad, sunny walk; my Arthur supporting the feebler steps of her little Helen, and sagaciously pointing out to her the brightest beauties of the border as they passed, with semi-articulate prattle that did as well for her as any other mode of discourse. From laughing at the pretty sight, we began to talk of the children's future life; and that made us thoughtful. We both relapsed into silent musing as we slowly proceeded up the walk; and I suppose Milicent by a train of associations was led to think of her sister.

'Helen,' said she, 'you often see Esther, don't you?'

'Not very often.'

'But you have more frequent opportunities of meeting her than I have: and she loves you I know, and reverences you too: there is nobody's opinion she thinks so much of, and she says you have more sense than mamma.'

'That is because she is self-willed, and my opinions more generally coincide with her own than your mamma's. But what then, Milicent?'

'Well, since you have so much influence with her, I wish you would seriously impress it upon her, never, on any account, or for any body's persuasion, to marry for the sake of money, or rank, or establishment, or any earthly thing, but true affection and well-grounded esteem.'

'There is no necessity for that,' said I: 'for we have had some discourse on that subject already, and I assure you her ideas of love and matrimony are as romantic as any one could desire.'

'But romantic notions will not do: I want her to have true notions.'

'Very right, but in my judgment, what the world stigmatizes as romantic, is often more nearly allied to the truth than is commonly supposed; for, if the generous ideas of youth are too often over-clouded by the sordid views of after-life, that scarcely proves them to be false.'

'Well, but if you think her ideas are what they ought to be, strengthen them, will you? and confirm them, as far as you can; for *I* had romantic notions once, and – I don't mean to say that I regret my lot, for I am quite sure I don't – but –'

'I understand you,' said I; 'you are contented for yourself, but you would not have your sister to suffer the same as you.'

'No – or worse. She might have far worse to suffer than I – for I *am really* contented, Helen, though you mayn't think it: I speak the solemn truth in saying that I would not exchange my husband for any man on earth, if I might do it by the plucking of this leaf.'

'Well, I believe you: now that you have him, you would not exchange *him* for another; but then you would gladly exchange some of his qualities for those of better men.'

'Yes; just as I would gladly exchange some of my own qualities for those of better women; for neither he nor I are perfect, and I desire his improvement as earnestly as my own. And he will improve – don't you think so Helen? – he's only six and twenty yet.'

'He may,' I answered.

'He will – he WILL!' repeated she.

'Excuse the faintness of my acquiescence, Milicent; I would not discourage your hopes for the world, but mine have been so often disappointed, that I am become as cold and doubtful in my expectations as the flattest of octogenarians.'

'And yet you do hope, still – even for Mr Huntingdon?'

'I do, I confess – "even" for *him*; for it seems as if life and hope must cease together. And is he so *much* worse, Milicent, than Mr Hattersley?'

'Well, to give you my candid opinion, I think there is no comparison between them. But you mustn't be offended, Helen, for you know I always speak my mind; and you may speak yours too. I shan't care.'

'I am not offended, love; and *my* opinion is that if there *be* a comparison made between the two, the difference, for the most part, is certainly in Hattersley's favour.'

Milicent's own heart told her how much it cost me to make this acknowledgment; and, with a childlike impulse, she expressed her sympathy by suddenly kissing my cheek, without a word of reply, and then turning quickly away caught up her baby, and hid her face in its frock. How odd it is that we so often weep for each other's distresses, when we shed not a tear for our own! Her heart had been full enough of her own sorrows, but it overflowed at the idea of mine; – and I too, shed tears at the sight of her sympathetic emotion, though I had not wept for myself for many a week.

But Milicent's satisfaction in her choice, is not entirely feigned: she really loves her husband; and it is too true that he loses nothing by comparison with mine. Either he is less un-bridled in his excesses, or owing to his stronger, hardier frame, they produce a much less deleterious effect upon him; for he never reduces himself to a state in any degree bordering on imbe-cility, and with him the worst effect of a night's debauch is a slight increase of irascibility, or it may be a season of sullen ferocity on the following morning: there is nothing of that lost, depressing appearance – that peevish, ignoble fretfulness, that wears one out with very shame for the transgressor. But then, it was not for-merly so with Arthur: he can bear less now than he could at Hattersley's age; and if the latter does not reform, his powers of endurance may be equally impaired when he has tried them as long. He has five years the advantage of his friend, and his vices have not mastered him yet: he has not folded them to him and made them a part of himself. They seem to sit loose upon him, like a cloak that he could throw aside at any moment if he would – but how long will that option be left him? – Though a creature of passion and sense, regardless of the duties and the higher privileges of intelligent beings, he is no voluptuary: he prefers the more active and invigorating animal enjoyments, to those of a more relaxing, enervating kind. He does not make a *science* of the gratification of his appetites either in the pleasures of the table or anything else; he eats heartily what is set before him, without demeaning himself by any of that abandonment to the palate and the eye – that unbecoming particularity in approval or disapproval which it is so hateful to witness in those we would esteem. Arthur, I fear, would give himself up to luxury as the chief good, and might ultimately plunge into the grossest excesses, but for the fear of irremediably blunting his appetites, and destroying his powers of further enjoyment. For Hattersley, graceless ruffian as he is, I believe there is more reasonable ground of hope; and – far be it from me to blame poor Milicent for his delinquencies – but I do think that if she had the courage or the will to speak her mind about them, and maintain her point unflinchingly, there would be more chance of his reclamation, and he would be likely to treat her better, and love her more, in the end. I am partly led to think so by what he said to me himself, not many days ago – I purpose to give her a little advice on the subject some time; but still, I hesitate from the consciousness that her ideas and disposition are both against it, and if my counsels failed to do good, they would do harm by making her more unhappy.

It was one rainy day last week: most of the company were killing time in the billiard-room, but Milicent and I were with little Arthur and Helen in the library, and between our books, our children, and each other, we expected to make out a very agreeable morning. We had not been thus secluded above two hours, however, when Mr Hattersley came in attracted, I suppose, by the voice of his child as he was crossing the hall, for he is prodigiously fond of her, and she of him.

He was redolent of the stables, where he had been regaling himself with the company of his fellow-creatures, the horses, ever since breakfast. But that was no matter to my little namesake: as soon as the colossal person of her father darkened the door, she uttered a shrill scream of delight, and, quitting her mother's side, ran crowing towards him – balancing her course with out-stretched arms, – and, embracing his knee, threw back her head and laughed in his face. He might well look smilingly down upon those small, fair features radiant with innocent mirth, those clear, blue, shining eyes, and that soft flaxen hair cast back upon the little ivory neck and shoulders. Did he not think how unworthy he was of such a possession? I fear no such idea crossed his mind. He caught her up, and there followed some minutes of very rough play, during which it is difficult to say whether the father or the daughter laughed and shouted the loudest. At length, however, the boisterous pastime terminated – suddenly, as might be expected: the little one was hurt and began to cry; and its ungentle play-fellow tossed it into its mother's lap, bidding her 'make all straight.' As happy to return to that gentle comforter as it had been to leave her, the child nestled in her arms and hushed its cries in a moment; and, sinking its little weary head on her bosom, soon dropped asleep.

Meantime, Mr Hattersley strode up to the fire, and, interposing his height and breadth between us and it, stood, with arms akimbo, expanding his chest, and gazing round him as if the house and all its appurtenances and contents were his own undisputed possessions.

'Deuced bad weather this!' he began. 'There'll be no shooting to-day, I guess.' Then, suddenly lifting up his voice, he regaled us with a few bars of a rollicking song, which abruptly ceasing, he finished the tune with a whistle, and then continued, – 'I say Mrs Huntingdon, what a fine stud your husband has! – not large but good – I've been looking at them a bit this morning; and upon my word, Black Bess, and Grey Tom, and that young Nimrod are the finest animals I've seen for many a day!' Then followed a particular discussion of their various merits, succeeded by a sketch of the great things *he* intended to do in the horse-jockey line when his old governor thought proper to quit the stage. – 'Not that I wish him to close his accounts,' added he; 'the old Trojan is welcome to keep his books open as long as he pleases for me.'

'I hope so, *indeed*, Mr Hattersley!'

'Oh yes! It's only my way of talking. The event must come, sometime, and so I look to the bright side of it – that's the right plan, isn't it, Mrs H.? – What are you two doing here, by the by – where's Lady Lowborough?'

'In the billiard-room.'

'What a splendid creature she *is*!' continued he, fixing his eyes on his wife, who changed colour, and looked more and more disconcerted as he proceeded. 'What a noble figure she has! and what magnificent black eyes; and what a fine spirit of her own; – and what a tongue of her own, too, when she likes to use it – I perfectly adore her! – But never mind, Milicent; I wouldn't have her for my wife – not if she'd a kingdom for her dowry! I'm better satisfied with the one I have. – Now, *then*! what do you look so sulky for? don't you believe me?'

'Yes, I believe you,' murmured she, in a tone of half sad, half sullen resignation, as she turned away to stroke the hair of her sleeping infant, that she had laid on the sofa beside her.

'Well *then*, what makes you so cross? Come here Milly, and tell me why you can't be satisfied with my assurance.'

She went, and, putting her little hand within his arm, looked up in his face, and said softly, –

'What does it amount to Ralph? Only to this, that though you admire Annabella so much, and for qualities that I don't possess, you would still rather have me than her for your wife, which merely proves that you don't think it necessary to love your wife: you are satisfied if she can keep your house and take care of your child. But I'm not cross; I'm only sorry; for,' added she in a low, tremulous accent, withdrawing her hand from his arm, and bending her looks on the rug, 'if you don't love me, you don't, and it can't be helped.'

'Very true: but who told you I didn't? Did I say I loved Annabella?'

'You said you adored her.'

'True, but adoration isn't love. I adore Annabella, but I don't love her; and I love thee Milicent, but I don't adore thee.' In proof of his affection, he clutched a handful of her light brown ringlets and appeared to twist them unmercifully.

'Do you really, Ralph?' murmured she with a faint smile beaming through her tears, just putting up her hand to his, in token that he pulled *rather* too hard.

'To be sure I do,' responded he: 'only you bother me rather, sometimes.'

'*I* bother you!' cried she in very natural surprise.

'Yes, *you* – but only by your exceeding goodness – when a boy has been cramming raisins and sugar-plums all day, he longs for a squeeze of sour orange by way of a change. And did you never, Milly, observe the sands on the sea-shore; how nice and smooth they look, and how soft and easy they feel to the foot? But if you plod along, for half an hour, over this soft, easy carpet – giving way at every step, yielding the more the harder you press, – you'll find it rather wearisome work, and be glad enough to come to a bit of good, firm rock, that won't budge an inch whether you stand, walk, or stamp upon it; and, though it be hard as the nether millstone, you'll find it the easier footing after all.'

'I know what you mean, Ralph,' said she, nervously playing with her watch-guard and tracing the figure on the rug with the point of her tiny foot, 'I know what you mean, but I thought you always liked to be yielded to; and I can't alter now.'

'I do like it,' replied he, bringing her to him by another tug at her hair. 'You mustn't mind my talk Milly. A man must have something to grumble about; and if he can't complain that his wife harries him to death with her perversity and ill-humour, he must complain that she wears him out with her kindness and gentleness.'

'But why complain at all, unless, because you are tired and dissatisfied?'

'To excuse my own failings, to be sure. Do you think I'll bear all the burden of my sins on my own shoulders, as long as there's another ready to help me, with none of her own to carry?'

'There is no such one on earth,' said she seriously; and then, taking his hand from her head, she kissed it with an air of genuine devotion, and tripped away to the door.

'What now?' said he. 'Where are you going?'

'To tidy my hair,' she answered, smiling through her disordered locks: 'you've made it all come down.'

'Off with you then! – An excellent little woman,' he remarked when she was gone, 'but a thought too soft – she almost melts in one's hands. I positively think I ill-use her sometimes, when I've taken too much – but I can't help it, for she never complains, either at the time or after. I suppose she doesn't mind it.'

'I can enlighten you on that subject, Mr Hattersley,' said I: 'she *does* mind it; and some other things she minds still more, which, yet, you may never hear her complain of.'

'How do you know? – does she complain to you?' demanded he, with a sudden spark of fury ready to burst into a flame if I should answer 'Yes.'

'No,' I replied; 'but I have known her longer and studied her more closely than you have done. – And I can tell you, Mr Hattersley, that Milicent loves you more than you deserve, and that you have it in your power to make her very happy, instead of which you are her evil genius, and, I will venture to say, there is not a single day passes in which you do not inflict upon her some pang that you might spare her if you would.'

'Well – it's not *my* fault,' said he, gazing carelessly up at the ceiling and plunging his hands into his pockets: 'if my ongoings don't suit her, she should tell me so.'

'Is she not exactly the wife you wanted? Did you not tell Mr Huntingdon you must have one that would submit to anything without a murmur, and never blame you, whatever you did?'

'True, but we shouldn't always have what we want: it spoils the best of us, doesn't it? How can I help playing the deuce when I see it's all one to her whether I behave like a Christian or like a scoundrel such as nature made me? – and how can I help teasing her when she's so invitingly meek and mim – when she lies down like a spaniel at my feet and never so much as squeaks to tell me that's enough?'

'If you are a tyrant by nature, the temptation is strong, I allow; but no generous mind delights to oppress the weak, but rather to cherish and protect.'

'I *don't* oppress her; but it's so confounded flat to be always cherishing and protecting; – and then how can I tell that I *am* oppressing her when she "melts away and makes no sign"? I sometimes think she has no feeling at all; and then I go on till she cries – and that satisfies me.'

'Then you *do* delight to oppress her.'

'I don't, I tell you! – only when I'm in a bad humour – or a particularly good one, and want to afflict for the pleasure of comforting; or when she looks flat and wants shaking up a bit. And sometimes, she provokes me by crying for nothing, and won't tell me what it's for; and then, I allow, it enrages me past bearing – especially, when I'm not my own man.'

'As is no doubt generally the case on such occasions,' said I. 'But in future, Mr Hattersley, when you see her looking flat or crying for "nothing" (as you call it), ascribe it all to yourself: be assured it is something you have done amiss, or your general misconduct that distresses her.'

'I don't believe it. If it were, she should tell me so: I don't like that way of moping and fretting in silence, and saying nothing – it's not honest. How can she expect me to mend my ways at that rate?'

'Perhaps she gives you credit for having more sense than you possess, and deludes herself with the hope that you will one day see your own errors and repair them, if left to your own reflection.'

'None of your sneers, Mrs Huntingdon! I *have* the sense to see that I'm not always quite correct – but sometimes I think that's no great matter, as long as I injure nobody but myself –'

'It *is* a great matter,' interrupted I, 'both to yourself (as you will hereafter find to your cost) and to all connected with you – most especially your wife – but indeed, it is nonsense to talk about injuring no one but yourself; it is impossible to injure yourself – especially by such acts as we allude to – without injuring hundreds, if not thousands, besides, in a greater or less degree, either by the evil you do or the good you leave undone.'

'And as I was saying,' continued he – 'or would have said if you hadn't taken me up so short – I sometimes think I should do better if I were joined to one that would always remind me when I was wrong, and give me a motive for doing good and eschewing evil by decidedly showing her approval of the one, and disapproval of the other.'

'If you had no higher motive than the approval of your fellow mortal, it would do you little good.'

'Well, but if I had a mate that would not always be yielding, and always equally kind, but that would have the spirit to stand at bay now and then, and honestly tell me her mind at all times – such a one as yourself for instance – now if I went on with you as I do with her when I'm in London, you'd make the house too hot to hold me at times, I'll be sworn.'

'You mistake me: I'm no termagant.'

'Well, all the better for that, for I can't stand contradiction – in a general way – and I'm as fond of my own will as another: only I think too much of it doesn't answer for any man.'

'Well, I would never contradict you without a cause, but certainly I would always let you know what I thought of your conduct; and if you oppressed me, in body, mind, or estate, you should at least have no reason to suppose "I didn't mind it." '

'I know that my lady; and I think if my little wife were to follow the same plan it would be better for us both.'

'I'll tell her.'

'No, no, let her be; there's much to be said on both sides – and, now I think upon it, Huntingdon often regrets that you are not more like her – scoundrelly dog that he is – and you see, after all, you can't reform *him*: he's *ten* times worse than I. – He's afraid of you, to be sure – that is, he's always on his best behaviour in your presence – but –'

'I wonder what his worst behaviour is like, then?' I could not forbear observing.

'Why, to tell you the truth, it's very bad indeed – isn't it, Hargrave?' said he, addressing that gentleman, who had entered the room unperceived by me, for I was now standing near the fire with my back to the door. 'Isn't Huntingdon,' he continued, 'as great a reprobate as ever was d——d?'

'His lady will not hear him censured with impunity,' replied Mr Hargrave, coming forward, 'but I must say, I thank God I am not such another.'

'Perhaps it would become you better,' said I, 'to look at what you are, and say, "God be merciful to me a sinner." '

'You are severe,' returned he, bowing slightly and drawing himself up with a proud yet injured air. Hattersley laughed, and clapped him on the shoulder. Moving from under his hand with a gesture of insulted dignity, Mr Hargrave took himself away to the other end of the rug.

'Isn't it a shame, Mrs Huntingdon?' cried his brother-in-law – 'I struck Walter Hargrave when I was drunk, the second night after we came, and he's turned a cold shoulder on me ever since; though I asked his pardon the very morning after it was done!'

'Your manner of asking it,' returned the other, 'and the clearness with which you remembered the whole transaction, showed you were not too drunk to be fully conscious of what you were about, and quite responsible for the deed.'

'You wanted to interfere between me and my wife,' grumbled Hattersley, 'and that is enough to provoke any man.'

'You justify it then?' said his opponent, darting upon him a most vindictive glance.

'No, I tell you I wouldn't have done it if I hadn't been under excitement; and if you choose to bear malice for it, after all the handsome things I've said – do so and be damned!'

'I *would* refrain from such language in a *lady's* presence, at least,' said Mr Hargrave, hiding his anger under a mask of disgust.

'What have I said?' returned Hattersley. 'Nothing but Heaven's truth – he will be damned, won't he, Mrs Huntingdon, if he doesn't forgive his brother's trespasses?'

'You ought to forgive him, Mr Hargrave, since he asks you,' said I.

'Do you say so? Then I will!' And, smiling almost frankly, he stepped forward and offered his hand. It was immediately clasped in that of his relative, and the reconciliation was apparently cordial on both sides.

'The affront,' continued Hargrave, turning to me, 'owed half its bitterness to the fact of its being offered in your presence; and since you bid me forgive it, I will – and forget it too.'

'I guess the best return I can make, will be to take myself off,' muttered Hattersley, with a broad grin. His companion smiled; and he left the room. This put me on my guard. Mr Hargrave turned seriously to me, and earnestly began –

'Dear Mrs Huntingdon, how I have longed for, yet dreaded this hour! Do not be alarmed,' he added, for my face was crimson with anger: 'I am not about to offend you with any useless entreaties or complaints. I am not going to presume to trouble you with the mention of my own feelings or your perfections, but I have something to reveal to you which you ought to know, and which, yet, it pains me inexpressibly –'

'Then don't trouble yourself to reveal it!'

'But it is of importance –'

'If so, I shall hear it soon enough – especially if it is bad news, as you seem to consider it. At present, I am going to take the children to the nursery.'

'But can't you ring, and send them?'

'No; I want the exercise of a run to the top of the house. – Come Arthur.'

'But you will return?'

'Not yet; don't wait.'

'Then, when may I see you again?'

'At lunch,' said I, departing with little Helen in one arm, and leading Arthur by the hand.

He turned away, muttering some sentence of impatient censure or complaint, in which 'heartless' was the only distinguishable word.

'What nonsense is this Mr Hargrave?' said I, pausing in the doorway. 'What do you mean?'

'Oh, nothing – I did not intend you should hear my soliloquy. But the fact is, Mrs Huntingdon, I have a disclosure to make – painful for me to offer as for you to hear – and I want you to give me a few minutes of your attention in private, at any time and place you like to appoint. It is from no selfish motive that I ask it, and not for any cause that could alarm your super-human purity; therefore you need not kill me with that look of cold and pitiless disdain. I know too well the feelings with which the bearers of bad tidings are commonly regarded, not to –'

'What *is* this wonderful piece of intelligence?' said I, impatiently interrupting him. 'If it is anything of real importance, speak it in three words before I go.'

'In three words I cannot. Send those children away, and stay with me.'

'No; keep your bad tidings to yourself. I know it is something I don't want to hear, and something you would displease me by telling.'

'You have divined too truly I fear; but still since I know it, I feel it my duty to disclose it to you.'

'Oh, spare us both the infliction – and I will exonerate you from the duty. You have offered to tell; I have refused to hear: my ignorance will not be charged on you.'

'Be it so – you shall not hear it from me. But if the blow fall too suddenly upon you when it comes, remember – I wished to soften it!'

I left him. I was determined his words should not alarm me. What could *he* of all men, have to reveal that was of importance for *me* to hear? It was no doubt some exaggerated tale about my unfortunate husband, that he wished to make the most of to serve his own bad purposes.

6th. He has not alluded to this momentous mystery since; and I have seen no reason to repent of my unwillingness to hear it. The threatened blow has not been struck yet; and I do not greatly fear it. At present I am pleased with Arthur: he has not positively disgraced himself for upwards of a fortnight, and all this last week, has been so very moderate in his indulgence at table, that I can perceive a marked difference in his general temper and appearance. Dare I hope this will continue?

CHAPTER XXXIII

TWO EVENINGS

SEVENTH. Yes, I *will* hope! To-night, I heard Grimsby and Hattersley grumbling together, about the inhospitality of their host. They did not know I was near, for I happened to be standing behind the curtain, in the bow of the window, watching the moon rising over the clump of tall, dark elm-trees below the lawn and wondering why Arthur was so sentimental as to stand without, leaning against the outer pillar of the portico, apparently watching it too.

'So, I suppose we've seen the last of our merry carousals in this house,' said Mr Hattersley; 'I *thought* his good-fellowship wouldn't last long. – But,' added he, laughing, 'I didn't expect it would meet its end this way. I rather thought our pretty hostess would be setting up her porcupine quills, and threaten-ing to turn us out of the house, if we didn't mind our manners.'

'You didn't foresee *this*, then?' answered Grimsby with a guttural chuckle. 'But he'll change again when he's sick of her. If we come here a year or two hence, we shall have all our own way, you'll see.'

'I don't know,' replied the other: 'she's not the style of woman you soon tire of – but be that as it may, it's devilish provoking now, that we can't be jolly, because he chooses to be on his good behaviour.'

'It's all these cursed women!' muttered Grimsby. 'They're the very bane of the world! They bring trouble and discomfort wherever they come, with their false, fair faces and their d—d deceitful tongues.'

At this juncture, I issued from my retreat, and smiling on Mr Grimsby as I passed, left the room and went out in search of Arthur. Having seen him bend his course towards the shrub-bery, I followed him thither, and found him just entering the shadowy walk. I was so light of heart, so overflowing with affection, that I sprang upon him and clasped him in my arms. This startling conduct had a singular effect upon him: first, he murmured, 'Bless you darling!' and returned my close embrace with a fervour like old times, and *then* he started, and in a tone of absolute terror, exclaimed –

'Helen! – what the devil is this!' and I saw, by the faint light gleaming through the overshadowing tree, that he was positively pale with the shock.

How strange that the instinctive impulse of affection should come first, and then the shock of the surprise! It shows at least that the affection is genuine: he is not sick of me yet.

'I startled you, Arthur,' said I, laughing in my glee. 'How nervous you are!'

'What the deuce did you do it for?' cried he, quite testily, extricating himself from my arms, and wiping his forehead with his handkerchief. 'Go back, Helen – go back directly! You'll get your death of cold!'

'I won't – till I've told you what I came for. They are blaming you, Arthur, for your temperance and sobriety, and I'm come to thank you for it. They say it is all "these cursed women," and that we are the bane of the world; but don't let them laugh, or grumble you out of your good resolutions, or your affection for me.'

He laughed. I squeezed him in my arms again, and cried in tearful earnest –

'Do – do persevere! – and I'll love you better than ever I did before!'

'Well, well, I will!' said he, hastily kissing me. 'There now, go. – You mad creature, how *could* you come out in your light evening dress, this chill autumn night?'

'It is a glorious night,' said I.

'It is a night that will give you your death, in another minute. Run away, do!'

'Do you see my death among those trees, Arthur?' said I, for he was gazing intently at the shrubs, as if he saw it coming, and I was reluctant to leave him, in my new-found happiness and revival of hope and love. But he grew angry at my delay, so I kissed him and ran back to the house.

I was in such a good humour that night: Milicent told me I was the life of the party, and whispered she had never seen me so brilliant. Certainly, I talked enough for twenty, and smiled upon them all. Grimsby, Hattersley, Hargrave, Lady Lowborough – all shared my sisterly kindness. Grimsby stared and wondered; Hattersley laughed and jested (in spite of the little wine he had been suffered to imbibe), but still behaved as well as he knew how; Hargrave and Annabella, from different motives and in different ways emulated me, and doubtless both surpassed me, the former in his discursive versatility and eloquence, the latter in boldness and animation at least. Milicent, delighted to see her husband, her brother and her over-estimated friend acquitting themselves so well, was lively and gay too, in her quiet way. Even Lord Lowborough caught the general contagion: his dark greenish eyes were lighted up beneath their moody brows; his sombre countenance was beautified by smiles; all traces of gloom, and proud or cold reserve had vanished for the time; and he astonished us all, not only by his general cheerfulness and animation, but by the positive flashes of true force and brilliance he emitted from time to time. Arthur did not talk much, but he laughed, and listened to the rest, and was in perfect good-humour, though not excited by wine. So that, altogether we made a very merry, innocent and entertaining party.

9th. Yesterday, when Rachel came to dress me for dinner, I saw that she had been crying. I wanted to know the cause of it, but she seemed reluctant to tell. Was she unwell? No. Had she heard bad news from her friends? No. Had any of the servants vexed her?

'Oh, no Ma'am!' she answered. – 'It's not for myself.'

'What then, Rachel? Have you been reading novels?'

'Bless you, no!' said she with a sorrowful shake of the head; and then she sighed and continued, 'But to tell you the truth, Ma'am, I don't like master's ways of going on.'

'What do you mean Rachel? – He's going on very properly – at present.'

'Well ma'am, if you think so, it's right.'

And she went on dressing my hair, in a hurried way, quite unlike her usual calm, collected manner, – murmuring, half to herself, she was sure it was beautiful hair: she 'could like to see 'em match it.' When it was done, she fondly stroked it and gently patted my head.

'Is that affectionate ebullition intended for my hair, or myself, nurse?' said I, laughingly turning round upon her; – but a tear was even now in her eye.

'What *do* you mean, Rachel?' I exclaimed.

'Well, ma'am, I don't know, – but if –'

'If what?'

'Well, if I was you, I wouldn't have that Lady Lowborough in the house another minute – not another *minute* I wouldn't!'

I was thunderstruck; but before I could recover from the shock sufficiently to demand an explanation, Milicent entered my room – as she frequently does, when she is dressed before me; and she stayed with me till it was time to go down. She must have found me a very unsociable companion this time, for Rachel's last words rang in my ears. But still, I hoped – I trusted they had no foundation but in some idle rumour of the servants from what they had seen in Lady Lowborough's manner last month; or, perhaps, from something that had passed between their master and her during her former visit. At dinner, I narrowly observed both her and Arthur, and saw nothing extraordinary in the conduct of either – nothing calculated to excite suspicion, except in distrustful minds – which mine was not, and therefore I would not suspect.

Almost immediately after dinner, Annabella went out with her husband to share his moonlight ramble, for it was a splendid evening like the last. Mr Hargrave entered the drawing-room a little before the others, and challenged me to a game of chess. He did it without any of that sad, but proud humility he usually assumes in addressing me, unless he is excited with wine. I looked at his face to see if that was the case now. His eye met mine keenly, but steadily: there was something about him I did not understand, but he seemed sober enough. Not choosing to engage with him, I referred him to Milicent.

'She plays badly,' said he: 'I want to match my skill with yours. Come now! – you can't pretend you are reluctant to lay down your work – I know you never take it up except to pass an idle hour, when there is nothing better you can do.'

'But chess players are so unsociable,' I objected; 'they are no company for any but themselves.'

'There is no one here – but Milicent, and she –'

'Oh, I shall be delighted to watch you!' cried our mutual

friend. – 'Two *such* players – it will be quite a treat! I wonder which will conquer.'

I consented.

'Now Mrs Huntingdon,' said Hargrave, as he arranged the men on the board, speaking distinctly, and with a peculiar emphasis as if he had a double meaning to all his words, 'you are a good player, – but I am a better: we shall have a long game, and you will give me some trouble; but I can be as patient as you, and, in the end, I shall certainly win.' He fixed his eyes upon me with a glance I did not like – keen, crafty, bold, and almost impudent; already half triumphant in his anticipated success.

'I hope not, Mr Hargrave!' returned I, with a vehemence that must have startled Milicent at least; but *he* only smiled and murmured, –

'Time will shew.'

We set to work; he, sufficiently interested in the game, but calm and fearless in the consciousness of superior skill; I, intensely eager to disappoint his expectations, for I considered this the type of a more serious contest – as I imagined he did – and I felt an almost superstitious dread of being beaten: at all events, I could ill endure that present success should add one tittle to his conscious power (his insolent self-confidence, I ought to say), or encourage, for a moment, his dream of future conquest. His play was cautious and deep, but I struggled hard against him. For some time the combat was doubtful; at length, to my joy, the victory seemed inclining to my side: I had taken several of his best pieces, and manifestly baffled his projects. He put his hand to his brow and paused, in evident perplexity. I rejoiced in my advantage, but dared not glory in it yet. At length, he lifted his head, and, quietly making his move, looked at me and said, calmly, –

'Now you think you will win, don't you?'

'I hope so,' replied I, taking his pawn, that he had pushed into the way of my bishop with so careless an air that I thought it was an oversight, but was not generous enough, under the circumstances, to direct his attention to it, and too heedless, at the moment, to foresee the after consequences of my move.

'It is those bishops that trouble me,' said he; 'but the bold knight can overleap the reverend gentlemen,' taking my last bishop with his knight; – 'and now, those sacred persons once removed, I shall carry all before me.'

'Oh Walter, how you talk!' cried Milicent. – 'She has far more pieces than you still.'

'I intend to give you some trouble yet,' said I; 'and perhaps, sir, you will find yourself checkmated before you are aware. Look to your queen.'

The combat deepened. The game was a long one, and I *did* give him some trouble: but he *was* a better player than I.

'What keen gamesters you are!' said Mr Hattersley, who had now entered, and been watching us for some time. 'Why, Mrs Huntingdon, your hand trembles as if you had staked your all upon it! and Walter – you dog – you look as deep and cool as if you were certain of success, – and as keen and cruel as if you would drain her heart's blood! – But if I were you, I wouldn't beat her, for very fear: she'll hate you if you do – she will, by Heaven! – I see it in her eye.'

'Hold your tongue, will you?' said I – his talk distracted me, for I was driven to extremities. A few more moves and I was inextricably entangled in the snare of my antagonist.

'Check,' – cried he: I sought in agony some means of escape – 'mate!' he added, quietly but with evident delight. He had suspended the utterance of that last fatal syllable the better to enjoy my dismay. I was foolishly disconcerted by the event. Hattersley laughed; Milicent was troubled to see me so disturbed. Hargrave placed his hand on mine that rested on the table, and squeezing it with a firm but gentle pressure, murmured 'Beaten – beaten!' and gazed into my face with a look where exultation was blended with an expression of ardour and tenderness yet more insulting.

'*No, never*, Mr Hargrave!' exclaimed I, quickly withdrawing my hand.

'Do you deny?' replied he, smilingly pointing to the board.

'No, no,' I answered, recollecting how strange my conduct must appear; 'you have beaten me in that game.'

'Will you try another, then?'

'No.'

'You acknowledge my superiority?'

'Yes – as a chess-player.'

I rose to resume my work.

'Where is Annabella?' said Hargrave, gravely, after glancing round the room.

'Gone out with Lord Lowborough,' answered I, for he looked at me for a reply.

'And not yet returned!' he said seriously.

'I suppose not.'

'Where is Huntingdon?' looking round again.

'Gone out with Grimsby – as you know,' said Hattersley suppressing a laugh, which broke forth as he concluded the sentence.

Why did he laugh? Why did Hargrave connect them thus together? Was it true, then? – And was this the dreadful secret he had wished to reveal to me? I must know – and that quickly. I instantly rose and left the room to go in search of Rachel, and demand an explanation of her words; but Mr Hargrave followed me into the ante-room, and before I could open its outer door, gently laid his hand upon the lock.

'May I tell you something, Mrs Huntingdon?' said he, in a subdued tone, with serious, downcast eyes.

'If it be anything worth hearing,' replied I, struggling to be composed, for I trembled in every limb.

He quietly pushed a chair towards me. I merely leant my hand upon it, and bid him go on.

'Do not be alarmed,' said he: 'what I wish to say is nothing in itself, and I will leave you to draw your own inferences from it. You say that Annabella is not yet returned?'

'Yes, yes – go on!' said I, impatiently, for I feared my forced calmness would leave me before the end of his disclosure, whatever it might be.

'And you hear,' continued he, 'that Huntingdon is gone out with Grimsby?'

'Well?'

'I heard the latter say to your husband – or the man who calls himself so –'

'Go on, sir!'

He bowed submissively, and continued, 'I heard him say, – "I shall manage it, you'll see! They're gone down by the water; I shall meet them there, and tell him I want a bit of talk with him about some things that we needn't trouble the lady with; and she'll say she can be walking back to the house; and then I shall apologize, you know, and all that, and tip her a wink to take the way of the shrubbery. I'll keep him talking there, about those matters I mentioned, and anything else I can think of, as long as I can, and then bring him round the other way, stopping to look at the trees, the fields, and anything else I can find to discourse of."' Mr Hargrave paused, and looked at me.

Without a word of comment or further questioning, I rose, and darted from the room and out of the house. The torment of suspense was not to be endured: I would not suspect my husband falsely, on this man's accusation, and I would not trust him unworthily – I must know the truth at once. I flew to the shrubbery. Scarcely had I reached it, when a sound of voices arrested my breathless speed.

'We have lingered too long; he will be back,' said Lady Lowborough's voice.

'Surely not, dearest!' was *his* reply, 'but you can run across the lawn, and get in as quietly as you can: I'll follow in a while.'

My knees trembled under me; my brain swam round: I was ready to faint. She must not see me thus. I shrunk among the bushes, and leant against the trunk of a tree to let her pass.

'Ah, Huntingdon!' said she reproachfully, pausing where

I had stood with him the night before – 'it was here you kissed that woman!' She looked back into the leafy shade. Advancing thence, he answered, with a careless laugh –

'Well, dearest, I couldn't help it. You know I must keep straight with her as long as I can. Haven't I seen you kiss your dolt of a husband, scores of times? – and do *I* ever complain?'

'But tell me, don't you love her still – a *little?*' said she placing her hand on his arm and looking earnestly in his face – for I could see them plainly, the moon shining full upon them from between the branches of the tree that sheltered me.

'Not *one bit*, by all that's sacred!' he replied, kissing her glowing cheek.

'Good Heavens, I *must* be gone!' cried she, suddenly breaking from him, and away she flew.

There he stood before me; but I had not strength to confront him now; my tongue cleaved to the roof of my mouth, I was well nigh sinking to the earth, and I almost wondered he did not hear the beating of my heart above the low sighing of the wind, and the fitful rustle of the falling leaves. My senses seemed to fail me, but still I saw his shadowy form pass before me, and through the rushing sound in my ears, I distinctly heard him say, as he stood looking up the lawn –

'There goes the fool! Run Annabella, run! There – in with you! Ah, he didn't see! That's right Grimsby, keep him back!' And even his low laugh reached me as he walked away.

'God help me now!' I murmured, sinking on my knees among the damp weeds and brushwood that surrounded me, and looking up at the moonlit sky, through the scant foliage above. It seemed all dim and quivering now to my darkened sight. My burning, bursting heart strove to pour forth its agony to God, but could not frame its anguish into prayer; until a gust of wind swept over me, which, while it scattered the dead leaves, like blighted hopes, around, cooled my forehead, and seemed a little to revive my sinking frame. Then, while I lifted up my soul in speechless, earnest supplication, some heavenly influence seemed to strengthen me within: I breathed more freely; my vision cleared; I saw distinctly the pure moon shining on, and the light clouds skimming the clear, dark sky; and then, I saw the eternal stars twinkling down upon me; I knew their God was mine, and He was strong to save and swift to hear. 'I will never leave thee, nor forsake thee,' seemed whispered from above their myriad orbs. No, no; I felt He would not leave me comfortless: in spite of earth and hell I should have strength for all my trials, and win a glorious rest at last!

Refreshed, invigorated if not composed, I rose and returned to the house. Much of my newborn strength and courage forsook me, I confess, as I entered it, and shut out the fresh wind and the glorious sky: everything I saw and heard seemed to sicken my heart – the hall, the lamp, the staircase, the doors of the different apartments, the social sound of talk and laughter from the drawing-room. How could I bear my future life? In this house, among those people – oh, how could I endure to live! John just then entered the hall, and seeing me, told me he had been sent in search of me, adding that he had taken in the tea, and master wished to know if I were coming.

'Ask Mrs Hattersley to be so kind as to make the tea, John,' said I. 'Say I am not well to-night, and wish to be excused.'

I retired into the large, empty dining-room, where all was silence and darkness, but for the soft sighing of the wind without, and the faint gleam of moonlight that pierced the blinds and curtains; and there I walked rapidly up and down, thinking my bitter thoughts alone. How different was this from the evening yesterday! *That* it seems, was the last expiring flash of my life's happiness. Poor, blinded fool that I was, to be so happy! I could now see the reason of Arthur's strange reception of me in the shrubbery: the burst of kindness was for his paramour, the start of horror for his wife. Now, too, I could better understand the conversation between Hattersley and Grimsby: it was doubtless of his love for *her* they spoke, not for me.

I heard the drawing-room door open: a light quick step came

out of the ante-room, crossed the hall, and ascended the stairs. It was Milicent, poor Milicent, gone to see how I was – no one else cared for me; but *she* still was kind. I had shed no tears before, but now they came – fast and free. Thus she did me good, without approaching me. Disappointed in her search, I heard her come down – more slowly than she had ascended. Would she come in there, and find me out? No; she turned in the opposite direction and re-entered the drawing-room. I was glad, for I knew not how to meet her, or what to say. I wanted no confidante in my distress. I deserved none – and I wanted none. I had taken the burden upon myself: let me bear it alone.

As the usual hour of retirement approached, I dried my eyes, and tried to clear my voice and calm my mind. I must see Arthur to-night, and speak to him; but I would do it calmly: there should be no scene – nothing to complain or to boast of to his companions – nothing to laugh at with his lady love. When the company were retiring to their chambers, I gently opened the door, and just as he passed, beckoned him in.

'What's to do with *you*, Helen?' said he. 'Why couldn't you come to make tea for us? and what the deuce are you here for, in the dark? What ails you, young woman – you look like a ghost!' he continued, surveying me by the light of his candle.

'No matter,' I answered – 'to you – you have no longer any regard for me, it appears; and I have no longer any for you.'

'Hal-low! what the devil is this?' he muttered.

'I would leave you to-morrow,' continued I, 'and never again come under this roof, but for my child' – I paused a moment to steady my voice.

'What in the devil's name *is* this, Helen?' cried he. 'What can you be driving at?'

'You know, perfectly well. Let us waste no time in useless explanation, but tell me, will you –'

He vehemently swore he knew nothing about it, and insisted upon hearing what poisonous old woman had been blackening his name, and what infamous lies I had been fool enough to believe.

'Spare yourself the trouble of forswearing yourself and racking your brains to stifle truth with falsehood,' I coldly replied. 'I have trusted to the testimony of no third person. I was in the shrubbery this evening, and I saw and heard for myself.'

This was enough. He uttered a suppressed exclamation of consternation and dismay, and muttering, 'I *shall* catch it now!' set down his candle on the nearest chair, and, rearing his back against the wall, stood confronting me with folded arms.

'Well! – what then?' said he, with the calm insolence of mingled shamelessness and desperation.

'Only this,' returned I; 'will you let me take our child and what remains of my fortune, and go?'

'Go where?'

'Anywhere, where he will be safe from your contaminating influence, and I shall be delivered from your presence – and you from mine.'

'No – by *Jove* I won't!'

'Will you let me have the child then, without the money?'

'No – nor yourself without the child. Do you think I'm going to be made the talk of the country, for your fastidious caprices?'

'Then I must stay here, to be hated and despised. – But henceforth, we are husband and wife only in the name.'

'Very good.'

'I am your child's mother, and *your* housekeeper – nothing more. So you need not trouble yourself any longer, to feign the love you cannot feel: I will exact no more heartless caresses from you – nor offer – nor endure them either – I will not be mocked with the empty husk of conjugal endearments, when you have given the substance to another!'

'Very good – if *you* please. We shall see who will tire first, my lady.'

'If I tire, it will be of living in the world with you; not of living without your mockery of love. When *you* tire of your sinful ways, and show yourself truly repentant, I will forgive you – and, perhaps, try to love you again, though that will be hard indeed.'

'Humph! – and meantime, you will go and talk me over to Mrs Hargrave, and write long letters to aunt Maxwell to complain of the wicked wretch you have married?'

'I shall complain to no one. Hitherto, I have struggled hard to hide your vices from every eye, and invest you with virtues you never possessed – but now you must look to yourself.'

I left him – muttering bad language to himself, and went up stairs.

'You are poorly Ma'am,' said Rachel, surveying me with deep anxiety.

'It is too true, Rachel!' said I, answering her sad looks rather than her words.

'I knew it – or I wouldn't have mentioned such a thing.'

'But don't *you* trouble yourself about it,' said I, kissing her pale, time-wasted cheek – 'I can bear it – better than you imagine.'

'Yes, you were always for "bearing." – But if I was you I wouldn't bear it – I'd give way to it, and cry right hard! – and I'd talk too, I just *would* – I'd let him know what it was to –'

'I have talked,' said I: 'I've said enough.'

'Then I'd cry,' persisted she. 'I wouldn't look so white and so calm, and burst my heart with keeping it in!'

'I *have* cried,' said I, smiling in spite of my misery; 'and I *am* calm now, really, so don't discompose me again, nurse: let us say no more about it – and *don't* mention it to the servants. – There, you may go now. Good night; – and don't disturb your rest for me: I shall sleep well – if I can.'

Notwithstanding this resolution, I found my bed so intolerable that, before two o'clock, I rose, and, lighting my candle by the rushlight that was still burning, I got my desk and sat down in my dressing-gown to recount the events of the past evening. It was better to be so occupied than to be lying in bed torturing my brain with recollections of the far past and anticipations of the dreadful future. I have found relief in describing the very circumstances that have destroyed my peace, as well as the little trivial details attendant upon their discovery. No sleep I could have got this night would have done so much towards composing my mind, and preparing me to meet the trials of the day – I fancy so, at least; – and yet, when I cease writing, I find my head aches terribly; and when I look into the glass I am startled at my haggard, worn appearance.

Rachel has been to dress me, and says I have had a sad night of it, she can see. Milicent has just looked in to ask me how I was. I told her I was better, but to excuse my appearance admitted I had had a restless night. – I wish this day were over! I shudder at the thoughts of going down to breakfast – how shall I encounter them all? – Yet let me remember it is not *I* that am guilty: *I* have no cause to fear; and if *they* scorn me as a victim of their guilt, I can pity their folly and despise their scorn.

CHAPTER XXXIV

CONCEALMENT

EVENING. Breakfast passed well over, I was calm and cool throughout. I answered composedly all enquiries respecting my health; and whatever was unusual in my look or manner, was generally attributed to the trifling indisposition that had occasioned my early retirement last night. But how am I to get over the ten or twelve days that must yet elapse before they go? Yet why so long for their departure? When they are gone how shall I get through the months or years of my future life, in company with that man – my greatest enemy – for none could injure me as he has done? Oh! when I think how fondly, how foolishly I have loved him, how madly I have trusted him, how constantly I have laboured, and studied, and prayed, and struggled for his advantage; and how cruelly he has trampled on my love, betrayed my trust, scorned my prayers and tears, and efforts for his preservation – crushed my hopes, destroyed my youth's best feelings, and doomed me to a life of hopeless misery – as far as man can do it – it is not enough to say that I no longer love my husband – I HATE him! The word stares me in the face like a guilty confession, but it is true: I hate him – I hate him! – But God have mercy on his miserable soul! – and make him see and feel his guilt – I ask no other vengeance! If he could but fully know and truly feel my wrongs, I should be well avenged; and I could freely pardon all; but he is so lost, so hardened in his heartless depravity that, in this life, I believe he never will. But it is useless dwelling on this theme: let me seek once more to dissipate reflection in the minor details of passing events.

Mr Hargrave has annoyed me all day long with his serious, sympathizing, and (as *he* thinks) unobtrusive politeness – if it were more obtrusive it would trouble me less, for then I could snub him; but, as it is, he contrives to appear so really kind and thoughtful that I cannot do so without rudeness and seeming ingratitude. I sometimes think I ought to give him credit for the good feeling he simulates so well; and then again, I think it is my *duty* to suspect him under the peculiar circumstances in which I am placed. His kindness may not all be feigned, but still, let not the purest impulse of gratitude to him, induce me to forget myself; let me remember the game of chess, the expressions he used on the occasion, and those indescribable looks of his, that so justly roused my indignation, and I think I shall be safe enough. I have done well to record them so minutely.

I think he wishes to find an opportunity of speaking to me alone: he has seemed to be on the watch all day, but I have taken care to disappoint him; not that I fear anything he could say, but I have trouble enough without the addition of his insulting consolations, condolences, or whatever else he might attempt; and, for Milicent's sake, I do not wish to quarrel with him. He excused himself from going out to shoot with the other gentlemen in the morning, under the pretext of having letters to write; and instead of retiring for that purpose into the library, he sent for his desk into the morning-room where I was seated with Milicent and Lady Lowborough. They had betaken themselves to their work; I, less to divert my mind than to deprecate conversation, had provided myself with a book. Milicent saw that I wished to be quiet, and accordingly let me alone. Annabella, doubtless, saw it too; but that was no reason why she should restrain her tongue, or curb her cheerful spirits: *she* accordingly chatted away, addressing herself almost exclusively to me, and with the utmost assurance and familiarity, growing the more animated and friendly, the colder and briefer my answers became. Mr Hargrave saw that I could ill endure it; and, looking up from his desk, he answered her questions and observations for me, as far as he could, and attempted to transfer her social attentions from me to himself; but it would not do. Perhaps, she thought I had a headache and could not bear to talk – at any rate, she saw that her loquacious vivacity annoyed me as I could tell by the malicious pertinacity with which she persisted. But I checked it, effectually, by putting into her hand the book I had been trying to read, on the fly leaf of which I had hastily scribbled, –

'I am too well acquainted with your character and conduct to feel any real friendship for you, and, as I am without your talent for dissimulation, I cannot assume the appearance of it. I must, therefore, beg that hereafter, all familiar intercourse may cease between us; and if I still continue to treat you with civility, as if you were a woman worthy of consideration and respect, understand that it is out of regard for your cousin Milicent's feelings, not for yours.'

Upon perusing this, she turned scarlet and bit her lip. Covertly tearing away the leaf, she crumpled it up and put it in the fire, and then employed herself in turning over the pages of the book and, really or apparently, perusing its contents. In a little while Milicent announced it her intention to repair to the nursery, and asked if I would accompany her.

'Annabella will excuse us,' said she, 'she's busy reading.'

'No, I won't,' cried Annabella, suddenly looking up and throwing her book on the table. 'I want to speak to Helen a minute. You may go Milicent, and she'll follow in a while.' (Milicent went.) 'Will you oblige me, Helen?' continued she.

Her impudence astounded me; but I complied, and followed her into the library. She closed the door, and walked up to the fire.

'Who told you this?' said she.

'No one: I am not incapable of seeing for myself.'

'Ah, you are suspicious!' cried she, smiling with a gleam of hope – hitherto, there had been a kind of desperation in her hardihood; now she was evidently relieved.

'If I *were* suspicious,' I replied, 'I should have discovered your infamy long before. No, Lady Lowborough, I do not found my charge upon suspicion.'

'On what *do* you found it then?' said she, throwing herself into an arm-chair, and stretching out her feet to the fender, with an obvious effort to appear composed.

'I enjoy a moonlight ramble as well as you,' I answered, steadily fixing my eyes upon her: 'and the shrubbery happens to be one of my favourite resorts.'

She coloured again excessively, and remained silent, pressing her finger against her teeth, and gazing into the fire. I watched her a few moments with a feeling of malevolent gratification; then, moving towards the door, I calmly asked if she had anything more to say.

'Yes, yes!' cried she eagerly, starting up from her reclining posture. 'I want to know if you will tell Lord Lowborough?'

'Suppose I do?'

'Well, if you are disposed to publish the matter, *I* cannot dissuade you, of course – but there will be terrible work if you do – and if you don't, I shall think you the most generous of mortal beings – and if there is anything in the world I can do for you – anything short of –' she hesitated.

'Short of renouncing your guilty connection with my husband, I suppose you mean,' said I.

She paused, in evident disconcertion and perplexity, mingled with anger she dared not show.

'I cannot renounce what is dearer than life,' she muttered in a low, hurried tone. Then, suddenly raising her head and fixing her gleaming eyes upon me, she continued earnestly, 'But Helen – or Mrs Huntingdon, or whatever you would have me call you – *will* you tell him? If you are generous, here is a fitting opportunity for the exercise of your magnanimity: if you are proud, here am I – your rival – ready to acknowledge myself your debtor for an act of the most noble forbearance.'

'I shall not tell him.'

'You will not!' cried she delightedly. 'Accept my sincere thanks, then!'

She sprang up, and offered me her hand. I drew back.

'Give me no thanks; it is not for *your* sake that I refrain. Neither is it an act of any forbearance: I have no wish to publish your shame. I should be sorry to distress your husband with the knowledge of it.'

'And Milicent? will you tell her?'

'No, on the contrary I shall do my utmost to conceal it from her. I would not for much that she should know the infamy and disgrace of her relation!'

'You use hard words, Mrs Huntingdon – but I can pardon you.'

'And now, Lady Lowborough,' continued I, 'let me counsel you to leave this house as soon as *possible*. You must be aware that your continuance here is excessively disagreeable to me –

not for Mr Huntingdon's sake,' said I, observing the dawn of a malicious smile of triumph on her face – 'you are welcome to him, if you like him, as far as *I* am concerned – but because it is painful to be always disguising my true sentiments respecting you, and straining to keep up an appearance of civility and respect towards one for whom I have not the most distant shadow of esteem; and because, if you stay, your conduct cannot possibly remain concealed much longer from the only two persons in the house who do not know it already. And, for your husband's sake, Annabella, and even for your own, I wish – I earnestly advise and *entreat* you to break off this unlawful connection at once, and return to your duty while you may, before the dreadful consequences –'

'Yes, yes, of course,' said she, interrupting me with a gesture of impatience. – 'But I cannot go, Helen, before the time appointed for our departure. What possible pretext could I frame for such a thing? Whether I proposed going back alone – which Lowborough would not hear of – or taking him with me, the very circumstance itself, would be certain to excite suspicion – and when our visit is so *nearly* at an end too – little more than a week – surely, you can endure my presence *so* long! I will not annoy you with any more of my friendly impertinences.'

'Well! I have nothing more to say to you.'

'Have you mentioned this affair to Huntingdon?' asked she, as I was leaving the room.

'How dare you mention his name to me!' was the only answer I gave.

No words have passed between us since, but such as outward decency or pure necessity demanded.

CHAPTER XXXV

PROVOCATIONS

NINETEENTH. – In proportion as Lady Lowborough finds she has nothing to fear from me, and as the time of departure draws nigh, the more audacious and insolent she becomes. She does not scruple to speak to my husband with affectionate familiarity in my presence, when no one else is by, and is particularly fond of displaying her interest in his health and welfare, or in anything that concerns him, as if for the purpose of contrasting her kind solicitude with my cold indifference. And he rewards her by such smiles and glances, such whispered words, or boldly spoken insinuations, indicative of his sense of her goodness and my neglect, as make the blood rush into my face, in spite of myself – for I would be utterly regardless of it all – deaf and blind to everything that passes between them, since the more I show myself sensible of their wickedness, the more she triumphs in her victory, and the more he flatters himself that I love him devotedly still, in spite of my pretended indifference. On such occasions I have sometimes been startled by a subtle, fiendish suggestion inciting me to show him the contrary by a seeming encouragement of Hargrave's advances; but such ideas are banished in a moment with horror and self-abasement; and then I hate him tenfold more than ever, for having brought me to this! – God pardon me for it – and all my sinful thoughts! Instead of being humbled and purified by my afflictions, I feel that they are turning my nature into gall. This must be my fault as much as theirs that wrong me. No true Christian could cherish such bitter feelings as I do against him and her – especially the latter: him, I still feel that I could pardon – freely, gladly – on the slightest token of repentance; but *she* – words cannot utter my abhorrence. Reason forbids, but passion urges strongly; and I must pray and struggle long ere I subdue it.

It is well that she is leaving to-morrow, for I could not well endure her presence for another day. This morning, she rose earlier than usual. I found her in the room alone, when I went down to breakfast.

'Oh Helen! is it you?' said she, turning as I entered.

I gave an involuntary start back on seeing her, at which she uttered a short laugh, observing, –

'I think we are *both* disappointed.'

I came forward and busied myself with the breakfast-things.

'This is the last day I shall burden your hospitality,' said she, as she seated herself at the table. 'Ah, here comes one that will not rejoice at it!' she murmured, half to herself, as Arthur entered the room.

He shook hands with her and wished her good morning: then, looking lovingly in her face, and still retaining her hand in his, murmured pathetically, –

'The last – last day!'

'Yes,' said she with some asperity; 'and I rose early to make the best of it – I have been here alone this half hour, and *you*, – you lazy creature –'

'Well, I thought I was early too,' said he – 'but,' dropping his voice almost to a whisper, 'you see we are not alone.'

'We never are,' returned she. But they were almost as good as alone, for I was now standing at the window, watching the clouds, and struggling to suppress my wrath.

Some more words passed between them, which, happily, I did not overhear; but Annabella had the audacity to come and place herself beside me, and even to put her hand upon my shoulder and say softly, –

'You need not grudge him to me, Helen, for I love him more than ever you could do.'

This put me beside myself. I took her hand and violently dashed it from me, with an expression of abhorrence and indignation that could not be suppressed. Startled, almost appalled, by this sudden outbreak, she recoiled in silence. I would have given way to my fury and said more, but Arthur's low laugh recalled me to myself. I checked the half-uttered invective, and scornfully turned away, regretting that I had given him so much amusement. He was still laughing when Mr Hargrave made his appearance. How much of the scene he had witnessed I do not know, for the door was ajar when he entered. He greeted his host and his cousin both coldly, and me with a glance intended to express the deepest sympathy mingled with high admiration and esteem.

'How much allegiance do you owe to that man?' he asked below his breath, as he stood beside me at the window, affecting to be making observations on the weather.

'None,' I answered. And immediately returning to the table, I employed myself in making the tea. He followed, and would have entered into some kind of conversation with me, but the other guests were now beginning to assemble and I took no more notice of him, except to give him his coffee.

After breakfast, determined to pass as little of the day as possible in company with Lady Lowborough, I quietly stole away from the company and retired to the library. Mr Hargrave followed me thither, under pretence of coming for a book; and first, turning to the shelves, he selected a volume; and then, quietly, but by no means timidly, approaching me, he stood beside me, resting his hand on the back of my chair, and said softly, –

'And so you consider yourself free, at last?'

'Yes,' said I, without moving, or raising my eyes from my book, 'free to do anything but offend God and my conscience.'

There was a momentary pause.

'Very right,' said he; 'provided your conscience be not too morbidly tender, and your ideas of God not too erroneously severe; but can you suppose it would offend that benevolent Being to make the happiness of one who would die for yours? – to raise a devoted heart from purgatorial torments to a state of heavenly bliss when you could do it without the slightest injury to yourself or any other?'

This was spoken in a low, earnest, melting tone as he bent over me. I now raised my head; and, steadily confronting his gaze, I answered calmly, –

'Mr Hargrave, do you mean to insult me?'

He was not prepared for this. He paused a moment to recover the shock; then, drawing himself up and removing his hand from my chair, he answered, with proud sadness, –

'That was not my intention.'

I just glanced towards the door, with a slight movement of the head, and then returned to my book. He immediately withdrew. This was better than if I had answered with more words, and in the passionate spirit to which my first impulse would have prompted. What a good thing it is to be able to command one's temper! I must labour to cultivate this inestimable quality: God, only, knows how often I shall need it in this rough, dark road that lies before me.

In the course of the morning, I drove over to the Grove with the two ladies, to give Milicent an opportunity for bidding farewell to her mother and sister. They persuaded her to stay with them the rest of the day, Mrs Hargrave promising to bring her back in the evening and remain till the party broke up on the morrow. Consequently, Lady Lowborough and I had the pleasure of returning *tête-à-tête* in the carriage together. For the first mile or two, we kept silence, I looking out of my window, and she leaning back in her corner. But I was not going to restrict myself to any particular position for her: when I was tired of leaning forward, with the cold, raw wind in my face; and surveying the russet hedges, and the damp, tangled grass of their banks, I gave it up, and leant back too. With her usual impudence, my companion then made some attempts to get up a conversation; but the monosyllables 'yes,' or 'no,' or 'humph,' were the utmost her several remarks could elicit from me. At last, on her asking my opinion upon some immaterial point of discussion, I answered, –

'Why do you wish to talk to me, Lady Lowborough? – you must know what I think of you.'

'Well, if you *will* be so bitter against me,' replied she, 'I can't help it; – but *I'm* not going to sulk for anybody.'

Our short drive was now at an end. As soon as the carriage door was opened, she sprang out, and went down the park to meet the gentlemen, who were just returning from the woods. Of course I did not follow.

But I had not done with her impudence yet: – after dinner, I retired to the drawing-room, as usual, and she accompanied me, but I had the two children with me, and I gave them my whole attention, and determined to keep them till the gentlemen came, or till Milicent arrived with her mother. Little Helen, however, was soon tired of playing, and insisted upon going to sleep; and while I sat on the sofa with her on my knee, and Arthur seated beside me, gently playing with her soft, flaxen hair, – Lady Lowborough composedly came and placed herself on the other side.

'To-morrow, Mrs Huntingdon,' said she, 'you will be delivered from my presence, which, no doubt, you will be very glad of – it is natural you should; – but do you know I have rendered you a great service? – Shall I tell you what it is?'

'I shall be glad to hear of any service you have rendered me,' said I, determined to be calm, for I knew by the tone of her voice she wanted to provoke me.

'Well,' resumed she, 'have you not observed the salutary change in Mr Huntingdon? Don't you see what a sober, temperate man he is become? You saw with regret the sad habits he was contracting, I know; and I know you did your utmost to deliver him from them, – but without success, until I came to your assistance. I told him, in few words, that I could not bear to see him degrade himself so, and that I should cease to – no matter what I told him, – but you see the reformation I have wrought; and you ought to thank me for it.'

I rose, and rang for the nurse.

'But I desire no thanks,' she continued, 'all the return I ask is, that you will take care of him when I am gone, and not, by harshness and neglect, drive him back to his old courses.'

I was almost sick with passion, but Rachel was now at the door: I pointed to the children, for I could not trust myself to speak: she took them away, and I followed.

'Will you, Helen?' continued the speaker.

I gave her a look that blighted the malicious smile on her face – or checked it, at least for a moment – and departed. In the ante-room I met Mr Hargrave. He saw I was in no humour to be spoken to, and suffered me to pass without a word; but when, after a few minutes' seclusion in the library, I had regained my composure, and was returning, to join Mrs Hargrave and Milicent, whom I had just heard come down stairs and go into the drawing-room, – I found him there still, lingering in the dimly lighted apartment, and evidently waiting for me.

'Mrs Huntingdon,' said he as I passed, 'will you allow me one word?'

'What is it then? – be quick if you please.'

'I offended you this morning; and I cannot live under your displeasure.'

'Then go, and sin no more,' replied I, turning away.

'No, no!' said he hastily, setting himself before me – 'pardon me, but I must have your forgiveness. I leave you to-morrow, and I may not have an opportunity of speaking to you again. I was wrong, to forget myself – and you, as I did; but let me implore you to forget and forgive my rash presumption, and think of me as if those words had never been spoken; for, believe me, I regret them deeply, and the loss of your esteem is too severe a penalty – I cannot bear it.'

'Forgetfulness is not to be purchased with a wish; and I cannot bestow my esteem on all who desire it, unless they deserve it too.'

'I shall think my life well spent in labouring to deserve it, if you will but pardon this offence – Will you?'

'Yes.'

'Yes? but that is coldly spoken. Give me your hand and I'll believe you. – You won't? Then, Mrs Huntingdon, you do *not* forgive me!'

'Yes – here it is, and my forgiveness with it: only *sin no more*.'

He pressed my cold hand with sentimental fervour, but said nothing, and stood aside to let me pass into the room, where all the company were now assembled. Mr Grimsby was seated near the door: on seeing me enter almost immediately followed by Hargrave, he leered at me, with a glance of intolerable significance, as I passed. I looked him in the face, till he sullenly turned away, if not *ashamed*, at least *confounded* for the moment. Meantime, Hattersley had seized Hargrave by the arm, and was whispering something in his ear – some coarse joke, no doubt, for the latter neither laughed nor spoke in answer, but, turning from him with a slight curl of the lip, disengaged himself and went to his mother, who was telling Lord Lowborough how many reasons she had to be proud of her son.

Thank Heaven, they are all going to-morrow.

CHAPTER XXXVI

DUAL SOLITUDE

DECEMBER 20TH, 1824. – This is the third anniversary of our felicitous union. It is now two months since our guests left us to the enjoyment of each other's society; and I have had nine weeks' experience of this new phase of conjugal life – two persons living together, as master and mistress of the house, and father and mother of a winsome, merry little child, with the mutual understanding that there is no love, friendship, or sympathy between them. As far as in me lies, I endeavour to live peaceably with him: I treat him with unimpeachable civility, give up my convenience to his, wherever it may reasonably be done, and consult him in a business-like way on household affairs, deferring to his pleasure and judgment, even when I know the latter to be inferior to my own.

As for him: for the first week or two, he was peevish and low – fretting, I suppose, over his dear Annabella's departure – and particularly ill-tempered to me: everything I did was wrong; I was cold-hearted, hard, insensate; my sour, pale face was perfectly repulsive; my voice made him shudder; he knew not how he could live through the winter with me; I should kill him by inches. Again I proposed a separation, but it would not do: he was not going to be the talk of all the old gossips in the neighbourhood: he would not have it said that he was such a brute his wife could not live with him; – no; he must contrive to bear with me.

'I must contrive to bear with *you* you mean,' said I, 'for so long as I discharge my functions of steward and housekeeper, so conscientiously and well, without pay and without thanks, you cannot afford to part with me. I shall therefore remit these duties when my bondage becomes intolerable.' This threat, I thought, would serve to keep him in check, if anything would.

I believe he was much disappointed that I did not feel his offensive sayings more acutely, for when he had said anything particularly well calculated to hurt my feelings, he would stare me searchingly in the face, and then grumble against my 'marble heart,' or my 'brutal insensibility.' If I had bitterly wept, and deplored his lost affection, he would, perhaps, have condescended to pity me, and taken me into favour for a while, just to comfort his solitude and console him for the absence of his beloved Annabella, until he could meet her again, or some more fitting substitute. Thank Heaven, I am not so weak as that! I was infatuated once, with a foolish, besotted affection, that clung to him in spite of his unworthiness, but it is fairly gone now – wholly crushed and withered away; and he has none but himself and his vices to thank for it.

At first (in compliance with his sweet lady's injunctions, I suppose), he abstained wonderfully well from seeking to solace his cares in wine; but at length he began to relax his virtuous efforts, and now and then exceeded a little, and still continues to do so – nay, sometimes, *not* a little. When he is under the exciting influence of these excesses, he sometimes fires up and attempts to play the brute; and then I take little pains to suppress my scorn and disgust: when he is under the *depressing* influence of the after consequences, he bemoans his sufferings and his errors, and charges them both upon me; he knows such indulgence injures his health, and does him more harm than good; but he says I drive him to it by my unnatural, unwomanly conduct; it will be the ruin of him in the end, but it is all my fault; – and *then*, *I* am roused to defend myself – sometimes, with bitter recrimination. This is a kind of injustice I cannot patiently endure. Have I not laboured long and hard to save him from this very vice? Would I not labour still, to deliver him from it, if I could? But could I do so by fawning upon him and caressing him when I know that he scorns me? Is it *my* fault that I have lost my influence with him, or that he has forfeited every claim to my regard? And should I seek a reconciliation with him, when I feel that I abhor him, and that he despises me? – and while he continues still to correspond with Lady Lowborough, as I know he does? No, never, never, never! – he may drink himself dead, but it is NOT my fault!

Yet I do my part to save him still: I give him to understand that drinking makes his eyes dull, and his face red and bloated; and that it tends to render him imbecile in body and mind; and if Annabella were to see him as often as I do, she would speedily be disenchanted; and that she certainly will withdraw her favour from him, if he continues such courses. Such a mode of admonition wins only coarse abuse for me – and indeed I almost feel as if I deserved it, for I hate to use such arguments, but they sink into his stupefied heart, and make him pause, and ponder, and abstain, more than anything else I could say.

At present, I am enjoying a temporary relief from his presence: he is gone with Hargrave to join a distant hunt, and will probably not be back before to-morrow evening. How differently I used to feel his absence!

Mr Hargrave is still at the Grove. He and Arthur frequently meet to pursue their rural sports together: he often calls upon us here, and Arthur not unfrequently rides over to him. I do not think either of these soi-disant friends is overflowing with love for the other; but such intercourse serves to get the time on, and I am very willing it should continue, as it saves me some hours of discomfort in Arthur's society, and gives him some better employment than the sottish indulgence of his sensual appetites. The only objection I have to Mr Hargrave's being in the neighbourhood, is that the fear of meeting him at the Grove, prevents me from seeing his sister so often as I otherwise should; for, of late, he has conducted himself towards me with such unerring propriety that I have almost forgotten his former conduct. I suppose he is striving to 'win my esteem.' If he continue to act in this way, he *may* win it; – but what then? The moment he attempts to demand anything more, he will lose it again.

February 10th. – It is a hard, embittering thing to have one's kind feelings and good intentions cast back in one's teeth. I was beginning to relent towards my wretched partner – to pity his forlorn, comfortless condition, unalleviated as it is by the consolations of intellectual resources and the answer of a good conscience towards God – and to think I ought to sacrifice my pride, and renew my efforts once again to make his home agreeable and lead him back to the path of virtue; not by false professions of love, and not by pretended remorse, but by mitigating my habitual coldness of manner, and commuting my frigid civility into kindness wherever an opportunity occurred; and not only was I beginning to think so, but I had already begun to act upon the thought – and what was the result? No answering spark of kindness – no awakening penitence, but an unappeasable ill-humour and a spirit of tyrannous exaction that increased with indulgence, and a lurking gleam of self-complacent triumph, at every detection of relenting softness in my manner, that congealed me to marble again as often as it recurred; and this morning he finished the business: – I think the petrifaction is so completely effected at last, that nothing can melt me again. Among his letters was one which he perused with symptoms of unusual gratification, and then threw it across the table to me, with the admonition, –

'There! read that, and take a lesson by it!'

It was in the free, dashing hand of Lady Lowborough. I glanced at the first page; it seemed full of extravagant protestations of affection; impetuous longings for a speedy reunion; and impious defiance of God's mandates, and railings against His providence for having cast their lot asunder, and doomed them both to the hateful bondage of alliance with those they could not love. He gave a slight titter on seeing me change colour. I folded up the letter, rose, and returned it to him, with no remark but, –

'Thank you – I *will* take a lesson by it!'

My little Arthur was standing between his knees, delightedly playing with the bright, ruby ring on his finger. Urged by a sudden, imperative impulse to deliver my son from that con-taminating influence, I caught him up in my arms and carried him with me out of the room. Not liking this abrupt removal, the child began to pout and cry. This was a new stab to my already tortured heart. I would not let him go; but, taking him with me into the library, I shut the door, and, kneeling on the floor beside him, I embraced him, kissed him, wept over him with passionate fondness. Rather frightened than consoled by this, he turned struggling from me and cried out aloud for his papa. I released him from my arms, and never were more bitter tears than those that now concealed him from my blinded, burning eyes. Hearing his cries, the father came to the room. I instantly turned away lest he should see and misconstrue my emotion. He swore at me, and took the now pacified child away.

It is hard that my little darling should love him more than me; and that, when the well-being and culture of my son is all I have to live for, I should see my influence destroyed by one whose selfish affection is more injurious than the coldest in-difference or the harshest tyranny could be. If I, for his good, deny him some trifling indulgence, he goes to his father, and the latter, in spite of his selfish indolence, will even give himself some trouble to meet the child's desires: if I attempt to curb his will, or look gravely on him for some act of childish disobedi-ence, he knows his other parent will smile and take his part against me. Thus, not only have I the father's spirit in the son to contend against, the germs of his evil tendencies to search out and eradicate, and his corrupting intercourse and example in after life to counteract, but already *he* counteracts my arduous labour for the child's advantage, destroys my influence over his tender mind, and robs me of his very love; – I had no earthly hope but this, and he seems to take a diabolical delight in tearing it away.

But it is wrong to despair; I will remember the counsel of the inspired writer to him 'that feareth the Lord and obeyeth the voice of his servant, that *sitteth in darkness and hath no light*; – let him trust in the name of the Lord, and stay upon his God!'

CHAPTER XXXVII

THE NEIGHBOUR AGAIN

DECEMBER 20TH, 1825. – Another year is past; and I am weary of this life. And yet, I cannot wish to leave it: whatever afflictions assail me here, I cannot wish to go and leave my darling in this dark and wicked world alone, without a friend to guide him through its weary mazes, to warn him of its thousand snares, and guard him from the perils that beset him on every hand. I am not well fitted to be his only companion, I know; but there is no other to supply my place. I am too grave to minister to his amusements and enter into his infantile sports as a nurse or a mother ought to do, and often his bursts of gleeful merriment trouble and alarm me; I see in them his father's spirit and temperament, and I tremble for the consequences; and, too often, damp the innocent mirth I ought to share. That father on the contrary has no weight of sadness on his mind – is troubled with no fears, no scruples concerning his son's future welfare; and at evenings especially, the times when the child sees him the most and the oftenest, he is always particularly jocund and open-hearted: ready to laugh and to jest with anything or anybody – but me – and I am particularly silent and sad: therefore, of course, the child dotes upon his seemingly joyous, amusing, ever indulgent papa, and will at any time gladly exchange my company for his. This disturbs me greatly; not so much for the sake of my son's affection (though I do prize that highly, and though I feel it is my right, and know I have done much to earn it), as for that influence over him which, for his own advantage, I would strive to purchase and retain, and which for very spite his father delights to rob me of, and, from motives of mere idle egotism, is pleased to win to himself, making no use of it but to torment me, and ruin the child. My only consolation is, that he spends comparatively little of his time at home, and, during the months he passes in London or elsewhere, I have a chance of recovering the ground I had lost, and overcoming with good the evil he has wrought by his wilful mismanagement. But then it is a bitter trial to behold him, on his return, doing his utmost to subvert my labours and transform my innocent, affectionate, tractable darling into a selfish, disobedient, and mischievous boy; thereby preparing the soil for those vices he has so successfully cultivated in his own perverted nature.

Happily, there were none of Arthur's 'friends' invited to Grassdale last autumn: he took himself off to visit some of them instead. I wish he would always do so, and I wish his friends were numerous and loving enough to keep him amongst them all the year round. Mr Hargrave, considerably to my annoyance, did not go with him; but I think I have done with that gentleman at last.

For seven or eight months he behaved so remarkably well, and managed so skilfully too, that I was almost completely off my guard, and was really beginning to look upon him as a friend, and even to treat him as such, with certain prudent restrictions (which I deemed scarcely necessary); when, presuming upon my unsuspecting kindness, he thought he might venture to overstep the bounds of decent moderation and propriety that had so long restrained him. It was on a pleasant evening at the close of May: I was wandering in the park, and he, on seeing me there as he rode past, made bold to enter and approach me, dismounting and leaving his horse at the gate. This was the first time he had ventured to come within its inclosure since I had been left alone, without the sanction of his mother's or sister's company, or at least the excuse of a message from them. But he managed to appear so calm and easy, so respectful and self-possessed in his friendliness, that, though a little surprised, I was neither alarmed nor offended at the unusual liberty, and he walked with me under the ash trees and by the water-side, and talked, with considerable animation, good taste, and intelligence, on many subjects, before I began to think about getting rid of him. Then, after a pause, during which we both stood gazing on the calm, blue water; I revolving in my mind the best means of politely dismissing my companion, he, no doubt, pondering other matters equally alien to the sweet sights and sounds that alone were present to his senses, – he suddenly electrified me by beginning, in a peculiar tone, low, soft, but perfectly distinct, to pour forth the most unequivocal expressions of earnest and passionate love; pleading his cause with all the bold yet artful eloquence he could summon to his aid. But I cut short his appeal, and repulsed him so determinately, so decidedly, and with such a mixture of scornful indignation tempered with cool, dispassionate sorrow and pity for his benighted mind, that he withdrew, astonished, mortified, and discomforted; and, a few days after, I heard that he had departed for London. He returned however in eight or nine weeks – and did not entirely keep aloof from me, but comported himself in so remarkable a manner that his quick-sighted sister could not fail to notice the change.

'What have you done to Walter, Mrs Huntingdon?' said she one morning, when I had called at the Grove, and he had just left the room after exchanging a few words of the coldest civility. 'He has been so extremely ceremonious and stately of late,

I can't imagine what it is all about, unless you have desperately offended him. Tell me what it is, that I may be your mediator, and make you friends again.'

'I have done nothing willingly to offend him,' said I. 'If he is offended, he can best tell you himself what it is about.'

'I'll ask him,' cried the giddy girl, springing up and putting her head out of the window; 'he's only in the garden – Walter!'

'No, no, Esther! you will seriously displease me if you do; and I shall leave you immediately, and not come again for months – perhaps years.'

'Did you call, Esther?' said her brother, approaching the window from without.

'Yes; I wanted to ask you –'

'Good morning, Esther,' said I, taking her hand and giving it a severe squeeze.

'To ask you,' continued she, 'to get me a rose for Mrs Huntingdon.' He departed. 'Mrs Huntingdon,' she exclaimed, turning to me and still holding me fast by the hand, 'I'm quite shocked at you – you're just as angry, and distant, and cold as he is: and I'm determined you shall be as good friends as ever, before you go.'

'Esther, how can you be so rude!' cried Mrs Hargrave, who was seated gravely knitting in her easy chair. 'Surely, you never *will* learn to conduct yourself like a lady!'

'Well mamma, you said, yourself –' But the young lady was silenced by the uplifted finger of her mamma, accompanied with a very stern shake of the head.

'Isn't she cross?' whispered she to me; but, before I could add my share of reproof, Mr Hargrave reappeared at the window with a beautiful moss rose in his hand.

'Here, Esther, I've brought you the rose,' said he, extending it towards her.

'Give it her yourself, you blockhead!' cried she, recoiling with a spring from between us.

'Mrs Huntingdon would rather receive it from you,' replied

he in a very serious tone, but lowering his voice that his mother might not hear. His sister took the rose and gave it to me.

'My brother's compliments, Mrs Huntingdon, and he hopes you and he will come to a better understanding by and by. – Will that do, Walter?' added the saucy girl, turning to him and putting her arm round his neck, as he stood leaning upon the sill of the window – 'or should I have said that you are sorry you were so touchy? or that you hope she will pardon your offence?'

'You silly girl! you don't know what you are talking about,' replied he gravely.

'Indeed I don't; for I'm quite in the dark.'

'Now Esther,' interposed Mrs Hargrave, who, if equally benighted on the subject of our estrangement, saw at least that her daughter was behaving very improperly, 'I must insist upon your leaving the room!'

'Pray don't, Mrs Hargrave, for I'm going to leave it myself,' said I, and immediately made my adieux.

About a week after, Mr Hargrave brought his sister to see me. He conducted himself, at first, with his usual cold, distant, half-stately, half-melancholy, altogether injured air; but Esther made no remark upon it this time; she had evidently been schooled into better manners. She talked to me, and laughed and romped with little Arthur, her loved and loving playmate. He, somewhat to my discomfort, enticed her from the room to have a run in the hall; and, thence, into the garden. I got up to stir the fire. Mr Hargrave asked if I felt cold, and shut the door – a very unseasonable piece of officiousness, for I had meditated following the noisy playfellows, if they did not speedily return. He then took the liberty of walking up to the fire himself, and asking me if I were aware that Mr Huntingdon was now at the seat of Lord Lowborough, and likely to continue there some time.

'No; but it's no matter,' I answered carelessly; and if my cheek glowed like fire, it was rather at the question than the information it conveyed.

'You don't object to it?' he said.

'Not at all, if Lord Lowborough likes his company.'

'You have no love left for him, then?'

'Not the least.'

'I knew that – I knew you were too high-minded and pure in your own nature to continue to regard one so utterly false and polluted, with any feelings but those of indignation and scornful abhorrence!'

'Is he not your friend?' said I, turning my eyes from the fire to his face, with perhaps a slight touch of those feelings he assigned to another.

'He *was*,' replied he, with the same calm gravity as before, 'but do not wrong me by supposing that I could continue my friendship and esteem to a man who could so infamously – so impiously forsake and injure one so transcendently – well, I won't speak of it. But tell me, do you never think of revenge?'

'Revenge! No – what good would that do? – it would make him no better, and me no happier.'

'I don't know how to talk to you, Mrs Huntingdon,' said he smiling; 'you are only half a woman – your nature must be half human, half angelic. Such goodness overawes me; I don't know what to make of it.'

'Then sir, I fear you must be very much worse than you should be, if I, a mere ordinary mortal, am by your own confession, so vastly your superior; – and since there exists so little sympathy between us, I think we had better each look out for some more congenial companion.' And forthwith moving to the window, I began to look out for my little son and his gay young friend.

'No, *I* am the ordinary mortal, I maintain,' replied Mr Hargrave. 'I will not allow myself to be worse than my fellows; but *you*, Madam – I equally maintain there is nobody like you. But are you happy?' he asked in a serious tone.

'As happy as some others, I suppose.'

'Are you as happy as you desire to be?'

'No one is so blest as that comes to, on this side eternity.'

'One thing I know,' returned he, with a deep, sad sigh; 'you are immeasurably happier than I am.'

'I am very sorry for you, then,' I could not help replying.

'Are you *indeed*? – No – for if you were, you would be glad to relieve me.'

'And so I should, if I could do so, without injuring myself or any other.'

'And can you suppose that I should wish you to injure yourself? – No; on the contrary, it is your own happiness I long for more than mine. You are miserable now, Mrs Huntingdon,' continued he, looking me boldly in the face. 'You do not complain, but I see – and feel – and know that you are miserable – and must remain so, as long as you keep those walls of impenetrable ice about your still warm and palpitating heart; – and I am miserable too. Deign to smile on me, and I am happy: trust me, and you shall be happy also, for if you *are* a woman, I can make you so – and I *will* do it in spite of yourself!' he muttered between his teeth, 'and as for others, the question is between ourselves alone: you cannot injure your husband, you know; and no one else has any concern in the matter.'

'I have a son, Mr Hargrave, and you have a mother,' said I, retiring from the window, whither he had followed me.

'They need not know,' he began, but before anything more could be said on either side, Esther and Arthur re-entered the room. The former glanced at Walter's flushed, excited countenance, and then at mine – a little flushed and excited too, I dare say, though from far different causes. She must have thought we had been quarrelling desperately, and was evidently perplexed and disturbed at the circumstance; but she was too polite, or too much afraid of her brother's anger to refer to it. She seated herself on the sofa, and putting back her bright, golden ringlets, that were scattered in wild profusion over her face, she immediately began to talk about the garden and her little playfellow, and continued to chatter away in her usual strain till her brother summoned her to depart.

'If I have spoken too warmly, forgive me,' he murmured on taking his leave, 'or I shall never forgive myself.' Esther smiled and glanced at me: I merely bowed, and her countenance fell. She thought it a poor return for Walter's generous concession, and was disappointed in her friend. Poor child, she little knows the world she lives in!

Mr Hargrave had not an opportunity of meeting me again in private for several weeks after this; but when he did meet me, there was less of pride and more of touching melancholy in his manner than before. Oh, *how* he annoyed me! I was obliged, at last almost entirely to remit my visits to the Grove, at the expense of deeply offending Mrs Hargrave and seriously afflicting poor Esther, who really values my society – for want of better, and who ought not to suffer for the fault of her brother. But that indefatigable foe was not yet vanquished: he seemed to be always on the watch. I frequently saw him riding lingeringly past the premises, looking searchingly round him as he went – or, if *I* did not, Rachel did. That sharp-sighted woman soon guessed how matters stood between us, and descrying the enemy's movements from her elevation at the nursery window, she would give me a quiet intimation, if she saw me preparing for a walk when she had reason to believe he was about, or to think it likely that he would meet or overtake me in the way I meant to traverse. I would then defer my ramble, or confine myself for that day to the park and gardens – or if the proposed excursion was a matter of importance, such as a visit to the sick or afflicted, I would take Rachel with me, and then I was never molested.

But one mild, sunshiny day, early in November, I had ventured forth alone, to visit the village school and a few of the poor tenants, and on my return, I was alarmed at the clatter of a horse's feet behind me approaching at a rapid, steady trot. There was no stile or gap at hand, by which I could escape into the fields: so I walked quietly on, saying to myself –

'It may not be he after all; and if it is, and if he *do* annoy me – it shall be for the last time – I am determined, if there be power in words and looks against cool impudence and mawkish sentimentality so inexhaustible as his.'

The horse soon overtook me, and was reined up close beside me. It *was* Mr Hargrave. He greeted me with a smile intended to be soft and melancholy, but his triumphant satisfaction at having caught me at last, so shone through, that it was quite a failure. After briefly answering his salutation and inquiring after the ladies at the Grove, I turned away and walked on; but he followed, and kept his horse at my side: it was evident he intended to be my companion all the way.

'Well! I don't much care. If you want another rebuff, take it – and welcome,' was my inward remark. 'Now sir, what next?'

This question, though unspoken, was not long unanswered: after a few passing observations upon indifferent subjects, he began, in solemn tones, the following appeal to my humanity: –

'It will be four years next April since I first saw you, Mrs Huntingdon, – *you* may have forgotten the circumstance, but *I* never can – I admired you then, most deeply, but I dared not love you: in the following autumn, I saw so much of your perfections that I could not fail to love you, though I dared not show it. For upwards of three years, I have endured a perfect martyrdom. From the anguish of suppressed emotions, intense and fruitless longings, silent sorrow, crushed hopes, and trampled affections, – I have suffered more than I can tell, or you imagine – and you were the cause of it – and not, altogether, the innocent cause. My youth is wasting away; my prospects are darkened; my life is a desolate blank; I have no rest day or night: I am become a burden to myself and others; – and you might save me by a word – a glance, and will not do it. – Is this right?'

'In the first place, I don't believe you,' answered I; 'in the second, if you will be such a fool, I can't hinder it.'

'If you affect,' replied he earnestly, 'to regard as folly, the best, the strongest, the most godlike impulses of our nature, – *I* don't believe *you* – I know you are not the heartless, icy being you pretend to be – you had a heart once, and gave it to your husband. When you found him utterly unworthy of the treasure you reclaimed it; – and you will not *pretend* that you loved that sensual, earthly minded profligate so deeply, so devotedly that you can never love another? – I know that there are feelings in your nature that have never yet been called forth – I know, too, that in your present neglected, lonely state you are, and *must* be miserable. You have it in your power to raise two human beings from a state of actual suffering to such unspeakable beatitude as only generous, noble self-forgetting love can give (for you *can* love me if you will; you may tell me that you scorn and detest me, but – since you have set me the example of plain speaking – I will answer that *I do not believe you!*), but you will not do it! you choose rather to leave us miserable; and you coolly tell me it is the will of God that we should remain so. *You* may call this religion, but *I* call it wild fanaticism!'

'There is another life both for you and for me,' said I. 'If it be the will of God that we should sow in tears, now, it is only that we may reap in joy, hereafter. It is His will that we should not injure others by the gratification of our own earthly passions; and you have a mother, and sisters, and friends, who would be seriously injured by your disgrace; and I too have friends, whose peace of mind shall never be sacrificed to my enjoyment – or yours either, with my consent – and if I were alone in the world, I have still my God and my religion, and I would sooner die than disgrace my calling and break my faith with Heaven to obtain a few brief years of false and fleeting happiness – happiness sure to end in misery, even here – for myself or any other!'

'There need be no disgrace – no misery or sacrifice in any quarter,' persisted he. 'I do not ask you to leave your home or defy the world's opinion.' – But I need not repeat all his arguments. I refuted them to the best of my power; but that power was provokingly small, at the moment, for I was too much flurried with indignation – and even shame – that he should thus dare to address me, to retain sufficient command of thought and language to enable me adequately to contend against his powerful sophistries. Finding, however, that he could not be silenced by reason, and even covertly exulted in his seeming advantage, and ventured to deride those assertions I had not the coolness to prove, I changed my course and tried another plan.

'Do you really love me?' said I seriously, pausing and looking him calmly in the face.

'Do I love you!' cried he.

'*Truly?*' I demanded.

His countenance brightened; he thought his triumph was at hand. He commenced a passionate protestation of the truth and fervour of his attachment which I cut short by another question: –

'But is it not a selfish love? – have you enough disinterested affection to enable you to sacrifice your own pleasure to mine?'

'I would give my life to serve you.'

'I don't want your life – but have you enough real sympathy for my afflictions to induce you to make an effort to relieve them, at the risk of a little discomfort to yourself?'

'Try me, and see.'

'If you have – *never mention this subject again*. You cannot recur to it in any way, without doubling the weight of those sufferings you so feelingly deplore. I have nothing left me but the solace of a good conscience and a hopeful trust in Heaven, and you labour continually to rob me of these. If you persist, I must regard you as my deadliest foe.'

'But hear me a moment –'

'No, sir! you said you would give your life to serve me: I only ask your *silence* on one particular point. I have spoken plainly; and what I say I mean. If you torment me in this way any more, I must conclude that your protestations are entirely false, and that you hate me in your heart as fervently as you profess to love me!'

He bit his lip and bent his eyes upon the ground in silence for a while.

'Then I must leave you,' said he at length, looking steadily upon me, as if with the last hope of detecting some token of irrepressible anguish or dismay awakened by those solemn words. 'I must leave you. I cannot live here, and be for ever silent on the all-absorbing subject of my thoughts and wishes.'

'Formerly, I believe, you spent but little of your time at home,' I answered: 'it will do you no harm to absent yourself again, for a while – if that be really necessary.'

'If that be really *possible*,' he muttered – 'and can you bid me go so coolly? Do you really wish it?'

'Most certainly I do. If you cannot see me without torment-ing me as you have lately done, I would gladly say farewell and never see you more.'

He made no answer, but, bending from his horse, held out his hand towards me. I looked up at his face, and saw, therein, such a look of genuine agony of soul that, whether bitter dis-appointment, or wounded pride, or lingering love, or burning wrath were uppermost, I could not hesitate to put my hand in his as frankly as if I bade a friend farewell. He grasped it very hard, and immediately put spurs to his horse and galloped away. Very soon after, I learned that he was gone to Paris, where he still is, and the longer he stays there the better for me.

I thank God for this deliverance!

END OF VOL. II

CHAPTER XXXVIII

THE INJURED MAN

DECEMBER 20TH, 1826. – The fifth anniversary of my wedding day, and I trust, the last I shall spend under this roof. My resolution is formed, my plan concocted, and already partly put in execution. My conscience does not blame me, but while the purpose ripens, let me beguile a few of these long winter evenings in stating the case for my own satisfaction – a dreary amusement enough, but having the air of a useful occupation, and being pursued as a task, it will suit me better than a lighter one.

In September, quiet Grassdale was again alive with a party of ladies and gentlemen (so called) consisting of the same individuals as those invited the year before last, with the addition of two or three others, among whom were Mrs Hargrave and her younger daughter. The gentlemen and Lady Lowborough were invited for the pleasure and convenience of the host; the other ladies, I suppose for the sake of appearances, and to keep me in check and make me discreet and civil in my demeanour. But the ladies stayed only three weeks, the gentlemen, with two exceptions, above two months, for their hospitable entertainer was loath to part with them and be left alone with his bright intellect, his stainless conscience, and his loved and loving wife.

On the day of Lady Lowborough's arrival, I followed her into her chamber, and plainly told her that, if I found reason to believe that she still continued her criminal connection with Mr Huntingdon, I should think it my absolute duty to inform her husband of the circumstance – or awaken his suspicions at least – however painful it might be, or however dreadful the consequences. She was startled at first, by the declaration, so unexpected, and so determinately yet calmly delivered; but rallying in a moment, she coolly replied that if I saw anything at all reprehensible or suspicious in her conduct, she would freely give me leave to tell his lordship all about it. Willing to be satisfied with this, I left her; and certainly I saw nothing thenceforth particularly reprehensible or suspicious in her demeanour towards her host; but then I had the other guests to attend to, and I did not watch them narrowly – for to confess the truth, I *feared* to see anything between them. I no longer regarded it as any concern of mine, and if it was my duty to enlighten Lord Lowborough, it was a painful duty, and I dreaded to be called to perform it.

But my fears were brought to an end, in a manner I had not anticipated. One evening, about a fortnight after the visitors' arrival, I had retired into the library to snatch a few minutes' respite from forced cheerfulness and wearisome discourse – for after so long a period of seclusion, dreary indeed, as I had often found it, I could not always bear to be doing violence to my feelings, and goading my powers to talk, and smile and listen, and play the attentive hostess – or even the cheerful friend: – I had just ensconced myself within the bow of the window, and was looking out upon the west where the darkening hills rose sharply defined against the clear amber light of evening, that gradually blended and faded away into the pure, pale blue of the upper sky, where one bright star was shining through, as if to promise – 'When that dying light is gone, the world will not be left in darkness, and they who trust in God – whose minds are unbeclouded by the mists of unbelief and sin, are never wholly comfortless,' – when I heard a hurried step approaching, and Lord Lowborough entered – this room was still his favourite resort. He flung the door to with unusual violence, and cast his hat aside regardless where it fell. What could be the matter with him? His face was ghastly pale; his eyes were fixed upon the ground; his teeth clenched; his forehead glistened with the dews of agony. It was plain he knew his wrongs at last!

Unconscious of my presence, he began to pace the room in a state of fearful agitation, violently wringing his hands and uttering low groans or incoherent ejaculations. I made a movement to let him know that he was not alone; but he was too pre-occupied to notice it. Perhaps, while his back was towards me, I might cross the room and slip away unobserved; I rose to make the attempt, but then he perceived me. He started and stood still a moment; then wiped his streaming forehead, and advancing towards me, with a kind of unnatural composure, said in a deep, almost sepulchral tone –

'Mrs Huntingdon, I must leave you to-morrow.'

'To-morrow!' I repeated, 'I do not ask the cause.'

'You know it then – and you can be so calm!' said he, surveying me with profound astonishment, not unmingled with a kind of resentful bitterness, as it appeared to me.

'I have so long been aware of –' I paused in time, and added, 'of my husband's character, that nothing shocks me.'

'But *this* – how long have you been aware of this?' demanded he, laying his clenched hand on the table beside him, and looking me keenly and fixedly in the face.

I felt like a criminal.

'Not long,' I answered.

'You knew it!' cried he with bitter vehemence – 'and you did not tell me! You helped to deceive me!'

'My lord, I did *not* help to deceive you.'

'Then why did you not tell me?'

'Because, I knew it would be painful to you – I hoped she would return to her duty, and then there would be no need to harrow your feelings with such —'

'O God! how long has this been going on? how long has it been, Mrs Huntingdon? – Tell me – I MUST know!' he exclaimed with intense and fearful eagerness.

'Two years, I believe.'

'Great Heaven! and she has duped me all this time!' He turned away with a suppressed groan of agony, and paced the room again, in a paroxysm of renewed agitation. My heart smote me; but I would try to console him, though I knew not how to attempt it.

'She is a wicked woman,' I said. 'She has basely deceived and betrayed you. She is as little worthy of your regret as she was of your affection. Let her injure you no farther: abstract yourself from her, and stand alone.'

'And you, Madam,' said he sternly, arresting his walk and turning round upon me – 'you have injured me too, by this ungenerous concealment!'

There was a sudden revulsion in my feelings. Something rose within me, and urged me to resent this harsh return for my heartfelt sympathy, and defend myself with answering severity. Happily, I did not yield to the impulse. I saw his anguish as, suddenly smiting his forehead, he turned abruptly to the window, and, looking upward at the placid sky, murmured passionately, 'O God, that I might die!' – and felt that to add one drop of bitterness to that already overflowing cup, would be ungenerous indeed. And yet, I fear there was more coldness than gentleness in the quiet tone of my reply: –

'I might offer many excuses that some would admit to be valid, but I will not attempt to enumerate them –'

'I know them,' said he hastily, 'you would say that it was no business of yours – that I ought to have taken care of myself – that if my own blindness has led me into this pit of hell, I have no right to blame another for giving me credit for a larger amount of sagacity than I possessed –'

'I confess I was wrong,' continued I, without regarding this bitter interruption; 'but whether want of courage or mistaken kindness was the cause of my error, I think you blame me too severely. I told Lady Lowborough two weeks ago, the very hour she came, that I should certainly think it my duty to inform you if she continued to deceive you: she gave me full liberty to do so if I should see anything reprehensible or suspicious in her conduct – I have seen nothing; and I trusted she had altered her course.'

He continued gazing from the window while I spoke, and did not answer, but, stung by the recollections my words awakened, stamped his foot upon the floor, ground his teeth, and corrugated his brow, like one under the influence of acute physical pain.

'It was wrong – it was wrong!' he muttered, at length. 'Nothing can excuse it – nothing can atone for it, – for nothing can recall those years of cursed credulity – nothing obliterate them! – nothing, nothing!' he repeated in a whisper whose despairing bitterness precluded all resentment.

'When I put the case to myself, I own it *was* wrong,' I answered; 'but I can only now regret that I did not see it in this light before, and that, as you say, nothing can recall the past.'

Something in my voice or in the spirit of this answer seemed to alter his mood. Turning towards me and attentively surveying my face by the dim light, he said in a milder tone than he had yet employed, –

'You too have suffered, I suppose.'

'I suffered much, at first.'

'When was that?'

'Two years ago; and two years hence you will be as calm as I am now, – and far, far happier, I trust, for you are a man, and free to act as you please.'

Something like a smile, but a *very* bitter one, crossed his face for a moment.

'You have not been happy lately?' he said with a kind of effort to regain composure, and a determination to waive the further discussion of his own calamity.

'Happy?' I repeated, almost provoked at such a question. – 'Could I be so, with such a husband?'

'I have noticed a change in your appearance since the first years of your marriage,' pursued he: 'I observed it to – to that infernal demon,' he muttered between his teeth – 'and he said it

was your own sour temper that was eating away your bloom:
it was making you old and ugly before your time, and had
already made his fire-side as comfortless as a convent cell. – You
smile Mrs Huntingdon – nothing moves you. I wish my nature
were as calm as yours.'

'My nature was not originally calm,' said I: 'I have learned
to appear so by dint of hard lessons, and many repeated efforts.'

At this juncture Mr Hattersley burst into the room.

'Hallow, Lowborough!' he began. – 'Oh! I beg your pardon,'
he exclaimed on seeing me; 'I didn't know it was a *tête-à-tête*.
Cheer up, man!' he continued, giving Lord Lowborough a
thump on the back, which caused the latter to recoil from him
with looks of ineffable disgust and irritation. 'Come, I want to
speak with you a bit.'

'Speak, then.'

'But I'm not sure it would be quite agreeable to the lady,
what I have to say.'

'Then it would not be agreeable to me,' said his lordship,
turning to leave the room.

'Yes, it would,' cried the other, following him into the hall.
'If you've the heart of a man it would be the very ticket for you.
It's just this, my lad,' he continued, rather lowering his voice,
but not enough to prevent me from hearing every word he said,
though the half-closed door stood between us: 'I think you're
an ill-used man – nay, now, don't flare up – I don't want to
offend you: it's only my rough way of talking. I must speak
right out you *know*, or else not at all; – and I'm come – stop
now! let me explain – I'm come to offer you my services, for
though Huntingdon is my friend, he's a devilish scamp as we
all know, and I'll be *your* friend for the nonce. I know what it
is you want, to make matters straight: it's just to exchange a
shot with him, and then you'll feel yourself all right again; and
if an accident happens – why, that'll be all right too, I dare say,
to a desperate fellow like you. – Come now! give me your hand,

and don't look so black upon it. Name time and place, and I'll manage the rest.'

'That,' answered the more low, deliberate voice of Lord Lowborough, 'is just the remedy my own heart – or the devil within it, suggested – to meet him, and *not to sever without blood*. Whether I or he should fall – or both, it would be an *inexpressible* relief to me, if –'

'Just so! Well then –'

'No!' exclaimed his lordship with deep, determined emphasis. 'Though I hate him from my heart, and should rejoice at any calamity that could befall him – I'll leave him to God; and though I abhor my own life, I'll leave that too, to Him that gave it.'

'But you see, in this case,' pleaded Hattersley –

'I'll not hear you!' exclaimed his companion, hastily turning away. 'Not another word! I've enough to do against the fiend within me.'

'Then you're a white livered fool, and I wash my hands of you,' grumbled the tempter as he swung himself round and departed.

'Right, right, Lord Lowborough!' cried I, darting out and clasping his burning hand, as he was moving away to the stairs. 'I begin to think the world is not worthy of you!'

Not understanding this sudden ebullition, he turned upon me with a stare of gloomy, bewildered amazement that made me ashamed of the impulse to which I had yielded; but soon a more humanized expression dawned upon his countenance, and, before I could withdraw my hand, he pressed it kindly, while a gleam of genuine feeling flashed from his eyes as he murmured, –

'God help us both!'

'Amen!' responded I; and we parted.

I returned to the drawing-room, where, doubtless, my presence would be expected by most, desired by one or two. In the ante-room was Mr Hattersley, railing against Lord Low-borough's poltroonery before a select audience, viz. Mr Hun-tingdon, who was lounging against the table exulting in his own treacherous villainy and laughing his victim to scorn, and Mr Grimsby, standing by, quietly rubbing his hands and chuckling with fiendish satisfaction. At the glance I gave them in passing, Hattersley stopped short in his animadversions and stared like a bull calf, Grimsby glowered upon me with a leer of malignant ferocity, and my husband muttered a coarse and brutal malediction.

In the drawing-room I found Lady Lowborough, evidently in no very enviable state of mind, and struggling hard to conceal her discomposure by an overstrained affectation of unusual cheerfulness and vivacity, very uncalled for under the circum-stances, for she had herself given the company to understand that her husband had received unpleasant intelligence from home, which necessitated his immediate departure, and that he had suffered it so to bother his mind that it had brought on a bilious headache, owing to which and the preparations he judged neces-sary to hasten his departure, she believed they would not have the pleasure of seeing him to-night. However, she asserted, it was only a business concern, and so she did not intend it should trouble *her*. She was just saying this as I entered, and she darted upon me such a glance of hardihood and defiance as at once astonished and revolted me.

'But I *am* troubled,' continued she, 'and vexed too, for I think it my duty to accompany his lordship, and of course I am very sorry to part with all my kind friends, so unexpectedly and so soon.'

'And yet, Annabella,' said Esther, who was sitting beside her, 'I never saw you in better spirits in my life.'

'Precisely so, my love; because I wish to make the best of your society, since it appears this is to be the last night I am to enjoy it, till Heaven knows when; and I wish to leave a good impression on you all,' – she glanced round, and seeing her aunt's eye fixed upon her, rather too scrutinizingly, as she probably thought, she started up and continued, – 'to which end I'll give you a song – shall I, aunt? shall I, Mrs Huntingdon? shall I, ladies and gentlemen – all? – Very well, I'll do my best to amuse you.'

She and Lord Lowborough occupied the apartments next to mine. I know not how *she* passed the night, but I lay awake the greater part of it listening to his heavy step pacing monotonously up and down his dressing-room, which was nearest my chamber. Once I heard him pause and throw something out of the window, with a passionate ejaculation; and in the morning, after they were gone, a keen-bladed clasp-knife was found on the grass-plot below; a razor, likewise was snapped in two and thrust deep into the cinders of the grate, but partially corroded by the decaying embers. So strong had been the temptation to end his miserable life, so determined his resolution to resist it.

My heart bled for him as I lay listening to that ceaseless tread. Hitherto, I had thought too much of myself, too little of him: now I forgot my own afflictions, and thought only of his – of the ardent affection so miserably wasted, the fond faith so cruelly betrayed, the – no, I will not attempt to enumerate his wrongs, – but I hated his wife and my husband more intensely than ever, and not for my sake, but for his.

'That man,' I thought, 'is an object of scorn to his friends and the nice-judging world. The false wife and the treacherous friend who have wronged him are not so despised and degraded as he; and his refusal to avenge his wrongs has removed him yet farther beyond the range of sympathy, and blackened his name with a deeper disgrace. He knows this; and it doubles his burden of wo. He sees the injustice of it, but he cannot bear up against it; he lacks that sustaining power of self-esteem which leads a man, exulting in his own integrity, to defy the malice of traducing foes and give them scorn for scorn – or, better still, which raises him above earth's foul and turbulent vapours, to repose in Heaven's eternal sunshine. He knows that God is just, but cannot see His justice now: he knows this life is short, and yet death seems insufferably far away; he believes there is a future state, but so absorbing is the agony of this that he cannot realize its rapturous repose. He can but bow his head to the storm, and cling, blindly, despairingly, to what he knows to be right. Like the shipwrecked mariner cleaving to a raft, blinded, deafened, bewildered, he feels the waves sweep over him, and sees no prospect of escape; and yet he knows he has no hope but this, and still, while life and sense remain, concentrates all his energies to keep it. Oh, that I had a friend's right to comfort him, and tell him that I never esteemed him so highly as I do this night!'

They departed early in the morning before any one else was down, except myself, and just as I was leaving my room, Lord Lowborough was descending to take his place in the carriage where his lady was already ensconced; and Arthur (or Mr Huntingdon as I prefer calling him, for the other is my child's name) had the gratuitous insolence to come out in his dressing-gown to bid his 'friend' good-bye.

'What, going already, Lowborough?' said he. 'Well, good morning.' He smilingly offered his hand.

I think the other would have knocked him down, had he not instinctively started back before that bony fist quivering with rage and clenched till the knuckles gleamed white and glistening through the skin. Looking upon him with a countenance livid with furious hate, Lord Lowborough muttered between his closed teeth, a deadly execration he would not have uttered had he been calm enough to choose his words, and departed.

'I call that an unchristian spirit now,' said the villain. 'But I'd never give up an old friend for the sake of a wife. You may have mine if you like, and I call that handsome – I *can* do no more than offer restitution, can I?'

But Lowborough had gained the bottom of the stairs, and was now crossing the hall; and Mr Huntingdon, leaning over the banisters, called out, – 'Give my love to Annabella! – and I wish you both a happy journey,' and withdrew laughing to his chamber.

He subsequently expressed himself rather glad she was gone: 'She was so deuced imperious and exacting,' said he: 'now I shall be my own man again, and feel rather more at my ease.'

I know nothing more of Lord Lowborough's subsequent proceedings but what I have heard from Milicent, who, though she is ignorant of the cause of his separation from her cousin, has informed me that such is the case; that they keep entirely separate establishments; that she leads a gay, dashing life in town and country, while he lives in strict seclusion at his old castle in the north. There are two children, both of whom he keeps under his own protection. The son and heir is a promising child nearly the age of my Arthur, and no doubt a source of some hope and comfort to his father; but the other, a little girl between one and two, with blue eyes and light auburn hair, he probably keeps from consciencious motives alone, thinking it wrong to abandon her to the teaching and example of such a woman as her mother. That mother never loved children, and has so little natural affection for her own that I question whether she will not regard it as a relief to be thus entirely separated from them, and delivered from the trouble and responsibility of their charge.

Not many days after the departure of Lord and Lady Lowborough, the rest of the ladies withdrew the light of their presence from Grassdale. Perhaps they might have stayed longer, but neither host nor hostess pressed them to prolong their visit – in fact, the former showed too plainly that he should be glad to get rid of them; – and Mrs Hargrave retired with her daughters and her grand-children (there are three of them now) to the Grove. But the gentlemen remained: Mr Huntingdon, as I intimated before, was determined to keep them as long as he could; and, being thus delivered from restraint, they gave a loose to all their innate madness, folly, and brutality, and made the house night after night one scene of riot, uproar, and confusion.

Who among them behaved the worst, or who the best, I can not distinctly say; for, from the moment I discovered how things would be, I formed the resolution of retreating upstairs or locking myself into the library the instant I withdrew from the dining-room, and not coming near them again till breakfast; – but this I must say for Mr Hargrave, that from all *I* could see of him, he was a model of decency, sobriety, and gentlemanly manners *in comparison* with the rest.

He did not join the party till a week or ten days after the arrival of the other guests; for he was still on the continent when they came, and I cherished the hope that he would not accept the invitation. Accept it he did, however, but his conduct towards me, for the first few weeks, was exactly what I should have wished it to be – perfectly civil and respectful without any affectation of despondency or dejection, and sufficiently distant without haughtiness, or any of such remarkable stiffness or iciness of demeanour as might be calculated to disturb or puzzle his sister, or call forth the investigation of his mother.

CHAPTER XXXIX

A SCHEME OF ESCAPE

M Y GREATEST SOURCE of uneasiness, in this time of trial, was my son, whom his father and his father's friends delighted to encourage in all the embryo vices a little child can show, and to instruct in all the evil habits he could acquire – in a word, to 'make a man of him' was one of their staple amusements; and I need say no more to justify my alarm on his account, and my determination to deliver him at any hazard from the hands of such instructors. I first attempted to keep him always with me or in the nursery, and gave Rachel particular injunctions never to let him come down to dessert as long as these 'gentlemen' stayed; but it was no use; these orders were immediately countermanded and over-ruled by his father: he was not going to have the little fellow moped to death between an old nurse and a cursed fool of a mother. So the little fellow came down every evening, in spite of his cross mamma, and learnt to tipple wine like papa, to swear like Mr Hattersley, and to have his own way like a man, and sent mamma to the devil when she tried to prevent him. To see such things done with the roguish naïveté of that pretty little child and hear such things spoken by that small infantile voice, was as peculiarly piquant and irresistibly droll to them as it was inexpressibly distressing and painful to me; and when he had set the table in a roar, he would look round delightedly upon them all, and add his shrill laugh to theirs. But if that beaming blue eye rested on me, its light would vanish for a moment, and he would say, in some concern, – 'Mamma, why don't *you* laugh? Make her laugh, papa – she never will.'

Hence, was I obliged to stay among these human brutes, watching an opportunity to get my child away from them, instead of leaving them immediately after the removal of the cloth, as I should always otherwise have done. He was never willing to go, and I frequently had to carry him away by force; for which he thought me very cruel and unjust; and sometimes his father would insist upon my letting him remain; – and then, I would leave him to his kind friends, and retire to indulge my bitterness and despair alone or to rack my brains for a remedy to this great evil.

But here again, I must do Mr Hargrave the justice to acknowledge that I never saw *him* laugh at the child's misdemeanours, nor heard him utter a word of encouragement to his aspirations after manly accomplishments. But when anything very extraordinary was said or done by the infant profligate, I noticed, at times, a peculiar expression in his face, that I could neither interpret nor define – a slight twitching about the muscles of the mouth – a sudden flash in the eye, as he darted a sudden glance at the child and then at me; and then, I could fancy there arose a gleam of hard, keen, sombre satisfaction in his countenance at the look of impotent wrath and anguish he was too certain to behold in mine. But on one occasion, when Arthur had been behaving particularly ill, and Mr Huntingdon and his guests had been particularly provoking and insulting to me in their encouragement of him, and I particularly anxious to get him out of the room, and on the very point of demeaning myself by a burst of uncontrollable passion – Mr Hargrave suddenly rose from his seat, with an aspect of stern determination, lifted the child from his father's knee, where he was sitting half tipsy, cocking his head and laughing at me, and execrating me with words he little knew the meaning of – handed him out of the room, and setting him down in the hall, held the door open for me, gravely bowed as I withdrew, and closed it after me. I heard high words exchanged between him and his already half-inebriated host as I departed, leading away my bewildered and disconcerted boy.

But this should not continue; my child must not be abandoned to this corruption: better far that he should live in poverty and obscurity with a fugitive mother, than in luxury and affluence with such a father. These guests might not be with us long, but they would return again; and he, the most injurious of the whole, his child's worst enemy, would still remain. I could endure it for myself, but for my son it must be borne no longer: the world's opinion and the feelings of my friends must be alike unheeded here, at least, alike unable to deter me from my duty. But where should I find an asylum, and how obtain subsistence for us both? Oh, I would take my precious charge at early dawn, take the coach to M—, flee to the port of —, cross the Atlantic, and seek a quiet, humble home in New England, where I would support myself and him by the labour of my hands. The palette

and the easel, my darling playmates once, must be my sober
toil-fellows now. But was I sufficiently skilful as an artist to
obtain my livelihood in a strange land, without friends and
without recommendation? No; I must wait a little; I must
labour hard to improve my talent and to produce something
worth while as a specimen of my powers, something to speak
favourably for me, whether as an actual painter or a teacher.
Brilliant success, of course, I did not look for, but some degree
of security from positive failure was indispensable – I must not
take my son to starve. And then I must have money for the
journey, the passage, and some little to support us in our retreat
in case I should be unsuccessful at first; and not too little either,
for who could tell how long I might have to struggle with the
indifference or neglect of others, or my own inexperience, or
inability to suit their tastes?

What should I do then? Apply to my brother, and explain
my circumstances and my resolves to him? No, no; even if I told
him *all* my grievances, which I should be very reluctant to do,
he would be certain to disapprove of the step: it would seem
like madness to him, as it would to my uncle and aunt, or to
Milicent. No; I must have patience and gather a hoard of my
own. Rachel should be my only confidant – I thought I could
persuade her into the scheme; and she should help me, first to
find out a picture dealer in some distant town; then, through
her means, I would privately sell what pictures I had on hand
that would do for such a purpose, and some of those I should
thereafter paint. Besides this, I would contrive to dispose of
my jewels – not the family jewels, but the few I brought with
me from home, and those my uncle gave me on my marriage.
A few months' arduous toil might well be borne by me, with
such an end in view; and in the interim, my son could not be
much more injured than he was already.

Having formed this resolution, I immediately set to work to
accomplish it. I might possibly have been induced to wax cool
upon it afterwards, or perhaps, to keep weighing the pros and

cons in my mind till the latter overbalanced the former, and I was driven to relinquish the project altogether, or delay the execution of it to an indefinite period, – had not something occurred to confirm me in that determination to which I still adhere, which I still think I did well to form, and shall do better to execute.

Since Lord Lowborough's departure, I had regarded the library as entirely my own, a secure retreat at all hours of the day. None of our gentlemen had the smallest pretensions to a literary taste, except Mr Hargrave; and he, at present, was quite contented with the newspapers and periodicals of the day. And if, by any chance, he should look in here, I felt assured he would soon depart on seeing me, for instead of becoming less cool and distant towards me, he had become decidedly more so since the departure of his mother and sisters, which was just what I wished. Here, then, I set up my easel, and here I worked at my canvass from daylight till dusk, with very little intermission saving when pure necessity, or my duties to little Arthur called me away – for I still thought proper to devote some portion of every day exclusively to his instruction and amusement. But contrary to my expectation, on the third morning, while I was thus employed, Mr Hargrave *did* look in, and did *not* immediately withdraw on seeing me. He apologized for his intrusion, and said he was only come for a book; but when he had got it, he condescended to cast a glance over my picture. Being a man of taste, he had something to say on this subject as well as another, and having modestly commented on it, without much encouragement from me, he proceeded to expatiate on the art in general. Receiving no encouragement in that either, he dropped it, but did not depart.

'You don't give us much of your company, Mrs Huntingdon,' observed he, after a brief pause, during which I went on coolly mixing and tempering my colours; 'and I cannot wonder at it, for you must be heartily sick of us all. I myself am so thoroughly ashamed of my companions, and so weary of their irrational

conversation and pursuits – now that there is no one to human-
ize them and keep them in check, since you have justly abandoned us to our own devices – that I think I shall presently
withdraw from amongst them – probably within this week –
and I cannot suppose you will regret my departure.'

He paused. I did not answer.

'Probably,' he added, with a smile, 'your only regret on the
subject will be, that I do not take all my companions along with
me. I flatter myself, at times, that though among them, I am
not of them; but it is natural that you should be glad to get rid
of me. I may regret this, but I cannot blame you for it.'

'I shall not rejoice at *your* departure, for you *can* conduct
yourself like a gentleman,' said I, thinking it but right to make
some acknowledgment for his good behaviour, 'but I must confess I shall rejoice to bid adieu to the rest, inhospitable as it may
appear.'

'No one can blame you for such an avowal,' replied he gravely:
'not even the gentlemen themselves, I imagine. I'll just tell you,'
he continued, as if actuated by a sudden resolution, 'what was
said last night in the dining-room, after you left us – perhaps
you will not mind it as you're so *very* philosophical on certain
points,' he added with a slight sneer. 'They were talking about
Lord Lowborough and his delectable lady, the cause of whose
sudden departure is no secret amongst them; and her character
is so well known to them all, that, nearly related to me as she
is, I could not attempt to defend it – God curse me,' he
muttered, *par parenthèse*, 'if I don't have vengeance for this!
If the villain *must* disgrace the family, must he blazon it abroad
to every low-bred knave of his acquaintance? – I beg your
pardon, Mrs Huntingdon. Well, they were talking of these
things, and some of them remarked that, as she was separated
from her husband, he might see her again when he pleased.'

' "Thank you," said he; "I've had enough of her for the
present: I'll not trouble to see her, unless she comes to me."

' "Then what do you mean to do, Huntingdon, when we're

gone?" said Ralph Hattersley. "Do you mean to turn from the error of your ways, and be a good husband, a good father, and so forth – as I do, when I get shut of you and all these rollicking devils you call your friends? I think it's time; and your wife is fifty times too good for you, you *know* –"

'And he added some praise of you, which you would not thank me for repeating – or him for uttering; proclaiming it aloud, as he did, without delicacy or discrimination, in an audience where it seemed profanation to utter your name – himself utterly incapable of understanding or appreciating your real excellencies. Huntingdon meanwhile, sat quietly drinking his wine, or looking smilingly into his glass and offering no interruption or reply, till Hattersley shouted out, –

' "Do you hear me, man?"

' "Yes, go on," said he.

' "Nay, I've done," replied the other: "I only want to know if you intend to take my advice."

' "What advice?"

' "To turn over a new leaf, you double-dyed scoundrel," shouted Ralph, "and beg your wife's pardon, and be a good boy for the future."

' "My wife! what wife? I have no wife," replied Huntingdon, looking innocently up from his glass – "or if I have, look you gentlemen, I value her so highly that any one among you, that can fancy her, may have her and welcome – you may, by Jove and my blessing into the bargain!"

'I – hem – some one asked if he really meant what he said, upon which, he solemnly swore he did, and no mistake. – What do you think of that, Mrs Huntingdon?' asked Mr Hargrave, after a short pause, during which I had felt he was keenly examining my half-averted face.

'I say,' replied I, calmly, 'that what he prizes so lightly, will not be long in his possession.'

'You cannot mean that you will break your heart and die for the detestable conduct of an infamous villain like that!'

'By no means: my heart is too thoroughly dried to be broken in a hurry, and I mean to live as long as I can.'

'Will you leave him then?'

'Yes.'

'When – and how?' asked he, eagerly.

'*When* I am ready, and *how* I can manage it most effectually.'

'But your child?'

'My child goes with me.'

'He will not allow it.'

'I shall not ask him.'

'Ah, then, it is a secret flight you meditate! – but with whom, Mrs Huntingdon?'

'With my son – and, possibly, his nurse.'

'Alone – and unprotected! But where can you go? What can you do? He will follow you and bring you back.'

'I have laid my plans too well for that. Let me once get clear of Grassdale, and I shall consider myself safe.'

Mr Hargrave advanced one step towards me, looked me in the face, and drew in his breath to speak; but that look, that heightened colour, that sudden sparkle of the eye made my blood rise in wrath: I abruptly turned away, and, snatching up my brush, began to dash away at my canvass with rather too much energy for the good of the picture.

'Mrs Huntingdon,' said he with bitter solemnity, 'you are cruel – cruel to me – cruel to yourself.'

'Mr Hargrave, remember your promise.'

'I *must* speak – my heart will burst if I don't! I have been silent long enough – and you *must* hear me!' cried he boldly intercepting my retreat to the door. 'You tell me you owe no allegiance to your husband; he openly declares himself weary of you, and calmly gives you up to any body that will take you; you are about to leave him; no one will believe that you go alone – all the world will say, "She has left him at last, and who can wonder at it? Few can blame her, fewer still can pity him; but who is the companion of her flight?" Thus you will have no credit for your virtue (if you call it such): even your best friends will not believe in it; because, it is monstrous, and not to be credited – but by those who suffer from the effects of it, such cruel torments that they know it to be indeed reality. – But what can you do in the cold, rough world alone? you, a young and inexperienced woman, delicately nurtured, and utterly –'

'In a word, you would advise me to stay where I am,' interrupted I. 'Well, I'll see about it.'

'By *all means*, leave him!' cried he earnestly, 'but NOT alone! Helen! let *me* protect you!'

'Never! – while Heaven spares my reason,' replied I, snatching away the hand he had presumed to seize and press between his own. But he was in for it now; he had fairly broken the barrier: he was completely roused, and determined to hazard all for victory.

'I must not be denied!' exclaimed he vehemently; and seizing both my hands, he held them very tight, but dropped upon his knee, and looked up in my face with a half-imploring, half-imperious gaze. 'You have no reason now: you are flying in the face of Heaven's decrees. God has designed me to be your comfort and protector – I feel it – I know it as certainly as if a voice from Heaven declared, "Ye twain shall be one flesh" – and you spurn me from you –'

'Let me go, Mr Hargrave!' said I sternly. But he only tightened his grasp.

'Let me go!' I repeated, quivering with indignation.

His face was almost opposite the window as he knelt. With a slight start, I saw him glance towards it; and then a gleam of malicious triumph lit up his countenance. Looking over my shoulder, I beheld a shadow just retiring round the corner.

'That is Grimsby,' said he deliberately. 'He will report what he has seen to Huntingdon and all the rest, with such embellishments as he thinks proper. He has no love for you, Mrs Huntingdon – no reverence for your sex – no belief in virtue – no admiration for its image. He will give such a version of this story as will leave no doubt at all, about your character, in the minds of those who hear it. Your fair fame is gone; and nothing that I or you can say can ever retrieve it. But give me the power to protect you, and show me the villain that dares to insult!'

'No one has ever dared to insult me as you are doing now!' said I, at length releasing my hands, and recoiling from him.

'I do not insult you,' cried he: 'I worship you. You are my angel – my divinity! I lay my powers at your feet – and you must and shall accept them!' he exclaimed impetuously, starting to his feet – 'I *will* be your consoler and defender! and if your conscience upbraid you for it, say I overcame you and you could not choose but yield!'

I never saw a man so terribly excited. He precipitated himself towards me. I snatched up my palette-knife and held it against him. This startled him: he stood and gazed at me in astonishment; I dare say I looked as fierce and resolute as he. I moved to the bell and put my hand upon the cord. This tamed him still more. With a half-authoritative, half-deprecating wave of the hand, he sought to deter me from ringing.

'Stand off, then!' said I. He stepped back. – 'And listen to me. – I don't like you,' I continued, as deliberately and emphatically as I could, to give the greater efficacy to my words; 'and if I were divorced from my husband – or if he were dead, I would not marry you. There now! I hope you're satisfied.'

His face grew blanched with anger.

'I *am* satisfied,' he replied with bitter emphasis, 'that you are the most cold-hearted, unnatural, ungrateful woman I ever yet beheld!'

'Ungrateful sir?'

'Ungrateful.'

'No, Mr Hargrave; I am not. For all the good you ever did me, or ever wished to do, I most sincerely thank you: for all the evil you have done me, and all you would have done, I pray God to pardon you, and make you of a better mind.'

Here the door was thrown open, and Messrs Huntingdon and Hattersley appeared without. The latter remained in the hall, busy with his ram-rod and his gun; the former walked in, and stood with his back to the fire, surveying Mr Hargrave and me, particularly the former, with a smile of insupportable meaning, accompanied as it was, by the impudence of his brazen brow and the sly, malicious twinkle of his eye.

'Well, sir?' said Hargrave interrogatively, and with the air of one prepared to stand on the defensive.

'Well, sir,' returned his host.

'We want to know if you're at liberty to join us in a go at the pheasants, Walter,' interposed Hattersley from without. 'Come! there shall be nothing shot besides, except a puss or two; *I'll* vouch for that.'

Walter did not answer, but walked to the window to collect his faculties. Arthur uttered a low whistle, and followed him with his eyes. A slight flush of anger rose to Hargrave's cheek; but in a moment, he turned calmly round, and said carelessly –

'I came here to bid farewell to Mrs Huntingdon, and tell her I must go to-morrow.'

'Humph! You're mighty sudden in your resolution. What takes you off so soon, may I ask?'

'Business,' returned he, repelling the other's incredulous sneer with a glance of scornful defiance.

'Very good,' was the reply; and Hargrave walked away. There-upon, Mr Huntingdon, gathering his coat laps under his arms, and setting his shoulder against the mantel-piece, turned to me, and, addressing me in a low voice, scarcely above his breath, poured forth a volley of the vilest and grossest abuse it was possible for the imagination to conceive or the tongue to utter. I did not attempt to interrupt him; but my spirit kindled within me, and when he had done, I replied –

'If your accusation were true, Mr Huntingdon, how *dare you* blame me?'

'She's hit it, by Jove!' cried Hattersley, rearing his gun against the wall; and, stepping into the room, he took his precious friend by the arm, and attempted to drag him away. 'Come, my lad,' he muttered; 'true or false, *you've* no right to blame her, you *know* – nor him either; after what you said last night. So come along.'

There was something implied here that I could not endure.

'Dare you suspect me, Mr Hattersley?' said I, almost beside myself with fury.

'Nay, nay, I suspect nobody. It's all right – it's all right. So come along Huntingdon, you blackguard.'

'She can't deny it!' cried the gentleman thus addressed, grinning in mingled rage and triumph. 'She can't deny it if her life depended on it!' and muttering some more abusive language, he walked into the hall, and took up his hat and gun from the table.

'I scorn to justify myself to you!' said I. 'But you,' turning to Hattersley, 'if you presume to have any doubts on the subject, ask Mr Hargrave.'

At this, they simultaneously burst into a rude laugh that made my whole frame tingle to the finger's ends.

'Where is he? I'll ask him myself!' said I, advancing towards them.

Suppressing a new burst of merriment, Hattersley pointed to the outer door. It was half open. His brother-in-law was standing on the front without.

'Mr Hargrave, will you please to step this way?' said I.

He turned and looked at me in grave surprise.

'Step this way, if you please!' I repeated, in so determined a manner that he could not, or did not choose to resist its authority. Somewhat reluctantly he ascended the steps and advanced a pace or two into the hall.

'And tell those gentlemen,' I continued – 'these *men* whether or not I yielded to your solicitations.'

'I don't understand you, Mrs Huntingdon.'

'You *do* understand me, sir; and I charge you upon your honour as a gentleman (if you have any), to answer truly. Did I, or did I not?'

'No,' muttered he, turning away.

'Speak up sir; they can't hear you. Did I grant your request?'

'You did not.'

'No, I'll be sworn she didn't,' said Hattersley, 'or he'd never look so black.'

'I'm willing to grant you the satisfaction of a gentleman, Huntingdon,' said Mr Hargrave, calmly addressing his host, but with a bitter sneer upon his countenance.

'Go to the deuce!' replied the latter, with an impatient jerk of the head. Hargrave withdrew with a look of cold disdain, saying, –

'You know where to find me, should you feel disposed to send a friend.'

Muttered oaths and curses were all the answer this intimation obtained.

'Now Huntingdon, you see!' said Hattersley, 'clear as the day.'

'I don't care *what* he sees,' said I, 'or what he imagines; but you, Mr Hattersley, when you hear my name belied and slandered, will you defend it?'

'I will. Blast me if I don't!'

I instantly departed, and shut myself into the library. What could possess me to make such a request of such a man? I cannot tell, but drowning men catch at straws: they had driven me desperate between them; I hardly knew what I said. There was no other to preserve my name from being blackened and aspersed among this nest of boon companions, and through them, perhaps into the world; and beside my abandoned wretch of a husband, the base, malignant Grimsby, and the false villain Hargrave, this boarish ruffian, coarse and brutal as he was, shone like a glow-worm in the dark, among its fellow worms.

What a scene was this! Could I ever have imagined that I should be doomed to bear such insults under my own roof – to hear such things spoken in my presence – nay spoken *to* me and *of* me – and by those who arrogated to themselves the name of gentlemen? And could I have imagined that I should have been able to endure it as calmly, and to repel their insults as firmly and as boldly as I had done? A hardness such as this, is taught by rough experience and despair alone.

Such thoughts as these, chased one another through my mind, as I paced to and fro the room, and longed – oh, *how* I longed to take my child and leave them now, without an hour's delay! But it could not be: there was work before me – hard work, that must be done.

'Then let me do it,' said I, 'and lose not a moment in vain repinings, and idle chafings against my fate, and those who influence it.'

And conquering my agitation with a powerful effort, I immediately resumed my task, and laboured hard all day.

Mr Hargrave did depart on the morrow; and I have never seen him since. The others stayed on for two or three weeks longer; but I kept aloof from them as much as possible, and still continued my labour, and have continued it, with almost unabated ardour, to the present day. I soon acquainted Rachel with my design, confiding all my motives and intentions to her ear, and much to my agreeable surprise, found little difficulty in persuading her to enter into my views. She is a sober, cautious woman, but she so hates her master, and so loves her mistress and her nursling, that after several ejaculations, a few faint objections, and many tears and lamentations that I should be brought to such a pass, she applauded my resolution and consented to aid me with all her might – on one condition, only – that she might share my exile: otherwise, she was utterly inexorable, regarding it as perfect madness for me and Arthur to go alone. With touching generosity, she modestly offered to aid me with her little hoard of savings, hoping I would 'excuse her for the liberty, but really if I would do her the favour to accept it as a loan, she should be very happy.' Of course I could not think of such a thing; – but now, thank Heaven, I have gathered a little hoard of my own, and my preparations are so far advanced, that I am looking forward to a speedy emancipation. Only let the stormy severity of this winter weather be somewhat abated, and then, some morning Mr Huntingdon will come down to a solitary breakfast-table, and perhaps be clamouring through the house for his invisible wife and child, when they are some fifty miles on their way to the western world – or it may be more, for we shall leave him hours before the dawn, and it is not probable he will discover the loss of both, until the day is far advanced.

I am fully alive to the evils that may, and must result upon the step I am about to take; but I never waver in my resolution, because I never forget my son. It was only this morning – while I pursued my usual employment, he was sitting at my feet, quietly playing with the shreds of canvass I had thrown upon the carpet – but his mind was otherwise occupied, for, in a while, he looked up wistfully in my face, and gravely asked –

'Mamma, why are you wicked?'

'Who told you I was wicked, love?'

'Rachel.'

'No, Arthur, Rachel never said so, I am certain.'

'Well then, it was papa,' replied he thoughtfully. Then, after a reflective pause, he added, 'At least, I'll tell you how it was I got to know: when I'm with papa, if I say mamma wants me, or mamma says I'm not to do something that he tells me to do – he always says, "Mamma be damned," – and Rachel says it's only wicked people that are damned. So, mamma, that's why I think you must be wicked – and I wish you wouldn't.'

'My dear child, I am not. Those are bad words, and wicked people often say them of others better than themselves. Those words cannot make people be damned, nor show that they deserve it. God will judge us by our own thoughts and deeds, not by what others say about us. And when you hear such words spoken, Arthur, remember never to repeat them: it is wicked to say such things of others, not to have them said against you.'

'Then it's papa that's wicked,' said he, ruefully.

'Papa is wrong to say such things, and you will be very wrong to imitate him, now that you know better.'

'What *is* imitate?'

'To do as he does.'

'Does *he* know better?'

'Perhaps he does; but that is nothing to you.'

'If he doesn't, you ought to tell him, mamma.'

'I *have* told him.'

The little moralist paused and pondered. I tried in vain to divert his mind from the subject.

'I'm sorry papa's wicked,' said he mournfully, at length, 'for I don't want him to go to hell.' And so saying he burst into tears.

I consoled him with the hope that perhaps his papa would alter and become good before he died – but is it not time to deliver him from such a parent?

CHAPTER XL

A MISADVENTURE

JAN. 10TH, 1827. While writing the above, yesterday evening, I sat in the drawing-room. Mr Huntingdon was present, but, as I thought, asleep on the sofa behind me. He had risen however, unknown to me, and, actuated by some base spirit of curiosity, been looking over my shoulder for I know not how long; for when I had laid aside my pen, and was about to close the book, he suddenly placed his hand upon it, and saying – 'With your leave, my dear, I'll have a look at this,' forcibly wrested it from me, and, drawing a chair to the table, composedly sat down to examine it – turning back leaf after leaf to find an explanation of what he had read. Unluckily for me, he was more sober that night than he usually is at such an hour.

Of course I did not leave him to pursue this occupation in quiet: I made several attempts to snatch the book from his hands, but he held it too firmly for that; I upbraided him in bitterness and scorn for his mean and dishonourable conduct, but that had no effect upon him; and, finally, I extinguished both the candles, but he only wheeled round to the fire, and raising a blaze sufficient for his purposes, calmly continued the investigation. I had serious thoughts of getting a pitcher of water and extinguishing that light too; but it was evident his curiosity was too keenly excited to be quenched by that, and the more I manifested my anxiety to baffle his scrutiny, the greater would be his determination to persist in it – besides it was too late.

'It seems very interesting, love,' said he, lifting his head and turning to where I stood wringing my hands in silent rage and anguish; 'but it's rather long; I'll look at it some other time; – and meanwhile, I'll trouble you for your keys, my dear.'

'What keys?'

'The keys of your cabinet, desk, drawers, and whatever else you possess,' said he, rising and holding out his hand.

'I've not got them,' I replied. The key of my desk, in fact, was, at that moment, in the lock, and the others were attached to it.

'Then you must send for them,' said he; 'and if that old bitch, Rachel, doesn't immediately deliver them up, she tramps bag and baggage to-morrow.'

'She doesn't know where they are,' I answered, quietly placing my hand upon them, and taking them from the desk, as I thought, unobserved. '*I* know, but I shall not give them up without a reason.'

'And *I* know, too,' said he, suddenly seizing my closed hand and rudely abstracting them from it. He then took up one of the candles and relighted it by thrusting it into the fire.

'Now, then,' sneered he, 'we must have a confiscation of property. But first, let us take a peep into the studio.'

And putting the keys into his pocket, he walked into the library. I followed, whether with the dim idea of preventing mischief or only to know the worst I can hardly tell. My painting materials were laid together on the corner table, ready for to-morrow's use, and only covered with a cloth. He soon spied them out, and putting down the candle, deliberately proceeded to cast them into the fire – palette, paints, bladders, pencils, brushes, varnish – I saw them all consumed – the palette-knives snapped in two – the oil and turpentine sent hissing and roaring up the chimney. He then rang the bell.

'Benson, take those things away,' said he, pointing to the easel, canvass, and stretcher; 'and tell the housemaid she may kindle the fire with them: your mistress won't want them any more.'

Benson paused aghast and looked at me.

'Take them away, Benson,' said I; and his master muttered an oath.

'And this and all, sir?' said the astonished servant referring to the half-finished picture.

'That and all,' replied the master; and the things were cleared away.

Mr Huntingdon then went up stairs. I did not attempt to follow him, but remained seated in the arm-chair, speechless, tearless, and almost motionless, till he returned about half an hour after, and walking up to me, held the candle in my face and peered into my eyes with looks and laughter too insulting to be borne. With a sudden stroke of my hand, I dashed the candle to the floor.

'Hal-lo!' muttered he, starting back. – 'She's the very devil for spite! Did *ever* any mortal see such eyes? – they shine in the dark like a cat's. *Oh*, you're a sweet one!' So saying, he gathered up the candle and the candlestick. The former being broken as well as extinguished, he rang for another.

'Benson, your mistress has broken the candle: bring another.'

'You expose yourself finely,' observed I as the man departed.

'I didn't say *I'd* broken it, did I?' returned he. He then threw my keys into my lap, saying, – 'There! you'll find nothing gone but your money, and the jewels – and a few little trifles I thought it advisable to take into my own possession, lest your mercantile spirit should be tempted to turn them into gold. I've left you a few sovereigns in your purse, which I expect to last you through the month – at all events, when you want more you will be so good as to give me an account of how that's spent. I shall put you upon a small monthly allowance, in future, for your own private expenses; and you needn't trouble yourself any more about my concerns; I shall look out for a steward, my dear; I won't expose you to the temptation. And as for the household matters, Mrs Greaves must be very particular in keeping her accounts: we must go upon an entirely new plan –'

'What great discovery have you made *now*, Mr Huntingdon? Have I attempted to defraud you?'

'Not in money matters, exactly, it seems, but it's best to keep out of the way of temptation.'

Here Benson entered with the candles, and there followed a brief interval of silence – I sitting still in my chair, and he standing with his back to the fire, silently triumphing in my despair.

'And so,' said he at length, 'you thought to disgrace me, did you, by running away and turning artist, and supporting yourself by the labour of your hands, forsooth? And you thought to rob me of my son too, and bring him up to be a dirty Yankee tradesman, or a low, beggarly painter?'

'Yes, to obviate his becoming such a gentleman as his father.'

'It's well you couldn't keep your own secret – ha, ha! It's well these women must be blabbing – if they haven't a friend to talk to, they must whisper their secrets to the fishes, or write them on the sand or something; and it's well too I wasn't over full to-night, now I think of it, or I might have snoozed away and never dreamt of looking what my sweet lady was about – or I might have lacked the sense or the power to carry my point like a man, as I have done.'

Leaving him to his self-congratulations, I rose to secure my manuscript, for I now remembered it had been left upon the drawing-room table, and I determined, if possible, to save myself the humiliation of seeing it in his hands again. I could not bear the idea of his amusing himself over my secret thoughts and recollections; though, to be sure, he would find little good of himself therein indited, except in the former part – and oh, I would sooner burn it all than he should read what I had written when I was such a fool as to love him!

'And by the by,' cried he as I was leaving the room, 'you'd better tell that d——d old sneak of a nurse to keep out of my way for a day or two – I'd pay her her wages and send her packing to-morrow, but I know she'd do more mischief out of the house than in it.'

And as I departed, he went on cursing and abusing my faithful friend and servant with epithets I will not defile this paper with repeating. I went to her as soon as I had put away my book, and told her how our project was defeated. She was as much distressed and horrified as I was – and more so than I was that night, for I was partly stunned by the blow, and partly excited and supported against it by the bitterness of my wrath. But in the morning, when I woke without that cheering hope that had been my secret comfort and support so long, and all this day, when I have wandered about restless and objectless, shunning my husband, shrinking even from my child – knowing that I am unfit to be his teacher or companion, hoping nothing for his future life, and fervently wishing he had never been born – I felt the full extent of my calamity – and I feel it now. I know that day after day such feelings will return upon me: I am a slave, a prisoner – but that is nothing; if it were myself alone, I would not complain, but I am forbidden to rescue my son from ruin, and what was once my only consolation, is become the crowning source of my despair.

Have I no faith in God? I try to look to Him and raise my heart to Heaven, but it will cleave to the dust: I can only say –

'He hath hedged me about, that I cannot get out: He hath made my chain heavy. He hath filled me with bitterness, He hath made me drunken with wormwood:' – I forget to add – 'But though He cause grief, yet will He have compassion according to the multitude of His mercies. For He doth not afflict willingly nor grieve the children of men.' I ought to think of this; and if there be nothing but sorrow for me in this world, what is the longest life of misery to a whole eternity of peace? And for my little Arthur – has he no friend but me? Who was it said, 'It is not the will of your Father which is in Heaven that one of these little ones should perish'?

CHAPTER XLI

'HOPE SPRINGS ETERNAL IN THE HUMAN BREAST'

MARCH 20TH. – Having now got rid of Mr Huntingdon for a season, my spirits begin to revive. He left me early in February; and the moment he was gone, I breathed again, and felt my vital energy return; not with the hope of escape – he has taken care to leave me no visible chance of that – but with a determination to make the best of existing circumstances. Here was Arthur left to me at last; and rousing from my despondent apathy, I exerted all my powers to eradicate the weeds that had been fostered in his infant mind, and sow again the good seed they had rendered unproductive. Thank Heaven, it is not a barren or a stony soil; if weeds spring fast there, so do better plants. His apprehensions are more quick, his heart more overflowing with affection than ever his father's could have been; and it is no hopeless task to bend him to obedience and win him to love and know his own true friend, as long as there is no one to counteract my efforts.

I had much trouble at first in breaking him of those evil habits his father had taught him to acquire, but already that difficulty is nearly vanquished now: bad language seldom defiles his mouth, and I have succeeded in giving him an absolute disgust for all intoxicating liquors, which I hope not even his father or his father's friends will be able to overcome. He was inordinately fond of them for so young a creature, and, remembering my unfortunate father as well as his, I dreaded the consequences of such a taste. But if I had stinted him in his usual quantity of wine or forbidden him to taste it altogether, that would only have increased his partiality for it, and made him regard it as a greater treat than ever. I therefore gave him quite as much as his father was accustomed to allow him – as much indeed, as he desired to have, but into every glass I surreptitiously introduced a small quantity of tartar-emetic – just enough to produce inevitable nausea and depression without positive sickness. Finding such disagreeable consequences invariably to result from this indulgence, he soon grew weary of it, but the more he shrank from the daily treat the more I pressed it upon him, till his reluctance was strengthened to perfect abhorrence. When he was thoroughly disgusted with every kind of wine, I allowed him, at his own request, to try brandy and water and then gin and water; for the little toper was familiar with them all, and I was determined that all should be equally hateful to him. This I have now effected; and since he declares that the taste, the smell, the sight of any one of them is sufficient to make him sick, I have given up teasing him about them, except now and then as objects of terror in cases of misbehaviour: 'Arthur, if you're not a good boy I shall give you a glass of wine,' or 'Now Arthur, if you say that again you shall have some brandy and water,' is as good as any other threat; and, once or twice, when he was sick, I have obliged the poor

child to swallow a little wine and water *without* the tartar-
emetic, by way of medicine; and this practice I intend to continue for some time to come; not that I think it of any real
service in a physical sense, but because I am determined to enlist
all the powers of association in my service: I wish this aversion
to be so deeply grounded in his nature that nothing in after life
may be able to overcome it.

Thus, I flatter myself, I shall secure him from this one vice;
and for the rest, if on his father's return I find reason to apprehend that my good lessons will be all destroyed – if Mr Huntingdon commence again the game of teaching the child to hate
and despise his mother and emulate his father's wickedness,
I will yet deliver my son from his hands. I have devised another
scheme that might be resorted to in such a case, and if I could
but obtain my brother's consent and assistance, I should not
doubt of its success. The old Hall where he and I were born and
where our mother died, is not now inhabited, nor yet quite sunk
into decay, as I believe. Now if I could persuade him to have
one or two rooms made habitable and to let them to me as a
stranger, I might live there, with my child, under an assumed
name, and still support myself by my favourite art. He should
lend me the money to begin with, and I would pay him back,
and live in lowly independence and strict seclusion, for the
house stands in a lonely place, and the neighbourhood is thinly
inhabited, and he himself should negotiate the sale of my
pictures for me. I have arranged the whole plan in my head; and
all I want, is to persuade Frederick to be of the same mind as
myself. He is coming to see me soon, and then I will make the
proposal to him, having first enlightened him upon my circumstances sufficiently to excuse the project.

Already, I believe, he knows much more of my situation than
I have told him. I can tell this by the air of tender sadness pervad-
ing his letters; and by the fact of his so seldom mentioning my
husband, and generally evincing a kind of covert bitterness
when he does refer to him; as well as by the circumstances of

his never coming to see me when Mr Huntingdon is at home. But he has never openly expressed any disapprobation of him or sympathy for me; he has never asked any questions, or said anything to invite my confidence. Had he done so, I should probably have had but few concealments from him. Perhaps he feels hurt at my reserve. He is a strange being – I wish we knew each other better. He used to spend a month at Staningley every year, before I was married; but, since our father's death, I have only seen him once, when he came for a few days while Mr Huntingdon was away. He shall stay many days this time, and there shall be more candour and cordiality between us than ever there was before, since our early childhood: my heart clings to him more than ever; and my soul is sick of solitude.

April 16th. – He is come and gone. He would not stay above a fortnight. The time passed quickly, but very, very happily, and it has done me good. I must have a bad disposition, for my misfortunes have soured and embittered me exceedingly: I was beginning insensibly to cherish very unamiable feelings against my fellow mortals – the male part of them especially; but it is a comfort to see there is at least one among them worthy to be trusted and esteemed; and doubtless there are more, though I have never known them – unless I except poor Lord Lowborough, and he was bad enough in his day; but what would Frederick have been, if he had lived in the world, and mingled from his childhood with such men as these of my acquaintance? and what *will* Arthur be, with all his natural sweetness of disposition, if I do not save him from that world and those companions? I mentioned my fears to Frederick and introduced the subject of my plan of rescue on the evening after his arrival, when I presented my little son to his uncle.

'He is like you, Frederick,' said I, 'in some of his moods: I sometimes think he resembles you more than his father; and I am glad of it.'

'You flatter me, Helen,' replied he, stroking the child's soft, wavy locks.

'No, – you will think it no compliment when I tell you I would rather have him to resemble *Benson* than his father.'

He slightly elevated his eyebrows, but said nothing.

'Do you know what sort of man Mr Huntingdon is?' said I.

'I think I have an idea.'

'Have you so clear an idea that you can hear, without surprise or disapproval, that I meditate escaping with that child to some secret asylum where we can live in peace, and never see him again?'

'Is it really so?'

'If you have not,' continued I, 'I'll tell you something more about him' – and I gave a sketch of his general conduct, and a more particular account of his behaviour with regard to his child, and explained my apprehensions on the latter's account, and my determination to deliver him from his father's influence.

Frederick was exceedingly indignant against Mr Huntingdon, and very much grieved for me; but still, he looked upon my project as wild and impracticable; he deemed my fears for Arthur disproportioned to the circumstances, and opposed so many objections to my plan, and devised so many milder methods for ameliorating my condition, that I was obliged to enter into further details to convince him that my husband was utterly incorrigible, and that nothing could persuade him to give up his son whatever became of me, he being as fully determined the child should not leave him, as I was not to leave the child; and that, in fact, nothing would answer but this, unless I fled the country as I had intended before. To obviate that, he at length consented to have one wing of the old Hall put into a habitable condition, as a place of refuge against a time of need; but hoped I would not take advantage of it, unless circumstances should render it really necessary, which I was ready enough to promise; for though, for my own sake, such a hermitage appears like paradise itself compared with my present situation, yet for my friends' sakes – for Milicent and Esther, my sisters in heart and affection, for the poor tenants of Grassdale, and above all for my aunt – I will stay if I possibly can.

July 29th. – Mrs Hargrave and her daughter are come back from London. Esther is full of her first season in town; but she is still heart-whole and unengaged. Her mother sought out an excellent match for her, and even brought the gentleman to lay his heart and fortune at her feet; but Esther had the audacity to refuse the noble gifts. He was a man of good family and large possessions, but the naughty girl maintained he was old as Adam, ugly as sin, and hateful as — one who shall be nameless.

'But, indeed, I had a hard time of it,' said she: 'mamma was very greatly disappointed at the failure of her darling project, and very, very angry at my obstinate resistance to her will, – and is so still; but I can't help it. And Walter, too, is so seriously displeased at my perversity and absurd caprice, as he calls it, that I fear he will never forgive me – I did not think he *could* be so unkind as he has lately shown himself. But Milicent begged me not to yield, and I'm sure, Mrs Huntingdon, if you had seen the man they wanted to palm upon me, you would have advised me not to take him too.'

'I should have done so whether I had seen him or not,' said I. 'It is enough that you dislike him.'

'I knew you would say so; though mamma affirmed you would be quite shocked at my undutiful conduct – you can't imagine how she lectures me – I am disobedient and ungrateful; I am thwarting her wishes, wronging my brother, and making myself a burden on her hands – I sometimes fear she'll overcome me after all. I have a strong will, but so has she, and when she says such bitter things, it provokes me to such a pass that I feel inclined to do as she bids me, and then break my heart and say, "There, mamma, it's all your fault!" '

'Pray don't!' said I. 'Obedience from such a motive would be positive wickedness, and certain to bring the punishment it deserves. Stand firm, and your mamma will soon relinquish her persecution; – and the gentleman himself will cease to pester you with his addresses if he finds them steadily rejected.'

'Oh, no! mamma will weary all about her before she tires herself with her exertions; and as for Mr Oldfield, she has given him to understand that I have refused his offer, not from any dislike of his person, but merely because I am giddy and young, and cannot at present reconcile myself to the thoughts of marriage under any circumstances: but, by next season, she has no doubt, I shall have more sense, and hopes my girlish fancies will be worn away. So she has brought me home, to school me into a proper sense of my duty, against the time comes round again – indeed, I believe she will not put herself to the expense of taking me up to London again, unless I surrender: she cannot afford to take me to town for pleasure and nonsense, she says, and it is not *every* rich gentleman that will consent to take me without a fortune, whatever exalted ideas I may have of my own attractions.'

'Well, Esther, I pity you; but still, I repeat, stand firm. You might as well sell yourself to slavery at once, as marry a man you dislike. If your mother and brother are unkind to you, you may leave them, but remember you are bound to your husband for life.'

'But I cannot leave them unless I get married, and I cannot get married if nobody sees me. I saw one or two gentlemen in London, that I might have liked, but they were younger sons, and mamma would not let me get to know them – one especially, who I believe rather liked me, but she threw every possible obstacle in the way of our better acquaintance – wasn't it provoking?'

'I have no doubt you would feel it so, but it is possible that if you married him, you might have more reason to regret it hereafter, than if you married Mr Oldfield. When I tell you not to marry *without* love, I do not advise you to marry for love alone – there are many, many other things to be considered. Keep both heart and hand in your own possession, till you see good reason to part with them; and if such an occasion should never present itself, comfort your mind with this reflection: that, though in single life your joys may not be very many, your sorrows at least will not be more than you can bear. Marriage *may* change your circumstances for the better, but in my private opinion, it is far more likely to produce a contrary result.'

'So thinks Milicent, but allow me to say, *I* think otherwise. If I thought myself doomed to oldmaidenhood, I should cease to value my life. The thought of living on, year after year at the Grove – a hanger-on upon mamma and Walter – a mere cumberer of the ground (now that I know in what light they would regard it), is perfectly intolerable – I would rather run away with the butler.'

'Your circumstances are peculiar I allow; but have patience, love; do nothing rashly. Remember you are not yet nineteen, and many years are yet to pass before any one can set you down as an old maid: you cannot tell what Providence may have in store for you. And meantime, remember you have a *right* to the protection and support of your mother and brother, however they may seem to grudge it.'

'You are so grave, Mrs Huntingdon,' said Esther after a pause. 'When Milicent uttered the same discouraging sentiments concerning marriage, I asked if she was happy: she said she was; but I only half believed her; and now I must put the same question to you.'

'It is a very impertinent question,' laughed I, 'from a young girl to a married woman so many years her senior – and I shall not answer it.'

'Pardon me, dear *madam*,' said she, laughingly throwing herself into my arms, and kissing me with playful affection; but I felt a tear on my neck, as she dropped her head on my bosom and continued, with an odd mixture of sadness and levity, timidity and audacity, – 'I know you are not so happy as I mean to be, for you spend half your life alone at Grassdale, while Mr Huntingdon goes about enjoying himself where, and how he pleases. – I shall expect *my* husband to have no pleasures but what he shares with me; and if his greatest pleasure of all is not the enjoyment of my company – why – it will be the worse for him – that's all.'

'If such are your expectations of matrimony, Esther, you must indeed, be careful whom you marry – or rather, you must avoid it altogether.'

CHAPTER XLII

A REFORMATION

SEPT. IST. – No Mr Huntingdon yet. Perhaps he will stay among his friends till Christmas; and then, next spring, he will be off again. If he continue this plan, I shall be able to stay at Grassdale well enough – that is, I *shall* be able to stay, and that is enough; even an occasional bevy of friends at the shooting season, may be borne if Arthur get so firmly attached to me – so well established in good sense and principles, before they come, that I shall be able, by reason and affection, to keep him pure from their contaminations. Vain hope, I fear! but still, till such a time of trial comes, I will forbear to think of my quiet asylum in the beloved old Hall.

Mr and Mrs Hattersley have been staying at the Grove a fortnight; and as Mr Hargrave is still absent, and the weather was remarkably fine, I never passed a day without seeing my two friends, Milicent and Esther, either there or here. On one occasion, when Mr Hattersley had driven them over to Grassdale in the phaeton, with little Helen and Ralph, and we were all enjoying ourselves in the garden – I had a few minutes' conversation with that gentleman, while the ladies were amusing themselves with the children.

'Do you want to hear anything of your husband, Mrs Huntingdon?' said he.

'No, unless you can tell me when to expect him home.'

'I can't. – You don't want him, do you?' said he with a broad grin.

'No.'

'Well, I think you're better without him, sure enough – for my part, I'm downright weary of him. I told him I'd leave him if he didn't mend his manners – and he wouldn't; so I left him – you see I'm a better man than you think me; – and what's more, I have serious thoughts of washing my hands of him entirely, and the whole set of 'em, and comporting myself from this day forward, with all decency and sobriety as a Christian and the father of a family should do. – What do you think of that?'

'It is a resolution you ought to have formed long ago.'

'Well, I'm not thirty yet: it isn't too late, is it?'

'No; it is never too late to reform, as long as you have the sense to desire it, and the strength to execute your purpose.'

'Well, to tell you the truth, I've thought of it often and often before, but he's such devilish good company is Huntingdon, after all – you can't imagine what a jovial good-fellow he is when he's not fairly drunk, only just primed or half-seas-over – we all have a bit of a liking for him at the bottom of our hearts, though we can't respect him.'

'But should you wish yourself to be like him?'

'No, I'd rather be like myself, bad as I am.'

'You can't continue as bad as you are without getting worse – and more brutalized every day – and therefore more like him.'

I could not help smiling at the comical, half angry, half confounded look he put on at this rather unusual mode of address.

'Never mind my plain speaking,' said I; 'it is from the best of motives. But tell me, should you wish your sons to be like Mr Huntingdon – or even like yourself?'

'Hang it, no.'

'Should you wish your daughter to despise you – or, at least, to feel no vestige of respect for you, and no affection but what is mingled with the bitterest regret?'

'Oh, blast it, no! I couldn't stand that.'

'And finally, should you wish your wife to be ready to sink into the earth when she hears you mentioned; and to loathe the very sound of your voice, and shudder at your approach?'

'She never will; she likes me all the same, whatever I do.'

'Impossible, Mr Hattersley! you mistake her quiet submission for affection.'

'Fire and fury –'

'Now don't burst into a tempest at that – I don't mean to say she does not love you – she does, I know, a great deal better than you deserve – but I am quite sure, that if you behave better, she will love you more, and if you behave worse, she will love you less and less till all is lost in fear, aversion, and bitterness of soul, if not in secret hatred and contempt. But, dropping the subject of affection, should you wish to be the tyrant of her life – to take away all the sunshine from her existence, and make her thoroughly miserable?'

'Of course not; and I don't, and I'm not going to.'

'You have done more towards it than you suppose.'

'Pooh, pooh! she's not the susceptible, anxious, worriting creature you imagine: she's a little meek, peaceable, affectionate body; apt to be rather sulky at times, but quiet and cool in the main, and ready to take things as they come.'

'Think of what she was five years ago, when you married her, and what she is now.'

'I know – she was a little plump lassie then, with a pretty pink and white face: now, she's a poor little bit of a creature, fading and melting away like a snow-wreath – but hang it! – by Jupiter, that's not my fault!'

'What is the cause of it then? Not years, for she's only five and twenty.'

'It's her own delicate health, and – confound it, madam! what would you make of me? – and the children, to be sure, that worry her to death between them.'

'No, Mr Hattersley, the children give her more pleasure than pain: they are fine well dispositioned children –'

'I know they are – bless 'em!'

'Then why lay the blame on them? – I'll tell you what it is: it's silent fretting and constant anxiety on your account, mingled I suspect, with something of bodily fear on her own. When you behave well, she can only rejoice with trembling; she has no security, no confidence in your judgment or principles; but is continually dreading the close of such short-lived felicity: when you behave ill, her causes of terror and misery are more than any one can tell but herself. In patient endurance of evil, she forgets it is our duty to admonish our neighbours of their trans-gressions. – Since you *will* mistake her silence for indifference, come with me, and I'll show you one or two of her letters – no breach of confidence, I hope, since you are her other half.'

He followed me into the library. I sought out and put into his hands two of Milicent's letters; one dated from London and written during one of his wildest seasons of reckless dissipation; the other in the country during a lucid interval. The former was full of trouble and anguish; not accusing *him*, but deeply regret-ting his connection with his profligate companions, abusing Mr Grimsby and others, insinuating bitter things against Mr Huntingdon, and most ingeniously throwing the blame of her husband's misconduct on to other men's shoulders. The latter was full of hope and joy, yet with a trembling consciousness that this happiness would not last; praising his goodness to the skies, but with an evident, though but half expressed wish that it were based on a surer foundation than the natural impulses of the heart, and a half prophetic dread of the fall of that house so founded on the sand, – which fall had shortly after taken place, as Hattersley must have been conscious while he read.

Almost at the commencement of the first letter, I had the

unexpected pleasure of seeing him blush; but he immediately turned his back to me and finished the perusal at the window. At the second, I saw him, once or twice, raise his hand and hurriedly pass it across his face. Could it be to dash away a tear? When he had done, there was an interval spent in clearing his throat and staring out of the window, and then, after whistling a few bars of a favourite air, he turned round, gave me back the letters and silently shook me by the hand.

'I've been a cursed rascal, God knows,' said he as he gave it a hearty squeeze, 'but you see if I don't make amends for it – G—d d—n me if I don't!'

'Don't curse yourself, Mr Hattersley; if God had heard half your invocations of that kind, you would have been in hell long before now – and you *cannot* make amends for the past by doing your duty for the future, in as much as your duty is only what you *owe* to your Maker, and you cannot do *more* than fulfil it – another must make amends for your past delinquencies. If you intend to reform, invoke God's blessing, His mercy, and His aid; not His curse.'

'God help me, then – for I'm sure I need it. – Where's Milicent?'

'She's there, just coming in with her sister.'

He stepped out at the glass door, and went to meet them. I followed at a little distance. Somewhat to his wife's astonishment, he lifted her off from the ground and saluted her with a hearty kiss and a strong embrace; then, placing his two hands on her shoulders, he gave her, I suppose, a sketch of the great things he meant to do, for she suddenly threw her arms round him, and burst into tears, exclaiming, –

'Do, do, Ralph – we shall be so happy! How very, very good you are!'

'Nay, not I,' said he, turning her round and pushing her towards me. 'Thank *her*, it's her doing.'

Milicent flew to thank me, overflowing with gratitude. I disclaimed all title to it, telling her her husband was predisposed to amendment before I added my mite of exhortation and encouragement, and that I had only done what she might – and ought to – have done herself.

'Oh, no!' cried she, 'I couldn't have influenced him, I'm sure, by anything that I could have said. I should only have bothered him by my clumsy efforts at persuasion, if I had made the attempt.'

'You never tried me, Milly,' said he.

Shortly after, they took their leave. They are now gone on a visit to Hattersley's father. After that, they will repair to their country home. I hope his good resolutions will not fall through, and poor Milicent will not be again disappointed. Her last letter was full of present bliss and pleasing anticipations for the future; but no particular temptation has yet occurred to put his virtue to the test. Henceforth, however, she will doubtless be somewhat less timid and reserved, and he more kind and thoughtful. – Surely, then, her hopes are not unfounded; and I have one bright spot, at least, whereon to rest my thoughts.

CHAPTER XLIII

THE BOUNDARY PAST

OCTOBER 10TH. – Mr Huntingdon returned about three weeks ago. His appearance, his demeanour and conversation, and my feelings with regard to him, I shall not trouble myself to describe. The day after his arrival, however, he surprised me by the announcement of an intention to procure a governess for little Arthur: I told him it was quite unnecessary, not to say ridiculous, at the present season: I thought I was fully competent to the task of teaching him myself – for some years to come, at least: the child's education was the only pleasure and business of my life; and since he had deprived me of every other occupation, he might surely leave me that.

He said I was not fit to teach children, or to be with them: I had already reduced the boy to little better than an automaton, I had broken his fine spirit with my rigid severity; and I should freeze all the sunshine out of his heart, and make him as gloomy an ascetic as myself, if I had the handling of him much longer. And poor Rachel, too, came in for her share of abuse, as usual; he cannot endure Rachel, because he knows she has a proper appreciation of him.

I calmly defended our several qualifications as nurse and governess, and still resisted the proposed addition to our family; but he cut me short by saying it was no use bothering about the matter, for he had engaged a governess already, and she was coming next week; so that all I had to do was to get things ready for her reception. This was a rather startling piece of intelligence. I ventured to inquire her name and address, by whom she had been recommended, or how he had been led to make choice of her.

'She is a very estimable, pious young person,' said he; 'you needn't be afraid. Her name is Myers, I believe; and she was recommended to me by a respectable old dowager – a lady of high repute in the religious world. I have not seen her myself, and therefore cannot give you a particular account of her person and conversation, and so forth; but, if the old lady's eulogies are correct, you will find her to possess all desirable qualifications for her position – an inordinate love of children among the rest.'

All this was gravely and quietly spoken, but there was a laughing demon in his half-averted eye that boded no good I imagined. However, I thought of my asylum in —shire, and made no further objections.

When Miss Myers arrived, I was not prepared to give her a

very cordial reception. Her appearance was not particularly calculated to produce a favourable impression at first sight, nor did her manners and subsequent conduct, in any degree, remove the prejudice I had already conceived against her. Her attainments were limited, her intellect noways above mediocrity. She had a fine voice, and could sing like a nightingale, and accompany herself sufficiently well on the piano; but these were her only accomplishments. There was a look of guile and subtlety in her face, a sound of it in her voice. She seemed afraid of me, and would start if I suddenly approached her. In her behaviour, she was respectful and complaisant even to servility: she attempted to flatter and fawn upon me at first, but I soon checked that. Her fondness for her little pupil was overstrained, and I was obliged to remonstrate with her on the subject of over-indulgence and injudicious praise; but she could not gain his heart. Her piety consisted in an occasional heaving of sighs and uplifting of eyes to the ceiling, and the utterance of a few cant phrases. She told me she was a clergyman's daughter, and had been left an orphan from her childhood, but had had the good fortune to obtain a situation in a very pious family; and then she spoke so gratefully of the kindness she had experienced from its different members that I reproached myself for my uncharitable thoughts and unfriendly conduct, and relented for a time – but not for long; my causes of dislike were too rational, my suspicions too well founded for that; and I knew it was my duty to watch and scrutinize till those suspicions were either satisfactorily removed or confirmed.

I asked the name and residence of the kind and pious family. She mentioned a common name, and an unknown and distant place of abode, but told me they were now on the Continent, and their present address was unknown to her. I never saw her speak much to Mr Huntingdon; but he would frequently look into the school-room to see how little Arthur got on with his new companion, when I was not there. In the evening, she sat with us in the drawing-room, and would sing and play to amuse him – or *us*, as she pretended – and was very attentive to his wants, and watchful to anticipate them, though she only talked to me – indeed, he was seldom in a condition to be talked to. Had she been other than she was, I should have felt her presence a great relief to come between us thus, except, indeed, that I should have been thoroughly ashamed for any decent person to see him as he often was.

I did not mention my suspicions to Rachel; but she, having sojourned for half a century in this land of sin and sorrow, has learned to be suspicious herself. She told me from the first she was 'down of that new governess,' and I soon found she watched her quite as narrowly as I did; and I was glad of it, for I longed to know the truth: the atmosphere of Grassdale seemed to stifle me, and I could only live by thinking of Wildfell Hall.

At last, one morning, she entered my chamber with such intelligence that my resolution was taken before she had ceased to speak. While she dressed me, I explained to her my intentions and what assistance I should require from her, and told her which of my things she was to pack up, and what she was to leave behind for herself, as I had no other means of recompencing her for this sudden dismissal, after her long and faithful service – a circumstance I most deeply regretted but could not avoid.

'And what will you do, Rachel?' said I – 'will you go home, or seek another place?'

'I have no home, ma'am, but with you,' she replied; 'and if I leave you I'll never go into place again as long as I live.'

'But I can't afford to live like a lady now,' returned I: 'I must be my own maid and my child's nurse.'

'What *signifies*?' replied she in some excitement. 'You'll want somebody to clean and wash, and cook, won't you? I can do all that; and never mind the wages – I've my bits o' savings yet, and if you wouldn't take me, I should have to find my own board and lodging out of 'em somewhere, or else work among strangers – and it's what I'm not used to – so you can please yourself ma'am.' Her voice quavered as she spoke, and the tears stood in her eyes.

'I should like it above all things, Rachel, and I'd give you such wages as I could afford – such as I should give to any servant of all work I might employ; but don't you see I should be dragging you down with me, when you have done nothing to deserve it?'

'Oh, fiddle!' ejaculated she.

'And besides, my future way of living will be so widely different to the past – so different to all you have been accustomed to –'

'Do you think, ma'am, I can't bear what my missis can? – surely I'm not so proud and so dainty as that comes to – and my little master too, God bless him?'

'But I'm young, Rachel; I shan't mind it; and Arthur is young too – it will be nothing to him.'

'Nor me either: I'm not so old but what I can stand hard fare and hard work, if it's only to help and comfort them as I've loved like my own barns – for all I'm too old to bide the thoughts o' leaving 'em in trouble and danger, and going amongst strangers myself.'

'Then you shan't, Rachel!' cried I, embracing my faithful friend. 'We'll all go together, and you shall see how the new life suits you.'

'Bless you, honey!' cried she affectionately returning my embrace. 'Only let us get shut of this wicked house and we'll do right enough, you'll see.'

'So think I,' was my answer; – and so that point was settled.

By that morning's post, I despatched a few hasty lines to Frederick, beseeching him to prepare my asylum for my immediate reception – for I should probably come to claim it within a day after the receipt of that note, – and telling him in few words, the cause of my sudden resolution. I then wrote three letters of adieu: the first to Esther Hargrave, in which I told her that I found it impossible to stay any longer at Grassdale, or to leave my son under his father's protection; and, as it was of the last importance that our future abode should be unknown to him and his acquaintance, I should disclose it to no one but my brother, through the medium of whom I hoped still to correspond with my friends. I then gave her his address, exhorted her to write frequently, reiterated some of my former admonitions regarding her own concerns, and bade her a fond farewell.

The second was to Milicent; much to the same effect, but a little more confidential, as befitted our longer intimacy, and her greater experience and better acquaintance with my circumstances.

The third was to my aunt – a much more difficult and painful undertaking, and therefore I had left it to the last; but I must give her some explanation of that extraordinary step I had taken, – and that quickly, for she and my uncle would no doubt hear of it within a day or two after my disappearance, as it was probable that Mr Huntingdon would speedily apply to them to know what was become of me. At last however, I told her I was sensible of my error: I did not complain of its punishment, and I was sorry to trouble my friends with its consequences; but in duty to my son, I must submit no longer; it was absolutely necessary that he should be delivered from his father's corrupting influence. I should not disclose my place of refuge even to her, in order that she and my uncle might be able, with truth, to deny all knowledge concerning it; but any communications addressed to me under cover to my brother, would be certain to reach me. I hoped she and my uncle would pardon the step I had taken, for if they knew all, I was sure they would not blame me; and I trusted they would not afflict themselves on my account, for if I could only reach my retreat in safety and keep it unmolested, I should be very happy, but for the thoughts of them; and should be quite contented to spend my life in obscurity, devoting myself to the training up of my child, and teaching him to avoid the errors of both his parents.

These things were done yesterday: I have given two whole days to the preparation for our departure, that Frederick may have more time to prepare the rooms, and Rachel to pack up the things – for the latter task must be done with the utmost caution and secrecy, and there is no one but me to assist her. I can help to get the articles together, but I do not understand the art of stowing them into the boxes, so as to take up the smallest possible space; and there are her own things to do, as well as mine and Arthur's. I can ill afford to leave anything behind, since I have no money, except a few guineas in my purse; – and besides, as Rachel observed, whatever I left would most likely become the property of Miss Myers, and I should not relish that.

But what trouble I have had throughout these two days struggling to appear calm and collected – to meet him and her as usual, when I was obliged to meet them, and forcing myself to leave my little Arthur in her hands for hours together! But I trust these trials are over now: I have laid him in my bed for better security, and never more, I trust, shall his innocent lips be defiled by their contaminating kisses, or his young ears polluted by their words. But shall we escape in safety? Oh, that the morning were come, and we were on our way at least! This evening, when I had given Rachel all the assistance I could, and had nothing left me but to wait, and wish and tremble, I became so greatly agitated, that I knew not what to do. I went down to dinner, but I could not force myself to eat. Mr Huntingdon remarked the circumstance.

'What's to do with you *now*?' said he, when the removal of the second course gave him time to look about him.

'I am not well,' I replied: 'I think I must lie down a little – you won't miss me much?'

'Not the least; if you leave your chair, it'll do just as well – better a trifle,' he muttered as I left the room, 'for I can fancy somebody else fills it.'

'Somebody else *may* fill it to-morrow,' I thought – but did not say. 'There! I've seen the last of *you*, I hope,' I muttered as I closed the door upon him.

Rachel urged me to seek repose, at once, to recruit my strength for to-morrow's journey, as we must be gone before the dawn, but in my present state of nervous excitement, that was entirely out of the question. It was equally out of the question to sit, or wander about my room, counting the hours and the minutes between me and the appointed time of action, straining my ears and trembling at every sound lest some one should discover and betray us after all. I took up a book and tried to read. My eyes wandered over the pages, but it was impossible to bind my thoughts to their contents. Why not have recourse to the old expedient, and add this last event to my chronicle? I opened its pages once more, and wrote the above account – with difficulty, at first, but gradually my mind became more calm and steady. Thus several hours have past away: the time is drawing near; – and now my eyes feel heavy, and my frame exhausted: I will commend my cause to God, and then lie down and gain an hour or two of sleep; and *then*! –

Little Arthur sleeps soundly. All the house is still: there can be no one watching. The boxes were all corded by Benson, and quietly conveyed down the back stairs after dusk, and sent away in a cart to the M— coach-office. The name upon the cards was Mrs Graham, which appellation I mean henceforth to adopt. My mother's maiden name was Graham, and therefore I fancy I have some claim to it, and prefer it to any other, except my own, which I dare not resume.

CHAPTER XLIV

THE RETREAT

OCTOBER 24TH. – Thank Heaven, I am free and safe at last! – Early we rose, swiftly and quietly dressed, slowly and stealthily descended to the hall, where Benson stood ready with a light to open the door and fasten it after us. We were obliged to let one man into our secret on account of the boxes, &c. All the servants were but too well acquainted with their master's conduct, and either Benson or John would have been willing to serve me, but as the former was more staid and elderly, and a crony of Rachel's besides, I of course directed her to make choice of him as her assistant and confidant on the occasion, as far as necessity demanded. I only hope he may not be brought into trouble thereby, and only wish I could reward him for the perilous service he was so ready to undertake. I slipped two guineas into his hand, by way of remembrance, as he stood in the doorway, holding the candle to light our departure, with a tear in his honest grey eye and a host of good wishes depicted on his solemn countenance. Alas! I could offer no more: I had barely sufficient remaining for the probable expenses of the journey.

What trembling joy it was when the little wicket closed behind us, as we issued from the park! Then, for one moment, I paused, to inhale one draught of that cool, bracing air, and venture one look back upon the house. All was dark and still; no light glimmered in the windows; no wreath of smoke obscured the stars that sparkled above it in the frosty sky. As I bade farewell for ever to that place, the scene of so much guilt and misery, I felt glad that I had not left it before, for now there was no doubt about the propriety of such a step – no shadow of remorse for him I left behind: there was nothing to disturb my joy but the fear of detection; and every step removed us farther from the chance of that.

We had left Grassdale many miles behind us before the round, red sun arose to welcome our deliverance, and if any inhabitant of its vicinity had chanced to see us then, as we bowled along on the top of the coach, I scarcely think they would have suspected our identity. As I intend to be taken for a widow I thought it advisable to enter my new abode in mourning: I was therefore attired in a plain black silk dress and mantle, a black veil (which I kept carefully over my face for the first twenty or thirty miles of the journey), and a black silk bonnet, which I had been constrained to borrow of Rachel for want of such an article myself – it was not in the newest fashion, of course; but none the worse for that, under present circumstances. Arthur was clad in his plainest clothes, and wrapped in a coarse woollen shawl; and Rachel was muffled in a grey cloak and hood that had seen better days, and gave her more the appearance of an ordinary, though decent old woman, than of a lady's maid.

Oh, what delight it was to be thus seated aloft, rumbling along the broad, sunshiny road, with the fresh morning breeze in my face, surrounded by an unknown country all smiling – cheerfully, gloriously, smiling in the yellow lustre of those early beams, – with my darling child in my arms, almost as happy as myself and my faithful friend beside me; a prison and despair behind me, receding farther, farther back at every clatter of the horses' feet, – and liberty and hope before! I could hardly refrain from praising God aloud for my deliverance, or astonishing my fellow passengers by some surprising outburst of hilarity.

But the journey was a very long one, and we were all weary enough before the close of it. It was far into the night when we reached the town of L—, and still we were seven miles from our journey's end; and there was no more coaching – nor any conveyance to be had, except a common cart – and that with the greatest difficulty, for half the town was in bed. And a dreary ride we had of it that last stage of the journey, cold and weary as we were; sitting on our boxes, with nothing to cling to, nothing to lean against, slowly dragged and cruelly shaken over the rough, hilly roads. But Arthur was asleep in Rachel's lap, and between us we managed pretty well to shield him from the cold night air.

At last we began to ascend a terribly steep and stony lane which, in spite of the darkness, Rachel said she remembered well: she had often walked there with me in her arms, and little thought to come again so many years after, under such circumstances as the present. Arthur being now awakened by the jolting and the stoppages, we all got out and walked. We had not far to go; but what if Frederick should not have received my letter? or if he should not have had time to prepare the rooms for our reception; and we should find them all dark, damp, and comfortless; destitute of food, fire, and furniture, after all our toil?

At length the grim, dark pile appeared before us. The lane conducted us round by the back way. We entered the desolate court, and in breathless anxiety surveyed the ruinous mass. Was it all blackness and desolation? No; one faint red glimmer cheered us from a window where the lattice was in good repair. The door was fastened, but after due knocking and waiting, and some parleying with a voice from an upper window, we were admitted, by an old woman who had been commissioned to air and keep the house till our arrival, – into a tolerably snug little apartment, formerly the scullery of the mansion, which Frederick had now fitted up as a kitchen. Here she procured us a light, roused the fire to a cheerful blaze, and soon prepared a simple repast for our refreshment; while we disencumbered ourselves of our travelling gear, and took a hasty survey of our new abode. Besides the kitchen there were two bedrooms, a good sized parlour, and another smaller one, which I destined for my studio, all well aired and seemingly in good repair, but only partly furnished with a few old articles, chiefly of ponderous black oak – the veritable ones that had been there before, and which had been kept as antiquarian relics in my brother's present residence, and now in all haste, transported back again.

The old woman brought my supper and Arthur's into the parlour, and told me, with all due formality, that 'The master desired his compliments to Mrs Graham, and he had prepared the rooms as well as he could upon so short a notice, but he would do himself the pleasure of calling upon her to-morrow, to receive her further commands.'

I was glad to ascend the stern-looking stone staircase, and lie down in the gloomy old-fashioned bed, beside my little Arthur. He was asleep in a minute; but, weary as I was, my excited feelings and restless cogitations kept me awake till dawn began to struggle with the darkness; but sleep was sweet and refreshing when it came, and the waking was delightful beyond expression. It was little Arthur that roused me, with his gentle kisses: – he was here, then – safely clasped in my arms, and many leagues away from his unworthy father! – Broad daylight illumined the apartment, for the sun was high in heaven, though obscured by rolling masses of autumnal vapour.

The scene, indeed, was not remarkably cheerful in itself, either within or without. The large bare room with its grim old furniture, the narrow, latticed windows, revealing the dull, grey sky above and the desolate wilderness below, where the dark stone walls and iron gate, the rank growth of grass and weeds, and the hardy ever-greens of preternatural forms, alone remained to tell that there had been once a garden, – and the bleak and barren fields beyond might have struck me as gloomy enough at another time, but now, each separate object seemed to echo back my own exhilarating sense of hope and freedom: indefinite dreams of the far past and bright anticipations of the future seemed to greet me at every turn. I should rejoice with more security, to be sure, had the broad sea rolled between my present and my former homes, but surely in this lonely spot I might remain unknown; and then, I had my brother here to cheer my solitude with his occasional visits.

He came that morning; and I have had several interviews with him since; but he is obliged to be very cautious when and how he comes: not even his servants, or his best friends must know of his visits to Wildfell – except on such occasions as a landlord might be expected to call upon a stranger tenant – lest suspicion should be excited against me, whether of the truth or of some slanderous falsehood.

I have now been here nearly a fortnight, and but for one disturbing care, the haunting dread of discovery, I am comfortably settled in my new home: Frederick has supplied me with all requisite furniture and painting materials: Rachel has sold most of my clothes for me, in a distant town, and procured me a wardrobe more suitable to my present position: I have a second hand piano, and a tolerably well-stocked book-case in my parlour; and my other room has assumed quite a professional, business-like appearance already. I am working hard to repay my brother for all his expenses on my account; not that there is the slightest necessity for anything of the kind, but it pleases me to do so: I shall have so much more pleasure in my labour, my earnings, my frugal fare, and household economy, when I know that I am paying my way honestly, and that what little I possess is legitimately all my own; and that no one suffers for my folly – in a pecuniary way at least. – I shall make him take the last penny I owe him, if I can possibly effect it without offending him too deeply. I have a few pictures already done, for I told Rachel to pack up all I had; and she executed her commission but too well, for among the rest, she put up a portrait of Mr Huntingdon that I had painted in the first year of my marriage. It struck me with dismay, at the moment, when I took it from the box and beheld those eyes fixed upon me in their mocking mirth, as if exulting, still, in his power to control my fate, and deriding my efforts to escape.

How widely different had been my feelings in painting that portrait to what they now were in looking upon it! How I had studied and toiled to produce something, as I thought, worthy of the original! what mingled pleasure and dissatisfaction I had had in the result of my labours! – pleasure for the likeness I had caught; dissatisfaction, because I had not made it handsome enough. Now, I see no beauty in it – nothing pleasing in any part of its expression; and yet it is far handsomer and far more agreeable – far less repulsive I should rather say – than he is now; for these six years have wrought almost as great a change upon himself as on my feelings regarding him. The frame, however, is handsome enough; it will serve for another painting. The picture itself I have not destroyed, as I had first intended; I have put it aside; not, I think, from any lurking tenderness for the memory of past affection, nor yet to remind me of my former folly, but chiefly that I may compare my son's features and countenance with this, as he grows up, and thus be enabled to judge how much or how little he resembles his father – if I may be allowed to keep him with me still, and never to behold that father's face again – a blessing I hardly dare reckon upon.

It seems Mr Huntingdon is making every exertion to discover the place of my retreat. He has been in person to Staningley, seeking redress for his grievances – expecting to hear of his victims, if not to find them there – and has told so many lies, and with such unblushing coolness, that my uncle more than half believes him, and strongly advocates my going back to him and being friends again; but my aunt knows better: she is too cool and cautious, and too well acquainted with both my husband's character and my own to be imposed upon by any specious falsehoods the former could invent. But he does not *want* me back; he wants my child; and gives my friends to understand that if I prefer living apart from him, he will indulge the whim and let me do so unmolested, and even settle a reasonable allowance on me, provided I will immediately deliver up his son. But, Heaven help me! I am not going to sell my child

for gold, though it were to save both him and me from starving:
it would be better that he should die with me, than that he
should live with his father.

Frederick showed me a letter he had received from that
gentleman, full of cool impudence such as would astonish any
one who did not know him, but such as, I am convinced, none
would know better how to answer than my brother. He gave
me no account of his reply, except to tell me that he had not
acknowledged his acquaintance with my place of refuge, but
rather left it to be inferred that it was quite unknown to him,
by saying it was useless to apply to him or any other of my
relations for information on the subject, as it appeared I had
been driven to such extremity that I had concealed my retreat
even from my best friends; but that if he *had* known it, or
should at any time be made aware of it, most certainly Mr
Huntingdon would be the last person to whom he should communicate the intelligence; and that he need not trouble himself
to bargain for the child, for he (Frederick) fancied he knew
enough of his sister to enable him to declare, that wherever she
might be, or however situated, no consideration would induce
her to deliver him up.

30th. – Alas! my kind neighbours will not let me alone. By
some means they have ferreted me out, and I have had to sustain
visits from three different families, all more or less bent upon
discovering who and what I am; whence I came, and why I have
chosen such a home as this. Their society is unnecessary to me,
to say the least, and their curiosity annoys and alarms me: if
I gratify it, it may lead to the ruin of my son, and if I am too
mysterious, it will only excite their suspicions, invite conjecture,
and rouse them to greater exertions – and perhaps be the means
of spreading my fame from parish to parish, till it reach the ears
of some one who will carry it to the lord of Grassdale Manor.

I shall be expected to return their calls, but if, upon enquiry,
I find that any of them live too far away for Arthur to accompany me, they must expect in vain for a while, for I cannot bear

to leave him, unless it be to go to church; and I have not attempted *that* yet, for – it may be foolish weakness, but I am under such constant dread of his being snatched away that I am never easy when he is not by my side; and I fear these nervous terrors would so entirely disturb my devotions, that I should obtain no benefit from the attendance. I mean, however, to make the experiment next Sunday, and oblige myself to leave him in charge of Rachel for a few hours. It will be a hard task, but surely no imprudence; and the vicar has been to scold me for my neglect of the ordinances of religion. I had no sufficient excuse to offer, and I promised, if all were well, he should see me in my pew next Sunday; for I do not wish to be set down as an infidel; and besides, I know I should derive great comfort and benefit from an occasional attendance at public worship, if I could only have faith and fortitude to compose my thoughts in conformity with the solemn occasion, and forbid them to be for ever dwelling on my absent child, and on the dreadful possibility of finding him gone when I return; and surely God in His mercy will preserve me from so severe a trial: for my child's own sake, if not for mine, He will not suffer him to be torn away.

November 3rd. – I have made some further acquaintance with my neighbours. The fine gentleman and beau of the parish and its vicinity (in his own estimation, at least) is a young...

Here it ended. The rest was torn away. How cruel – just when she was going to mention me! for I could not doubt it *was* your humble servant she was about to mention, though not very favourably of course – I could tell that, as well by those few words as by the recollection of her whole aspect and demeanour towards me in the commencement of our acquaintance. Well! I could readily forgive her prejudice against me, and her hard thoughts of our sex in general, when I saw to what brilliant specimens her experience had been limited.

Respecting me, however, she had long since seen her error,

and perhaps fallen into another in the opposite extreme; for if, at first, her opinion of me had been lower than I deserved I was convinced that now my deserts were lower than her opinion; and if the former part of this continuation had been torn away to avoid wounding my feelings, perhaps the latter portion had been removed for fear of ministering too much to my self-conceit. At any rate, I would have given much to have seen it all – to have witnessed the gradual change, and watched the progress of her esteem and friendship for me, – and whatever warmer feeling she might have – to have seen how much of love there was in her regard, and how it had grown upon her in spite of her virtuous resolutions and strenuous exertions to – but no, I had no right to see it: all this was too sacred for any eyes but her own, and she had done well to keep it from me.

CHAPTER XLV

RECONCILIATION

WELL HALFORD, WHAT do you think of all this? and while you read it, did you ever picture to yourself what my feelings would probably be during its perusal? Most likely not; but I am not going to descant upon them now: I will only make this acknowledgment, little honourable as it may be to human nature, and especially to myself: – that the former half of the narrative was, to me, more painful than the latter; not that I was at all insensible to Mrs Huntingdon's wrongs or unmoved by her sufferings, but, I must confess, I felt a kind of selfish gratification in watching her husband's gradual decline in her good graces, and seeing how completely he extinguished all her affection at last. The effect of the whole, however, in spite of all my sympathy for her and my fury against him, was to relieve my mind of an intolerable burden and fill my heart with joy, as if some friend had roused me from a dreadful night-mare.

It was now near eight o'clock in the morning, for my candle had expired in the midst of my perusal, leaving me no alternative but to get another, at the expense of alarming the house, or to go to bed and wait the return of daylight. On my mother's account, I chose the latter; but how *willingly* I sought my pillow, and how much sleep it brought me, I leave you to imagine.

At the first appearance of dawn I rose, and brought the manuscript to the window, but it was impossible to read it yet. I devoted half an hour to dressing, and then returned to it again. Now, with a little difficulty, I could manage; and with intense and eager interest, I devoured the remainder of its contents. When it was ended, and my transient regret at its abrupt conclusion was over, I opened the window and put out my head to catch the cooling breeze, and imbibe deep draughts of the pure morning air. A splendid morning it was; the half-frozen dew lay thick on the grass, the swallows were twittering round me, the rooks cawing and cows lowing in the distance; and early frost and summer sunshine mingled their sweetness in the air. But I did not think of that: a confusion of countless thoughts and varied emotions crowded upon me while I gazed abstractedly on the lovely face of nature. Soon, however, this chaos of thoughts and passions cleared away, giving place to two distinct emotions: joy unspeakable that my adored Helen was all I wished to think her – that through the noisome vapours of the world's aspersions and my own fancied convictions, her character shone bright, and clear, and stainless as that sun I could not bear to look on; and shame and deep remorse for my own conduct.

Immediately after breakfast, I hurried over to Wildfell Hall. Rachel had risen many degrees in my estimation since yesterday. I was ready to greet her quite as an old friend; but every kindly impulse was checked by the look of cold distrust she cast upon me on opening the door. The old virgin had constituted herself the guardian of her lady's honour, I suppose, and doubtless she saw in me another Mr Hargrave, only the more dangerous in being more esteemed and trusted by her mistress.

'Missis can't see any one to-day, sir – she's poorly,' said she in answer to my enquiry for Mrs Graham.

'But I must see her, Rachel,' said I, placing my hand on the door to prevent its being shut against me.

'Indeed, sir, you can't,' replied she, settling her countenance in still more iron frigidity than before.

'Be so good as to announce me.'

'It's no manner of use, Mr Markham; she's poorly, I tell you.'

Just in time to prevent me from committing the impropriety of taking the citadel by storm, and pushing forward un-announced, an inner door opened, and little Arthur appeared with his frolicsome playfellow the dog. He seized my hand between both his, and smilingly drew me forward.

'Mamma says you're to come in, Mr Markham,' said he, 'and I'm to go out and play with Rover.'

Rachel retired with a sigh, and I stepped into the parlour and shut the door. There, before the fire-place, stood the tall, grace-ful figure wasted with many sorrows. I cast the manuscript on the table, and looked in her face. Anxious and pale, it was turned towards me; her clear, dark eyes were fixed on mine with a gaze so intensely earnest that they bound me like a spell.

'Have you looked it over?' she murmured. The spell was broken.

'I've read it through,' said I, advancing into the room, – 'and I want to know if you'll forgive me – if you *can* forgive me?'

She did not answer, but her eyes glistened, and a faint red mantled on her lip and cheek. As I approached, she abruptly turned away, and went to the window. It was not in anger, I was well assured, but only to conceal or control her emotion. I therefore ventured to follow and stand beside her there, – but not to speak. She gave me her hand, without turning her head, and murmured, in a voice she strove in vain to steady, –

'Can *you* forgive *me*?'

It might be deemed a breach of trust, I thought, to convey that lily hand to my lips, so I only gently pressed it between my own, and smilingly replied, –

'I hardly can. You should have told me this before. It shows a want of confidence –'

'Oh, no,' cried she, eagerly interrupting me, 'it was not that! It was no want of confidence in you; but if I had told you anything of my history, I must have told you all, in order to excuse my conduct; and I might well shrink from such a disclosure, till necessity obliged me to make it. But you forgive me? – I have done very, very wrong, I know; but, as usual, I have reaped the bitter fruits of my own error, – and must reap them to the end.'

Bitter, indeed, was the tone of anguish, repressed by resolute firmness, in which this was spoken. Now, I raised her hand to my lips, and fervently kissed it again and again; for tears prevented any other reply. She suffered these wild caresses without resistance or resentment; then, suddenly turning from me, she paced twice or thrice through the room. I knew by the contraction of her brow, the tight compression of her lips, and wringing of her hands, that meantime a violent conflict between reason and passion, was silently passing within. At length she paused before the empty fire-place, and turning to me, said calmly – if that might be called calmness, which was so evidently the result of a violent effort –

'Now Gilbert, you must leave me – not this moment, but soon – and you must *never come again.*'

'Never again, Helen? just when I love you more than ever!'

'For that very reason, if it be so, we should not meet again. I thought *this* interview was necessary – at least, I persuaded myself it was so – that we might severally ask and receive each other's pardon for the past; but there can be no excuse for another. I shall leave this place, as soon as I have means to seek another asylum; but our intercourse must end here.'

'End here!' echoed I; and approaching the high, carved chimney-piece, I leant my hand against its heavy mouldings, and dropped my forehead upon it in silent, sullen despondency.

'You must not come again,' continued she. There was a slight tremor in her voice, but I thought her whole manner was provokingly composed, considering the dreadful sentence she pronounced. 'You must know why I tell you so,' she resumed; 'and you must see that it is better to part at once: – if it be hard to say adieu for ever, you ought to help me.' She paused. I did not answer. 'Will you promise not to come? – If you won't, and if you do come here again, you will drive me away before I know where to find another place of refuge – or how to seek it.'

'Helen,' said I, turning impatiently towards her, 'I cannot discuss the matter of eternal separation, calmly and dispassionately as you can do. It is no question of mere expedience with *me*; it is a question of life and death!'

She was silent. Her pale lips quivered, and her fingers trembled with agitation, as she nervously entwined them in the hair chain to which was appended her small gold watch – the only thing of value she had permitted herself to keep. I had said an unjust and cruel thing; but I must needs follow it up with something worse.

'But, Helen!' I began in a soft, low tone, not daring to raise my eyes to her face – 'that man is *not* your husband: in the sight of Heaven he has forfeited all claim to –' She seized my arm with a grasp of startling energy.

'*Gilbert, don't!*' she cried, in a tone that would have pierced a heart of adamant. 'For God's sake, don't *you* attempt these arguments! No *fiend* could torture me like this!'

'I won't, I won't!' said I, gently laying my hand on hers; almost as much alarmed at her vehemence, as ashamed of my own misconduct.

'Instead of acting like a true friend,' continued she, breaking from me and throwing herself into the old arm-chair – 'and helping me with all your might – or rather taking your own part in the struggle of right against passion – you leave all the burden to me; – and not satisfied with that, you do your utmost to fight against me – when you know that I —' She paused, and hid her face in her handkerchief.

'Forgive me, Helen!' pleaded I, 'I will never utter another word on the subject. But may we not still meet as friends?'

'It will not do,' she replied, mournfully shaking her head; and then she raised her eyes to mine, with a mildly reproachful look that seemed to say, 'You must know that as well as I.'

'Then what *must* we do?' cried I, passionately. But immediately I added in a quieter tone – 'I'll do whatever you desire; – only *don't* say that this meeting is to be our last.'

'And why not? Don't you know that every time we meet, the thoughts of the final parting will become more painful? Don't you *feel* that every interview makes us dearer to each other than the last?'

The utterance of this last question was hurried and low, and the downcast eyes and burning blush too plainly showed that *she*, at least, had felt it. It was scarcely prudent to make such an admission, or to add – as she presently did – 'I have power to bid you go, now: another time it might be different,' – but I was not base enough to attempt to take advantage of her candour.

'But we may write,' I timidly suggested – 'You will not deny me that consolation?'

'We can hear of each other through my brother.'

'Your brother!' A pang of remorse and shame shot through me. She had not heard of the injury he had sustained at my hands; and I had not the courage to tell her. 'Your brother will not help us,' I said: 'he would have all communion between us to be entirely at an end.'

'And he would be right, I suppose. As a friend of both, he would wish us both well; and every friend would tell us it was our interest, as well as our duty, to forget each other, though we might not see it ourselves. But don't be afraid, Gilbert,' she added, smiling sadly at my manifest discomposure, 'there is little chance of my forgetting you. But I did not mean that Frederick should be the means of transmitting messages between us, only that each might know, through him, of the other's welfare; – and more than this ought not to be; for you are young, Gilbert, and you ought to marry – and will some time, though you may think it impossible now: – and though I hardly can say I wish you to forget me, I know it is right that you should, both for your own happiness and that of your future wife; – and therefore I must and will wish it,' she added resolutely.

'And you are young too, Helen,' I boldly replied, 'and when that profligate scoundrel has run through his career, you will give your hand to me – I'll wait till then.'

But she would not leave me this support. Independently of the moral evil of basing our hopes upon the death of another, who, if unfit for this world, was at least no less so for the next, and whose amelioration would thus become our bane and his greatest transgression our greatest benefit, – she maintained it to be madness: many men of Mr Huntingdon's habits had lived to a ripe though miserable old age; – 'and if I,' said she, 'am young in years I am old in sorrow; but even if trouble should fail to kill me before vice destroys him, think, if he reached but fifty years or so, would you wait twenty or fifteen – in vague uncertainty and suspense – through all the prime of youth and manhood – and marry at last a woman faded and worn as I shall be – without ever having seen me from this day to that? – You would not,' she continued, interrupting my earnest protestations of unfailing constancy, – 'or if you would you should not. Trust me, Gilbert; in this matter I know better than you. You think me cold and stony hearted, and you may, but –'

'I don't Helen.'

'Well, never mind; you might if you would – but I have not spent my solitude in utter idleness, and I am not speaking now from the impulse of the moment as you do: I have thought of all these matters again and again; I have argued these questions with myself, and pondered well our past, and present, and future career; and, believe me, I have come to the right conclusion at last. Trust my words rather than your own feelings, now, and in a few years you will see that I was right – though at present I hardly can see it myself,' she murmured with a sigh as she rested her head on her hand. – 'And don't argue against me any more: all you can say has been already said by my own heart and refuted by my reason. It was hard enough to combat those suggestions as they were whispered within me; in your mouth they are ten times worse, and if you knew how much they pain me you would cease at once, I know. If you knew my present feelings, you would even try to relieve them at the expense of your own.'

'I will go – in a minute, if *that* can relieve you – and NEVER return!' said I with bitter emphasis. – 'But, if we may never meet, and never hope to meet again, is it a crime to exchange our thoughts by letter? May not kindred spirits meet, and mingle in communion whatever be the fate and circumstances of their earthly tenements?'

'They may, they may!' cried she with a momentary burst of glad enthusiasm. 'I thought of that too, Gilbert, but I feared to mention it, because I feared you would not understand my views upon the subject – I fear it even now – I fear any kind friend would tell us we are *both* deluding ourselves with the idea of keeping up a spiritual intercourse without hope or prospect of anything further – without fostering vain regrets and hurtful aspirations, and feeding thoughts that should be sternly and pitilessly left to perish of inanition –'

'Never mind our kind friends: if they can part our bodies, it is enough; in God's name, let them not sunder our souls!' cried I, in terror lest she should deem it her duty to deny us this last remaining consolation.

'But no letters can pass between us here,' said she, 'without giving fresh food for scandal; and when I departed, I had intended that my new abode should be unknown to you as to the rest of the world; not that I should doubt your word if you promised not to visit me, but I thought you would be more tranquil in your own mind if you knew you could not do it; and likely to find less difficulty in abstracting yourself from me if you could not picture my situation to your mind. But listen,' said she, smilingly putting up her finger to check my impatient reply: 'in six months you shall hear from Frederick precisely where I am; and if you still retain your wish to write to me, and think you can maintain a correspondence all thought, all spirit – such as disembodied souls or unimpassioned friends, at least, might hold, – write, and I will answer you.'

'Six months!'

'Yes, to give your present ardour time to cool and try the truth and constancy of your soul's love for mine. And now, enough has been said between us. – Why can't we part at once!' exclaimed she almost wildly, after a moment's pause, as she suddenly rose from her chair with her hands resolutely clasped together. I thought it was my duty to go without delay; and I approached and half extended my hand as if to take leave; she grasped it in silence. But this thought of final separation was too intolerable: it seemed to squeeze the blood out of my heart; and my feet were glued to the floor.

'And must we never meet again?' I murmured in the anguish of my soul.

'We shall meet in Heaven. Let us think of that,' said she in a tone of desperate calmness; but her eyes glittered wildly, and her face was deadly pale.

'But not as we are now,' I could not help replying. 'It gives me little consolation to think I shall next behold you as a dis-embodied spirit, or an altered being, with a frame perfect and glorious, but not like this! – and a heart, perhaps, entirely estranged from me.'

'No Gilbert, there is perfect love in Heaven!'

'*So* perfect, I suppose, that it soars above distinctions, and you will have no closer sympathy with me than with any one of the ten thousand thousand angels and the innumerable multitude of happy spirits round us.'

'Whatever I am, you will be the same, and therefore, cannot possibly regret it; and whatever that change may be, we know it must be for the better.'

'But if I am to be so changed that I shall cease to adore you with my whole heart and soul, and love you beyond every other creature, I shall not be myself, and though, if ever I win Heaven at all, I must, I know, be infinitely better and happier than I am now, my earthly nature cannot rejoice in the anticipation of such beatitude, from which itself and its chief joy must be excluded.'

'Is your love *all* earthly then?'

'No, but I am supposing we shall have no more intimate communion with each other, than with the rest.'

'If so, it will be because we love them more and not each other less. Increase of love brings increase of happiness, when it is mutual, and pure as that will be.'

'But can *you*, Helen, contemplate with delight this prospect of losing me in a sea of glory?'

'I own I cannot; but we know not that it will be so; – and I do know that to regret the exchange of earthly pleasures for the joys of Heaven, is as if the grovelling caterpillar should lament that it must one day quit the nibbled leaf to soar aloft and flutter through the air, roving at will from flower to flower, sipping sweet honey from their cups or basking in their sunny petals. If these little creatures knew how great a change awaited them, no doubt they would regret it; but would not all such sorrow be misplaced? And if that illustration will not move you, here is another: – We are children now; we feel as children, and we understand as children; and when we are told that men and women do not play with toys, and that our companions will one day weary of the trivial sports and occupations that interest them and us so deeply now, we cannot help being sad-dened at the thoughts of such an alteration, because we cannot conceive that as we grow up, our own minds will become so enlarged and elevated that we ourselves shall then regard as trifling those objects and pursuits we now so fondly cherish, and that, though our companions will no longer join us in those childish pastimes, they will drink with us at other fountains of delight, and mingle their souls with ours in higher aims and nobler occupations beyond our present comprehension, but not less deeply relished or less truly good for that, – while yet both we and they remain essentially the same individuals as before. But, Gilbert, can you really derive no consolation from the thought that we may meet together where there is no more pain and sorrow, no more striving against sin, and struggling of the spirit against the flesh; where both will behold the same glorious truths, and drink exalted and supreme felicity from the same fountain of light and goodness – that Being whom both will worship with the same intensity of holy ardour, and whose pure and happy creatures both will love with the same divine affection? If you cannot, never write to me!'

'Helen, I can, if faith would never fail.'

'Now, then,' exclaimed she, 'while this hope is strong within us –'

'We will part,' I cried. 'You shall not have the pain of another effort to dismiss me: I will go at once; but –'

I did not put my request in words: she understood it instinctively and *this* time she yielded too – or rather, there was nothing so deliberate as requesting or yielding in the matter: there was a sudden impulse that neither could resist. One moment I stood and looked into her face, the next I held her to my heart, and we seemed to grow together in a close embrace from which no physical or mental force could rend us. A whispered 'God bless you!' and 'Go – go!' was all she said; but while she spoke, she held me so fast that, without violence, I could not have obeyed her. At length, however, by some heroic effort, we tore ourselves apart, and I rushed from the house.

I have a confused remembrance of seeing little Arthur running up the garden walk to meet me, and of bolting over the wall to avoid him – and subsequently running down the steep fields, clearing the stone fences and hedges as they came in my way, till I got completely out of sight of the old Hall and down to the bottom of the hill; and then of long hours spent in bitter tears and lamentations, and melancholy musings in the lonely valley, with the eternal music in my ears, of the west wind rushing through the over-shadowing trees, and the brook babbling and gurgling along its stony bed – my eyes, for the most part, vacantly fixed on the deep, checkered shades restlessly playing over the bright sunny grass at my feet, where now and then a withered leaf or two would come dancing to share the revelry, but my heart was away up the hill in that dark room where she was weeping desolate and alone – she whom I was not to comfort, not to see again, till years or suffering had overcome us both, and torn our spirits from their perishing abodes of clay.

There was little business done that day, you may be sure. The farm was abandoned to the labourers, and the labourers were left to their own devices. But one duty must be attended to: I had not forgotten my assault upon Frederick Lawrence; and I must see him to apologize for the unhappy deed. I would fain have put it off till the morrow; but what if he should denounce me to his sister in the mean time? No, no, I must ask his pardon to-day, and intreat him to be lenient in his accusation, if the revelation must be made. I deferred it however, till the evening, when my spirits were more composed and when – oh, wonderful perversity of human nature! – some faint germs of indefinite hopes were beginning to rise in my mind; not that I intended to cherish them after all that had been said on the subject, but there they must lie for a while, uncrushed though not encouraged, till I had learnt to live without them.

Arrived at Woodford, the young squire's abode, I found no little difficulty in obtaining admission to his presence. The servant that opened the door told me his master was very ill, and seemed to think it doubtful whether he would be able to see me. I was not going to be baulked however. I waited calmly in the hall to be announced, but inwardly determined to take no denial. The message was such as I expected – a polite intimation that Mr Lawrence could see no one; he was feverish and must not be disturbed.

'I shall not disturb him long,' said I; 'but I must see him for a moment: it is on business of importance that I wish to speak to him.'

'I'll tell him, sir,' said the man. And I advanced farther into the hall and followed him nearly to the door of the apartment where his master was – for it seemed he was not in bed. The answer returned, was that Mr Lawrence hoped I would be so good as to leave a message or a note with the servant, as he could attend to no business at present.

'He may as well see me as you,' said I; and, stepping past the astonished footman, I boldly rapped at the door, entered, and closed it behind me. The room was spacious and handsomely furnished – very comfortably, too, for a bachelor. A clear, red fire was burning in the polished grate: a superannuated greyhound, given up to idleness and good living lay basking before it on the thick, soft rug, on one corner of which, beside the sofa, sat a smart young springer, looking wistfully up in its master's face; perhaps, asking permission to share his couch, or, it might be, only soliciting a caress from his hand or a kind word from his lips. The invalid himself looked very interesting as he lay reclining there, in his elegant dressing-gown, with a silk handkerchief bound across his temples. His usually pale face was flushed and feverish; his eyes were half closed, until he became sensible of my presence – and then he opened them wide enough; – one hand was thrown listlessly over the back of the sofa, and held a small volume with which, apparently, he had been vainly attempting to beguile the weary hours. He dropped it, however, in his start of indignant surprise as I advanced into the room and stood before him on the rug. He raised himself on his pillows and gazed upon me with equal degrees of nervous horror, anger, and amazement depicted on his countenance.

'Mr Markham, I scarcely expected this!' he said; and the blood left his cheek as he spoke.

'I know you didn't,' answered I; 'but be quiet a minute, and I'll tell you what I came for.' Unthinkingly I advanced a step or two nearer. He winced at my approach, with an expression of aversion and instinctive physical fear anything but conciliatory to my feelings. I stepped back, however.

'Make your story a short one,' said he, putting his hand on the small silver bell that stood on the table beside him, – 'or I shall be obliged to call for assistance. I am in no state to bear your brutalities now, or your presence either.' And in truth the moisture started from his pores and stood on his pale forehead like dew.

Such a reception was hardly calculated to diminish the difficulties of my unenviable task. It must be performed, however, in some fashion; and so I plunged into it at once, and floundered through it as I could.

'The truth is, Lawrence,' said I, 'I have not acted quite correctly towards you of late – especially on this last occasion; and I'm come to – in short, to express my regret for what has been done, and to beg your pardon. – If you don't choose to grant it,' I added hastily, not liking the aspect of his face, 'it's no matter – only *I've* done *my* duty – that's all.'

'It's easily done,' replied he, with a faint smile bordering on a sneer: 'to abuse your friend and knock him on the head, without any assignable cause, and then tell him the deed was not quite correct, but it's no matter whether he pardons it or not.'

'I forgot to tell you that it was in consequence of a mistake,' muttered I. 'I should have made a very handsome apology, but you provoked me so confoundedly with your ——. Well, I suppose it's my fault. The fact is, I didn't know that you were Mrs Graham's brother, and I saw and heard some things respecting your conduct towards her, which were calculated to awaken unpleasant suspicions, that allow me to say, a little candour and confidence on your part might have removed; and at last,

I chanced to overhear a part of a conversation between you and her that made me think I had a right to hate you.'

'And how came you to know that I was her brother?' asked he, in some anxiety.

'She told me herself. She told me all. She knew I might be trusted. But you needn't disturb yourself about *that*, Mr Lawrence, for I've seen the last of her!'

'The last! Is she gone then?'

'No; but she has bid adieu to me; and I have promised never to go near that house again while she inhabits it.' I could have groaned aloud at the bitter thoughts awakened by this turn in the discourse. But I only clenched my hands and stamped my foot upon the rug. My companion however, was evidently relieved.

'You have done right!' he said in a tone of unqualified approbation, while his face brightened into almost a sunny expression. 'And as for the mistake, I am sorry for both our sakes that it should have occurred. Perhaps you can forgive my want of candour, and remember, as some partial mitigation of the offence, how little encouragement to friendly confidence you have given me of late.'

'Yes, yes I remember it all: nobody can blame me more than I blame myself in my own heart – at any rate, nobody can regret more sincerely than I do the result of my *brutality* as you rightly term it.'

'Never mind that,' said he, faintly smiling; 'let us forget all unpleasant words on both sides, as well as deeds, and consign to oblivion everything that we have cause to regret. Have you any objection to take my hand – or you'd rather not?' It trembled through weakness, as he held it out, and dropped before I had time to catch it and give it a hearty squeeze, which he had not the strength to return.

'How dry and burning your hand is Lawrence,' said I. 'You are really ill, and I have made you worse by all this talk.'

'Oh, it is nothing: only a cold got by the rain.'

'My doing, too.'

'Never mind that – but tell me, did you mention this affair to my sister?'

'To confess the truth, I had not the courage to do so; but when you tell her, will you just say that I deeply regret it, and –'

'Oh, never fear! I shall say nothing against you, as long as you keep your good resolution of remaining aloof from her. She has not heard of my illness then, that you are aware of?'

'I think not.'

'I'm glad of that, for I have been all this time tormenting myself with the fear that somebody would tell her I was dying, or desperately ill, and she would be either distressing herself on account of her inability to hear from me or do me any good, or perhaps committing the madness of coming to see me. I must contrive to let her know something about it, if I can,' continued he, reflectively, 'or she will be hearing some such story. Many would be glad to tell her such news, just to see how she would take it; and then she might expose herself to fresh scandal.'

'I wish I had told her,' said I. 'If it were not for my promise, I would tell her now.'

'By no means! I am not dreaming of that; – but if I were to write a short note, now – not mentioning you, Markham, but just giving a slight account of my illness, by way of excuse for my not coming to see her, and to put her on her guard against any exaggerated reports she may hear, – and address it in a disguised hand – would you do me the favour to slip it into the post-office as you pass? for I dare not trust any of the servants in such a case.'

Most willingly I consented, and immediately brought him his desk. There was little need to disguise his hand, for the poor fellow seemed to have considerable difficulty in writing at all, so as to be legible. When the note was done, I thought it time to retire, and took leave after asking if there was anything in the world I could do for him, little or great, in the way of alleviating his sufferings, and repairing the injury I had done.

'No,' said he; 'you have already done much towards it; you

have done more for me than the most skilful physician could do; for you have relieved my mind of two great burdens – anxiety on my sister's account, and deep regret upon your own, for I do believe these two sources of torment have had more effect in working me up into a fever, than anything else; and I am persuaded I shall soon recover now. There is one more thing you can do for me, and that is, come and see me now and then – for you see I am very lonely here, and I promise your entrance shall not be disputed again.'

I engaged to do so, and departed with a cordial pressure of the hand. I posted the letter on my way home, most manfully resisting the temptation of dropping in a word from myself at the same time.

CHAPTER XLVI

FRIENDLY COUNSELS

I FELT STRONGLY tempted, at times, to enlighten my mother and sister on the real character and circumstances of the persecuted tenant of Wildfell Hall; and at first I greatly regretted having omitted to ask that lady's permission to do so; but, on due reflection, I considered that if it were known to them, it could not long remain a secret to the Millwards and Wilsons, and such was my present appreciation of Eliza Millward's disposition, that, if once she got a clue to the story, I should fear she would soon find means to enlighten Mr Huntingdon upon the place of his wife's retreat. I would therefore wait patiently till these weary six months were over, and then, when the fugitive had found another home, and I was permitted to write to her, I would beg to be allowed to clear her name from these vile calumnies: at present I must content myself with simply asserting that I knew them to be false, and would prove it some day, to the shame of those who slandered her. I don't think anybody believed me: but everybody soon learned to avoid insinuating a word against her, or even mentioning her name in my presence. They thought I was so madly infatuated by the seductions of that unhappy lady that I was determined to support her in the very face of reason; and meantime I grew insupportably morose and misanthropical from the idea that every one I met was harbouring unworthy thoughts of the supposed Mrs Graham, and would express them if he dared. My poor mother was quite distressed about me; but I couldn't help it – at least I thought I could not; though sometimes I felt a pang of remorse for my undutiful conduct to her, and made an effort to amend, attended with some partial success – and indeed I was generally more humanized in my demeanour to her than to any one else, Mr Lawrence excepted. Rose and Fergus usually shunned my presence; and it was well they did, for I was not fit company for them, nor they for me, under the present circumstances.

Mrs Huntingdon did not leave Wildfell Hall till above two months after our farewell interview. During that time she never appeared at church, and I never went near the house: I only knew she was still there by her brother's brief answers to my many and varied enquiries respecting her. I was a very constant and attentive visiter to him throughout the whole period of his illness and convalescence; not only from the interest I took in his recovery, and my desire to cheer him up and make the utmost possible amends for my former 'brutality,' but from my growing attachment to himself, and the increasing pleasure I found in his society – partly, from his increased cordiality to me, but chiefly on account of his close connection – both in blood and in affection – with my adored Helen. I loved him for it better than I liked to express; and I took a secret delight in pressing those slender, white fingers, so marvellously like her own, considering he was not a woman, and in watching the passing changes in his fair, pale features, and observing the intonations of his voice – detecting resemblances which I wondered had never struck me before. He provoked me at times, indeed, by his evident reluctance to talk to me about his sister, though I did not question the friendliness of his motives in wishing to discourage my remembrance of her.

His recovery was not quite so rapid as he had expected it to be: he was not able to mount his pony till a fortnight after the date of our reconciliation; and the first use he made of his returning strength, was to ride over by night to Wildfell Hall, to see his sister. It was a hazardous enterprise both for him and for her, but he thought it necessary to consult with her on the subject of her projected departure, if not to calm her apprehensions respecting his health, and the worst result was a slight relapse of his illness; for no one knew of the visit, but the inmates of the old Hall – except myself; and I believe it had not been his intention to mention it to me, for when I came to see him the next day, and observed he was not so well as he ought to have been, he merely said he had caught cold by being out too late in the evening.

'You'll *never* be able to see your sister, if you don't take care of yourself,' said I, a little provoked at the circumstance on her account, instead of commiserating him.

'I've seen her already,' said he, quietly.

'You've seen her!' cried I, in astonishment.

'Yes.' And then he told me what considerations had impelled him to make the venture, and with what precautions he had made it.

'And how was she?' I eagerly asked.

'As usual,' was the brief though sad reply.

'As usual – that is, far from happy and far from strong.'

'She is not positively ill,' returned he; 'and she will recover her spirits in a while I have no doubt – but so many trials have been almost too much for her. How threatening those clouds look!' continued he, turning towards the window. 'We shall have thunder-showers before night, I imagine; and they are just in the midst of stacking my corn. Have you got yours all in yet?'

'No. – And Lawrence, did she – did your sister mention me?'

'She asked if I had seen you lately.'

'And what else did she say?'

'I cannot tell you all she said,' replied he with a slight smile, 'for we talked a good deal, though my stay was but short; but our conversation was chiefly on the subject of her intended departure, which I begged her to delay till I was better able to assist her in her search after another home.'

'But did she say no more about me?'

'She did not say much about you, Markham. I should not have encouraged her to do so, had she been inclined; but happily she was not: she only asked a few questions concerning you, and seemed satisfied with my brief answers; wherein she showed herself wiser than her friend – and I may tell you too, that she seemed to be far more anxious lest you should think too much of her, than lest you should forget her.'

'She was right.'

'But I fear *your* anxiety is quite the other way, respecting her.'

'No, it is not: I wish her to be happy; but I don't wish her to forget me altogether. She knows it is impossible that I should forget *her*; and she is right to wish me not to remember her too well. I should not desire her to regret me *too* deeply; but I can scarcely imagine she will make herself very unhappy about me, because I know I am not worthy of it, except in my appreciation of her.'

'You are neither of you worthy of a broken heart, – nor of all the sighs, and tears, and sorrowful thoughts that have been, and I fear will be wasted upon you both; but at present, each has a more exalted opinion of the other than, I fear, he or she deserves; and my sister's feelings are naturally full as keen as yours, and I believe *more* constant; but she has the good sense and fortitude to strive against them in this particular; and I trust she will not rest till she has entirely weaned her thoughts –' he hesitated.

'From me,' said I.

'And I wish you would make the like exertions,' continued he.

'Did she *tell* you that that was her intention?'

'No; the question was not broached between us: there was no necessity for it, for I had no doubt that such was her determination.'

'To forget me?'

'Yes Markham! Why not?'

'Oh! well,' was my only audible reply; but I internally answered, – 'No, Lawrence, you're wrong there, she is *not* determined to forget me. It would be *wrong* to forget one so deeply and fondly devoted to her, who can so thoroughly appreciate her excellencies and sympathize with all her thoughts as I can do, and it would be wrong in me to forget so excellent and divine a piece of God's creation as she, when I have once so truly loved and known her.' But I said no more to him on that subject. I instantly started a new topic of conversation, and soon took leave of my companion, with a feeling of less cordiality towards him than usual. Perhaps I had no right to be annoyed at him, but I was so nevertheless.

In little more than a week after this, I met him returning from a visit to the Wilsons; and I now resolved to do *him* a good turn, though at the expense of his feelings, and, perhaps, at the risk of incurring that displeasure which is so commonly the reward of those who give disagreeable information or tender their advice unasked. In this, believe me, I was actuated by no motives of revenge for the occasional annoyances I had lately sustained from him, – nor yet by any feeling of malevolent enmity towards Miss Wilson, but purely by the fact that I could not endure that such a woman should be Mrs Huntingdon's sister, and that, as well for his own sake as for hers, I could not bear to think of his being deceived into a union with one so unworthy of him, and so utterly unfitted to be the partner of his quiet home, and the companion of his life. He had had uncomfortable suspicions on that head himself, I imagined, but such was his inexperience, and such were the lady's powers of attraction and her skill in bringing them to bear upon his young imagination, that they had not disturbed him long, and I believe the only effectual cause of the vacillating indecision that had preserved him hitherto from making an actual declaration of love, was the consideration of her connections, and especially of her mother, whom he could not abide. Had they lived at a distance, he might have surmounted the objection, but within two or three miles of Woodford, it was really no light matter.

'You've been to call on the Wilsons, Lawrence,' said I as I walked beside his pony.

'Yes,' replied he, slightly averting his face: 'I thought it but civil to take the first opportunity of returning their kind attentions, since they have been so very particular and constant in their enquiries, throughout the whole course of my illness.'

'It's all Miss Wilson's doing.'

'And if it is,' returned he, with a very perceptible blush, 'is that any reason why I should not make a suitable acknowledgment?'

'It is a reason why you should not make the acknowledgment she looks for.'

'Let us drop that subject if you please,' said he in evident displeasure.

'No, Lawrence, with your leave we'll continue it a while longer; and I'll tell you something, now we're about it, which you may believe or not as you choose – only please to remember that it is not my custom to speak falsely, and that in this case, I can have no motive for misrepresenting the truth –'

'Well, Markham! what now?'

'*Miss Wilson hates your sister.* It may be natural enough that, in her ignorance of the relationship, she should feel some degree of enmity against her, but no good or amiable woman would be capable of evincing that bitter, cold-blooded, designing malice towards a fancied rival that I have observed in her.'

'Markham!!'

'Yes – and it is my belief that Eliza Millward and she, if not the very originators of the slanderous reports that have been propagated, were designedly the encouragers and chief disseminators of them. She was not desirous to mix up *your* name in the matter, of course, but her delight was, and still is, to blacken your sister's character to the utmost of her power without risking too greatly the exposure of her own malevolence!'

'I cannot believe it,' interrupted my companion, his face burning with indignation.

'Well, as I cannot prove it, I must content myself with asserting that it is so to the best of my belief, but as you would not willingly marry Miss Wilson if it *were* so, you will do well to be cautious, till you have proved it to be otherwise.'

'I never told you, Markham, that I *intended* to marry Miss Wilson,' said he proudly.

'No, but whether you do or not, she intends to marry you.'

'Did she tell you so?'

'No, but –'

'Then you have no right to make such an assertion respecting her.' He slightly quickened his pony's pace, but I laid my hand on its mane, determined he should not leave me yet.

'Wait a moment, Lawrence, and let me explain myself; and don't be so very – I don't know what to call it – *inaccessible* as you are. – I know what you think of Jane Wilson; and I believe I know how far you are mistaken in your opinion: you think she is singularly charming, elegant, sensible, and refined: you are not aware that she is selfish, cold-hearted, ambitious, artful, shallow-minded –'

'Enough, Markham, enough.'

'No; let me finish. – You don't know that, if you married her, your home would be rayless and comfortless; and it would break your heart at last to find yourself united to one so wholly incapable of sharing your tastes, feelings, and ideas – so utterly destitute of sensibility, good feeling, and true nobility of soul.'

'Have you done?' asked my companion quietly.

'Yes; – I know you hate me for my impertinence, but I don't care if it only conduces to preserve you from that fatal mistake.'

'Well!' returned he, with a rather wintry smile – 'I'm glad you have overcome, or forgotten your own afflictions so far as to be able to study so deeply the affairs of others, and trouble your head, so unnecessarily, about the fancied or possible calamities of their future life.'

We parted – somewhat coldly again; but still we did not cease to be friends; and my well-meant warning, though it might have been more judiciously delivered, as well as more thankfully received, was not wholly unproductive of the desired effect: his visit to the Wilsons was not repeated, and though, in our subsequent interviews, he never mentioned her name to me, nor I to him, – I have reason to believe he pondered my words in his mind, eagerly though covertly sought information respecting the fair lady from other quarters, secretly compared my character of her with what he had himself observed and what he heard from others, and finally came to the conclusion that, all things considered, she had much better remain Miss Wilson of Ryecote Farm, than be transmuted into Mrs Lawrence of Woodford Hall. I believe, too, that he soon learned to contemplate with secret amazement his former predilection, and to congratulate himself on the lucky escape he had made; but he never confessed it to me, or hinted one word of acknowledgment for the part I had had in his deliverance – but this was not surprising to any one that knew him as I did.

As for Jane Wilson, she, of course, was disappointed and embittered by the sudden cold neglect, and ultimate desertion of her former admirer. Had I done wrong to blight her cherished hopes? I think not; and certainly my conscience has never accused me, from that day to this, of any evil design in the matter.

CHAPTER XLVII

STARTLING INTELLIGENCE

ONE MORNING, ABOUT the beginning of November, while I was inditing some business letters, shortly after breakfast, Eliza Millward came to call upon my sister. Rose had neither the discrimination nor the virulence to regard the little demon as I did, and they still preserved their former intimacy. At the moment of her arrival, however, there was no one in the room but Fergus and myself, my mother and sister being both of them absent, 'on household cares intent;' but *I* was not going to lay myself out for her amusement, whoever else might so incline: I merely honoured her with a careless salutation and a few words of course, and then went on with my writing, leaving my brother to be more polite if he chose. But she wanted to tease me.

'What a pleasure it is to find you at home, Mr Markham!' said she, with a disingenuously malicious smile. 'I so seldom see you now, for you never come to the vicarage. Papa is quite offended I can tell you,' she added playfully, looking into my face with an impertinent laugh, as she seated herself, half beside and half before my desk, off the corner of the table.

'I have had a good deal to do of late,' said I, without looking up from my letter.

'Have you indeed! Somebody said you had been strangely neglecting your business these last few months.'

'Somebody said wrong, for, these last *two* months especially, I have been particularly plodding and diligent.'

'Ah! Well, there's nothing like active employment, I suppose, to console the afflicted; – and, excuse me, Mr Markham, but you look so very far from well, and have been, by all accounts, so moody and thoughtful of late, – I could almost think you have some secret care preying on your spirits. *Formerly*,' said she timidly, 'I could have ventured to ask you what it was, and what I could do to comfort you: I dare not do it now.'

'You're very kind, Miss Eliza. When I think you can do anything to comfort me, I'll make bold to tell you.'

'Pray do! – I suppose I mayn't guess what it is that troubles you?'

'There's no necessity, for I'll tell you plainly. The thing that troubles me the most at present, is a young lady sitting at my elbow, and preventing me from finishing my letter, and thereafter, repairing to my daily business.'

Before she could reply to this ungallant speech, Rose entered the room; and Miss Eliza rising to greet her, they both seated themselves near the fire, where that idle lad, Fergus, was standing, leaning his shoulder against the corner of the chimney-piece, with his legs crossed and his hands in his breeches pockets.

'Now, Rose, I'll tell you a piece of news – I hope you've not heard it before, for good, bad, or indifferent, one always likes to be the first to tell. – It's about that sad Mrs Graham —'

'Hush – sh – sh!' whispered Fergus, in a tone of solemn import. ' "We never mention her; her name is never heard." ' And glancing up, I caught him with his eye askance on me, and his finger pointed to his forehead; then, winking at the young lady with a doleful shake of the head, he whispered – 'a monomania – but don't mention it – all right but that.'

'I should be sorry to injure any one's feelings,' returned she, speaking below her breath, 'another time, perhaps.'

'Speak out, Miss Eliza!' said I, not deigning to notice the other's buffooneries, 'you needn't fear to say anything in my presence – that is *true*.'

'Well,' answered she, 'perhaps you know already that Mrs Graham's husband is not really dead, and that she had run away from him?' I started, and felt my face glow; but I bent it over my letter, and went on folding it up as she proceeded, 'but perhaps you did *not* know that she is now gone back to him again, and that a perfect reconciliation has taken place between them? Only think,' she continued, turning to the confounded Rose, 'what a fool the man must be!'

'And who gave you this piece of intelligence, Miss Eliza?' said I, interrupting my sister's exclamations.

'I had it from a very authentic source, sir.'

'From whom, may I ask?'

'From one of the servants at Woodford.'

'Oh! I was not aware that you were on such intimate terms with Mr Lawrence's household.'

'It was not from the man himself, that I heard it; but he told it in confidence to our maid Sarah, and Sarah told it to me.'

'In confidence, I suppose; and you tell it in confidence to us; but *I* can tell *you* that it is but a lame story after all, and scarcely one half of it true.'

While I spoke, I completed the sealing and direction of my letters, with a somewhat unsteady hand, in spite of all my efforts to retain composure, and in spite of my firm conviction that the story *was* a lame one – that the supposed Mrs Graham, most certainly, had not *voluntarily* gone back to her husband, or dreamt of a reconciliation. Most likely, she was gone away, and the tale-bearing servant, not knowing what was become of her, had *conjectured* that such was the case, and our fair visiter had detailed it as a certainty, delighted with such an opportunity of tormenting me. But it was possible – barely possible, that some one might have betrayed her, and she had been taken away by force. Determined to know the worst, I hastily pocketed my two letters, and muttering something about being too late for the post, left the room, rushed into the yard and vociferously called for my horse. No one being there, I dragged him out of the stable myself, strapped the saddle on to his back and the bridle on to his head, mounted, and speedily galloped away to Woodford. I found its owner pensively strolling in the grounds.

'Is your sister gone?' were my first words as I grasped his hand, instead of the usual enquiry after his health.

'Yes; she's gone,' was his answer, so calmly spoken, that my terror was at once removed.

'I suppose I mayn't know where she is?' said I, as I dismounted and relinquished my horse to the gardener, who, being the only servant within call, had been summoned by his master, from his employment of raking up the dead leaves on the lawn, to take him to the stables.

My companion gravely took my arm, and leading me away to the garden, thus answered my question: –

'She is at Grassdale Manor, in —shire.'

'Where?' cried I, with a convulsive start.

'At Grassdale Manor.'

'How was it?' I gasped. 'Who betrayed her?'

'She went of her own accord.'

'Impossible, Lawrence!! She *could* not be so frantic!' exclaimed I, vehemently grasping his arm, as if to force him to unsay those hateful words.

'She did,' persisted he in the same grave, collected manner as before – 'and not without reason,' he continued, gently disengaging himself from my grasp: 'Mr Huntingdon is ill.'

'And so she went to nurse him?'

'Yes.'

'Fool!' I could not help exclaiming – and Lawrence looked up with a rather reproachful glance. 'Is he dying then?'

'I think not, Markham.'

'And how many more nurses has he? – How many ladies are there besides, to take care of him?'

'None: he was alone, or she would not have gone.'

'Oh, confound it! this is intolerable!'

'What is? That he should be alone?'

I attempted no reply, for I was not sure that this circumstance did not partly conduce to my distraction. I therefore continued to pace the walk in silent anguish, with my hand pressed to my forehead; then suddenly pausing and turning to my companion, I impatiently exclaimed,

'Why did she take this infatuated step? What fiend persuaded her to it?'

'Nothing persuaded her but her own sense of duty.'

'Humbug!'

'I was half inclined to say so myself, Markham, at first. I assure you it was not by my advice that she went, for I detest that man as fervently as you can do – except, indeed, that his reformation would give me much greater pleasure than his death: – but all I did was to inform her of the circumstance of his illness (the consequence of a fall from his horse in hunting), and to tell her that that unhappy person, Miss Myers, had left him some time ago.'

'It was ill done! Now, when he finds the convenience of her presence, he will make all manner of lying speeches and false, fair promises for the future, and she will believe him, and then her condition will be ten times worse and ten times more irremediable than before.'

'There does not appear to be much ground for such apprehensions at present,' said he, producing a letter from his pocket: 'from the account I received this morning, I should say –'

It was *her* writing! By an irresistible impulse, I held out my hand, and the words – 'Let me see it,' involuntarily passed my lips. He was evidently reluctant to grant the request, but while he hesitated, I snatched it from his hand. Recollecting myself, however, the minute after, I offered to restore it.

'Here, take it,' said I, 'if you don't want me to read it.'

'No,' replied he, 'you may read it if you like.'

I read it and so may you.

Grassdale, Nov. 4th.

Dear Frederick,

I know you will be anxious to hear from me: and I will tell you all I can. Mr Huntingdon is very ill, but not dying, or in any immediate danger; and he is rather better at present than he was when I came. I found the house in sad confusion: Mrs Greaves, Benson, every decent servant had left, and those that were come to supply their places were a negligent, disorderly set, to say no worse – I must change them again if I stay. A professional nurse, a grim, hard old woman, had been hired to attend the wretched invalid. He suffers much, and has no fortitude to bear him through. The immediate injuries he sustained from the accident, however, were not very severe, and would, as the doctor says, have been but trifling to a man of temperate habits; but with *him* it is very different. On the night of my arrival, when I first entered his room, he was lying in a kind of half delirium. He did not notice me till I spoke; and then, he mistook me for another.

'Is it you, Alice, come again?' he murmured. 'What did you leave me for?'

'It is I, Arthur – it is Helen, your wife,' I replied.

'My wife!' said he, with a start. – 'For Heaven's sake, don't mention her! – I have none. – Devil take her,' he cried, a moment after, – 'and you too! What did you do it for?'

I said no more; but observing that he kept gazing towards the foot of the bed, I went and sat there, placing the light so as to shine full upon me; for I thought he might be dying, and I wanted him to know me. For a long time, he lay silently looking upon me, first with a vacant stare, then with a fixed gaze of strange, growing intensity. At last he startled me by suddenly raising himself on his elbow and demanding in a horrified whisper, with his eyes still fixed upon me, – 'Who is it?'

'It is Helen Huntingdon,' said I, quietly, rising, at the same time, and removing to a less conspicuous position.

'I must be going mad,' cried he, – 'or something – delirious perhaps – but leave me, whoever you are – I can't bear that white face, and those eyes – for God's sake go, and send me somebody else, that doesn't look like that!'

I went, at once, and sent the hired nurse. But next morning,

I ventured to enter his chamber again; and, taking the nurse's place by his bedside, I watched him and waited on him for several hours, showing myself as little as possible, and only speaking when necessary, and then not above my breath. At first he addressed me as the nurse, but, on my crossing the room to draw up the window-blinds, in obedience to his directions, he said –

'No, it isn't nurse; it's Alice. Stay with me, do! that old hag will be the death of me.'

'I mean to stay with you,' said I. And after that, he would call me Alice – or some other name almost equally repugnant to my feelings. I forced myself to endure it for a while, fearing a contradiction might disturb him too much: but when, having asked for a glass of water, while I held it to his lips, he murmured 'Thanks, dearest!' – I could not help distinctly observing – 'You would not say so if you knew me,' intending to follow that up with another declaration of my identity, but he merely muttered an incoherent reply, so I dropped it again, till some time after, when, as I was bathing his forehead and temples with vinegar and water to relieve the heat and pain in his head, he observed, after looking earnestly upon me for some minutes –

'I have such strange fancies – I can't get rid of them, and they won't let me rest; and the most singular and pertinacious of them all, is your face and voice; they seem just like hers. I could swear at this moment, that she was by my side.'

'She is,' said I.

'That seems comfortable,' continued he, without noticing my words; 'and while you do it, the other fancies fade away – but *this* only strengthens. Go on – go on, till it vanishes, too. I can't stand such a mania as this; it would kill me!'

'It never will vanish,' said I distinctly, 'for it is the truth.'

'The truth!' he cried, starting as if an asp had stung him. 'You don't mean to say that you are really she!'

'I do; but you needn't shrink away from me, as if I were your greatest enemy: I am come to take care of you, and do what none of *them* would do.'

'For God's sake, don't torment me now!' cried he in pitiable agitation; and then he began to mutter bitter curses against me, or the evil fortune that had brought me there; while I put down the sponge and basin, and resumed my seat at the bed-side.

'Where are they?' said he – 'have they all left me – servants and all?'

'There are servants within call, if you want them; but you had better lie down now and be quiet: none of them could or would attend you as carefully as I shall do.'

'I can't understand it at all,' said he, in bewildered perplexity. 'Was it a dream that —' and he covered his eyes with his hands, as if trying to unravel the mystery.

'No Arthur, it was not a dream, that your conduct was such as to oblige me to leave you; but I heard that you were ill and alone, and I am come back to nurse you. You need not fear to trust me: tell me all your wants, and I will try to satisfy them. There is no one else to care for you; and I shall not upbraid you now.'

'Oh! I see,' said he with a bitter smile; 'it's an act of Christian charity, whereby you hope to gain a higher seat in Heaven for yourself, and scoop a deeper pit in hell for me.'

'No; I came to offer you that comfort and assistance your situation required; and if I could benefit your soul as well as your body, and awaken some sense of contrition and —'

'Oh, yes; if you could overwhelm me with remorse and confusion of face, now's the time. What have you done with my son?'

'He is well, and you may see him some time, if you will compose yourself, but not now.'

'Where is he?'

'He is safe.'

'Is he here?'

'Wherever he is, you will not see him till you have promised to leave him entirely under my care and protection, and to let me take him away whenever and wherever I please, if I should hereafter judge it necessary to remove him again. But we will talk of that to-morrow: you must be quiet now.'

'No, let me see him now. I promise, if it *must* be so.'

'No –'

'I swear it, as God is in Heaven! Now then, let me see him.'

'But I cannot trust your oaths and promises: I must have a written agreement, and you must sign it in presence of a witness – but not to-day, to-morrow.'

'No, to-day – now,' persisted he: and he was in such a state of feverish excitement, and so bent upon the immediate gratification of his wish, that I thought it better to grant it at once, as I saw he would not rest till I did. But I was determined my son's interest should not be forgotten; and having clearly written out the promise I wished Mr Huntingdon to give upon a slip of paper, I deliberately read it over to him, and made him sign it in the presence of Rachel. He begged I would not insist upon this: it was a useless exposure of my want of faith in his word, to the servant. I told him I was sorry, but since he had forfeited my confidence, he must take the consequence. He next pleaded inability to hold the pen. 'Then we must wait until you can hold it,' said I. Upon which, he said he would try; but then, he could not see to write. I placed my finger where the signature was to be, and told him he might write his name in the dark, if he only knew where to put it. But he had not power to form the letters. 'In that case, you must be too ill to see the child,' said I; and finding me inexorable, he at length managed to ratify the agreement; and I bade Rachel send the boy.

All this may strike you as harsh, but I felt I must not lose my present advantage, and my son's future welfare should not be sacrificed to any mistaken tenderness for this man's feelings. Little Arthur had not forgotten his father, but thirteen months of absence, during which he had seldom been permitted to hear a word about him, or hardly to whisper his name, had rendered him somewhat shy; and when he was ushered into the darkened room where the sick man lay, so altered from his former self, with fiercely flushed face and wildly gleaming eyes – he instinctively clung to me, and stood looking on his father with a countenance expressive of far more awe than pleasure.

'Come here, Arthur,' said the latter, extending his hand towards him. The child went, and timidly touched that burning hand, but almost started in alarm, when his father suddenly clutched his arm and drew him nearer to his side.

'Do you know me?' asked Mr Huntingdon, intently perusing his features.

'Yes.'

'Who am I?'

'Papa.'

'Are you glad to see me?'

'Yes.'

'You're *not!*' replied the disappointed parent, relaxing his hold, and darting a vindictive glance at me.

Arthur, thus released, crept back to me and put his hand in mine. His father swore I had made the child hate him, and abused and cursed me bitterly. The instant he began I sent our son out of the room; and when he paused to breathe, I calmly assured him that he was entirely mistaken; I had never once attempted to prejudice his child against him.

'I did indeed desire him to *forget* you,' I said, 'and especially to forget the lessons you taught him; and for that cause, and to lessen the danger of discovery, I own I have generally discouraged his inclination to talk about you; – but no one can blame me for that, I think.'

The invalid only replied by groaning aloud and rolling his head on a pillow in a paroxysm of impatience.

'I am in hell, already!' cried he. 'This cursed thirst is burning my heart to ashes! Will *nobody* –'

Before he could finish the sentence, I had poured out a glass of some acidulated, cooling drink that was on the table, and brought it to him. He drank it greedily, but muttered, as I took away the glass, –

'I suppose you're heaping coals of fire on my head – you think.'

Not noticing this speech, I asked if there was anything else I could do for him.

'Yes; I'll give you another opportunity of shewing your Christian magnanimity,' sneered he: – 'set my pillow straight, – and these confounded bed-clothes.' I did so. 'There – now, get me another glass of that slop.' I complied. 'This is delightful! isn't it?' said he with a malicious grin, as I held it to his lips – 'you never hoped for such a glorious opportunity?'

'Now, shall I stay with you?' said I, as I replaced the glass on the table – 'or will you be more quiet if I go, and send the nurse?'

'Oh, yes, you're wondrous gentle and obliging! – But you've driven me mad with it all!' responded he, with an impatient toss.

'I'll leave you, then,' said I, and I withdrew, and did not trouble him with my presence again that day, except for a minute or two at a time, just to see how he was and what he wanted.

Next morning, the doctor ordered him to be bled; and after that, he was more subdued and tranquil. I passed half the day in his room at different intervals. My presence did not appear to agitate or irritate him as before, and he accepted my services quietly, without any bitter remarks – indeed he scarcely spoke at all, except to make known his wants, and hardly then. But on the morrow – that is, to-day – in proportion as he recovered from the state of exhaustion and stupefaction – his ill-nature appeared to revive.

'Oh, this sweet revenge!' cried he, when I had been doing all I could to make him comfortable and to remedy the carelessness of his nurse. 'And you can enjoy it with such a quiet conscience too, because it's all in the way of duty.'

'It is well for me that I *am* doing my duty,' said I, with a bitterness I could not repress, 'for it is the only comfort I have; and the satisfaction of my own conscience, it seems, is the only reward I need look for!'

He looked rather surprised at the earnestness of my manner. 'What reward *did* you look for?' he asked.

'You will think me a liar if I tell you – but I *did* hope to benefit you: as well to better your mind, as to alleviate your present sufferings; but it appears I am to do neither – your own bad spirit will not let me. As far as *you* are concerned, I have sacrificed my own feelings, and all the little earthly comfort that was left me, to no purpose; – and every little thing I do for you is ascribed to self-righteous malice and refined revenge!'

'It's all very fine, I dare say,' said he, eyeing me with stupid amazement; 'and of course I ought to be melted to tears of penitence and admiration at the sight of so much generosity and superhuman goodness, – but you see I can't manage it. However, pray do me all the good you can, if you do really find any pleasure in it; for you perceive I am almost as miserable just now as you need wish to see me. Since you came, I confess, I have had better attendance than before, for these wretches neglected me shamefully, and all my old friends seem to have fairly forsaken me. I've had a dreadful time of it, I assure you: I sometimes thought I should have died – do you think there's any chance?'

'There's always a chance of death; and it is always well to live with such a chance in view.'

'Yes, yes – but do you think there's any likelihood that this illness will have a fatal termination?'

'I cannot tell; but, supposing it should, how are you prepared to meet the event?'

'Why, the doctor told me I wasn't to think about it, for I was sure to get better, if I stuck to his regimen and prescriptions.'

'I hope you may, Arthur, but neither the doctor nor I can speak with certainty in such a case: there is internal injury, and it is difficult to know to what extent.'

'There now! you want to scare me to death.'

'No; but I don't want to lull you to false security. If a con-sciousness of the uncertainty of life can dispose you to serious and useful thoughts, I would not deprive you of the benefit of such reflections, whether you do eventually recover or not. Does the idea of death appal you *very* much?'

'It's just the only thing I can't bear to think of, so if you've any –'

'But it must come sometime,' interrupted I; 'and if it be years hence, it will as certainly overtake you as if it came to-day, – and no doubt be as unwelcome then as now, unless you –'

'Oh, hang it! don't torment me with your preachments now, unless you want to kill me outright – I can't stand it, I tell you – I've sufferings enough without that. If you think there's danger, save me from it; and then, in gratitude, I'll hear whatever you like to say.'

I accordingly dropped the unwelcome topic. And now, Frederick, I think I may bring my letter to a close. From these details you may form your own judgment of the state of my patient, and of my own position and future prospects. Let me hear from you soon, and I will write again to tell you how we get on; but now that my presence is tolerated – and even required in the sick-room, I shall have but little time to spare between my husband and my son, – for I must not entirely neglect the latter: it would not do to keep him always with Rachel, and I dare not leave him for a moment with any of the other servants, or suffer him to be alone, lest he should meet them. If his father get worse, I shall ask Esther Hargrave to take charge of him for a time, till I have re-organized the household at least; but I greatly prefer keeping him under my own eye.

I find myself in rather a singular position: I am exerting my utmost endeavours to promote the recovery and reformation of my husband, and if I succeed what shall I do? My duty, of course, – but how? – No matter; I can perform the task that is before me now, and God will give me strength to do whatever He requires hereafter. – Good-bye, dear Frederick.

Helen Huntingdon.

'What do you think of it?' said Lawrence as I silently refolded the letter.

'It seems to me,' returned I, 'that she is casting her pearls before swine. May they be satisfied with trampling them under their feet, and not turn again and rend her! But I shall say no more against her: I see that she was actuated by the best and noblest motives in what she has done; and if the act is not a wise one, may Heaven protect her from its consequences! May I keep this letter, Lawrence? – you see she has never once mentioned me throughout – or made the most distant allusion to me; therefore, there can be no impropriety or harm in it.'

'And therefore, why should you wish to keep it?'

'Were not these characters written by her hand? and were not these words conceived in her mind, and many of them spoken by her lips?'

'Well,' said he. And so I kept it; otherwise, Halford, you could never have become so thoroughly acquainted with its contents.

'And when you write,' said I, 'will you have the goodness to ask her if I may be permitted to enlighten my mother and sister on her real history and circumstance, just so far as is necessary to make the neighbourhood sensible of the shameful injustice they have done her? I want no tender messages, but just ask her that, and tell her it is the greatest favour she could do me; and tell her – no, nothing more. – You see I know the address, and I might write to her myself, but I am so virtuous as to refrain.'

'Well, I'll do this for you, Markham.'

'And as soon as you receive an answer, you'll let me know?'

'If all be well, I'll come myself and tell you, immediately.'

CHAPTER XLVIII

FURTHER INTELLIGENCE

FIVE OR SIX days after this, Mr Lawrence paid us the honour of a call; and when he and I were alone together – which I contrived as soon as possible, by bringing him out to look at my cornstacks – he showed me another letter from his sister. This one he was quite willing to submit to my longing gaze: he thought, I suppose, it would do me good. The only answer it gave to my message was this: –

'Mr Markham is at liberty to make such revelations concerning me as he judges necessary. He will know that I should wish but little to be said on the subject. I hope he is well; but tell him he must not think of me.'

I can give you a few extracts from the rest of the letter, for I was permitted to keep this also – perhaps, as an antidote to all pernicious hopes and fancies.

He is decidedly better, but very low from the depressing effects of his severe illness and the strict regimen he is obliged to observe – so opposite to all his previous habits. It is deplorable to see how completely his past life has degenerated his once noble constitution, and vitiated the whole system of his organization. But the doctor says he may now be considered out of danger, if he will only continue to observe the necessary restrictions. Some stimulating cordials he must have, but they should be judiciously diluted and sparingly used; and I find it very difficult to keep him to this. At first, his extreme dread of death rendered the task an easy one; but in proportion as he feels his acute suffering abating and sees the danger receding, the more intractable he becomes. Now also, his appetite for food is beginning to return; and here too, his long habits of self-indulgence are greatly against him. I watch and restrain him as well as I can, and often get bitterly abused for my rigid severity; and sometimes he contrives to illude my vigilance, and sometimes acts in open opposition to my will. But he is now so completely reconciled to my attendance in general that he is never satisfied when I am not by his side. I am obliged to be a little stiff with him sometimes, or he would make a complete slave of me; and I know it would be unpardonable weakness to give up all other interests for him. I have the servants to overlook and my little Arthur to attend to, – and my own health too, all of which would be entirely neglected were I to satisfy his exorbitant demands. I do not generally sit up at nights, for I think the nurse who has made it her business, is better qualified for such undertakings than I am; but still, an unbroken night's rest is what I but seldom enjoy, and never can venture to reckon upon; for my patient makes no scruple of calling me up at an hour when his wants or his fancies require my presence. But he is manifestly afraid of my displeasure; and if at one time he tries my patience by his unreasonable exactions, and fretful complaints and reproaches, at another, he depresses me by his abject submission and deprecatory self-abasement when he fears he has gone too far. But all this I can readily pardon; I know it is chiefly the result of his enfeebled frame and disordered nerves – what annoys me the most, is his occasional attempts at affectionate fondness that I can neither credit nor return; not that I hate him: his sufferings and my own laborious care have given him some claim to my regard – to my affection even, if he would only be quiet and sincere, and content to let things remain as they are, but the more he tries to conciliate me the more I shrink from him and from the future.

'Helen, what do you mean to do when I get well?' he asked this morning. 'Will you run away again?'

'It entirely depends upon your own conduct.'

'Oh, I'll be very good.'

'But if I find it necessary to leave you, Arthur, I shall not "run away:" you know I have your own promise that I may go whenever I please, and take my son with me.'

'Oh, but you shall have no cause.' And then followed a variety of professions, which I rather coldly checked.

'Will you not forgive me, then?' said he.

'Yes, – I *have* forgiven you; but I know you cannot love me as you once did – and I should be very sorry if you were to, for I could not pretend to return it: so let us drop the subject, and never recur to it again. By what I *have* done for you, you may judge of what I *will* do – if it be not incompatible with the higher duty I owe to my son (higher, because he never forfeited his claims, and because I hope to do more good to him than I can ever do to you); and if you wish me to feel kindly towards you, it is *deeds* not *words* which must purchase my affection and esteem.'

His sole reply to this was a slight grimace, and a scarcely perceptible shrug. Alas unhappy man! words, with him, are so much cheaper than deeds; it was as if I had said, 'Pounds, not pence, must buy the article you want.' And then he sighed a querulous, self-commiserating sigh, as if in pure regret that he, the loved and courted of so many worshippers, should be now abandoned to the mercy of a harsh, exacting, cold-hearted woman like that, and even glad of what kindness she chose to bestow.

'It's a pity, isn't it?' said I; and whether I rightly divined his musings or not, the observation chimed in with his thoughts, for he answered – 'It can't be helped,' with a rueful smile at my penetration.

I have seen Esther Hargrave twice. She is a charming creature, but her blithe spirit is almost broken, and her sweet temper almost spoiled, by the still unremitting persecutions of her mother, in behalf of her rejected suitor – not violent, but wearisome and unremitting like a continual dropping. The unnatural parent seems determined to make her daughter's life a burden if she will not yield to her desires.

'Mamma does all she can,' said she, 'to make me feel myself a burden and incumbrance to the family, and the most ungrateful, selfish, and undutiful daughter that ever was born; and Walter, too, is as stern and cold, and haughty as if he hated me outright. I believe I should have yielded at once if I had known, from the beginning, how much resistance would have cost me; but now, for very obstinacy's sake, I *will* stand out!'

'A bad motive for a good resolve,' I answered. 'But however, I know you have better motives, really, for your perseverance: and I counsel you to keep them still in view.'

'Trust me, I will. I threaten mamma sometimes, that I'll run away, and disgrace the family by earning my own livelihood, if she torments me any more; and then that frightens her a little. But I *will* do it, in good earnest, if they don't mind.'

'Be quiet and patient a while,' said I, 'and better times will come.'

Poor girl! I wish somebody that was worthy to possess her would come and take her away – don't you, Frederick?

If the perusal of this letter filled me with dismay for Helen's future life and mine, there was one great source of consolation: it was now in my power to clear her name from every foul aspersion. The Millwards and the Wilsons should see with their own eyes, the bright sun bursting from the cloud – and they should be scorched and dazzled by its beams; – and my own friends too should see it – they whose suspicions had been such gall and wormwood to my soul. To effect this, I had only to drop the seed into the ground, and it would soon become a stately, branching herb: a few words to my mother and sister, I knew, would suffice to spread the news throughout the whole neighbourhood, without any further exertion on my part.

Rose was delighted; and as soon as I had told her all I thought proper – which was all I affected to know – she flew with alacrity to put on her bonnet and shawl, and hasten to carry the glad tidings to the Millwards and Wilsons – glad tidings I suspect, to none but herself and Mary Millward – that steady, sensible girl, whose sterling worth had been so quickly perceived and duly valued by the supposed Mrs Graham, in spite of her plain outside; and who, on her part, had been better able to see and appreciate that lady's true character and qualities than the brightest genius among them.

As I may never have occasion to mention her again, I may as well tell you here, that she was at this time privately engaged to Richard Wilson – a secret, I believe to every one but their two selves. That worthy student was now at Cambridge, where his most exemplary conduct and his diligent perseverance in the pursuit of learning carried him safely through, and eventually brought him with hard-earned honours and an untarnished reputation, to the close of his collegiate career. In due time, he became Mr Millward's first and only curate – for that gentleman's declining years forced him at last to acknowledge that the duties of his extensive parish were a little too much for those vaunted energies which he was wont to boast over his younger and less active brethren of the cloth. This was what the patient, faithful lovers had privately planned, and quietly waited for years ago; and in due time they were united, to the astonishment of the little world they lived in, that had long since declared them both born to single blessedness; affirming it impossible that the pale, retiring bookworm should ever summon courage to seek a wife, or be able to obtain one if he did, and equally impossible that the plain-looking, plain-dealing, unattractive, unconciliating Miss Millward should ever find a husband.

They still continued to live at the vicarage, the lady dividing her time between her father, her husband, and their poor parish-ioners, – and subsequently, her rising family; and now that the Reverend Michael Millward has been gathered to his fathers, full of years and honours, the Reverend Richard Wilson has succeeded him to the vicarage of Lindenhope, greatly to the satisfaction of its inhabitants, who had so long tried and fully proved his merits, and those of his excellent and well-loved partner.

If you are interested in the after fate of that lady's sister, I can only tell you – what perhaps you have heard from another quarter – that some twelve or thirteen years ago, she relieved the happy couple of her presence by marrying a wealthy trades-man of L—; and I don't envy him his bargain. I fear she leads him a rather uncomfortable life, though, happily he is too dull to perceive the extent of his misfortune. I have little enough to do with her myself: we have not met for many years; but, I am well assured, she has not yet forgotten or forgiven either her former lover or the lady whose superior qualities first opened his eyes to the folly of his boyish attachment.

As for Richard Wilson's sister, she, having been wholly un-able to re-capture Mr Lawrence or obtain any partner rich and elegant enough to suit her ideas of what the husband of Jane Wilson ought to be, is yet in single blessedness. Shortly after the death of her mother, she withdrew the light of her presence from Ryecote Farm, finding it impossible any longer to endure the rough manners and unsophisticated habits of her honest brother Robert and his worthy wife, or the idea of being identi-fied with such vulgar people in the eyes of the world, – and took lodgings in — the county town, where she lived, and still lives, I suppose, in a kind of closefisted, cold, uncomfortable gentility, doing no good to others and but little to herself; spending her days in fancy-work and scandal; referring fre-quently to her 'brother the vicar' and her 'sister the vicar's lady,' but never to her brother the farmer and her sister the farmer's wife; seeing as much company as she can without too much expense, but loving no one and beloved by none – a cold-hearted, supercilious, keenly, insidiously censorious old maid.

CHAPTER XLIX

'The rain descended, and the floods came, and the winds blew, and beat upon that house; and it fell: and great was the fall of it.'

THOUGH MR LAWRENCE'S health was now quite re-established, my visits to Woodford were as unremitting as ever; though often less protracted than before. We seldom *talked* about Mrs Huntingdon; but yet we never met without mentioning her, for I never sought his company but with the hope of hearing something about her, and he never sought mine at all, because he saw me often enough without. But I always began to talk of other things, and waited first to see if *he* would introduce the subject. If he did not, I would casually ask, 'Have you heard from your sister lately?' If he said 'No,' the matter was dropped: if he said 'Yes,' I would venture to enquire, 'How is she?' but never 'How is her husband?' though I might be burning to know; because, I had not the hypocrisy to profess any anxiety for his recovery, and I had not the face to express any desire for a contrary result. Had I any such desire? – I fear I must plead guilty: but since you have heard my confession, you must hear my justification as well – a few of the excuses, at least, wherewith I sought to pacify my own accusing conscience: –

In the first place, you see, his life did harm to others, and evidently no good to himself; and though I wished it to terminate, I would not have hastened its close if, by the lifting of a finger, I could have done so, or if a spirit had whispered in my ear that a single effort of the will would be enough, – unless, indeed, I had the power to exchange him for some other victim of the grave, whose life might be of service to his race, and whose death would be lamented by his friends. But was there any harm in wishing that, among the many thousands whose souls would certainly be required of them before the year was over, this wretched mortal might be one? I thought not; and therefore I wished with all my heart that it might please Heaven to remove him to a better world, or if that might not be, still, to take him out of this, for if he were unfit to answer the summons now, after a warning sickness, and with such an angel by his side, it seemed but too certain that he never would be – that, on the contrary, returning health would bring returning lust and villainy, and as he grew more certain of recovery, more accustomed to her generous goodness, his feelings would become more callous, his heart more flinty and impervious to her persuasive arguments – but God knew best. Meantime, however, I could not but be anxious for the result of His decrees; knowing, as I did, that (leaving myself entirely out of the question) however Helen might feel interested in her husband's welfare, however she might deplore his fate, still, while he lived, she *must* be miserable.

A fortnight passed away, and my enquiries were always answered in the negative. At length a welcome 'yes' drew from me the second question. Lawrence divined my anxious thoughts, and appreciated my reserve. I feared at first, he was going to torture me by unsatisfactory replies, and either leave me quite in the dark concerning what I wanted to know, or force me to drag the information out of him, morsel by morsel, by direct enquiries – 'and serve you right,' you will say; but he was more merciful; and in a little while, he put his sister's letter into my hand. I silently read it, and restored it to him without comment or remark. This mode of procedure suited him so well that thereafter he always pursued the plan of showing me her letters at once, when I enquired after her, if there were any to show: it was so much less trouble than to tell me their contents; and I received such confidences so quietly and discreetly that he was never induced to discontinue them.

But I devoured those precious letters with my eyes, and never let them go till their contents were stamped upon my mind; and when I got home, the most important passages were entered in my diary among the remarkable events of the day.

The first of these communications brought intelligence of a serious relapse in Mr Huntingdon's illness, entirely the result of his own infatuation in persisting in the indulgence of his appetite for stimulating drink. In vain had she remonstrated, in vain she had mingled his wine with water: her arguments and entreaties were a nuisance, her interference was an insult so intolerable that at length, on finding she had covertly diluted the pale port that was brought him, he threw the bottle out of the window, swearing he would not be cheated like a baby, ordered the butler, on pain of instant dismissal, to bring a bottle of the strongest wine in the cellar, and, affirming that he should have been well long ago if he had been let to have his own way, but she wanted to keep him weak in order that she might have him under her thumb – but by the Lord Harry, he would have no more humbug – seized a glass in one hand and the bottle in the other, and never rested till he had drunk it dry. Alarming symptoms were the immediate result of this 'imprudence' as she mildly termed it – symptoms which had rather increased than diminished since; and this was the cause of her delay in writing to her brother. Every former feature of his malady had returned with augmented virulence: the slight external wound, half-healed, had broken out afresh; internal inflammation had taken place, which might terminate fatally if not soon removed. Of course, the wretched sufferer's temper was not improved by this calamity – in fact, I suspect it was well nigh insupportable, though his kind nurse did not complain; but she said she had been obliged, at last, to give her son in charge to Esther Hargrave, as her presence was so constantly required in the sick-room that she could not possibly attend to him herself; and though the child had begged to be allowed to continue with her there, and to help her to nurse his papa, and though she had no doubt he would have been very good and quiet, – she could not think of subjecting his young and tender feelings to the sight of so much suffering, or of allowing him to witness his father's impatience, or hear the dreadful language he was wont to use in his paroxysms of pain or irritation.

'The latter,' continued she, 'most deeply regrets the step that has occasioned his relapse, – but, as usual, he throws the blame upon me. If I had reasoned with him like a rational creature, he says, it never would have happened; but to be treated like a baby or a fool, was enough to put any man past his patience, and drive him to assert his independence even at the sacrifice of his own interest – he forgets how often I had *reasoned* him "past his patience" before. He appears to be sensible of his danger; but nothing can induce him to behold it in the proper light. The other night while I was waiting on him, and just as I had brought him a draught to assuage his burning thirst – he observed, with a return of his former sarcastic bitterness, –

' "Yes, you're mighty attentive *now*! – I suppose there's *nothing* you wouldn't do for me now?"

' "You know," said I, a little surprised at his manner, "that I am willing to do anything I can to relieve you."

' "Yes, *now*, my immaculate angel; but when once you have secured your reward, and find yourself safe in Heaven, and me howling in hell-fire, catch you lifting a finger to serve me *then*! – No, you'll look complacently on, and not so much as dip the tip of your finger in water to cool my tongue!"

' "If so, it will be because of the great gulf over which I cannot pass; and if I *could* look complacently on in such a case, it would be only from the assurance that you were being purified from your sins, and fitted to enjoy the happiness I felt. – But are you *determined*, Arthur, that I shall not meet you in Heaven?"

' "Humph! What should I do there, I should like to know?"

' "Indeed, I cannot tell; and I fear it is too certain that your tastes and feelings must be widely altered before you can have any enjoyment there. But do you prefer sinking, without an effort, into the state of torment you picture to yourself?"

' "Oh, it's all a fable," said he, contemptuously.

' "Are you sure, Arthur? are you *quite* sure? Because if there is any doubt, and if you *should* find yourself mistaken after all, when it is too late to turn –"

' "It would be rather awkward, to be sure," said he; "but don't bother me now – I'm not going to die yet. – I can't and won't," he added vehemently, as if suddenly struck with the appalling aspect of that terrible event, "Helen, you *must* save me!" And he earnestly seized my hand, and looked into my face with such imploring eagerness that my heart bled for him, and I could not speak for tears.'

The next letter brought intelligence that the malady was fast increasing; and the poor sufferer's horror of death was still more distressing than his impatience of bodily pain. *All* his friends had not forsaken him, for Mr Hattersley, hearing of his danger, had come to see him from his distant home in the north. His wife had accompanied him, as much for the pleasure of seeing her dear friend, from whom she had been parted so long, as to visit her mother and sister.

Mrs Huntingdon expressed herself glad to see Milicent once more, and pleased to behold her so happy and well. 'She is now at the Grove,' continued the letter, 'but she often calls to see me. Mr Hattersley spends much of his time at Arthur's bedside. With more good feeling than I gave him credit for, he evinces considerable sympathy for his unhappy friend, and is far more willing than able to comfort him. Sometimes he tries to joke and laugh with him, but that will not do: sometimes he endeavours to cheer him with talk about old times; and this, at one time, may serve to divert the sufferer from his own sad thoughts; at another, it will only plunge him into deeper melancholy than before; and then Hattersley is confounded, and knows not what to say, – unless it be a timid suggestion that the clergyman might be sent for. But Arthur will never consent to that: he knows he has rejected the clergyman's well-meant admonitions with scoffing levity at other times, and cannot dream of turning to him for consolation now.

'Mr Hattersley sometimes offers his services instead of mine, but Arthur will not let me go: that strange whim still increases, as his strength declines – the fancy to have me always by his side. I hardly ever leave him, except to go into the next room, where I sometimes snatch an hour or so of sleep when he is quiet; but even then, the door is left ajar that he may know me to be within call. I am with him now, while I write; and I fear my occupation annoys him; though I frequently break off to attend to him, and though Mr Hattersley is also by his side. That gentleman came, as he said, to beg a holiday for me, that I might have a run in the park, this fine, frosty morning, with Milicent, and Esther, and little Arthur, whom he had driven over to see me. Our poor invalid evidently felt it a heartless proposition, and would have felt it still more heartless in me to accede to it. I therefore said I would only go and speak to them a minute, and then come back. I did but exchange a few words with them, just outside the portico – inhaling the fresh, bracing air as I stood – and then, resisting the earnest and eloquent entreaties of all three to stay a little longer, and join them in a walk round the garden, – I tore myself away and returned to my patient. I had not been absent five minutes, but he reproached me bitterly for my levity and neglect. His friend espoused my cause: –

' "Nay, nay, Huntingdon," said he, "you're too hard upon her – she must have food and sleep, and a mouthful of fresh air now and then, or she can't stand it I tell you. Look at her, man, she's worn to a shadow already."

' "What are her sufferings to mine?" said the poor invalid. "You don't grudge me these attentions, do you, Helen?"

' "No, Arthur, if I could really serve you by them. I would give my life to save you, if I might."

' "Would you, *indeed* ? – No!"

' "Most willingly I would."

' "Ah! that's because you think yourself more fit to die!"

'There was a painful pause. He was evidently plunged in gloomy reflections, but while I pondered for something to say, that might benefit without alarming him, Hattersley, whose mind had been pursuing almost the same course, broke silence with, –

' "I say, Huntingdon, I *would* send for a parson, of some sort. – If you didn't like the vicar, you know, you could have his curate, or somebody else."

' "No; none of them can benefit me if *she* can't," was the answer. And the tears gushed from his eyes as he earnestly exclaimed, – "Oh, Helen, if I had listened to you, it never would have come to this! And if I had heard you long ago – oh, God! how different it would have been!"

' "Hear me now, then, Arthur," said I, gently pressing his hand.

' "It's too late now," said he despondingly. And after that another paroxysm of pain came on; and then his mind began to wander, and we feared his death was approaching; but an opiate was administered, his sufferings began to abate, he gradually became more composed, and at length sank into a kind of slumber. He has been quieter since; and now Hattersley has left him, expressing a hope that he shall find him better when he calls to-morrow.

' "Perhaps, I *may* recover," he replied; "who knows? – this may have been the crisis. What do *you* think, Helen?"

'Unwilling to depress him, I gave the most cheering answer I could, but still recommended him to prepare for the possibility of what I inly feared was but too certain. But he was determined to hope. Shortly after, he relapsed into a kind of doze – but now he groans again.

'There is a change. Suddenly he called me to his side, with such a strange, excited manner that I feared he was delirious – but he was not. "That *was* the crisis, Helen!" said he delightedly. – "I had an infernal pain here – it is quite gone now; I never was so easy since the fall. – Quite gone, by Heaven!" and he clasped and kissed my hand in the very fullness of his heart;

but, finding I did not participate his joy, he quickly flung it from him, and bitterly cursed my coldness and insensibility. How could I reply? Kneeling beside him, I took his hand and fondly pressed it to my lips – for the first time since our separation – and told him as well as tears would let me speak, that it was not *that* that kept me silent; it was the fear that this sudden cessation of pain was not so favourable a symptom as he supposed. – I immediately sent for the doctor. We are now anxiously awaiting him: I will tell you what he says. There is still the same freedom from pain – the same deadness to all sensation where the suffering was most acute.

'My worst fears are realized – mortification has commenced. The doctor has told him there is no hope – no words can describe his anguish – I can write no more.'

The next was still more distressing in the tenor of its contents. The sufferer was fast approaching dissolution – dragged almost to the verge of that awful chasm he trembled to contemplate, from which no agony of prayers or tears could save him. Nothing could comfort him now: Hattersley's rough attempts at consolation were utterly in vain. The world was nothing to him: life and all its interests, its petty cares and transient pleasures were a cruel mockery. To talk of the past, was to torture him with vain remorse; to refer to the future, was to increase his anguish; and yet to be silent, was to leave him a prey to his own regrets and apprehensions. Often he dwelt with shuddering minuteness on the fate of his perishing clay – the slow, piecemeal dissolution already invading his frame; the shroud, the coffin, the dark, lonely grave, and all the horrors of corruption.

'If I try,' said his afflicted wife, 'to divert him from these things – to raise his thoughts to higher themes, it is no better: – "Worse and worse!" he groans. "If there be really life beyond the tomb, and judgment after death, how *can* I face it?" – I cannot do him any good; he will neither be enlightened, nor roused, nor comforted by anything I say; and yet he clings to me with unrelenting pertinacity – with a kind of childish desperation, as if *I* could save him from the fate he dreads. He keeps me night and day beside him. He is holding my left hand now, while I write; he has held it thus for hours: sometimes quietly, with his pale face upturned to mine: sometimes clutching my arm with violence – the big drops starting from his forehead, at the thoughts of what he sees, or thinks he sees before him. If I withdraw my hand for a moment it distresses him: –

' "Stay with me, Helen," he says; "let me hold you so: it seems as if harm could not reach me while you are here. But death *will* come – it is coming now – fast, fast! – and – oh, if I *could* believe there was nothing after!"

' "Don't try to believe it, Arthur; there is joy and glory after, if you will but try to reach it!"

' "What, for *me*?" he said, with something like a laugh. "Are we not to be judged according to the deeds done in the body? Where's the use of a probationary existence, if a man may spend it as he pleases, just contrary to God's decrees, and then go to Heaven with the best – if the vilest sinner may win the reward of the holiest saint, by merely saying, 'I repent!' "

' "But if you *sincerely* repent –"

' "I *can't* repent; I only fear."

' "You only regret the past for its consequences to yourself?"

' "Just so – except that I'm sorry to have wronged you Nell, because you're so good to me."

' "Think of the goodness of God, and you cannot but be grieved to have offended Him."

' "What *is* God? – I cannot see Him or hear Him. – God is only an idea."

' "God is Infinite Wisdom, and Power, and Goodness – and LOVE; but if this idea is too vast for your human faculties – if your mind loses itself in its overwhelming infinitude, fix it on Him who condescended to take our nature upon Him, who was raised to Heaven even in His glorified human body, in whom the fullness of the Godhead shines."

' "But he only shook his head and sighed. Then, in another paroxysm of shuddering horror, he tightened his grasp on my hand and arm, and groaning and lamenting, still clung to me with that wild, desperate earnestness so harrowing to my soul, because I know I cannot help him. I did my best to soothe and comfort him.

' "Death is so terrible," he cried, "I cannot bear it! *You* don't know, Helen – you can't imagine what it is, because you haven't it before you; and when I'm buried, you'll return to your old ways and be as happy as ever, and all the world will go on just as busy and merry as if I had never been; while I —" He burst into tears.

' "You needn't let *that* distress you," I said; "we shall all follow you soon enough."

' "I wish to God I could take you with me now!" he exclaimed: "you should plead for me."

' "No man can deliver his brother, nor make agreement unto God for him," I replied: " 'it cost more to redeem their souls' – it cost the blood of an incarnate God, perfect and sinless in Himself, to redeem us from the bondage of the evil one; – let *Him* plead for you."

'But I seem to speak in vain. He does not now, as formerly, laugh these blessed truths to scorn: but still he cannot trust, or will not comprehend them. He cannot linger long. He suffers dreadfully, and so do those that wait upon him – but I will not harass you with further details: I have said enough, I think, to convince you that I did well to go to him.'

Poor, poor Helen! dreadful indeed her trials must have been! And I could do nothing to lessen them – nay, it almost seemed as if I had brought them upon her myself, by my own secret desires; and whether I looked at her husband's sufferings or her own, it seemed almost like a judgment upon myself for having cherished such a wish.

The next day but one, there came another letter. That too was put into my hands without a remark, and these are its contents: –

DEC. 5th.

He is gone at last. I sat beside him all night, with my hand fast locked in his, watching the changes of his features and listening to his failing breath. He had been silent a long time, and I thought he would never speak again, when he murmured, faintly but distinctly –

'Pray for me, Helen!'

'I do pray for you – every hour and every minute, Arthur; but you must pray for yourself.'

His lips moved but emitted no sound; – then his looks became unsettled; and, from the incoherent half-uttered words that escaped him from time to time, supposing him to be now unconscious, I gently disengaged my hand from his, intending to steal away for a breath of air, for I was almost ready to faint; but a convulsive movement of the fingers, and a faintly whispered 'Don't leave me!' immediately recalled me: I took his hand again, and held it till he was no more – and then I fainted; it was not grief; it was exhaustion that, till then, I had been enabled successfully to combat. Oh Frederick! none can imagine the miseries, bodily and mental, of that death bed! How could I endure to think that that poor trembling soul was hurried away to everlasting torment? it would drive me mad! But thank God I have hope – not only from a vague dependence on the possibility that penitence and pardon might have reached him at the last, but from the blessed confidence that, through whatever purging fires the erring spirit may be doomed to pass – whatever fate awaits it, still, it is not lost, and God, who hateth nothing that He hath made, *will* bless it in the end!

His body will be consigned on Thursday to that dark grave he so much dreaded; but the coffin must be closed as soon as possible. If you will attend the funeral come quickly, for I need help.

HELEN HUNTINGDON.

CHAPTER L

DOUBTS AND DISAPPOINTMENTS

ON READING THIS, I had no reason to disguise my joy and hope from Frederick Lawrence, for I had none to be ashamed of. I felt no joy but that his sister was at length released from her afflictive, overwhelming toil – no hope but that she would in time recover from the effects of it, and be suffered to rest in peace and quietness, at least, for the remainder of her life. I experienced a painful commiseration for her unhappy husband (though fully aware that he had brought every particle of his sufferings upon himself, and but too well deserved them all), and a profound sympathy for her own afflictions, and deep anxiety for the consequences of those harassing cares, those dreadful vigils, that incessant and deleterious confinement beside a living corpse – for I was persuaded she had not hinted half the sufferings she had had to endure.

'You will go to her, Lawrence?' said I, as I put the letter into his hand.

'Yes, immediately.'

'That's right! I'll leave you, then, to prepare for your departure.'

'I've done that, already, while you were reading the letter, and before you came; and the carriage is now coming round to the door.'

Inly approving his promptitude, I bade him good morning, and withdrew. He gave me a searching glance as we pressed each other's hands at parting; but whatever he sought in my countenance, he saw there nothing but the most becoming gravity, it might be, mingled with a little sternness in momentary resentment at what I suspected to be passing in his mind.

Had I forgotten my own prospects, my ardent love, my pertinacious hopes? It seemed like sacrilege to revert to them now, but I had not forgotten them. It was, however, with a gloomy sense of the darkness of those prospects, the fallacy of those hopes, and the vanity of that affection, that I reflected on those things as I remounted my horse and slowly journeyed homewards. Mrs Huntingdon was free now; it was no longer a crime to think of her – but did she ever think of *me*? – not *now* – of course it was not to be expected – but would she, when this shock was over? – In all the course of her correspondence with her brother (our mutual friend, as she herself had called him), she had never mentioned me but once – and that was from necessity. This, alone, afforded strong presumption that I was already forgotten; yet this was not the worst: it might have been her sense of duty that had kept her silent, she might be only *trying* to forget; but in addition to this, I had a gloomy conviction that the awful realities she had seen and felt, her reconciliation with the man she had once loved, his dreadful sufferings and death, must eventually efface from her mind all traces of her passing love for me. She might recover from these horrors so far as to be restored to her former health, her tranquillity, her cheerfulness even – but never to those feelings which would appear to her, henceforth, as a fleeting fancy, a vain, illusive dream; especially as there was no one to remind her of my existence – no means of assuring her of my fervent constancy, now that we were so far apart, and delicacy forbade me to see her or to write to her, for months to come at least. And how could I engage her brother in my behalf? how could I break that icy crust of shy reserve? Perhaps he would disapprove of my attachment now, as highly as before; perhaps he would think me too poor – too lowly born, to match with his sister. Yes, there was another barrier: doubtless there was a wide distinction between the rank and circumstances of Mrs Huntingdon, the lady of Grassdale Manor, and those of Mrs Graham the artist, the tenant of Wildfell Hall; and it might be deemed presumption in me to offer my hand to the former – by the world, by her friends – if not by herself – a penalty I might brave, if I were certain she loved me; but otherwise, how could I? And, finally, her deceased husband, with his usual selfishness, might have so constructed his will as to place restrictions upon her marrying again. So that you see I had reasons enough for despair if I chose to indulge it.

Nevertheless, it was with no small degree of impatience that I looked forward to Mr Lawrence's return from Grassdale – impatience that increased in proportion as his absence was prolonged. He stayed away some ten or twelve days. All very right that he should remain to comfort and help his sister, but he might have written to tell me how she was, – or at least to tell me when to expect his return; for he might have known I was suffering tortures of anxiety for her, and uncertainty for my own future prospects. And when he did return, all he told me about her, was that she had been greatly exhausted and worn by her unremitting exertions in behalf of that man who had been the scourge of her life, and had dragged her with him nearly to the portals of the grave, – and was still much shaken and depressed by his melancholy end and the circumstances attendant upon it; but no word in reference to me – no intimation that my name had ever passed her lips, or even been spoken in her presence. To be sure, I asked no questions on the subject: I could not bring my mind to do so, believing, as I did, that Lawrence was indeed averse to the idea of my union with his sister.

I saw that he expected to be further questioned concerning his visit, and I saw too, with the keen perception of awakened jealousy, or alarmed self-esteem – or by whatever name I ought to call it – that he rather shrank from that impending scrutiny, and was no less pleased than surprised to find it did not come. Of course, I was burning with anger, but pride obliged me to suppress my feelings, and preserve a smooth face – or at least, a stoic calmness throughout the interview. It was well it did, for, reviewing the matter in my sober judgment, I must say it would have been highly absurd and improper to have quarrelled with him on such an occasion: I must confess too that I wronged him in my heart: the truth was, he liked me very well, but he was fully aware that a union between Mrs Huntingdon and me would be what the world calls a mésalliance; and it was not in his nature to set the world at defiance; – especially in such a case as this, for its dread laugh, or ill opinion, would be far more terrible to him directed against his sister than himself. Had he believed that a union was necessary to the happiness of both, or of either, or had he known how fervently I loved her, he would have acted differently; but seeing me so calm and cool, he would not for the world disturb my philosophy; and though refraining entirely from any active opposition to the match, he would yet do nothing to bring it about, and would much rather take the part of prudence, in aiding us to overcome our mutual predilections, than that of feeling, to encourage them. 'And he was in the right of it,' you will say. Perhaps he was – at any rate, I had no business to feel so bitterly against him as I did; but I could not then regard the matter in such a moderate light; and, after a brief conversation upon indifferent topics, I went away, suffering all the pangs of wounded pride and injured friendship, in addition to those resulting from the fear that I was indeed forgotten, and the knowledge that she I loved was alone and afflicted, suffering from injured health and dejected spirits, and I was forbidden to console or assist her – forbidden even to assure her of my sympathy, for the transmission of any such message through Mr Lawrence was now completely out of the question.

But what should I do? I would wait, and see if she would notice me – which of course she would not, unless by some kind message intrusted to her brother, that, in all probability, he would not deliver, and then – dreadful thought! – she would think me cooled and changed for not returning it – or perhaps, he had already given her to understand that I had ceased to think of her! I would wait, however, till the six months after our parting were fairly passed (which would be about the close of February), and then I would send her a letter modestly reminding her of her former permission to write to her at the close of that period, and hoping I might avail myself of it, at least to express my heart-felt sorrow for her late afflictions, my just appreciation of her generous conduct, and my hope that her health was now completely re-established, and that she would, some time, be permitted to enjoy those blessings of a peaceful, happy life, which had been denied her so long, but which none could more truly be said to merit than herself, – adding a few words of kind remembrance to my little friend Arthur, with a hope that he had not forgotten me, and, perhaps, a few more in reference to by-gone times – to the delightful hours I had passed in her society, and my unfading recollection of them, which was the salt and solace of my life, – and a hope that her recent troubles had not entirely banished me from her mind. – If she did not answer this, of course I should write no more: if she did (as surely she would, in *some* fashion) my future proceedings should be regulated by her reply.

Ten weeks was long to wait in such a miserable state of un-certainty, but courage! it must be endured; – and meantime I would continue to see Lawrence now and then, though not so often as before, and I would still pursue my habitual enquiries after his sister – if he had lately heard from her, and how she was, but nothing more.

I did so, and the answers I received were always provokingly limited to the letter of the enquiry: She was much as usual: She made no complaints, but the tone of her last letter evinced great depression of mind: – She said she was better: – and, finally: – She said she was well, and very busy with her son's education, and with the management of her late husband's property and the regulation of his affairs. The rascal had never told me how that property was disposed, or whether Mr Huntingdon had died intestate or not; and I would sooner die than ask him, lest he should misconstrue into covetousness my desire to know. He never offered to show me his sister's letters now; and I never hinted a wish to see them. February, however, was approaching; December was past; January, at length, was almost over – a few more weeks, and then, certain despair or renewal of hope would put an end to this long agony of suspense.

But alas! it was just about that time she was called to sustain another blow in the death of her uncle – a worthless old fellow enough, in himself, I dare say, but he had always shown more kindness and affection to her than to any other creature, and she had always been accustomed to regard him as a parent. She was with him when he died, and had assisted her aunt to nurse him during the last stage of his illness. Her brother went to Staningley to attend the funeral, and told me, upon his return, that she was still there, endeavouring to cheer her aunt with her presence, and likely to remain some time. This was bad news for me, for while she continued there, I could not write to her, as I did not know the address, and would not ask it of him. But week followed week, and every time I enquired about her she was still at Staningley.

'Where *is* Staningley?' I asked at last.

'In —shire,' was the brief reply: and there was something so cold and dry in the manner of it, that I was effectually deterred from requesting a more definite account.

'When will she return to Grassdale?' was my next question.

'I don't know.'

'Confound it!' I muttered.

'Why, Markham?' asked my companion, with an air of innocent surprise. But I did not deign to answer him, save by a look of silent, sullen contempt, at which he turned away, and contemplated the carpet with a slight smile, half pensive, half amused; but quickly looking up, he began to talk of other subjects, trying to draw me into a cheerful and friendly conversation; but I was too much irritated to discourse with him, and soon took leave.

You see Lawrence and I somehow could not manage to get on very well together. The fact is, I believe, we were both of us a little too touchy. It is a troublesome thing Halford, this susceptibility to affronts where none are intended. I am no martyr to it now, as you can bear me witness: I have learned to be merry and wise, to be more easy with myself and more indulgent to my neighbours, and I can afford to laugh at both Lawrence and you.

Partly from accident, partly from wilful negligence on my part (for I was really beginning to dislike him), several weeks elapsed before I saw my friend again. When we did meet, it was *he* that sought *me* out. One bright morning early in June, he came into the field where I was just commencing my hay harvest.

'It is long since I saw you, Markham,' said he after the first few words had passed between us. 'Do you never mean to come to Woodford again?'

'I called once, and you were out.'

'I was sorry: but that was long since; I hoped you would call again; and now, *I* have called, and *you* were out – which you generally are, or I would do myself the pleasure of calling more frequently – but being determined to see you this time, I have left my pony in the lane, and come over hedge and ditch to join you; for I am about to leave Woodford for a while, and may not have the pleasure of seeing you again for a month or two.'

'Where are you going?'

'To Grassdale first,' said he, with a half-smile he would will-ingly have suppressed if he could.

'To Grassdale! Is she there, then?'

'Yes, but in a day or two she will leave it to accompany Mrs Maxwell to F— for the benefit of the sea air; and I shall go with them.' (F— was at that time a quiet but respectable watering place: it is considerably more frequented now.)

Lawrence seemed to expect me to take advantage of this circumstance to intrust him with some sort of a message to his sister; and I believe he would have undertaken to deliver it without any material objections, if I had had the sense to ask him; though of course he would not *offer* to do so, if I was content to let it alone. But I could not bring myself to make the request; and it was not till after he was gone, that I saw how fair an opportunity I had lost; – and then, indeed, I deeply regretted my stupidity and my foolish pride; but it was now too late to remedy the evil.

He did not return till towards the latter end of August. He wrote to me twice or thrice from F——; but his letters were most provokingly unsatisfactory, dealing in generalities or in trifles that I cared nothing about, or replete with fancies and reflections equally unwelcome to me at the time, – saying next to nothing about his sister, and little more about himself. I would wait, however, till he came back: perhaps I could get something more out of him then. At all events, I would not write to her now, while she was with him and her aunt, who doubtless would be still more hostile to my presumptuous aspirations than himself. When she was returned to the silence and solitude of her own home it would be my fittest opportunity.

When Lawrence came, however, he was as reserved as ever on the subject of my keen anxiety. He told me that his sister had derived considerable benefit from her stay at F——, that her son was quite well, and – alas! that both of them were gone, with Mrs Maxwell, back to Staningley; – and there they stayed at least three months. But instead of boring you with my chagrin, my expectations and disappointments, my fluctuations of dull despondency and flickering hope, my varying resolutions, now to drop it, and now to persevere – now to make a bold push, and now to let things pass and patiently abide my time, – I will employ myself in settling the business of one or two of the characters, introduced in the course of this narrative, whom I may not have occasion to mention again.

Sometime before Mr Huntingdon's death, Lady Lowborough eloped with another gallant to the continent, where, having lived awhile in reckless gaiety and dissipation, they quarrelled and parted. She went dashing on for a season, but years came and money went: she sunk, at length, in difficulty and debt, disgrace and misery; and died at last, as I have heard, in penury, neglect, and utter wretchedness. But this might be only a report: she may be living yet for anything I, or any of her relatives or former acquaintances can tell; for they have all lost sight of her long years ago, and would as thoroughly forget her if they could. Her husband, however, upon this second misdemeanour, immediately sought and obtained a divorce, and, not long after, married again. It was well he did, for Lord Lowborough, morose and moody as he seemed, was not the man for a bachelor's life. No public interests, no ambitious projects, or active pursuits, – or ties of friendship even (if he had had any friends), could compensate to him for the absence of domestic comforts and endearments. He had a son and a nominal daughter, it is true, but they too painfully reminded him of their mother, and the unfortunate little Annabella was a source of perpetual bitterness to his soul. He had obliged himself to treat her with paternal kindness: he had forced himself not to hate her, and even, perhaps, to feel some degree of kindly regard for her, at last, in return for her artless and unsuspecting attachment to himself, but the bitterness of his self-condemnation for his inward feelings towards that innocent being, his constant struggles to subdue the evil promptings of his nature (for it was not a generous one), though partly guessed at by those who knew him, could be known to God and his own heart alone; – so also was the hardness of his conflicts with the temptation to return to the vice of his youth, and seek oblivion for past calamities, and deadness to the present misery of a blighted heart, a joyless, friendless life, and a morbidly disconsolate mind, by yielding again to that insidious foe to health, and sense, and virtue, which had so deplorably enslaved and degraded him before.

The second object of his choice was widely different from the first. Some wondered at his taste; some even ridiculed it – but in this their folly was more apparent than his. The lady was about his own age – i.e. between thirty and forty – remarkable neither for beauty nor wealth, nor brilliant accomplishments;

nor any other thing that I ever heard of, except genuine good sense, unswerving integrity, active piety, warmhearted benevolence, and a fund of cheerful spirits. These qualities however, as you may readily imagine, combined to render her an excellent mother to the children, and an invaluable wife to his lordship. *He*, with his usual self-depreciation (or *ap*preciation?) thought her a world too good for him, and while he wondered at the kindness of Providence in conferring such a gift upon him, and even at her taste in preferring him to other men, he did his best to reciprocate the good she did him, and so far succeeded that she was, and I believe still is, one of the happiest and fondest wives in England; and all who question the good taste of either partner may be thankful if *their* respective selections afford them half the genuine satisfaction in the end, or repay their preference with affection half as lasting and sincere.

If you are at all interested in the fate of that low scoundrel, Grimsby, I can only tell you that he went from bad to worse, sinking from bathos to bathos of vice and villainy, consorting only with the worst members of his club and the lowest dregs of society – happily for the rest of the world – and at last met his end in a drunken brawl from the hands, it is said, of some brother scoundrel he had cheated at play.

As for Mr Hattersley, he had never wholly forgotten his resolution to 'come out from among them,' and behave like a man and a Christian, and the last illness and death of his once jolly friend Huntingdon, so deeply and seriously impressed him with the evil of their former practices, that he never needed another lesson of the kind. Avoiding the temptations of the town, he continued to pass his life in the country immersed in the usual pursuits of a hearty, active country gentleman; his occupations being those of farming, and breeding horses and cattle, diversified with a little hunting and shooting, and enlivened by the occasional companionship of his friends (better friends than those of his youth), and the society of his happy little wife (now cheerful and confiding as heart could wish) and his fine family of stalwart sons and blooming daughters. His father, the banker, having died some years ago and left him all his riches, he has now full scope for the exercise of his prevailing tastes, and I need not tell you that Ralph Hattersley, Esqr, is celebrated throughout the country for his noble breed of horses.

CHAPTER LI

AN UNEXPECTED OCCURRENCE

WE WILL NOW turn to a certain still, cold, cloudy afternoon about the commencement of December, when the first fall of snow lay thinly scattered over the blighted fields and frozen roads, or stored more thickly in the hollows of the deep cart ruts and footsteps of men and horses, impressed in the now petrified mire of last month's drenching rains. I remember it well, for I was walking home from the vicarage, with no less remarkable a personage than Miss Eliza Millward by my side. I had been to call upon her father, – a sacrifice to civility undertaken entirely to please my mother, not myself, for I hated to go near the house; not merely on account of my antipathy to the once so bewitching Eliza, but because I had not half forgiven the old gentleman himself for his ill opinion of Mrs Huntingdon; for though now constrained to acknowledge himself mistaken in his former judgment, he still maintained that she had done wrong to leave her husband; it was a violation of her sacred duties as a wife, and a tempting of Providence by laying herself open to temptation; and nothing short of bodily ill-usage (and that of no trifling nature) could excuse such a step – nor even that, for in such a case she ought to appeal to the laws for protection. But it was not of him I intended to speak; it was of his daughter Eliza. Just as I was taking leave of the vicar, she entered the room, ready equipped for a walk.

'I was just coming to see your sister, Mr Markham,' said she; 'and so, if you have no objection, I'll accompany you home. I like company when I'm walking out – don't you?'

'Yes, when it's agreeable.'

'That of course,' rejoined the young lady, smiling archly. So we proceeded together.

'Shall I find Rose at home, do you think?' said she, as we closed the garden gate, and set our faces towards Linden-car.

'I believe so.'

'I trust I shall, for I've a little bit of news for her – if you haven't forestalled me.'

'I?'

'Yes: do you know what Mr Lawrence is gone for?' She looked up anxiously for my reply.

'*Is* he gone?' said I, and her face brightened.

'Ah! then he hasn't told you about his sister?'

'What of *her*?' I demanded, in terror lest some evil should have befallen her.

'Oh, Mr Markham, how you blush!' cried she with a tormenting laugh. 'Ha, ha, you have not forgotten her yet! But you had better be quick about it, I can tell you, for – alas, alas! – she's going to be married next Thursday!'

'No, Miss Eliza, that's false.'

'Do you charge me with a falsehood, sir?'

'You are misinformed.'

'Am I? Do you know better then?'

'I think I do.'

'What makes you look so pale then?' said she, smiling with delight at my emotion. 'Is it anger at poor me for telling such a fib? Well, I only "tell the tale as 'twas told to me:" I don't vouch for the truth of it; but at the same time, I don't see what reason Sarah should have for deceiving me, or her informant for deceiving her; and that was what she told me the footman told her: – that Mrs Huntingdon was going to be married on Thursday, and Mr Lawrence was gone to the wedding. She did tell me the name of the gentleman, but I've forgotten that. Perhaps you can assist me to remember it. Is there not some one that lives near – or frequently visits the neighbourhood, that has long been attached to her? a Mr – oh dear! – Mr –'

'Hargrave?' suggested I, with a bitter smile.

'You're right!' cried she, 'that was the very name.'

'Impossible, Miss Eliza!' I exclaimed in a tone that made her start.

'Well, you know, that's what they told me,' said she, composedly staring me in the face. And then she broke out into a long shrill laugh that put me to my wit's end with fury.

'Really, you must excuse me,' cried she: 'I know it's very rude, but ha, ha, ha! – did you think to marry her yourself? Dear, dear, what a pity! ha, ha, ha! – Gracious, Mr Markham! are you going to faint? O mercy! shall I call this man? Here, Jacob –' But checking the word on her lips, I seized her arm and gave it, I think, a pretty severe squeeze, for she shrank into herself with a faint cry of pain or terror; but the spirit within her was not subdued: instantly rallying, she continued, with well feigned concern –

'What can I do for you? Will you have some water – some brandy? – I dare say they have some in the public-house down there, if you'll let me run.'

'Have done with this nonsense!' cried I sternly. She looked confounded – almost frightened again, for a moment. 'You know I hate such jests,' I continued.

'*Jests* indeed! I wasn't *jesting*!'

'You were laughing, at all events; and I don't like to be laughed at,' returned I, making violent efforts to speak with proper dignity and composure, and to say nothing but what was coherent and sensible. 'And since you are in such a merry mood, Miss Eliza, you must be good enough company for yourself, and therefore I shall leave you to finish your walk alone – for, now I think of it, I have business elsewhere; so good evening.'

With that I left her (smothering her malicious laughter) and turned aside into the fields, springing up the bank, and pushing through the nearest gap in the hedge. Determined at once to prove the truth – or rather the falsehood of her story, I hastened to Woodford as fast as my legs could carry me – first, veering round by a circuitous course, but the moment I was out of sight of my fair tormentor, cutting away across the country, just as a bird might fly – over pasture-land and fallow, and stubble, and lane – clearing hedges and ditches, and hurdles, till I came to the young squire's gates. Never till now had I known the full fervour of my love – the full strength of my hopes, not wholly crushed even in my hours of deepest despondency, always tenaciously clinging to the thought that one day she might be mine – or if not that, at least that something of my memory, some slight remembrance of our friendship and our love would be for ever cherished in her heart. I marched up to the door, determined if I saw the master, to question him boldly concerning his sister, to wait and hesitate no longer, but cast false delicacy and stupid pride behind my back, and know my fate at once.

'Is Mr Lawrence at home?' I eagerly asked of the servant that opened the door.

'No sir, master went yesterday,' replied he, looking very alert.

'Went where?'

'To Grassdale, sir – wasn't you aware, sir? He's very close, is master,' said the fellow with a foolish, simpering grin. 'I suppose, sir –'

But I turned and left him, without waiting to hear what he supposed. I was not going to stand there to expose my tortured feelings to the insolent laughter and impertinent curiosity of a fellow like that.

But what was to be done now? Could it be possible that she had left me for *that* man? I could not believe it. Me she might forsake, but *not* to give herself to him! Well, I would know the truth – to no concerns of daily life could I attend, while this tempest of doubt and dread, of jealousy and rage distracted me. I would take the morning coach from L— (the evening one would be already gone), and fly to Grassdale, I *must* be there before the marriage. And why? Because a thought struck me, that *perhaps* I might prevent it – that if I did not, she and I might both lament it to the latest moment of our lives. It struck me that some one might have belied me to her: perhaps her brother – yes, no doubt her brother had persuaded her that I was false and faithless, and taking advantage of her natural indignation, and perhaps her desponding carelessness about her future life, had urged her, artfully, cruelly on, to this other marriage in order to secure her from me. If this *was* the case, and if she should only discover her mistake when too late to repair it – to what a life of misery and vain regret might she be doomed as well as me! and what remorse for me, to think my foolish scruples had induced it all! Oh, I *must* see her – she must know my truth even if I told it at the church door! I might pass for a madman or an impertinent fool – even she might be offended at such an interruption, or at least might tell me it was now too late – but if I *could* save her! if she *might* be mine – it was too rapturous a thought!

Winged by this hope, and goaded by these fears, I hurried homewards to prepare for my departure on the morrow. I told my mother that urgent business which admitted no delay, but which I could not then explain, called me away to — (the last large town through which I had to pass). My deep anxiety and serious preoccupation, could not be concealed from her maternal eyes; and I had much ado to calm her apprehensions of some disastrous mystery.

That night there came a heavy fall of snow, which so retarded the progress of the coaches on the following day, that I was almost driven to distraction. I travelled all night of course, for this was Wednesday: to-morrow morning, doubtless, the marriage would take place. But the night was long and dark; the snow heavily clogged the wheels and balled the horses' feet; the animals were consumedly lazy, the coachmen most execrably cautious, the passengers confoundedly apathetic in their supine indifference to the rate of our progression. Instead of assisting me to bully the several coachmen and urge them forward, they merely stared and grinned at my impatience: one fellow even ventured to rally me upon it – but I silenced him with a look that quelled him for the rest of the journey; – and when, at the last stage, I would have taken the reins into my own hand, they all with one accord opposed it.

It was broad daylight when we entered M— and drew up at the Rose and Crown. I alighted and called aloud for a post-chaise to Grassdale. There was none to be had: the only one in the town was under repair. 'A gig then – a fly – car – anything – only be quick!' There was a gig but not a horse to spare. I sent into the town to seek one; but they were such an intolerable time about it that I could wait no longer: I thought my own feet would carry me sooner, and bidding them send the confounded conveyance after me, if it were ready within an hour, I set off as fast as I could walk. The distance was little more than six miles, but the road was strange, and I had to keep stopping to enquire my way – hallooing to carters and clod-hoppers, and frequently invading the cottages, for there were few abroad that winter's morning, – sometimes knocking up the lazy people from their beds, for where so little work was to be done – perhaps so little food and fire to be had, they cared not to curtail their slumbers. I had no time to think of *them*, however: aching with weariness and desperation, I hurried on. The gig did not overtake me: it was well I had not waited for it – vexatious, rather, that I had been fool enough to wait so long.

At length however, I entered the neighbourhood of Grassdale. I approached the little rural church – but lo! there stood a train of carriages before it – it needed not the white favours bedecking the servants and horses, nor the merry voices of the village idlers assembled to witness the show, to apprize me that there was a wedding within. I ran in among them, demanding, with breathless eagerness, had the ceremony long commenced? They only gaped and stared. In my desperation I pushed past them, and was about to enter the church-yard gate, when a group of ragged urchins, that had been hanging like bees to the window, suddenly dropped off and made a rush for the porch, vociferating in the uncouth dialect of their county, something which signified, 'It's over – they're coming out!'

If Eliza Millward had seen me then, she might indeed have been delighted. I grasped the gate-post for support, and stood intently gazing towards the door to take my last look on my soul's delight, my first on that detested mortal who had torn her from my heart, and doomed her, I was certain, to a life of misery and hollow, vain repining – for what happiness could she enjoy with him? I did not wish to shock her with my presence now, but I had not power to move away. Forth came the bride and bridegroom. Him I saw not; I had eyes for none but her. A long veil shrouded half her graceful form, but did not hide it; I could see that while she carried her head erect, her eyes were bent upon the ground, and her face and neck were suffused with a crimson blush; but every feature was radiant with smiles, and, gleaming through the misty whiteness of her veil, were clusters of golden ringlets! O Heavens! it was *not* my Helen! The first glimpse made me start – but my eyes were darkened with exhaustion and despair – dare I trust them? Yes – it *is* not she! It was a younger, slighter, rosier beauty – lovely, indeed, but with far less dignity and depth of soul – without that indefinable grace, that keenly *spirituel* yet gentle charm, that ineffable power to attract and subjugate the heart – *my* heart at least. I looked at the bridegroom – it was Frederick Lawrence! I wiped away the cold drops that were trickling down my forehead, and stepped back as he approached; but, his eyes fell upon me, and he knew me, altered as my appearance must have been.

'Is that you Markham?' said he, startled and confounded at the apparition – perhaps, too, at the wildness of my looks.

'Yes, Lawrence – is that you?' I mustered the presence of mind to reply.

He smiled and coloured, as if half-proud and half-ashamed of his identity; and if he had reason to be proud of the sweet lady on his arm, he had no less cause to be ashamed of having concealed his good fortune so long.

'Allow me to introduce you to my bride,' said he, endeavouring to hide his embarrassment by an assumption of careless gaiety. 'Esther, this is Mr Markham, my friend Markham, Mrs Lawrence, late Miss Hargrave.'

I bowed to the bride, and vehemently wrung the bridegroom's hand.

'Why did you not tell me of this?' I said reproachfully, pretending a resentment I did not feel (for in truth I was almost wild with joy to find myself so happily mistaken, and overflowing with affection to him for this and for the base injustice I felt that I had done him in my mind – he might have wronged me, but not to *that* extent; and as I had hated him like a demon for the last forty hours, the reaction from such a feeling was so great that I could pardon all offences for the moment – and love him in spite of them too).

'I *did* tell you,' said he, with an air of guilty confusion, 'you received my letter?'

'What letter?'

'The one announcing my intended marriage.'

'I never received the most distant hint of such an intention.'

'It must have crossed you on your way then – it should have reached you yesterday morning – it was rather late, I acknowledge. But what brought you here then, if you received no information?'

It was now *my* turn to be confounded; but the young lady, who had been busily patting the snow with her foot during our short, sotto voce colloquy, very opportunely came to my assistance by pinching her companion's arm and whispering a suggestion that his friend should be invited to step into the carriage and go with them; it being scarcely agreeable to stand there among so many gazers, and keeping their friends waiting, into the bargain.

'And so cold as it is too!' said he, glancing with dismay at her slight drapery, and immediately handing her into the carriage. 'Markham, will you come? We are going to Paris, but we can drop you anywhere between this and Dover.'

'No, thank you. Good-bye – I needn't wish you a pleasant journey; but I shall expect a very handsome apology, some time, mind, and scores of letters, before we meet again.'

He shook my hand and hastened to take his place beside his lady. This was no time or place for explanation or discourse: we had already stood long enough to excite the wonder of the village sight-seers, and perhaps the wrath of the attendant bridal party; though, of course, all this passed in a much shorter time than I have taken to relate or even than you will take to read it. I stood beside the carriage, and, the window being down, I saw my happy friend fondly encircle his companion's waist with his arm, while she rested her glowing cheek on his shoulder, looking the very impersonation of loving, trusting bliss. In the interval between the footman's closing the door and taking his place behind, she raised her smiling brown eyes to his face, observing, playfully –

'I fear you must think me very insensible, Frederick: I know it is the custom for ladies to cry on these occasions, but I couldn't squeeze a tear for my life.'

He only answered with a kiss, and pressed her still closer to his bosom.

'But what is this?' he murmured. 'Why, Esther, you're crying now!'

'Oh, it's nothing – it's only too much happiness – and the wish,' sobbed she, 'that our dear Helen were as happy as ourselves.'

'Bless you for that wish!' I inwardly responded as the carriage rolled away – 'and Heaven grant it be not wholly vain!'

I thought a cloud had suddenly darkened her husband's face as she spoke. What did *he* think? Could he grudge such happiness to his dear sister and his friend as he now felt himself? At *such* a moment it was impossible. The contrast between her fate and his *must* darken his bliss for a time. Perhaps too he thought of me: perhaps he regretted the part he had had in preventing our union, by omitting to help us, if not by actually plotting against us – I exonerated him from *that* charge, now, and deeply lamented my former ungenerous suspicions; but he *had* wronged us, still – I hoped, I trusted that he had. He had not attempted to check the course of our love by actually damming up the streams in their passage, but he had passively watched the two currents wandering through life's arid wilderness, declining to clear away the obstructions that divided them, and secretly hoping that both would lose themselves in the sand before they could be joined in one. And meantime, he had been quietly proceeding with his own affairs: perhaps his heart and head had been so full of his fair lady that he had had but little thought to spare for others. Doubtless he had made his first acquaintance with her – his first intimate acquaintance at least – during his three months' sojourn at F——, for I now recollected that he had once casually let fall an intimation that his aunt and sister had a young friend staying with them at the time, and this accounted for at least one half his silence about all transactions there. Now too I saw a reason for many little things that had slightly puzzled me before; among the rest, for sundry departures from Woodford, and absences more or less prolonged, for which he never satisfactorily accounted, and concerning which he hated to be questioned on his return. Well might the servant say his master was 'very close.' But why this strange reserve to *me*? Partly, from that remarkable idiosyncrasy to which I have before alluded; partly, perhaps, from tenderness to my feelings, or fear to disturb my philosophy by touching upon the infectious theme of love.

CHAPTER LII

FLUCTUATIONS

THE TARDY GIG had overtaken me at last. I entered it, and bade the man who brought it drive to Grassdale Manor – I was too busy with my own thoughts to care to drive it myself. I would see Mrs Huntingdon – there could be no impropriety in that now that her husband had been dead above a year – and by her indifference or her joy at my unexpected arrival, I could soon tell whether her heart was truly mine. But my companion, a loquacious, forward fellow, was not disposed to leave me to the indulgence of my private cogitations.

'There they go!' said he as the carriages filed away before us. 'There'll be brave doings on yonder *to-day*, as what come to-morra. – Know anything of that family, sir? or you're a stranger in these parts?'

'I know them by report.'

'Humph! – There's the best of 'em gone anyhow. And I suppose the old missis is agoing to leave after this stir's gotten overed, and take herself off, somewhere, to live on her bit of a jointure; and the young 'un – at least the new 'un (she's none so very young) is coming down to live at the Grove.'

'Is Mr Hargrave married, then?'

'Ay sir, a few months since. He should a been wed afore, to a widow lady, but they couldn't agree over the money: she'd a rare long purse, and Mr Hargrave wanted it all to his-self; but she wouldn't let it go, and so then they fell out. This one isn't quite as rich – nor as handsome either, but she hasn't been married before. She's very plain they say, and getting on to forty or past, and so, you know, if she didn't jump at this hopportunity, she thought she'd never get a better. I guess she thought such a handsome young husband was worth all 'at ever she had, and he might take it and welcome; but I lay she'll rue her bargain afore long. They say she begins already to see 'at he isn't not altogether that nice, generous, perlite, delightful gentleman 'at she thought him afore marriage – he begins a being careless, and masterful already. Ay, and she'll find him harder and care-lesser nor she thinks on.'

'You seem to be well acquainted with him,' I observed.

'I am, sir; I've known him since he was quite a young gentle-man; and a proud'un he was, and a wilful. I was servant yonder for several years; but I couldn't stand their niggardly ways – she got ever longer and worse did Missis, with her nipping and screwing, and watching and grudging; so I thought I'd find another place as *what* came.'

And then he discoursed upon his present position as ostler at the Rose and Crown, and how greatly superior it was to his former one, in comfort and freedom, though inferior in out-ward respectability; and entered into various details respecting the domestic economy at the Grove, and the characters of Mrs Hargrave and her son, – to which I gave no heed, being too much occupied with my own anxious, fluttering anticipations and with the character of the country through which we passed, that, in spite of the leafless trees and snowy ground, had for some time begun to manifest unequivocal signs of the approach to a gentleman's country seat.

'Are we not near the house?' said I, interrupting him in the middle of his discourse.

'Yes, sir; yond's the park.'

My heart sank within me to behold that stately mansion in the midst of its expansive grounds – the park as beautiful now, in its wintry garb, as it could be in its summer glory; the majestic sweep, the undulating swell and fall, displayed to full advantage in that robe of dazzling purity, stainless and printless – save one long, winding track left by the trooping deer – the stately timber-trees with their heavy laden branches gleaming white against the dull, grey sky; the deep, encircling woods; the broad expanse of water sleeping in frozen quiet; and the weeping ash and willow drooping their snowclad boughs above it – all presented a picture, striking, indeed, and pleasing to an un-encumbered mind, but by no means encouraging to me. There was one comfort, however, – all this was entailed upon little Arthur, and could not under any circumstances, strictly speak-ing, be his mother's. But how was she situated? Overcoming with a sudden effort my repugnance to mention her name to my garrulous companion, I asked him if he knew whether her late husband had left a will, and how the property had been disposed of. Oh, yes, he knew all about it; and I was quickly informed that to her had been left the full control and manage-ment of the estate during her son's minority, besides the abso-lute, unconditional possession of her own fortune (but I knew that her father had not given her much), and the small addi-tional sum that had been settled upon her before marriage.

Before the close of the explanation, we drew up at the park gates. Now for the trial – if I should find her within – but alas! she might be still at Staningley: her brother had given me no intimation to the contrary. I enquired at the porter's lodge if Mrs Huntingdon were at home. No, she was with her aunt in —shire, but was expected to return before Christmas. She usually spent most of her time at Staningley, only coming to Grassdale occasionally, when the management of affairs, or the interest of her tenants and dependants required her presence.

'Near what town is Staningley situated?' I asked. The requis-ite information was soon obtained. 'Now then, my man, give me the reins, and we'll return to M—. I must have some break-fast at the Rose and Crown, and then away to Staningley by the first coach for ****.'

'You'll not get there to-day, sir.'

'No matter, I don't want to get there to-day; I want to get there to-morrow, and pass the night on the road.'

'At an inn, sir? You'd better by half stay at *our* house; and then start fresh to-morrow, and have the whole day for your journey.'

'What, and lose twelve hours? not I.'

'Perhaps, sir, you're *related* to Mrs Huntingdon?' said he, seeking to indulge his curiosity since his cupidity was not to be gratified.

'I have not that honour.'

'Ah! well,' returned he with a dubious, sidelong glance at my splashed, grey trousers and rough P jacket. 'But,' he added, encouragingly, 'there's many a fine lady like that 'at has kinsfolks poorer nor what you are, sir, I should think.'

'No doubt, – and there's many a fine gentleman would esteem himself vastly honoured to be able to claim kindred with the lady you mention.'

He now cunningly glanced at my face. 'Perhaps, sir, you *mean* to –'

I guessed what was coming, and checked the impertinent conjecture with, – 'Perhaps you'll be so good as to be quiet a moment. I'm busy.'

'Busy, sir?'

'Yes, in my mind, and don't want to have my cogitations disturbed.'

'Indeed, sir!'

You will see that my disappointment had not *very* greatly affected me, or I should not have been able so quietly to bear with the fellow's impertinence. The fact is I thought it as well – nay better, all things considered, that I should not see her to-day, – that I should have time to compose my mind for the interview – to prepare it for a heavier disappointment, after the intoxicating delight experienced by this sudden removal of my former apprehensions; not to mention that, after travelling a night and a day without intermission, and rushing in hot haste through six miles of new-fallen snow, I could not possibly be in a very presentable condition.

At M— I had time before the coach started to replenish my forces with a hearty breakfast, and to obtain the refreshment of my usual morning's ablutions, and the amelioration of some slight change in my toilet, – and also to dispatch a short note to my mother (excellent son that I was) to assure her that I was still in existence and to excuse my non-appearance at the expected time. It was a long journey to Staningley for those slow travelling days; but I did not deny myself needful refreshment on the road, nor even a night's rest at a way-side inn; choosing rather to brook a little delay than to present myself worn, wild, and weatherbeaten before my mistress and her aunt, who would be astonished enough to see me without that. Next morning, therefore, I not only fortified myself with as substantial a breakfast as my excited feelings would allow me to swallow, but I bestowed a little more than usual time and care upon my toilet; and, furnished with a change of linen from my small carpet-bag, well brushed clothes, well polished boots, and neat new gloves, – I mounted 'the Lightning,' and resumed my journey. I had nearly two stages yet before me, but the coach, I was informed, passed through the neighbourhood of Staningley, and, having desired to be set down as near the Hall as possible, I had nothing to do but to sit with folded arms and speculate upon the coming hour.

It was a clear, frosty morning. The very fact of sitting exalted aloft, surveying the snowy landscape and sweet, sunny sky, inhaling the pure, bracing air, and crunching away over the crisp, frozen snow, was exhilarating enough in itself; but add to this the idea of to what goal I was hastening, and whom I expected to meet, and you may have some faint conception of my frame of mind at the time – only a *faint* one though, for my heart swelled with unspeakable delight, and my spirits rose almost to madness – in spite of my prudent endeavours to bind them down to a reasonable platitude by thinking of the undeniable difference between Helen's rank and mine; of all that she had passed through since our parting; of her long, unbroken silence; and, above all, of her cool, cautious aunt, whose counsels she would doubtless be careful not to slight again. These considerations made my heart flutter with anxiety, and my chest heave with impatience to get the crisis over, but they could not dim her image in my mind, or mar the vivid recollection of what had been said and felt between us – or destroy the keen anticipation of what was to be – in fact, I could not realize their terrors now. Towards the close of the journey, however, a couple of my fellow passengers kindly came to my assistance, and brought me low enough.

'Fine land this,' said one of them, pointing with his umbrella to the wide fields on the right, conspicuous for their compact hedgerows, deep, well-cut ditches, and fine timber-trees, growing sometimes on the borders, sometimes in the midst of the enclosure; – '*very* fine land, if you saw it in the summer or spring.'

'Ay,' responded the other – a gruff elderly man, with a drab greatcoat buttoned up to the chin and a cotton umbrella between his knees. 'It's old Maxwell's I suppose.'

'It *was* his, sir, but he's dead now, you're aware, and has left it all to his niece.'

'All?'

'Every rood of it, – and the mansion-house and all, – every hatom of his worldly goods! – except just a trifle, by way of remembrance to his nephew down in —shire and an annuity to his wife.'

'It's strange, sir!'

'It is sir. And she wasn't his own niece neither; but he had no near relations of his own – none but a nephew he'd quarrelled with – and he always had a partiality for this one. And then his wife advised him to it, they say: she'd brought most of the property, and it was her wish that this lady should have it.'

'Humph! – She'll be a fine catch for somebody.'

'She will so. She's a widow, but quite young yet, and uncommon handsome – a fortune of her own, besides, and only one child – and she's nursing a fine estate for him in ✳✳✳✳. There'll be lots to speak for her! – 'fraid there's no chance for uz' – (facetiously jogging me with his elbow, as well as his companion) – 'ha, ha, ha! No offence, sir, I hope?' (to me) 'Ahem! I should think she'll marry none but a nobleman myself. Look ye sir,' resumed he, turning to his other neighbour, and pointing past me with his umbrella, 'that's the Hall – grand park, you see – and all them woods – plenty of timber there, and lots of game – hallo! what now?'

This exclamation was occasioned by the sudden stoppage of the coach at the park gates.

'Gen'leman for Staningley Hall?' cried the coachman; and I rose and threw my carpet-bag on to the ground, preparatory to dropping myself down after it.

'Sickly, sir?' asked my talkative neighbour, staring me in the face (I dare say it was white enough).

'No. Here, coachman.'

'Thank'ee, sir. – All right!'

The coachman pocketed his fee and drove away, leaving me not walking up the park, but pacing to and fro before its gates, with folded arms and eyes fixed upon the ground – an overwhelming force of images, thoughts, impressions crowding on my mind, and nothing tangibly distinct but this: – My love had been cherished in vain; my hope was gone for ever; I must tear myself away at once, and banish or suppress all thoughts of her like the remembrance of a wild, mad dream. Gladly would I have lingered round the place for hours, in the hope of catching, at least one distant glimpse of her before I went, but it must not be: I must not suffer her to see me; for what could have brought me hither but the hope of reviving her attachment, with a view, hereafter to obtain her hand? And could I bear that she should think me capable of such a thing? – of presuming upon the acquaintance – the *love* if you will – accidentally contracted, or rather forced upon her against her will, when she was an unknown fugitive, toiling for her own support, apparently without fortune, family, or connections – to come upon her now, when she was re-instated in her proper sphere, and claim a share in her prosperity, which, had it never failed her, would most certainly have kept her unknown to me for ever? and this, too, when we had parted sixteen months ago, and she had expressly forbidden me to hope for a re-union in this world – and never sent me a line or a message from that day to this? No! The very idea was intolerable.

And even if she should have a lingering affection for me still, ought I to disturb her peace by awakening those feelings? to subject her to the struggles of conflicting duty and inclination – to whichsoever side the latter might allure, or the former imperatively call her – whether she should deem it her duty to risk the slights and censures of the world, the sorrow and displeasure of those she loved, for a romantic idea of truth and constancy to me, or to sacrifice her individual wishes to the feelings of her friends and her own sense of prudence and the fitness of things? No – and I would not! I would go at once, and she should never know that I had approached the place of her abode; for though I might disclaim all idea of ever aspiring to her hand, or even of soliciting a place in her friendly regard, her peace should not be broken by my presence, nor her heart afflicted by the sight of my fidelity.

'Adieu then, dear Helen, for ever! – For ever adieu!'

So said I – and yet I could not tear myself away. I moved a few paces, and then looked back, for one last view of her stately home, that I might have its outward form, at least, impressed upon my mind as indelibly as her own image, which alas! I must not see again – then, walked a few steps farther; and then lost in melancholy musings, paused again and leant my back against a rough old tree that grew beside the road.

CHAPTER LIII

CONCLUSION

WHILE STANDING THUS, absorbed in my gloomy reverie, a gentleman's carriage came round the corner of the road. I did not look at it; and had it rolled quietly by me, I should not have remembered the fact of its appearance at all; but a tiny voice from within it roused me by exclaiming –

'Mamma, mamma, here's Mr Markham!'

I did not hear the reply, but presently the same voice answered –

'It is indeed, mamma – look for yourself.'

I did not raise my eyes, but I suppose mamma looked, for a clear melodious voice, whose tones thrilled through my nerves, exclaimed –

'Oh, aunt! here's Mr Markham – Arthur's friend! – Stop, Richard!'

There was such evidence of joyous though suppressed excitement in the utterance of those few words – especially that tremulous, 'Oh, aunt –' that it threw me almost off my guard. The carriage stopped immediately, and I looked up and met the eye of a pale, grave, elderly lady surveying me from the open window. She bowed and so did I, and then she withdrew her head, while Arthur screamed to the footman to let him out; but before that functionary could descend from his box, a hand was silently put forth from the carriage window. I knew that hand, though a black glove concealed its delicate whiteness and half its fair proportions, and quickly seizing it, I pressed it in my own – ardently for a moment, but instantly recollecting myself, I dropped it, and it was immediately withdrawn.

'Were you coming to see us, or only passing by?' asked the low voice of its owner, who, I felt, was attentively surveying my countenance from behind the thick, black veil which with the shadowing panels, entirely concealed her own from me.

'I – I came to see the place,' faltered I.

'The *place*,' repeated she, in a tone which betokened more displeasure or disappointment than surprise. 'Will you not enter it then?'

'If you wish it.'

'Can you doubt?'

'Yes, yes! he *must* enter,' cried Arthur running round from the other door; and seizing my hand in both his, he shook it heartily.

'Do you remember me, sir?' said he.

'Yes, full well, my little man, altered though you are,' replied I, surveying the comparatively tall, slim young gentleman with his mother's image visibly stamped upon his fair, intelligent features, in spite of the blue eyes beaming with gladness, and the bright locks clustering beneath his cap.

'Am I not grown?' said he, stretching himself up to his full height.

'Grown! three inches upon my word!'

'I was *seven* last birthday,' was the proud rejoinder. 'In seven years more, I shall be as tall as you, nearly.'

'Arthur,' said his mother, 'tell him to come in. Go on Richard.'

There was a touch of sadness as well as coldness in her voice, but I knew not to what to ascribe it. The carriage drove on and entered the gates before us. My little companion led me up the park, discoursing merrily all the way. Arrived at the Hall door, I paused on the steps and looked round me, waiting to recover my composure, if possible – or at any rate, to remember my new formed resolutions and the principles on which they were founded; and it was not till Arthur had been for some time gently pulling my coat, and repeating his invitations to enter, that I at length consented to accompany him into the apartment where the ladies awaited us.

Helen eyed me as I entered with a kind of gentle, serious scrutiny and politely asked after Mrs Markham and Rose. I respectfully answered her enquiries. Mrs Maxwell begged me to be seated, observing it was rather cold, but she supposed I had not travelled far that morning.

'Not quite twenty miles,' I answered.

'Not on foot!'

'No, Madam, by coach.'

'Here's Rachel, sir,' said Arthur, the only truly happy one amongst us, directing my attention to that worthy individual, who had just entered to take her mistress's things. She vouchsafed me an almost friendly smile of recognition – a favour that demanded, at least, a civil salutation on my part, which was accordingly given and respectfully returned – she had seen the error of her former estimation of my character.

When Helen was divested of her lugubrious bonnet and veil, her heavy winter cloak &c. she looked so like herself that I knew not how to bear it. I was particularly glad to see her beautiful black hair unstinted still and unconcealed in its glossy luxuriance.

'Mamma has left off her widow's cap in honour of uncle's marriage,' observed Arthur, reading my looks with a child's mingled simplicity and quickness of observation. Mamma looked grave and Mrs Maxwell shook her head. 'And aunt Maxwell is never going to leave off hers,' persisted the naughty boy; but when he saw that his pertness was seriously displeasing and painful to his aunt, he went and silently put his arm round her neck, kissed her cheek, and withdrew to the recess of one of the great bay windows, where he quietly amused himself with his dog while Mrs Maxwell gravely discussed with me the interesting topics of the weather, the season, and the roads. I considered her presence very useful as a check upon my natural impulses – an antidote to those emotions of tumultuous excitement which would otherwise have carried me away against my reason and my will, but *just then* I felt the restraint almost intolerable, and I had the greatest difficulty in forcing myself to attend to her remarks and answer them with ordinary politeness; for I was sensible that Helen was standing within a few feet of me beside the fire. I dared not look at her, but I felt her eye was upon me, and from one hasty, furtive glance, I thought her cheek was slightly flushed, and that her fingers, as she played with her watch chain, were agitated with that restless, trembling motion which betokens high excitement.

'Tell me,' said she, availing herself of the first pause in the attempted conversation between her aunt and me, and speaking fast and low with her eyes bent on the gold chain – for I now ventured another glance – 'Tell me how you all are at Linden-hope – has nothing happened since I left you?'

'I believe not.'

'Nobody dead? nobody married?'

'No.'

'Or – or expecting to marry? – No old ties dissolved or new ones formed? no old friends forgotten or supplanted?'

She dropped her voice so low in the last sentence that no one could have caught the concluding words but myself, and at the same time turned her eyes upon me with a dawning smile, most sweetly melancholy, and a look of timid though keen enquiry that made my cheeks tingle with inexpressible emotions.

'I believe not,' I answered. – 'Certainly not, if others are as little changed as I.' Her face glowed in sympathy with mine.

'And you really did not mean to call?' she exclaimed.

'I feared to intrude.'

'To intrude!' cried she, with an impatient gesture. – 'What' – but as if suddenly recollecting her aunt's presence, she checked herself and turning to that lady continued – 'Why aunt, this man is my brother's close friend and was my own intimate acquaintance (for a few short months at least), and professed a great attachment to my boy – and when he passes the house, so many scores of miles from his home, he declines to look in for fear of intruding!'

'Mr Markham is over-modest,' observed Mrs Maxwell.

'Over ceremonious rather,' said her niece – 'over – well, it's no matter.' And turning from me, she seated herself in a chair beside the table, and pulling a book to her by the cover, began to turn over the leaves in an energetic kind of abstraction.

'If I had known,' said I, 'that you would have honoured me by remembering me as an intimate acquaintance, I most likely should not have denied myself the pleasure of calling upon you, but I thought you had forgotten me long ago.'

'You judged of others by yourself,' muttered she without raising her eyes from the book, but reddening as she spoke and hastily turning over a dozen leaves at once.

There was a pause of which Arthur thought he might venture to avail himself to introduce his handsome young setter and show me how wonderfully it was grown and improved, and to ask after the welfare of its father Sancho. Mrs Maxwell then withdrew to take off her things. Helen immediately pushed the book from her and after silently surveying her son, his friend, and his dog for a few moments, she dismissed the former from the room under pretence of wishing him to fetch his last new book to show me. The child obeyed with alacrity; but I continued caressing the dog. The silence might have lasted till its master's return had it depended on me to break it, but, in half a minute or less, my hostess impatiently rose, and taking her former station on the rug between me and the chimney corner, earnestly exclaimed –

'Gilbert, what *is* the matter with you? – why are you so changed? – It is a very indiscreet question I know,' she hastened to add: 'perhaps, a very rude one – don't answer it if you think so – but I hate mysteries and concealments.'

'I am not changed, Helen – unfortunately I am as keen and passionate as ever – it is not I, it is circumstances that are changed.'

'What circumstances? *Do* tell me!' Her cheek was blanched

with the very anguish of anxiety – could it be with the fear that I had rashly pledged my faith to another?

'I'll tell you at once,' said I. 'I will confess that I came here for the purpose of seeing you (not without some monitory misgivings at my own presumption, and fears that I should be as little welcome as expected when I came), but I did not know that this estate was yours, until enlightened on the subject of your inheritance by the conversation of two fellow passengers in the last stage of my journey; and then, I saw at once the folly of the hopes I had cherished and the madness of retaining them a moment longer; and though I alighted at your gates, I determined not to enter within them; I lingered a few minutes to see the place, but was fully resolved to return to M— without seeing its mistress.'

'And if my aunt and I had not been just returning from our morning drive, I should have seen and heard no more of you?'

'I thought it would be better for both that we should not meet,' replied I as calmly as I could, but not daring to speak above my breath from conscious inability to steady my voice, and not daring to look in her face lest my firmness should forsake me altogether: 'I thought an interview would only disturb your peace and madden me. But I am glad, now, of this opportunity of seeing you once more and knowing that you have not forgotten me, and of assuring you that I shall never cease to remember you.'

There was a moment's pause. Mrs Huntingdon moved away, and stood in the recess of the window. Did she regard this as an intimation that modesty alone prevented me from asking her hand? and was she considering how to repulse me with the smallest injury to my feelings? Before I could speak to relieve her from such a perplexity, she broke the silence herself by suddenly turning towards me and observing –

'You might have had such an opportunity before – as far I mean as regards assuring me of your kindly recollections, and yourself of mine, if you had written to me.'

'I would have done so, but I did not know your address, and did not like to ask your brother, because I thought he would object to my writing – but this would not have deterred me for a moment, if I could have ventured to believe that you expected to hear from me, or even wasted a thought upon your unhappy friend; but your silence naturally led me to conclude myself forgotten.'

'Did you expect me to write to *you* then?'

'No, Helen – Mrs Huntingdon,' said I, blushing at the implied imputation, 'certainly not; but if you had sent me a message through your brother, or even asked him about me now and then –'

'I did ask about you, frequently. I was not going to do more,' continued she, smiling, 'so long as you continued to restrict yourself to a few polite enquiries about my health.'

'Your brother never told me that you had mentioned my name.'

'Did you ever ask him?'

'No; for I saw he did not wish to be questioned about you, or to afford the slightest encouragement or assistance to my too obstinate attachment.' Helen did not reply. 'And he was perfectly right,' added I. But she remained in silence looking out upon the snowy lawn. 'Oh, I will relieve her of my presence!' thought I; and immediately I rose and advanced to take leave, with a most heroic resolution – but pride was at the bottom of it, or it could not have carried me through.

'Are you going already?' said she, taking the hand I offered, and not immediately letting it go.

'Why should I stay any longer?'

'Wait till Arthur comes, at least.'

Only too glad to obey, I stood and leant against the opposite side of the window.

'You told me you were not changed,' said my companion: 'you *are* – very much so.'

'No, Mrs Huntingdon, I only *ought* to be.'

'Do you mean to maintain that you have the same regard for me that you had when last we met?'

'I have, but it would be wrong to talk of it now.'

'It was wrong to talk of it *then*, Gilbert; it would *not* now – unless to do so would be to violate the truth.'

I was too much agitated to speak; but, without waiting for an answer, she turned away her glistening eye and crimson cheek, and threw up the window and looked out, whether to calm her own excited feelings or to relieve her embarrassment, – or only to pluck that beautiful half-blown Christmas rose that grew upon the little shrub without, just peeping from the snow, that had hitherto, no doubt, defended it from the frost, and was now melting away in the sun. Pluck it however, she did, and having gently dashed the glittering powder from its leaves, approached it to her lips and said, –

'This rose is not so fragrant as a summer flower, but it has stood through hardships none of *them* could bear: the cold rain of winter has sufficed to nourish it, and its faint sun to warm it; the bleak winds have not blanched it, or broken its stem, and the keen frost has not blighted it. Look, Gilbert, it is still fresh, and blooming as a flower can be, with the cold snow even now on its petals. – Will you have it?'

I held out my hand: I dared not speak lest my emotion should overmaster me. She laid the rose across my palm, but I scarcely closed my fingers upon it, so deeply was I absorbed in thinking what might be the meaning of her words, and what I ought to do or say upon the occasion; whether to give way to my feelings or restrain them still. Misconstruing this hesitation into indifference – or reluctance even – to accept her gift, Helen suddenly snatched it from my hand, threw it out on to the snow, shut down the window with an emphasis, and withdrew to the fire.

'Helen! what means this?' I cried, electrified at this startling change in her demeanour.

'You did not understand my gift,' said she, – 'or, what is

worse, you despised it: I'm sorry I gave it you; but since I did make such a mistake, the only remedy I could think of, was to take it away.'

'You misunderstood me, cruelly,' I replied, and in a minute I had opened the window again, leaped out, picked up the flower, brought it in, and presented it to her, imploring her to give it me again, and I would keep it for ever for her sake, and prize it more highly than anything in the world I possessed.

'And will this content you?' said she as she took it in her hand.

'It shall,' I answered.

'There, then; take it.'

I pressed it earnestly to my lips, and put it in my bosom, Mrs Huntingdon looking on with a half sarcastic smile.

'Now, are you going?' said she.

'I will if – if I must.'

'You *are* changed,' persisted she – 'you are grown either very proud or very indifferent.'

'I am neither, Helen – Mrs Huntingdon. If you could see my heart –'

'You *must* be one, – if not both. And why Mrs Huntingdon? – why not Helen, as before?'

'Helen, then – dear Helen!' I murmured. I was in an agony of mingled love, hope, delight, uncertainty, and suspense.

'The rose I gave you was an emblem of my heart,' said she; 'would you take it away and leave me here alone?'

'Would you give me your hand too, if I asked it?'

'Have I not said enough?' she answered with a most enchanting smile. I snatched her hand and would have fervently kissed it, but suddenly checked myself and said, –

'But have you considered the consequences?'

'Hardly, I think, or I should not have offered myself to one too proud to take me, or too indifferent to make his affection outweigh my worldly goods.'

Stupid blockhead that I was! – I trembled to clasp her in my arms, but dared not believe in so much joy, and yet restrained myself to say, –

'But if you *should* repent!'

'It would be your fault,' she replied: 'I never shall, unless you bitterly disappoint me. If you have not sufficient confidence in my affection to believe this, let me alone.'

'My darling angel – my *own Helen*,' cried I, now passionately kissing the hand I still retained, and throwing my left arm around her, 'you never shall repent, if it depend on me alone. – But have you thought of your aunt?' I trembled for the answer and clasped her closer to my heart in the instinctive dread of losing my new-found treasure.

'My aunt must not know of it yet,' said she. 'She would think it a rash, wild step, because she could not imagine how well I know you; but she must know you herself, and learn to like you. You must leave us now, after lunch, and come again in spring, and make a longer stay, and cultivate her acquaintance; and I know you will like each other.'

'And then you will be mine,' said I printing a kiss upon her lips, and another, and another – for I was as daring and impetuous now as I had been backward and constrained before.

'No – in another year,' replied she, gently disengaging herself from my embrace, but still fondly clasping my hand.

'Another year! Oh, Helen, I could not wait so long!'

'Where is your fidelity?'

'I mean I could not endure the misery of so long a separation.'

'It would not be a separation: we will write every day: my spirit shall be always with you; and sometimes you shall see me with your bodily eye. I will not be such a hypocrite as to pretend that I desire to wait so long myself, but as my marriage is to please myself alone, I ought to consult my friends about the time of it.'

'Your friends will disapprove.'

'They will not greatly disapprove, dear Gilbert,' said she, earnestly kissing my hand – 'they cannot, when they know you –

or if they could, they would not be true friends; I should not care for their estrangement. – Now are you satisfied?' She looked up in my face with a smile of ineffable tenderness.

'Can I be otherwise, with your love? And you *do* love me, Helen?' said I, not doubting the fact, but wishing to hear it confirmed by her own acknowledgment.

'If you loved as *I* do,' she earnestly replied, 'you would not have so nearly lost me – these scruples of false delicacy and pride would never thus have troubled you – you would have seen that the greatest worldly distinctions and discrepancies of rank, birth, and fortune are as dust in the balance compared with the unity of accordant thoughts and feelings, and truly loving, sympathizing hearts and souls.'

'But this is too much happiness,' said I, embracing her again; 'I have not deserved it Helen – I dare not believe in such felicity: and the longer I have to wait, the greater will be my dread that something will intervene to snatch you from me – and think, a thousand things may happen in a year! – I shall be in one long fever of restless terror and impatience all the time. And besides, winter is such a dreary season.'

'I thought so too,' replied she gravely: 'I would not be married in winter – in December, at least,' she added with a shudder – for in that month had occurred both the ill-starred marriage that had bound her to her former husband and the terrible death that released her – 'and therefore, I said another year in spring.'

'*Next* spring?'

'No, no – next autumn, perhaps.'

'Summer, then?'

'Well, the close of summer. There now! be satisfied.'

While she was speaking, Arthur re-entered the room – good boy for keeping out so long.

'Mamma, I couldn't find the book in either of the places you told me to look for it' (there was a conscious something in mamma's smile that seemed to say, 'No, dear, I knew you could not'), 'but Rachel got it for me at last. Look, Mr Markham, a natural history with all kinds of birds and beasts in it, and the reading as nice as the pictures!'

In great good humour, I sat down to examine the book and drew the little fellow between my knees. Had he come a minute before, I should have received him less graciously, but now I affectionately stroked his curling locks, and even kissed his ivory forehead: he was my own Helen's son, and therefore mine; and as such I have ever since regarded him. That pretty child is now a fine young man: he has realized his mother's brightest expectations, and is at present residing in Grassdale Manor with his young wife, the merry little Helen Hattersley, of yore.

I had not looked through half the book, before Mrs Maxwell appeared to invite me into the other room to lunch. That lady's cool, distant manners rather chilled me at first; but I did my best to propitiate her, and not entirely without success I think, even in that first short visit; for when I talked cheerfully to her, she gradually became more kind and cordial, and when I departed she bade me a gracious adieu, hoping erelong to have the pleasure of seeing me again.

'But you must not go till you have seen the conservatory, my aunt's winter garden,' said Helen, as I advanced to take leave of her, with as much philosophy and self-command as I could summon to my aid.

I gladly availed myself of such a respite, and followed her into a large and beautiful conservatory, plentifully furnished with flowers considering the season – but of course, I had little attention to spare for *them*. It was not however for any tender colloquy that my companion had brought me there: –

'My aunt is particularly fond of flowers,' she observed, 'and she is fond of Staningley too: I brought you here to offer a petition in her behalf that this may be her home as long as she lives, and – if it be not our home likewise – that I may often see her and be with her; for I fear she will be sorry to lose me; and, though she leads a retired and contemplative life, she is apt to get low-spirited if left too much alone.'

'By all means, dearest Helen! – do what you will with your own. I should not dream of wishing your aunt to leave the place under any circumstances; and we will live either here or elsewhere as you and she may determine, and you shall see her as often as you like. I know she must be pained to part with you, and I am willing to make any reparation in my power. I love her for your sake, and her happiness shall be as dear to me as that of my own mother.'

'Thank you, darling! you shall have a kiss for that. Goodbye. There now – there Gilbert – let me go – here's Arthur, don't astonish his infantile brain with your madness.'

But it is time to bring my narrative to a close – any one but you would say I had made it too long already; but for *your* satisfaction, I will add a few words more; because, I know you will have a fellow-feeling for the old lady, and will wish to know the last of her history. I did come again in spring, and agreeably to Helen's injunctions, did my best to cultivate her acquaintance. She received me very kindly, having been doubtless, already prepared to think highly of my character, by her niece's too favourable report. I turned my best side out of course, and we got along marvellously well together. When my ambitious intentions were made known to her, she took it more sensibly than I had ventured to hope. Her only remark on the subject, in my hearing, was –

'And so Mr Markham, you are going to rob me of my niece I understand. Well! I hope God will prosper your union, and make my dear girl happy at last. Could she have been contented to remain single, I own I should have been better satisfied; but if she must marry again, I know of no one, now living and of a suitable age, to whom I would more willingly resign her than yourself, or who would be more likely to appreciate her worth and make her truly happy, as far as I can tell.'

Of course I was delighted with the compliment, and hoped to show her she was not mistaken in her favourable judgment.

'I have, however, one request to offer,' continued she. 'It seems I am still to look on Staningley as my home: I wish you to make it yours likewise, for Helen is attached to the place and to me – as I am to her. There are painful associations connected with Grassdale, which she cannot easily overcome; and I shall not molest you with my company or interference here: I am a very quiet person, and shall keep my own apartments and attend to my own concerns, and only see you now and then.'

Of course I most readily consented to this; and we lived in the greatest harmony with our dear aunt until the day of her death, which melancholy event took place a few years after – melancholy, not to herself (for it came quietly upon her, and she was glad to reach her journey's end), but only to the few loving friends and grateful dependants she left behind.

To return, however, to my own affairs: I was married in summer, on a glorious August morning. It took the whole eight months, and all Helen's kindness and goodness to boot, to over-come my mother's prejudices against my bride elect, and to reconcile her to the idea of my leaving Linden-car and living so far away. Yet she was gratified at her son's good fortune after all, and proudly attributed it all to his own superior merits and endowments. I bequeathed the farm to Fergus, with better hopes of its prosperity than I should have had a year ago under similar circumstances; for he had lately fallen in love with the Vicar of L—'s eldest daughter, a lady whose superiority had roused his latent virtues and stimulated him to the most surpris-ing exertions, not only to gain her affection and esteem, and to obtain a fortune sufficient to enable him to aspire to her hand, but to render himself worthy of her, in his own eyes, as well as in those of her parents; and in the end he was successful, as you already know. As for myself, I need not tell you how happily my Helen and I have lived and loved together, and how blessed we still are in each other's society, and in the promising young scions that are growing up about us. We are just now looking forward to the advent of you and Rose, for the time of your annual visit draws nigh, when you must leave your dusty, smoky, noisy, toiling, striving city for a season of invigorating relaxation and social retirement with us.

Till then, farewell,

GILBERT MARKHAM.

Staningley, June 10th, 1847.

THE END

ABOUT THE INTRODUCER

LUCY HUGHES-HALLETT is a cultural historian and critic. She is the author of *Cleopatra: Queen, Lover, Legend* and *Heroes: Saviours, Traitors and Supermen*. She reviews regularly for the *Sunday Times* Books Section.

This book is set in GARAMOND, the first typeface in
the ambitious programme of matrix production
undertaken by the Monotype Corporation
under the guidance of Stanley Morrison
in 1922. Although named after the
great French royal typographer,
Claude Garamond (1499–
1561), it owes much to
Jean Jannon of Sedan
(1580–1658).